THE WORLD'S CLASSICS
NOTRE-DAME DE PARIS

VICTOR HUGO was born in Besançon in 1802, the youngest of three sons of an officer (eventually a general), who took his family with him from posting to posting, as far as Italy and Spain. In 1812 his parents separated, and Madame Hugo settled in Paris with her sons. Victor's prolific literary career began with publication of poems (1822), a novel (1823), and a drama, *Cromwell* (1827), the preface of which remains a major manifesto of French Romanticism. The riot occasioned at the first performance of his drama *Hernani* (1830) established him as a leading figure among the Romantics, and *Notre-Dame* (1831) added to his prestige at home and abroad. Favoured by Louis-Philippe (1830–48), he chose exile rather than live under Napoleon III (President 1848, Emperor 1851). In exile in Brussels (1851), Jersey (1853), and Guernsey (1855) he wrote some of his finest work, notably the satirical poems *Les Châtiments* (1853), the first of the series of epic poems, *Légende des siècles* (1859), and the lengthy novel *Les Misérables* (1862). Only with Napoleon III's defeat and replacement by the Third Republic did Hugo return, to be elected deputy, and later senator. His opposition to tyranny and continuing immense literary output established him as a national hero. When he died in 1885 he was honoured by interment in the Panthéon.

A. J. KRAILSHEIMER is Emeritus Student and was Tutor in French at Christ Church, Oxford from 1957 until his retirement in 1988. His published work is mostly on the sixteenth and seventeenth centuries, but among his translations are Flaubert's *Three Tales* (also in the World's Classics), *Salammbô*, and *Bouvard et Pécuchet*.

D1025754

THE WORLD'S CLASSICS

VICTOR HUGO

Notre-Dame de Paris

Translated with an Introduction
and Notes by
ALBAN KRAILSHEIMER

Oxford   New York
OXFORD UNIVERSITY PRESS
1993

Oxford University Press, Walton Street, Oxford OX2 6DP
Oxford New York Toronto
Delhi Bombay Calcutta Madras Karachi
Kuala Lumpur Singapore Hong Kong Tokyo
Nairobi Dar es Salaam Cape Town
Melbourne Auckland Madrid
and associated companies in
Berlin Ibadan

Oxford is a trade mark of Oxford University Press

British Library Cataloguing in Publication
Data available

Library of Congress Cataloging in Publication Data
Hugo, Victor, 1802–1885
[Notre-Dame de Paris. English]
Notre-Dame de Paris / Victor Hugo ; translated with an introduction
and notes by Alban Krailsheimer.
p. cm.
1. France—History—Louis XI, 1461–1483—Fiction.
2. Paris (France)—History—To 1515—Fiction.
I. Krailsheimer, A. J. II. Title.
PQ2288.A35 1993 843'.7—dc20 92-38259
ISBN 0-19-282911-4

1 3 5 7 9 10 8 6 4 2

Typeset by Pure Tech Corporation, Pondicherry, India
Printed in Great Britain by
BPCC Paperbacks Ltd
Aylesbury, Bucks

CONTENTS

INTRODUCTION

(NOTE: Readers who do not want to know beforehand
the plot of *Notre-Dame de Paris* might prefer to read this
Introduction after the book itself.)

TODAY, more than a hundred years after Hugo's death, it
is difficult, if not impossible, to approach the man and his
work with an open mind. His remains were enthusiastically
borne to the Panthéon in 1885, to join those of such other
great men as Voltaire and Rousseau; he endured exile for
nearly twenty years for speaking his mind against Napoleon
III; he fought a spirited campaign all his life against capital
punishment. His vast literary output includes some of the
most notable poetry in French in both the lyric and the epic
mode. His dramatic work was an integral part of the Romantic movement: although his plays are of very varying
quality, the preface to the virtually unactable *Cromwell*
(1827) is probably better known than any other manifesto
of Romanticism, while *Hernani* literally caused a riot in the
theatre at its first performance in February 1830. More to
the immediate point, his two best-known novels have inspired several film versions of *The Hunchback of Notre-Dame*
(a title, incidentally, going back to the English translation
of the novel in 1833) and stage, as well as film, versions of
parts of *Les Misérables*, the most recent of which has proved
a commercial success as a musical. On the subject of music,
it is worth noting that as early as 1851 Verdi took Hugo's
drama *Le Roi s'amuse* (banned as subversive after its first
performance in 1832) as the basis for his opera *Rigoletto*
(another hunchback hero . . .). The sheer energy and range
of Hugo's writings, and indeed of the man himself in his life
from day to day, should not be allowed to obscure the fact
that all is by no means sound and fury: his poetry includes
many examples of a more reflective, elegiac lyricism.

It would be misleading here to treat *Notre-Dame* in
the light of Hugo's later novels, or as a stage in his long

development as man and writer. What matters is the book itself, the experiences, literary and other, which helped to shape it, and, not least, features of the novel's structure and composition which are by no means obvious to an uninitiated reader.

The first Note, introducing the text published in March 1831, but apparently composed only after completion of that text, explains that the inspiration for the book was an inscription, incised deeply into the wall of one of the towers of Notre-Dame by an identifiably medieval hand, but erased since the author first came upon it while exploring the building: the single Greek word 'ANÁΓKH. This brief Note, despite specific references to crime and misfortune, souls in anguish, and so on, is curiously vague and uncertain as to why the inscription can no longer be seen. More than half-way through the novel (Book Seven, Ch. IV), the reader meets the word again, first in the chapter heading, then actually being incised with a pair of compasses into the wall by Claude Frollo, whose state of mind at that moment matches the description given in Hugo's introductory Note. Such careful mystification and ambiguity is a recurrent feature of Hugo's narrative technique, but in this case is uniquely prominent because the implications of the Greek inscription go far beyond anything Frollo could have foreseen when he wrote it. The author alone holds the secret of his book, and reveals it to the reader as and when he chooses. That reader (in 1831) would have had to wait for the definitive edition of 1832 for an explanation of the emphasis in the second half of the Note on demolition, erasure, destruction—not just of individuals, but of the seemingly most solid and beautiful works of human hands.

The second Note addressed to the reader, dated October 1832, is much longer and as well as explaining, after a fashion, why three previously unpublished chapters are only now appearing, goes on to amplify in detail, and with examples, the brief general statements on the destruction of medieval architecture already included in the earlier Note. The aesthetic and philosophical considerations which Hugo touches on in the Note of 1832 were of great importance to him, and need comment, but it is necessary first to explain why chapters already composed were not published with the rest in 1831.

As early as November 1828 Hugo had signed a contract with the publisher Gosselin for a novel on the lines of those of Walter Scott, wildly popular at the time in France. This was originally due to be delivered the following year, but was constantly deferred. His theatrical work, especially *Hernani*, a more public and tempting arena for someone of Hugo's combative temperament, and domestic preoccupations distracted him until an ultimatum from the publisher, giving him until December 1830 to deliver the promised novel or suffer heavy financial penalty, finally spurred him to make a start. On 25 July Hugo, in serious need of cash, began to write, two days later the brief but decisive July Revolution ('the Three Glorious Days') broke out, and on 28 July his wife Adèle presented him with their fifth child, a daughter. Nothing daunted (and by then there were enough problems to daunt anyone of meaner stamp) Hugo grimly went about his task, and by October foresaw that his original plan was likely to exceed the two volumes stipulated. He imprudently asked Gosselin how much extra he would be paid for the third volume which seemed necessary to accommodate the novel as he now envisaged it. Gosselin was in no mood to temporize, and all that Hugo extracted from him was a few weeks' extension to the deadline—even publishers have to recognize the distraction of a revolution as a valid excuse for delay—and a bleak refusal to entertain the idea of a third volume, let alone pay extra for it. In the event, the chapters Hugo held back are the two comprising the present Book Five. A third chapter, only one page long, rounding off Book Four with a description of Frollo and Quasimodo together, seems to have been added shortly before the definitive edition came out. Whether the Book Five dossier was at any stage lost or mislaid in the course of moving house, as Hugo claims in his Note, is irrelevant; he knew very well that the content would be, so to speak, 'caviare to the general'.

By the time Hugo had settled his accounts with Gosselin he had moved to another publisher, Renduel. That is why the definitive edition of 1832 makes much of the two classes of reader: those who seek no more than 'a good read', or, as Hugo more elegantly puts it, 'who looked in *Notre-Dame de Paris* only for the drama, the novel'; and those other readers 'who have not found it a waste of time to study the aesthetic and philosophical ideas hidden within the book . . . It is especially for those readers that the chapters added to this edition will make *Notre-Dame de Paris* complete . . .'. There follows a condemnation of contemporary architecture, with a catalogue of the acts of vandalism accomplished or threatened against medieval buildings. The Note of 1832 affirms Hugo's passionate commitment to the cause of conservation, which he describes as one of the chief aims in his life, with a specific statement to the effect that the novel was intended to serve that cause. If more evidence were needed, it is worth mentioning that already in the first edition a chapter added at the last moment, 'Bird's-Eye View of Paris', contains a brief but withering attack on post-medieval architecture in Paris.

All this emphasis on architecture, the pleas for conservation, and the diatribes against contemporary lack of taste and blatant vandalism, seem to have little enough to do with a novel on the lines of Walter Scott, or indeed with any novel designed primarily to attract readers seeking no more than dramatic and narrative entertainment. Be that as it may, it would be a serious mistake to dismiss Hugo's claim to be crusading for Gothic architecture as mere rhetoric, or at best as the expression of an amateur interest, however genuine. He wanted to achieve results, and from all accounts succeeded. As early as 1824 his ode 'La Bande noire' had denounced vandalism in general, and in March 1832, that is between the first and definitive editions of *Notre-Dame*, he had published a vigorous article in the *Revue des deux mondes* entitled 'Guerre aux démolisseurs!' ['War on the Demolishers!']. From 1835 until 1848 he served continuously and actively on a government committee for ancient monuments. At first he was one of eight members, then, from 1838, with a more specific brief, the committee was enlarged to number sixteen, including Méri-mée and Montalembert. In the opinion of Montalembert, an influential figure at the time, the success of *Notre-Dame* had made a decisive contribution to the cause of the con-servationists. The reader may well not share Hugo's priorities, or indeed have the slightest interest in architec-ture, but the recital of these bare facts (and there are of course many more) should be enough to show that in the Notes just considered he wrote about architecture from deep conviction, and deserves to be taken seriously.

The novel's opening sentences pose a problem of a dif-ferent order. The precision of the dating is of twofold importance: 'the sixth of January 1482', like the book's sub-title '1482', seems to announce a historical novel, more or less on the lines of Scott's *Quentin Durward*, set in 1468, which Hugo had reviewed quite favourably in 1823, but the date 25 July 1830, which a moment's calculation reveals as the 'today' designated by the very precise lapse of time, is no ordinary date. The Revolution which broke out two days later swept away the restored Bourbon monarchy in the person of the increasingly repressive Charles X, and put on the throne Louis-Philippe of the junior Orléans branch as constitutional monarch. Thus every reflection throughout the book on kingship, popular insurrection, and the Bourbon family (powerful in 1482 but still a good hundred years from the throne) is liable to be coloured by recent nineteenth-century events as much as by the fif-teenth-century context, and prophecies made by characters in 1482 are inevitably conditioned by the reader's know-ledge and the author's interpretation of happenings in 1789 and 1830.

Where specific events, great or small, in the narrative are concerned one should not expect a historian's accuracy or consistent chronology, for the book is fiction and artistic demands are paramount in chronology as in everything else. At the very beginning of the story, for example, it is true to say that the feast of the Epiphany always falls on 6 January, but it is quite untrue that the Feast of Fools coincided with it 'from time immemorial', or at all. The fact that the Flemish embassy adds a new strand to the festivities, and that thanks to them a face-pulling competition gives yet another theme to this particular day, is of minor importance in terms of chronology, but essential to the narrative. More significant is the change Hugo effected in Pierre Gringoire's dates: the writer was in fact born in 1475 and thus 7 years old in 1482, but he is none the less chosen by Hugo for a leading role in the story, and is made twenty years older to that end. When we read, in the second chapter of the book, that he announced his name to the chattering girls as proudly as if he had said 'Pierre Corneille' (1606–84), we realize that it is only the name and some anachronistic details that have anything to do with the real Pierre Gringoire of history.

Towards the end of his life Hugo categorically denied ever having written a historical novel, by which he meant, it seems, a novel based on historical persons and events, into which fictional characters and situations are inserted. While generally appreciative of Scott's work, as early as the review of *Quentin Durward* in 1823, Hugo regretted the absence of a truly epic dimension, a broadly sweeping view which would give the narrative some deeper meaning. At the same time he was fascinated by the odd minutiae of bygone ages. This flexible attitude to chronology on the one hand and an eagerness to share with the reader a mass of curious and esoteric information on the other gives much of the book a paradoxically realistic quality. The fact that Paris is the scene of most of the action explains why two of Hugo's main sources are early historians of the city: Jacques Du Breul (1528–1614), whose *Théâtre des antiquités de Paris* was published in 1612, and Henri Sauval (1623–76) whose *Histoire et recherches des antiquités de la ville de Paris* came out in 1724 in three large folio volumes, the third of which was devoted to printing the accounts for the Provostry of Paris, covering the period of the novel. Sauval in particular is a mine of curious and often improbable information on topography, etymology of street names, strange happenings, popular sayings, even the Court of Miracles. Sauval indeed, a zealous rather than a discriminating collector of antiquarian facts, devotes three pages to the 'visions', as he puts it, concerning various statues and figures in Notre-Dame and other buildings which the 'seekers after the philosophers' stone', or alchemists, associate with their mystery; treasure trove indeed for Hugo. Sauval, two hundred years and more after the event, also enables Hugo to give chapter and verse for the trial and condemnation (and cost) of animals connected with witchcraft.

The accumulation of specific details about the period, authenticated by quotations of the kind just mentioned from Sauval and similar collections of curious facts, is an effective way of presenting the reader, however ignorant of history, with a series of insights into the quite alien culture of the waning Middle Ages. Perhaps equally effective are the chapters devoted to synthesis of a particular theme. Such subjects as the administration of justice, the bird's-eye view of Paris, the physical description of the cathedral, the place of anchorites in medieval urban society, are more important for Hugo's sense of history than are chronological accuracy or the reconstruction of political situations. The hideous description (Book Ten, Ch. V) of the cage in the Bastille in which the Bishop of Verdun is incarcerated, the details of its construction and cost, the king's indifference to human suffering and anger at wasteful expenditure, all tell the reader more than could any historical discussion of the prisoner's alleged treachery. On a less elevated plane, the animated dialogue attributed to the students in the opening chapters is full of allusions, plays on words, and gibes at authority, much of which must have been as obscure to most readers in Hugo's day as to those of today, but such exchanges set the scene and convey something of the atmosphere of Paris in the late fifteenth century.

All these details are so much décor; for the deeper philosophy of history to which Hugo subscribed one must turn to the chapters of Book Five which were omitted from the first published version. In narrative terms the chapter describing the visit of the transparently disguised Louis XI, in the company of his physician Coictier, is vaguely assigned to 'about the same time' as Claude Frollo's refusal to meet the king's daughter, Madame de Beaujeu, when she came on a visit to Notre-Dame in December 1481. This refusal is linked to what is stated to be an intensified misogyny pushed to the point of obsession, linked with a similarly obsessive campaign against gypsies, especially dancers. The reader does not have to be particularly alert to see in this development the sign that Frollo's passion for Esmeralda has finally unhinged his reason. Thus, when in the chapter describing the king's clandestine visit, Frollo's successive denunciations of medicine and astrology as futile provoke Coictier's furious asides 'He's mad!', we already know this to be the case, but for reasons of which Coictier is quite unaware. Coictier's hold over the king, who is in genuinely bad health as well as incurably superstitious, depends on his own expertise in medicine and astrology; Frollo appeals to an equally powerful feature of Louis's notoriously avaricious character by indicating that the quest for gold, though long and arduous, is ultimately worth pursuing: 'to make gold is to be God. That is the only science.' (p. 187.) Thus far the course of the conversation is consistent with what has already been revealed, and which in Book Seven is to be confirmed, that the hermetic science of such men as Nicolas Flamel had long held Frollo's interest and that numerous architectural features, in the cathedral of Notre-Dame and elsewhere in Paris, pointed the way to the hidden treasure—indeed Sauval lists these clues, as we have already noted. It comes therefore as no surprise when Frollo tells the king that if, at his age, he really wants to learn the rudiments of the hermetic science, it is from these local buildings that he can be taught the alphabet. What is novel is the list of ancient and distant buildings which Frollo has not seen himself, but which he associates with the book of true wisdom. The king then asks the crucial question: 'What are these books of yours?', which is answered by Frollo who points to the vast bulk of the cathedral all around them, and then enigmatically remarks, with one hand indicating Notre-Dame and the other a printed book on his table: 'This will kill that.' The curfew puts an end to the interview, but not before the king concedes to Coictier that Frollo may indeed be mad, though we are told that he formed so good an opinion of him that they subsequently often met again.

The following chapter, entitled 'This Will Kill That', abandons the narrative for an essay on the respective roles of architecture and printing in the history of mankind, with Hugo addressing the reader directly. According to him, from the beginning of human history until the fifteenth century, architecture was *the* book of mankind, evolving from single standing stones (letters of the alphabet), to groups (such as dolmens) making up syllables, to complexes like that of Carnac, representing whole sentences. Then came buildings, and he cites Indian temples of marble, Solomon's temple in Jerusalem, and the temples of Egypt. Not only temples arose, for 'Every civilization begins with theocracy and ends with democracy.' Passing rapidly to the Middle Ages, Hugo contrasts Romanesque architecture, representative of the dogmatic authority of the Church, with the pointed arch brought back from the Crusades,—'a great popular movement'—through which the feudal nobles challenged the power of the Church, and were soon followed by the people claiming their share of power. Thus he sees Gothic architecture as coming to embody all the main ideas of a people, rather than of a caste, perpetuated in stone.

The fifteenth century put an end to this, he maintains, with the arrival of printing. The death of Gothic architecture and—a familiar theme—the decadence of all that came after was balanced by the overwhelming growth of the printing press, a second tower of Babel reaching far into the heavens, ceaselessly raised ever higher by the whole of mankind working together: popular, because so much cheaper than buildings, more durable, because no longer dependent on single, perishable manuscripts, available to all because numerous copies could be produced. Hugo stresses that ancient literary monuments, such as the work of Homer, the Vedas, and the *Nibelungen*, are also beneficiaries of printing, having now been made secure for posterity. 'The invention of printing is the greatest event in history. It is the mother of revolutions' (p. 200). Thus unambiguously Hugo nails his colours to the mast.

Frollo's gloomy vision, for it is his priestly dominion that will suffer most, may well have seemed madness in 1482, but Hugo's interpretation of 'this will kill that' is, with its social implications, offered as retrospective fact. The attack on the cathedral by the truands, marginalized members of society, is a vivid fictional representation of a challenge to established authority of a very different kind from that which won independence for the first Swiss confederation. In France the spark of rebellion from below was as yet nothing compared to the savage repression exercised by central authority; but by 1482 feudalism had run its course, and a new, though not necessarily better, system was to come.

In the original 1831 version the reader was led directly from Gringoire's disconsolate wanderings on the evening of the fiasco of his play to the Court of Miracles and his 'marriage' to Esmeralda, and on to a Book Three combining a description of Notre-Dame and the panoramic view of Paris with what is now Book Four, except for the last brief chapter. In other words the building and its setting lead straight on to chapters describing in turn the 4-year-old foundling soon to be christened Quasimodo, his adoptive father Claude Frollo, and Claude's baby brother Jehan, sole object of the already austere and learned priest's human affection. The sixteen years between the two opening books, set in 1482, and the evolution of these three characters, and their relationship to each other and to the outside world, are thus seen in reverse order. The mischievous and unruly Jehan du Moulin, the deaf and deformed Quasimodo, Pope of Fools, the sinister archdeacon, mad enough to attempt abduction of the gypsy girl by whom he is obsessed, are given a personal history only when the reader knows what they have become. In 1831 what followed was the present Book Six, composed in fact before the chapters in Books Three and Four just mentioned.

In real time the whole of Book Six takes place the morning after the events of the opening books, but a story told by a provincial visitor, from Reims, neatly links topography (the Place de Grève) with history. The farcical trial of Quasimodo for the affray caused by the attempted abduction of Esmeralda the night before consigns him to the pillory in the Grève that morning; the *sachette* is introduced only after a chapter describing the Rat-hole; and on the way to see this as one of the local sights, mention of a gypsy girl sets off a train of ideas linking fear of the gypsies as child-stealers, the *sachette*'s fear of gypsies, and finally the tale related by Mahiette, the visitor from Reims.

This story has as its fixed point the coronation of Louis XI at Reims in 1461, when the girl Paquette la Chantefleurie was 14 years old and had begun her brief career of shame. In 1466 she gave birth to a daughter on whom she doted, but before the baby Agnès was a year old, gypsies stole her, substituting a monster child, about 4 years old. All Paquette had left of her own child was a little embroidered shoe she had made herself. In the best Romantic tradition, the mother disappeared soon afterwards; whether she fled to Paris or committed suicide by drowning no one quite knew. As for the little monster, he was sent to Paris for the foundlings' bed, and thus can be identified as Quasimodo. Moments after ending her story Mahiette is able to identify the *sachette* as the vanished Paquette, as soon as she catches sight of the little shoe at which the recluse is gazing. At this point, half-way through the narrative, the exposition is at last complete, and dramatic irony intensifies. The *sachette*, immured in her cell, wildly curses Esmeralda as a child-stealer, when she is in fact the child stolen; Quasimodo, borne only the day before to the Place de Grève in triumphant procession as Pope of Fools, is flogged and pilloried in the same place for an offence ordered by his master, Claude Frollo, who puts in an appearance, but makes no attempt to help him; the gypsy, alone of the crowd, answers the wretched Quasimodo's plea for a drink of water, when it was she whom he had tried to seize the previous night; while the *sachette* only curses the girl the more, predicting a shameful end for her on that same ladder.

The only character of any importance still to be integrated into the story is the handsome young officer who rescued Esmeralda from abduction, and about whom she has been dreaming ever since. He was the last character Hugo introduced, and though he is clearly a type his creator despised, from Book Seven on he is the unwitting instrument of Esmeralda's destruction, while remaining the object of her blind adoration. It is ironic that the murder with witchcraft of which she is accused later should be that of a man whom she actually sees alive as she is taken to the scaffold for the first time, when Quasimodo snatches her into sanctuary at the last moment, and the sight of whom causes her to betray herself fatally in the end only minutes after being reunited with her mother after a lifetime's separation. Vain and shallow as Phoebus is, he represents the absence of any moral or rational justification for the dreadful consequences of Esmeralda's obsession with him. There are no star-crossed lovers, no Romeo and Juliet or Tristram and Iseult, in this story, only the endless irony of human beings unable to match their uncontrollable passions to the reality of the world around them. The alchemists' quest for gold, their belief that a sunbeam could be buried and gold extracted from it, which had animated Frollo until his obsession with the gypsy girl drove all other interests from his mind—that vain hope is no more real than the girl's pathetic belief that her sun, her Phoebus, her protector, would rescue her.

The first four chapters of Book Seven see the tragic knot tied. Esmeralda's command performance in the Gondelaurier mansion marks her out as a kind of circus freak beyond the social pale, until the goat's betrayal of her secret brands her as a witch. Gringoire's interview with Frollo, and his revelation that in the eyes of the truands he is married to Esmeralda for the next four years, though in name only, just serves to inflame the priest's passion, while his explanation of the goat's apparently magic tricks proves both girl and goat innocent of sorcery. It is the fourth chapter, with its title 'ΑΝΑΓΚΗ, set in Frollo's secret laboratory, that takes the reader back to the introductory Note at the very beginning.

It was at that point that Hugo paused in his narrative to compose the two chapters that became Book Five. Once he had completed the chapter describing the king's visit (to his cell in the cloister, not the laboratory in the tower), followed by the chapter 'This Will Kill That', he was able very rapidly to go back to the visit of Charmolue, already expected when brother Jehan inconveniently arrives and has to hide, and amplify the sense of the inscription Frollo has just carved on the wall. Irony is yet again evident: Charmolue reports that the case against Esmeralda is already prepared, and despite Gringoire's full explanation of a day or two before that witchcraft has nothing to do with her act, there can be no doubt that the charge will be taken as proved in the sort of society where Quasimodo's deafness earns him extra punishment from a deaf judge. At this point the inscription is reflected in the little drama of the spider and the fly. The web, several times compared to a rose-window, exemplifies the inevitability of what Frollo sees as the fate of the girl and himself. Part of that fatality is the victim's helpless struggle when caught in the trap. Only a few hours later, through a series of coincidences, Frollo witnesses as a voyeur the amorous scene between the mysterious Phoebus, whom he at last identifies, and the girl, and in a fit of jealous frenzy stabs his rival, fatally, as he believes, and escapes to let the girl pay the price for his crime.

From then on to the end of the book one misunderstanding after another provokes some of the most striking scenes in the book, alternating horror with hope. The trial, the torture, the death sentence, the condemned cell in the bowels of the prison, finally the grim spectacle of the liturgy and *amende honorable* at the door of the cathedral, follow their inexorable course up to the point when Quasimodo intervenes to snatch the girl to sanctuary. All he wants is to make her happy and keep her safe. Thus, when Frollo comes one night to her sanctuary cell and tries to take her by force, he is stopped by Quasimodo and all but stabbed by the girl. From that moment on Frollo is jealous of the hunchback, who for the first time wavers between his loyalty to master and to idol.

After the momentary lull of sanctuary comes the last act of the drama, a set piece so spectacular, occupying some hundred pages, that it is easy to see why film producers have been repeatedly attracted to it, but which is also dense with misunderstanding. The tempo of the narrative changes with the revelation that the judicial authorities propose to breach sanctuary (unusual, but not unknown) and that less than three days remain to take the girl to a secret and safer refuge. It is Gringoire, meeting Frollo by chance, who proposes using the truands to create a diversion under cover of which she can be removed to a new sanctuary. Frollo assents to the plan, and is so absorbed by it that for the first time he dismisses his brother's plea for money (though he relents at the last moment) and even his threat to become a truand. They never meet again.

The description of the truands' tavern, their silent march on Notre-Dame at midnight, the gathering momentum of the action, all takes place in the dark, and latterly even the moon disappears behind the clouds. The whole set piece is typical of the chiaroscuro so dear to the Romantics, but leads to a fatal misunderstanding. Keeping watch for the girl's safety, all that Quasimodo knows is that he is surrounded by an armed crowd attempting to break in, and thus, as he supposes, hostile to Esmeralda. His heroic and single-handed defence is based so utterly on this mistake that when the king's men turn up to put down the insurrection and seize the alleged witch he hails them as rescuers.

However, before Phoebus and his men arrive to crush the truands, they have to be sent there. Once again the king holds the stage, but this time not at all incognito. In his royal fortress of the Bastille, busily dispatching affairs of State, his presence tacitly invites the reader of Hugo's day to look into what was an indefinite future in 1482 but an immediate past in 1831. The usual themes are all there: the king's obsessive concern for cheeseparing in expenses, the casual infliction of torture on objects of his displeasure, the superstition. All are as much trademarks of Louis XI as his pet oath '*Pasquedieu!*' and his false bonhomie in addressing members of his entourage as 'Compère'. All this, of course, runs parallel in time with the preparation and mounting of the truands' assault, and leaves the reader uncertain about what will happen. News of the insurrection reaches the king in bits; at first it is his physician, Coictier, who reports a popular uprising against the bailiff of the Palais. The news that the people are helping to bring about Louis's ambition to curb the power of the numerous feudal lords in favour of centralized royal government gives him a momentary explosion of delight, which lasts long enough to save Gringoire, arrested and brought in as a suspected truand, from execution.

Throughout the chapter, witnessing all that takes place, including the visit to the cage, are two of the men from Ghent, Guillaume Rym and Jacques Coppenole, part of the Flemish embassy described at length at the beginning of the book, and here presented as agents of Louis's policy. By now the fire lit by Quasimodo is clearly visible from the Bastille, and Louis leads the Flemings into a discussion on revolution. Coppenole, rather than the more cautious Rym, speaks his mind. He reminds the king that only six years earlier Swiss peasants had defeated the flower of Burgundian nobility at Grandson, so class has nothing to do with victory. Louis objects that the Swiss were fighting a battle, whereas this is a popular insurrection which he can crush whenever he chooses. Coppenole replies that if this is so, the hour of the people in France has not yet struck. Pressed by the king, and speaking in and of the fortress whose destruction gave the name Bastille a different resonance for ever on 14 July 1789, he answers firmly in prophetic terms. Pressed to explain how to organize a revolt, he, who had already humiliated the Lady of Flanders by having two of her highest dignitaries publicly executed at Ghent, speaks of finding a popular grievance and then exploiting it. As always he speaks as a man of the people who knows how they feel. Louis's remedy for everything is repression, and he cannot believe that the common people can ever defeat central authority. The irony of such sentiments in 1831 hardly needs comment.

The king's mood abruptly changes when more recent information reaches him about the disturbance. He learns that it is the very cathedral of his patroness, Notre-Dame, which is being besieged, and that it is thus not the bailiff but he himself who is under attack. His response is to order immediate and ruthless repression by the forces available. When the Provost of Paris mistakenly says that the people want to violate the gypsy's sanctuary in order to hang her themselves, the royal solution is simple: destroy the people, hang the witch, do not delay. It is at this point that the royal troops are hailed by Quasimodo as rescuers.

Irony and misunderstanding continue. Gringoire persuades the girl to flee from the sanctuary cell (with her goat). Quasimodo and the royal searchers find the cell empty, and Esmeralda only realizes that she is victim of a subterfuge when Gringoire makes off with the goat, leaving her alone with Frollo, and the rescue takes her no further than the Grève. Frollo, now raving mad and made more so by the news of Jehan's death, indirectly caused by his rejection of his brother, has to bear the mark of Cain to add to all his other crimes.

The last act of the drama is bloody; trusting in the *sachette*'s well-known hatred of gypsies, Frollo hands Esmeralda over to her while he goes off to report to the soldiers where she is to be found. He too is mistaken. Hatred gives way to mutual recognition as mother and daughter are at last reunited, for a few minutes only, after fifteen years' of separation. The last misunderstanding is fatal: hearing the voice of her beloved and totally indifferent Phoebus, Esmeralda gives herself away by crying out to him. As the sun comes up after all the violence of the long night before, she is hanged; her mother, breaking out of her cell for the first time in fifteen years, dies at the foot of the scaffold; Frollo, watching from a tower of Notre-Dame, exults, only to be pushed to his death by Quasimodo, who sees everything from a vantage point nearby; and all this within a few moments. The poetic epilogue at Montfaucon adds nothing to the story except to confirm the fidelity and humble devotion of the hunchback.

The dismal concept of 'ΑΝΑΓΚΗ excludes any notion of justice; things happen because they must. The image of spider and fly is adequate for what Frollo feels to be his situation, but hungry spiders catching food in the way they have been programmed to do so command little human sympathy. There is no question of tragic flaws in otherwise virtuous characters, like that of an Oedipus, which can, however painfully, in the end be redeemed. Human justice, in small things and in large, is shown in the book to be a cruel and arbitrary farce, punishment a spectacle, poverty a crime. The most notable omission from the book is Christianity: odd, to say the least, in a long work with a specifically Christian title. There are plenty of references to Scripture, to the liturgy, to things ecclesiastical in general, but they are as little relevant to a God of mercy and goodness as are the lawyers and their procedure to equity and justice. Any kind of spiritual content there may have been in fifteenth-century religion is totally obscured in the book by talk of placating Notre-Dame with a fine silver statue or putting the little baby shoes on a statue of the infant Jesus in some church. Even the kind souls, the *haudriettes*, gloat at the thought of burning the infant Quasimodo. Christianity and Catholicism, when they are not actually denounced, are so much décor. For the liberal Catholic and fervent monarchist the young Hugo had been, this is a more important development than for a genuine sceptic such as, for example, the fictional Gringoire is made out to be. Frollo's final dying cry of 'Damnation!' is a shorter version of the *sachette*'s bewildered railing at a supposedly good God as the hangman comes to take away her daughter after their brief reunion. In dramatic terms there are many occasions throughout the book when a *deus ex machina* intervenes to prevent imminent disaster, but it is precisely these temporary reprieves which are shown in the end to have been literary devices rather than steps to a less gloomy ending.

From the very first the element in the book which attracted most attention was the grotesque figure of Quasimodo.

Apart from the inherent improbability that gypsies, or anyone else, would in the late Middle Ages have kept such a monster baby alive for four years, he is the only one of the principal characters to evolve in a positive way. The single tear he sheds on the pillory, the first in his life, is a reaction to a wholly gratuitous act of kindness. He owes his very life to Claude Frollo, who adopted him out of kindness and whose devoted slave he became, but to Esmeralda he owes the first stirrings of moral autonomy. Rescuing her, defending her, he develops a human dignity of which his physical ugliness had wholly deprived him hitherto. The second time he weeps is a flood, not a single tear, as he sees the death of the only two persons he had ever loved. The Romantics, particularly Hugo in the preface to *Cromwell*, had made much of the grotesque as an integral part of real life, and thus of literature, as against Classical insistence on propriety, *bienséance*. It would be hard to create a figure more grotesque than Quasimodo, and it is pointless to protest if readers have been more impressed by him than by other aspects of the novel, or if it is he who has inspired popular versions for stage and screen.

Popularity, an appeal to the more basic emotions of as large a public as possible, was something Hugo could not afford to despise and for which he had a natural gift. The drama or novel—and in particular Quasimodo—are, however, only part of what *Notre-Dame de Paris* offers, as Hugo himself underlines in his Note to the edition of 1832. The ideas and 'message' of this long novel are much richer than the more obviously striking and melodramatic plot suggests. The cathedral itself is the focus for studying what Hugo sees as the inevitable and recurrent cycles of human evolution—repression, by religious or secular authority, giving way to freedom as the people's hour strikes. It would be as wrong to see in the social and historical ideas expressed in the book its real purpose as it would be to go no deeper than the story. Unlike the cathedral, the book is not the work of many hands, over many years, but the fusion of many disparate elements from many sources into a creation of great density and complexity, into which a poet has breathed life. The unifying factor is Hugo himself, and the epic dimension he missed in Walter Scott is his own vision of mankind's destiny, subsequently presented in prose and poetry for the rest of his working life. *Notre-Dame de Paris* is a monument to Romanticism at its most colourful and vigorous.

NOTE ON THE TEXT

THE text used for this translation is that of the definitive, or eighth, edition of 1832, as it appears in the excellent edition by Jacques Seebacher, published in the *Bibliothèque de la Pléiade* collection by Gallimard (Paris, 1975). (The volume also contains *Les Travailleurs de la mer*.) The critical apparatus is particularly valuable, presenting clearly the chronology of the novel's composition as well as the *reliquat*, that is, Hugo's notes on the reading he undertook in preparation for the book, now preserved at the Bibliothèque Nationale in Paris. Seebacher's own notes and table of variants have been indispensable.

SELECT BIBLIOGRAPHY

1. *Life and Works*

J. P. Houston, *Victor Hugo*, Twayne's World Author Series, revised edition (G. K. Hall, Boston, Mass., 1988).

André Maurois, *Victor Hugo* (Cape, London, 1956).

Joanna Richardson, *Victor Hugo* (Weidenfeld & Nicolson, London, 1976).

2. *The Novels*

Victor Brombert, *Victor Hugo and the Visionary Novel* (Harvard UP, Cambridge, Mass. and London, 1984).

Kathryn M. Grossman, *The Early Novels of Victor Hugo* (Droz, Geneva, 1986).

3. *Specific Aspects*

Jean Mallion, *Victor Hugo et l'art architectural* (PUF, Paris, 1962).

C. W. Thompson, *Victor Hugo and the Graphic Arts* (Droz, Geneva, 1970).

See also two recent volumes in the World's Classics series:

Victor Hugo, *The Last Day of a Condemned Man*, translated and edited by G. Woollen.

Walter Scott, *Quentin Durward*, edited by Susan Manning.

A CHRONOLOGY OF VICTOR HUGO

1802   26 February: born at Besançon.

1822   Marries Adèle Foucher.

1823   Publication of first novel, *Han d'Islande*. Publishes review of Scott's *Quentin Durward*, translated into French soon after first publication in English.

1824   Publication of ode 'La bande noire' against vandalism in general.

1825   Attends coronation of Charles X at Reims; on the way deplores ruinous state of cathedral and abbey at Soissons.

1826   Publication of novel *Bug-Jargal* and of collection *Odes et ballades*.

1827   Publication of unactable play *Cromwell*, with its long preface, a stirring manifesto of Romanticism.

1828   Contract with Gosselin for *Notre-Dame*.

1829   Publication of *Les Orientales*, followed by *Dernier jour d'un condamné*.

1830   February: first night of *Hernani* provokes a riot in the theatre. 25 July: work finally begins on *Notre-Dame*, interrupted almost at once by July Revolution (27–9 July), which sends Charles X into exile, and by the birth of a daughter (28 July). In full production by September.

1831   16 March: publication of *Notre-Dame* (less the eventual Book Five).

1832   March: publishes article 'Guerre aux démolisseurs!' November: *Le Roi s'amuse* banned as seditious after one performance (finally performed 1882). December: definitive edition of *Notre-Dame* published by Renduel.

1835   January: appointed to eight-man committee on monuments set up by the government.

1836   November: *La Esmeralda* performed at Paris Opéra, with libretto by Hugo and music by Louise Bertin.

1838   Appointed to new sixteen-man committee on monuments and arts, together with Prosper Mérimée and Montalembert, and remains a very active member until 1848. The preservation of the Hôtel de Sens and acquisition of the Hôtel de Cluny are attributed to him (in 1843).

1841   Elected to Académie Française (after four unsuccessful attempts).

1843   Failure of play *Les Burgraves* ends his theatrical career. Accidental drowning of his favourite daughter Léopoldine and her husband at Villequier the same year causes him such grief that he writes nothing creative for nine years.

1845   Created a peer of France.

1848   Revolution expels Louis-Philippe.

1851   December: Hugo, at first favourable to the Republic, flees to Brussels as he becomes more and more hostile to Louis-Napoleon (who proclaimed himself President and a year later Emperor Napoleon III).

1852   Leaves Brussels for Jersey.

1853   Publishes *Les Châtiments*, biting satirical poems against Napoleon III.

1855   Obliged to leave Jersey after imprudent political activity; moves to Guernsey.

1859   Publication of first series of epic *Légende des siècles*.

1862   Publication of *Les Misérables*.

1864   Publication of critical study *William Shakespeare*.

1866   Publication of *Les Travailleurs de la mer*, a novel set in the Channel Islands.

1868   Adèle, his long-separated wife, dies in Brussels.

1869   Publication of *L'Homme qui rit*, a novel set in seventeenth-century England.

1870   5 September: Hugo returns from exile the day after the proclamation of the Third Republic, following the defeat at Sedan and eventual exile of Napoleon III.

1871   Communards pull down the column in the Place Vendôme despite Hugo's protests; he continues to campaign for an amnesty for the communards.

1874   Publication of *Quatre-vingt-treize*, a novel on the Terror of 1793.

1876   Elected senator.

1877   Publication of second series of *Légende des siècles* and *Histoire d'un crime, i*, a violent attack on Napoleon III, written in 1851.

1878   Publication of *Histoire d'un crime, ii*.

1883   Publication of *Légende des siècles, iii*.
1884   Last recorded intervention in favour of conserva-
       tion, this time of Mont Saint-Michel.
1885   22 May: dies in Paris. 1 June: interred in the
       Panthéon with great public ceremony.

The events and publications recorded above take almost no
account of the collections of poems which were published
throughout his life, but do, on the other hand, stress his
interest in conservation and politics.

Notre-Dame de Paris

TABLE OF CONTENTS

BOOK FIVE

BOOK SIX

BOOK SEVEN

BOOK EIGHT

BOOK NINE

NOTE TO THE FIRST EDITION

SOME years ago the author of this book was going round Notre-Dame, or, more exactly, prying about, when he found in an obscure recess in one of the towers this word carved by hand on the wall: ΑΝΑΓΚΗ.*

These Greek capitals, black with age and quite deeply incised into the stone, certain characteristics of Gothic calligraphy somehow stamped on their form and attitude, as if to reveal that it was a medieval hand that had written them, above all the dismal sense of inevitability conveyed by them, made a deep impression on the author.

He wondered, he tried to guess, who might have been the soul in anguish unwilling to leave this world before branding the mark of crime or misfortune on the old church's brow.

Since then the wall has been distempered or scraped (I forget now which) and the inscription has disappeared. That is how the wonderful churches of the Middle Ages have been treated for nearly two hundred years now. Mutilations have come upon them from every side, from within and without. The priest distempers them, the architect scrapes them, then the people arrive and pull them down.

So, apart from the fragile memory which the author of this book devotes to it here, nothing today remains of the mysterious word carved on the gloomy tower of Notre-Dame, nothing of the unknown destiny which it summed up with such melancholy. The man who wrote that word on the wall has been erased, several centuries ago, from the midst of the generations, the word in its turn has been erased from the wall of the church, the church itself may soon perhaps be erased from the earth.

This book was written about that word.

February 1831

NOTE ADDED TO
THE DEFINITIVE EDITION (1832)

THIS edition was mistakenly announced as due to be expanded by several *new* chapters. They should have been called *unpublished*. Indeed, if by new is understood *newly written*, the chapters added to this edition are not *new*. They were written at the same time as the rest of the work, they date from the same period and originated from the same thinking; they have always been part of the manuscript of *Notre-Dame de Paris*. Moreover, it would be beyond the author's comprehension that new chapters should later be added to a work of this kind. That cannot be done at will. A novel, according to him, is born, necessarily as it were, with all its chapters; a drama is born with all its scenes. You must not suppose that there is anything arbitrary about the number of parts of which this whole is composed, the mysterious microcosm you call drama or novel. Grafts or welds do not take well on works of this nature, which must spring forth in a single burst and stay just as they are. Once the work is complete, there must be no second thoughts, no touching up. Once the sex of the work, virile or not, has been recognized and proclaimed, once the child has uttered its first cry, it is born, there it is, that is how it is made, neither father nor mother can do anything about it, it belongs to the air and sunlight, let it live or die as it is. Is your book a failure? Too bad. Do not add a chapter to a book that is a failure. Is it incomplete? It should have been made complete at its begetting. Is your tree gnarled? You will never straighten it. Is your novel consumptive? Is your novel not viable? You will never give it the breath it lacks. Was your drama born lame? Believe me, do not put a wooden leg on it.

The author, then, considers it particularly important that the public should be aware that the chapters added here were not written specially for this reprinting. If they were not published in previous editions of this book, the reason is quite simple. At the moment when *Notre-Dame de Paris* was being printed for the first time, the file containing these three chapters went astray. They had either to be rewritten or dispensed with. The author considered that the only two of these chapters of significant length were chapters on art and history, which in no way affected the basic drama or novel, that the public would not notice their absence, and that he alone, as author, would be party to the secret of the omission. He decided to let it go. Also, if all is to be admitted, his laziness recoiled from the task of rewriting three missing chapters. He would have found it quicker to write a new novel.

Today these chapters have turned up again, and he takes this first opportunity to put them back where they belong.

So here now is his work in its entirety, as he imagined it, as he wrote it, good or bad, lasting or flimsy, but as he wants it to be.

No doubt these rediscovered chapters will be deemed of little worth in the eyes of those people, otherwise most judicious, who looked in *Notre-Dame de Paris* only for the drama, for the novel. But there may be other readers who have not found it a waste of time to study the aesthetic and philosophical ideas hidden within the book, and who, while reading *Notre-Dame de Paris*, have taken willing pleasure in sorting out beneath the novel something other than the novel and following, if we may be allowed the somewhat ambitious expressions, the historian's system and the artist's aim through the poet's creation, such as it is.

It is especially for those readers that the chapters added to this edition will make *Notre-Dame de Paris* complete, always supposing that *Notre-Dame de Paris* is worth completing.

The author expresses and develops in one of these chapters, on the present decadence of architecture and the death, according to him, today almost inevitable, of that sovereign art, an opinion, unfortunately, deeply rooted within him and the subject of much reflection. He feels a need, however, to say here that he dearly wishes that the future should one day prove him wrong. He knows that art, in all its forms, can have every hope in the new generation, whose still-budding genius can be heard springing up in our studios. The seed is in the furrow, the harvest will certainly be rich. His only fear is, and the reason will be seen in the second volume of this edition, that the sap may have withdrawn from this old soil of architecture which for so many centuries was that art's richest ground.

There is, though, in young artists today so much life, power, and, so to speak, predestination, that at the present time, particularly in our schools of architecture, the teachers, who are odious, are producing, not only without realizing it, but even quite despite themselves, pupils who are excellent: just the opposite of Horace's potter, who dreamed of amphorae and produced cooking-pots. *Currit rota, urceus exit* [The wheel turns, out comes a pot].*

But in any case, whatever the future of architecture may be, however our young architects may one day resolve the question of their art, while we wait for new monuments, let us preserve the old ones. Let us inspire the nation, if possible, with a love of our national architecture. Such, the author declares, is one of the main aims of this book; such is one of the main aims of his life.

Notre-Dame de Paris may have opened up some true perspectives on the art of the Middle Ages, on that wonderful art unknown up till now to some or, what is still worse, misunderstood by others. But the author is far from regarding as accomplished the task which he has voluntarily imposed on himself. On more than one occasion he has already pleaded the cause of our old architecture, he has already spoken out loudly to denounce many a profanation, many a demolition, many an impiety. He will not tire in so doing. He has pledged himself to return frequently to this subject, and he will return to it. He will be as tireless in defending our historic buildings as the iconoclasts in our schools and academies are relentless in attacking them. For it is distressing to see into what hands the architecture of the Middle Ages has fallen, and the way in which the plaster-sloppers of the present day treat the ruin of that great art. It is even shameful for us, intelligent men, who can see what they are doing and are content just to boo. We are not speaking here simply of what goes on in the provinces, but of what is being done in Paris, on our own doorsteps, beneath our windows, in this great town, this cultured town, in the city of the press, the spoken word, ideas. In conclusion to this Note, we cannot resist the need to report a few of these acts of vandalism which every day are planned, debated, begun, continued, and quietly completed before our eyes, before the eyes of the artistic public in Paris, in the face of criticism disconcerted by such audacity. They have just demolished the archbishop's palace,* a building in poor taste, no great harm done; but together with the archbishop's palace they demolished that of the bishop, a rare fourteenth-century fragment which the demolition architect was unable to distinguish from the rest. He tore out the wheat with the tares; it is all the same to him. There is talk of razing the admirable chapel at Vincennes, so that the stones can be used to build some fortification or other, which Daumesnil* never needed for all that. While they repair and restore at vast expense the Palais Bourbon,* that wretched barn, they let the equinoctial gales smash in the magnificent stained-glass windows of the Sainte-Chapelle. For some days now there has been scaffolding on the tower of Saint-Jacques-de-la-Boucherie;* and one of these mornings the pickaxe will set to. They found some mason to build a little white house between the venerable towers of the Palais de Justice. They found another to castrate Saint-Germain-des-Prés,* the feudal abbey with its three steeples. They will find another, have no doubt about it, to pull down Saint-Germain-l'Auxerrois.* All these masons claim to be architects, they are paid by the prefecture or the privy purse, and wear green coats.* Any harm that false taste can do to true taste, they do. At the moment of writing—deplorable sight!—one of them is in charge of the Tuileries, one of them is slashing Philibert Delorme* right in the middle of his face, and it is assuredly not one of the lesser scandals of our time to see how shamelessly this gentleman's lumpish architecture is sprawled right across one of the most delicate façades of the Renaissance!

Paris, 20 October 1832

BOOK ONE

I

THE GREAT HALL

JUST three hundred and forty-eight years, six months, and nineteen days ago today* Parisians woke to the sound of all the bells pealing out within the triple precinct of City, University, and Town.

The sixth of January 1482 is not, however, a day commemorated by history. There was nothing very special about the event which thus launched the bells and the people of Paris into movement from early in the morning. It was not an attack by Picards or Burgundians,* not a procession of relics, not a student revolt in the Laas vineyard,* not 'our aforesaid most dread sovereign Lord the King' making his entry, not even the fine spectacle of men and women being hanged for robbery at the Palais de Justice in Paris. Nor was it the arrival of some embassy, a frequent occurrence in the fifteenth century, all bedizened and plumed. It was hardly two days since the last cavalcade of that kind, the Flemish embassy sent to conclude the marriage of the Dauphin and Marguerite of Flanders, had entered Paris, much to the annoyance of the Cardinal de Bourbon, who, to please the King, had had to put on a welcoming smile for this rustic bunch of Flemish burgomasters and treat them, in his Hôtel de Bourbon, to 'a very fine morality, satire, and farce', while torrential rain soaked the magnificent tapestries hung at his door.

What, in the words of Jean de Troyes,* 'excited all the people of Paris' on 6 January was the twofold celebration, combined since time immemorial, of the Feast of the Epiphany and the Feast of Fools.*

That day there was to be a bonfire on the Place de Grève, a maypole set up at the chapel of Braque,* and a mystery play at the Palais de Justice. The news had been publicly proclaimed with trumpet calls at all the crossroads by the Provost's men, in their handsome tunics of purple camlet,* with big white crosses on the front.

From early morning the crowd of townsfolk, men and women, had begun to come in from all directions, leaving houses and shops closed up, making their way towards one of the three appointed places. Everyone had made a choice, some for the bonfire, some for the maypole, some for the mystery. It must be said, in praise of the age-old good sense of curious Parisians, that the majority of this crowd was making for the bonfire, which came very seasonably, or the mystery, to be performed in the sheltered and enclosed Great Hall of the Palais, and that, by common consent, the curious left the poor maypole, with its scanty garlands, to shiver all alone under the January sky in the cemetery of the chapel of Braque.

The flood of people was particularly dense in the roads leading to the Palais de Justice, because it was known that the Flemish ambassadors, who had arrived two days earlier, intended to be present at the performance of the mystery play and the election of the Pope of Fools, which was also to take place in the Great Hall.

It was no easy matter that day to gain admission to the Great Hall, though at the time it was reputed to be the largest enclosed and covered space in the world. (It is true that Sauval had not yet measured the great hall of the castle at Montargis.) To onlookers watching from their windows the Place du Palais, blocked with people, presented the appearance of a vast sea into which a dozen streets, like so many river mouths, continually disgorged fresh streams of heads. The waves of this human flood, constantly spreading, broke against the corners of houses projecting here and there like headlands into the irregular basin formed by the Place. In the centre of the tall, Gothic[1] façade of the Palais

---

[1] The word *Gothic* in the sense in which it is generally used is quite improper, but firmly established. We accept it therefore and adopt it, like everyone else, to denote the architecture of the second half of the Middle Ages, of which the pointed arch is the principle, in succession to the architecture of the earlier period, which derived from the round arch. V.H.

was the grand staircase; up and down it flowed continuously a double stream, breaking on the central flight of steps,
and then spreading out in broad waves over its two lateral
flights. This grand staircase, as I say, poured ceaselessly
into the Place like a cascade into a lake. The shouts of
laughter, the tramping of these thousands of feet, set up a
great noise and clamour. Now and then this noise and
clamour grew louder, the current driving the whole crowd
towards the grand staircase ebbed, broke into turbulence
and eddies. It was an archer thumping somebody, or the
horse of one of the provost-sergeants kicking out to restore
order—an admirable tradition bequeathed by the Provost's
men to the constabulary, by the constabulary to the
mounted police, and by the mounted police to our modern
Paris gendarmerie.

At doors, windows, skylights, on the roofs, swarmed thousands of citizens, with good, solid, honest faces, just looking
at the Palais, looking at the throng, and perfectly satisfied
to do so, for plenty of people in Paris are quite content with
the spectacle of spectators, and curiosity is easily aroused by
a wall behind which something is going on.

If it could be given to us, men of 1830, to mingle in
thought with these fifteenth-century Parisians and join
them as they go, tugged, jostled, shoved into this immense
hall in the Palais, so cramped on that 6 January 1482, the
spectacle would not prove to be without interest or appeal,
and everything around us would be so old as to strike us as
a novelty.

With the reader's permission we shall try to recreate in
imagination the impression he would have shared with us
as he crossed the threshold of the Great Hall amid this
throng of people dressed in surcoat, tunic, and kirtle.

First of all we feel a buzzing in our ears, our eyes are
dazzled. Above our heads a double ogive vault, panelled
with wooden carvings, painted sky-blue, sprinkled with
golden fleurs-de-lys, beneath our feet a marble pavement
with alternate slabs of black and white. A few paces away
stands an enormous pillar, then another and another; seven
pillars in all down the length of the hall, supporting in the

middle of its width the springing of the double vaults.
Round the first four pillars stand traders' stalls, sparkling
with glass and tinsel; round the last three are set oaken
benches, worn smooth and polished by the breeches of
litigants and the robes of lawyers. All round the hall, along
the lofty walls, between the doors, between the windows,
between the pillars, is an endless range of statues of every
king of France since Pharamond;* the do-nothing kings,
arms slack and eyes downcast; the valorous warrior kings,
head and hands raised boldly up to heaven. Then, in the
tall pointed windows, stained glass of countless hues; at the
spacious arches leading to the hall, finely carved and splendid doors; and the whole, vaults, pillars, walls, window
frames, panelling, doors, statues, all covered from top to
bottom with splendid gold and blue illumination, already
slightly faded by the time we are looking at it, and almost
completely hidden beneath dust and cobwebs in the year
of grace 1549 when Du Breul* still admired it as tradition
demanded.

Now imagine this vast oblong hall, lit by the wan light of
a January day, invaded by a motley, noisy crowd drifting
round the walls and swirling round the pillars, and you will
already have a vague idea of the whole scene which we shall
try to depict in more precise and curious detail.

It is certain that if Ravaillac* had not assassinated Henri
IV there would have been no documents from Ravaillac's
trial to be deposited in the registry of the Palais de Justice;
no accomplices with an interest in making the said documents disappear; hence no arsonists obliged, for want of
any better method, to burn down the registry in order to
burn the documents and to burn down the Palais de Justice
in order to burn the registry; in short, therefore, no great
fire in 1618. The old Palais would still be standing with its
old Great Hall; I could say to the reader 'Go and see it',
and we should both be spared the trouble, I of composing,
he of reading, any detailed description of it. Which proves
a new truth: great events have incalculable consequences.

It is true that Ravaillac may quite possibly have had no
accomplices, and then that his accomplices, if perchance he

had any, had nothing to do with the fire of 1618. There are two other, quite plausible explanations for it. First, the great fiery star, a foot wide and a cubit high, which fell, as everyone knows, from the sky on to the Palais, after midnight on 7 March. Secondly Théophile's* quatrain:

> Certes ce fut un triste jeu,
> Quand à Paris Dame Justice,
> Pour avoir mangé trop d'épice,
> Se mit tout le palais en feu.

[It was indeed poor sport when Dame Justice in Paris took too much spicy food/in bribes and set all her palate/Palais ablaze.]

Whatever one may think of this triple explanation, political, physical, poetical, for the conflagration of the Palais de Justice in 1618, the one unfortunately certain fact is the conflagration. Very little remains today, thanks to that catastrophe, and above all thanks to the different and successive restorations, which finished off what had been spared of that first residence of the kings of France, of that palace older than the Louvre, already so old in the time of Philippe le Bel* that a search was made for traces of the magnificent buildings put up by King Robert and described by Helgaldus. Almost everything has disappeared. What has become of the bedroom in the chancellery where St Louis 'consummated his marriage'? The garden where he dispensed justice, 'wearing a camlet tunic, a sleeveless linsey-woolsey surcoat, with a black sendal cloak on top, reclining on carpets with Joinville'? Where is the Emperor Sigismond's room? That of Charles IV? Of John Lackland? Where is the staircase from which Charles VI promulgated his Edict of Mercy? The slab on which Marcel, in the Dauphin's presence, murdered Robert de Clermont and the maréchal de Champagne? The wicket where the bulls of the anti-pope Benedict* were torn up, and from whence those who had brought them set out again, mockingly decked in cope and mitre, to make *amende honorable* right through Paris? And the Great Hall, with its gilding, its azure colouring, pointed arches, statues, pillars, the immense vault fretted with carvings? And the Gilded Chamber? And the stone lion standing at the door, head down and tail between his legs, like the lions of Solomon's throne, in the humbly submissive posture befitting strength before justice? And the fine doors? And stained-glass windows? And the chased ironwork which made Biscornette* lose heart? And the delicate joinery of Du Hancy?* What have the years, what have men done to these marvels? What have they given us in place of it all, all that Gaulish history, all that Gothic art? The heavy surbased arches of Monsieur de Brosse,* the clumsy architect of the Portail Saint-Gervais, so much for art; and as for history, we have the garrulous memories of the great pillar, still echoing with the Patrus'* gossip.

It is not very much—let us return to the real Great Hall of the real old Palais.

One end of this gigantic parallelogram contained the famous marble table, so long, broad, and thick, according to the old registers, in a style to whet Gargantua's appetite, that never had there been seen 'such a slab of marble anywhere in the world'. The other end contained the chapel where Louis XI had had himself sculptured kneeling before the Virgin, and to which he had transferred, heedless of the two niches left empty in the row of royal statues, those of Charlemagne and St Louis, two saints who, he supposed, must enjoy much favour in heaven as kings of France. This chapel, still new, its construction dating from barely six years before, was all conceived with that delightful taste for delicate architecture, wonderful sculpture, precise and deeply incised tracery which in France marks the end of the Gothic age and survives until about the middle of the six-teenth century in the magical fantasies of the Renaissance. The little open-work rose-window pierced over the door-way was in particular a masterpiece of lightness and grace; it looked like a star woven from lace.

In the middle of the hall, opposite the great door, a tribune of gold brocade had been set up against the wall, with its own entrance contrived through a window in the passage leading to the Gilded Chamber; this was for the Flemish envoys and other important persons invited to the performance of the mystery play.

According to custom the mystery was to be performed actually on the marble table. It had been prepared to that end early that morning; its rich slab of marble, scored by the heels of the law clerks, bore a frame of scaffolding of a considerable height, the upper surface of which, visible from every part of the hall, was to serve as the stage, while the inside, screened by tapestries, was to be used as a dressing room for the actors. A ladder, artlessly placed outside, afforded communication between stage and dressing room, and its steep rungs had to serve for exits as well as entrances. No character so unexpected, no twist of plot, no dramatic suspense but had to climb this ladder. Innocent and venerable infancy of art and stage machinery!

Four sergeants of the bailiff of the Palais, whose duty was to stand guard over all popular entertainments, whether holidays or executions, stood at the four corners of the marble table.

The play was not due to commence until the last stroke of twelve came from the great clock in the Palais. That was certainly late for a theatrical performance, but the time had to be set to suit the ambassadors.

Now all this multitude had been waiting since morning. A good number of these honest spectators had been shivering since daybreak in front of the great steps of the Palais; some even claimed to have spent the night lying in the great doorway to be sure of entering first. The crowd grew denser all the time, and like water overflowing its level, began rising up the walls, surging round the pillars, spilling over the entablatures, cornices, window ledges, over all the architectural projections, all the protrusions of the sculptures. So discomfort, impatience, boredom, the liberated feeling of a day devoted to licence and folly, the quarrels continually breaking out over too sharp a nudge or a kick from a hob-nailed boot, the tedium of a long wait, all this well before the hour appointed for the ambassadors' arrival, lent a sour and bitter note to the clamour of this mass of people cribbed, cabined, confined, trampled, suffocated. All that could be heard were curses on the Flemings, the Provost of Merchants, Cardinal de Bourbon, the bailiff of the Palais, Madame

Marguerite of Austria, the sergeants with their wands, the cold, the heat, the bad weather, the Bishop of Paris, the Pope of Fools, the pillars, the statues, this closed door, that open window, all to the great amusement of the bands of students and lackeys scattered through the mass, who stirred into all this discontent their own teasing and mischief, adding pinpricks to exacerbate the general ill humour.

Among others there was a group of these merry devils who, after smashing the glass, had boldly ensconced themselves on the entablature of a window, and thence stared and jeered outside and inside in turn at the crowd in the hall and the crowd in the Place outside. From their gestures of mimicry, their roars of laughter, the banter and jeering cries they exchanged with one another from one end of the hall to the other, it was obvious that these young clerks did not share the boredom and weariness of those present, and knew very well how to turn the sight before their eyes into an entertainment for their private pleasure which gave them patience to wait for the other.

'Upon my soul, it's you, *Joannes Frollo de Molendino*,' one of them cried out to a little fair-haired devil, with a comely, mischievous face, clinging to the carved acanthus leaves of a capital. 'You are well named Jehan of the Mill; your arms and legs look like four mill-sails turning in the wind. How long have you been here?'

'By the devil's mercy,' Joannes Frollo replied; 'more than four hours now, and I have every hope of having them counted against my time in purgatory. I heard the eight singing-men of the King of Sicily* intone the opening verse of the seven o'clock High Mass from the Sainte-Chapelle.'

'Fine singers,' retorted the other; 'their voices are even sharper than their pointed caps! Before he endowed a mass for St John, the King should have found out whether the worthy St John enjoys Latin chanted with a Provençal accent.'

'He did it to give work to those damned singers of the King of Sicily!' screeched an old woman in the crowd below the window. 'I ask you! A thousand *livres parisis* for a mass! And paid for from the tax on salt-water fish sold in the Paris market, what's more!'

'Hold your peace, old woman,' put in a stout and stately individual holding his nose as he stood beside the fishwife; 'a mass certainly had to be endowed. Surely you didn't want the King to fall sick again?'

'Bravely spoken, Sir Gilles Lecornu, master skinner and furrier of the King's wardrobe!' cried the little student clinging to the capital.

A roar of laughter from all the students greeted the unfortunate name of the poor skinner-furrier of the King's wardrobe.

'Lecornu! Gilles Lecornu!' said some.

'*Cornutus et hirsutus* [Horned and hairy],' added another.

'Eh, no doubt,' went on the little demon on the capital. 'What is there to laugh at? There is his Honour Gilles Lecornu, brother of Maître Jacques Lecornu, provost of the King's household, son of Maître Mahiet Lecornu, head porter of the Bois de Vincennes, all burghers of Paris, all married from father to son!'

The merriment increased. The stout furrier, without answering a word, strove to escape the eyes gazing at him from every side, but he sweated and puffed in vain; like a wedge being driven into wood, the only result of his efforts was to clamp still more tightly between his neighbours' shoulders his great apoplectic face, purple with vexation and rage.

Finally one of these neighbours, short, stout, and respectable like him, came to his aid:

'How abominable! Students talking like that to a respectable citizen! In my time they would have been thrashed with a big stick and then burned with it.'

The whole band burst out: 'Ho there! Who is singing that song? Who is that screechowl of ill omen?'

'There, I know who he is,' said one; 'he's Maître Andry Musnier.'

'Because he's one of the four official booksellers of the University!' said the other.

'Everything in that dump goes in fours,' cried a third; 'four nations, four faculties, four holidays, four proctors, four electors, four booksellers.'

'Well then,' Jehan Frollo put in, 'we'll have to play four kinds of merry hell with them.'

'Musnier, we'll burn your books.'

'Musnier, we'll thrash your lackey.'

'Musnier, we'll rumple your wife.'

'Good stout Mademoiselle Oudarde.'

'As fresh and merry as if she were a widow.'

'Devil take you!' muttered Maître Andry Musnier.

'Maître Andry,' Jehan went on, still hanging on to his capital, 'shut up, or I'll drop on your head!'

Maître Andry looked up, seemed for a moment to be gauging the height of the pillar, the weight of the young rascal, mentally multiplied that weight by the square of the velocity, and shut up.

Jehan, master of the battlefield, pressed on in triumph: 'I'd do it too, even if I am an archdeacon's brother!'

'Fine fellows, our University people! Didn't even see that our privileges were respected on a day like this! Why, there's a maypole and a bonfire in the Town; a mystery play, Pope of Fools, and a Flemish embassy in the City; and in the University not a thing!'

'Yet the Place Maubert is big enough!' replied one of the clerks stationed on the window ledge.

'Down with the rector, the electors and the proctors!' cried Joannes.

'We must make a bonfire this evening in the Champ-Gaillard,' the other continued, 'with Maître Andry's books.'

'And the scribes' desks!'

'And the beadles' wands!'

'And the deans' spittoons!'

'And the proctors' sideboards!'

'And the electors' chests!'

'And the rector's stools!'

'Down with them all!' little Jehan chimed in with the chorus; 'down with Maître Andry, the beadles and the scribes, the theologians, doctors, and canon lawyers; the proctors, the electors, and the rector!'

'This is the end of the world then,' murmured Andry, stopping up his ears.

'Talk of the rector! Here he comes, down in the Place!' cried one of those on the window ledge.

Everyone tried to turn round and face the Place.

'Is that really our venerable rector, Maître Thibaut?' asked Jehan Frollo du Moulin, who could not see what was going on outside from the inside pillar to which he clung.

'Yes, yes,' all the others answered, 'it's him, it's him all right, Maître Thibaut, the rector.'

It was indeed the rector and all the University dignitaries going in procession to meet the embassy, and at that moment crossing the Place du Palais. The students, pressing at the window, greeted them as they passed by with sarcastic sallies and ironic applause. The rector, riding at the head of his company, took the first broadside: it was a rough one.

'Good-day, Monsieur le Recteur! Hello there! Good-day to you!'

'How did he manage to be here, the old gambler? Did he leave his dice behind?'

'Look at him trotting along on his mule! Its ears aren't as long as his!'

'Hey there! Good-day, Monsieur le Recteur Thibaut! *Thybalde aleator*! [Thibaut the gambler] Silly old fool! Old gambler!'

'God save you! Did you throw many double sixes last night?'

'Oh! what a decrepit sight! his face all grey and drawn and hollow-eyed because he's so fond of gambling and dice!'

'Where are you going then, *Tybalde ad dados* [Thibaut the dice], turning your back on the University and trotting off towards the Town?'

'He's probably going to look for lodgings in the rue Thibautodé,'* cried Jehan du Moulin.

The whole band repeated the pun in thunderous tones, with frenzied clapping.

'You are off to look for lodgings in the rue Thibautodé, aren't you, Monsieur le Recteur, the man who gambles with the devil?'

Then came the turn of the other dignitaries.

'Down with the beadles! Down with the mace-bearers!'

'Tell me, Robin Poussepain, who's that fellow?'

'That's Gilbert de Suilly, *Gilbertus de Soliaco*, chancellor of the Collège d'Autun.'

'Here, here's my shoe; you are better placed than I am, throw it in his face.'

'*Saturnalitias mittimus ecce nuces* [Here we send some Saturnalian nuts].'*

'Down with the six theologians in their white surplices!'

'Are they theologians there? I thought they were the six white geese Sainte-Geneviève* pays the town for the fief of Roogny.'

'Down with the doctors!'

'Down with all disputations, the regular ones and the occasional ones* too.'

'Here's my cap for you, chancellor of Sainte-Geneviève! You did me down—yes, it's quite true! He gave my place in the Norman nation to little Ascanio Falzaspada, who belongs to the province of Bourges, since he's Italian.'

'That's not fair,' said all the students. 'Down with the chancellor of Sainte-Geneviève!'

'Hey there! Maître Joachim de Ladehors! Hey! Louis Dahuille! Hey! Lambert Hoctement!'

'Devil choke the proctor of the German nation!'

'And the chaplains of the Sainte-Chapelle with their grey amices, *cum tunicis grisis*!'

'*Seu de pellibus grisis fourratis*! [Or lined with grey fur!]'

'Hey there! masters of arts! Look at all those fine black copes! all those fine red copes!'

'That makes a fine tail for the rector.'

'It's like the Doge of Venice going to wed the sea.'

'I say, Jehan! the canons of Sainte-Geneviève!'

'Devil take the canonry!'

'Abbot Claude Choart! Doctor Claude Choart! Are you looking for Marie la Giffarde?'

'She's in the rue de Glatigny.'

'Making the bed for the chief inspector of bawds.'

'Paying her fourpence: *quattuor denarios*.'

'*Aut unum bombum* [Or a fart].'

'Do you want her to pay you on the nose?'

'Comrades! Maître Simon Sanguin, elector of Picardy, with his wife on the pillion.'

'*Post equitem sedet atra cura* [Dark care sits behind the rider].'*

'Bold man, Maître Simon!'

'Good-day, Monsieur the Elector!'

'Good-night, Madame the Electress!'

'Aren't they lucky to be able to see it all,' said Joannes de Molendino with a sigh, still perched up on the foliage of his capital.

Meanwhile the University's official bookseller, Maître Andry Musnier, bent to whisper in the ear of the furrier of the King's wardrobe, Maître Gilles Lecornu.

'I tell you, monsieur, it's the end of the world. The students' behaviour has never been so outrageous. It's all these damnable modern inventions that are the ruin of everything. Artillery, serpentines, bombards, and especially printing, that other plague from Germany. It's the end of manuscripts, the end of books! Printing is killing off the book trade. The end of the world is at hand!'

'I can see that from the way velvet material is coming in,' said the furrier.

At that moment the clock struck twelve.

'Ah!' said the whole crowd with one voice. The students fell silent, then there was a great bustling about, a great moving of heads and feet, a great explosion of coughs and nose-blowing; everyone settled in their chosen positions, stood on tiptoe, bunched together; then a great silence fell; every neck remained outstretched, every mouth open, every eye turned to the marble table. Nothing appeared. The bailiff's four sergeants still stood there, stiff and motionless as four painted statues. All eyes turned to the tribune reserved for the Flemish envoys. The door remained closed, the tribune empty. This crowd had been waiting since early morning for three things: noon, the embassy from Flanders, the mystery play. Only noon had been punctual.

This was really too much.

They waited one, two, three, five minutes, a quarter of an hour; nothing came. The tribune stayed empty, the stage silent. Meanwhile impatience gave way to anger. People were expressing annoyance, still quietly, it is true. 'The mystery! The mystery!' came a subdued murmur. The mood was one of ferment. A storm, as yet only rumbling, hovered over the surface of the crowd. It was Jehan du Moulin who struck the first spark.

'The mystery, and to hell with the Flemings!' he yelled with all the strength of his lungs, writhing like a serpent round his capital.

The crowd clapped their hands. 'The mystery!' they repeated, 'and to hell with Flanders!'

'We want the mystery, and we want it now,' went on the student, 'or methinks we should hang the bailiff of the Palais by way of comedy and morality.'

'Well spoken,' cried the people; 'let's start the hanging with his sergeants.'

This met with loud cheers. The four poor devils began to go pale and looked at each other. The mob moved towards them, and they could already see the flimsy wooden balustrade separating them from it begin to bend and bulge under pressure from the crowd.

The moment was critical.

'String them up! string them up!' rose the cry on every side.

At that moment the curtain of the dressing room described earlier parted, and through it came an individual whose mere appearance stopped the crowd and as if by magic changed its anger into curiosity.

'Silence! silence!'

This person, by no means reassured and shaking in every limb, came up to the edge of the marble table, with frequent bows, and the nearer he came the more they looked like genuflexions.

Meanwhile calm had been gradually restored. All that remained was the slight murmur always given off by a silent crowd.

'Gentlemen,' he said, 'and ladies, citizens of this town, we are to have the honour of declaiming and performing before his Eminence Monsieur le Cardinal a very fine morality play entitled: *The Good Judgement of Our Lady the Virgin*

Mary. I play Jupiter. His Eminence is at this moment accompanying the most honourable embassy of Monsieur the Duke of Austria; which is being delayed at the present moment while they listen to the address of Monsieur the Rector of the University at the Porte Baudets. As soon as the most eminent cardinal appears we shall begin.'

It is certain that nothing less than Jupiter's intervention could have saved the four unfortunate sergeants of the bailiff of the Palais. If we had been fortunate enough to invent this most truthful story and consequently to have to answer for it before Our Lady of Criticism, we could not at this moment be charged with the Classical precept: *Ne deus intersit* [Let there be no divine intervention].* Besides, Lord Jupiter's costume was most handsome and had helped considerably in calming the crowd by attracting all its attention. Jupiter wore a coat of mail covered in black velvet, with gilt studs; on his head was a bycocket decorated with silver-gilt buttons; and but for the rouge and bushy beard which each covered half his face; but for the scroll of gilded pasteboard, sprinkled with sequins and bristling with strips of tinsel, in his hand, easily recognized by expert eyes as thunderbolts; but for his flesh-coloured feet, sporting ribbons in the Grecian style, he might have borne comparison, for the severity of his appearance, with a Breton archer of Monsieur de Berry's corps.

II

PIERRE GRINGOIRE

IN the course of his oration, however, the satisfaction and admiration unanimously aroused by his costume diminished as he spoke, and when he reached the unfortunate conclusion: 'As soon as the most eminent cardinal arrives we shall begin', his voice was drowned by thunderous booing.

'Start right away! The mystery! The mystery right away!' cried the people. And above all the other voices that of Joannes de Molendino could be heard, cutting through the hubbub like the fife in a charivari* at Nîmes: 'Start right away!' the student was yelping.

'Down with Jupiter and the Cardinal de Bourbon!' bawled Robin Poussepain and the other clerks perched on the window.

'The morality now!' repeated the crowd. 'At once! Right now! String up the players and the cardinal!'

Poor Jupiter, gaunt, aghast, pale under his rouge, dropped his thunderbolt, took his helmet in his hand; then bowing and trembling he stammered: 'His Eminence . . . the ambassadors . . . Madame Marguerite of Flanders . . .'. He did not know what to say. Truth to tell, he was afraid of being hanged. Hanged by the crowd for waiting, hanged by the cardinal for not waiting, all he could see on either side of him was an abyss that is a gallows.

Fortunately someone came to rescue him and assume responsibility.

An individual, who stood within the balustrade in the space left clear round the marble table, had so far gone unnoticed, so completely was his long, slender person protected from every line of sight by the diameter of the pillar on which he was leaning. This individual, we repeat, tall, lean, pallid, fair-haired, still young, though already showing wrinkles on his forehead and cheeks, with bright eyes and a smile on his lips, dressed in black serge, worn shiny with age, came up to the marble table and made a sign to the poor victim. But the other was too stunned to notice.

The newcomer took another step forward: 'Jupiter!' he said, 'my dear Jupiter!'

The other did not hear.

Finally the tall, fair-haired man lost patience, and shouted almost directly into his face:

'Michel Giborne!'

'Who's calling me?' said Jupiter, as if waking up with a start.

'I am,' answered the man in black.

'Ah!' said Jupiter.

'Start at once,' the other went on. 'Satisfy the crowd. I'll take care of placating Monsieur the Bailiff, and he'll placate the cardinal.'

Jupiter breathed again.

'Worshipful citizens,' he shouted with all the power in his lungs to the crowd which went on booing, 'we are starting at once.'

'*Evoe, Iuppiter! Plaudite cives!* [Bravo Jupiter! Applaud citizens!]' cried the students.

'Noël! Noël!' cried the people.

They clapped their hands in deafening applause, and the hall was still rocking with cheers by the time Jupiter had retired behind his curtain.

Meanwhile, the unknown man who had so magically changed 'the storm into calm' as our dear old Corneille* puts it, had modestly returned to the obscurity of his pillar, where he could no doubt have remained invisible, motionless and silent as before, had he not been drawn away by two young women who, from their place in the front row of spectators, had observed his conversation with Michel Giborne/Jupiter.

'Maître,' said one of them, beckoning him closer . . .

'Do be quiet, my dear Liénarde,' said her neighbour, pretty, fresh-faced, and a brave sight in her best clothes. 'He's not a clerk, he's a layman. You mustn't call him "maître" but "messire".'

'Messire,' said Liénarde.

The stranger approached the balustrade. 'What can I do for you, mademoiselle?' he asked, as if anxious to oblige.

'Oh! nothing,' said Liénarde in embarrassment, 'it's my neighbour, Gisquette-la-Gencienne, who wants a word with you.'

'No, no,' replied Gisquette, blushing, 'it was Liénarde who said: maître; I told her she should say: messire.'

The two girls dropped their eyes. The man, who asked for nothing better than to engage them in conversation, looked at them with a smile.

'So you have nothing to say to me, mesdemoiselles?'

'Oh! nothing at all,' replied Gisquette.

'No, nothing,' said Liénarde.

The tall, fair young man took a step back, but the two girls were curious and did not want to let him go.

'Messire,' burst out Gisquette eagerly, with a rush, like a lock-gate opening or a woman making up her mind, 'so you know that soldier who is to play the part of Our Lady the Virgin in the mystery?'

'You mean Jupiter's part?' the nameless man replied.

'Oh, yes,' said Liénarde, 'isn't she stupid! So you know Jupiter?'

'Michel Giborne?' answered the nameless one. 'Yes, I do, madame.'

'He has a fine beard!' said Liénarde.

'Is it going to be lovely, what they are going to say up there?' Gisquette asked timidly.

'Very lovely, mademoiselle,' the nameless one replied without the slightest hesitation.

'What will it be?' said Liénarde.

'*The Good Judgement of Our Lady the Virgin*, a morality, if you please, mademoiselle.'

'Ah, that's different,' answered Liénarde.

A brief silence ensued. The stranger broke it. 'It's a brand new morality, never been used before.'

'So it's not the same,' said Gisquette, 'as the one they put on two years ago, the day Monsieur the Legate* made his entry, when they had three lovely girls representing . . .'

'Sirens,' said Liénarde.

'And stark naked,' added the young man.

Liénarde modestly dropped her eyes. Gisquette looked at her and did the same. He went on with a smile: 'It was a most agreeable sight. Today it's a morality specially composed for Madame the Princess of Flanders.'

'Will they sing *bergerettes*?'* asked Gisquette.

'Come now!' said the stranger, 'in a morality? You must not confuse different kinds of play. If it was a farce, that would be fine.'

'That's a pity,' Gisquette replied. 'That day, at the Ponceau fountain, there were wild men and women* fighting and striking different attitudes while they sang little motets and *bergerettes*.'

'What is suitable for a legate,' the stranger said rather dryly, 'is not suitable for a princess.'

'And by them,' Liénarde went on, 'several bass instruments were playing most tunefully.'

'And for the refreshment of passers-by,' continued Gisquette, 'the fountain had three spouts pouring out wine, milk, and hippocras,* for anyone to help themselves.'

'And a bit down from the Ponceau,' Liénarde went on, 'at the Trinité, there was a Passion play without words.'

'Don't I remember!' cried Gisquette: 'God on the Cross, and the two thieves to left and right!'

At this the young gossips, becoming excited at the memory of the legate's entry, both began talking at once.

'And further on, at the Porte-aux-Peintres, there were some other people in sumptuous clothes.'

'And at the Holy Innocents' fountain that huntsman chasing a deer with a great noise of hounds and hunting horns!'

'And at the Paris Boucherie those scaffolds representing the fortress of Dieppe!'*

'And when the legate went by, you know, Gisquette, they launched their assault and all the English had their throats cut!'

'And at the Châtelet, against the gate, there were some other lovely-looking actors!'

'And on the Pont-au-Change, which was all covered in hangings!'

'And when the legate went past they released more than two hundred dozen birds of every kind; it was really lovely, Liénarde.'

'It will be lovelier still today,' their interlocutor finally put in, his patience apparently tried as he listened to them.

'Do you promise it will be a fine mystery today?' said Gisquette.

'Absolutely,' he answered; then he added with some emphasis, 'Mesdemoiselles, I am the author.'

'Really?' said the girls, quite astounded.

'Really!' the poet answered, rather preening himself: 'That is there are two of us: Jehan Marchand who sawed the boards and put up the framework for the theatre and all the woodwork, and I, who wrote the play. My name is Pierre Gringoire.'*

The author of *The Cid* could not have said 'Pierre Corneille' more proudly.

Our readers may have observed that some time must have elapsed between the moment when Jupiter went behind the curtain and that when the author of the new morality play so abruptly revealed himself to the simple admiration of Gisquette and Liénarde. Remarkably enough, all the crowd, which had been in such an uproar a few minutes before, was now quite docile as it waited, trusting in the actor's word, which goes to prove the eternal truth, still a matter of daily experience in our modern theatres, that the best way to get the public to wait patiently is to assure them that the play is about to begin at once.

However, the student Joannes was not asleep.

'Hey there!' he suddenly cried amid the expectant calm which had followed the commotion, 'Jupiter, Our Lady the Virgin, you devil's tumblers! Are you having us on? The play! the play! Start now, or we'll start up again!'

That was all it needed.

From inside the scaffolding came the sound of music from instruments both treble and bass; the curtain was raised; four characters in motley and make-up emerged, climbed the steep ladder up to the stage, and once on the upper platform lined up before the public, to whom they bowed low; at that the music stopped. The mystery was about to begin.

The four characters, their bows amply rewarded by applause, embarked, amid a religious silence, on a prologue, which we gladly spare our readers. Besides, as still happens today, the public was much more interested in the costumes worn by the actors than in the part they were reciting; and indeed this was only right. All four wore robes half yellow and half white, differing only in the kind of material of which they were made; the first was of gold and silver brocade, the second silk, the third wool, the fourth coarse linen. The first character held a sword in his right hand, the second two golden keys, the third a pair of scales, the fourth a spade; and to help those of sluggish intelligence who had failed to see clearly through such transparent attributes, one could read embroidered in big black letters: at the bottom of the brocade robe MY NAME IS NOBILITY; at the bottom of the silk robe MY NAME IS CLERGY; at the bottom of the woollen robe MY NAME IS TRADE; and at the bottom of the linen robe MY NAME IS HUSBANDRY. The sex of the two male allegories was clearly indicated to every discerning spectator by their shorter robes and the 'cramignole'* caps they wore, while the two female allegories, whose dresses were not so short, wore hoods.

It would have needed a lot of ill will not to grasp, through the poetry of the prologue, that Husbandry was married to Trade and Clergy to Nobility, and that the two happy couples were the joint owners of a magnificent golden dolphin (*dauphin*) which they intended to award only to the most beautiful of women. So they were going round the world in a search and quest for this beauty, and having rejected successively the Queen of Golconda, the Princess of Trebizond, the Grand Khan of Tartary's daughter etc., etc., Husbandry and Trade, Nobility and Clergy had come to rest themselves on the marble table of the Palais de Justice, while they uttered before the worthy audience all the sentences and maxims which could at that time be dispensed in the Faculty of Arts in the examinations, sophisms, determinations, figures, and acts at which masters were capped for their degrees.

This was indeed all very fine.

However, in this crowd over which the four allegories competed in pouring out streams of metaphor, no ear was more attentive, no heart palpitated with more emotion, no eye was more distraught, no neck more intently craned than the eye, ear, heart, and neck of the author, the poet, the good Pierre Gringoire, who a moment before had not been able to resist the pleasure of telling two pretty girls his name. He had returned to a position a few yards from them, behind his pillar, where he listened, watched, relished. The warm applause which had greeted the beginning of his prologue still resounded in his inmost heart, and he was completely absorbed in the kind of ecstatic contemplation with which an author sees his ideas drop one by one from the actor's lips into the silence of a vast audience. Worthy Pierre Gringoire!

It pains us to say so, but this initial ecstasy was very soon disturbed. Gringoire had scarcely raised to his lips this heady cup of joy and triumph when a dash of bitterness was mixed into it.

A ragged beggar, unable to ply his trade, lost as he was amidst the crowd, and who had no doubt failed to find sufficient compensation in his neighbours' pockets, had conceived the idea of perching in some conspicuous spot so as to attract attention and alms. He had therefore, during the opening lines of the prologue, hoisted himself up by means of the pillars of the reserved tribune as far as the cornice running along the lower edge of its balustrade, and had sat down there, soliciting the attention and pity of the multitude with his rags and a hideous sore covering his right arm. For the rest, he uttered not a word.

His silence allowed the prologue to proceed without hindrance, and no noticeable disorder would have occurred had not mischance caused the student Joannes, high up on his pillar, to catch sight of the beggar and his grimaces. Helpless laughter overcame the young rascal, and unconcerned at interrupting the play and disturbing everyone's concentration he cheerfully bawled: 'Look at that fellow, faking sickness and asking for alms!'

Anyone who has ever tossed a stone into a pond full of frogs or fired a gun at a flock of birds can imagine the effect of such unseemly words when the attention of all was fixed elsewhere. Gringoire started as if from an electric shock. The prologue was stopped short, and amid uproar all heads turned towards the beggar, who, far from being disconcerted, saw in this incident a good opportunity to reap a profit, and began with doleful look and half-closed eyes to call: 'Charity, please!'

'Well now, upon my soul,' Joannes went on, 'it's Clopin Trouillefou. Hey there, my friend, was that sore on your leg so uncomfortable that you moved it to your arm?'

So saying, he threw, deft as a monkey, a small coin into the greasy hat that the beggar held out with his affected arm. The beggar accepted the alms and the gibe without flinching, and went on crying mournfully: 'Charity, please!'

This episode had seriously distracted the audience, and a good number of spectators, with Robin Poussepain and all the clerks in the lead, merrily applauded the weird duet improvised in the middle of the prologue by the student with his strident voice and the beggar with his imperturbable chant.

Gringoire was extremely put out. Recovering from his initial stupefaction, he cried with all his might to the four characters on stage: 'Go on! Damn it all, go on!' without even deigning to spare a scornful glance at the two interrupters.

At that moment he felt someone tug at the hem of his surcoat; he turned round in some annoyance, and had some difficulty in smiling. He had to, however. It was Gisquette-la-Gencienne's comely arm pushed through the balustrade which thus invited his attention.

'Monsieur,' the girl said, 'will they be going on?'

'Certainly,' Gringoire answered, rather taken aback by the question.

'In that case, messire,' she went on, 'would you be kind enough to explain . . .'

'What they are going to say?' Gringoire broke in. 'Well, just listen.'

'No,' said Gisquette, 'what they've said so far.'

Gringoire jumped like someone touched on an open wound. 'A plague on the stupid, dim-witted girl!' he said between clenched teeth.

From that moment on he dismissed Gisquette from his mind.

Meanwhile the actors had obeyed his injunction, and the public, seeing them speaking again, had begun again to listen, not without the loss of much beautiful poetry in the sort of soldered patch effected to join the two parts of the piece so abruptly cut off. Gringoire reflected on this bitterly in an undertone. However, calm had gradually been restored, the student was quiet, the beggar was counting coins in his hat, and the play once more had the upper hand.

It was in fact a very fine piece of work, and in our view might well be turned to good account even today, subject to a few alterations. The exposition, rather long and rather hollow, that is to say within the rules, was simple, and Gringoire, in the candid sanctuary of his inmost heart, admired its clarity. As may well be supposed, the four allegorical characters were rather weary after travelling three parts around the world without managing to dispose acceptably of their golden dolphin. Whereupon came a eulogy of the marvellous fish, with numerous delicate allusions to Marguerite of Flanders' young fiancé, then in dreary seclusion at Amboise, scarcely suspecting that Husbandry and Clergy, Nobility and Trade had just gone round the world for his sake. The aforesaid dolphin, then, was young, handsome, strong, and above all (magnificent origin of all the royal virtues!) he was the son of the lion of France. I declare this bold metaphor to be admirable, and maintain that natural history in the theatre, on a day of allegory and royal epithalamium, has no cause for offence in a dolphin being son of a lion. It is precisely such rare, Pindaric hybrids which prove real enthusiasm. None the less, to give criticism its due as well, the poet could have developed this fine idea in something less than two hundred lines. It is true that the mystery was meant to last from noon until four in the afternoon, according to Monsieur the Provost's decree, and the actors had to say something. Besides, the audience were listening patiently.

Suddenly, in the middle of a quarrel between Mademoiselle Trade and Madame Nobility, just as Maître Husbandry was pronouncing the wonderful line:

'You never saw a more triumphant beast in all the woods'

the door of the reserved tribune, which had so far remained inconveniently closed, was still more inconveniently opened, and the usher's resounding voice abruptly announced: 'His Eminence Monseigneur the Cardinal de Bourbon.'

III

MONSIEUR LE CARDINAL

POOR Gringoire! The crash of all the great double petards on St John's day, a volley from a score of arquebuses, the detonation of that famous serpentine in the Billy tower, which killed seven Burgundians in one go on Sunday, 29 December 1465 during the siege of Paris, the explosion of all the gunpowder in the magazine at the Porte du Temple, none of that could have split his eardrums more brutally at that solemn and dramatic moment than those few words from an usher's mouth: 'His Eminence Monseigneur the Cardinal de Bourbon.'

Not that Pierre Gringoire felt any fear, or contempt, for the cardinal. He was neither so weak nor so arrogant. A genuine eclectic, as we should say today, Gringoire was one of those spirits, at once elevated, firm, moderate, and calm, who always manage to preserve a balance (*stare in dimidio rerum*) full of reason and liberal philosophy, while paying cardinals their due. Wisdom, like a second Ariadne, seems to have given this precious, unbroken line of philosophers a ball of thread which they have been unwinding since the world began through the labyrinth of human affairs. They are to be found in every age, always the same, that is always in tune with the age. Setting aside our Pierre Gringoire, who would be their representative in the fifteenth century if we succeeded in restoring to him the renown he deserves, it was certainly their spirit which inspired Father Du Breul in the sixteenth century when he wrote these sublimely simple words, worthy of any century: 'I am a Parisian by nation and a parrhesian by speech, since *parrhesia* in Greek means liberty of speech; thus have I dealt even with my lords the cardinals, uncle and brother of my lord the Prince de Conti; albeit respecting their greatness and without offending anyone in their entourage, no mean feat.'*

There was thus no dislike of the cardinal, nor scorn for his presence, in the disagreeable impression it made on Pierre Gringoire. Quite the contrary; our poet had too much common sense and too threadbare a smock not to feel particularly keen that many of the allusions in his prologue, especially the glorification of the dolphin, son of the lion of France, should be picked up by so eminent an ear. But self-interest is not the ruling factor in the noble nature of poets. If we assume that the poet's entity is represented by the number ten, it is certain that a chemist, analysing and, as Rabelais puts it, pharmacopolizing it, would find it composed of one part of self-interest to nine of self-esteem. Now, at the moment when the door opened for the cardinal, Gringoire's nine parts of self-esteem, inflated and puffed up by the breath of popular admiration, were in a state of prodigious enlargement, causing that imperceptible molecule of self-interest which we identified a moment ago in the constitution of poets, to disappear as if smothered; a precious ingredient, moreover a ballast of reality and humanity without which poets' feet would never touch the ground. Gringoire was enraptured at feeling, seeing, fingering, so to speak, a whole assembly (of the baser sort, true, but what does that matter?) being stunned, petrified, as though asphyxiated by the immeasurable tirades continually erupting from every part of his epithalamium. I can assert that he himself shared the general beatitude, and unlike La Fontaine, who asked during a performance of his comedy *The Florentine*:* 'What bumpkin wrote that rhapsodic mess?' Gringoire would gladly have asked his neighbour: 'Who wrote this masterpiece?' You can now judge the effect on him of the cardinal's abrupt and untimely arrival.

All his worst fears were only too well realized. His Eminence's entrance had a shattering effect on the audience. Every head turned towards the tribune. You could no longer hear yourself speak. 'The cardinal! the cardinal!' everyone repeated. The unfortunate prologue was cut short for the second time.

The cardinal paused for a moment at the entrance to the tribune. As he cast a somewhat indifferent eye round the audience, the uproar increased. Everyone wanted a better view of him. Each one strained to crane his head over his neighbour's shoulder.

He was indeed an exalted personage, the sight of whom was worth any stage spectacle. Charles, Cardinal de Bourbon, Archbishop Count of Lyons, primate of the Gauls, was related both to Louis XI, through his brother, Pierre, Lord of Beaujeu, who had married the King's daughter, and to Charles the Bold, through his mother, Agnes of Burgundy. Now the ruling feature, the characteristic and distinctive aspect of the primate of the Gauls' character was his courtier's instinct and his devotion to those in power. One can imagine the countless problems which these double family connections had caused him, and all the temporal shoals through which his spiritual barque had had to tack, lest it be wrecked either on Louis or on Charles, that Scylla and Charybdis which had swallowed up the Duke of Nemours and the Constable of Saint-Pol.* Heaven be praised, he had survived the passage rather well, and arrived in Rome without mishap. But though he was in harbour, and precisely because he was in harbour, he never recalled without disquiet the diverse fortunes of his political life, so long filled with danger and toil. Thus he used to say that 1476 had been 'a black and white' year for him; meaning that in one year he had lost his mother, the Duchess of Bourbonnais, and his cousin, the Duke of Burgundy, one bereavement consoling him for the other.

For the rest he was a good fellow. He enjoyed a cardinal's life, liked getting merry on the royal wine of Challuau [Chaillot], was not averse to Richarde la Garmoise and Thomasse la Saillarde, gave alms to pretty girls rather than to old women, and for all these reasons went down very well with the ordinary people of Paris. He went about always surrounded by a little court of bishops and abbots of noble lineage, gallant, bawdy, and good trenchermen if need be; and more than once the pious ladies of Saint-Germain d'Auxerre, passing in the evening beneath the brightly lit windows of the Bourbon residence, had been scandalized to hear the same voices which had sung them

vespers in the daytime chanting to the clink of glasses
the Bacchic motto of Benedict XII, the Pope who added
a third crown to the tiara: '*Bibamus papaliter*' [Let us
drink papally].

It was no doubt this well-deserved popularity which saved
him, as he entered, from any hostile reception from the
throng, which had been so disgruntled only a moment
before and not at all in the mood to show respect for a
cardinal on the very day when they were going to elect a
pope. But Parisians rarely harbour a grudge; and then, by
having the performance begin on their own authority, the
good citizens had scored over the cardinal, and that triumph
was enough for them. Besides, Monsieur le Cardinal de
Bourbon was a fine figure of a man, he had a fine red robe
and wore it very well; in other words, he had all the women
on his side, and consequently the better part of the audience.
It would certainly be unfair and in poor taste to boo a
cardinal for keeping everyone waiting at the show, when he
is a fine-looking man and wears his red robe so well.

He came in then, greeted the audience with the hereditary smile which the great bestow on the people, and advanced with measured step towards his scarlet armchair,
looking as though his thoughts were elsewhere. His train,
what would today be called his staff of bishops and abbots,
poured on to the tribune in his wake, exciting increased
tumult and curiosity among the groundlings. Everyone was
trying to point them out to his neighbour, put a name to
them, be acquainted with at least one of them; for one it
was the Lord Bishop of Marseilles, Alaudet, if memory
serves aright; another the dean of Saint-Denis; another,
Robert de Lespinasse, abbot of Saint-Germain-des-Prés,
libertine brother of one of Louis XI's mistresses: all this
with numerous errors and cacophony. As for the students,
they were swearing. It was their day, their Feast of Fools,
their Saturnalia, annual orgy of law clerks and students. On
that day their entitlement to the vilest behaviour was something sacred. And then there were some wild gossips in the
crowd, Simone Quatre-livres, Agnès la Gadine, Robine
Piédebou. Couldn't they at least be left to swear in peace

and utter the odd profanity on such a fine day, in the
excellent company of churchmen and harlots? So they went
to it with a will; and amid the general clamour came a
fearful chorus of blasphemies and obscenities from all these
unbridled tongues of clerks and students, restrained for the
rest of the year by fear of Saint Louis's* branding irons on
their tongues. Poor Saint Louis, how they derided him in
his own Palais de Justice! Each of them had marked out a
target among those who had just arrived on the tribune, a
black, or grey, or white, or violet cassock. As for Joannes
Frollo de Molendino, as an archdeacon's brother it was on
the red cassock that he launched his bold assault, and he
sang at the top of his voice, staring shamelessly at the
cardinal: '*Cappa repleta mero*' [A cope filled with wine].

All these details, here exposed for the reader's edification,
were so submerged in the general tumult as to be lost before
they reached the reserved tribune. Besides, the cardinal
would not have been much upset, for the licence on that
day was quite taken for granted. In any case, as his preoccupied expression showed, he had another cause for concern, which followed hard on his heels and came on to the
tribune almost at the same time as he did. That was the
embassy from Flanders.

Not that he was a profound politician, fussing about the
possible consequences of the marriage of Madame his
cousin, Marguerite of Burgundy, to Monsieur his cousin,
Charles, Dauphin of Vienne; how long the understanding
patched up between the Duke of Austria and the King of
France would last,* how the King of England would take
this slight to his daughter, that worried him very little, and
every evening he paid tribute to wine from the royal vineyard at Chaillot without ever suspecting that a few flasks of
that same wine (slightly revised and amended, it is true, by
the physician Coictier) cordially presented to Edward IV
by Louis XI would one fine morning rid Louis XI of Edward IV.* 'The most honoured embassy of the Duke of
Austria' brought the cardinal no such worries, but bothered
him in another way. It was indeed a bit hard, as we have
already mentioned on the second page of this book, that

he, Charles de Bourbon, should be obliged to entertain and welcome mere burghers: he, a cardinal, they échevins[sheriffs]; he, a Frenchman, fond of the table, they Flemish beer-swillers; and in public at that. This was, to be sure, one of the most irksome smiles he had ever had to assume for the sake of the King's good pleasure.

He turned towards the door, then, with the utmost graciousness (so well did he apply himself), when the usher resoundingly announced: 'Messieurs the envoys of Monsieur the Duke of Austria.' Needless to say the entire audience followed suit.

At that there filed in, two by two, with a gravity strongly contrasting with the exuberant ecclesiastical suite of Charles de Bourbon, Maximilian of Austria's ambassadors, led by the reverend Father in God Jehan, abbot of Saint-Bertin, chancellor of the Golden Fleece, and Jacques de Goy, sieur Dauby, high bailiff of Ghent. A profound silence fell on the assembly, with some laughter, though muffled so that they could listen to all the ludicrous names and civic titles that each individual transmitted imperturbably to the usher, who then tossed names and titles in any order and much mangled down to the crowd. There was Maître Loys Roelof, échevin of the town of Louvain; Messire Clays d'Étuelde, échevin of Brussels; Messire Paul de Baeust, sieur de Voirmizelle, presiding magistrate of Flanders; Maître Jehan Coleghens, burgomaster of Antwerp; Maître George de la Moere, first échevin of the *kuere* [court] of Ghent; Maître Gheldof van der Hage, first échevin of the *parchons** of the aforesaid town; and the sieur de Bierbecque, and Jehan Pinnock, and Jehan Dymaerzelle, etc., etc., etc.: bailiffs, échevins, burgomasters; burgomasters, échevins, bailiffs; all stiff, formal, starchy in their best velvet and damask, wearing cramignole caps of black velvet with huge tassels of Cyprus gold thread; good Flemish heads after all, dignified, severe features belonging to the same family as that which Rembrandt brings out so powerfully and gravely against the black background of the 'Night Watch'; personages every one of whom bore graven on his brow that Maximilian of Austria had been right, as his manifesto ran: 'to have full confidence in their prudence, valour, experience, loyalty, and integrity'.

With one exception, however. This was a shrewd, intelligent, cunning face, a sort of cross between a monkey and a diplomat, towards which the cardinal advanced three paces and bowed low, and yet whose name was just Guillaume Rym, counsellor and pensionary of the town of Ghent.

Few then knew what manner of man was Guillaume Rym. A rare genius, who in time of revolution would have made a dazzling appearance on the surface of events, but who in the fifteenth century was reduced to subterranean intrigue and 'living in the saps', as the duc de Saint-Simon puts it. For the rest, he was appreciated by the chief 'sapper' of Europe, he was familiarly involved in Louis XI's machinations, and often lent a hand with the King's secret operations. All of which was quite unknown to this crowd, which marvelled at the courtesies paid by the cardinal to this weedy-looking Flemish bailiff.

MAÎTRE JACQUES COPPENOLE

WHILE the pensionary of Ghent and His Eminence were exchanging low bows and a few words in an even lower voice, a tall man with a broad face and powerful shoulders came up so that he entered abreast with Guillaume Rym, looking like a mastiff beside a fox. His felt bycocket and leather jerkin stood out conspicuously amid the silk and velvet around him. Assuming that he was some groom who had lost his way, the usher stopped him.

'Hey, my friend! You can't go through there.'

The man in the leather jerkin shouldered him aside. 'What does this fellow think he's doing?' he roared in a voice which drew the attention of the entire hall to this strange altercation. 'Can't you see that I am one of them?'

'Your name?' asked the usher.

'Jacques Coppenole.'

'Your titles?'

'Hosier, at the sign of the Three Little Chains at Ghent.'

The usher recoiled. Announcing échevins and burgomasters was one thing, but a hosier ... that was hard. The cardinal was in torment. All the people were looking and listening. For two days now His Eminence had been striving to lick these Flemish bears into rather better shape for public appearances, and this piece of bad manners went too far. Meanwhile Guillaume Rym, with his crafty smile, went up to the usher:

'Announce Maître Jacques Coppenole, clerk to the échevins of the town of Ghent,' he said in a very low whisper.

'Usher,' the cardinal said aloud,' announce Maître Jacques Coppenole, clerk to the échevins of the illustrious town of Ghent.'

That was a mistake. Guillaume Rym left to himself could have evaded the difficulty, but Coppenole had heard the cardinal. 'No, by the Holy Rood!' he thundered. 'Jacques

Coppenole, hosier. Do you hear, usher? No more, and no less. By the Rood! hosier is fine enough! My lord archduke has gone looking more than once for his gauntlet [Ghent-let] in my hose.'

Applause and laughter broke out. In Paris a pun is picked up at once, and thus always applauded.

It should be added that Coppenole was a man of the people, and the audience around him was of the people. So communication between him and them had been rapid, electric, and, so to speak, on an equal footing. The Flemish hosier's proud outburst, by humiliating the courtiers, had stirred up in all those plebeian souls a certain sense of dignity, in the fifteenth century as yet vague and undefined. This hosier, who had just stood up to Monsieur le Cardinal, was their equal—a comforting thought indeed for poor devils accustomed to show respect and obedience to the servants of the bailiff of the abbot of Sainte-Geneviève, the cardinal's train-bearer.

Coppenole bowed proudly to His Eminence, who bowed back to this all-powerful burgher so feared by Louis XI. Then, while Guillaume Rym, 'a wise and crafty man' as Philippe de Commines puts it, followed both of them with a mocking and superior smile, they each went to their place, the cardinal quite put out and pensive, Coppenole calm and haughty, reflecting no doubt that after all his title of hosier was as good as any other, and Mary of Burgundy, mother of the Marguerite whom Coppenole was marrying off that day, would have feared him less as a cardinal than as a hosier: for no cardinal would have stirred up the people of Ghent against the favourites of Charles the Bold's daughter; no cardinal would have steeled the crowd with a word against her tears and entreaties when the lady of Flanders came to the very foot of the scaffold to beg her people for mercy on their behalf; while the hosier had only to lift his leather elbow to make both your heads roll, my most illustrious lords Guy d'Hymbercourt and chancellor Guillaume Hugonet!*

However, that was not yet the end of it for the poor cardinal and he had to drain to the dregs the cup of finding himself in such bad company.

The reader has perhaps not forgotten the shameless beggar who had come to cling to the fringes of the cardinal's tribune once the prologue began. The arrival of the illustrious guests had by no means made him let go, and while prelates and ambassadors packed into the stalls of the tribune, as tightly as real Flemish herrings in a barrel, he had made himself comfortable, boldly crossing his legs on the architrave. This exceptional piece of insolence had at first gone quite unnoticed, since the attention of all was directed elsewhere. He, for his part, noticed nothing in the hall; he kept nodding his head, as unconcerned as any Neapolitan, repeating from time to time, amid the general noise, as if from mechanical habit: 'Charity, please!' And indeed he was probably the only person out of all those present who had not deigned to turn his head towards the altercation between Coppenole and the usher. Now, as luck would have it, the master hosier from Ghent, with whom the people already felt such sympathy and on whom all eyes were fixed, came to sit down in the front row of the tribune, precisely above the beggar; they were not a little amazed to see the Flemish ambassador inspect the rascal perched beneath him and then give him a friendly tap on his ragged shoulder. The beggar turned round; surprise, recognition, broad smiles on the two faces, etc.; then, totally heedless of the spectators, the hosier and the supposed victim of sickness began chatting in low voices, clasping each other by the hand, while Clopin Trouillefou's rags spread over the cloth of gold on the tribune looked like a caterpillar on an orange.

The novelty of this unusual scene aroused a wave of such wild merriment in the hall that the cardinal was soon aware of it; he half leaned forward, but from the point at which he was sitting he had only the most imperfect view of Trouillefou's disreputable mantle and quite naturally assumed that the beggar was asking for alms; outraged at such a liberty he cried: 'Monsieur the bailiff of the Palais, have this rascal thrown into the river.'

'By the Rood! Monseigneur le Cardinal,' Coppenole said without loosing Coppenole's hand, 'he's a friend of mine.'

'Noël! Noël!' cried the audience. From that moment on Maître Coppenole enjoyed in Paris, as he did in Ghent, 'high esteem with the people; for men of such stature do so,' says Philippe de Commines, 'when they are thus unruly.'

The cardinal bit his lip. He leaned over to his neighbour, the abbot of Sainte-Geneviève, and said in an undertone: 'Monsieur the Archduke has sent us a fine lot of ambassadors to herald Madame Marguerite!'

'Your Eminence,' the abbot replied, 'is wasting his courtesies on these Flemish snouts. *Margaritas ante porcos* [Pearls before swine].'

'Say rather,' answered the cardinal with a smile: '*Porcos ante Margaritam* [Swine before Marguerite/pearl].'

The whole of this little court swooned in their cassocks with ecstasy over this pun. The cardinal's spirits rose a little; he had now got even with Coppenole, and also won applause for his pun.

Now we should like permission from those of our readers with the power to generalize an image or idea, as the modern style puts it, to ask whether they have a clear picture of the scene presented by the vast parallelogram of the Great Hall of the Palais at the moment on which our attention is focused. In the middle of the hall, set up against the western wall, a large and magnificent tribune of gold brocade, which a procession of solemn personages, announced in turn by the strident voice of an usher, is entering through a small Gothic doorway. In the front rows numerous venerable figures are already seated, in their ermine, velvet, and scarlet hoods. Around the tribune, where quiet and dignity prevail, below, in front, everywhere, a great crowd and a great buzz of noise. From the crowd countless eyes gaze at every face on the tribune, countless comments are whispered over every name. The spectacle is indeed a curious one, well worthy of the spectators' attention. But over there, at the far end, whatever can that be, that sort of trestle with four motley puppets on top and four more beneath? Whoever can that be, standing beside the trestle with his black smock and pale face? Alas! dear reader, it is Pierre Gringoire and his prologue.

We had all completely forgotten him. Which is exactly what he had feared.

From the moment the cardinal had made his entrance Gringoire had been constantly busy trying to save his prologue. First he had instructed the actors, who had remained in suspended animation, to go on, and to speak more loudly. Then, seeing that no one was listening, he had stopped them, and during the quarter-hour or so that the interruption lasted, he had been ceaselessly tapping his foot, jumping about, hailing Gisquette and Liénarde, encouraging his neighbours to have the prologue resumed; all in vain. No one could be diverted from the cardinal, the embassy, and the tribune, the single centre of this immense circle of visual radii. It also seems likely, and we say so with regret, that the audience was beginning to be slightly bored with the prologue just as His Eminence came in to divert attention so drastically from it. After all, on the tribune as on the marble table, it was all the same spectacle: the conflict of Husbandry and Clergy, of Nobility and Trade. And many people simply preferred to see them living, breathing, moving, jostling, in flesh and blood, in this Flemish embassy, this episcopal court, in the cardinal's robes, in Coppenole's jerkin, rather than painted and dressed up, speaking in verse and, so to speak, stuffed like dummies beneath the yellow and white tunics in which Gringoire had rigged them up.

However, when our poet saw that calm had been partially restored, he conceived a stratagem which might have saved the day.

'Monsieur,' he said, turning to one of his neighbours, a stout, patient-looking worthy, 'supposing they began again?'

'Began what?' said the neighbour.

'Why, the mystery,' said Gringoire.

'Just as you like,' replied the neighbour.

This half-approval was enough for Gringoire, and taking matters into his own hands he began crying out, merging as much as possible into the crowd: 'Start the mystery again! Start again!'

'Devil take it,' said Joannes de Molendino, 'what are they chanting there, down at the end?' (For Gringoire was making enough noise for four people.) 'What about it, comrades? Isn't the mystery ended? They want to start it up again. That's not right.'

'No! no!' cried all the students. 'Down with the mystery! Down with it!'

But Gringoire only tried harder and cried still more loudly: 'Start again! Start again!'

All this clamour attracted the cardinal's attention.

'Monsieur the Bailiff of the Palais,' he said to a tall, dark man standing near him. 'Why are those rascals making that infernal noise, like men possessed?'

The bailiff of the Palais was a kind of amphibious magistrate, a sort of bat in the judicial order, a cross between rat and bird, judge and soldier.

He approached His Eminence, very much afraid of his displeasure, and stammered out an explanation for the people's unseemly behaviour; noon had arrived before His Eminence, and the players had been forced to begin without waiting for His Eminence.

The cardinal burst out laughing. 'Upon my soul, the rector of the University should have done the same. What say you, Maître Guillaume Rym?'

'Monseigneur,' Guillaume Rym replied, 'let's be content with having been let off half the comedy. There's that much at least to our credit.'

'Can these rogues go on with their farce?' asked the bailiff.

'Go on, go on,' said the cardinal, 'it's all the same to me. I'll be reading my breviary the while.'

The bailiff came forward to the edge of the tribune, silenced them with a gesture and cried: 'Citizens, villeins, inhabitants, to satisfy those who want it to start again and those who want it done with, His Eminence orders the play to continue.'

Both parties had to put up with that. However author and public for long afterwards felt resentment towards the cardinal.

The characters on the stage resumed their commentary, and Gringoire hoped that at least the remainder of his text would be heard. This hope soon went the way of his other illusions; silence in the audience had indeed been more or less restored, but Gringoire had failed to notice that at the moment when the cardinal gave the order to continue, the tribune was far from full, and after the Flemish envoys had come other persons belonging to the procession, whose names and titles, intermittently projected by the usher's cry amid the continuing dialogue, was wreaking considerable havoc with it. Try indeed to imagine, in the middle of a theatrical performance, a yelping usher interjecting between two rhymes, and often between two hemistichs, such parentheses as these: 'Maître Jacques Charmolue, the King's attorney in the ecclesiastical court!—Jehan de Harlay, esquire, keeper of the office of Chevalier of the Night Watch of the Town of Paris!—Messire Galiot de Genoilhac, knight, seigneur de Brussac, Master of the King's Artillery!—Maître Dreux-Raguier, Inspector of Waters and Forests of our lord the King for the Île-de-France, Champagne, and Brie!—Messire Louis de Graville, knight, counsellor, and chamberlain to the King, admiral of France, guardian of the forest of Vincennes!—Maître Denis le Mercier, Keeper of the Hospital for the Blind of Paris!— etc., etc.' It was becoming intolerable.

This strange accompaniment, which made it hard to follow the play, made Gringoire all the more indignant as he could not disguise from himself the fact that it was becoming more interesting all the time and the only thing wrong with his work was that no one was listening to it. It would indeed be hard to imagine a more ingenious and dramatic construction. The four characters of the prologue were bemoaning their insoluble predicament, when Venus in person, *vera incessu patuit dea** [a true goddess was evident in her step] appeared before them, wearing a fine cotehardie emblazoned with the ship of the town arms of Paris. She came herself to claim the dolphin promised to the most beautiful of women. Jupiter, whose thunder could be heard rumbling from the dressing room, supported her, and the goddess was about to win the prize, that is, in plain terms, to marry Monsieur le Dauphin, when a little girl, dressed in white damask and holding in her hand a marguerite daisy (a transparent personification of the Princess of Flanders) had come to contend with Venus. Dramatic surprise, reversal of fortune. After some debate, Venus, Marguerite, and those in the wings had agreed to abide by the judgement of the Holy Virgin. There was another fine part, that of Dom Pedro, King of Mesopotamia. But with so many interruptions it was hard to work out what he was there for. They had all climbed the ladder to come up on stage.

But the play was done for. None of these beauties had been felt or understood. At the cardinal's entrance it seemed as though a magic, invisible thread had suddenly drawn every eye from the marble table to the tribune, from the southern end of the hall to its western side. Nothing could break the spell put on the audience. Every eye remained riveted there, and the new arrivals, their cursed names, their faces, and their costumes constituted a continual distraction. It was heart-rending. Except for Gisquette and Liénarde, who turned away from time to time when Gringoire pulled at their sleeves, except for the stout, patient neighbour, no one was facing the poor abandoned morality. All Gringoire could see were faces in profile.

How bitterly he saw the piecemeal collapse of his whole edifice of fame and poetry! And just to think that these people had been on the point of rebellion against Monsieur the bailiff, so impatient were they to hear his work! Now that they had it, no one cared about it. The same performance which had begun with such unanimous applause! Eternal ebb and flow of popular favour! To think that they had come close to hanging the bailiff's sergeants! What would he not have given to return to that hour of sweetness!

The usher's brutal monologue, however, came to an end. All had now arrived and Gringoire breathed again. The actors went bravely on. But what should happen but that Maître Coppenole, the hosier, suddenly stands up, and Gringoire hears him deliver, amid the attention of all, this abominable harangue:

'Messieurs, burghers and squires of Paris, I don't know, by the Rood! what we are doing here. I can quite clearly see over there, in that corner, on that trestle, some people who look as if they want a fight. I don't know if that's what you call a "mystery", but it's not much fun. They go for each other with their tongues, and that's all. For quarter of an hour I've been waiting for the first blow, nothing happens. They are cowards, and they only scratch each other with insults. They should have brought over some fighters from London or Rotterdam; and then, my goodness! there would have been punches you could hear out in the street! But this lot are pathetic. They ought at least to give us a Morris dance or some other mummery! This isn't what they told me. They promised us a Feast of Fools, with the election of a pope. We have our Pope of Fools in Ghent too, and we don't lag behind anyone when it comes to that, by the Rood! This is what we do. We get together a crowd, like here. Then everyone in turn sticks his head through a hole and pulls faces at the others. The one who pulls the ugliest face, by general acclamation, is elected pope. There you are. Most entertaining. Would you like us to make your pope as we do at home? At least it wouldn't be as dull as listening to those windbags. If they want to come and pull a face at the hole they'll be in the competition. What do you say, Messieurs the burghers? There's a good enough choice of gargoyles of both sexes for us to have a good Flemish laugh, and enough ugly mugs to hope for a splendid grimace.'

Gringoire would have liked to reply. Stupefaction, anger, indignation left him speechless. Besides, the popular hosier's motion was greeted with such enthusiasm by these burghers, who felt flattered to be addressed as squires, that resistance was pointless. There was nothing for it but to go along with the torrent. Gringoire buried his face in his hands, not being fortunate enough to have a cloak to hide his head like Timanthes'* Agamemnon.

V

QUASIMODO

IN less than no time everything was ready for carrying out
Coppenole's idea. Townsfolk, students, and law clerks had
set to work. The small chapel facing the marble table was
chosen as the scene for the face-pulling. Where glass had
been broken from the pretty rose-window it had left open
a stone circle through which, it was agreed, the contestants
would stick their heads. All they had to do to reach it was
to clamber up a couple of barrels, which had been brought
from somewhere and precariously balanced one on top of
the other. It was laid down that every candidate, man or
woman (for a female pope might be chosen) should
preserve the impression of their grimace unspoiled and
intact by covering their faces and staying out of sight in the
chapel until it was time for them to make their appearance.
In a moment the chapel was full of contestants and the door
was closed behind them.

From his place on the tribune Coppenole organized, directed, and arranged everything. During the commotion
the cardinal, no less put out than Gringoire, had taken
himself off with all his suite on the pretext of having business and vespers to attend to, without the crowd, which
had been so excited by his arrival, taking the slightest notice
of his departure. Guillaume Rym was the only one to notice
His Eminence put to flight. The attention of the people,
like the sun, pursued its revolution; starting at one end of
the hall, after pausing for a time in the middle, it was now
at the other end. The marble table, the brocaded tribune
had had their moment; it was now the turn of Louis XI's
chapel. From now on the field was clear for unbridled folly.
Only the Flemings and the rabble remained.

The face-pulling began. The first face to appear at the
hole, with eyelids turned inside out with rouge, mouth
agape like a monster's jaws, and brows all wrinkled like our

Empire cavalry boots, set off such peals of uncontrollable laughter that Homer would have taken all these villeins for gods. However, the Great Hall was anything but Olympus, as Gringoire's poor Jupiter knew better than anyone. A second, and a third ugly face followed, then another and yet another, and each time there was renewed laughter and delighted stamping of feet. The spectacle provoked a special kind of giddy elation, it had a certain power of intoxication and fascination, of which it would be hard to convey any idea to a modern reader and modern drawing-room society. Imagine a series of faces successively presenting every geometrical shape, from the triangle to the trapezium, from the cone to the polyhedron—every human expression, from anger to lust—every age of man, from the wrinkles of the new-born baby to the wrinkles of the dying old crone; every religious phantasmagoria, from Faunus to Beelzebub; every animal profile, from jaw to beak, from snout to muzzle. Picture all the grotesque heads carved on the Pont-Neuf, those nightmares turned to stone under the hand of Germain Pilon,* taking on life and breath, and coming one by one to stare at you with burning eyes; all the masks from the Venice carnival passing one after the other before your spyglass; in a word, a human kaleidoscope.

The orgy was becoming more and more Flemish. Teniers* could give only a very imperfect idea of it. Imagine Salvator Rosa's* battle picture turned into Bacchanalia. There were no more students, ambassadors, burghers, men, women; no more Clopin Trouillefou, Gilles Lecornu, Marie Quatre-livres, Robin Poussepain. All was eclipsed in the common licence. The Great Hall was now just a vast furnace of shameless merriment, where every mouth was a shout, every eye a sparkle, every face a grimace, every individual a posture. It was all shouting and bawling. The strange faces which came one after another to grind their teeth at the rose-window were so many brands thrown on the fire. From all this seething throng rose, like steam from a furnace, a sharp, shrill, piercing, high-pitched buzz like the wings of a gnat.

'Hey! Blast!'

'Just look at that face!'

'That one's no good.'

'And the next!'

'Guillemette Maugerepuis, just look at that bull's muzzle, it's got everything but horns. It can't be your husband, then.'

'Next!'

'By the Pope's belly! what sort of grimace is that?'

'Hey! that's cheating. You may only show your face.'

'That damned Perrette Callebotte! She's quite capable of that.'

'Noël! Noël!'

'I'm choking!'

'There's one can't get his ears through!'

Etc., etc.

We must, however, give our friend Jehan his due. Amid all this witches' sabbath he could still be seen up on his pillar, like a cabin boy in the crow's nest. He was throwing himself about in an incredible frenzy. His mouth was wide open, and from it emerged a cry that no one could hear, not that it was lost in the general clamour, intense though that was, but because it had surely gone to the limit of high-pitched audible sounds, the twelve thousand vibrations of Sauveur or the eight thousand of Biot.*

As for Gringoire, once his initial depression had passed, he had recovered his composure. He had braced himself against adversity. 'Go on!' he had told his actors, his talking machines, for the third time. Then striding round in front of the marble table he had a notion to go in his turn and appear at the chapel window, if only for the pleasure of pulling faces at these ungrateful people. 'No, that would be unworthy of us; no revenge! Fight on to the end,' he kept telling himself. 'The power of poetry over the people is great; I'll bring them back. We'll see which will win, face-pulling or the literary arts.'

Alas! he was the only spectator of his play left.

It was much worse than it had been shortly before. Now all he could see was backs.

I am mistaken. The patient, stout man, whom he had already consulted at a critical moment, still faced the stage. As for Gisquette and Liénarde, they had long since deserted.

Gringoire was deeply moved by the loyalty of his sole spectator. He went up and spoke to him, gently shaking him by the arm; for the good man was leaning on the balustrade in a light doze.

'Monsieur,' said Gringoire, 'thank you.'

'Monsieur,' the stout man answered with a yawn, 'what for?'

'I can see what's bothering you,' the poet went on; 'with all this noise you can't hear properly. But don't worry, your name will go down to posterity. What is your name, if you please?'

'Renault Château, keeper of the seal at the Châtelet, in Paris, at your service.'

'Monsieur, you are the only representative of the Muses here,' said Gringoire.

'You are too kind, monsieur,' answered the keeper of the seal at the Châtelet.

'You are the only one to have given the play a proper hearing. What do you think of it?'

'Eh, eh!' the stout magistrate answered, 'pretty lively, to be sure.'

Gringoire had to be content with this word of praise, for thunderous applause, accompanied by a tremendous burst of cheering, cut short their conversation. The Pope of Fools had been elected.

'Noël! Noël! Noël!' cried people on every side.

It was indeed a quite marvellous grimace that was just then beaming through the hole in the rose-window. After all the faces, pentagonal, hexagonal, and irregular, which had succeeded each other at the window without ever achieving the grotesque ideal that imaginations fevered by the orgy had composed, it took nothing less to carry their vote than the sublime grimace which had just dazzled the assembly. Maître Coppenole himself applauded; and Clopin Trouillefou, who had been a competitor, and goodness knows the intense degree of ugliness his face could attain, confessed himself beaten. We shall do likewise. We shall not attempt to give the reader an idea of that tetrahedral nose, that horseshoe mouth, that tiny left eye obscured by a shaggy red eyebrow, while the right eye lay completely hidden beneath an enormous wart. Those irregular teeth, with gaps here and there like the battlements of a fortress, that calloused lip, over which one of those teeth protruded like an elephant's tusk, that cleft chin, and above all the facial expression extending over the whole, a mixture of malice, amazement, and sadness. Conjure up, if you can, this overall effect.

The acclamation was unanimous. Everyone rushed to the chapel. From it they brought in triumph the blessed Pope of Fools. But it was then that surprise and wonder reached their peak. The grimace was his ordinary face.

Or rather his whole person was grimace. A large head bristling with red hair; between his shoulders an enormous hump, the effects of which were also visible in front; an assemblage of thighs and legs so strangely distorted that they touched only at the knees and, from the front, looked like two sickle blades joined at the handle; big feet, monstrous hands; and with all that deformity a certain air of fearsome energy, agility, and courage; a strange exception to the eternal rule which says that strength, like beauty, results from harmony. Such was the pope whom the fools had just given themselves.

He looked like a giant, broken into pieces and then badly mended.

When this kind of Cyclops appeared at the entrance to the chapel, motionless, squat, and almost as broad as he was tall, 'squared by the base' as a great man* put it, his surcoat, half red, half violet, sprinkled with silver bells, and above all his quite perfect ugliness, at once enabled the people to recognize him, and they cried with one voice:

'It's Quasimodo, the bell-ringer! It's Quasimodo the hunchback of Notre-Dame! One-eyed Quasimodo! Bandy-legged Quasimodo! Noël! Noël!'

The poor devil clearly had a choice of nicknames.

'Watch out, any pregnant women!' shouted the students.

'Or any who want to be,' Joannes put in.

The women were indeed hiding their faces.

'Oh! the ugly monkey,' said one.

'As wicked as he's ugly,' put in another.

'He is the devil,' added a third.

'I'm unlucky enough to live near Notre-Dame; all night long I hear him prowling about in the guttering.'

'With the cats.'

'He's always up on our roofs.'

'He casts spells on us down the chimney.'

'The other evening he came to make faces at me through my attic window. I thought it was some man. I was so scared!'

'I'm sure he goes to the witches' sabbath. Once he left a broomstick on my roof-leads.'

'Oh! what a horrid-looking hunchback!'

'Oh! the evil soul!'

'Ugh!'

The men, on the contrary, were delighted and applauded.

Quasimodo, object of the uproar, still stood at the chapel door, sombre and serious, letting them admire him.

A student, Robin Poussepain, I think, went up to laugh in his face, but came too near. Quasimodo contented himself with seizing him round the waist and hurling him ten yards into the crowd. All without uttering a word.

Maître Coppenole, struck with wonder, approached him. 'By the Rood! Holy Father, you are the most beautifully ugly thing I've ever seen in my life. You deserve to be pope in Rome as well as Paris.'

So saying he cheerfully clapped him on the shoulder. Quasimodo did not stir. Coppenole went on. 'You're a fellow I'm longing to share a feast with, even if it cost me one of those big new *douzains*.* What say you?'

Quasimodo made no reply.

'By the Rood!' said the hosier; 'are you deaf?'

He was indeed deaf.

However, he was beginning to get tired of Coppenole's behaviour, and suddenly turned on him, grinding his teeth so fearfully that the Flemish giant retreated, like a bulldog before a cat.

Then terror and respect cleared round this strange personage a circle at least fifteen geometrical paces in radius. An old woman explained to Maître Coppenole that Quasimodo was deaf.

'Deaf!' said the hosier with his coarse Flemish laugh. 'Holy Rood! He's the perfect pope!'

'Eh! I know who he is,' cried Jehan, who had finally come down from his capital for a closer look at Quasimodo; 'he's my brother the archdeacon's bell-ringer. Hello, Quasimodo!'

'Devil of a man!' said Robin Poussepain, still aching and bruised all over from his fall. 'He appears: he's a hunchback. He walks: he's bandy-legged. He looks at you: he's one-eyed. You speak to him: he's deaf. Well then, what's his tongue for, this Polyphemus?'

'He speaks when he wants to,' said the old woman. 'He went deaf from ringing the bells. He's not dumb.'

'That's one defect missing,' observed Jehan.

'And he has one eye too many,' added Robin Poussepain.

'No he hasn't,' said Jehan judiciously. 'A man with one eye is more imperfect than a completely blind one. He knows what he hasn't got.'

Meanwhile all the beggars, all the lackeys, all the cutpurses had joined the students and gone in procession to fetch from the lawyers' wardrobe the pasteboard tiara and mock chimer kept for the Pope of Fools. Quasimodo let them robe him without a flicker of protest and with a kind of proud docility. Then they seated him on a gaudy litter. Twelve officers of the confraternity of fools lifted him on to their shoulders; and a kind of bitter, contemptuous pleasure spread over the Cyclops' sullen face as he saw beneath his misshapen feet the heads of handsome, straight-limbed, well-made men. Then the yelling, ragged procession moved off on the traditional inner circuit of the galleries of the Palais before parading through the streets and crossroads.

VI

LA ESMERALDA

WE are delighted to be able to inform our readers that during the whole of this scene Gringoire and his play had stood fast. His actors, with him spurring them on, had not left off declaiming his comedy, and he had not left off listening. He had come to terms with the din, and was determined to go on to the end, not abandoning the hope of regaining the people's attention. This glimmer of hope revived when he saw Quasimodo, Coppenole, and the deafening procession escorting the Pope of Fools noisily leave the hall. The crowd rushed eagerly after them. 'Good,' he thought, 'there go all the trouble-makers.' Unfortunately all the trouble-makers were all the public. In a twinkling the Great Hall was empty.

Some spectators did in fact still remain, some scattered about, others grouped round the pillars, women, old folk, and children, who had had their fill of uproar and commotion. A few students had stayed astride the window ledges and were looking out on to the Place.

'Well,' thought Gringoire, 'there are still enough left to hear the end of my mystery. There are only a few, but it is a superior kind of audience, an educated audience.'

After a moment a symphony, intended to produce a striking effect as the Holy Virgin arrived, failed to materialize. Gringoire realized that his band had been taken off by the procession of the Pope of Fools. 'Carry on,' he said stoically.

He approached a group of citizens who, he thought, were discussing his play. He caught the following scrap of conversation:

'You know, Maître Cheneteau, the Hôtel de Navarre, which used to belong to Monsieur de Nemours?'

'Yes, opposite the chapel of Braque.'

'Well, the tax people have just let it to Guillaume Alixandre, the decorator, for 6 *livres* 8 *sous* a year.'

'How rents are going up!'

'Come!' Gringoire said to himself with a sigh, 'the others are listening.'

'Comrades!' one of the young rascals on the window suddenly cried, 'La Esmeralda! La Esmeralda's in the Place!'

These words had a magical effect. All those left in the hall rushed to the windows, climbing up the walls to see, and repeated: 'La Esmeralda! la Esmeralda!'

At the same time loud applause could be heard from outside.

'What does that mean—la Esmeralda?' said Gringoire, clasping his hands in despair. 'Oh goodness, it seems to be the turn of the windows now.'

He turned round towards the marble table, and saw that the performance had been interrupted. This was just the moment when Jupiter was meant to appear with his thunderbolt. But Jupiter stood motionless below the stage.

'Michel Giborne,' the poet cried angrily, 'what are you doing there? Is that your part? Get up there, will you!'

'Alas!' said Jupiter, 'one of the students has just taken the ladder.'

Gringoire looked. It was only too true. All communication had been severed between his dramatic knot and its resolution.

'The rogue!' he muttered. 'And why did he take the ladder?'

'To go and see la Esmeralda,' Jupiter pathetically replied. 'He said: "Well now, here's a ladder no one is using!" and took it.'

This was the final blow. Gringoire accepted it with resignation. 'Devil take you!' he said to the actors; 'and if I get paid you will be.'

Then he retreated, head bowed, but the last to go, like a general who has fought well.

And as he went down the winding stairs of the Palais he grumbled between his teeth: 'These Parisians are a fine lot of asses and boors; they come to see a mystery play, and don't listen to a word! They took an interest in everyone, Clopin Trouillefou, the cardinal, Coppenole, Quasimodo, the devil! but not a bit of interest in Our Lady the Virgin Mary. If I'd known, I'd have given you Virgin Marys, you nosy idlers! As for me, I come expecting to see faces and see nothing but backs! To be a poet and have as much success as an apothecary! It's true Homerus went round the Greek villages begging, and Naso* died in exile among the Muscovites. But may the devil flay me if I understand what they mean with their Esmeralda! What sort of word is that anyhow? It's Egyptiac!'

BOOK TWO

I

FROM CHARYBDIS TO SCYLLA

NIGHT comes early in January. The streets were already
dark when Gringoire left the Palais. He was pleased that
night had fallen; he was longing to find some dark lonely
alley where he could ponder at leisure and where the philosopher could apply first aid to the wound suffered by the
poet. Philosophy was in any case his only refuge, for he did
not know where he could stay. After the shattering fiasco
of his first attempt at drama he did not dare go back to his
previous lodgings in the rue Grenier-sur-l'Eau, opposite the
Port-au-Foin, having counted on what Monsieur the Provost was to give him for the epithalamium to pay Maître
Guillaume Doulx-Sire, who farmed the tax on cloven-
footed beasts in Paris, the six months' rent he owed, that
is, 12 *sols parisis*; twelve times more than the value of all his
worldly possessions, including his breeches, shirt, and bycocket hat. After a moment's reflection, while he took temporary shelter beneath the small wicket-gate of the treasurer
of the Sainte-Chapelle's prison, as to where he might decide to spend the night, with all the cobblestones in Paris
to choose from, he remembered having noticed the week
before, in the rue de la Savaterie, in front of a parliamentary
counsellor's door, a mounting block for mule riders, which,
he had thought, might, on occasion, provide an excellent
pillow for a beggar or a poet. He thanked providence for
sending him such a good idea, but as he was about to cross
the Place du Palais to reach the tortuous labyrinth of the
City, through which wind all those serpentine old sisters,
the rues de la Barillerie, de la Vieille-Draperie, de la Savaterie, de la Juiverie etc., still standing today with their
nine-storey houses, he saw the Pope of Fools' procession

also leaving the Palais and rushing across his path, with loud shouts, bright torchlight, and his, Gringoire's, band. The sight opened up again the lacerating injuries inflicted on his self-esteem: he fled. In the bitterness of his dramatic misadventures, anything that reminded him of the day's celebration soured him and made his wound bleed again.

He intended to take the Pont Saint-Michel; children were running about on the bridge with squibs and rockets.

'A plague on all fireworks!' said Gringoire and fell back on the Pont-au-Change. On the houses at the approach to the bridge had been hung three banners representing the King, the Dauphin and Marguerite of Flanders, and six smaller banners portraying the Duke of Austria, the Cardinal de Bourbon, Monsieur de Beaujeu, Madame Jeanne de France, Monsieur the Bastard of Bourbon, and someone or other besides; all lit up by torches. The crowd was full of admiration.

'He's a lucky painter, that Jehan Fourbault!' said Gringoire with a deep sigh, and turned his back on the banners, large and small. A street opened in front of him; he found it so dark and deserted that he hoped to escape there from all the echoes and illuminations of the festival. He plunged down it. After a moment or two he stubbed his foot on an obstacle; he stumbled and fell. It was the May bundle* which the law clerks had put down that morning at the door of a parliamentary president in honour of the feast day. Gringoire heroically endured this new encounter. He picked himself up and reached the water's edge. Leaving behind him the Tournelle *civile* and the Tour *criminelle*, and following the great wall of the king's gardens along the unpaved river bank where the mud came up to his ankles, he came to the westernmost tip of the City, and stayed for a while looking at the little island of the cow-ferryman, *passeur-aux-vaches*, which has since disappeared beneath the bronze horse and the Pont-Neuf. The little island appeared in the shadows like a dark mass on the far side of the pale strip of water separating him from it. One could just make out by the beams of a little light a sort of hut, shaped like a beehive, where the ferryman sheltered at night.

'Lucky cow-ferryman!' thought Gringoire: 'You don't have dreams of glory and you don't write epithalamia! What do kings' weddings and duchesses of Burgundy matter to you! The only marguerites you know are the daisies that your April meadow gives your cows to graze on! And I, a poet, am booed, and stand shivering with cold, and owe 12 *sous*, and the soles of my shoes have worn so thin that they are transparent enough to serve as glass for your lantern. Thank you, cow-ferryman, your cabin is a restful sight and makes me forget Paris!'

He was woken out of his almost lyrical ecstasy by a great double petard suddenly exploding from the blessed cabin. It was the ferryman contributing to the day's celebrations and letting off a firework. This petard made Gringoire bristle.

'Cursed festival!' he cried. 'Are you going to pursue me everywhere? Oh God! even to the ferryman's!'

Then he looked down at the Seine at his feet, and was seized with a horrible temptation.

'Oh!' he said, 'how gladly would I drown myself if the water weren't so cold!' Then he came to a desperate decision. It was this: since he could not escape the Pope of Fools, Jehan Fourbault's banners, May bundles, squibs, and petards, he would boldly plunge into the very heart of the festivities and go to the Place de Grève.

'At least,' he thought,' I may find there a brand from the bonfire to warm me up, and find a crumb for supper from the three great coats of arms worked in royal sugar they are bound to have set up there on the buffet offered to the public by the Town.'

II

THE PLACE DE GRÈVE

TODAY there remains only one quite imperceptible trace of the Place de Grève as it then existed. That is the charming turret which occupies the northern corner of the Place and which, already buried beneath the ignoble coats of distemper which clog the bold lines of its carvings, will perhaps soon have disappeared, submerged by the rising flood of new buildings so rapidly swallowing up all the old façades of Paris.

Those who, like ourselves, never pass by the Place de Grève without sparing a look of pity and sympathy for that poor turret, squeezed between two ramshackle Louis XIV buildings, can easily reconstruct in their mind's eye the whole collection of buildings to which it belonged and thus recreate in its entirety the old Gothic Place of the fifteenth century.

It formed, as it does today, an irregular trapezium, bounded on one side by the river quay, and on the other three by a series of tall, narrow, gloomy houses. In the daytime one could admire the variety of its buildings, all carved in stone or wood, and already offering complete samples of the different types of medieval domestic architecture, going back from the fifteenth through to the eleventh century, from the casement which was beginning to oust the ogive, back to the round Romanesque arch which the ogive had supplanted, and which still occupied, beneath the ogive, the first floor of that ancient house of the Tour-Roland, in the corner of the Place giving on to the Seine, on the rue de la Tannerie side. At night all that could be distinguished of this mass of buildings was the dark serrated outline of the roofs unfolding their chain of acute angles round the Place. For one of the basic differences between towns then and now is that today it is the façades which look on to squares and streets, while then it was the gables. For the past two centuries houses have turned about.

In the centre of the eastern side of the Place rose a heavy, heterogeneous construction consisting of three houses in juxtaposition. It was known by three names, explaining its history, purpose, and architecture: the *Maison du Dauphin*, because Charles V as Dauphin had lived there; the *Marchandise*, because it served as the Town Hall; the *Maison-aux-Piliers* (*domus ad piloria*), because of a series of large pillars supporting its three storeys. There the town could find everything that a good town like Paris needs: a chapel, for prayer; a courtroom, for hearing pleas, and, if necessary, putting the King's men in their place; and in the loft, an arsenal full of artillery. For the burghers of Paris know that it is not enough in every contingency to pray or to plead for the freedoms of the City, and always have in reserve in a loft of the Hôtel de Ville some good old rusty arquebus.

The Grève then already had the sinister aspect still preserved today by the execrable image it evokes, and Dominique Boccador's* gloomy Hôtel de Ville, which has replaced the Maison-aux-Piliers. It must be said that a permanent gallows and pillory, a 'justice' and a 'ladder' as they were then called, standing side by side in the middle of the paving, contributed not a little to making people avert their gaze from this fatal site, where so many beings full of life and health had breathed their last; where fifty years later was to be born that Saint-Vallier's* fever, that sickness which is a terror of the scaffold, the most monstrous of all sicknesses, because it comes not from God but from man.

It is a comforting thought, be it said in passing, that the death penalty which, three hundred years ago still cluttered up with its iron wheels, its stone gibbets, its whole apparatus of punishment permanently fixed into the pavement, the Grève, the Halles, the Place Dauphine, the Croix-du-Trahoir, the Marché-aux-Pourceaux, the hideous Montfaucon, the Barrière des Sergents, the Place-aux-Chats, the Porte Saint-Denis, Champeaux, the Porte Baudets, the Porte Saint-Jacques, not to mention the countless 'ladders' of the provosts, the bishop, the chapter, the abbots, the priors with rights of jurisdiction; not to speak of judicial execution by drowning in the river Seine; it is comforting to think that today, having lost one by one all the pieces of her armour, her profusion of torments, her imaginative and fanciful punishments, her torture for which she had a new leather bed made every five years at the Grand Châtelet, that old sovereign ruler of feudal society, almost expelled from our laws and our towns, hunted from code to code, driven from place to place, has nothing left in all our vast city of Paris but one dishonoured corner of the Grève, one wretched guillotine, furtive, anxious, ashamed, seemingly always afraid of being caught red-handed, to judge by the haste with which it disappears once it has done its job.

III

BESOS PARA GOLPES*

BY the time Pierre Gringoire reached the Place de Grève he was numb with cold. He had gone by way of the Pont-aux-Meuniers to avoid the throng at the Pont-au-Change and Jehan Fourbault's banners; but the wheels of all the bishop's water-mills had splashed him as he went by and his smock was wringing wet. Moreover, the failure of his play seemed to have made him feel the cold much more. So he hurried to get near the splendid bonfire blazing in the middle of the square. But a considerable crowd was massed all round it.

'Damned Parisians!' he said to himself, for Gringoire, like any true dramatic poet, was given to monologues; 'now they're blocking me from the fire! Yet I could really do with a fireside corner. My shoes leak and all those blasted mill-wheels have given me a cold shower! Devil take the Bishop of Paris and his water-mills! I'd like to know what use a mill is to a bishop! Does he expect to change from being a bishop into a miller? If all he needs for that is my curse, then I freely give it to him, his cathedral, and his mills! Just see whether these idlers will move aside! What are they doing there, I ask you? They are having a warm; fine way to enjoy yourself! They're watching a hundred faggots burn; a fine entertainment!'

Looking more closely, he realized that the circle was much wider than it needed to be for enjoying the warmth of the bonfire and that such a mass of spectators had not been attracted merely by the beauty of a hundred faggots blazing away.

In the huge open space left between the crowd and the fire, a girl was dancing.

Whether this girl was a human being, a fairy, or an angel was something that Gringoire, sceptical philosopher, ironic poet though he was, could not decide straight away, so fascinated was he by the dazzling vision.

She was not very tall, but her slim figure stood so boldly straight that she seemed to be so. She was dark, but one could see that in daylight her skin would have the fine golden glow of Andalusian and Roman women. Her small foot too was Andalusian, for it fitted both snugly and easily into her dainty shoe. She was dancing, turning, whirling on an old Persian carpet, thrown down carelessly beneath her feet; and each time her radiant face passed before you as she spun round her great, dark eyes flashed lightning.

Around her everyone gazed open-mouthed; and in truth, while she danced like that, to the thrumming of a tambourine held above her head by her two pure, shapely arms, slim, frail, lively as a wasp, with her golden unpleated bodice, her brightly coloured dress swirling out, her bare shoulders, her slender legs uncovered now and then by her skirt, her dark hair, her blazing eyes, she was a supernatural creature.

'Truly,' thought Gringoire, 'she's a salamander,* a nymph, a goddess, a Bacchante from Mount Maenalus!'*

Just then one of the braids of the 'salamander's' hair came undone, and a small brass coin that was attached to it rolled on to the ground.

'Oh no!' he said, 'she's a gypsy.'

Every illusion had been dispelled.

She started to dance again. She picked up two swords from the ground, balanced them by the tips on her forehead and made them turn in one direction while she turned in the other. She was indeed quite simply a gypsy. But disenchanted though Gringoire was, the overall scene was not without glamour and magic: the bonfire cast a harsh red glare which flickered brightly over the circle of faces in the crowd, over the girl's brown forehead, and on the square behind cast a pale reflection mingled with their wavering shadows, on one side upon the black, wrinkled old façade of the Maison-aux-Piliers, on the other on the stone arms of the gibbet.

Among the hundreds of faces stained scarlet by this glow, there was one which seemed even more absorbed than all the others in contemplating the dancer. It was a man's face, austere, calm, sombre. This man, whose clothes were concealed by the crowd around him, did not look more than 35 years old; yet he was bald; at his temples he had scarcely more than a few scanty tufts of hair already grey; his broad, high forehead was beginning to be furrowed with wrinkles; but in his deep-set eyes shone an extraordinary youthfulness, ardent vitality, intense passion. He never took his eyes off the gypsy girl, and while the wild 16-year-old danced and leaped about to the delight of all, his private reverie seemed to become more and more sombre. From time to time a smile and a sigh met on his lips, but the smile revealed more pain than the sigh.

Out of breath, the girl stopped at last, and the people applauded her warmly.

'Djali,' said the girl.

Then Gringoire saw a pretty little white she-goat come up, nimble, lively, glossy, with gilded horns, gilded hooves, a gilded collar; he had not noticed it before, for it had remained crouching up till then on a corner of the carpet, watching its mistress dance.

'Djali,' said the dancer, 'now it's your turn.'

And as she sat down, she gracefully held out her tambourine to the goat.

'Djali,' she continued, 'what month of the year is it?'

The goat raised its foreleg and struck the tambourine once. It was indeed the first month of the year. The crowd applauded.

'Djali,' the girl went on, turning the tambourine round, 'what day of the month is it?' Djali raised her little golden hoof and struck the tambourine six times.

'Djali,' the gypsy continued, once more moving the tambourine about, 'what hour of the day is it?'

Djali tapped seven times. At the same moment the clock on the Maison-aux-Piliers struck seven o'clock. The people marvelled.

'There's witchcraft behind that,' said a sinister voice in the crowd. It was that of the bald man who never took his eyes off the gypsy girl.

She shuddered and turned away; but applause broke out, drowning the peevish exclamation. The applause in fact so effectively wiped it from her mind that she continued her questioning of the goat.

'Djali, how does Maître Guichard Grand-Rémy, captain of the municipal pistoleers, behave in the Candlemas procession?'

Djali stood up on her hindlegs and began bleating as she marched, with such charming gravity that the entire circle of spectators burst out laughing at this parody of the self-centred piety of the pistoleer captain.

'Djali,' went on the girl, emboldened by her growing success, 'how does Maître Jacques Charmolue, the King's attorney in the ecclesiastical court, look when he preaches?'

The goat sat down on its rump and began bleating, waving its forelegs about so quaintly that, apart from the bad French and bad Latin, it was Jacques Charmolue to the life, gestures, accent, posture, and all.

And the crowd applauded even louder.

'Sacrilege! Profanation!' went on the bald man's voice.

The gypsy girl turned round again.

'Ah!' she said, 'it's that nasty man!' Then sticking out her lower lip, she pouted slightly in what seemed like a familiar expression with her, turned on her heel, and began collecting the crowd's contributions in a tambourine.

All sorts of small coins rained down, *grands blancs, petits blancs, targes, liards-à l'aigle.** Suddenly she passed in front of Gringoire. He stuck his hand in his pocket in such a daze that she stopped. 'Oh, hell!' said the poet, finding reality, that is emptiness, at the bottom of his pocket. Meanwhile the pretty girl was there, looking at him with her huge eyes, holding out the tambourine, waiting. Gringoire was dripping with perspiration.

If he had had all the riches of Peru in his pocket he would certainly have given it all to the dancer; but Gringoire did not have Peru, and anyhow America had not yet been discovered.

Fortunately an unexpected incident came to his rescue. 'Will you go away, you Egyptian locust?' cried a shrill voice

from the darkest corner of the Place. The girl turned round
in fright. This was not the bald man's voice now; it was a
woman's voice, pious and malicious.

However, this cry, which frightened the gypsy girl, delighted a band of children who were prowling about. 'It's
the recluse from the Tour-Roland,' they shouted, laughing
wildly, 'it's the *sachette*★ grumbling! Hasn't she had any
supper? Let's fetch her some scraps from the public buffet.'

They all rushed off to the Maison-aux-Piliers.

Meanwhile Gringoire had taken advantage of the
dancer's confusion to disappear. The children's shouts reminded him that he had not had any supper either. So he
ràn off to the buffet. But the little rascals ran faster than
he did; when he got there they had cleared the board. There
was not so much left as one of those wretched *camichons*★
that sell for five *sous* the pound. All that remained on the
wall were the delicate fleurs-de-lys, intertwined with rose
bushes, painted in 1434 by Mathurin Biterne. That was not
much of a supper.

Going to bed with no supper is tiresome enough; it is
even less fun to go without supper and no prospect of a bed
for the night. Gringoire had come to that. No bread, no
bed; he saw necessity hemming him in on every side, and
found necessity most unmannerly. He had long ago discovered the truth, that Jupiter created men in a fit of mis-
anthropy and throughout the wise man's life his fate lays
siege to his philosophy. As for him, he had never known
such a total blockade; he could hear his stomach rumbling
in surrender, and thought it very unfair that ill fate should
starve his philosophy into capitulation.

He was becoming more and more engrossed in this melancholy reverie when a song, strange but sweet, suddenly
tore him out of it. It was the gypsy girl singing.

The same qualities held good for her voice as for her
dancing and her beauty. It was indefinable and charming; something pure, resonant, airy, winged, so to speak.
It flowed continuously in passages of soaring lyricism,
melodies, unexpected cadences, then simple phrases sprinkled with sharp, sibilant notes, cascades of scales which

would have defeated a nightingale, but where the harmony was always present, then softly rippling octaves, rising and falling like the young singer's breast. Her lovely features followed every caprice of her song with peculiar mobility, from the wildest inspiration to the chastest dignity. At one moment she seemed like a mad woman, at the next a queen.

She sang words in a language unknown to Gringoire, and apparently unknown to her too, so little did the expression she gave to her song relate to the sense of the words. Thus these four lines in her mouth expressed wild gaiety:

> Un cofre de gran riqueza
> Hallaron dentro un pilar,
> Dentro del, nuevas banderas
> Con figuras de espantar.

And a moment later she gave this verse such a tone that Gringoire felt the tears spring to his eyes:

> Alarabes de cavallo
> Sin poderse menear,
> Con espadas, y los cuellos,
> Ballestas de buen echar.*

Yet her song breathed joy above all, and she seemed to sing, like a bird, out of serene and carefree happiness.

The gypsy's song had disturbed Gringoire's reflections, but in the same way as a swan disturbs the water. He listened to it in a kind of trance, as if oblivious of all else. It was the first time for many hours that he felt no pain.

The moment was brief.

The voice of the same woman who had interrupted the gypsy-girl's dance now interrupted her song.

'Will you shut up, you cicada from hell?' she cried, still from the same dark corner of the square.

The poor cicada stopped dead. Gringoire blocked up his ears. 'Oh!' he cried, 'cursed toothless saw, come to break the lyre!'

Meanwhile the other spectators were grumbling like him. 'Devil take the *sachette*!' more than one was saying. And the

invisible old spoil-sport might have had cause to regret her
attacks on the gypsy if at that very moment they had not
been distracted by the Pope of Fools' procession, which
after wending its way through many a street and crossing
was now debouching into the Place de Grève with all its
torches and clamour.

That procession, which our readers saw leaving the Palais, had been organized as it went along, and had recruited
all that Paris had to offer by way of rogues, idle thieves,
and available vagabonds, so that it was looking of respectable size when it reached the Grève.

First came Egypt. The Duke of Egypt at the head, on
horseback, with his counts on foot, holding his bridle and
stirrups; behind them the Egyptian men and women in no
particular order, with their small children yelling on their
shoulders; all of them, the duke, counts, ordinary people,
in rags and tinsel. Then came the realm of Argot, thieves'
cant; that is to say, all the thieves of France, ranked in order
of dignity, the lowest going first. There thus filed by in
column of four, wearing the different insignia of their degrees in this strange faculty, most of them disabled in some
way, some limping, some with only one arm, the *courtauds
de boutanche, coquillarts, hubins, sabouleux, calots, francs-
mitoux, polissons, piètres, capons, malingreux, rifodés, marcandiers, narquois*, orphans, *archisuppôts, cagoux*; an enumeration
to make Homer weary. In the midst of the conclave of
cagoux and *archisuppôts*, the King of Argot, or the great *coësre*,*
could just be made out, squatting in a little cart drawn by
two big dogs.* After the kingdom of the Argoteers came
the empire of Galilee. Guillaume Rousseau, Emperor of
Galilee,* marched majestically in his purple, wine-stained,
robe, preceded by mummers hitting each other and doing
a war dance, surrounded by his mace-bearers, his henchmen and clerks from his counting-house. Last came the law
clerks, the *basoche*,* with maypoles wreathed in flowers,
their black gowns, music fit for a witches' sabbath, and
great candles of yellow wax. In the middle of this crowd
the high officers of the confraternity of Fools bore on their
shoulders a litter more heavily laden with candles than the

reliquary of Sainte-Geneviève* in time of plague. And upon this litter shone in splendour, decked in cross, cope, and mitre, the new Pope of Fools, the bell-ringer of Notre-Dame, Quasimodo the Hunchback.

Each section of this grotesque procession had its own particular music. The Egyptians banged away on their balafos* and African tambourines. The Argoteers, an unmusical race, had progressed no further than the viol, the buccina, and the Gothic rebec of the twelfth century. The empire of Galilee was hardly more advanced; one could just make out in its music some wretched rebec from the infancy of the musical art, still confined to *re–la–mi.* But it was around the Pope of Fools that all the musical riches of the period were displayed in magnificent cacophony. It was all treble rebecs, counter-tenor rebecs, tenor rebecs, not to mention flutes and brass. Alas! our readers will recall that this was Gringoire's orchestra!

It is hard to convey any idea of the degree of proud and blissful satisfaction which the hideous, mournful features of Quasimodo had come to express in the course of the journey from the Palais to the Grève. It was the first time he had ever enjoyed any feeling of self-esteem. Hitherto all he had known was humiliation, contempt for his condition, disgust for his person. Thus, stone-deaf as he was, he was relishing, like a real pope, the acclamations of this crowd which he hated because he felt hated by them. His people might be a collection of fools, cripples, thieves, and beggars, no matter! They were for all that a people, and he was their sovereign. And he took seriously all these ironic cheers, all this mock respect mingled, we must add, with a little very real fear on the crowd's part. For the hunchback was robust; the bow-legs were nimble; the deaf man was spiteful; three qualities to temper ridicule.

However, that the new Pope of Fools realized inwardly the feelings he experienced or those which he inspired is something we find it hard to believe. The mind lodged in that misshapen body was itself inevitably incomplete and deaf. Thus what it felt at that moment was absolutely vague, indistinct, and confused. Only joy came through, pride was dominant. That gloomy, unhappy face beamed radiantly.

It caused, therefore, no little surprise and alarm when just as Quasimodo, in this state of semi-intoxication, was passing triumphantly before the Maison-aux-Piliers, a man was seen suddenly to dart from the crowd, and with an angry gesture tear from Quasimodo's hands the gilded wooden crozier, emblem of his Fools' papacy.

The man who had acted so rashly was the individual with the bald forehead who, a moment before, blending with the group round the gypsy girl, had chilled the poor girl with his menacing and hateful words. He was in ecclesiastical dress. Just as he emerged from the crowd Gringoire, who had not noticed him until then, recognized him: 'My word!' he cried in amazement, 'it's my master in Hermes, Dom Claude Frollo the archdeacon! What the devil is he up to with that ugly one-eyed creature? He'll be eaten up alive.'

A cry of terror did indeed go up. The formidable Quasimodo had plunged down from his litter, and women averted their gaze so that they would not see him tear the archdeacon to pieces.

He reached the priest in one bound, looked at him, and fell on his knees.

The priest tore off the tiara, smashed the crozier, ripped the tinsel cope.

Quasimodo remained kneeling, with head bowed and hands clasped.

There then took place between them a strange dialogue of signs and gestures, for neither spoke. The priest, upright, angry, menacing, imperious: Quasimodo prostrate, humble, suppliant. Yet it is certain that Quasimodo could have squashed the priest just with his thumb.

At length the archdeacon, roughly shaking Quasimodo's powerful shoulder, signed to him to rise and follow him.

Quasimodo rose.

Then the confraternity of Fools, recovering from their initial stupefaction, tried to defend their pope, who had been so rudely dethroned. The Egyptians, the Argoteers, and all the law clerks came yelping round the priest.

Quasimodo placed himself in front of the priest, flexed the muscles of his athletic fists and looked at the assailants, grinding his teeth like an angry tiger.

The priest resumed his look of sombre gravity, made a sign to Quasimodo, and silently withdrew.

Quasimodo walked in front of him, scattering the crowd as he went along.

When they had passed through the crowd out of the square, a horde of curious and idle people tried to follow them. Quasimodo then took up the rearguard, and followed the archdeacon walking backwards, squat, snarling, monstrous, bristling, flexing his limbs, licking his boar-like tusks, growling like a wild beast, and sending huge ripples through the crowd with a mere look or gesture.

The two of them were allowed to plunge into a dark, narrow street, where no one dared venture after them. The nightmare image of Quasimodo grinding his teeth was itself enough to bar entry.

'That's all very wonderful,' said Gringoire, 'but where the devil am I going to find some supper?'

IV

THE DISADVANTAGES OF FOLLOWING A PRETTY
WOMAN THROUGH THE STREETS AT NIGHT

GRINGOIRE, trusting entirely to luck, had begun following the gypsy girl. He had seen her and her goat take the rue de la Coutellerie; he had taken the rue de la Coutellerie.

'Why not?' he had said to himself.

Gringoire, as a practical philosopher of the Paris streets, had noticed that nothing is more conducive to reverie than following a pretty woman without knowing where she is going. In this voluntary abdication of one's own free will, in this fancy submitting to another's quite unsuspecting fancy, there is a mixture of capricious independence and blind obedience, an indefinable middle term between slavery and freedom, which was to Gringoire's liking, with his essentially mixed, indecisive and complex mind, holding tenuously to every extreme, suspended between every human propensity, cancelling out one by another. He liked to compare himself to Mahomet's tomb, attracted in opposite directions by two lodestones, eternally hesitating between high and low, ceiling and floor, falling and rising, zenith and nadir.

If Gringoire were living in our day, what a fine balance he would have struck between Classic and Romantic!

But he was not primitive enough to live for three hundred years, more's the pity! His absence leaves a vacuum which is felt only too keenly today.

However, for following passers-by (especially female ones) through the streets, something Gringoire enjoyed doing, there is no better frame of mind.

He was therefore in reflective mood as he walked behind the girl, who quickened her pace and made her pretty goat fairly trot along as she saw the townsfolk going home and the taverns closing, for no other shops had been open that day.

'After all,' ran his thoughts, more or less, 'she must live somewhere; gypsy women are kind-hearted—who knows?'

And the row of dots which followed his mental reticence implied some rather pleasing vague ideas.

Meanwhile, as he passed from time to time the last groups of townsfolk closing their doors, he caught some scraps of their conversations which broke the thread of his attractive hypotheses.

Now it was two old men meeting.

'Maître Thibaut Fernicle, it's cold, don't you know?'

(Gringoire had known that since the beginning of winter.)

'Yes, indeed, Maître Boniface Disome! Are we going to have another winter like the one three years ago, in '80, when wood cost 8 *sous* a bundle?'

'Bah! that's nothing, Maître Thibaut, compared to the winter of 1407, when it froze from Martinmas to Candlemas! And so hard that the parliamentary clerk's pen froze, in the Great Chamber, with every three words! They couldn't go on recording the proceedings.'

Further on it was two women at neighbouring windows, their candles sputtering in the fog.

'Did your husband tell you about the accident, Mademoiselle La Boudraque?'

'No. What happened then, Mademoiselle Turquant?'

'The horse belonging to Monsieur Gilles Godin, notary at the Châtelet, took fright at the Flemings and their procession and knocked down Maître Philippot Avrillot, a Celestine* oblate.'

'Really?'

'Just like that.'

'A civilian horse! That's going a bit far. If it had been a cavalry horse, all well and good!'

And the windows closed. But not without breaking Gringoire's train of thought.

Fortunately he soon recovered it, and easily picked up the thread again, thanks to the gypsy girl, and thanks to Djali, who were walking in front of him: two finely made, delicate, charming creatures, whose dainty feet, shapely form, graceful demeanour he admired, almost mixing them up as he watched; in their understanding and close friendship he saw them both as two girls, in their light, nimble, surefooted step they both seemed like little goats.

The streets meanwhile were with every moment becoming darker and lonelier. The curfew had sounded long ago, and it was only at rare intervals that anyone passed by on the pavement or that a light shone at a window. Gringoire, following the gypsy, had entered the impenetrable maze of alleys, crossroads, and cul-de-sacs surrounding the ancient burial place of the Holy Innocents, which resembled nothing so much as a skein of thread tangled up by a cat. 'There's not much logic to these streets!' said Gringoire, lost in the innumerable twists and turns, continually doubling back on themselves, but through which the girl followed a path which she seemed to know well, without hesitating and walking ever faster and faster. As for him, he would not have had the slightest idea where he was had he not noticed in passing, at a bend in the street, the octagonal bulk of the pillory in the Halles, its open-work top boldly silhouetted against a window where a light still showed in the rue Verdelet.

For the past few moments he had attracted the girl's attention; she had looked round at him uneasily several times; once she had even stopped dead, and taken advantage of a ray of light emerging from a half-closed baker's shop to stare at him from head to foot; then, after this searching look, Gringoire had seen her make the little pout he had noticed already, and she had gone on.

This little pout incited Gringoire's reflection. There was certainly an element of scorn and mockery in the graceful little grimace. So he was beginning to hang his head, count the cobble stones, and follow the girl at a slightly greater distance when, as she turned into a street where he lost her from sight, he heard her give a piercing shriek.

He quickened his step.

The street was quite dark. However, a wick of tow soaked in oil, burning in an iron cage at the feet of the Blessed Virgin at the street corner, enabled Gringoire to make out the gypsy girl struggling in the arms of two men who were trying to muffle her cries. The poor little goat, frightened to death, dropped its horns and bleated.

'Help, gentlemen of the watch!' cried Gringoire, and stepped forward boldly. One of the men holding the girl turned towards him. It was the formidable figure of Quasimodo.

Gringoire did not take to his heels, but nor did he advance another step.

Quasimodo came up to him, flung him to the ground four paces away with a backhanded blow, and swiftly plunged into the shadows, carrying the girl hanging limply over his arm like a silk scarf. His companion followed, and the poor goat ran after them, bleating piteously.

'Murder! murder!' cried the unfortunate gypsy girl.

'Stop right there, you wretches, and let go of that wench!' cried in a voice of thunder a horseman who suddenly emerged from a crossroads nearby.

It was a captain of the archers of the King's troop,* armed from head to foot, broadsword in his hand.

He snatched the gypsy girl from the astounded Quasimodo's grasp, put her across his saddle, and just as the redoubtable hunchback, recovering from his surprise, rushed at him to take back his prey, fifteen or sixteen archers appeared, following close behind their captain, their great swords at the ready. It was a squadron of the King's troop on counter-patrol by order of Robert d'Estouteville, keeper of the Provostry of Paris.

Quasimodo was surrounded, seized, trussed up. He bellowed, foamed at the mouth, bit, and, if it had been daytime, there can be no doubt that his face alone, made even more hideous by anger, would have put the whole squadron to flight. But the dark deprived him of his most fearful weapon: his ugliness.

His companion had disappeared during the struggle.

The gypsy sat up gracefully on the officer's saddle, rested her hands on the young man's shoulders and gazed at him for a few seconds, as though enchanted by his good looks and the timely assistance he had just brought her. Then, the first to break the silence, she said, making her sweet voice sweeter still: 'What is your name, Monsieur le gendarme?'*

'Captain Phoebus de Châteaupers, at your service, my beauty!' replied the officer, drawing himself up.

'Thank you,' she said.

And while Captain Phoebus was twirling his Burgundian moustache, she slipped down from the horse, like an arrow dropping to the ground, and made off.

She disappeared faster than a streak of lightning.

'By the Pope's navel!' said the captain, getting them to tighten Quasimodo's bonds, 'I'd rather have kept the wench.'

'What do you expect, captain?' said one of the troopers. 'The linnet has flown, we're left with the bat.'

V

THE DISADVANTAGES
(CONTINUED)

GRINGOIRE, stunned by his fall, still lay on the ground in front of the good Virgin at the street corner. He gradually came to his senses; at first he floated for a short time in a kind of half-somnolent daydream, not wholly unpleasant, in which the airy figures of the gypsy girl and the goat blended with the solid weight of Quasimodo's fist. This state did not last long. A very lively impression of cold in that part of his body which was in contact with the ground all at once woke him up and brought his mind back up to the surface. 'What's making me so chilly?' he suddenly asked himself. He noticed then that he was lying pretty well in the middle of the gutter.

'Devil take that one-eyed hunchback!' he muttered between his teeth and tried to get up. But he was too dizzy and too bruised. He had to stay where he was. His hand, however, moved quite freely; he held his nose and resigned himself.

'Paris mud,' he thought (for he was now pretty sure that the gutter was definitely going to be his room for the night, 'and what is there to do in a room but dream?')* 'Paris mud has a particularly nasty stench. It must contain a lot of nitre and sal volatile. At any rate, that is the opinion of Maître Nicolas* and the hermetics. . . .'

The word 'hermetics' suddenly brought to his mind the image of Archdeacon Claude Frollo. He recalled the violent scene of which he had caught just a glimpse, the gypsy girl struggling with two men, the fact that Quasimodo had had a companion, and the grim, haughty face of the archdeacon passed vaguely through his memory.

'That would be strange!' he thought. And he began with that datum and on that basis to construct a fantastic assembly of hypotheses, the philosophers' house of cards, then suddenly, coming back to reality again: 'Oh! oh! I'm freezing!' he cried.

His position was indeed becoming less and less tenable. Every molecule of water in the gutter removed a molecule of the caloric radiating around Gringoire's waist, and the process of establishing equilibrium between his body's temperature and that of the gutter water had painfully begun.

Trouble of a quite different kind suddenly assailed him.

A group of children, those little barefoot savages who have always run around the Paris streets under the eternal name of urchins, *gamins*, and who, when we were children too, threw stones at all of us when we came out of school in the afternoon, because our trousers were not ragged, a swarm of these young rascals ran to the crossroads where Gringoire lay, laughing and shouting as though unconcerned about the neighbours trying to sleep. They dragged after them some kind of shapeless sack; and were making enough noise with their clogs alone to wake the dead. Gringoire, who had not yet quite reached that state, half rose.

'Hey! Hennequin Dandèche! Hey! Jehan Pincebourde!' they yelled at the top of their voices, 'old Eustache Moubon, the ironmonger on the corner, has just died. We've got his palliasse, we're going to make a bonfire with it! It's the Flemings today!'

And with that they threw the palliasse right over Gringoire, whom they had come upon without seeing him. At the same time one of them took a handful of straw which he went to light from the wick in front of the good Virgin.

'Christ's death!' muttered Gringoire, 'am I going to be too hot now?'

The moment was critical. He was about to be caught between fire and water; he made a superhuman effort, like a counterfeiter about to be boiled alive trying to escape. He rose to his feet, threw the palliasse back at the urchins and fled.

'Holy Virgin!' cried the children; 'the ironmonger's ghost!' And they ran off too.

The palliasse remained master of the battlefield. Belleforêt, Father le Juge, and Corrozet* assure us that next day

it was collected with great ceremony by the local clergy and
borne to the treasury of the church of Sainte-Opportune,*
where up to 1789 the sacristan made a tidy income from
the great miracle of the statue of the Virgin on the corner
of the rue Mauconseil who had, by the mere fact of her
presence, on the memorable night of 6 to 7 January 1482
exorcized the deceased Eustache Moubon who, to trick the
devil, had, as he died, cunningly hidden his soul in his
palliasse.

THE BROKEN PITCHER

AFTER running at full pelt for some time, with no idea where he was going, rushing round many a street corner, stepping over many a gutter, crossing many an alley, cul-de-sac, crossroads, seeking an escape route and passage through all the twists and turns of the old cobbles of the Halles, exploring in his panic what the beautiful Latin of the charters calls *tota via, cheminum et viaria* [every road, pathway, and thoroughfare], our poet suddenly stopped, first because he was out of breath, then because he was pulled up short by a dilemma which had just occurred to him. 'It seems to me, Maître Pierre Gringoire,' he said to himself, pressing a finger to his forehead, 'that you are running away like a featherbrain. The little rascals were just as scared of you as you were of them. It seems to me, I tell you, that you heard the clatter of their clogs running off to the south, while you ran north. Now one of two things must have happened: either they have made themselves scarce, in which case the palliasse they must have forgotten in their terror is precisely that hospitable bed you have been chasing after since this morning, and which Our Lady the Virgin miraculously sent you as a reward for composing in her honour a morality accompanied by triumphs and mummeries; or the children have not made themselves scarce, in which case they have set the palliasse alight, and there you will find the excellent fire you need to cheer you up, dry you, and warm you. In either case, good fire or good bed, the palliasse is a gift from heaven. The Blessed Virgin Mary, at the corner of the rue Mauconseil, may well have caused Eustache Moubon to die just to that end, and it's silly of you to run away like that, helter-skelter like a Picard with a Frenchman after him, leaving behind the very thing you were chasing after; and you are a fool!'

Then he retraced his steps, trying to find his bearings, ferreting around, sniffing the wind, ears alert, making every effort to find the blessed palliasse. But in vain. There was nothing but rows of houses intersecting, blind alleys, multiple crossroads, amidst which he was constantly hesitating and doubtful, more baffled and stuck in this tangle of dark alleys than he would have been in the actual maze of the Hôtel des Tournelles. In the end he lost patience and solemnly exclaimed: 'A curse on crossroads! It's the devil who made them in the image of his fork!'

This outburst made him feel a bit better, and a kind of reddish reflection which he noticed just then at the end of a long, narrow alley completed the restoration of his morale. 'Praise God!' he said. 'There it is! That's my palliasse burning.' And comparing himself to the sailor foundering in the darkness: '*Salve*,' he added piously, '*salve maris stella* [Hail, star of the sea].'*

Was he addressing this fragment of the litany to the Blessed Virgin or to the palliasse? We have absolutely no idea.

He had gone scarcely more than a few steps down the long alley, which was on a slope, unpaved and increasingly steep and muddy, when he noticed something rather peculiar. It was not empty. Here and there along its length vague, shapeless masses crawled, all moving towards the light flickering at the end of the street, like those heavy insects which at night drag themselves along from one blade of grass to the next towards a shepherd's fire.

Nothing makes a man more adventurous than an empty feeling behind his waistband. Gringoire kept on, and had soon caught up with the most sluggish of these larva-like shapes, which trailed behind the others. As he approached he saw that it was quite simply a wretched cripple with no legs, hopping along on his hands, like a maimed daddy-long-legs with only two feet left. Just as he passed this species of spider with a human face, it lifted up to him a piteous voice:

'*La buona mancia, signor! la buona mancia!* [Alms, sir! alms!]'*

'The devil take you,' said Gringoire, 'and me with you, if I know what you mean!'

And he passed on.

He caught up with another of these moving shapes and examined it. It was a cripple, short of both a leg and an arm, and so mutilated that the complicated system of crutches and wooden legs which held him up made him look like a builder's scaffolding on the move. Gringoire, ready with noble Classical comparisons, mentally compared him with Vulcan's living tripod.

The living tripod saluted him as he went by, but by raising his hat no higher than Gringoire's chin, like a shaving-dish, and crying in his ear: '*Señor caballero, para comprar un pedaso de pan!* [Noble sir, to buy a crust of bread!]'*

'It seems,' said Gringoire, 'that this one talks too; but it's a harsh tongue, and he is more fortunate than I if he understands it.'

Then, striking his forehead at a sudden switch of ideas: 'Come to think of it, what the devil did they mean this morning with their *Esmeralda*?'

He tried to walk faster; but for the third time something obstructed his path. This something, or rather someone, was a blind man, a little blind man with a bearded Jewish face, who, as he swept the area round him with a stick, with a big dog towing him along, said in a nasal Hungarian accent: '*Facitote caritatem!* [Give of your charity!].'

'That's good!' said Pierre Gringoire; 'here at last is one who speaks a Christian language. I must have a very eleemosynary look about me for anyone to ask for my charity with my purse as lean as it is. My friend,' and he turned towards the blind man, 'I sold my last shirt last week; that is, since you only understand Cicero's language: *Vendidi hebdomada nuper transita meam ultimam chemisam.*'*

Saying which, he turned his back on the blind man and continued on his way; but the blind man began to lengthen his stride at the same time as he did, and then up came the cripple, up came the legless man, in great haste and with a great din from the wooden bowl holding the stump of the one and from the crutches supporting the other, clattering

over the stones. Then all three, jostling close behind Gringoire, began singing their song at him:

'*Caritatem!*' sang the blind man.

'*La buona mancia!*' sang the legless man.

And the cripple took up the musical phrase as he repeated: '*Un pedaso de pan!*'

Gringoire stopped up his ears. 'Oh, Tower of Babel!'
he cried.

He started to run. The blind man ran. The cripple ran.
The legless man ran.

And then, as he plunged further down the street, legless
men, blind men, cripples, swarmed round him, and men
with one arm, or with one eye, and lepers with their sores,
some coming out of the houses, some from little side
streets, some from the cellar openings, shouting, bellowing,
yelping, all hobbling, bobbing along, hurrying towards the
light, wallowing in the mire like slugs after rain.

Gringoire, still followed by his three persecutors, and not
too sure what was going to come of all this, walked in
dismay among the others, turning the cripples aside, stepping over the ones with no legs, getting his feet tangled in
this anthill of the disabled, like the English captain who was
sucked under by an army of crabs.

It occurred to him to try to retrace his steps. But it was
too late. The whole legion had closed ranks behind him,
and his three beggars held him fast. So he went on, driven
at once by this irresistible tide, by fear, and by a dizziness
which made it all seem to him like a horrible dream.

At last he reached the end of the street. It opened on to
a huge square, where a thousand scattered lights flickered
in the hazy night fog. Gringoire rushed into it, hoping that
his fleetness of foot would enable him to escape from the
three infirm spectres clinging on to him.

'*Onde vas, hombre?* [Where are you going, man?]' cried
the cripple, throwing away his crutches and running after
him on the best two legs that ever measured a full stride on
the Paris pavements.

Meanwhile the legless man, standing on his own two
feet, stuck his heavy iron-shod bowl over Gringoire's

head, and the blind man looked straight at him with blazing eyes.

'Where am I?' asked the terrified poet.

'In the Court of Miracles,' replied a fourth spectre who had accosted them.

'Upon my soul,' went on Gringoire, 'I can see the blind watching and the lame running; but where is the Saviour?'

They answered with a burst of sinister laughter.

The poor poet looked around him. He was indeed in that redoubtable Court of Miracles, where no honest man had ever penetrated at such an hour; a magic circle where the officers of the Châtelet and the sergeants of the Provostry who ventured in disappeared in small bits; the thieves' city, a hideous wen on the face of Paris; a sewer from which there seeped every morning and to which returned every night to stagnate that gutter stream of vice, beggary, and vagrancy which is always overflowing in the streets of capital cities; a monstrous hive to which all the hornets of the social order bring back their booty every evening; a counterfeit hospital where the gypsy, the unfrocked monk, the ruined student, the dregs of every nation, Spaniards, Italians, Germans, of every religion, Jews, Christians, Muslims, idolaters, covered in simulated sores, were beggars by day and at night transformed themselves into robbers; an immense changing room, in a word, where at that time all the actors dressed and undressed for the endless drama of robbery, prostitution, and murder played out in the Paris streets.

It was a vast open square, irregular and badly paved like all the Paris squares at that time. Fires, around which strange groups swarmed, glowed brightly here and there. Everything was hustle and bustle and shouting. Shrill laughter, small children squalling, women's voices. The hands and heads of the people in this crowd, standing out dark against the luminous background, were silhouetted in one weird gesture after another. At times on the ground, where the light from the fires flickered and merged with great amorphous shadows, a dog could be seen going by, looking like a man, or a man, looking like a dog. Boundaries

between races and species seemed to be erased in this city
as in a pandemonium. Men, women, animals, sex, health,
sickness, everything seemed to be held in common by these
people; everything went together, mingled, merged, superimposed; everyone shared in everything.

The wavering, feeble illumination from the fires enabled
Gringoire to make out, confused as he was, all round
the vast square a hideous frame of old houses, whose rotten, shrivelled, stunted façades, each pierced by one or
two lighted attic windows, looked to him in the darkness
like the heads of old women, standing in a circle, monstrous and baleful, watching the witches' sabbath with
blinking eyes.

It was like a new world, unknown, unheard of, misshapen, reptilian, teeming, fantastic.

Gringoire, more and more frightened, gripped by the
three beggars as though by three sets of pincers, deafened
by a crowd of other faces barking all round him in a ceaseless swell, the unfortunate Gringoire tried to collect his wits
together and remember whether it was a sabbath, a Saturday. But his efforts were in vain; the thread of his memory
and his thoughts was broken; and doubting everything,
drifting from what he saw to what he felt, he asked himself
the insoluble question: 'If I am, does this exist? If this
exists, am I?'

At that moment a distinct cry went up from the buzzing
throng that surrounded him: 'Take him to the King! Take
him to the King!'

'Holy Virgin!' muttered Gringoire, 'the King of this place
must be a he-goat.'

'To the King! the King!' every voice repeated.

They dragged him off. They vied with each other to
get their clutches on him. But the three beggars would not
let him go, and tore him away from the others, shouting:
'He's ours!'

The poet's already ailing doublet gave its last gasp in the
struggle.

As he crossed this awful square his dizziness cleared.
After a few steps he had regained a sense of reality. He

began to adjust to the atmosphere of the place. At the start fumes, a vapour, so to speak, had risen from his poet's head, or perhaps, quite simply and prosaically, from his empty stomach and this, interposed between objects and himself, had let him glimpse them only through the incoherent haze of nightmare, through the obscurity of those dreams which blur every edge, distort every shape, piling up objects into disproportionate groups, inflating things into chimeras and people into phantoms. Gradually these hallucinations were succeeded by a vision less distraught and less exaggerating. Reality dawned around him, touched his sight, touched his feet, and bit by bit dismantled all the poetry of terror with which he had at first believed himself to be surrounded. He was forced to realize that he was not walking in the Styx but in the mire, that he was not being jostled by devils but by robbers; that it was not his soul that was at stake but quite simply his life (since he lacked the precious intermediary which so effectively conciliates thief and honest man: a purse). Finally, as he examined the orgy more closely and coolly, he fell from a witches' sabbath to a tavern.

The Court of Miracles was in fact just a tavern, but a thieves' tavern, as red with blood as with wine.

The sight that met his eyes, once his ragged escort delivered him at his destination, was not such as to bring him back to poetry, not even the poetry of hell. It was more than ever the prosaic, brutal reality of the tavern. If we were not in the fifteenth century, we should say that Gringoire had descended from Michelangelo to Callot.*

Round a great fire burning on a large round flagstone, with flames licking at the red-hot legs of a trivet which for the moment was empty, were set some worm-eaten tables, here and there, at random, without any pot-boy with an orderly eye having bothered to arrange them in parallel, or at least see that they did not intersect at too unusual an angle. On these tables glistened pots dripping wine and beer, and round these pots were gathered numerous Bacchic countenances, flushed from the fire and the wine. There was a jovial-looking man with a big belly loudly kissing a fleshy, thick-set harlot. There was a kind of sham soldier, *narquois* as they are called in argot, whistling as he unwound the dressing from his sham wound, and stretching his sound, healthy knee, wrapped up since morning in countless bindings; as the other side of the coin, a *malingreux* was getting his 'God's leg'* ready for the morning with celandine and ox-blood. Two tables away a *coquillart*, in full pilgrim's garb, was spelling out the complaint of Sainte-Reine, not forgetting the chant and the nasal whine. Elsewhere a young *hubin* was having an epilepsy lesson from an old *sabouleux*, who was teaching him the art of foaming at the mouth by chewing a bit of soap. Beside them a dropsy sufferer was deflating himself, and making four or five women thieves hold their noses as they squabbled at the same table over a child they had stolen that evening. All these circumstances, two centuries later, 'seemed so ridiculous to the Court,' as Sauval says, 'that they were served up as a pastime to the King and an introduction to the royal ballet *Night*, divided into four parts and danced at the Petit-Bourbon theatre.' 'Never,' adds an eye-witness of 1653, 'have the sudden metamorphoses of the Court of Miracles been more felicitously depicted. Benserade prepared us for it with some very racy verses.'*

From all sides guffaws of laughter and obscene songs could be heard. Everyone played his own game, with comments and oaths, paying no heed to his neighbour. Pots banged together, rows broke out as they clashed, and when a pot was chipped from the impact rags were torn.

A big dog sat on its rump, looking at the fire. There were some children involved in this orgy. The stolen child cried and yelled. Another, a big lad of 4, sat with his legs dangling on a bench that was too high for him, with the table coming up to his chin, never saying a word. A third was solemnly using his finger to spread over the table the melted tallow dripping from a candle. A fourth small boy, squatting in the mud, was almost lost in a cauldron which he was scraping with a tile, producing a sound to make Stradivarius swoon.

A barrel stood by the fire, and on the barrel sat a beggar. It was the King on his throne.

Gringoire's three captors led him before this barrel, and the whole Bacchanalia fell silent for a moment, except for the cauldron with the child inside.

Gringoire did not dare breathe or raise his eyes.

'*Hombre, quita tu sombrero* [Man, take your hat off],' said one of the three rogues who had claimed him; and before he had understood what that meant, the other had taken off his hat. A wretched bycocket, it is true, but still good for a day of sunshine or a day of rain. Gringoire sighed.

Meanwhile the King, from the top of his cask, addressed him: 'What sort of rogue is this?'

Gringoire gave a start. That voice, although full of menace, recalled to him another voice which had that morning struck the first blow at his mystery play with its nasal whine in the midst of the audience: 'Charity, please!' He raised his head. It was indeed Clopin Trouillefou.

Clopin Trouillefou, dressed up in his royal insignia, was no more and no less ragged; the sore on his arm had already disappeared. In his hand he carried one of those whips with white leather thongs used at that time by the sergeants of the wand for pushing back the crowd, and which were called *boullayes*. On his head he wore a kind of circular headgear, closed on top; but it was hard to tell whether it was a child's padded bonnet or a king's crown, the two are so much alike.

Meanwhile Gringoire, without knowing why, felt somewhat more hopeful at recognizing in the King of the Court of Miracles his cursed beggar from the Great Hall.

'Maître,' he stammered, 'My lord . . . Sire . . . How should I address you?' he said in the end, having reached the top note of his crescendo, and at a loss to know how to go still higher or come down again.

'My lord, Majesty, comrade, address me as you please. But hurry up. What have you to say in your defence?'

'In your defence,' thought Gringoire. 'I don't like that.' He replied, stuttering: 'I am the man who this morning . . .'

'By the devil's nails!' Clopin intervened, 'your name, rogue, and no more. You stand before three mighty sovereigns: me, Clopin Trouillefou, King of Tunis, successor to the great *coësre*, supreme suzerain of the kingdom of Argot; Matthias Hunyadi Spicati, Duke of Egypt and Bohemia, that yellow old chap you see over there with a duster round his head; Guillaume Rousseau, Emperor of Galilee, that fat fellow who isn't listening to us, there fondling a harlot. We are your judges. You entered the kingdom of Argot without being an Argoteer, you violated the privileges of our city. You must be punished, unless you are a *capon*, a *franc-mitou* or a *rifodé*, that is in the argot of honest men, a thief, a beggar, or a vagrant. Are you anything of that sort? Justify yourself. State your occupation.'

'Alas!' said Gringoire, 'I do not have that honour. I am the author . . .'

'That'll do,' Trouillefou broke in, without letting him finish. 'You'll be hanged. It's quite simple, messieurs, all you respectable citizens, we treat your people in our city just as you treat ours in yours. The same law that you apply to truands, the truands apply to you. It's your fault if it's a bad law. Now and then we need to see an honest man grimacing above the hempen collar; it makes the whole business honourable. Come on, friend, share out your rags gladly with these ladies. I'm going to have you hanged to amuse the truands and you're going to give them your purse to drink to it. If you have some mumbo-jumbo to get through first, over there in that mortar there is a very fine stone God the Father which we stole from Saint-Pierre-aux-Bœufs. You've got four minutes to cast your soul at his head.'

It was a formidable harangue.

'Well said, upon my soul! Clopin Trouillefou preaches like our Holy Father the Pope,' cried the Emperor of Galilee, smashing his pot to prop up his table.

'My lords, emperors and kings,' said Gringoire coolly, for somehow he had recovered his firmness and spoke resolutely, 'you can't be serious. My name is Pierre Gringoire, and I am the poet whose morality play was performed this morning in the Great Hall of the Palais.'

'Ah! so it's you, maître!' said Clopin. 'I was there, by God! Very well! Comrade, is there any reason, because you bored us this morning, for not hanging you this evening?'

'I'm going to have a hard job getting out of this,' Gringoire thought. All the same he made one more effort. 'I don't see why,' he said, 'poets shouldn't be included among the truands. A vagabond, Aesop was; a beggar, Homer was; a thief, Mercury was . . .'

Clopin interrupted him: 'I think you are trying to hoodwink us with your patter. By God, let them hang you and don't make such a fuss!'

'Pardon me, my lord King of Tunis,' replied Gringoire, fighting every inch of the ground. 'It's well worth it . . . One moment! . . . Listen to me . . . You're not going to condemn me without giving me a hearing.'

His unhappy voice was indeed drowned by the din going on around him. The small boy was scraping his cauldron more vigorously than ever; and to cap it all, an old woman had just put a pan full of fat on top of the red-hot trivet, and it sputtered over the fire with a noise like a band of children running after a masker.

Meanwhile Clopin Trouillefou seemed to be briefly conferring with the Duke of Egypt and the Emperor of Galilee, who was completely drunk. Then he cried out sharply: 'Silence!' and as the cauldron and the frying pan were not listening but continued their duet, he jumped down from his barrel, gave the cauldron a mighty kick, which sent it rolling ten yards away with the boy inside, kicked over the frying pan, spilling all the fat on to the fire, and then solemnly climbed back on his throne, paying no heed to the child's muffled sobs nor to the old woman's grumbling at the sight of her supper going up in a fine sheet of white flame.

Trouillefou made a sign, and the duke, the emperor, the *archisuppôts*, and the *cagoux* formed a horseshoe round him, with Gringoire, still held bodily in rough hands, at the centre. It was a semicircle of rags, tatters, tinsel, pitchforks, hatchets, legs unsteady with wine, great bare arms, sordid, lacklustre, besotted faces. In the middle of this round table of beggary, Clopin Trouillefou, like the doge of this senate, like the king of this peerage, like the pope of this conclave, dominated, first from being perched aloft on his barrel, then with an indefinable look, proud, fierce, and formidable, which made his eyes glint and refined on his savage profile the brutish character of the truand race. He was like a wild boar's head among pigs' snouts.

'Listen,' he said to Gringoire, stroking his misshapen chin with a horny hand, 'I don't see why you shouldn't be hanged. It's true that the idea seems to repel you; and that's simply because you ordinary citizens are not used to it. You are making far too much of the whole thing. After all, we wish you no harm. Here's a way of getting off for the moment. Are you willing to be one of us?'

The effect of this proposal on Gringoire can easily be imagined; he had seen his life running out and had begun to let it go. He energetically took a new grip on it.

'I am indeed, to be sure,' he said.

'You agree,' Clopin went on, 'to be enrolled among the people of the *petite flambe*?'*

'The *petite flambe*. Quite so,' answered Gringoire.

'You acknowledge yourself to be a member of the *franche-bourgeoisie*?'* the King of Tunis went on.

'The *franche-bourgeoisie*.'

'Subject of the kingdom of Argot?'

'Of the kingdom of Argot.'

'Truand?'

'Truand.'

'In your soul?'

'In my soul.'

'I would like you to note,' the King went on, 'that all that will make no difference to your being hanged.'

'The devil!' said the poet.

'It's just,' Clopin continued imperturbably, 'that you'll be hanged later, more ceremoniously, at the expense of the good city of Paris, on a fine stone gibbet, and by honest men. That's some consolation.'

'As you say,' Gringoire answered.

'There are other advantages. As a *franc-bourgeois* you won't have to pay the rates for the streets, the poor, or the lighting to which ordinary citizens are liable.'

'So be it,' said the poet. 'I agree. I am a truand, an Argoteer, a *franc-bourgeois*, a *petite-flambe*, anything you like. And I was all those things before, monsieur, King of Tunis, for I am a philosopher: and *omnia in philosophia, omnes in philosopho continentur* [all things are contained in philosophy, all men in the philosopher], as you know.'

The King of Tunis frowned.

'Who do you take me for, friend? What Hungarian Jewish lingo are you singing now? I don't know Hebrew. Being a robber doesn't make you a Jew. I don't even steal any more, I'm above all that, I kill. Cutthroat, yes, cutpurse, no.'

Gringoire tried to slip in some excuse amid these brief words, which anger made increasingly staccato. 'I beg your pardon, my lord. It isn't Hebrew, it's Latin.'

'I tell you,' Clopin went on in a rage, 'that I'm not a Jew, and I'll have you hanged, by the synagogue's belly! Like that little *marcandier* from Judaea beside you, and whom I hope one day to see nailed to a counter like the counterfeit coin he is!'

Saying which he pointed his finger at the little bearded Hungarian, who had accosted Gringoire with his '*facitote caritatem*' and who, knowing no other language, observed with surprise the bad temper of the King of Tunis venting itself on him.

At length Monseigneur Clopin calmed down.

'Rogue!' he said to our poet, 'so you do want to be a truand?'

'Quite certainly,' answered the poet.

'Wanting isn't everything,' said Clopin gruffly. 'Good will never put an extra onion in the soup, and its only use is for getting into paradise; now paradise and Argot are two quite different things. To be accepted into Argot you've got to prove that you are some use, and to do that you'll have to search the dummy.'

'I'll search anything you like,' said Gringoire.

Clopin made a sign. Some Argoteers left the circle and returned after a moment. They were carrying two posts, with two wooden feet on their lower end so that they stood firm on the ground. On the upper end of the two posts they fitted a crossbar, the whole forming a very neat portable gallows, which Gringoire had the satisfaction of seeing erected before him in the twinkling of an eye. There was nothing lacking, not even the rope, which swung gracefully from the crossbar.

'What are they up to?' Gringoire wondered rather uneasily. A tinkling of bells that he heard at that moment allayed his anxiety. It came from a dummy which the truands were suspending with the rope round its neck, a kind of scarecrow, dressed in red, and laden with enough jingling, tinkling little bells to provide the harness for thirty Castilian mules. These hundreds of little bells jingled for a while as the rope swung, gradually becoming fainter, and in the end fell silent, when the dummy had returned to a point of rest in accordance with the law of the pendulum which has ousted the clepsydra or water-clock and hourglass.

Then Clopin, pointing to a rickety old stool placed beneath the dummy, told Gringoire: 'Get up there.'

'Hell's teeth,' Gringoire objected, 'I'll break my neck. Your stool limps as badly as one of Martial's distichs: one foot is a hexameter, the other a pentameter.'

'Up,' Clopin repeated.

Gringoire got up on the stool, and managed, not without some wobbling of head and arms, to find his centre of gravity.

'Now,' the King of Tunis continued, 'turn your right foot round your left leg, and stand on tiptoe on your left foot.'

'My lord,' said Gringoire, 'are you absolutely set on having me break a limb?'

Clopin shook his head.

'Listen, friend, you talk too much. Here in short is what it's all about. You will stand on tiptoe, as I said; that will bring you within reach of the dummy's pocket; you'll search it; you'll pull out a purse that's in there; and if you do all that without anyone hearing one of the bells tinkle, that's fine; you'll be a truand. All we have to do then is thrash you for a week.'

'God's belly! I'll take care not to. And if I make the bells jingle?'

'Then you'll be hanged. Understand?'

'I don't understand at all,' Gringoire answered.

'Listen once more. You're going to search the dummy and take its purse from it; if a single bell moves while you're doing so you'll be hanged. Do you understand that much?'

'Right,' said Gringoire, 'I understand that much. And then?'

'If you succeed in removing the purse without the bells jingling, you are a truand, and you'll be thrashed every day for a week. Now perhaps you understand?'

'No, my lord, that's where I stop understanding. Where's the benefit for me? Hanged in one case, beaten in the other . . .'

'And truand?' put in Clopin, 'and truand? Isn't that worth something? It's in your interest that we thrash you, so as to harden you against beatings.'

'Many thanks,' the poet replied.

'Come on, hurry up,' said the King, banging his foot against the barrel, which boomed like a big drum. 'Search the dummy, and have done. I warn you for the last time that if I hear a single little bell you'll take the dummy's place.'

The band of Argoteers applauded Clopin's words and formed a circle round the gallows, laughing so unmercifully that Gringoire saw that he was providing them with too much sport not to have everything to fear from them. So he had no hope left, except the slim chance of succeeding in the fearful exercise imposed on him. He decided to risk it, but not without first addressing a fervent prayer to the dummy which he was about to rob and which would have been easier to soften up than the truands. These thousands of little bells with their little brass tongues seemed to him like so many asps' jaws open, ready to bite and hiss.

'Oh!' he said in a whisper, 'can it be possible that my life should depend on the slightest vibration of the least of these bells? Oh!' he added, with hands clasped together, 'bells, don't bell! chimes, don't chime! tinklers, don't tinkle!'

He made one more effort with Trouillefou. 'Suppose there's a sudden puff of wind?' he asked.

'You'll be hanged,' the other replied without hesitation.

Seeing that there was no possibility of respite, delay, or prevarication, he bravely set to. He turned his right foot round his left leg, stood on tiptoe on his left foot, and stretched out his arm; but just as he touched the dummy, his body, now balanced only on one foot, swayed on the stool which had only three; he tried automatically to steady himself on the dummy, lost his balance, and fell heavily to the ground, deafened by the fatal vibrations of the hundreds of bells on the dummy, which, under the impulse from his hand, first turned on its own axis, and then swung majest-ically between the two posts.

'Curse it!' he cried as he fell, and lay like a dead man with his face to the ground.

Meanwhile he heard the dread carillon above his head, and the truands' diabolical laughter, and Trouillefou's voice saying: 'Pick up that rascal and hang him smartly.'

He stood up. The dummy had already been taken down to make room for him.

The Argoteers made him stand on the stool. Clopin came up to him, put the noose round his neck and clapped him on the shoulder: 'Goodbye, friend! You can't escape now, even if you had the Pope's bowels to digest with.'

The word 'mercy' expired on Gringoire's lips. He looked round. But it was hopeless; they were all laughing.

'Bellevigne de l'Étoile,' the King of Tunis said to a huge truand who stepped forward, 'get up on the crossbar.'

Bellevigne de l'Étoile nimbly climbed up on the beam, and Gringoire looked up a moment later in terror to see him squatting on the crossbar above his head.

'Now,' Clopin Trouillefou went on, 'as soon as I clap my hands, Andry-le-Rouge, you push the stool over with your knee; François Chante-Prune, you hang on to the rogue's feet; and you, Bellevigne, jump on his shoulders; all at the same time, do you hear?'

Gringoire shivered.

'Ready?' Clopin Trouillefou said to the three Argoteers, all set to pounce on Gringoire like three spiders on a fly. The poor victim had a moment of awful expectation, while Clopin calmly used the tip of his foot to push back into the fire a few twigs which the flames had not reached. 'Ready?' he repeated, and opened his hands to clap. One second more and it would all be over.

But he stopped, as though struck by a sudden idea. 'One minute!' he said; 'I was forgetting . . . It's our custom not to hang a man without asking if there's a woman who wants him. Comrade, it's your last resort. You have either got to wed a truand woman or the rope.'

This Bohemian law, weird though it may seem to the reader, is still today written down in full in the old English statute books. See *Burington's Observations*.*

Gringoire breathed again. It was the second time he had come back to life in half an hour. So he did not dare rely on it too much.

'Hallo there!' cried Clopin, back on top of his cask; 'hallo! women, females, is there any one among you, from the witch to her cat, any bawdy wench would like to have this bawdy fellow? Hey there, Colette la Charonne! Elisabeth Trouvain! Simone Jodouyne! Marie Piédebon! Thonne la Longue! Bérarde Fanouel! Michelle Genaille! Claude Ronge-Oreille! Mathurine Girorou! Hey! Isabeau la Thierrye! Come up and look! A man for nothing! Who wants him?'

Gringoire, in this wretched state, was no doubt not very attractive. The women truands showed no great interest in the offer. The unfortunate man heard them reply: 'No! No! Hang him, then we can all have some fun.'

Three, however, emerged from the crowd and came to sniff at him. The first was a big, slab-faced girl. She carefully examined the philosopher's deplorable doublet. The smock was threadbare and had more holes in it than a chestnut roasting-pan. The girl pulled a face. 'Bit of old rag,' she muttered, and, turning to Gringoire: 'Let's see your cape!'

'I've lost it,' said Gringoire.

'Your hat?'

'It's been stolen.'

'Your shoes?'

'The soles are beginning to wear away.'

'Your purse?'

'Alas!' Gringoire stammered, 'I haven't got so much as a *denier parisis*.'

'Let him hang, and say thank you for it!' the truande replied, turning her back on him.

The second one, old, dark, wrinkled, hideous, ugly enough to be noticeable even in the Court of Miracles, walked all round Gringoire. He was almost trembling for fear that she might want him. But she mumbled: 'He's too skinny,' and went away.

The third was a young girl, fresh enough, and not too ugly. 'Save me!' the poor devil said to her in a low voice. She looked at him for a moment with pity, then dropped her eyes, made a pleat in her skirt and remained undecided. His eyes followed her every movement; it was his last ray of hope. 'No,' the girl said at last; 'no! Guillaume Longuejoue would beat me.' She went back into the crowd.

'Comrade,' said Clopin, 'your luck's out.'

Then, standing up on his barrel: 'Nobody wants him?' he cried, imitating an auctioneer's tones, to the great delight of all: 'Nobody wants him? Going, going, going!' And turning towards the gallows with a sign of his head: 'Gone!'

Bellevigne de l'Étoile, Andry le Rouge, François Chante-Prune came closer to Gringoire.

At that moment a cry went up from the Argoteers: 'La Esmeralda! la Esmeralda!'

Gringoire started, and turned in the direction of the shouting. The crowd opened, and let through a pure, dazzling figure.

It was the gypsy girl.

'La Esmeralda!' said Gringoire, stunned, in the midst of all his emotions, at how suddenly that magic word knitted together all his memories of that day.

This rare creature seemed to extend even over the Court of Miracles the sovereign power of her charm and beauty. The men and women of the Argot gently stood back to let her through and their brutish countenances lit up as she looked at them.

She approached the victim with her graceful step. Her pretty Djali followed her. Gringoire was more dead than alive. She contemplated him for a moment in silence.

'You are going to hang this man?' she gravely asked Clopin.

'Yes, sister,' the King of Tunis answered, 'unless you take him for a husband.'

She stuck out her lower lip in her pretty little pout.

'I'll take him,' she said.

At this point Gringoire firmly believed that ever since that morning he had just been in a dream, and that this was a continuation of the same dream.

The turn of fortune, though delightful, was indeed violent.

They undid the slip-knot, took the poet down from the stool. He was obliged to sit down, so intense was his shock.

The Duke of Egypt, without uttering a word, brought up a clay pitcher. The gypsy girl presented it to Gringoire. 'Throw it on the ground,' she said.

The pitcher broke into four pieces.

'Brother,' the Duke of Egypt said then, placing his hands on their foreheads, 'she is your wife; sister, he is your husband. For four years. On your way!'

The Hunchback of Notre Dame 107

'You are going to hang this man?' the gypsy asked Clopin.

'Yes, sister,' the King of Tunis answered, 'unless you take him for a husband.'

She struck her pretty nether lip with her little pout.

'I'll take him,' she said.

VII

A WEDDING NIGHT

A FEW moments later our poet found himself in a little Gothic vaulted room, nicely private and warm, sitting in front of a table which looked as if it would be only too pleased to borrow one or two things from a meatsafe hanging nearby, with the prospect of a decent bed, and alone in the company of a pretty girl. The adventure had a touch of magic about it. He was beginning to take himself seriously as a character in a fairy tale; from time to time he looked around as if to see whether the fiery chariot hitched to two winged chimeras, for nothing else could have conveyed him so swiftly from hell to paradise, was still there. At times too he riveted his gaze on the holes in his doublet, in order to cling to reality and not completely to lose contact with the earth. His reason, bouncing around in imaginary space, was now secured only by that thread.

The girl seemed to be taking no notice of him; she came and went, moved a stool, talked to her goat, pouted now and then. At length she came to sit by the table and Gringoire was able to contemplate her at leisure.

You were once a child, reader, and perhaps you are fortunate enough to be one still. You must then more than once (and speaking for myself, I have spent whole days at it, the most profitable of my life) have followed from bush to bush, beside a running brook, on a sunny day, some lovely green or blue dragonfly, darting in zigzag flight, kissing the tip of every branch. You will recall the loving curiosity with which your mind and eyes fastened on that little whirlwind, humming and whirring on its purple and azure wings, in the midst of which floated an elusive shape, veiled by the very speed of its movement. The aerial creature whose shape could be vaguely discerned through the vibrating wings seemed to you chimerical, imaginary, impossible to touch, impossible to see. But when at last the dragonfly rested on the tip of a reed and you were able to examine with bated breath the long gauzy wings, the long enamel body, the two crystal globes, how utterly astonished you were and how afraid to see the form once more disappear into shadow and the living creature into a chimera! Recall these impressions, and you will easily realize what Gringoire felt as he contemplated in visible and palpable form that Esmeralda of whom, up till then, he had caught only a glimpse through a whirlwind of dance, song, and excitement.

Plunging deeper and deeper into his reverie: 'So that,' he said to himself, following her vaguely with his eyes, 'is what *la Esmeralda* is! A celestial creature! A street dancer! So much and so little! It was she who dealt the final blow to my mystery play this morning, she who saved my life this evening. My evil genius! My good angel! A pretty woman, upon my word—and who must love me madly to have taken me as she did. Come to think,' he said, suddenly standing, with that feeling for the authentic which formed the basis of his character and philosophy, 'I am not too sure how it has come about, but I am her husband!'

With this idea in his mind and in his eyes he approached the girl in so military and gallant a manner that she drew back.

'What do you want with me?' she said.

'How can you ask, adorable Esmeralda?' Gringoire replied in such passionate tones that he himself was astonished to hear himself speak like that.

The gypsy opened wide her large eyes. 'I don't know what you mean!'

'Come now,' Gringoire went on, getting more and more worked up, and thinking that after all he was only dealing with a Court of Miracles virtue, 'am I not yours, sweetheart? Are you not mine?'

And in all innocence he took her by the waist.

The gypsy girl's bodice slipped through his hands like an eelskin. With one bound she leaped to the far end of the cell, stooped, and straightened up again with a small dagger in her hand before Gringoire even had time to see where the dagger had come from; angry and proud, her lips puffed out, nostrils flaring, cheeks apple-red, eyes flashing lightning. At the same time the little goat put itself in front of her, and confronted Gringoire in battle order, bristling with two pretty, gilded, and very sharp horns. This all happened in less than no time.

The dragonfly had become a wasp and would be only too happy to sting.

Our philosopher stood dumbfounded, his eyes passing bemused from the goat to the girl in turn.

'Holy Virgin!' he said finally when he had recovered sufficiently from his surprise to speak; 'there's a sporting pair!'

The gypsy girl broke silence in her turn.

'You must be a very bold rascal!'

'Forgive me, mademoiselle,' Gringoire said with a smile, 'but why did you take me for a husband?'

'Ought I to have let them hang you?'

Gringoire bit his lips. 'Well then, 'he said, 'I am not yet as successful in Cupid as I thought. But what was the point, then, of breaking that poor pitcher?'

Meanwhile Esmeralda's dagger and the goat's horns stayed on the defensive.

'Mademoiselle Esmeralda,' said the poet, 'let's come to terms. I'm not clerk of the court at the Châtelet, and I'm not going to quibble at your carrying a dagger in Paris in defiance of the ordinances and prohibitions of Monsieur the Provost. All the same, you will be aware that Noël Lescripvain was fined a week ago 10 *sols parisis* for carrying a short sword. Now that's none of my business, and I'll come to the point. I swear by my share of paradise that I won't come near you without your leave and permission; but give me some supper.'

Basically Gringoire, like Monsieur Despréaux,* was 'not a very passionate man'. He was not one of those swash-buckling military braggarts who take girls by storm. In love as in everything else he was all for temporizing and the middle course; and a good supper, in friendly intimacy, seemed to him, especially when he was hungry, an excellent interlude between the prologue and dénouement of an amorous adventure.

The gypsy girl made no reply. She made her scornful little pout, cocked her head like a bird, then burst out laughing, and the dainty little dagger disappeared as it had emerged, without Gringoire being able to see where the bee hid its sting.

A moment later a loaf of rye bread, a slice of bacon, some shrivelled apples, and a jug of beer lay on the table. Gringoire began eating ravenously. To hear the furious clinking of his iron fork on the earthenware plate, anyone would have thought that his love had all turned into appetite.

The girl sitting in front of him watched him in silence, obviously preoccupied with some other thought, at which she smiled from time to time, while her hand gently stroked the goat's intelligent head, pressed softly between her knees.

A yellow wax candle lit up this scene of voracity and reflection.

Meanwhile, the first mewlings of his stomach quietened, Gringoire felt a certain false shame at seeing that all that remained was one apple. 'Aren't you eating, Mademoiselle Esmeralda?'

She replied with a negative nod of her head, and her pensive gaze fixed on the room's vaulted ceiling.

'What the devil is she so interested in?' wondered Gringoire, looking at what she was looking at: 'It can't be that grinning dwarf carved on the keystone that's absorbing all her attention. Devil take it! I can stand that comparison!'

He raised his voice: 'Mademoiselle!'

She did not seem to hear.

He went on still louder: 'Mademoiselle Esmeralda!'

A waste of time. The girl's mind was somewhere else, and Gringoire's voice was quite unable to bring it back again. Fortunately the goat took a hand. It began gently tugging its mistress's sleeve. 'What do you want, Djali?' the gypsy girl said sharply, as though waking up with a start.

'She's hungry,' said Gringoire, delighted to have started some conversation.

La Esmeralda began crumbling some bread, which Djali ate gracefully from the hollow of her hand.

However, Gringoire did not give her time to resume her reverie. He ventured a delicate question.

'So you don't want me for a husband?'

The girl stared at him and said: 'No.'

'For a lover?' Gringoire went on.

She pouted, and answered: 'No.'

'For a friend?' continued Gringoire.

She stared at him again, and after a moment's thought: 'Perhaps.'

This 'perhaps', so dear to philosophers, emboldened Gringoire.

'Do you know what friendship is?' he asked.

'Yes,' the gypsy answered. 'It means being brother and sister, two souls touching but not merging, two fingers of the same hand.'

'And love?' Gringoire continued.

'Oh! love!' she said, her voice trembling and her eyes radiant. 'That is being two and yet only one. A man and a woman fusing into an angel. It's heaven.'

As the street dancer said this, Gringoire was particularly struck by her beauty, which seemed to be in perfect harmony with the almost oriental exaltation of the words. Her pure, rose-red lips were half smiling; her calm, innocent forehead was at times overclouded by her thoughts, like a mirror by a breath; and from her long, dark, lowered eyelashes shone a kind of ineffable light which gave her profile that ideal sweetness which Raphael* later found at the mystic point of intersection of virginity, maternity, and divinity.

Gringoire pressed on none the less.

'What must one be to please you?'

'A man.'

'And what am I then?' he asked.

'A man has a helmet on his head, a sword in his hand, and golden spurs on his heels.'

'Right,' said Gringoire, 'without a horse you can't be a man. Do you love anyone?'

'As a lover?'

'As a lover.'

She remained thoughtful for a moment, then she said with an odd expression: 'I shall soon know.'

'Why not this evening?' the poet went on fondly. 'Why not me?'

She looked at him gravely. 'I can only love a man able to protect me.'

Gringoire went red and took the point. It was obvious that the girl was referring to his feeble support in the critical situation in which she had been two hours earlier. That memory, effaced by his other adventures that evening, came back to him. He smote his forehead.

'Talking of which, mademoiselle, that is where I should have begun. Forgive me for being so foolishly distracted. How did you manage, then, to escape from Quasimodo's clutches?'

The question startled the gypsy girl. 'Oh! the horrible hunchback!' she said, burying her face in her hands, and shivering as though bitterly cold.

'Horrible indeed!' said Gringoire, who was not giving up his idea, 'but how were you able to escape from him?'

La Esmeralda smiled, sighed, and remained silent.

'Do you know why he followed you?' Gringoire went on, trying to revert to his question in a roundabout way.

'I don't know,' said the girl. And added sharply: 'But you were following me too, why was that?'

'To tell the truth,' Gringoire answered, 'I don't know either.'

There was silence. Gringoire slashed at the table with his knife, the girl smiled and seemed to be looking at something through the wall. Suddenly she began singing in a scarcely articulate voice:

> Quando las pintadas aves
> Mudas estas y la tierra . . .

[When the coloured birds are silent and the earth . . .]*

She broke off abruptly and started fondling Djali.

'That's a pretty animal you have there,' said Gringoire.

'She's my sister,' she answered.

'Why do they call you *la Esmeralda*?' asked the poet.

'I have no idea.'

'Come now!'

She pulled from her bosom a sort of little oblong sachet, which hung round her neck on a chain of adrezarach seeds. The sachet gave off a strong smell of camphor. It was covered in green silk, and at its centre had a large, green, glass bead, in imitation of an emerald.

'Perhaps because of this,' she said.

Gringoire tried to take the sachet. She drew back.

'Don't touch it. It's an amulet; you would hurt the charm, or the charm would hurt you.'

The poet grew increasingly curious. 'Who gave it to you?'

She put a finger to her lip and hid the amulet in her bosom. He tried some other questions but she barely answered.

'What does the word *la Esmeralda* mean?'

'I don't know,' she said.

'What language is it?'

'Egyptian, I think.'

'I suspected as much,' said Gringoire.' You don't come from France?'

'I've no idea.'

'Are your parents alive?'

She began singing to an old tune:

> My father's a bird—my mother's another,
> I can cross the water without a skiff,
> I can cross the water without a boat,
> My mother's a bird—my father's another.

'Very good,' said Gringoire. 'How old were you when you came to France?'

'Very young.'

'To Paris?'

'Last year. Just as we entered by the Porte-Papale I saw the reed-warbler on the wing; it was the end of August; I said: "It will be a hard winter." '

'It has been,' said Gringoire, delighted to have started some conversation; 'I have spent it blowing on my fingers. So you have the gift of prophecy?'

She became monosyllabic again: 'No.'

'That man you call the Duke of Egypt, is he the chief of your tribe?'

'Yes.'

'But he's the one who married us,' the poet timidly observed.

She made her usual pretty pout. 'I don't even know your name.'

'My name? If you want to know, it's Pierre Gringoire.'

'I know a finer one,' she said.

'That's unkind!' the poet went on. 'No matter, you won't make me angry. Look, perhaps you'll like me when you know me better, and anyhow you told me your story so trustingly that I owe you a bit of mine. You must know, then, that my name is Pierre Gringoire, and I'm the son of the tax-farmer for the Gonesse district. My father was hanged by the Burgundians and my mother ripped open by the Picards at the time of the siege of Paris twenty years ago. So I was an orphan at 6, with nothing beween my bare feet and the pavements of Paris. I don't know how I filled in the time between 6 and 16. Here a fruit seller would give me a plum, there a baker would throw me a crust; at night I would get myself picked up by the watch, who would put me in prison, and there I'd find a bundle of straw. All that didn't stop me growing up tall and thin, as you can see. In winter I'd warm myself in the sun, under the porch of the Hôtel de Sens, and I thought it quite absurd that the great bonfire on Midsummer's Eve should be kept for the dogdays. At 16 I tried to find a trade. I sampled them all, one after another. I became a soldier, but I wasn't brave enough. I became a monk, but I wasn't devout enough. And I can't drink too much either. In despair I went in as an apprentice carpenter in the timber trade; but I wasn't strong enough. I felt more inclined to be a schoolmaster; it's true I couldn't read; but that's no bar. After a while I realized that I lacked something whatever I tried; and when I saw that I was good for nothing, of my own free will I became a poet and composer of rhymes. That's a trade you can always take up when you are a vagrant, and it's better than stealing, as some of my larcenous young friends advised me to do.

'One fine day I was lucky enough to meet Dom Claude Frollo, the reverend archdeacon of Notre-Dame. He took an interest in me, and it's thanks to him that today I am a real scholar, knowing Latin from Cicero's *Offices* to the *Mortuology* of the Celestine fathers, and no barbarian in scholastics, poetics, rhythmics, or even hermetics, the wisdom of wisdoms. I am the author of the mystery performed today, with great success and attended by a great throng of people in the Great Hall of the Palais, no less. I have also written a book which will run to six hundred pages on the prodigious comet of 1465, which drove one man mad. I have had other successes as well. Being something of an armourer, I worked on that great bombard of Jean Maugue, which, as you know, burst on the Pont de Charenton the day they tried it out, and killed twenty-four spectators. You see I am by no means such a bad match. I know lots of very attractive tricks to teach your goat; for instance, how to mimic that damned Pharisee the Bishop of Paris, whose mill-wheels splash passers-by the whole length of the Pont-aux-Meuniers. And then my mystery will bring me in a lot of hard cash, if they ever pay me for it. In short I am at your service, I, my wit, my knowledge, and my learning, ready to live with you, mademoiselle, as it may please you, in chastity or mutual enjoyment, husband and wife, if that suits you, brother and sister, if that suits you better.'

Gringoire fell silent, waiting to see the effect of his harangue on the girl. Her eyes were fixed on the ground.

'*Phoebus*,' she said in an undertone. Then, turning to the poet: 'What does it mean, *Phoebus*?'

Gringoire, unsure what connection there might be between his speech and this question, was not averse to showing off his erudition. He preened himself as he replied: 'It's a Latin word meaning *sun*.'

'Sun,' she repeated.

'It's the name of a certain handsome archer, who was a god,' Gringoire added.

'A god!' repeated the gypsy girl. And her tone had something both thoughtful and passionate about it.

At that moment one of her bracelets came undone and dropped on the ground. Gringoire swiftly stooped to pick it up. When he stood up again the girl and the goat had disappeared. He heard the sound of a bolt. A small door, no doubt giving access to a neighbouring cell, was being closed from the outside.

'Has she at least left me a bed?' said our philosopher.

He made a tour of the cell. The only piece of furniture suitable for sleeping on was a fairly long wooden chest, though it had a carved lid, as a result of which when Gringoire stretched out on it he felt somewhat like Micromegas* lying down full length across the Alps.

'Come on,' he said, adjusting himself as best he could. 'One must take what comes. But this is an odd wedding night. It's a pity. That wedding with the broken pitcher had something artless and old-fashioned about it that I rather liked.'

BOOK THREE

I

NOTRE-DAME

No doubt the church of Notre-Dame de Paris is still today a sublime and majestic building. But for all the beauty it has preserved in ageing, it is hard to repress a sigh, to repress indignation over the countless degradations and mutilations which time and men have simultaneously inflicted on the venerable monument, showing no respect for Charlemagne, who laid its first stone, or for Philip-Augustus,* who laid the last.

On the face of this old queen of our cathedrals, beside each wrinkle you will find a scar. *Tempus edax, homo edacior* [Time devours, man devours still more].* Which I should like to translate thus: 'Time is blind, man is stupid.'

If we had the leisure to examine with the reader one by one the various traces of destruction imprinted on the ancient church, time's share would be the least, that of men the worst, especially men of the art. I have to say 'men of the art' since there have been individuals in the past two centuries who have assumed the title of architect.

First of all, to give only a few major examples, there are assuredly few finer pages in architecture than that façade where successively and simultaneously the three recessed, pointed doorways, the embroidered and serrated band of the twenty-eight royal niches; the immense central rose-window, flanked by the two side windows like the priest by deacon and sub-deacon, the lofty, slender gallery of tre-foiled arches supporting a heavy platform on its delicate small columns; finally the two dark, massive towers with their slate eaves, harmonious parts of a magnificent whole, rising one above the other in five gigantic storeys, all unfold before one's eye, multitudinous and unconfused with their innumerable details of statuary, sculpture, and carvings, adding powerfully to the calm grandeur of the whole; a vast symphony in stone, so to speak; the colossal work of a man and a people, at the same time one and complex, like its sisters the *Iliads* and the *Romanceros*; the prodigious result of contributions made from all the resources of an age, where every stone displays in hundreds of ways the work-man's imagination disciplined by the artist's genius; a kind of human creation, in a word, as mighty and fruitful as the divine creation whose dual character it seems to have ab-stracted: variety, eternity.

And what we are saying here about the façade must be said of the entire church; and what we are saying about the cathedral church of Paris must be said of all the churches of Christendom in the Middle Ages. Everything coheres in this art, self-generating, logical, and well proportioned. To measure a toe is to measure the giant.

Let us come back to the façade of Notre-Dame, as it still appears at the present day, when we go piously to admire the solemn and mighty cathedral which, accord-ing to its chroniclers, inspires terror: *quae mole sua terrorem incutit spectantibus* [which by its mass strikes spectators with terror].*

Three important things are today missing from that fa-çade. First, the flight of eleven steps which once raised it above ground level; then the lower series of statues which occupied the niches in the three doorways; and lastly the upper series of the twenty-eight earliest kings of France, which filled the first-floor gallery, from Childebert* to Philip-Augustus, each holding in his hand 'the imperial apple'.

As to the steps, it is time which has caused them to disappear, by slowly and irresistibly raising the ground level of the City. But time, while causing the rising tide of Paris pavements to devour one by one the eleven steps which added to the majestic height of the building, has perhaps given the church more than it has taken away, for it is time which has spread over the façade that sombre colouring of centuries which makes the old age of monuments the age of their beauty.

But who cast down the two rows of statues? Who left the niches empty? Who cut that new and bastard ogive right in the middle of the central doorway? Who dared set within it that heavy, tasteless, wooden door carved in Louis XV style, next to Biscornette's arabesques? The men, the architects, the artists of our own day.

And, going inside the building, who overthrew that colossal Saint Christopher, proverbial among statues just as the great hall of the Palais was among halls, the spire of Strasbourg among steeples? And those myriads of statues which thronged every space between the columns of nave and choir, kneeling, standing, riding, men, women, children, kings, bishops, soldiers, in stone, marble, gold, silver, brass, even in wax, who swept them all brutally away? Not time.

And who substituted for the old Gothic altar, with its splendid clutter of shrines and reliquaries, that heavy marble sarcophagus with angels' heads and clouds, looking like some spare sample from the Val-de-Grâce or the Invalides? Who stupidly fixed that heavy stone anachronism into Hercandus'* Carolingian pavement? Was it not Louis XIV fulfilling the vow of Louis XIII?

And who put in those cold, white windows in place of the 'richly coloured' stained glass which made our forebears' eyes hesitate in wonder between the rose of the great doorway and the ogive windows of the apse? And what would a succentor of the sixteenth century say at the sight of the fine yellow distemper which our archiepiscopal vandals have daubed over their cathedral? He would remember that that was the colour which the public executioner smeared over *infamous* buildings; he would recall the Hôtel du Petit-Bourbon, plastered with yellow too after the Constable de Bourbon's treason,* 'a yellow, besides, of such good quality,' says Sauval, 'and so highly recommended, that more than a century has passed without its colour fading.' He would think that the holy place had become infamous, and run away.

And if we go up on top of the cathedral, without paying attention to countless acts of barbarity of every kind, what have they done with that delightful little steeple which used to stand at the mid-point of the crossing and which, no less slender and no less bold than the neighbouring spire (also destroyed) of the Sainte-Chapelle, pierced even more deeply into the sky than the towers, slim, pointed, sonorous, fretted? An architect of good taste (1787) amputated it and thought it enough to conceal the wound with that large leaden patch that looks like a saucepan lid.

That is how the marvellous art of the Middle Ages has been treated in almost every country, especially in France. Three sorts of damage can be distinguished on the ruins, and they all affect it at different depths: first is time, which has chipped it away imperceptibly here and there and left rust all over its surface; then political and religious revolutions which, blind and angry by their very nature, have hurled themselves upon it in tumult, rent its rich array of sculptures and carvings, smashed its rose-windows, broken its necklaces of arabesques and figurines, torn down its statues, sometimes for wearing a mitre, sometimes a crown; finally fashions, increasingly silly and absurd, which after the splendidly anarchic deviations of the Renaissance, have succeeded one another in the inevitable decline of architecture. Fashions have done more harm than revolutions. They have cut into the living flesh, attacked the bone-structure of the art underneath, they have hewn, hacked, dislocated, killed the building, in its form as in its symbolism, in its logic as in its beauty. And then they remade it; a claim that at least neither time nor revolutions had advanced. Brazenly, in the name of 'good taste', they stuck over the wounds of Gothic architecture their wretched baubles of a day, their marble ribbons, their metal pompoms, a veritable leprosy of ovolos, scrolls, surrounds, draperies, garlands, fringes, stone flames, bronze clouds, chubby cupids, bloated cherubs, which started eating away the face of art in the oratory of Catherine de' Medici, and caused its death, two centuries later, in a tortured grimace, in the Dubarry's boudoir.*

Thus, to sum up the points just mentioned, Gothic architecture is today disfigured by three kinds of ravage. Wrinkles and warts on its skin are the work of time; marks of violence, brutality, contusions, fractures, the work of re-volutions from Luther to Mirabeau. Mutilations, amputa-tions, dislocation of its limbs, 'restorations', are the Greek, Roman, and barbaric work of professors quoting Vitruvius* and Vignolo*. The magnificent art produced by the Van-dals was killed by the academies. To the centuries and revolutions, which at least devastated impartially and on the grand scale, has been added the swarm of architects from the schools, licensed, sworn, and accredited, degrading with all the discernment and choice of bad taste, substitut-ing Louis XV chicory for Gothic lace to the greater glory of the Parthenon. It is the ass kicking the dying lion. It is the old oak decaying, as a final blow being stung, bitten, and gnawed by caterpillars.

How far it is from this to the age when Robert Cenalis, comparing Notre-Dame de Paris to that famous temple of Diana at Ephesus, 'so celebrated by the pagans of an-tiquity', which immortalized Erostratus,* found the Gallic cathedral 'more excellent in length, breadth, height, and structure'![1]

Notre-Dame de Paris is not, however, what can be called a complete, definite, classifiable monument. It is no longer a Romanesque church, nor yet a Gothic one. The building is not typical. Notre-Dame de Paris does not have, like the abbey of Tournus, the solemn, massive build, the broad, circular vaulting, the chilly bareness, the majestic simplicity of buildings whose generating principle is the round arch. It is not, like the cathedral of Bourges, the magnificent, light, multiform, involved, spiky, flowery product of the pointed arch. It cannot be ranked among that ancient fam-ily of dark, mysterious, low-roofed churches, crushed, as it were, by the round arch; almost Egyptian, but for their ceilings; all hieroglyphic, priestly, symbolic; decorated more profusely with lozenges and zigzags than flowers, with flowers more than animals, with animals more than with human beings; not so much the work of the architect as of

[1] (*Histoire gallicane, liv. II, period III, fo. 130, p. 1*) [V. H.]

the bishop; the first transformation of the art, stamped all over with theocratic, military discipline, rooted back in the Late Empire and ending with William the Conqueror. Nor can our cathedral be placed in that other family of lofty, airy churches, rich with stained glass and sculpture; of pointed forms and bold attitudes; communal and civic as political symbols, free, fanciful and unrestrained as works of art; a second transformation of architecture, no longer hieroglyphic, immutable, and priestly, but artistic, progressive, and popular, which begins with the return from the Crusades and ends with Louis XI. Notre-Dame de Paris is not of pure Roman stock like the first, nor of pure Arab stock like the second.

It is a transitional building. The Saxon architect was just completing the first pillars of the nave when the pointed arch arriving from the Crusades installed itself victoriously on those broad Romanesque capitals designed only for round arches. The pointed arch, dominant from then on, constructed the rest of the church. However, inexperienced and diffident to start with, it opened, broadened out, contained itself, and did not dare soar up into spires and lancets as it did later in so many marvellous cathedrals. It is as though it was conscious of the presence of the heavy Romanesque pillars nearby.

In any case, these buildings which mark the transition from Romanesque to Gothic repay study no less than the pure types. They express a nuance of the art which would be lost without them, that is to say the grafting of the pointed on to the round arch.

Notre-Dame de Paris in particular is a curious example of that variety. Each face, each stone of the venerable monument is a page not only of the history of France, but also of the history of science and art. Thus, to indicate here only the main details, while the little Porte-Rouge goes almost to the limits of fifteenth-century Gothic delicacy, the nave pillars, by their volume and weightiness, go back to the Carolingian abbey of Saint-Germain-des-Prés. Anyone would think that there were six centuries between that door and those pillars. Even the hermetics find in the symbolism of that great doorway a satisfying summary of their science, of which the church of Saint-Jacques-de-la-Boucherie was so complete a hieroglyph. So the Roman-esque abbey, the philosophical church, Gothic art, Saxon art, the heavy round pillar recalling Gregory VII,* the her-metic symbolism which made Nicolas Flamel the precursor of Luther, papal unity, schism, Saint-Germain-des-Prés, Saint-Jacques-de-la-Boucherie, everything is merged, com-bined, amalgamated in Notre-Dame. This central, gener-ative church is a kind of chimera among the old churches of Paris; it has the head of one, the limbs of another, the rear of a third; something of all of them.

We repeat, these hybrid constructions are not the least interesting for the artist, the antiquary, the historian. They make one feel how primitive a thing architecture is by demonstrating, as the Cyclopean remains, Egyptian pyr-amids, gigantic Hindu temples also demonstrate, that archi-tecture's greatest productions are not so much the works of individuals as of societies; the fruit of whole peoples in labour rather than the inspiration of men of genius; the deposit left by a nation; the accumulation of centuries; the residue from successive evaporations of human society; in a word, types of formation. Each wave of time lays its alluvium on top, each race lays down its stratum, each individual brings his stone. That is the way of beavers, that is the way of bees, that is the way of men. The great symbol of architecture, Babel, is a beehive.

Great buildings, like great mountains, are the work of centuries. Art often undergoes a transformation while they are pending: *pendent opera interrupta* [interrupted works remain in suspense];* they are quietly continued in accord-ance with the art transformed. The new art takes the monu-ment as it finds it, forms a crust upon it, assimilates it, develops it as it pleases, and completes it if it can. It all takes place without trouble, without strain, without reac-tion, according to a tranquil law of nature. A graft occurs, sap circulates, vegetation continues. To be sure, there is material for massive tomes, and often for the universal history of mankind, in these successive weldings of several arts at several levels on the same monument. The man, the artist, the individual are erased from these great masses with no author's name; they are a summary of human intelligence and represent its sum total. Time is the architect, the whole people the builder.

Considering here only European, Christian architecture, younger sister of the great masonries of the Orient, it strikes the eye as a huge formation divided into three clearly distinct zones superimposed one upon the other: the Romanesque zone,[1] the Gothic, the Renaissance, which we should like to call Graeco-Roman. The Romanesque stratum, the oldest and deepest, is occupied by the round arch, which reappears carried on the Greek column in the higher, more recent stratum of the Renaissance. The pointed arch is between the two. Buildings belonging exclusively to one of these three strata are perfectly distinct, unified, and complete. Such are the abbey of Jumièges, the cathedral of Reims, Sainte-Croix at Orléans. But the three zones merge and amalgamate at their edges, like the colours in the solar spectrum. Whence the complex monuments, buildings of nuance and transition. One such may have Romanesque feet, a Gothic middle, a Graeco-Roman head. That is because it took six hundred years to build it. That variety is rare. The keep at Étampes is an example. But monuments of two formations are more frequent. Such is Notre-Dame de Paris, a pointed-arch building, but with its earliest pillars going down into that Romanesque zone where the doorway of Saint-Denis and the nave of Saint-Germain-des-Prés are deeply plunged. Such is the charming half-Gothic chapter house of Boscherville, where the Romanesque stratum goes half-way up the body. Such is the cathedral of Rouen, which would be entirely Gothic if the tip of its central spire did not dip into the Renaissance zone.[2]

[1] This is the same that is also called, according to place, climate, and type, Lombard, Saxon, and Byzantine. These are four sisters, parallel architectures, each with its own particular character, but all deriving from the same principle, the round arch: *Facies non omnibus una/Non diversa tamen, qualem* . . . [They do not all have one face, nor yet a different one . . .].*

[2] That part of the spire which was timber is precisely that which was consumed by lightning in 1823. [V. H.]

However, all these nuances, all these differences affect only the surface of the buildings. Art has changed its skin. The actual constitution of the Christian church has not been touched by it. It is still the same inner framework, the same logical disposition of the parts. Whatever may be the carved or decorated envelope of a cathedral, there will always be found under it, at least in germ or rudimentary form, the Roman basilica. It develops on the ground eternally according to the same law. There are invariably two naves crossing at right angles, the upper end of which is rounded into an apse and forms the choir; there are always side aisles for processions inside the church, for chapels, a kind of lateral ambulatory into which the main nave empties through the bays. That granted, the number of chapels, doorways, steeples, spires can be endlessly modified, according to the fancy of the age, the people, the art. Once the needs of worship have been met and ensured, architecture can do whatever it chooses. Statues, stained glass, rose-windows, arabesques, indentations, capitals, bas-reliefs: all such objects of imagination can be combined according to whichever logarithm is appropriate. Whence the prodigious external variety of these buildings where so much order and unity are essentially lodged. The tree trunk never varies, the foliage is a matter of caprice.

A BIRD'S-EYE VIEW OF PARIS

WE have just tried to repair for the reader the admirable church of Notre-Dame de Paris. We have briefly indicated most of the beauties it had in the fifteenth century and has no longer today, but we omitted the chief of them: the view of Paris revealed at that time from the top of its towers.

Indeed, when after groping one's way up the long, dark spiral staircase, pierced vertically through the thickness of the tower walls, one at last emerged on to one of the two lofty platforms, flooded with light and air, it was a fine picture that on every side at once unfolded before the eye; a sight *sui generis*, which can be readily visualized by those of our readers who have been lucky enough to see a Gothic town intact, complete, homogeneous, such as the few still remaining, Nuremberg in Bavaria, Vittoria in Spain, or even smaller specimens, so long as they are well preserved, Vitré in Brittany, Nordhausen in Prussia.

The Paris of three hundred and fifty years ago, the Paris of the fifteenth century, was already an enormous city. We Parisians are generally mistaken in thinking how much ground we have acquired since then. Paris since Louis XI has not grown by much more than a third. It has, to be sure, lost more in beauty than it has gained in size.

Paris was born, as we all know, on that old island of the City shaped like a cradle. Its first enclosure was the shore-line of that island, the Seine its first moat. For several hundred years Paris remained an island, with two bridges, one to the north, the other to the south, and two bridge-heads, at once gates and fortresses, the Grand Châtelet on the right bank, the Petit Châtelet on the left. Then, from the time of the first line of kings, Paris, too constricted on the island, no longer with room enough to turn round, crossed the water. Then, beyond the Grand and beyond the Petit Châtelet a first ring of walls and towers began to encroach on the countryside on both banks of the Seine. Some traces of that ancient enclosure still existed into the last century; today all that remains is the memory, here and there a tradition, the Porte Baudets or Baudoyer, *Porta Bagauda*. Gradually the flood of houses, constantly driven outwards from the heart of the town, overflowed this enclosure, eroded it, wore it down, erased it. Philip-Augustus built a new containing dyke. He imprisoned Paris within a circular chain of massive, solid, high towers. For more than a century the houses pressed and piled up one upon another, their level rising like water in a reservoir. They began to grow deeper, put storey upon storey, climbed one upon another, spurted upwards like any sap under pressure, and each strove to lift its head higher than its neighbours for the sake of a little fresh air. The streets grew deeper and narrower; every open space was filled up and disappeared. At last the houses leaped over Philip-Augustus's wall, and joyfully scattered over the plain in ragged disorder, as though escaping from captivity. There they settled, hacked gardens out of the fields, took their ease. From 1367 the town had spread so far into the suburbs that a new enclosure was needed, especially on the right bank. Charles V built it. But a town like Paris is in perpetual spate. Only such towns ever become capital cities. They are like funnels into which drain all the geographical, political, moral, intellectual slopes of a nation, all the natural inclinations of a people; wells of civilization, so to speak, but also sewers, where trade, industry, intelligence, population, all the sap, the life, all the soul of a nation is constantly filtered and collected, drop by drop, century by century. Charles V's wall, then, had the same fate as that of Philip-Augustus. From the end of the fifteenth century it was encroached upon, superseded, and the suburbs ran still further out. In the sixteenth century the wall seemed to be visibly withdrawing, buried deeper and deeper in the old town, so dense already was the new one beyond it. Thus from the fifteenth century, to go no further, Paris had already worn out the three concentric ring-walls which at the time of Julian the Apostate* were, so to speak, in embryonic existence in the Grand and Petit Châtelets. The mighty city had burst successively four rings of walls like a growing child splitting its last year's clothes. Under Louis XI one could in places see sticking out amid this sea of houses a few groups of ruined towers from the ancient enclosures like the tips of hills from a flood, like archipelagos of old Paris submerged beneath the new.

Since then Paris has been further transformed, unfortunately for our eyes; but it has burst out of only one more enclosure, that of Louis XV, that wretched wall of mud and spittle, worthy of the king who built it, worthy of the poet who sang of it:

> Le mur murant Paris rend Paris murmurant.*

In the fifteenth century Paris was still divided into three quite distinct and separate towns, each with its own physiognomy, specialities, way of life, customs, privileges, history: the City, the University, the Town. The City, which occupied the island of that name, was the oldest, the smallest, and mother of the other two, squeezed between them, if we may be allowed the comparison, like a little old woman between her two tall beautiful daughters. The University covered the left bank of the Seine, from the Tournelle to the Tour de Nesle, corresponding in the Paris of today respectively to the Halle-aux-Vins [Wine Market] and the Monnaie [Mint]. Its boundary scooped a large piece out of the countryside where Julian had built his Baths. The mount of Sainte-Geneviève was enclosed by it. The highest point of this arc of walls was the Porte Papale, more or less the present site of the Panthéon. The Town, the largest of the three portions of Paris, had the right bank. Its quayside, though broken or interrupted in several places, ran along the Seine, from the Tour de Billy to the Tour du Bois, that is from the place where the Grenier d'Abondance stands today to where the Tuileries are. These four points at which the Seine cut the capital's ring-wall, the Tournelle and the Tour de Nesle on the left, the Tour de Billy and the Tour du Bois on the right, were called *par excellence* 'the four towers of Paris'. The Town penetrated even further into the countryside than the University. The extreme point of the Town's enclosure (that of Charles V) was at the Porte Saint-Denis and the Porte Saint-Martin, whose site has not changed.

As we have just said, each of these three great divisions of Paris was a town, but too special a town to be complete, a town which could not do without the other two. Whence three absolutely different aspects. In the City churches abounded, in the Town palaces, in the University colleges. Leaving aside here the less important peculiarities of old Paris, and the caprices of right of way, we may say in general, taking only the overall pattern and major features in the chaos of communal jurisdiction, that the island belonged to the bishop, the right bank to the Provost of merchants, the left bank to the rector of the University. The Provost of Paris, a royal, not a municipal official, had jurisdiction over the whole. The City had Notre-Dame, the Town the Louvre and the Hôtel de Ville, the University the Sorbonne. The Town had the Halles, the City the Hôtel-Dieu, the University the Pré-aux-Clercs. Offences committed by students on the left bank, in their own Pré-aux-Clercs, were tried on the island, in the Palais de Justice, and punished on the right bank, at Montfaucon. Unless the rector, sensing that the University was strong and the king weak, intervened; for it was the students' privilege to be hanged in their own part of Paris.

(Most of these privileges, be it noted in passing, and there were better ones than that, had been wrung out of the King by revolts and mutinies. That is the immemorial way things go. The King only loosens his hold when the people snatch. There is an old charter which expresses it artlessly, on the subject of loyalty: *fidelitas in reges, quae tamen aliquoties seditionibus interrupta, multa peperit privilegia* [Loyalty to kings, although interrupted by a certain number of insurrections, has won many privileges].)

In the fifteenth century the Seine washed five islands within the walls of Paris: the Île Louviers, where there were then trees and now only timber; the Île-aux-Vaches and the Île Notre-Dame, both deserted, apart from one hovel, both fiefs of the bishop (in the seventeenth century these two islands were made into one, which was then built upon and is now called the Île Saint-Louis); finally the Île de la Cité, the City, with at its tip the cow-ferryman's islet, since buried beneath the esplanade of the Pont-Neuf. The City then had five bridges: three on the right, the Pont Notre-Dame and the Pont-au-Change of stone, the Pont-aux-Meuniers of wood; two on the left, the stone Petit-Pont and the wooden Pont Saint-Michel; all with houses on them. The University had six gates built by Philip-Augustus; namely, starting from the Tournelle, the Porte Saint-Victor, the Porte Bordelle, the Porte Papale, the Porte Saint-Jacques, the Porte Saint-Michel, the Porte Saint-Germain. The Town had six gates built by Charles V; namely, starting from the Tour de Billy, the Porte Saint-Antoine, the Porte du Temple, the Porte Saint-Martin, the Porte Saint-Denis, the Porte Montmartre, the Porte Saint-Honoré. All these gates were strong and beautiful too, for beauty does not detract from strength. A broad, deep moat, fast-flowing during the winter floods, washed the foot of the walls all round Paris; the Seine provided the water. At night the gates were closed, the river at each end of the town was barred with great iron chains, and Paris slept peacefully.

Seen from a bird's-eye view, then, these three townships of City, University, and Town each appeared as an inextricable web of weirdly tangled streets. However, it was apparent from the first glance that these three fragments of city formed a single body. You saw at once two long, parallel streets, running without a break, without disturbance, almost in a straight line, crossing each of the townships from end to end, from south to north, at right angles to the Seine, connecting and mingling, then, constantly infusing, pouring, and decanting the people from one into the walls of another, and making the three into one. The first of these two streets ran from the Porte Saint-Jacques to the Porte Saint-Martin, and was called rue Saint-Jacques in the University, rue de la Juiverie in the City, rue Saint-Martin in the Town; it crossed the river twice under the name of Petit-Pont and Pont Notre-Dame. The second, called rue de la Harpe on the left bank, rue de la Barillerie on the island, rue Saint-Denis on the right bank, Pont Saint-Michel over one arm of the Seine, Pont-au-Change over the other, ran from the Porte Saint-Michel in the University to the Porte Saint-Denis in the Town. However, under so many different names, they were still only two streets, but two parent streets, the two generators and arteries of Paris. All the other veins of the triple town were fed from them or emptied into them.

Independently of these two main streets, diametrically cutting across the width of Paris from side to side, common to the whole capital, Town and University each had their own particular main street, running lengthways across them, parallel with the Seine, intersecting the two arterial streets at right angles. Thus in the Town you could go in a straight line from the Porte Saint-Antoine to the Porte Saint-Honoré; in the University from the Porte Saint-Victor to the Porte Saint-Germain. These two great thoroughfares, intersecting with the first two, formed the canvas backing on which lay the labyrinthine street network of Paris, knotted and pulled in every direction. With careful scrutiny one might further discern within the unintelligible pattern of this network what looked like two outspread wheatsheaves, one in the University, the other in the Town, two bundles of broad streets fanning out as they led from the bridges to the gates.

Something of this ground plan still remains today.

Now, what did the whole view look like from the top of the towers of Notre-Dame in 1482? That is what we shall try to say.

The spectator arriving breathless at this summit was met first by a dizzy confusion of roofs, chimneys, streets, bridges, squares, spires, steeples. Everything caught the eye at once, the carved gable, the steep roof, the turret suspended at the corner of the walls, the stone pyramid of the eleventh century, the slate obelisk of the fifteenth, the bare, round tower of the castle keep, the square decorated tower of the church, the big, the small, the massive, the airy. The eye lingered at every level of this labyrinth, where there was nothing without its originality, its reason, its genius, its beauty, nothing which did not derive from art, from the humblest house with carved and painted front, external timbers, low doorway, overhanging storeys, to the royal Louvre, which at that time had a colonnade of towers. But the principal masses discernible to the eye, once it began to adjust to this jumble of buildings, are as follows.

First the City. The Île de la Cité, in the words of Sauval, whose muddled writing contains the occasional felicity of style, 'the Île de la Cité is made like a great ship stuck in the mud and stranded with the current near the middle of the Seine.' We have just explained that in the fifteenth century this ship was moored to the two riverbanks by five bridges. This outline of a vessel had also struck the heraldic scribes; for that, and not the siege of the Normans, according to Favyn and Pasquier, is the origin of the ship emblazoned on the old arms of Paris. For anyone who knows how to read it, heraldry is an algebra, a language. The entire history of the second half of the Middle Ages is written in heraldry, just as the history of the first half is written in the symbolism of the Romanesque churches. They are the hieroglyphs of feudalism, following those of theocracy.

The City, then, first struck the eye with its stern to the east and its prow to the west. Turning towards the prow you had before you an innumerable flock of old roofs with the leaded apse of the Sainte-Chapelle rising broad and round above them, like an elephant carrying its tower on its hindquarters. Only here the tower was the boldest, the most finely worked and carved, the most skilfully fretted spire which ever showed the sky through its lacy cone. Directly in front of Notre-Dame three streets debouched on to the Parvis, a fine square of old houses. On the south side of this square leaned the wrinkled, scowling façade of the Hôtel-Dieu, its roof covered seemingly with boils and warts. Then, to right, to left, to east, to west, within the bounds of the City, narrow though they were, rose the steeples of its twenty-one churches, of every date, shape and size, from the low, decaying Romanesque campanile of Saint-Denys-du-Pas, *carcer Glaucini* [prison of Glaucinus], to the delicate spires of Saint-Pierre-aux-Bœufs and Saint-Landry. Behind Notre-Dame extended, to the north, its cloister with its Gothic galleries; to the south the semi-Romanesque Bishop's Palace; to the east, the island's empty tip, known as the Terrain. Amid this pile of houses one could also make out, by the tall, open-work stone mitres on the roof itself which then crowned the topmost windows of palaces, the Hôtel given by the Town, under Charles VI, to Juvénal des Ursins; a little further on the tarred sheds of the Marché-Palus; elsewhere again the new apse of Saint-Germain-le-Vieux, extended in 1458 by taking in a bit from the rue-aux-Febves; and then, here and there, a crossroads thronged with people, a pillory standing at a street corner, a fine section of Philip-Augustus pavement, magnificent flagstones scored in the middle to stop horses' hooves slipping, and so poorly replaced in the sixteenth century by those wretched cobbles known as 'League paving', a deserted backyard with one of those transparent staircases they used to build in the fifteenth century, one of which can still be seen in the rue des Bourdonnais. Finally, to the right of the Sainte-Chapelle, towards the west, the Palais de Justice sat at the water's edge with its group of towers. The groves of the king's garden, which covered the western tip of the City, concealed the cow-ferryman's islet. As for the water, from the top of the towers of Notre-Dame it was scarcely visible on either side of the City. The Seine was lost to sight under the bridges, the bridges under their houses.

And when you looked past the bridges, on which the roofs were plainly turning green, mouldering before their time in the vapours from the water, and turned your gaze to the left, towards the University, the first building to strike the eye was a large, low bunch of towers, the Petit Châtelet, whose yawning gateway swallowed up the end of the Petit-Pont. Then, if you looked along the bank from east to west, from the Tournelle to the Tour de Nesle, there ran a long string of houses with carved beams, coloured windows, overhanging the pavement with one storey projecting above another, an endless zigzag of comfortable citizens' gables, cut frequently by the end of some street, and also now and then by the front or angle of some great stone mansion, ensconced comfortably with its courtyards and gardens, its wings and main buildings, amid this rabble of cramped, narrow houses like some great lord amid a mob of yokels. There were five or six of these mansions on the quay, from the Logis de Lorraine, which shared with the Bernardins* the great enclosure adjacent to the Tournelle, to the Hôtel de Nesle, whose main tower marked the boundary of Paris, and whose pointed roofs were privileged for three months in the year to interpose their black triangles upon the scarlet disc of the setting sun.

That side of the Seine was, for the rest, the less commercial of the two; noise and crowds came from the students rather than the artisans, and the quay, strictly speaking, ran only from the Pont Saint-Michel to the Tour de Nesle. Otherwise along the bank of the Seine ran either a bare strand, as it was beyond the Bernardins, or a clutter of houses with their feet in the water, as between the two bridges. The washerwomen made a lot of noise there, shouting, talking, singing from morning to night along the water's edge, and banging away at their washing as they do today. They offer by no means the least of Paris entertainments.

The University looked like one single block. From one end to the other it formed a homogeneous and compact whole. Those hundreds of roofs, dense, angular, tightly packed together, almost all consisting of the same geometric element seen from above, looked like a crystallization of the same one substance. The capricious cracks formed by the ravine of the streets divided this mass of houses into slices that were not too disproportionate. The forty-two colleges were distributed fairly evenly, and were to be found everywhere; the varied and amusing summits of these fine buildings were products of the same art as the simple roofs they dominated, and amounted to no more than the same geometrical figure multiplied by its square or its cube. They thus added complexity to the whole without disrupting it, completed it without overloading it. Geometry is a matter of harmony. Some fine mansions also projected magnificently over the picturesque attics of the left bank, the Logis de Nevers, the Logis de Rome, the Logis de Reims which have since disappeared; the Hôtel de Cluny, which still remains for the artist's consolation, and whose tower was so stupidly pollarded a few years ago. Near Cluny, that Roman palace, with lovely round arches, were Julian's Baths. There were also a goodly number of abbeys whose beauty was more religious and grandeur more solemn than the mansions, but no less beautiful nor less grand for that. Those which first excited notice were the Bernardins, with its three steeples; Sainte-Geneviève, whose square tower, still existing, makes one grieve for the loss of the rest; the Sorbonne, half college, half monastery, of which such an admirable nave survives; the beautiful quadrilateral cloister of the Mathurins; its neighbour, the cloister of Saint-Benoît, within whose walls they have had time to botch together a theatre between the seventh and eighth editions of this book; the Cordeliers, with three enormous gables side by side; the Augustins, whose graceful spire was, after the Tour de Nesle, the second sharp projection on that side of Paris, counting from the west. The colleges, which were in fact the intermediate link between the cloister and the world, stood midway in the series of monuments between the mansions and the abbeys, with a severity full of elegance, less frivolous sculptures than the palaces, less earnest architecture than the convents. Unfortunately hardly anything remains of these monuments in which Gothic art drew the line so precisely between riches and economy. The churches—which were numerous and splendid in the University and ranged too through every period of architecture from the round arches of Saint-Julien to the pointed ones of Saint-Séverin—the churches dominated the whole, and, as one more harmony among this mass of harmonies, constantly punctuated the jagged outline of these countless gables with slashed spires, open-work steeples, delicate spires whose line was just one more magnificent exaggeration of the steep angle of the roofs.

The University was built on hilly ground. To the south-east the Montagne Sainte-Geneviève formed an immense bulge, and it was a sight to see from the top of Notre-Dame that throng of narrow winding streets (the Latin Quarter of today), those clusters of houses, spread out in all directions from the summit of that eminence, tumbling in disorder, almost vertically, down its slopes to the water's edge, looking as if some were falling and others climbing back again, all holding on to each other. A continual stream of hundreds of black dots crossing one another on the pavement gave the impression that everything was in motion. This was how the people looked, from high up and at a distance.

Finally, in the intervals between these roofs, these spires, these uneven contours of the innumerable buildings which bent, twisted, and indented so oddly the outer line of the University, one caught a glimpse here and there of some great section of wall, overgrown with moss, a thick round tower, a crenellated city-gate, representing the fortress; this was Philip-Augustus's enclosure. Beyond, the green meadows stretched away, beyond, the roads ran off, with a few suburban houses still trailing along them, ever thinner on the ground as the distance increased. Some of these suburbs had a certain importance. First, starting from the Tournelle, came the Bourg Saint-Victor, with its single-arched bridge over the Bièvre, its abbey, where one could read the epitaph of Louis the Fat, *epitaphium Ludovici Grossi*, and its church with an octagonal steeple, flanked by four eleventh-century turrets (there is one like it to be seen at Étampes; it has not been pulled down yet); then the Bourg Saint-Marceau, which already then had three churches and a convent. Then, leaving on the left the Gobelins mill with its four white walls, you came to the Faubourg Saint-Jacques, with the handsome carved cross at the crossroads, the church of Saint-Jacques, which was then a Gothic one, pointed and charming, Saint-Magloire, with a fine fourteenth-century nave used by Napoleon as a hay barn, Notre-Dame des Champs, with some Byzantine mosaics. Finally, leaving behind in the open fields the Carthusian monastery, a sumptuous building contemporaneous with the Palais de Justice, with its little compartmented gardens and the haunted ruins of Vauvert, the eye fell to the west on the three Romanesque spires of Saint-Germain-des-Prés. The Bourg Saint-Germain, already a substantial commune, extended over some fifteen or twenty streets behind. The pointed steeple of Saint-Sulpice marked one of the corners of the Bourg. Close by you could make out the quadrilateral enclosure of the Saint-Germain fair, where the market is today; then the abbot's pillory, a pretty little round tower neatly capped with a lead cone. The tile kiln lay further away, and the rue du Four which led to the communal oven [*four*], and the mill on its mound, and the leper house, an isolated little building shunned by all. But what particularly drew the eye, and held it long fixed on that spot, was the abbey itself. It is certain that this monastery, of imposing appearance both as a church and as a manorial seat, this abbatial palace, where the bishops of Paris counted themselves lucky to spend even one night, this refectory on which the architect had conferred the appearance, the beauty, and the splendid rose-window of a cathedral, this elegant Lady Chapel, this monumental dormitory, vast gardens, portcullis, drawbridge, enveloping battlements, cutting out notches from the view of the green meadows around them, courtyards where men in shining armour mingled with gold copes, all grouped and gathered round the three tall Romanesque spires set firmly on a Gothic apse, made an altogether magnificent figure on the horizon.

When at last, after lengthy contemplation of the University, you turned towards the right bank, towards the Town, the sight before you suddenly changed in character. The Town, indeed, much larger than the University, was also less unified. At first sight it could be seen to divide into several peculiarly distinct masses. First, to the east, in the part of the Town still named after the marsh, Marais, where Camulogenus bogged down Caesar, there was a dense collection of palaces. This mass came down to the water's edge. Four mansions almost touching, the Hôtels de Jouy, de Sens, de Barbeau, and the Logis de la Reine were mirrored in the Seine, their slate roofs punctuated by slender turrets. These four buildings filled up the space from the rue des Nonaindières to the abbey of the Celestines, whose graceful spire set off their line of gables and battlements. A few greenish hovels leaning out over the water in front of these superb mansions did not impede the view of the fine angles of their façades, their broad, square windows with stone mullions, their Gothic porches heavily laden with statuary, the sharp groining of their still clean-cut walls, and all those delightful architectural features which make it seem as though Gothic art starts its combinations afresh with each new monument. Behind these palaces, there ran in every direction, now fenced, stockaded, crenellated like a citadel, now veiled with tall trees like a charterhouse, the vast, multi-form enclosure of the marvellous Hôtel de Saint-Pol, where the King of France could provide superb accommodation for twenty-two princes of the rank of the Dauphin or the Duke of Burgundy, with their servants and suites, not to mention great nobles, and the Emperor when he came to look at Paris, and the lions, who had their separate residence within the royal residence. We should say here that at that time a prince's apartment consisted of no fewer than eleven rooms, from the audience room to the oratory, not to mention the galleries, baths, steam rooms, and other 'superfluous places' with which each apartment was provided; not to mention the private gardens of each of the King's guests; not to mention kitchens, storerooms, pantries, general household refectories; backyards, with twenty-two general workshops, from the bakehouse to the butlery; games of innumerable kinds, mall, tennis, tilting at the ring; aviaries, fishponds, menageries, stables, cattle-sheds; libraries, arsenals, and foundries. Such was a king's palace at the time, a Louvre, a Hôtel Saint-Pol. A city within a city.

From the tower where we are standing the Hôtel Saint-Pol, almost half of it hidden by the four large residences we have just mentioned, was still a very considerable and wonderful sight. Clearly distinguishable within it, though skilfully attached to the main building by long galleries with stained-glass windows and rows of pillars, were the three mansions which Charles V had amalgamated with his palace, the Hôtel du Petit-Muce, its roof trimmed with a graceful, lacy balustrade, the Hôtel of the abbot of Saint-Maur, with the lines of a fortress, a massive tower, machicolations, loopholes, iron *moineaux* [bastions], and over its wide Saxon gateway the abbot's coat of arms between the two grooves for the drawbridge; the Hôtel of the comte d'Étampes, the top of its round keep in ruins and jagged like a coxcomb; here and there three or four old oaks, clumped together like huge cauliflowers, swans disporting themselves in the clear waters of the fishponds, all striped with light and shade; numerous courtyards revealing picturesque corners; the lion house, with low Gothic arches on short Saxon pillars, its iron portcullises, and continual roaring; cutting across the whole the scaly spire of the Ave-Maria; to the left, the residence of the Provost of Paris flanked by four delicately hollowed-out turrets; in the centre, at the back, the Hôtel Saint-Pol proper, with its multiple façades, its successive enrichments since Charles V's time, the hybrid excrescences piled on it over two centuries by the fancies of architects, with all the apses of its chapels, the gables of its galleries, hundreds of weathervanes, and two lofty, contiguous towers, whose conical roofs, with crenellations round their base, looked like pointed hats with the brim turned up.

Continuing up the successive levels of this amphitheatre of palaces unfolding in the distance over the ground, after crossing a deep ravine cut through the roofs of the Town, which marked the line of the rue Saint-Antoine, the eye reached—and we are still confining ourselves to the principal monuments—the Logis d'Angoulême, a vast structure from several different periods, some parts of which were quite new and very white, blending with the whole scarcely better than a red patch on a blue doublet. However, the peculiarly high and steeply pitched roof of the modern palace, bristling with carved gargoyles, covered in lead sheets over which glittering incrustations of gilded copper twisted in a thousand fantastic arabesques, this oddly damascened roof sprang gracefully from amid the brown ruins of the ancient building, whose massive old towers, bulging with the years like casks collapsing with age and splitting from top to bottom, looked like fat bellies released from the support of buttons. Behind rose the forest of slender spires of the Tournelles palace. There was no spectacle in the world, not Chambord, nor the Alhambra, more magical, more ethereal, more marvellous than this cluster of spires, turrets, chimneys, weathervanes, spiral staircases, open-work lanterns, looking as though they had been stamped out with a punch, pavilions, spindle-shaped turrets or, as they were then called, *tournelles*, all of different shapes, height, and altitude. It was like some gigantic stone chessboard.

To the right of the Tournelles, that enormous bundle of inky-black towers, running one into another, and lashed together, so to speak, by a circular moat, that keep with far more loopholes than windows, that drawbridge kept always raised, that portcullis always lowered, that is the Bastille. Those things projecting like black beaks between the battlements, which you might from a distance take for waterspouts, are cannon.

Within their range, at the foot of the formidable building, lies the Porte Saint-Antoine, hidden between its two towers.

Beyond the Tournelles, and up as far as Charles V's wall, stretched a velvety carpet of gardens and royal parks, with rich compartments of greenery and flowers, in the midst of which could be identified, from its labyrinth of trees and paths, the famous Daedalus garden which Louis XI had given to Coictier. The doctor's observatory rose above the maze like a massive isolated column with a little house in place of a capital. Some terrible astrological predictions had originated in that laboratory.

The Place Royale* is there today.

As we have just said, the palace quarter, of which we have tried to give the reader some idea, while pointing out only the highlights, filled the angle formed by Charles V's wall

meeting the Seine to the east. The centre of the Town was
occupied by a heap of houses for ordinary folk. That indeed
is where the three bridges from the City discharged on the
right bank, and bridges produce houses before palaces.
This pile of ordinary dwellings, packed together like cells
in a beehive, had a beauty of its own. The roofs of a capital
city, like the waves of the sea, have a certain grandeur. In
the first place, the streets, intersecting and tangled, formed
numerous diverting patterns in the mass. Around the Halles
it was like a many-pointed star. The rues Saint-Denis and
Saint-Martin, with their countless ramifications, rose side
by side like two great trees mingling their branches. Then
tortuous lines, the rues de la Plâtrerie, de la Verrerie, de la
Tixanderie, coiled over the whole. There were, too, some
fine buildings breaking through the petrified waves of this
sea of gables. At the head of the Pont-aux-Changeurs,
behind which one could see the Seine foaming beneath the
mill-wheels of the Pont-aux-Meuniers, stood the Châtelet,
no longer a Roman tower as it was under Julian the Apostate, but a thirteenth-century feudal tower, of stone so hard
that in three hours with a pickaxe you could not chip away
a hand's thickness. There was the sumptuous square
steeple of Saint-Jacques-de-la-Boucherie, its angles all
rounded with sculptures, already admirable in the fifteenth
century though still unfinished.* In particular it lacked the
four monsters which still today, perched at the corners of
its roof, look like four sphinxes inviting new Paris to solve
the riddle of the old; the sculptor Rault did not put them
there till 1526, and was paid 20 francs for his trouble.
There was the Maison-aux-Piliers, opening on to the Place
de Grève, of which we have already given the reader
some idea. There was Saint-Gervais, since spoiled by a
doorway 'in good taste'; Saint-Méry, whose old Gothic
arches were still almost round Romanesque ones; Saint-
Jean, whose magnificent spire was a byword; there were
a score of other monuments which did not disdain to bury
their marvels amid this chaos of dark, narrow, cavernous
streets. Add the carved stone crosses even more generously
distributed at crossroads than the gibbet; the cemetery of

the Innocents, whose architectural enclosure was visible in the distance above the roofs; the pillory of the Halles, whose top showed between two chimneys in the rue de la Cossonière; the gallows of the Croix-du-Trahoir at the crossroads there, always black with people; the circular shacks of the Halle-au-Blé [Corn Market]; fragments of the old enclosure of Philip-Augustus to be seen here and there, submerged among the houses, the towers eaten away by ivy, gateways in ruins, crumbling and shapeless sections of wall; the quay with its hundreds of shops and bloody skinners' yards; the Seine crammed with boats from the Pont-au-Foin to For-l'Évêque; with that you will have a rough picture of how the central trapezium of the Town looked in 1482.

With these two quarters, one of mansions, the other of dwelling houses, the third feature of the Town's appearance was a long belt of abbeys which ran almost right round it, from east to west, forming behind the ring of fortifications enclosing Paris a second inner ring of convents and chapels. Thus, directly beside the park of the Tournelles, between the rue Saint-Antoine and the rue vieille du Temple, lay Sainte-Catherine, with its vast area of cultivation, bounded only by the city wall of Paris. Between the rue vieille and the rue neuve du Temple lay the Temple, a sinister cluster of towers, tall, upright, and isolated amid a huge crenellated enclosing wall. Between the rue neuve du Temple and the rue Saint-Martin lay the abbey of Saint-Martin, amid its gardens, a superb fortified church, with a girdle of towers and a triple crown of steeples, surpassed in strength and splendour only by Saint-Germain-des-Prés. Between the rues Saint-Martin and Saint-Denis extended the enclosure of the Trinité. Finally, between the rue Saint-Denis and the rue Montorgueil, the Filles-Dieu. Beside it could be made out the decaying roofs and unpaved precinct of the Court of Miracles. It was the only profane link to combine with this pious chain of monastic establishments.

Last, the fourth compartment which stood out from the agglomeration of roofs on the right bank and occupied the

western corner of the enclosure and the riverbank downstream was a new knot of palaces and mansions packed
together at the feet of the Louvre. The old Louvre of
Philip-Augustus, that building out of all proportion whose
massive tower grouped around it twenty-three major towers,
not counting turrets, seemed from a distance to be inset
into the Gothic rooftops of the Hôtel d'Alençon and the
Petit-Bourbon. That hydra of towers, a giant keeping guard
over Paris, with its two dozen heads always alert, its monstrous hindquarters sheathed in lead or scales of slate, glis-
tening with metallic reflections, came as a surprising
conclusion to the Town's western configuration.

Thus an immense mass, what the Romans called *insula*,
an island, of private dwellings, flanked to right and left by
two blocks of palaces, one crowned by the Louvre, the
other by the Tournelles, bordered on the north by a long
belt of abbeys and cultivated enclosures, the whole amalgamated and fused as one watched; above these hundreds
of buildings whose roofs of tiles and slates stood out against
one another to form so many strange ridges and chains, the
tattooed, embossed, guilloched* steeples of the forty-four
churches on the right bank; innumerable streets criss-
crossing; bounded on one side by an enclosure of high walls
with square towers (that of the University had round towers); on the other by the Seine, which was intersected by
bridges and bore a heavy traffic of boats: such was the
Town in the fifteenth century.

Beyond the walls a few suburbs pressed around the gates,
but they were fewer and more scattered than those of the
University. Behind the Bastille a score of poor cottages
huddled round the curious sculptures of the Croix-Faubin
and the flying buttresses of the abbey of Saint-Antoine-des-
Champs; then came Popincourt, lost among the cornfields;
then la Courtille, a merry village full of taverns; the Bourg
Saint-Laurent, with its church, the steeple from a distance
looking like an addition to the pointed towers of the Porte
Saint-Martin; the Faubourg Saint-Denis, with the vast enclosure of Saint-Ladre;* outside the Porte Montmartre, the
Grange-Batelière girdled with white walls; behind, with its

chalky slopes, Montmartre, which at that time had as many
churches as windmills, but has kept only the windmills,
for all that society now demands is bread for the body.
Finally, beyond the Louvre, one could see the already quite
considerable Faubourg Saint-Honoré running out into the
meadows, la Petite-Bretagne in all its greenery, the Marché-
aux-Pourceaux spreading out, with, at its centre, the horrible round furnace in which counterfeiters were boiled
alive. Between la Courtille and Saint-Laurent, on the summit of some high ground squatting above the empty plains,
your eye had already noticed a structure of some sort,
looking from a distance like a ruined colonnade standing
on an exposed base. This was no Parthenon, nor Temple
of Olympian Jupiter. It was Montfaucon.*

Now, if this enumeration of so many buildings, succinct
as we have tried to make it, has not shattered as fast as we
put it together the general picture of old Paris in the
reader's mind, we shall resume it in a few words. In the
centre the Île de la Cité, looking like a huge tortoise in
shape and thrusting out its bridges, scaled with tiles, like
paws from beneath its grey carapace of roofs. To the left
the monolithic, firm, dense, compacted, bristling trapezium
of the University. To the right the vast semicircle of the
Town, much more of a mixture with its gardens and monuments. The three blocks, City, University, Town, veined
with countless streets. Running through it all the Seine, 'the
nutritive Seine' as Father Du Breul puts it, obstructed by
islands, bridges, and boats. All around an immense plain,
a patchwork of innumerable kinds of cultivation, sprinkled
with attractive villages; to the left Issy, Vanves, Vaugirard,
Montrouge, Gentilly, with its round tower and its square
tower, etc.; to the right a score of others from Conflans to
Ville-l'Évêque. On the horizon a circular fringe of hills like
the rim of the basin. Finally, far off to the east, Vincennes
and its seven quadrangular towers; to the south, Bicêtre and
its pointed turrets; to the north Saint-Denis and its slim
spire; to the west Saint-Cloud and its keep. Such was the
Paris which crows living in 1482 could see from the top of
the towers of Notre-Dame.

Yet this was the town of which Voltaire said 'before Louis XIV it possessed only four fine monuments':* the dome of the Sorbonne, Val de Grâce, the modern Louvre, and a fourth that I forget, perhaps the Luxembourg. Fortunately, Voltaire none the less wrote *Candide,* and of all those who have followed one another in the long line of mankind he is the man with the most diabolical laugh. That also proves that one can be a real genius and still lack all understanding of an art which is not one's own. Did not Molière think he was paying Raphael and Michelangelo a handsome tribute when he called them 'the Mignards* of their age'?

Let us return to Paris and the fifteenth century.

It was not merely a fine town at that time; it was a homogeneous town, the architectural and historical product of the Middle Ages, a chronicle in stone. It was a city formed of two strata only, the Romanesque and the Gothic, for the Roman stratum had long since disappeared, except for Julian's Baths, where it still broke through the thick medieval crust. As for the Celtic stratum, no more examples of it were being found then, even when wells were dug.

Fifty years later, when the Renaissance arrived to add to that unity, so austere and yet so varied, the dazzling profusion of its fantasies and systems, its riot of rounded Roman arches, Greek columns and Gothic surbasements, its sculpture full of such idealized tenderness, its special taste for arabesques and acanthus, the paganism of its architecture, in an age when Luther too was alive, Paris was perhaps even more beautiful, though less harmonious to the eye and the mind. But that splendid moment did not last. The Renaissance was not impartial; it was not content with putting up, it wanted also to pull down. It is true that it needed room. So Gothic Paris was complete only for a minute. Saint-Jacques-de-la-Boucherie was hardly finished before they began demolishing the old Louvre.

Since then the great city has suffered more and more disfigurement, day by day. The Gothic Paris beneath which Romanesque Paris disappeared has disappeared in its turn. But can we say what sort of Paris has taken its place?

There is the Paris of Catherine de' Medici at the Tuileries,[1] the Paris of Henri II at the Hôtel de Ville, two buildings still in excellent taste; the Paris of Henri IV in the Place Royale: brick façades with stone quoins and slate roofs, tricolour houses; the Paris of Louis XIII at Val-de-Grâce: a squat, compressed architecture, vaults like basket handles, something paunchy about the columns and hump-backed about the dome; the Paris of Louis XIV at the Invalides: grand, ornate, gilded and cold; the Paris of Louis XV at Saint-Sulpice: scrolls, knots of ribbon, clouds, vermicelli and chicory, all in stone; the Paris of Louis XVI, at the Panthéon: a poor copy of Saint Peter's in Rome (the building has settled awkwardly, which has not improved its lines); the Paris of the Republic, at the École de Médecine: a poor Graeco-Roman style as much like the Coliseum or the Parthenon as the Constitution of the Year III is like that of Minos, in architecture it is known as the 'Messidor style';* the Paris of Napoleon at the Place Vendôme: that is quite sublime, a bronze column made from cannon; the Paris of the Restoration at the Bourse: a very white colonnade supporting a very smooth frieze, the whole is square and cost 20 million.

Associated with each of these typical monuments by similarity of style, manner, and attitude are a certain number of houses scattered through different districts, which the connoisseur's eye can easily pick out and date. Anyone who knows how to look can recognize the spirit of an age and the physiognomy of a king even in a door-knocker.

---

[1] We have seen with grief mixed with indignation that they are thinking of enlarging, recasting, reshaping, that is, destroying this admirable palace. The architects of our day are too heavy-handed to touch these delicate works of the Renaissance. We still hope that they will not dare to do so. Besides, to demolish the Tuileries now would not merely be an assault brutal enough to make a drunken Vandal blush, it would be an act of betrayal. The Tuileries is no longer just a masterpiece of sixteenth-century art, it is also a part of nineteenth-century history. The palace no longer belongs to the king, but to the people. Leave it as it is. Our revolution has twice marked its brow. On one of its two façades it has the cannonballs of 10 August, on the other those of 29 July. It is sacred. Paris, 7 April 1831. (Note to the 5th ed.)

Present-day Paris has, then, no general physiognomy. It is a collection of examples from several centuries, and the finest have disappeared. The capital is increasing only in houses, and what houses! At the rate Paris is going it will be renewed every fifty years. So the historical significance of its architecture is being erased every day. Its monuments are becoming increasingly rare, and they are, as it seems, being gradually swallowed up before our eyes, drowned in the sea of houses. Our fathers had a Paris of stone; our sons will have a Paris of plaster.

As for the modern monuments of our new Paris, we shall gladly refrain from comment. Not that we withhold from them the admiration which is their due. Monsieur Soufflot's Sainte-Geneviève is certainly the finest sponge cake ever made out of stone. The Palais of the Légion d'Honneur is also a most distinguished piece of confectionery. The dome of the corn market is an English jockey cap on the grand scale. The towers of Saint-Sulpice are two huge clarinets, a shape as shapes go; the crooked, grinning telegraph makes a pleasant contrast on their roofline. Saint-Roch has a doorway that can be compared in magnificence only with Saint-Thomas d'Aquin. It has also a calvary sculpted in the round in a cellar and a sun made of gilded wood. These are all real marvels. The lantern in the maze at the Jardin des Plantes is also most ingenious. As for the palace of the Bourse, Greek in its colonnades, Roman in the rounded arches of its doors and windows, Renaissance in its great surbased ceiling, it is indisputably a monument in the purest and most correct style. To prove the point, it is crowned by an attic storey such as was never seen in Athens, a fine straight line, gracefully broken here and there by stove pipes. Let us add that it is the rule that a building's architecture should be so adapted to its intended function that that function should be self-evident simply from the appearance of the building. No admiration could be too great for a monument which might equally well be a king's palace, a house of commons, a town hall, a college, a riding school, an academy, a warehouse, a lawcourt, a museum, a barracks, a sepulchre, a temple, a theatre. For the moment it is a stock exchange. A monument should furthermore be appropriate to the climate. This one has obviously been constructed expressly for our cold, rainy skies. It has a roof almost as flat as in the East, with the result that in winter, when it snows, they sweep the roof, and roofs are assuredly made to be swept. As for the intended function just mentioned, it fulfils it wonderfully; it is a Bourse in France, as it would have been a temple in Greece. It is true that the architect found it quite hard to conceal the clock-face which would have destroyed the purity of the façade's fine lines; but to make up for that there is the colonnade going right round the building, beneath which on high days of religious solemnity the procession of stockbrokers and jobbers can wend its majestic way.

There can be no doubt that these are very splendid monuments. Add to them numerous fine streets as amusing and varied as the rue de Rivoli, and I am not without hope that Paris seen from a balloon may one day afford the sight of that amplitude of lines, that wealth of detail, that diversity of aspect, that indefinable element of grandiose simplicity and unexpected beauty which characterizes a draught-board.

However admirable though the Paris of the present day may seem to you, recreate the Paris of the fifteenth century, reconstruct it in your mind, look at the daylight coming through that astonishing hedge of spires, towers, and steeples, spread out the Seine through the midst of the immense town, with a tear at the tip of the islands, a fold at the arches of the bridges, the Seine with its wide pools of green and yellow, more changeable than a snake's skin; make the Gothic profile of old Paris stand out sharply against a blue horizon, make its contours float in the winter mist clinging to its countless chimneys; plunge it into deep night, and watch the strange play of darkness and points of light in this sombre labyrinth of buildings; cast upon it a ray of moonlight to shape its vague outline and bring out from the fog the great heads of the towers; or take that black silhouette again, underline with shadow the innumerable acute angles of spire and gable, and make it stand out, more jagged than a shark's jaws, against the copper sky at sunset—and then compare.

And if you want to have an impression of the old city such as the modern one can no longer offer, go up, on the morning of some great festival, at sunrise on Easter Day or Whitsun, go up to some high point overlooking the whole capital and experience the waking of the bells. See, at a signal from the heavens, for it is the sun that gives it, these hundreds of churches start as one from their sleep. At first scattered tinklings go from one church to the other, like musicians giving notice that they are about to start; then all of a sudden look, for at certain moments the ear too seems to see, look at how from every steeple at the same moment there rises a pillar of sound, a smoke-cloud of harmony. At first the vibration of each bell rises straight, pure, and, so to speak, in isolation from the others into the splendid morning sky. Then gradually as the sound increases they merge, blend, coalesce, all combine in one magnificent concert. It is now a single mass of sound-waves ceaselessly pouring from the countless steeples, floating, rippling, leaping, swirling over the city and extending far beyond the horizon the deafening eddies of its oscillations. However, this sea of harmony is by no means chaotic. Vast and deep as it is, it has not lost its transparency. You can see the separate undulations of each group of notes escaping from the peals; you can follow the dialogue, alternately deep and shrill, of the lightest and the heaviest bell, the rattle and the bourdon: you can see the octaves leap from one belfry to the next; you can watch them spring winged, light, and whistling from the silver bell, fall broken and lame from the wooden one; among them you can admire the rich gamut falling and rising ceaselessly from the seven bells of Saint-Eustache; you can see clear, rapid notes running across like three or four bright zigzags and vanishing like lightning flashes. Over there is the abbey of Saint-Martin, singing sharp and cracked; here the gruff, sinister voice of the Bastille; at the other end the great tower of the Louvre, with its bass-baritone. The royal carillon of the Palais casts in all directions respendent trills, on to which fall at regular intervals the heavy strokes from the belfry of Notre-Dame, striking sparks from them like the anvil under the hammer. Now and then you can see passing by sounds of every shape emanating from the triple peal of Saint-Germain-des-Prés. Then again from time to time this mass of sublime sounds leaves an opening through which comes the *stretta** of the Ave-Maria,* bursting and sparkling like a plume of stars. Below, in the depths of the concert, you can vaguely make out the singing from inside the churches, seeping through the vibrating pores of their vaulted ceilings. It is, to be sure, an opera worth listening to. Usually the murmur that comes from Paris in the daytime is the city speaking; at night it is the city breathing; here it is the city singing. Lend an ear, then, to this chorus from all the steeples, spread over the whole the murmur of half a million people, the everlasting plaint of the river, the infinite breathing of the wind, the deep and distant quartet of the four forests ranged over the hills on the horizon like immense organ cases, damp down as in a half-tone everything too raucous and shrill in the central peal, and then say whether you know anything in the world more rich, joyful, golden, dazzling than this tumult of bells and chimes; this furnace of music; these ten thousand brazen voices singing at once in stone flutes three hundred feet high; this city transformed into an orchestra; this symphony of tempestuous sound.

BOOK FOUR

I

KIND SOULS

It was sixteen years before the beginning of this story when one fine Quasimodo (or Low) Sunday morning a living creature had been left after mass in the church of Notre-Dame, on the bedstead fixed into the parvis on the left-hand side, facing the 'great image' of Saint Christopher at which the carved stone effigy of Messire Antoine des Essarts, knight, had been gazing on his knees ever since 1413, when it was decided to pull down both saint and devotee. It was on this bedstead that foundlings were customarily exposed to public charity. Whoever wished could take them. In front of the bedstead was a copper bowl for alms.

The sort of living creature which lay on those boards that Quasimodo morning in the year of Our Lord 1467 seemed to be arousing intense curiosity among the very considerable group collected round the bed. This group was mainly composed of persons of the fair sex. They were nearly all old women.

In the front row, bending most closely over the bed, could be seen four women who, from their grey cowls, a sort of cassock, presumably belonged to some religious sisterhood. I see no reason why history should not transmit to posterity the names of these four discreet and venerable ladies. They were Agnès la Herme, Jehanne de la Tarmè, Henriette la Gaultière, Gauchère la Violette, all four of them widows, all four *bonnes-femmes* or religious from the Chapel of Étienne Haudry,* who had left their house with their superior's permission, and in accordance with Pierre d'Ailly's statutes, to come and hear the sermon.

However, if these *haudriettes* were for the moment observing Pierre d'Ailly's statutes, they were certainly transgress-

ing to their hearts' content those of Michel de Brache
and the Cardinal of Pisa which so harshly laid down silence
for them.

'Whatever is that, sister?' said Agnès to Gauchère, looking at the little creature exposed there, which was squealing
and wriggling about on the bed, frightened by so many
onlookers.

'What are we coming to,' said Jehanne, 'if that's the way
they are making children nowadays?'

'I don't know much about children,' replied Agnès, 'but
looking at this one must be sinful.'

'That's not a child, Agnès.'

'It's a monkey gone wrong,' observed Gauchère.

'It's a miracle,' put in Henriette la Gaultière.

'In that case,' Agnès noted,' it is the third since Laetare
Sunday.* For less than a week ago we had the miracle of
divine punishment being visited by Our Lady of Aubervil-
lers on the man who scoffed at pilgrims, and that was the
second miracle this month.'

'It's a real monster of abomination, this so-called foundling,' Jehanne went on.

'He's yelling loud enough to deafen a cantor,' continued
Gauchère. 'Do be quiet, you little screamer!'

'Just imagine his Grace of Reims sending this monstrosity
to the Bishop of Paris!' La Gaultière added, clasping her
hands.

'I imagine,' said Agnès la Herme, 'that it's a beast, an
animal, the offspring of a Jew and a sow; in fact, something
that's not Christian and ought to be thrown into the water
or the flames.'

'I certainly hope,' la Gaultière went on, 'that no one will
apply for it.'

'Oh, my goodness!' exclaimed Agnès, 'those poor wet-
nurses in the foundlings' home, down at the bottom of the
lane as you go downstream, right next to my Lord Bishop;
just suppose someone brought them this little monster to
suckle! I'd rather give suck to a vampire.'

'How innocent she is, that poor la Herme!' Jehanne went
on. 'Can't you see, sister, that the little monster is at least

4 years old, and would find your teats much less appetizing than something off the spit.'

In fact this 'little monster' (we should ourselves be hard put to it to describe him otherwise) was no newborn babe. It was a very angular, very restless small mass, imprisoned in a canvas bag marked with the cipher of Messire Guillaume Chartier, then Bishop of Paris, with a head sticking out. That head was very deformed. All you could see was a thicket of red hair, an eye, a mouth, and some teeth. The eye was weeping, the mouth crying, and the teeth seemed only to want something to bite. The whole mass was struggling about in the bag, to the great amazement of the crowd of bystanders, which grew all the time and attracted new people.

Dame Aloïse de Gondelaurier, a rich noblewoman, holding a pretty little girl of about 6 by the hand, and whose coif had a long veil trailing from its golden horn, stopped as she passed in front of the bed, and looked for a moment at the unfortunate creature, while her charming little girl, Fleur-de-Lys de Gondelaurier, all dressed up in silk and velvet, spelled out with her pretty finger the label permanently attached to the bed: FOUNDLINGS.

'Really,' said the lady, turning away in disgust, 'I thought they only exposed children here.'

She turned her back, and threw into the bowl a silver florin which rang out among the *liards* and made the poor sisters of the Étienne Haudry chapel stare wide-eyed.

A moment later the grave and learned Robert Mistricole, protonotary to the king, went by with an enormous missal under one arm and on the other his wife (Damoiselle Guillemette la Mairesse), thus having on either side his two governors, spiritual and temporal.

'Foundling!' he said, after examining the object, 'found apparently on the parapet of the river Phlegethon!'*

'You can only see one of its eyes,' observed Mademoiselle Guillemette, 'there's a wart over the other.'

'That's not a wart,' replied Maître Robert Mistricole. 'It's an egg, with another devil, just like him, inside, with another little egg containing another devil and so on.'

'How do you know?' asked Guillemette La Mairesse.

'I know it for a fact,' replied the protonotary.

'Monsieur the protonotary,' asked Gauchère, 'what do you predict for this alleged foundling?'

'The greatest disasters,' answered Mistricole.

'Ah! my goodness!' said an old woman in the audience, 'on top of that bad outbreak of pestilence we had last year and talk of the English preparing to land in force at Harefleu [Harfleur].'

'Perhaps that will stop the queen coming to Paris in September,' put in another. 'Business is bad enough as it is!'

'It's my opinion,' exclaimed Jehanne de la Tarme, 'that the people of Paris would be better off with that little wizard lying on a faggot instead of a plank.'

'A nicely blazing faggot!' added the old woman.

'That would be wiser,' said Mistricole.

For some little time a young priest had been listening to the arguments of the *haudriettes* and the utterances of the protonotary. His face was austere, his forehead broad, his gaze piercing. He silently moved the crowd aside, examined the 'little wizard' and laid his hand on him. It was none too soon. For all the pious women were already licking their chops at the 'nicely blazing faggot'.

'I adopt this child,' said the priest.

He gathered him into his cassock and carried him off. They all watched him go with looks of alarm. A moment later he had disappeared through the Porte-Rouge, which then led from the church to the cloister.

Once the initial surprise had passed, Jehanne de la Tarme whispered in la Gaultière's ear:

'What did I tell you sister, that young cleric, Monsieur Claude Frollo, is a sorcerer.'

II

CLAUDE FROLLO

CLAUDE FROLLO was indeed not one of the common herd.

He belonged to one of those families of middle rank which, in the impertinent language of the last century, were called indifferently upper bourgeoisie or minor nobility. This family had inherited from the brothers Paclet the fief of Tirechappe, which came under the Bishop of Paris, and whose twenty-one houses had in the thirteenth century been the object of so many pleadings before the official. As possessor of this fief Claude Frollo was one of the 'seven score and one' lords claiming feudal dues in Paris and its suburbs, and his name could for a long time be seen inscribed in that capacity between the Hôtel de Tancarville, belonging to Maître François le Rez, and the Collège de Tours, in the cartulary deposited at Saint-Martindes-Champs.

Claude Frollo had been destined by his parents since childhood for the Church. He had learned to read in Latin. He had been brought up to keep his eyes downcast and his voice low. While he was still only a child, his father had cloistered him in the Collège de Torchi* in the University. There he had grown up on the missal and the Lexicon.

He was besides a cheerless, solemn, serious boy, who studied with fervour and learned quickly. He did not make a lot of noise during recreation, took little part in the revelries of the rue du Fouarre, did not know what it was to *dare alapas et capillos laniare* [to hit people and tear out their hair] and played no part in the mutiny of 1463 which the annalists gravely record under the heading: 'Sixth Disturbance at the University'. He seldom jeered at the poor scholars of Montaigu for the skimpy capes, *capettes*, for which they were nicknamed, or the scholarship boys of the Collège de Dormans for their shaven heads, and their tripartite surcoats of grey, blue, and purple, *azurini coloris et bruni*, in the words of the charter of the Cardinal des Quatre-Couronnes.

On the other hand he was assiduous in attending the schools, major and minor, of the rue Jean-de-Beauvais. The first student whom the abbot of Saint-Pierre de Val always noticed as he was about to begin his reading of canon law, was Claude Frollo, pressed against a pillar, facing his pulpit in the school of Saint-Vendregesile, armed with his ink-horn, chewing his pen, scribbling on his well-worn knee, and in winter blowing on his fingers. The first member of the audience whom Messire Miles d'Isliers, Doctor of Decretals, saw arriving every Monday morning, quite out of breath, when the doors opened at the School of Chef-Saint-Denis, was Claude Frollo. Thus, at 16 the young clerk could have held his own in mystical theology with a Father of the Church, in canonical theology with a conciliar father, and in scholastic theology with a doctor of the Sorbonne.

Once past theology he had plunged into the study of decretals. From the 'Master of the Sentences'* he had fallen on the *Capitularies of Charlemagne*. And in his thirst for knowledge he had successively devoured one set of decretals after another, those of Theodore [sc. Isidore] Bishop of Hispalis [Seville], of Burchard, Bishop of Worms, of Yves, Bishop of Chartres; then Gratian's *Decretum*, which succeeded Charlemagne's *Capitularies*; then the collection of Gregory IX; then Honorius III's Epistle *Super specula*. He clarified and familiarized himself with that vast, turbulent period when civil and canon law were struggling and labouring in the chaos of the Middle Ages, a period beginning with Bishop Theodore [Isidore] in 618 and ending with Pope Gregory in 1227.

With decretals digested, he threw himself into medicine and the liberal arts. He studied the science of herbs, the science of unguents. He became an expert on fevers and contusions, wounds and abscesses. Jacques d'Espars* would have admitted him as a physician, Richard Hellain* as a surgeon. He likewise passed through all the degrees in arts, from bachelor to master to doctor. He studied languages,

Latin, Greek, Hebrew, a threefold sanctuary at that time frequented by very few. He had a real fever for acquiring and hoarding knowledge. By the age of 18 he had gone through all four faculties.* It seemed to the young man that there was only one purpose in life: knowledge.

It was about this time that the excessively hot summer of 1466 caused an outbreak of the great plague which carried off more than forty thousand souls in the viscounty of Paris, among others, says Jean de Troyes,* 'Maître Arnoul, astrologer to the king, a most honest man, wise and pleasant'. The rumour went round the University that the rue Tirechappe had been especially devastated by the sickness. It was there, in the middle of their fief, that Claude's parents resided. The young student hurried in great alarm to the paternal home. When he entered, his father and mother had been dead since the day before. An infant brother, still in swaddling clothes, was still alive and crying, abandoned in his cradle. It was all that was left of Claude's family. The young man tucked the child under his arm and went away pensive. Up to then he had lived only in science, now he was beginning to live in life.

This catastrophe came as a crisis in Claude's existence. An orphan, an elder brother, head of the family at 19, he felt rudely recalled from his academic dreams to the realities of the world. So, moved to pity, he became passionately devoted to this child, his brother; human affection came as something strange and sweet to him, whose only love before had been his books.

This affection developed to an exceptional degree. In a soul so new it was like a first love. Separated since childhood from his parents, whom he had hardly known, cloistered and immured, as it were, in his books, eager above all to study and to learn, up till then concerned exclusively with his intellect, which expanded with knowledge, and his imagination, which grew with reading, the poor student had not yet had time to feel where his heart came in. This younger brother, with no father or mother, this little child, suddenly dropped from the heavens into his charge, made a new man of him. He realized that there were other things in the world besides the speculations of the Sorbonne and Homer's poetry, that man has a need for affection, that life without tenderness and love is just a dry, creaking, destructive piece of machinery; only he imagined, for he was at an age when illusions are still replaced only by other illusions, that the affections of blood and family were the only ones necessary, and that having a little brother to love was enough to fill up his whole existence.

He threw himself, then, into loving his little Jehan with all the passion of a character already profound, ardent, and single-minded. This poor, frail creature, pretty, fair, pink, and curly-haired, this orphan with no support but another orphan, moved him to the depths of his being; and, serious thinker that he was, he began to reflect about Jehan with infinite pity. He treated him with care and concern as something most fragile, especially entrusted to him. He was more than a brother to the child, he became a mother to it.

Little Jehan had lost his mother while he was still at the breast. Claude put him out to nurse. As well as the fief of Tirechappe, he had inherited from his father the fief of the Mill, *Moulin*, which was a dependency of the square tower of Gentilly. This mill stood on a hill, near the castle of Winchestre (Bicêtre). The miller's wife there was suckling a fine boy; it was not far from the University. Claude carried little Jehan to her himself.

From then on, feeling he had a burden to bear, he took life very seriously. The thought of his little brother became not merely a recreation from his studies, but their very goal. He resolved to devote himself entirely to a future, for which he would answer before God, and never to have any other spouse, any other child than the happiness and prosperity of his brother. He therefore became more than ever committed to his clerical vocation. His merit, his learning, his position as immediate vassal of the Bishop of Paris, opened wide for him the gates of the Church. At the age of 20,* by special dispensation of the Holy See, he was a priest, serving, as the junior chaplain of Notre-Dame, the altar known from the late mass celebrated there as the *altare pigrorum* [altar of the slothful].

There, absorbed more than ever in his beloved books, which he only left to hurry for an hour to the fief of the Mill, this blend of learning and austerity, so rare at his age, had soon won him the respect and admiration of the cloister. From the cloister his reputation for learning had reached the people, where it had become slightly distorted, as frequently happened at the time, into renown as a sorcerer.

He was just returning, on Quasimodo Sunday, from saying his mass for the lazy at their altar, which was beside the door in the choir leading to the nave, on the right, near the image of the Virgin, when his attention had been aroused by the group of old women yapping round the foundlings' bed.

Then it was that he had approached the unfortunate little creature, object of so much hatred and menaces. Such distress, such deformity, such abandonment, the thought of his young brother, the wild fancy that suddenly struck him that, were he to die, his dear little Jehan might well be cast wretchedly upon the foundlings' bed, this had all filled his heart at the same time; a great feeling of pity had stirred within him and he had carried the child away.

When he pulled the child out of the bag he found that it was indeed badly deformed. The poor little devil had a wart over his left eye, his head down between his shoulders, his spine all bent, his breastbone sticking out, his legs crooked; but he looked lively; and although it was impossible to tell what language he was mouthing, his cry betokened a certain health and strength. Claude's compassion was increased by such ugliness; and he vowed inwardly to bring up this child for love of his brother, so that, whatever faults Jehan might commit in the future, there should stand to his credit this act of charity, performed for his sake. It was a sort of investment of good works made on his young brother's account; a parcel of good deeds which he wanted to put together for him in advance, in case the young rascal might one day find himself short of such currency, the only one accepted at the toll gate of paradise.

He baptized his adopted child, and named him Quasimo-do, either because he wanted thereby to indicate the day on which he had found him, or because he wanted to signify by that name the degree to which the poor little creature was unfinished and incomplete. Indeed, Quasimodo, one-eyed, hunchbacked, bow-legged was hardly more than a 'more or less'.*

III

IMMANIS PECORIS CUSTOS IMMANIOR IPSE*
[OF A MONSTROUS FLOCK A STILL MORE MONSTROUS KEEPER]

NOW, in 1482, Quasimodo had grown up. Several years before he had become bell-ringer of Notre-Dame, thanks to his adoptive father Claude Frollo, who himself had become archdeacon of Josas,* thanks to his suzerain, Messire Louis de Beaumont, who had become Bishop of Paris in 1472, on the death of Guillaume Chartier, thanks to his patron Olivier le Daim, barber of Louis XI, King by the grace of God.

So Quasimodo was in charge of the peal at Notre-Dame.

With time an indefinable close bond had been formed uniting the bell-ringer and the church. Cut off for ever from the world by the double fatality of his unknown birth and his natural deformity, imprisoned since infancy within this double circle from which there was no escape, the poor unfortunate had become accustomed to seeing nothing of the world beyond the religious walls which had received him into their shadow. Notre-Dame had been successively, as he grew and developed, his egg, his nest, his home, his country, his universe.

And assuredly there was some sort of mysterious pre-existent harmony between that creature and the building. When, while still only small, he dragged himself tortuously and jerkily beneath the gloom of its vaults he seemed with his human face and animal's limbs to be the native reptile of the damp and sombre paving over which the shadows of the Romanesque capitals cast so many strange shapes.

Later, the first time he clung automatically to the rope in the towers, hung on it, and set the bell swinging, the effect it produced on Claude, his adoptive father, was of a child whose tongue is loosened and who begins to talk.

Thus it was that little by little, always developing in tune with the cathedral, living, sleeping there, almost never leaving it, subject at every moment to its mysterious pressures, he came to resemble it, to be encrusted on it, so to speak, to become an integral part of it. His protruding angles fitted, if we may be allowed the comparison, the concave angles of the building, and he seemed to be not just its denizen but its natural contents. You could almost say that he had taken its shape, as the snail takes the shape of its shell. It was his abode, his hole, his envelope. Between the old church and him there was an instinctive sympathy so profound and magnetic, and material affinities so numerous, that he somehow adhered to it like the tortoise to its shell. The rugged cathedral was his carapace.

There is no need to warn the reader not to take literally the metaphors we are obliged to use here to express the peculiar, symmetrical, immediate, almost consubstantial conjunction of a man and a building. It is equally needless to say how familiar the whole cathedral had become to him during so long and intimate a cohabitation. This dwelling place was his. It had no depth which Quasimodo had not penetrated, no height he had not scaled. Many times he had climbed up several elevations of the façade with no help other than the projections of the stone carving. The towers, on whose outer surfaces he could often be seen crawling like a lizard gliding over a perpendicular wall, those two twin giants, so tall, so threatening, so fearsome, never caused him vertigo, terror, or fits of giddiness; seeing them so docile to his hand, so easily scaled, you would have said he had tamed them. By dint of leaping, climbing, frolicking amid the abysses of the gigantic cathedral, he had become some kind of monkey and chamois, like the Calabrian child who swims before it can walk and from infancy plays with the sea.

Moreover, it was not only his body which seemed to have been fashioned to fit the cathedral, but his mind too. The state of that soul, the habits it had contracted, the shape it had taken beneath that constricting envelope, leading so unsociable a life, such questions would be hard to determine. Quasimodo had been born one-eyed, hunchbacked, lame. It took much trouble and much patience before Claude Frollo managed to teach him to talk. But a fatality dogged the poor foundling. Bell-ringer of Notre-Dame at 14, a new disability had come to make him complete: the bells had ruptured his eardrums; he had become deaf. The only door that nature had left open for him on to the outer world had suddenly been closed for ever.

In closing it had cut off the one ray of light and joy which still penetrated Quasimodo's soul. That soul fell into darkest night. The poor wretch's melancholy became as incurable and complete as his deformity. We should add that his deafness to some extent made him also dumb. For, so that others should have no occasion to laugh at him, from the moment that he realized he was deaf he firmly resolved to keep a silence which he hardly ever broke except when he was alone. He deliberately tied the tongue which Claude Frollo had taken such pains to loosen. As a result, when compelled by necessity to speak, his tongue was stiff, clumsy, like a door with rusty hinges.

Were we now to try to penetrate as far as Quasimodo's soul through that hard, thick crust; were we to plumb the depths of that misshapen organism; were it given to us to inspect with a torch behind those organs impermeable to light, to explore the dark interior of that opaque creature, to elucidate its obscure corners and absurd impasses, and suddenly to cast a bright light on the psyche chained up in the depths of that cavern, we should no doubt find the wretch in some pathetic, stunted, rachitic posture like those prisoners kept below the roof in Venice, growing old bent double in a stone box too low and too short for movement.

It is certain that the spirit atrophies in a defective body. Quasimodo was scarcely aware of the blind movements within him of a soul made in his own image. The impressions made on him by objects underwent considerable refraction before reaching his mind. His brain was a peculiar medium; the ideas which passed through it merged all twisted. The reflections resulting from such refraction were inevitably divergent and deviant.

Hence innumerable optical illusions, innumerable aberrations of judgement, innumerable diversions for his errant thoughts, now wild, now idiotic.

The first effect of this fatal organism was to disturb the way he looked at things. He had almost no direct perception of them. The outside world seemed much further away to him than to us.

The second effect of his misfortune was to make him vicious.

He was in fact vicious because he avoided people; he avoided people because he was ugly. There was a logic in his nature as there is in ours.

His strength, so extraordinarily developed, was a further cause of viciousness. '*Malus puer robustus*', says Hobbes.* 'The strong boy is vicious.'

Besides, to be fair to him, his viciousness was perhaps not innate. From his earliest steps among men he had felt, then seen himself the object of jeers, condemnation, rejection. Human speech for him always meant mockery or curses. As he grew older he had found nothing but hatred around him. He had caught it. He had acquired the general viciousness. He had picked up the weapon with which he had been wounded.

After all this he turned towards mankind only with reluctance. His cathedral was sufficient for him. It was peopled by marble figures, kings, saints, bishops, who at least did not burst out laughing in his face and looked on him only with serenity and benevolence. The other statues, of monsters and demons, showed no hatred for Quasimodo. He resembled them too closely for that. They kept their mockery rather for other men. The saints were his friends, and blessed him; the monsters were his friends, and protected him. So he would pour out his heart to them at length. So he would sometimes spend hours at a time squatting in front of one of these statues, in solitary conversation with it. If anyone happened to appear, he would flee like a lover surprised while serenading.

And the cathedral was not just society to him, but the universe as well, the whole of nature. He never dreamed of any other espaliers than those of the stained-glass windows always in bloom, any shade but that of the stone foliage, laden with birds, flowering in clumps on the Saxon capitals, any mountains but the colossal towers of the church, any ocean but Paris murmuring at their feet.

What he loved above all in the maternal building, what awoke his soul to spread out the poor wings which it kept so miserably folded in its cavern, were the bells. He loved them, fondled them, talked to them, understood them. From the peal in the slender spire over the crossing to the great bell over the doorway, he was fond of them all. The spire over the crossing, the two towers were for him like three great cages in which the birds, trained by him, would sing for no one else. Yet it was these same bells which had made him deaf; but mothers often show most love for the child who has made them suffer most.

It is true that their voice was the only one he could still hear. On that score, the great bell was his dearly beloved. That was the one he preferred out of that family of noisy girls which bobbed around him on feast days. This great bell was called Marie. She was alone in the south tower with her sister Jacqueline, a smaller bell, enclosed in a smaller cage beside her. This Jacqueline was so called after the wife of Jean de Montagu, who had given it to the church, but that had not prevented him from appearing without his head at Montfaucon.* In the second tower were six other bells, and finally the six smallest lived in the spire over the crossing with the wooden bell, rung only from the afternoon of Maundy Thursday until the morning of Easter Eve. Quasimodo thus had fifteen bells in his seraglio, but big Marie was his favourite.

You cannot imagine his joy on the days of a full peal. As soon as the archdeacon let him go, saying: 'Go on!', he would go up the spiral staircase in the bell tower faster than anyone else would have come down it. Quite out of breath he went into the great bell's airy chamber; gazed at it for a moment in loving reverence; then spoke softly to it, stroked it with his hand, like some good horse about to run a long race. He expressed his sympathy for the trouble she was about to suffer. After these preliminary caresses, he called out to his assistants, standing on the lower floor of the tower, to begin. They hung on the ropes, the capstan

creaked, and the huge metal capsule slowly moved. Quasimodo, shaking with excitement, followed it with his eyes.
The first impact of the clapper on the bronze wall made the
timber frame on which it was mounted quiver. Quasimodo
vibrated with the bell. 'Vah!' he cried with a bellow of crazy
laughter. Meanwhile the bourdon gathered speed in its
swing, and as it described a wider and wider angle, Quasimodo's eye grew also wider and wider, flaming like phosphorus. At last the full peal began, the whole tower
trembled, timbers, leads, stonework, everything rumbled at
the same time, from the foundation piles to the trefoils on
the roof ridge. Quasimodo was now in a lather of excitement; he went to and fro; he trembled from head to foot
with the tower. The bell, in unbridled frenzy, offered to
each side of the tower in turn its bronze throat, emitting
its tempestuous breath which could be heard four leagues
away. Quasimodo placed himself in front of this open
mouth; squatted down, rose again as the bell swung,
breathed in this shattering blast, looked alternately at the
Place, swarming with people two hundred feet below, and
the enormous brazen tongue which came second after second to shout in his ear. It was the only speech he could still
hear, the only sound which disturbed his universal silence.
It made him swell out like a bird in the sunshine. Suddenly
he caught the bell's frenzy; his eye became extraordinary;
he waited for the bourdon to come past, like a spider
waiting for a fly, and suddenly flung himself headlong upon
it. Then, suspended over the abyss, launched on the fearsome swinging of the bell, he seized the bronze monster by
its lugs, gripped it with both knees, spurred it on with both
heels and added the whole shock and weight of his body
to increase the frenzy of the peal. Meanwhile the tower
swayed; he shouted and ground his teeth, his red hair
bristled, his chest sounded like the bellows in a forge, his
eye flashed fire. The monstrous bell whinnied, panting beneath him, and then it was no longer the bourdon of Notre-
Dame or Quasimodo, it was a dream, a whirlwind, a
tempest; vertigo riding on sound; a spirit clinging to a flying
crupper; a strange centaur, half man, half bell; a kind of

horrible Astolfo* carried away on a prodigious hippogriff of living bronze.

The presence of this extraordinary being sent round the whole cathedral some indefinable breath of life. It seemed as though there came from him, so at least the exaggerating superstitions of the people held, some mysterious emanation which brought to life all the stones of Notre-Dame and stirred the inmost vitals of the old church. The knowledge that he was there was enough to make people believe they could see the hundreds of statues in the galleries and doorways living and stirring. And in fact the cathedral seemed to be a docile and obedient creature under his hand; it waited on his will to raise its great voice; it was possessed and filled by Quasimodo as by a familiar spirit. It was as if he made the immense building breathe. He was indeed everywhere, multiplying himself to be at every point in the monument at once. Now there would be the frightening sight of a bizarre dwarf on top of one of the towers, climbing, wriggling, crawling on all fours, coming down the outside over the abyss, leaping from projection to projection, delving into the belly of some sculptured Gorgon; it was Quasimodo dislodging crows. Now in some dim corner of the church you would collide with a kind of living chimera, squatting with a scowl; it was Quasimodo thinking. Now under a bell tower you would catch sight of a huge head and an untidy bundle of limbs swaying furiously on the end of a rope; it was Quasimodo ringing for vespers or the angelus. Often at night a hideous shape could be seen wandering along the flimsy open-work lacy balustrade which runs along the top of the towers and round the curve of the apse; once again it was the hunchback of Notre-Dame. Then, the women of the neighbourhood would say, the whole church took on some element of the fantastic, supernatural, horrible; eyes and mouths opened here and there; you could hear barking from the stone dogs, wyverns, tarasques* which keep watch day and night, neck outstretched and jaws open, round the monstrous cathedral; and if it was a Christmas night, while the great bell seemed to growl as it summoned the faithful to the blazing lights

of midnight mass, the atmosphere spread over the sombre
façade was such that the great doorway seemed to be swallowing up the crowd and the rose-window watching it. And
that all came from Quasimodo. In Egypt he would have
been taken for the temple's god; the Middle Ages thought
he was its demon; he was its soul.

So much so that for those who know Quasimodo once
existed, Notre-Dame today is deserted, inanimate, dead.
There is the feeling that something has gone. That immense
body is empty; it is a skeleton; the spirit has left it. You can
see where it was, and that is all. It is like a skull which has
eyeholes but no longer any eyes to see.

IV

THE DOG AND HIS MASTER

THERE was, however, one human being whom Quasimodo excepted from his malice and hatred for the rest, and whom he loved as much as his cathedral, and perhaps even more. That was Claude Frollo.

It was quite simple. Claude Frollo had taken him in, adopted him, fed him, brought him up. While he was still a small child it was by Claude Frollo's legs that he would take refuge when dogs and children snarled at him. Claude Frollo had taught him to talk, read, write. Claude Frollo finally had made him a bell-ringer. Now, giving the great bell in marriage to Quasimodo was like giving Juliet to Romeo.

Thus Quasimodo's gratitude was deep, passionate, unbounded; and although his adoptive father's face was often stern and overcast, although his speech was habitually curt, harsh, imperious, that gratitude had never faltered for a moment. In Quasimodo the archdeacon had the most obedient of slaves, the most docile of servants, the most vigilant of watchdogs. When the poor bell-ringer had gone deaf there was established between him and Claude Frollo a mysterious sign language understood by them alone. In that way the archdeacon was the only human being with whom Quasimodo had maintained communication. He was in touch with only two things in the world, Notre-Dame and Claude Frollo.

The power of the archdeacon over the bell-ringer, the bell-ringer's attachment to the archdeacon defy comparison. A sign from Claude, and the idea of pleasing him, would have been enough to make Quasimodo throw himself off the top of the towers of Notre-Dame. It was quite remarkable that with all that physical strength, developed to such an extraordinary degree, Quasimodo should have blindly put it at the disposal of another. There was in this no doubt filial devotion, domestic attachment; there was also the fascination of one mind by another. It was a poor, awkward, clumsy organism standing with bowed head and pleading eye before an intellect at once lofty and profound, powerful and superior. Finally, and above all, it was gratitude. Gratitude taken to such extreme limits that there is nothing with which we can compare it. It is not a virtue of which the finest examples are to be found among men. We shall say, then, that Quasimodo loved the archdeacon as no dog, no horse, no elephant ever loved its master.

V

CLAUDE FROLLO (CONTINUED)

IN 1482 Quasimodo was about 20, Claude Frollo about 36;
the one had grown up, the other had aged.

Claude Frollo was no longer the simple student of the
Collège de Torchi, loving protector of a little child, the
dreamy young philosopher who knew a lot of things and
was ignorant of many more. He was an austere, solemn,
morose priest; having the cure of souls; Monsieur the Archdeacon of Josas, second acolyte to the bishop, having
charge of the two deaneries of Montlhéry and Châteaufort
and a hundred and seventy-four rural incumbents. He was
a sombre and imposing person, before whom trembled the
choirboys in their alb and gown, the *machicots*,* the breth-
ren of Saint Augustine, the early morning clergy of Notre-
Dame, as he slowly passed beneath the high arches of the
choir, majestic, pensive, with his arms folded and his head
bent so low on his chest that all that could be seen of his
face was his great bald forehead.

Dom Claude Frollo had, however, abandoned neither
learning nor the education of his young brother, the two
occupations of his life. But with that a certain bitterness
had mingled with such sweet pleasures. In the long run,
says Paul the Deacon,* the best bacon goes rancid. Little
Jehan Frollo, nicknamed *du Moulin*, 'of the mill', from the
place where he had been put out to nurse, had not grown
up along the lines which Claude had tried to imprint upon
him. His big brother counted on a pious, docile, learned,
honourable pupil. Now the young brother, like those sap-
lings which defeat the gardener's efforts and turn obstinately towards the air and light, the young brother only
increased and multiplied, only put forth fine, luxuriant,
bushy branches towards idleness, ignorance, and debauchery. He was a proper devil, very unruly, which made
Dom Claude frown, but very droll and very crafty, which

made his big brother smile. Claude had entrusted him to the same Collège de Torchi where he had spent his own early years in study and meditation; and it grieved him that this sanctuary, once edified by the name of Frollo, should now be scandalized by it. He sometimes lectured Jehan severely and at length on the subject, and this was endured undaunted. After all, the young rascal had a good heart, as any play will illustrate. But once the lecture was over he none the less calmly resumed his lawless and outrageous ways. Now it was a *béjaune* (the name given to newcomers in the University) whom he had treated to a very rough welcome; a precious tradition which has been carefully perpetuated to our own day. Now he had stirred up a band of students, who had made a classic assault on a tavern, *quasi classico excitati** [as if roused by the trumpet call], had then beaten the innkeeper 'with offensive sticks', and joyfully plundered the tavern, even staving in the hogsheads of wine in the cellar. And then there was this fine report in Latin which the under-monitor of Torchi brought piteously to Dom Claude with the distressing marginal note: *Rixa, prima causa vinum optimum potatum* [Brawl, main cause: excellent wine drunk]. Finally it was said, a shocking thing for a boy of 16, that his excesses many a time led him even to the rue de Glatigny.*

All this had left Claude saddened and disheartened in his human affections, and he had thrown himself all the more enthusiastically into the arms of science, that sister who does at least not laugh in your face and always repays you, although sometimes in rather shortweight coin, for your attentions to her. He thus became more and more learned and at the same time, as a natural consequence, more and more rigid as a priest, more and more gloomy as a man. For each of us there are certain parallelisms between our intellect, our way of life, and our character which develop continuously and are broken only by the major disturbances of life.

As Claude Frollo had from his early youth completed the whole circle of positive, external, and lawful human knowledge, he was obliged, short of stopping *ubi defuit orbis* [where the circle came to an end], to go further and seek other food for the insatiable activity of his intellect. The ancient symbol of the serpent biting its own tail is particularly appropriate for science. It would seem that Claude Frollo had experienced it. A number of grave persons affirmed that having exhausted the *fas* [permissible] of human knowledge he had dared to penetrate the *nefas* [forbidden]. It was said that he had tasted successively all the apples from the tree of knowledge and, whether from hunger or disgust, had ended by biting the forbidden fruit. He had attended in turn, as our readers have seen, the theological lectures in the Sorbonne, the assemblies of the Faculty of Arts at the statue of Saint Hilary, the lawyers' disputations at the statue of Saint-Martin, the medical meetings at the stoup of Notre-Dame, *ad cupam Nostrae Dominae*; all the permitted and approved dishes which those four great kitchens called the four faculties could prepare and serve up to the intellect, he had devoured them, and had felt glutted before his hunger was appeased; he had then dug further, deeper, beneath all this finite, material, limited knowledge; he had perhaps put his soul at risk, and had sat down in the cavern at the mysterious table of the alchemists, astrologers, hermetics, at the head of which, in the Middle Ages, sat Averroes, Guillaume de Paris, and Nicolas Flamel, and which in the Orient, by the light of the seven-branched candlestick, extends as far as Solomon, Pythagoras, and Zoroaster.

So at least it was supposed, rightly or wrongly.

It is certain that the archdeacon often visited the cemetery of the Holy Innocents, where his father and mother had been buried, it is true, with the other victims of the plague of 1466; but he seemed to pay much less devotion to the cross on their grave than to the strange figures set upon the tomb of Nicolas Flamel and Claude Pernelle,* erected beside it.

It is certain that he had often been seen going along the rue des Lombards and furtively entering a small house at the corner of the rue des Écrivains and the rue Marivault. This was the house built by Nicolas Flamel, where he had

died in about 1417, and which, empty ever since, was already beginning to fall into ruin, thanks to all the hermetics
and alchemists of every land who had worn away the walls
just by carving their names upon them. Some of the neighbours even affirmed that they had once seen, through a
grating, archdeacon Claude digging, stirring, and turning
over the earth in the two cellars whose buttresses had been
daubed with countless verses and hieroglyphs by Nicolas
Flamel himself. Flamel was supposed to have buried the
philosophers' stone in these cellars and the alchemists for
two hundred years, from Magistri to Father Pacifique,* did
not cease from tossing the soil about until the house, so
roughly excavated and ransacked, finally turned to dust
beneath their feet.

It is certain too that the archdeacon had become gripped
by a singular passion for the symbolic doorway of Notre-
Dame, that page of sorcery written in stone by Bishop
Guillaume of Paris, who has doubtless been damned for
attaching such an infernal frontispiece to the sacred poem
chanted eternally by the rest of the building. Archdeacon
Claude was also believed to have made a thorough study of
the colossal statue of Saint Christopher and the long, enigmatic figure which then stood at the entrance from the
Parvis and which the people derisively called *Monsieur Legris.** But what everyone had been able to observe was the
interminable hours he often spent, sitting on the parapet of
the Parvis, contemplating the statues of the doorway, sometimes examining the foolish virgins with their lamps upside
down, sometimes the wise virgins with their lamps upright;
at other times calculating the angle of sight of the crow on
the left-hand doorway, looking at some mysterious point
inside the church where the philosophers' stone is surely
hidden, if it is not in Nicolas Flamel's cellar. It was, be it
said in passing, a strange destiny for the church of Notre-
Dame at that time to be thus loved to two different degrees
and so devotedly by two beings as dissimilar as Claude and
Quasimodo; loved by the one, a kind of instinctive and
savage half-man, for its beauty, its stature, the harmonies
emanating from its magnificent whole; loved by the other,

a man of learned and passionate imagination, for what it signified, its myth, for the meaning it contained, for the symbolism scattered beneath the sculptures of its façade like the original text beneath a later one in a palimpsest; in a word, for the enigma it offered eternally to the intellect.

Finally, it is certain that the archdeacon had fitted out for himself, in that one of the two towers that overlooks the Grève, right beside the bell cage, a very secret little cell which no one, not even the bishop, so it was said, could enter without his leave. In former times this cell had been constructed almost on top of the tower, among the crows' nests, by Bishop Hugo of Besançon,[1] who had practised the black arts there in his time. What the cell contained nobody knew; but at night, from the shore by the Terrain, there had often been seen, at a little window it had at the back of the tower, a strange, intermittent red glow, appearing, disappearing, reappearing at short, regular intervals, which seemed consistent with the puffing of a bellows and to come from a flame rather than a light. In the dark at that height, it produced a peculiar effect, and the good women would say: 'There's the archdeacon at his bellows, hell's sparking up there.'

All that, when all is said and done, did not add up to strong evidence of sorcery; but it was still as much smoke as was needed to assume some fire; and the archdeacon had a quite formidable reputation. We must say, however, that the sciences of Egypt, necromancy, magic, even of the whitest and most innocent kind, had no enemy more relentless, no one who denounced them more inexorably to the officiality of Notre-Dame. Whether this was from genuine horror or the play-acting of the thief shouting: 'Stop thief!', it did not prevent the archdeacon being regarded by the learned heads in the chapter as a soul who had ventured into the antechamber of hell, lost in the caverns of the Kabbala, groping in the darkness of the occult sciences. The people made no mistake about it either; for anyone with a little sense Quasimodo was the demon, Claude

---

[1] Hugo II de Bisuncio (1326–32). [V. H.]

Frollo the sorcerer. It was obvious that the bell-ringer had
to serve the archdeacon for a given time, at the end of which
he would carry off his soul by way of payment. Thus
the archdeacon, despite the excessive austerity of his life,
was in bad odour with God-fearing souls; and any devout
woman, however inexperienced, could sniff him out as
a magician.

And if, as he grew older, abysses had opened in his
sciences, they had opened too in his heart. That at least is
what there was reason to believe from an examination of
his face, where his soul shone only through a dark cloud.
Where did he get that broad, bare forehead, that head
always bent forward, that chest always heaving with sighs?
What secret thoughts brought such a bitter smile to his lips
at the same moment as his frowning brows came closer
together like two bulls about to fight? Why were his remaining hairs already grey? What was that inner fire which
sometimes flashed in his eyes, so much so that they looked
like holes pierced in a furnace wall?

These symptoms of some violent moral preoccupation
had reached a particularly high degee of intensity by the
time of our story. More than once a chorister, finding him
alone in the church, had fled in terror before such strangely
glaring eyes. More than once, in choir, during the office,
the occupant of the neighbouring stall had heard him mingling unintelligible parentheses into the plainchant *ad omnem
tonum* [in every tone]. More than once the washerwoman
of the Terrain whose job it was to 'wash the chapter' had
noticed, not without alarm, the marks left by nails and
clenched fingers on the surplice of Monsieur the Archdeacon of Josas.

He became, however, doubly severe and more exemplary
than ever. By his calling and by his character he had always
kept away from women; he seemed to hate them more than
ever. The mere rustle of a silk petticoat brought his hood
down over his eyes. On this point he was so jealous of his
austerity and reserve that when the Dame de Beaujeu, the
King's daughter, came in December 1481 to visit the cloister of Notre-Dame, he solemnly opposed her admission,

reminding the bishop of the statute in the Black Book, dated St Bartholomew's eve 1334, forbidding access to the cloister to any woman 'whatsoever, old or young, mistress or chambermaid'. Whereupon the bishop felt constrained to quote him the legate Odo's ordinance, making an exception for certain great ladies, *aliquae magnates mulieres, quae sine scandalo evitari non possunt* [some ladies of high rank, who cannot be shunned without scandal]. But the archdeacon still protested, objecting that the legate's ordinance, which went back to 1207, was a hundred and twenty-seven years earlier than the Black Book, and was consequently, as a matter of fact, abrogated by it. And he refused to appear before the princess.

It was further remarked that for some little time his horror of gypsy women and Zingari seemed to have intensified. He had solicited an edict from the bishop expressly forbidding gypsy women to dance and play their tambourines in the square before the cathedral, and at the same time had been going through the official's musty archives to collect cases of sorcerers and sorceresses condemned to the flames or the rope for complicity in witchcraft with he-goats, sows, or she-goats.

VI

UNPOPULARITY

THE archdeacon and the bell-ringer, as we have already said, were not greatly liked by the people, high or low, who lived near the cathedral. When Claude and Quasimodo went out together, which frequently occurred, and were seen in each other's company, the servant behind his master, passing through the cool, narrow, dark streets adjoining Notre-Dame, more than one spiteful remark, more than one ironic snatch of song, more than one rude gibe pestered them as they went by, unless, as rarely happened, Claude Frollo walked with head erect, showing his severe and almost august forehead to silence the mockers.

In their quarter both were like 'the poets' of whom Régnier speaks:

> All kinds of people follow behind poets
> As behind owls do songbirds in full cry.*

Now it was a stealthy brat risking skin and bones for the ineffable delight of sticking a pin into Quasimodo's hump. Now a pretty, buxom girl, bolder than she should have been, brushing against the priest's black robe and singing the sardonic refrain: 'Away, away, the devil's been caught.' Sometimes a group of squalid old women, spread out squatting over the steps of some shady porch, loudly grumbling as the archdeacon and bell-ringer went by, and mumbling their malice with some such encouraging welcome as: 'Hm! there goes one whose soul is just like the other's body!' Or it might be a band of students and soldiers playing hopscotch rising in a body and greeting them classically with some Latin jeer: '*Eia! eia! Claudius cum claudo!* [Come on! Claude with his limping companion!]*

But most often the insults went unnoticed by priest and bell-ringer. Quasimodo was too deaf and Claude too rapt in thought to take in all these gracious comments.

BOOK FIVE

I

ABBAS BEATI MARTINI
[THE ABBOT OF SAINT-MARTIN]

DOM CLAUDE'S fame had spread far and wide. At about
the same time that he refused to see Madame de Beaujeu
it earned him a visit which he long remembered.

It was evening. He had just retired after the office to
his canonical cell in the cloister of Notre-Dame. There
was nothing strange or mysterious about this cell, apart
perhaps from a few glass phials abandoned in a corner,
filled with a somewhat dubious powder closely resembling
the powder of projection.* Here and there, to be sure,
were some inscriptions on the walls, but they were simply
scientific or pious maxims taken from reliable authors.
The archdeacon had just sat down by the light from a
triple brass candleholder in front of a huge chest laden
with manuscripts. His elbow rested on an open volume
of the book of Honorius of Autun *De praedestinatione et
libero arbitrio* [*On Predestination and Free Will*], and he
was sunk in reflection as he turned the pages of a printed
folio volume he had just brought in, the only product of
the printing-press that his cell contained. In the midst of
his reverie there was a knock at the door. 'Who is it?'
cried the scholar in a tone as gracious as that of a hungry
mastiff disturbed at its bone. A voice answered from outside: 'Your friend, Jacques Coictier.' He went to open
the door.

It was indeed the King's doctor, a man of about 50,
whose hard features were tempered only by his crafty look.
Another man accompanied him. Both wore long, slate-grey
gowns, trimmed with grey squirrel fur, belted and fastened,
with caps of the same material and colour. Their hands

were hidden in their sleeves, their feet beneath their gowns, their eyes beneath their caps.

'God help me, gentlemen!' said the archdeacon as he let them in, 'I was not expecting such distinguished visitors at this late hour.' And while he spoke these courteous words he was uneasily scrutinizing the doctor and then his companion.

'It is never too late to pay a call on so notable a scholar as Dom Claude Frollo de Tirechappe,' replied Doctor Coictier, with a Franche-Comté accent which dragged out every sentence as majestically as a robe with a train.

The doctor and the archdeacon then began one of those introductory exchanges of compliments which at that time customarily preceded any conversation between men of learning and did not prevent them from cordially detesting each other. Besides, it is still the same today, the mouth of any scholar who pays compliments to another is a jar of honeyed venom.

Claude Frollo's congratulations to Jacques Coictier mainly concerned the numerous temporal advantages which the worthy doctor had been able to derive, in the course of his much-envied career, from each of the King's illnesses by practising a better and more reliable alchemy than the search for the philosopher's stone.

'Truly! Monsieur le docteur Coictier, I was delighted to learn that your nephew, my reverend lord Pierre Versé, had been appointed to a bishopric. He is Bishop of Amiens, is he not?'

'Yes, Monsieur Archdeacon; by God's gracious mercy.'

'You know, you looked very splendid on Christmas Day at the head of your company from the Exchequer, Monsieur le Président?'

'Vice-President, Dom Claude. Alas! that's all.'

'How is that superb house of yours in the rue Saint-André-des-Arcs coming along? It is another Louvre. I just love the apricot tree carved over the door with its amusing play on words: À L'ABRI-COTIER.'*

'Alas, Maître Claude, all that stone-masonry is costing me dear. As the house goes up I am being ruined.'

'Oh! don't you have your income from the gaol and palace bailiwicks, and the rent from all the houses, stalls, huts, and booths within the walls? That's a fine milch-cow for you.'

'My lordship of Poissy hasn't brought in anything this year.'

'But your toll dues at Triel, Saint-James, and Saint-Germain-en-Laye always give a good yield.'

'A hundred and twenty *livres*, and not even *parisis*.'*

'You have your post as King's counsellor. That's a fixed fee.'

'Yes, Claude, dear colleague, but that damned manor at Poligny that they talk about isn't worth 60 gold *écus* to me, taking one year with another.'

In the compliments Dom Claude paid to Jacques Coictier there was a sardonic, sour note of subdued derision, the sad, cruel smile of an unhappy but superior person amusing himself for a moment by playing with the solid prosperity of a vulgar man. The other did not notice.

'Upon my soul,' said Dom Claude at last, as he grasped the other man's hand, 'I am glad to see you looking so well.'

'Thank you, Maître Claude.'

'That reminds me,' exclaimed Dom Claude, 'how is your royal patient?'

'He doesn't pay his physician enough,' the doctor answered, with a sidelong glance at his companion.

'Do you think so, Compère Coictier?' said the companion.

These words, uttered in a tone of reproachful surprise, drew the attention of the archdeacon once more to this unknown stranger, from whom, truth to tell, it had not been fully diverted for a moment since he had crossed the cell's threshold. It was only because he had so many reasons for keeping on good terms with Doctor Coictier, Louis XI's all-powerful physician, that he had received him thus accompanied. So there was nothing really cordial in his expression when Jacques Coictier said: 'By the way, Dom Claude, I bring you a colleague who wanted to meet you on account of your reputation.'

'Monsieur is interested in science?' asked the archdeacon, fixing a penetrating stare on Coictier's companion. Beneath the stranger's brows he met a gaze no less piercing and mistrustful than his own.

He was, as far as the dim lamplight enabled one to judge, an elderly man of some 60 years, of average height, looking rather ill and bent. His profile, although its lines were in no way noble, had a certain power and severity, his very deep-set eyes sparkled like a light in the depths of a cave, and beneath the cap pulled low over his face one could sense a genius's brow turning over far-reaching plans.

He took it on himself to reply to the archdeacon's question in person. 'Reverend master,' he said gravely, 'your fame has reached even me, and I wanted to consult you. I am only a poor country gentleman who takes off his shoes before entering the home of scholars. But I must introduce myself. My name is Compère* Tourangeau.'

'An odd name for a gentleman!' thought the archdeacon. However, he felt something strong and serious confonting him. The instinct of his own lofty intelligence made him suspect another no less lofty beneath Compère Tourangeau's fur-trimmed cap; and as he looked at this grave figure, the ironic grin which Jacques Coictier's presence had brought to his sombre countenance disappeared like twilight on the night horizon. He had sat down again, in gloomy silence, in his big armchair, his elbow back in its usual position on the table, his forehead against his hand. After some moments' thought, he invited his two visitors with a sign to be seated, and addressed Compère Tourangeau.

'You have come to consult me, Maître, concerning which science?'

'Reverend sir,' replied Compère Tourangeau, 'I am a sick man, very sick. You are said to be a great Aesculapius* and I have come to ask you for some medical advice.'

'Medicine!' said the archdeacon, with a nod of his head. He seemed to be collecting his thoughts for a moment, then went on: 'Compère Tourangeau, since that is your name, turn your head. You will find my answer written on the wall.'

Compère Tourangeau obeyed, and read this inscription carved on the wall above his head: '*Medicine is the daughter of dreams*— JAMBLICHUS.'*

Meanwhile Jacques Coictier had heard his companion's question with a resentment which Dom Claude's reply only increased. He bent over and whispered in Compère Tourangeau's ear in a voice too low to be heard by the archdeacon: 'I warned you that he was mad. You would come and see him!'

'But he may very well be right, this madman, doctor Jacques!' the compère answered in the same low tones, with a bitter smile.

'As you please!' Coictier retorted drily. Then, addressing the archdeacon: 'You have a nimble touch, Dom Claude, and Hippocrates is hardly more of a problem to you than a nut to a monkey. Medicine a dream! I doubt whether the pharmacopolists and master apothecaries could keep themselves from stoning you if they were here. So you deny the influence of philtres on the blood, of unguents on the flesh! You deny that eternal pharmacy of flowers and metals called the world, created expressly for the eternal patient, called man!'

'I deny,' Dom Claude said coldly, 'neither the pharmacy nor the patient. I deny the physician.'

'So it's not true,' Coictier went on with some heat, 'that gout is internal herpes, that a gunshot wound can be cured by an application of roast mouse, that a proper infusion of young blood can restore youth to old veins; it's not true that two and two make four, and that emprosthotonos comes after opisthotonos?'*

The archdeacon replied unmoved: 'There are certain things which I think about in a certain way.'

Coictier went red with anger.

'Now, now, my good Coictier, let's keep our tempers,' said Compère Tourangeau, 'Monsieur the Archdeacon is our friend.'

Coictier calmed down, muttering under his breath: 'After all, he's mad.'

'*Pasquedieu*, Maître Claude,' went on Compère Tourangeau after a moment's silence, 'you are making me feel very embarrassed. I wanted to consult you on two points, one concerning my health, the other my stars.'

'Monsieur,' replied the archdeacon, 'if that is what is in your mind, you would have done better to have saved your breath by not climbing up my stairs. I do not believe in medicine. I do not believe in astrology.'

'Really!' said the compère in surprise.

Coictier gave a forced laugh.

'You can see now that he's mad,' he said in a very low voice to Compère Tourangeau. 'He doesn't believe in astrology.'

'How could anyone imagine,' continued Dom Claude, 'that every beam from a star is a thread attached to a man's head?'

'What do you believe in then?' exclaimed Compère Tourangeau.

The archdeacon stayed undecided for a moment; then gave a bleak smile which seemed to belie his answer: '*Credo in Deum.*'

'*Dominum nostrum,*'* added Compère Tourangeau, making the sign of the cross.

'Amen,' said Coictier.

'Reverend master,' the compère went on, 'my soul rejoices to see such sound religion in you. But great scholar that you are, are you so learned that you no longer believe in science?'

'No,' said the archdeacon, seizing Compère Tourangeau by the arm, a flash of enthusiasm rekindling in his dull eyes, 'no, I do not deny science. I have not crawled on my belly for so long with my nails in the earth through the cavern's countless ramifications without glimpsing far ahead, at the end of the dark tunnel, a light, a flame, something, no doubt a reflection from the dazzling central laboratory where wise and patient men have caught God unawares.'

'Then what do you consider true and certain?' Tourangeau broke in.

'Alchemy.'

Coictier exclaimed: 'By heaven, Dom Claude, alchemy no doubt has its point, but why blaspheme against medicine and astrology?'

'A nothing, your science of man! A nothing, your science of the heavens!' said the archdeacon imperiously.

'That's treating Epidaurus and Chaldea* very summarily,' replied the doctor with a sneer.

'Listen, Messire Jacques, I'm saying this in good faith. I am not the King's doctor, and His Majesty has not given me the Daedalus garden so that I can observe the constellations from it—don't lose your temper, listen to me—what truth have you drawn, I won't say from medicine, which is much too foolish, but from astrology? Tell me the virtues of the vertical boustrophedon, the discoveries made from the numbers ziruph and zephirod.'*

'Do you deny,' said Coictier, 'the sympathetic power of the Clavicula* and the fact that the Kabbala is derived from it?'

'Quite wrong, Messire Jacques! None of your formulas gives any real results, whereas alchemy has made discoveries. Do you question such results as these? Ice enclosed underground for a thousand years turns into rock crystal; lead is the ancestor of all metals (for gold is not a metal, gold is light)—it takes lead only four periods, each of two hundred years, to pass successively from the state of lead to that of red arsenic, from red arsenic to tin, from tin to silver. Are those facts? But to believe in the Clavicula, the full line, and the stars is as ridiculous as believing, like the inhabitants of Grand Cathay, that the oriole changes into a mole and grains of corn into fish of the genus cyprinidae!'*

'I have studied hermetics,' exclaimed Coictier, 'and I maintain . . .'

The hot-headed archdeacon did not let him finish: 'And I have studied medicine, astrology, and hermetics. Here alone lies truth' (as he spoke he had picked up from the chest a phial full of the powder mentioned earlier), 'here alone is light! Hippocrates, a dream, Urania, a dream, Hermes, an idea. Gold is the sun, to make gold is to be God. That is the only science. I have probed into medicine and astrology, I tell you! Nothing, nothing. The human body, darkness; the stars, darkness!'

And he fell back into his chair in an attitude of one powerful and inspired. Compère Tourangeau watched him in silence. Coictier tried hard to give a mocking laugh, shrugged his shoulders imperceptibly, and repeated in an undertone: 'A madman!'

'And the wonderful goal,' The Tourangeau said suddenly, 'have you attained it? Have you made gold?'

'If I had,' the archdeacon replied, pronouncing the words slowly, like a man reflecting, 'the King of France would be called Claude and not Louis.'

The compère frowned.

'What am I saying?' Dom Claude went on with a disdainful smile. 'What would the throne of France mean to me when I could rebuild the empire of the Orient!'

'And the best of luck!' said the compère.

'Oh, the poor fool!' murmured Coictier.

The archdeacon continued, now seemingly answering only his own thoughts: 'No, I am still crawling, scraping my face and knees on the stones of the underground path. I catch only a glimpse, I cannot gaze! I cannot read, only spell out the letters.'

'And once you can read,' asked the compère, 'will you make gold?'

'Who could doubt it?' said the archdeacon.

'In that case Our Lady knows that I badly need money, and I should very much like to learn how to read your books. Tell me, reverend master, is your science hostile or displeasing to Our Lady?'

To this question from the compère, Dom Claude was content to answer with lofty calm: 'Whose archdeacon I am?'

'That's true, master. Very well! Would you care to initiate me? Have me spell out the letters with you.'

Claude assumed the majestic and pontifical attitude of a Samuel.

'Old man, it would take more years than remain to you to undertake that journey through the things of mystery. Your head is very grey! One only comes out from the cavern with white hair, but only enters it with hair still black. Science all by itself is well able to emaciate, wither, and dry up human faces; it does not need old age to bring to it faces already wrinkled. However, if you are driven by a desire to put yourself to school at your age and decipher the fearsome alphabet of the sages, come to me, all right, I'll try. I won't tell you, poor old man that you are, to go and visit the burial chambers of the Pyramids, of which ancient Herodotus speaks, nor the brick tower of Babel, nor the immense white marble sanctuary of the Indian temple of Eklinga.* I have not seen, any more than you have, the Chaldean stone buildings constructed on the sacred model of the Sikra,* nor Solomon's Temple, now destroyed, nor the stone doors of the sepulchre of the kings of Israel, now shattered. We shall content ourselves with the fragments of Hermes' books that we have here. I shall explain the statue of St Christopher, the symbol of the Sower, and that of the two angels at the doorway of the Sainte-Chapelle, one of whom has his hand in a vase and the other in a cloud . . .'

At this point Jacques Coictier, who had been unseated by the archdeacon's fiery replies, put himself back in the saddle, and interrupted him with the triumphant tone of one scholar correcting another: 'Erras, amice Claudi [You are mistaken, friend Claude]. Symbols are not numbers. You are taking Orpheus for Hermes.'

'It is you who are mistaken,' the archdeacon gravely replied. 'Daedalus is the foundations, Orpheus the walls, Hermes the building. That is, the whole. You can come when you like,' he went on, turning to the Tourangeau, 'I'll show you the particles of gold left in the bottom of Nicolas Flamel's crucible, and you can compare them with the gold of Guillaume de Paris. I will teach you the occult virtues of the Greek word peristera.* But first of all I will make you read one by one the marble letters of the alphabet, the granite pages of the book. We'll go from Bishop Guillaume's doorway and Saint-Jean-le-Rond to the Sainte-Chapelle, then to Nicolas Flamel's house, in the rue Marivault, to his tomb, in the Holy Innocents' cemetery, to his two hospitals in the rue de Montmorency. I will make you read the hieroglyphs covering the four great andirons in the doorway of the Saint-Gervais hospital and in the rue de la Ferronnerie. We'll go on together to spell out the façades of Saint-Côme, Sainte-Geneviève-des-Ardents, Saint-Martin and Saint-Jacques-de-la-Boucherie . . .'

The Tourangeau, despite the intelligence in his eyes, had seemed for some time now no longer able to understand Dom Claude. He interrupted him.

'*Pasquedieu!* What are these books of yours then?'

'Here's one,' said the archdeacon.

And opening the window of his cell he pointed to the huge church of Notre-Dame which, with its twin towers standing out in silhouette against the starry sky, its stone ribs and monstrous crupper, looked like an enormous two-headed sphinx sitting there in the middle of the town.

The archdeacon silently contemplated the gigantic building for a while, then sighed as he stretched out his right hand towards the printed book lying open on his table and his left hand towards Notre-Dame, and looked sadly from the book to the church.

'Alas! he said, 'this will kill that.'

Coictier, who had eagerly come closer to the book, could not help exclaiming it: 'Well! but what is so awesome about this: GLOSSA IN EPISTOLAS D. PAULI. *Norimbergae. Antonius Koburger, 1474* [Gloss on St Paul's Epistles, Nuremberg]. That's not new. It's a book of Peter Lombard, the Master of the Sentences. Is it because it's printed?'

'That's right,' Claude answered, apparently absorbed in some profound reflection, standing with his index finger bent against the folio volume from the celebrated presses of Nuremberg. Then he added these mysterious words: 'Alas! alas! little things overcome great ones; a tooth triumphs over a whole body. The Nile rat kills the crocodile, the swordfish kills the whale, the book will kill the building.'

Curfew rang in the cloister just as Doctor Jacques was repeating to his companion in a very low voice his eternal refrain: 'He's mad.' To which his companion this time replied: 'Yes, I think so.'

It was the hour after which no stranger might remain in the cloister. The two visitors withdrew. 'Master,' said Compère Tourangeau as he took leave of the archdeacon, 'I like scholars and great minds, and I hold you in particular esteem. Come to the Palace of the Tournelles tomorrow and ask for the abbot of Saint-Martin of Tours.'

The archdeacon returned to his cell dumbfounded, finally realizing the identity of Compère Tourangeau, and recalling this passage from the cartulary of Saint-Martin of Tours:

Abbas beati Martini, SCILICET REX FRANCIAE, est canonicus de consuetudine et habet parvam prebendam quam habet sanctus Venantius et debet sedere in sede thesaurarii.

[The abbot of Saint-Martin, that is the King of France, is by custom a canon and holds the minor prebend held by Saint Venantius and should sit in the treasurer's seat].

It was asserted that from that time on the archdeacon frequently conferred with Louis XI when His Majesty came to Paris, and that Dom Claude's credit caused umbrage to Olivier le Daim and Jacques Coictier who, as was his wont, gave the King a piece of his mind on the subject.

THIS WILL KILL THAT

OUR lady readers will forgive us if we stop for a moment to look for what thought might lie hidden behind the archdeacon's enigmatic words: '*This will kill that, the book will kill the building.*'

In our view, that thought was twofold. First of all it was a priest's way of thinking. It was priestly dread in the face of a new agent: printing. It was the terror and confusion of the man of the sanctuary dazzled by the light shining from Gutenberg's press. It was the pulpit and the manuscript, the spoken and the written word, taking fright at the printed word; something like the stupefaction of a sparrow seeing the angel Legion spreading his six million wings. It was the cry of the prophet who already hears the clamorous swarming of emancipated mankind, who foresees intelligence undermining faith, opinion dethroning belief, the world shaking off Rome. The philosopher's forecast, as he sees human thought, volatilized by the printing press, evaporate out of its theological container. The soldier's terror as he examines the bronze battering ram and says: 'The tower will crumble.' It meant that one power would succeed another. It meant: the printing press will kill the Church.

But beneath that thought, no doubt the first and simplest one, there was in our view another, newer one, less easily perceived and more easily challenged, a view just as philosophical, no longer that of the priest alone, but of the scholar and the artist. It was the presentiment that in changing its form human thought was going to change its mode of expression, that the most important idea of each generation would no longer be written in the same material and in the same way, that the book of stone, so solid and durable, would give way to the book of paper, even more solid and durable. In that connection the archdeacon's vague formula had a second meaning; it signified that one art would dethrone another. It meant: printing will kill architecture.

In fact, from the origin of things up to the fifteenth century of the Christian era inclusive, architecture was the great book of mankind, the principal expression of man at his different stages of development, whether as strength or as intelligence.

When the memory of the earliest peoples felt overloaded, when mankind's store of memories became so heavy and confused that speech, bare and fleeting, risked losing some on the way, they were transcribed on the ground in what was at once the most visible, the most durable, and the most natural fashion. Each tradition was sealed beneath a monument.

The first monuments were simply chunks of rock 'which iron had not touched', as Moses puts it.* Architecture began like any system of writing. First it was an alphabet. A stone was set upright, and that was a letter, and each letter was a hieroglyph, and each hieroglyph carried a group of ideas like the capital on a column. That was what the earliest peoples did, everywhere, all at the same time, over the surface of the entire world. The 'standing stone' of the Celts is to be found in Asiatic Siberia, in the pampas of America.

Later on words were formed. Stone was laid upon stone, these granite syllables were joined, language tried out a few combinations. The Celtic dolmen and cromlech, the Etruscan tumulus, the Hebrew galgal, are words. Some, especially the tumulus, are proper names. Sometimes even, when there was plenty of stone and a wide level area, they wrote a sentence. The immense accumulation at Carnac is already a completed formula.

Finally they produced books. Traditions had given birth to symbols beneath which they disappeared like a tree trunk beneath its foliage; all these symbols, in which mankind put its faith, grew, multiplied, intersected, becoming more and more complex, so that the early monuments were no longer adequate to contain them and overflowed everywhere; these monuments scarcely still expressed the primitive tradition, which like them was simple, unadorned and rested on the ground. Symbolism needed to expand into a building. Architecture thus developed along with human thought; it became a giant with countless heads and arms, and fixed all this drifting symbolism in an eternal, visible, palpable form. While Daedalus, who is strength, took measurements, while Orpheus, who is intelligence, sang, the pillar, which is a letter, the arcade, which is a syllable, the pyramid, which is a word, set in motion at once by a geometrical and a poetic law, were grouping, combining, blending, rising, descending, lying in juxtaposition on the ground, rising in tiers into the sky, until they had written at the dictation of the general idea of an epoch those wonderful books which were also wonderful buildings: the pagodas of Eklinga, the Ramesseum of Egypt, the Temple of Solomon.

The idea that gave them birth, the word, was not merely in the foundations of all these buildings, but also in their form. Solomon's Temple, for instance, was not simply the binding of the sacred book, it was the sacred book itself. On each of its concentric enclosures the priests could read the word translated and made manifest to the eye, and could thus follow its transformations from sanctuary to sanctuary until in the final tabernacle they grasped it in its most concrete form, which was still architectural: the ark. Thus the word was enclosed in the building, but its image was on the envelope like the human figure on a mummy's coffin.

And not only the form of the buildings, but also the site chosen for them reveals the thought they represented. According to whether the symbol to be expressed was smiling or sombre, Greece crowned her mountains with a temple harmonious to the eye, India ripped open hers to carve out within them those shapeless underground pagodas borne by gigantic rows of granite elephants.

Thus, during the first six thousand years of the world's existence, from the most immemorial pagoda of Hindustan down to Cologne cathedral, architecture was the great script of the human race. And so true is this that not only every religious symbol, but every human thought has its page in this immense book and its monument.

Every civilization begins with theocracy and ends up with democracy. This law of liberty succeeding unity is written in architecture. For, let us stress the point, it must not be thought that masonry's power is limited to building the temple, to expressing myth and priestly symbolism, to transcribing in hieroglyphs on its stone pages the mysterious tables of the law. If that were the case, as there comes a moment in every human society when the sacred symbol is worn out and obliterated by free thought, when the man eludes the priest, when the outgrowth of philosophies and systems erodes the face of religion, then architecture would be unable to reproduce this new state of the human mind; its leaves, full on the recto side, would be empty on the verso, its work would be cut short, its book would be incomplete. But it is not so.

Take for example the Middle Ages, where we can see more clearly because they are closer to us. During the early medieval period, while theocracy was organizing Europe, while the Vatican was rallying and regarding around itself the elements of a Rome made from the Rome lying in ruins around the Capitol, while Christianity was busy searching through the debris of the earlier civilization for all the stages of society and rebuilding from the ruins a new hierarchical universe with the priesthood as its keystone; first you can hear welling up amid the chaos, then see rising bit by bit under the inspiration of Christianity, under the hand of barbarians, from the rubble of the dead architecture, Greek and Roman, that mysterious Romanesque architecture, sister to the theocratic masonries of Egypt and India, unalterable emblem of pure Catholicism, immutable hieroglyph of papal unity. All the thought of that time is in fact written in that sombre Romanesque style. Everywhere in it you can feel authority, unity, the impenetrable, the absolute, Gregory VII;* everywhere the priest, never the man; everywhere the caste, never the people. But then came the Crusades. It was a great popular movement, and every great popular movement, whatever its cause and its aim, always releases the spirit of freedom from its final precipitate. A new day was dawning. It was the beginning of the stormy

period of Jacqueries, Pragueries, Leagues.* Authority tot-
tered, unity was split. Feudalism demanded to share with
theocracy, pending the inevitable arrival of the people who
would, as always, take the lion's share. *Quia nominor leo*
[because I am called lion].* The nobility thus breaks
through beneath the priesthood, the commune beneath the
nobility. The face of Europe has changed. Very well! The
face of architecture changes too. Like civilization it has
turned the page, and the new spirit of the times finds it
ready to write at its dictation. Architecture came back from
the Crusades with the pointed arch, as the nations did with
their freedom. Then, while Rome gradually fell apart, Romanesque architecture died. The hieroglyphs deserted the
cathedral and went off to add prestige to the feudal nobility
by emblazoning the castle keep. The cathedral itself, once
so dogmatic a building, from now on invaded by the
citizens, by the commons, by liberty, escaped from the
priest and fell into the artist's power. The artist builds in
his own way. Farewell to mystery, myth, law. Enter fancy
and caprice. Provided the priest had his basilica and his
altar, he had no more say. Four walls belong to the artist.
The book of architecture belonged no more to the priesthood, religion, Rome, but to imagination, poetry, the
people. Whence the countless swift transformations of this
architecture, only three centuries old, so striking after the
stagnating immobility of Romanesque architecture, which
was six or seven centuries old. Art, however, took giant
strides. Popular genius and originality took on the task the
bishops used to perform. Each race as it passed by wrote
its line in the book; it erased the old Romanesque hieroglyphs on the frontispieces of the cathedrals, and at the very
most the dogma remains still visible here and there through
the new symbolism overlaying it. Popular drapery gives
scarcely a hint of the religious skeleton underneath. It is
impossible to imagine the liberties taken by architects of
that time, even towards the Church. There are capitals
interwoven with monks and nuns shamelessly coupling, as
in the Hall of Chimneys of the Palais de Justice in Paris.
There is Noah's misadventure carved *in explicit detail,* as in

the great doorway at Bourges. There is the Bacchic monk with ass's ears and glass in hand laughing in the face of a whole community, as over the lavabo at the abbey of Boscherville. At that time there existed for ideas written in stone a privilege fully comparable with our present freedom of the press. It was freedom of architecture.

That freedom was far-reaching. Sometimes a doorway, a façade, a whole church offers a symbolic meaning absolutely alien to worship, or even hostile to the Church. Going back to the thirteenth century, Guillaume de Paris,* and in the fifteenth Nicolas Flamel, wrote some of these subversive pages. Saint-Jacques-de-la-Boucherie was wholly an opposition church.

Thought at that time enjoyed no other kind of freedom, and was therefore written down in full only in those books which were called buildings. But for its form as a building it would have found itself being publicly burned at the hand of the executioner in the form of manuscript, had it been unwise enough to risk appearing thus. Thought in the form of church doorway would have attended the punishment of thought in book form. Thus, having no other way of declaring itself but in stone masonry, thought rushed to it from every direction. Whence the vast quantity of cathedrals all over Europe, so prodigious a number as to be hardly credible even when verified. All the material, all the intellectual forces of society converged on the same point: architecture. In this way, under the pretext of building churches to God, the art developed into one of magnificent proportions.

At that time anyone who was born a poet became an architect. The genius scattered among the masses, kept down everywhere under the feudal system as though by a *testudo** of bronze shields, finding no other outlet than architecture, emerged through that art, and its *Iliads* took the form of cathedrals. All the other arts were obedient and submitted to the discipline of architecture. They were workmen in the great work. The architect, the poet, the master summed up in his own person the sculpture carved over his façades, the painting illuminating his windows, the music which set his bells swinging and breathed through his organ. Even poor poetry, properly so-called, that which went on obstinately vegetating in manuscripts, found itself obliged, if it were to count for something, to become incorporated into the framework of the building in the form of hymn or prose sequence; that after all was the role played by Aeschylus' tragedies in the religious festivals of Greece, by the book of Genesis in Solomon's Temple.

Thus, until the coming of Gutenberg, architecture was the main, the universal form of writing. This book of granite was begun in the Orient, carried on by Greek and Roman antiquity, and the last page was written in the Middle Ages. Moreover, this phenomenon of a popular architecture succeeding a caste's architecture, which we have just observed in the Middle Ages, is repeated with every analogous movement of human intelligence in the other great periods of history. Thus, to give only a summary statement of a law which it would take volumes to develop, in the high Orient, cradle of primitive times, after Hindu architecture came Phoenician architecture, opulent mother of Arab architecture; in antiquity, after Egyptian architecture, of which the Etruscan style and the Cyclopean monuments are only a variation, came Greek architecture, of which the Roman style is simply an extension, with the Carthaginian dome put on top; in modern times, after Romanesque architecture came Gothic. And splitting these three series into two, you will find in the three elder sisters, Hindu, Egyptian, and Romanesque architecture, the same symbol: namely theocracy, caste, unity, dogma, myth, God; and in the three younger sisters, Phoenician, Greek, and Gothic architecture, whatever diversity of form may be inherent in their nature, there is also the same significance: freedom, the people, man.

Whether he be called Brahmin, magus, or pope, in the Hindu, Egyptian, or Romanesque masonry it is always the priest, nothing but the priest, of whom one is aware. It is not the same with popular forms of architecture. They are richer and less sacred. In Phoenician architecture one is aware of the merchant, in Greek of the republican, in Gothic of the citizen.

The general characteristics of any theocratic architecture are immutability, a horror of progress, preservation of traditional lines, consecration of primitive types, the constant bending of every form of man and nature to the incomprehensible whims of the symbol. They are books wrapped in obscurity which only initiates can decipher. Besides, every form, every deformity even, in them has a sense which renders it inviolable. Do not ask Hindu, Egyptian, Romanesque masonry for a corrected design or improved statuary. For them any attempt at improvement is impiety. In these forms of architecture it seems that dogmatic rigidity has spread over the stone like a second petrifaction. The general characteristics of popular masonry on the other hand are variety, progress, originality, opulence, perpetual motion. They are already sufficiently detached from religion to think of their own beauty, to take care over it, to adjust incessantly their adornment of statues and arabesques. They belong to their age. There is in them a human quality which they constantly blend with the divine symbol under which they are still produced. Whence buildings accessible to every soul, every intellect, every imagination, still symbolic, but as easy to understand as nature. Between theocratic architecture and this there is the difference between a sacred and a vulgar tongue, between a hieroglyph and art, between Solomon and Phidias.

To sum up what we have so far sketched very roughly, ignoring countless proofs and also countless objections of detail, it comes to this: architecture up to the fifteenth century was the principal record of mankind; during that time no concept of any complexity appeared in the world which was not made into a building; every popular idea like every religious law has had its monuments; finally, the human race never had an important thought which it did not write down in stone. And why? Because every thought, be it religious or philosophical, has an interest in perpetuating itself, an idea which has stirred one generation wants to stir others and leave its mark. Now, how precarious is the immortality of a manuscript! How much more solid, durable, and resistant a book is a building! All that it takes to destroy the written word is a lighted torch or a Turk. To demolish the constructed word it takes a social, a terrestrial revolution. The barbarians passed over the Coliseum, the Flood, perhaps, over the Pyramids.

With the fifteenth century everything changed.

Human thought discovered a means of perpetuating itself not only more durable and more resistant than architecture, but simpler and easier. Architecture was dethroned. Orpheus' letters of stone were succeeded by Gutenberg's letters of lead.

The book is going to kill the building.

The invention of printing is the greatest event in history. It is the mother of revolutions. It is humanity's mode of expression totally renewed, human thought discarding one form and putting on another, it is the complete and definitive change of skin of that symbolic serpent which, ever since Adam, has represented intelligence.

In the form of printing, thought is more imperishable than ever; it is volatile, elusive, indestructible. It blends with the air. In the time of architecture it became a mountain and took forceful possession of an age and a space. Now it becomes a flock of birds, scatters to the four winds and simultaneously occupies every point of air and space.

We repeat, who can fail to see that in that form it is much more indelible? It used to be solid, now it has become long-lived. It has passed from being durable to being immortal. A mass can be demolished, but how can ubiquity be eradicated? If a flood comes, the mountain will long since have disappeared beneath the waters while the birds are still flying overhead; and if there is but one ark still afloat on the surface of the cataclysm, they will settle on it, stay afloat with it, will be there with it to see the waters go down; and the new world emerging from this chaos will see as it awakes the thought of the drowned world hovering overhead, winged and alive.

And when you observe that this form of expression is not only the best for conservation, but also the simplest, the most convenient, the most universally available; when you think that it is not encumbered by baggage and requires the moving of no heavy apparatus; when you compare the way thought, before it can be translated into a building, has to set in motion four or five other arts and tons of gold, a whole mountain of stone, a whole forest of timber, a whole people of workmen; when you compare it with thought becoming a book, needing only a little paper, a little ink, and a pen, how can anyone be surprised if human intelligence has forsaken architecture for printing? If you suddenly cut across the bed of a river a canal dug at a lower level, the river will abandon its bed.

Look, then, at how since the discovery of printing architecture has gradually dried up, atrophied, and been stripped bare. What a feeling one has of waters falling, sap failing, the thought of ages and peoples withdrawing from it! This cooling-off is almost imperceptible in the fifteenth century, the printing press is as yet too feeble, and at the most draws off from mighty architecture some of its superfluous vigour. But already from the sixteenth century on, architecture's sickness is evident; it has already ceased to be the essential expression of society; it transforms itself miserably into classical art; once Gaulish, European, indigenous, it becomes Greek and Roman, once genuine and modern, it becomes pseudo-antique. This decadence is what is called Renaissance. A splendid decadence, though, for the old Gothic genius; the sun setting behind the gigantic printing press at Mainz still for a while sheds its final rays on that hybrid heap of Latin arcades and Corinthian colonnades.

This setting sun is what we take for a new dawn.

Yet once architecture became merely one art among others, once it ceased to be the total, sovereign, tyrannical art, it was no longer strong enough to hold on to the other arts. So they freed themselves, threw off the yoke of architecture and each went its own way. Each of them gained from this divorce. Isolation enlarged everything. Sculpture became statuary, imagery became painting, the canon became music. It was like dismembering an empire on the death of its Alexander, with all its provinces becoming kingdoms.

Whence Raphael, Michelangelo, Jean Goujon, Palestrina, those glories of the dazzling sixteenth century.

At the same time as the arts, thought set itself free on every side. The heresiarchs of the Middle Ages had already made large inroads into Catholicism. The sixteenth century shattered religious unity. Before printing, the Reformation would just have been a schism; printing made it a revolution. Take away the printing press and heresy is enervated. Be it fate or providence, Gutenberg was Luther's precursor.

Meanwhile, when the sun of the Middle Ages had finally set, when Gothic genius had faded away for ever on the horizon of art, architecture became ever more dull, colourless, nondescript. The printed word, gnawing like a worm at its buildings, sucked and devoured it. It grew bare, its leaves fell off, it wasted visibly away, it was mean, poor, of no account. It no longer expressed anything, not even the memory of the art of former days. Reduced to itself, abandoned by the other arts because abandoned by human thought, it called in labourers for want of artists. Plain glass replaced stained glass in the windows. The stonecutter succeeded the sculptor. Farewell to any vigour, originality, life, intelligence. It dragged itself along, pathetically begging its way round the studio from copy to copy. Michelangelo, who already in the sixteenth century no doubt felt that it was dying, had one last idea, an idea born of despair. This Titan of art had heaped the Pantheon on the Parthenon and created St Peter's, Rome: a great work which deserved to remain unique, architecture's last piece of originality, a giant artist's signature at the bottom of that colossal stone record which then closed. With the death of Michelangelo what did this wretched architecture do, living on as a spectre and shade of its former self? It took St Peter's, Rome, copied it, parodied it. It was an obsession. It was pitiful. Every century has its St Peter's, Rome; in the seventeenth century the Val-de-Grâce, in the eighteenth Sainte-Geneviève. Every country has its St Peter's, Rome. London has one, St Petersburg has one, Paris has two or three. A meaningless legacy, last ramblings of a great art fallen into decrepitude and second childhood before it expires.

If instead of characteristic monuments like those we have just mentioned we examine the general picture of architecture from the sixteenth to the eighteenth century, we observe the same phenomenon of decline and emaciation. From the time of François II the architectural form of the building becomes steadily less evident and makes the geometrical form stand out like the bone-structure of someone emaciated through illness. The beautiful lines of art give way to the cold, inexorable lines of the geometer. A building is no longer a building, it is a polyhedron. Architecture, however, took great pains to conceal its nakedness. Here is the Greek pediment inscribed in the Roman pediment, and vice versa. It is still the Pantheon in the Parthenon, St Peter's, Rome. Here you have the brick houses with stone quoins of Henri IV: the Place Royale, the Place Dauphine. Here the Louis XIII churches, heavy, squat, surbased, stocky, weighed down with a dome like a hump. Here Mazarin's architecture, the bad Italian pastiche of the Quatre-Nations.* Here Louis XIV's palaces, long barracks for courtiers, stiff, glacial, boring. Finally Louis XV style, with its chicory and vermicelli, and all the warts and all the tumours disfiguring that old architecture, a toothless, decaying, and still coquettish hag. From François II to Louis XV the disease has grown worse in geometrical progression. The art has become just skin and bones. It is dying wretchedly.

Meanwhile what has become of printing? That is where all the life ebbing out of architecture has gone. As architecture diminishes, so printing swells and grows. The capital reserves of strength which human thought once spent on buildings are henceforth spent on books. So as early as the sixteenth century the printing press, grown now to equal stature with declining architecture, fights and slays its rival. In the seventeenth century the printing press is already sufficiently supreme, sufficiently triumphant, sufficiently secure in its victory to entertain the world to a great age of literature. In the eighteenth, after its long years of repose at Louis XIV's court, it takes up once more Luther's old sword, arms Voltaire with it, and rushes tumultuously to attack the old Europe whose architectural expression it had already killed. By the time the eighteenth century draws to its close the printing press has destroyed everything. In the nineteenth century it will rebuild.

And now we put the question: which of the two arts has for the past three centuries really represented human thought? Which has translated it? Which has expressed, not only its literary and scholastic obsessions, but its vast, deep, universal movement? Which has constantly superimposed itself, without a break or a lapse, on advancing mankind, that monster of a thousand feet? Architecture or printing?

Printing. Make no mistake about it, architecture is dead, dead beyond recall, killed by the printed book, killed because it is less durable, killed because it costs more. Every cathedral is a thousand million francs. Try now to imagine what capital outlay would be needed to rewrite the book of architecture; to restore to the earth those teeming thousands of buildings; to return to the ages when the throng of monuments was such that in the words of an eye-witness: 'it was as though the world had shaken off its old garments to clothe itself in a white vestment of churches.' *Erat enim ut si mundus, ipse excutiendo semet, rejecta vetustate, candidam ecclesiarum vestem indueret* (GLABER RADULPHUS).*

A book is soon finished, costs so little and can go so far! Why be surprised that all human thought should flow down that slope? That does not mean that architecture will not produce here and there a fine monument, an isolated masterpiece. One might well still have now and then, under the reign of the printing press, a column made, I suppose, by a whole army out of cannon* all stuck together as, under the reign of architecture, one had *Iliads* and *Romanceros*, *Mahabharatas* and *Nibelungen*, made by a whole people from an accumulation and fusion of rhapsodies. The great accident of an architect of genius might occur in the twentieth century as did that of Dante in the thirteenth. But architecture will no longer be the social, the collective, the dominant art. The great poem, the great building, the great work of mankind will no longer be built, it will be printed.

And from now on, if architecture should accidentally revive, it will no longer be sovereign. It will be subject to the law of literature, to which it once laid down the law. The respective positions of the two arts will be reversed. Certainly during the age of architecture poems, though rare, it is true, were like the monuments. In India, Vyasa* is complex, strange, impenetrable as a pagoda. In the Egyptian East poetry has the same grandeur and tranquillity of line as the buildings; in ancient Greece beauty, serenity, calm; in Christian Europe the majesty of Catholicism, the simplicity of the people, the rich, luxuriant vegetation of an age of renewal. The Bible resembles the Pyramids, the *Iliad* the Parthenon, Homer Phidias. Dante in the thirteenth century is the last Romanesque church; Shakespeare in the sixteenth the last Gothic cathedral.

Thus, to sum up what we have said so far in an inevitably incomplete and abbreviated form, mankind has two books, two records, two testaments: masonry and printing, the stone Bible and the paper Bible. No doubt, looking at these two Bibles so widely open through the centuries, one may be permitted to regret the loss of the visible majesty of that granite writing, those gigantic alphabets formulated as colonnades, pylons, and obelisks, those man-made mountains, as it were, covering the earth and the past from the pyramid to the steeple, from Cheops to Strasbourg. The past must be reread on those marble pages. We must admire and ceaselessly leaf through the book written by architecture; but we must not deny the grandeur of the building raised in its turn by printing.

That building is colossal. Some statistician or other has calculated that if all the volumes printed since Gutenberg were piled one on top of another they would reach as far as the distance from the earth to the moon, but that is not the sort of grandeur we want to talk about. Yet, when you try to compose a full mental picture of the combined production of printing up to our own day, does not this look like an immense construction, based on the whole world,

at which humanity labours without respite, and whose monstrous head is lost in the profound mist of the future? It is
the ant-hill of all intellect. It is the hive to which the golden
bees of imagination bring their honey. The building has a
thousand storeys. Here and there you can see opening out
on the ramps around it the dark caves of science, which
intersect in its bowels. Everywhere on its surface art brings
forth a visible luxuriance of arabesques, rose-windows, and
tracery. There each individual work, however fanciful and
isolated it may seem, has its place and its projection. The
whole results in harmony. From the cathedral of Shakespeare to the mosque of Byron, countless turrets jostle in
disorder on this metropolis of universal thought. On its base
some ancient titles of humanity, unrecorded by architecture, have been rewritten. To the left of the entrance has
been fixed the old white marble bas-relief of Homer, to the
right the polyglot Bible raises its seven heads. The hydra of
the *Romanceros* bristles further on, with other hybrid forms,
the Vedas and the *Nibelungen*. For the rest the prodigious
edifice remains always unfinished. The printing press, that
giant machine, pumping without respite all the intellectual
sap of society, incessantly spews out fresh material for its
work. The entire human race is on the scaffolding. Every
mind is a mason. The very humblest stops up a hole or lays
a stone. Rétif de la Bretonne* brings up his hod full of
plaster. Every day a new course is added. Independently of
the original, individual contribution of each writer, there
are collective shares. The eighteenth century gives the *En-
cyclopédie*, the Revolution the *Moniteur*.* To be sure this too
is a construction which grows and rises in endless spirals;
there too is a medley of tongues, ceaseless activity, tireless
labour, unremitting assistance from the whole of mankind,
the refuge promised to intelligence against a new Flood,
against submersion by the barbarians. It is the second
Tower of Babel of the human race.

BOOK SIX

I

AN IMPARTIAL LOOK AT THE OLD MAGISTRACY

A MOST fortunate person in the year of grace 1482 was the noble gentleman Robert d'Estouteville,* knight, Sieur of Beyne, baron of Ivri and Saint-Andry in la Marche, counsellor and chamberlain to the King, keeper of the Provostry of Paris. It was already close on seventeen years since he had, on 7 November 1465, in the year of the comet,[1] received from the King this fine post of Provost of Paris, reputed more of a lordship than an office. *Dignitas*, says Joannes Loemnoeus, *quae non cum exigua potestate politiam concernente, atque praerogativis multis et juribus conjuncta est* [a dignity which is accompanied by no small power of police, and many prerogatives and rights]. A gentleman holding the King's commission with letters of appointment going back to the time of the marriage* of Louis XI's natural daughter to the Bastard of Bourbon was something wondrous in 1482. The same day that Robert d'Estouteville had replaced Jacques de Villiers as Provost of Paris, Maître Jean Dauvet replaced Messire Hélye de Thorettes as First President of the Court of Parliament, Jean Jouvenel des Ursins supplanted Pierre de Morvilliers in the office of Chancellor of France, Regnault des Dormans relieved Pierre Puy of the post of Master of Requests in Ordinary in the King's household. Now, upon how many heads had the presidency, the chancellorship, and the mastership fallen since Robert d'Estouteville had held the Provostship of Paris! It had been 'granted into his keeping' said the letters patent, and he had indeed kept it well. He had clung to it, embodied himself in it, identified himself with it. So much

---

[1] This comet, against which Pope Calixtus, uncle of Borgia, ordered public prayers, is the same as will reappear in 1835. [V. H.]

so that he had escaped the mania for change which possessed Louis XI, a distrustful, quarrelsome, hard-working
king, bent on preserving through frequent appointments
and dismissals the elasticity of his power. Moreover, the
gallant knight had obtained for his son the reversion of his
office, and for the past two years now the name of the noble
Jacques d'Estouteville, Esquire, figured beside his own at
the head of the register of the ordinary of the Provostry of
Paris. A rare and signal favour indeed! It is true that Robert
d'Estouteville was a good soldier, that he had loyally raised
his pennon against the 'League of the public weal',* and
had presented to the queen a most wonderful stag made of
preserves on the day of her entry into Paris in 14[67].* He
moreover enjoyed the friendship of Messire Tristan l'Hermite, Provost-Marshal of the King's household. So it was
a very agreeable and pleasant existence that Maître Robert
led. First there was an excellent salary, to which were
attached, hanging like extra bunches on his vine, the
revenue from the civil and criminal registries of the Provostry, plus the revenues, civil and criminal, from the lower
courts of the Châtelet, not to mention some small tolls from
the bridges of Mantes and Corbeil, profits from the duty
on blacksmiths' iron in Paris, and from the assizers of
firewood and inspectors of salt. Add to that the pleasure of
displaying as he rode about the town his fine fighting dress
(which you can still admire today carved on his tomb at the
abbey of Valmont in Normandy), and his helmet, badly
dented at Montlhéry,* all this contrasting with the half-red,
half-tan robes of the échevins and *quarteniers*. And then, did
it count for nothing to have supreme authority over the
sergeants of the *douzaine*, the keeper and watch of the
Châtelet, the two auditors of the Châtelet, *auditores Castel-
leti*, the sixteen commissioners of the sixteen districts, the
gaoler of the Châtelet, the four hereditary sergeants, the
hundred and twenty mounted sergeants, the hundred and
twenty sergeants of the wand, or catchpoles, the captain of
the watch with his watch, under-watch, counter-watch and
rear-watch? Was it nothing to exercise justice, high and low,
with the right to turn, hang, and draw, not to mention petty

jurisdiction of first instance, *in prima instantia*, as the charters have it, over this viscounty of Paris, so splendidly
appanaged with seven noble bailiwicks? Can any sweeter
pleasure be imagined than that of passing sentence and
judgement, as Messire Robert d'Estouteville did every day
in the Grand Châtelet, beneath Philip-Augustus's broad,
flattened arches? And to go every evening, as was his wont,
to that charming house in the rue Galilée, in the precincts
of the Palais-Royal, which he held in the right of his wife,
Madame Ambroise de Loré, to rest from the fatigue of
sending some poor devil to spend his night in 'that little
cell in the rue de l'Escorcherie, which the provosts and
échevins of Paris were wont to use as their prison; it being
11 feet long, 7 feet 4 inches wide and 11 feet high.'[1]

Not only did Messire Robert d'Estouteville have his personal right of justice as Provost and Viscount of Paris, he
also had a share, as spectator and participant, in the King's
high justice. There was no head of any distinction which
had not passed through his hands before falling to the
executioner. He it was who had gone to fetch Monsieur de
Nemours from the Bastille Saint-Antoine and bring him to
the Halles, and to bring Monsieur de Saint-Pol to the
Grève, despite the objections and protests of the same,
much to the delight of Monsieur the Provost, who was no
friend of Monsieur the Constable.*

That is certainly more than enough to make for a happy
and illustrious life, and one day to earn a notable page in
that interesting history of the Provosts of Paris, in which
we learn that Oudard de Villeneuve had a house in the rue
des Boucheries, that Guillaume de Hangest bought the
Great and Little Savoy, that Guillaume Thiboust donated
to the nuns of Sainte-Geneviève his houses in the rue
Clopin, that Hugues Aubriot lived at the Hôtel du Porc-
Épic, and other facts of a domestic nature.

However, with so many reasons for taking life with patience and enjoyment, Messire Robert d'Estouteville had
woken up on the morning of 7 January 1482 very grumpy

[1] Estate Accounts, 1383 [V. H.]

and in a vile temper. What had caused such a mood? He could not have explained it himself. Was it because the sky was grey? or because the buckle of his old swordbelt from Montlhéry had been pulled too tight, and constricted his provostial girth in too military a fashion? that he had seen in the street, passing by beneath his window, some ribald fellows making fun of him, a gang of four of them going along with no shirts under their doublets, no crowns to their hats, wallet and bottle at their side? Was it a vague premonition of the 370 *livres* 16 *sous* 8 *deniers* that the future King Charles VIII was going to cut from the income of the provostship? The reader can take his choice; for our part we should be inclined to believe quite simply that he was in a bad temper because he was in a bad temper.

Besides, it was the day following a holiday, a tiresome day for everyone, and above all for the magistrate responsible for clearing all the rubbish, literal and figurative, left by a holiday in Paris. Moreover he was due to hold a sitting at the Grand Châtelet. Now we have observed that judges generally arrange things so that the day when they are sitting is also the day when they are in a bad temper, in order always to have someone on whom to vent their spleen conveniently, in the name of the king, the law, and justice.

The hearing, however, had begun without him. His deputies for civil, criminal, and private cases were doing his job for him, as was customary, and since eight o'clock in the morning some scores of townsfolk, men and women, packed and squashed in a dark corner of the lower court of the Châtelet, between a stout oak barrier and the wall, had been blissfully looking at the varied and delightful spectacle of civil and criminal justice being dispensed by Maître Florian Barbedienne, auditor at the Châtelet, deputy to Monsieur the Provost, a little confusedly and quite at random.

The room was small, low, and vaulted. At the back was a table covered with fleurs-de-lys, with a great carved oak armchair, which was the Provost's, and empty, and a stool on the left for the auditor, Maître Florian. Below sat the clerk of the court, scribbling away. Facing them were the people, and in front of the door and the table numerous provost sergeants in purple camlet tunics with white crosses. Two sergeants from the Parloir-aux-Bourgeois, in their All Saints Day jacket, half red and half blue, stood guard before a low, closed door, visible at the back behind the table. A single pointed window, tightly set into the thick wall, let a wan beam of January daylight fall on two grotesque figures, the fanciful stone devil carved as a *cul-de-lampe* on the keystone of the vault, and the judge sitting at the far end of the room upon the fleurs-de-lys.

Imagine, indeed, sitting at the Provost's table, between two bundles of case documents, crouched down on his elbows, his foot on his robe of plain brown cloth, face buried in the white lambswool trimming, from which his eyebrows seemed to have been cut too, red-faced, surly, blinking, majestically carrying fat, fleshy cheeks which met beneath his chin, Maître Florian Barbedienne, auditor at the Châtelet.

Now the auditor was deaf—a slight defect in an auditor. Maître Florian none the less delivered his judgements without appeal and most appropriately. It is certainly enough for a judge to appear to be listening; and the venerable auditor fulfilled this condition, the only one essential to good justice, all the better for the fact that no noise could distract his attention.

For the rest, there was in the audience a merciless observer of his deeds and action in the person of our friend Jehan Frollo du Moulin, the young student of the day before, that rambler whom one was always sure to meet anywhere in Paris except in front of the professor's chair.

'Look,' he said in an undertone to his companion, Robert Poussepain, who sniggered beside him as he gave a commentary on the scenes being enacted before their eyes, 'there's Jehanneton du Buisson, the pretty daughter of that idle dog at the Marché Neuf. 'Pon my soul, the old man is finding her guilty. His sight's no better than his hearing. 15 *sous* 4 *deniers parisis* for wearing two sets of beads! That's a bit dear. *Lex duri carminis* [Law of the harsh formula]. Who's that? Robin Chief-de-Ville, hauberk maker!—for having been passed and admitted master of the said trade?—that's his entrance fee. Ha! two gentlemen among these rascals! Aiglet de Soins, Hutin de Mailly. Two esquires, *corpus Christi!* Oh! they've been playing dice. When shall I see our rector here?* A fine of a hundred *livres parisis* to the King! Old Barbedienne really lays it on—deaf to argument as he is! May I change places with my brother the archdeacon if that is going to stop me gambling, gambling day and night, living and dying a gambler, gambling away my soul when I've already lost my shirt! Holy Virgin, look at all those girls! One after another, my ewe lambs! Ambroise Lécuyère! Isabeau la Paynette! Bérarde Gironin! I know them all, by God! Fine them! fine them! That'll teach you to wear gold belts! Ten *sols parisis*! Flibbertigibbets!—Oh! what a snout on that deaf old idiot of a judge! O Florian, you oaf! O Barbedienne, you clod! He's making a meal of it! He gobbles up plaintiffs, gobbles up lawsuits, eats, chews, stuffs himself, crams himself to the brim. Fines, lost property, taxes, expenses, reasonable costs, wages, damages and interests, torture, prison, gaol, stocks with costs, are so much Christmas pie and midsummer marzipan for him! Look at the old pig! Right! good, another light of love! Thibaud la Thibaude, no less! For leaving the rue Glatigny!—Who is this fellow? Gieffroy Mabonne, crossbowman. He took the name of the Father in vain. Fine our Thibaude! Fine our Gieffroy! Fine them both! Deaf old fool! He must have mixed up the cases! Ten to one he makes the girl pay for swearing and the soldier for making love! Look out, Robert Poussepain! Who are they going to bring in? That's a lot of sergeants! By Jove! all the hounds in the pack are there! They must have bagged something really big! A wild boar! It is a boar! It is, it is! And a fine one at that! By Hercules! It's our prince from yesterday, our Pope of Fools, our bell-ringer, our one-eyed, grimacing hunchback! It's Quasimodo!'

It was none other.

It was Quasimodo roped, trussed, tied, and bound, and heavily guarded. The squad of sergeants surrounding him was attended by the captain of the watch in person, bearing the arms of France embroidered on his chest and those of the town on his back. There was, however, nothing about Quasimodo, apart from his deformity, to justify this display of halberds and arquebuses. He was sullen, silent, and calm. His single eye just occasionally cast a covert look of anger at the bonds holding him.

He looked around him too, but in so lifeless and sleepy a way that the women only pointed him out to each other to scoff.

Meanwhile Maître Florian, the auditor, attentively leafed through the dossier of the charges brought against Quasimodo, which the clerk handed him, and once he had glanced at it, seemed to be reflecting for a moment. Thanks to this precaution, which he always made sure of taking just before proceeding to an interrogation, he knew in advance the names, titles, and offences of the accused, made expected rejoinders to expected answers, and managed to negotiate successfully all the twists and turns of the interrogation without making his deafness too obvious. The dossier of the case was for him like a dog to a blind man. If it so happened that his infirmity was revealed now and then by some inconsequential comment or some unintelligible question, some took it for profundity, others for imbecility. In both cases the honour of the magistracy remained intact; for it is much better that a judge should be reputed imbecile or profound than deaf. He therefore took great pains to conceal his deafness from all eyes, and usually succeeded so well that he had ended by deceiving himself. Besides, that is easier than one might think. All hunchbacks go about with their heads high, all stammerers hold forth, all deaf people mumble. As for him, he thought that at the very most his hearing was a little refractory. This was the only concession on the matter that he made to public opinion, in his moments of frankness and self-examination.

Thus, having duly ruminated over Quasimodo's case, he threw back his head and half closed his eyes, to appear more majestic and impartial, with the result that at that moment he was at once deaf and blind—twin conditions without which no judge is perfect. It was in this magisterial attitude that he commenced his interrogation.

'Your name?'

Now here we have a case which had not been 'foreseen by the law', that of one deaf man having to interrogate another.

Quasimodo, wholly unaware of the question addressed to him, continued to stare at the judge and did not answer. The judge, deaf, and wholly unaware that the accused was deaf, thought that he had answered, as all accused persons generally did, and went on with his stupid and mechanical self-assurance.

'Right. Your age?'

Quasimodo did not answer this question either. The judge thought it had been answered, and continued:

'Now, your calling?'

The same silence as before. The audience, however, began to whisper and exchange looks.

'That will do,' went on the imperturbable auditor when he assumed that the accused had completed his third answer. 'You stand accused before us: *primo*, of causing nocturnal disturbance; *secundo*, of indecent assault against the person of a loose woman, *in praejudicium meretricis* [to the detriment of a harlot]; tertio, of rebellious and disloyal conduct towards the archers of the ordinance of the king, our master. Explain yourself on all these points— clerk, have you written down what the accused has said so far?'

At this unfortunate question a roar of laughter went up from the clerks to the public, so violent, uncontrollable, contagious, and universal that the two deaf men could not help noticing. Quasimodo turned round, scornfully shrugging his hump, while Maître Florian, as surprised as he was, and supposing the spectators' laughter to have been provoked by some disrespectful reply from the accused, made visible for him by that scornful shrug, addressed him indignantly:

'The answer you have just given, you rogue, deserves the halter! Do you know whom you are talking to?'

This outburst was not likely to halt an explosion of general mirth. It seemed so incongruous and irrelevant that the uncontrollable laughter spread even to the sergeants from the Parloir-aux-Bourgeois, like knaves of spades whose stupidity was part of the uniform. Quasimodo alone remained serious, for the good reason that he could understand none of what was going on around him. The judge, increasingly angry, thought that he ought to continue in the same tone, hoping thus to strike such terror into the accused that it would react on the public and instil some respect in them once more.

'That means then, master of perversity and violence that you are, that you presume to show disrespect for the auditor of the Châtelet, the magistrate appointed to police the people of Paris, responsible for investigating crimes, offences, and misconduct, for supervising all trades and preventing monopoly, for the upkeep of roadways, for preventing the regrating of poultry, fowl, and wildfowl, for assizing firewood and other sorts of wood, for cleansing the town of sludge and the air of contagious diseases, for being constantly concerned with the public good, in a word, without fee or hope of payment! Do you know that my name is Florian Barbedienne, Monsieur the Provost's own deputy, and, what is more, commissioner, investigator, comptroller and examiner with equal powers in the Provostry, Bailiwick, Conservancy* and presidial courts?'

There is no reason why one deaf man talking to another should ever stop. God knows where and when Maître Florian would have made landfall, thus launched in full sail on the high seas of eloquence, if the low door at the back had not suddenly opened to admit Monsieur the Provost in person.

At this entrance Maître Florian did not stop short, but turning round on his heel, and abruptly aiming at the Provost the harangue with which he had been bombarding Quasimodo a moment before: 'Monseigneur,' he said, 'I request such penalty as may please you against the accused here present for gross and wondrous contempt of court.'

And he sat down quite out of breath, wiping off great drops of sweat which fell from his brow like tears, soaking the parchments spread out before him. Messire Robert d'Estouteville frowned and gestured so imperiously and meaningfully to Quasimodo to pay attention, that the deaf man understood to some degree.

The Provost addressed him sternly: 'What have you done then to be here, scoundrel?'

The poor devil, assuming that the Provost was asking his name, broke his customary silence and answered in a hoarse, guttural voice: 'Quasimodo.'

The reply bore so little relevance to the question that the uncontrollable laughter began again, and Messire Robert cried out, red with fury: 'Are you scoffing at me too, you arrant rogue?'

'Bell-ringer of Notre-Dame,' answered Quasimodo, thinking that he was meant to explain to the judge who he was.

'Bell-ringer!' the Provost went on, having woken up that morning in such a bad temper, as we have said, that his fury did not need to be stirred up by such strange replies. 'Bell-ringer! I'll have you thrashed with a full peal of rods on your back through all the crossroads of Paris. Do you understand, you rascal?'

'If it's my age you want to know,' said Quasimodo,' I think I'll be 20 at Martinmas.'

This was really going too far; the Provost could stand no more.

'Ah! you scoff at the Provostship, you wretch! Sergeants of the wand, you'll take this rascal to the pillory of the Grève, you'll flog him, and turn him round for an hour. He'll pay for it, by God! and I want this present sentence publicly cried, with four sworn trumpeters in attendance, through the seven castellanies of the viscounty of Paris.'

The clerk at once began drafting the sentence.

'God's belly! that's a good sentence!' the young student Jehan Frollo du Moulin cried out from his corner.

The Provost turned round and again glared at Quasimodo: 'I believe the rascal said "God's belly!"—Clerk, add a fine of 12 *deniers parisis* for swearing, half of it to go to the fabric fund of Saint-Eustache. I have a particular devotion to Saint-Eustache.'

In a few minutes the sentence was drawn up. Its tenor was brief and simple. The customary of the Provostry and viscounty of Paris had not yet been worked on by President Thibaut Baillet and Roger Barmne, advocate to the King. It had not yet then been obstructed by the tall forest of chicanery and legal procedure which these two jurisconsults planted there at the beginning of the sixteenth century. Everything was clear, expeditious, explicit. It went straight to the point, and you could see at once, at the end of every path, without the complication of undergrowth or side-track, the wheel, the gibbet, or the pillory. At least you knew where you were going.

The clerk handed the sentence to the Provost, who affixed his seal to it, and left to continue his round of the courtrooms, in a frame of mind which must have filled up all the gaols of Paris that day. Jehan Frollo and Robert Poussepain were laughing up their sleeves. Quasimodo regarded it all with an air of indifference and surprise.

Meanwhile the clerk, just as Maître Florian Barbedienne was reading over the sentence in his turn before signing it, felt moved by pity for the poor devil who had been condemned and, in the hope of obtaining some mitigation of the punishment, came as close as he could to the auditor's ear and said to him, pointing to Quasimodo: 'That man is deaf.'

He hoped that this shared infirmity would arouse Maître Florian's interest in favour of the condemned man. But first of all we have already observed that Maître Florian did not like his deafness to be noticed. Then, he was so hard of hearing that he did not catch a word of what the clerk said; however, he wanted to give the impression that he had heard, and replied: 'Aha! that's different. I didn't know that. An extra hour in the pillory, in that case.'

And he signed the sentence thus modified.

'That serves him right,' said Robert Poussepain, who still bore a grudge against Quasimodo; 'that will teach him to be rough with people.'

II

THE RAT-HOLE

WITH the reader's permission, we shall now go back to the
Place de Grève, which we left yesterday with Gringoire in
order to follow la Esmeralda.

It is ten o'clock in the morning. There are signs everywhere of the day after a public holiday. The roadway is
covered with litter, ribbons, scraps of cloth, feathers from
plumes, drops of wax from torches, crumbs from the public
banquet. A good many townsfolk are strolling about, stirring the charred brands of the bonfire with their feet, going
into raptures before the Maison-aux-Piliers, recalling the
fine hangings of the previous day as they look this morning
at the nails, all that remains of that pleasure. The beer and
cider vendors are rolling their barrels among the groups of
people. A few passers-by come and go about their business.
Tradesmen chat and call out to each other from the doorway of their shops. The festivities, the ambassadors, Coppenole, the Pope of Fools, are on everyone's lips, each
trying to outdo the others in apt comment and hearty
laughter. Meanwhile, four mounted sergeants who have just
stationed themselves at the four corners of the pillory have
already concentrated around them a fair proportion of the
populace scattered across the square, who condemn themselves to boredom and immobility in the hope of seeing
some minor punishment executed.

If the reader, after contemplating the lively, noisy scene
being played out in every part of the square, will now turn
his eyes on to that ancient half-Gothic, half-Romanesque
house of the Tour-Roland, which stands at the western
corner of the quayside, he will observe in the angle of the
façade a large public breviary, richly illuminated, protected
from the rain by a little canopy, and from thieves by a grille,
which, however, leaves room to turn the pages. Beside this
breviary is a narrow, pointed window, closed by two inter-

secting iron bars, looking on to the square, the only opening which admits a little fresh air and daylight to a small doorless cell, set at ground level in the thickness of the old house's wall, and filled with a peace made all the more profound, a silence made all the more mournful by the fact that a public square, the noisiest and busiest in Paris, teems and yells all around.

This cell had been famous in Paris for nearly three centuries, ever since Madame Rolande of the Tour-Roland, in mourning for her father who had died on the Crusades, had had it hollowed out from the wall of her own house and there shut herself up for ever, retaining of her palace nothing but this dwelling, of which the door was walled up and the window open, winter and summer; all the rest she gave to the poor and to God. The desolate lady had in fact waited twenty years for death in this anticipated tomb, praying night and day for her father's soul, sleeping on ashes, without so much as a stone for a pillow, wearing a black sack, and subsisting only on whatever bread and water compassionate passers-by left on her window ledge, thus receiving charity after she had exercised it. At her death, at the moment of passing over to another tomb, she had bequeathed this one in perpetuity to women in affliction, mothers, widows, or daughters, who had much praying to do for others or for themselves, and wished to be buried alive in great grief or great penitence. The poor of her time had given her a fine funeral with their tears and blessings; but to their great regret the pious maid could not be canonized as a saint for want of patronage. Those among them who were not as pious as they ought to have been had hoped that the matter could be settled more easily in paradise than in Rome, and had simply prayed to God for the deceased, instead of to the Pope. Most people had been content to hold Rolande's memory sacred and make relics out of her rags. The town, for its part, had founded a public breviary in the lady's honour, and fastened it near the window of her cell, so that passers-by might stop there from time to time, if only to offer a prayer; that prayer might make them think of alms, and thus the poor recluses, heirs to Madame Rolande's tomb, should not perish completely from hunger and neglect.

This kind of tomb was in any case by no means rare in towns in the Middle Ages. One would often encounter, in the busiest streets, in the gaudiest and noisiest market, right in the middle, beneath the horses' hooves, virtually beneath the carts' wheels, a cellar, a well, a walled and barred cell, in the depths of which some human being prayed day and night, voluntarily dedicated to some endless lamentation, some great expiation. And all the reflections aroused in us today by such a strange spectacle, such a horrible cell, a kind of intermediate link between a home and a tomb, cemetery and city, this living creature cut off from human companionship and henceforth counted among the dead, this lamp burning its last drop of oil in the shadows, this remnant of life flickering in a grave, this breath, this voice, this unceasing prayer in a stone coffin, this face for ever turned towards another world, this eye lit already by another sun, this ear pressed to the walls of the tomb, this soul imprisoned in the body, this body imprisoned in its dungeon, and beneath the double envelope of flesh and granite the droning of that soul in distress, that all went unnoticed by the crowd. The piety of those days, little given to reasoning and none too subtle, could not see so many facets in a religious act. It took the thing as a whole, and honoured, venerated, if need be sanctified, but did not analyse the suffering involved and felt no particular pity for it. From time to time it brought a pittance to the wretched penitent, looked into the hole to see whether the person inside was still alive, did not know his name, hardly knew how many years it had been since he had begun to die, and to a stranger enquiring about the living skeleton rotting in this cellar, the neighbours would simply answer: 'He's the recluse', or if it were a woman: 'She's the recluse.'

That is how people saw everything in those days, without metaphysics, without exaggeration, without a magnifying glass, with the naked eye. The microscope had not yet been invented, either for material things of for those of the spirit.

Besides, although they aroused no great wonder, examples of this kind of claustration in the midst of towns were, in fact, frequent, as we have just said. In Paris there were quite a number of such cells for praying to God and doing penance; almost all were occupied. It is true that the clergy did not like to leave them empty, which would imply a lack of fervour among the faithful, and lepers were put in when there were no penitents. Apart from the cell on the Grève, there was one at Montfaucon, one at the charnel-house of the Innocents, another—just where I have forgotten—at the Logis Clichon, I believe. There were still more in many places where their traces can be found in traditions, in the absence of any monuments. The University too had its own. On the Montagne Sainte-Geneviève a kind of medieval Job spent thirty years on a dungheap, at the bottom of a cistern, singing the seven penitential psalms, and, once he had finished, starting all over again, chanting in a louder voice at night, *magna voce per umbras*, and the antiquary today still has the impression of hearing his voice as he turns into the rue du Puits-qui-parle [Talking-well].*

To limit ourselves to the cell in the Tour-Roland, we have to say that it had never been short of recluses. Since the death of Madame Rolande it had rarely been vacant for a year or two. Many women had come there to weep, until they died, for parents, lovers, sins. The malice of Parisians who interfere in everything, even what concerns them least, claimed that few widows had been seen there.

In accordance with the fashion of the time, a Latin inscription on the wall indicated to the literate passer-by the pious purpose of the cell. Up to the middle of the sixteenth century the custom was maintained of explaining a building by some brief device written over the door. Thus in France you can still read over the wicket of the seigneurial prison at Tourville: *Sileto et spera* [Be silent and hope]; in Ireland, under the shield placed on top of the main gate of the castle of Fortescue: *Forte scutum, salus ducum* [a strong shield, the safety of leaders]; in England, over the main entrance to the hospitable manor of the Earls Cowper: *Tuum est* [it is yours]. That is because at that time every building was an idea.

As there was no door to the walled-up cell of the Tour-Roland, someone had carved over the window in Romanesque capital letters the two words: TU, ORA [you, pray]

As a result, the people, whose good sense does not see the finer points of things and cheerfully translates *Ludovico Magno* [to Louis the Great] by *Porte Saint-Denis*, had given this dark, dismal, dank cavity the name *Trou-aux-Rats** [Rat-hole]—a less sublime description perhaps than the other, but on the other hand more picturesque.

III

THE STORY OF A MAIZE CAKE

AT the time of which we are writing the Tour-Roland cell
was occupied. If the reader wishes to know by whom, he
has only to listen in to the conversation of three worthy
gossips who, at the moment when we fixed our attention
on the Rat-hole, were proceeding in the very same direction
as they walked beside the river up from the Châtelet towards the Grève.

Two of these women were dressed like good townswomen
of Paris. Their fine white gorgets, their red-and-white
striped tiretaine skirts, their white knitted stockings, with
coloured embroidery at the ankles, pulled trimly over the
leg, their square shoes of fawn leather with black soles,
and especially their headdress, a sort of tinsel horn loaded
with ribbons and lace, such as women still wear in Champagne, in common with the grenadiers of the Russian Imperial Guard, proclaimed that they belonged to that class
of rich tradespeople which comes midway between what
servants call 'a woman' and what they call 'a lady'. They
did not wear rings, or gold crosses, and it was easy to
see that in their case this was due not to poverty but quite
simply for fear of incurring a fine. Their companion was
got up in much the same way, but there was something
about her dress and bearing which had a whiff of the
country lawyer's wife. You could see from the way her
belt came up above her hips that she had not been long
in Paris. Add to that a pleated gorget, ribbon-bows on
her shoes, the stripes on her skirt running horizontally
and not vertically, and countless other enormities offensive
to good taste.

The first two women walked with the step peculiar to
Parisians showing provincials around Paris. The provincial
woman held a stout lad by the hand, and he in turn held a
large cake.

It pains us to have to add that, given the rigours of the season, he was using his tongue as a handkerchief.

The boy had to be dragged along, *non passibus aequis* [not with even steps], as Virgil puts it, and kept stumbling, to his mother's loud protests. It is true that his eyes were more on the cake than the pavement. No doubt he had some serious reason for not biting into it (the cake), for he contented himself with gazing at it affectionately. But his mother ought to have carried the cake herself. It was cruel to make a Tantalus of the big, chubby lad.

Meanwhile the three *damoiselles* (for the title *dame* was at that time reserved for noblewomen) were all talking at once.

'Let's hurry, Damoiselle Mahiette,' said the youngest of the three, who was also the fattest, to the provincial woman. 'I'm very much afraid that we may get there too late. They told us at the Châtelet that they were taking him to the pillory straightaway.'

'Bah! what are you talking about, Damoiselle Oudarde Musnier?' replied the other Parisian. 'He'll stay two hours in the pillory. We've plenty of time. Have you ever seen anyone put in the pillory, my dear Mahiette?'

'Yes,' said the provincial lady, 'at Reims.'

'Bah! what's that, your pillory at Reims? A wretched cage where they only turn peasants. That's not up to much!'

'Only peasants!' said Mahiette. 'At the Marché-aux-Draps! At Reims! We've seen some really splendid criminals there; some had killed both father and mother! Peasants indeed! What do you take us for, Gervaise?'

The provincial was certainly about to lose her temper for the honour of her pillory. Fortunately the prudent Damoiselle Oudarde Musnier changed the subject in time.

'By the way, Damoiselle Mahiette, what do you think of our Flemish ambassadors? Do you have any as fine as that in Reims?'

'I admit,' answered Mahiette, 'that it's only in Paris that you see Flemings like that.'

'Did you see that tall one in the embassy who is a hosier?' asked Oudarde.

'Yes,' said Mahiette, 'he looked like a Saturn.'

'And that fat one with a face like a bare belly?' Gervaise went on, 'and the little one with little eyes, with red-rimmed eyelids, all plucked and jagged like a thistle-head?'

'It's their horses that are such a brave sight,' said Oudarde, 'all dressed up in the fashion of their country!'

'Ah! my dear,' broke in the provincial Mahiette, putting on a superior air in her turn, 'what would you have said then if you had seen, in '61, at the coronation in Reims, eighteen years ago,* the horses of the princes and the King's company! Hangings and caparisons of every kind; some of damask, fine cloth of gold, trimmed with sable fur; others of velvet, trimmed with ermine; others again covered with jewellery and great gold and silver bells! And the money it cost! And the handsome young pageboys riding them!'

'That doesn't alter the fact,' Damoiselle Oudarde replied drily,' that the Flemings have very fine horses, and they had a magnificent supper yesterday, given by the Provost of Merchants at the Hôtel de Ville, and were served sugared almonds, hippocras, spices and other delicacies.'

'What are you talking about, neighbour?' exclaimed Gervaise; 'it was with Monsieur the Cardinal, at the Petit-Bourbon, that the Flemings had supper.'

'No, they didn't. At the Hôtel de Ville!'

'Yes they did. At the Petit-Bourbon.'

'It was quite certainly at the Hôtel de Ville,' Oudarde retorted tartly, 'because Doctor Scourable gave them a Latin oration which pleased them greatly. My husband, who's a sworn bookseller, told me so.'

'It was certainly at the Petit-Bourbon,' Gervaise replied just as sharply, 'because this is what Monsieur the Cardinal's procurator gave them: 12 double quarts of hippocras, white, *clairet*,* and red; two dozen boxes of double gilt Lyons marzipan; the same number of torches of 2 pounds weight each, and 6 *demi-queues** of the best Beaune wine to be had, white and red. I hope that settles it. I have it from my husband, who is a *cinquantenier** at the Parloir-aux-Bourgeois, and this morning he was comparing the Flemish ambassadors with the ones from Prester John and the Emperor of Trebizond who came from Mesopotamia to Paris in our late King's time, and wore rings in their ears.'

'So true is it that they had supper at the Hôtel de Ville,' Oudadre rejoined, unmoved by this display, 'that there was such an array of viands and sugared sweets as has never been seen before.'

'I tell you that they were served by Le Sec, the town sergeant, at the Hôtel du Petit-Bourbon, and that's what misled you.'

'The Hôtel de Ville, I tell you.'

'The Petit-Bourbon, my dear! Because the word *Espérance*** which is written over the great doorway was all lit up with magic glasses.'

'The Hôtel de Ville! The Hôtel de Ville! Husson le Voir even played the flute there.'

'I tell you it wasn't!'

'I tell you it was!'

'I tell you it wasn't!'

Good fat Oudarde was getting ready to reply, and the quarrel might have led to blows, if Mahiette had not suddenly cried out: 'Just look at all those people flocking together there at the end of the bridge! There is something in the middle of them that they are all looking at.'

'Indeed,' said Gervaise, 'I can hear the sound of a tambourine. I think it's young Smeralda doing her mummeries with her goat. Quick, Mahiette! Hurry up there and pull your boy along. You came here to see the curiosities of Paris. Yesterday you saw the Flemings; today you must see the gypsy girl.'

'Gypsy girl!' said Mahiette, abruptly turning back and gripping her son's arm tightly. 'God preserve me! She would steal my child—come along, Eustache!'

And she began running along the quay towards the Grève until she had left the bridge far behind. However, the child she was dragging along fell over on his knees; she stopped, out of breath. Oudarde and Gervaise caught her up.

'That gypsy steal your child!' said Gervaise. 'That's a peculiar fancy you have.'

Mahiette shook her head thoughtfully.

'What is peculiar,' Oudarde observed, 'is that the *sachette* has the same idea about gypsies.'

'Who's the *sachette*?' asked Mahiette.

'Why!' said Oudarde, 'Sister Gudule.'

'Who's Sister Gudule?' Mahiette went on.

'Anyone can see you are from Reims if you don't know that!' Oudarde replied. 'She's the recluse in the Rat-hole.'

'What?' asked Mahiette, 'the poor woman we are taking the cake to?'

Oudarde nodded assent.

'Exactly. You'll see her in a minute or two at her little window on the Grève. She thinks the same as you about these gypsy vagabonds who play their tambourines and tell fortunes. No one knows why she has such a horror of Zingari and gypsies. But what about you, Mahiette, why do you run away like that at the mere sight of them?'

'Oh!' said Mahiette, clutching her son's round head in both hands, 'I didn't want what happened to Paquette la Chantefleurie to happen to me.'

'Ah! that's a story you'll have to tell us, my good Mahiette,' said Gervaise, taking her by the arm.

'I don't mind doing so,' replied Mahiette, 'but you must be real Parisians not to know it! Let me tell you then—but there's no need to stop while I tell you the tale—that Paquette la Chantefleurie was a pretty girl of 18 when I was the same age, that is eighteen years ago, and it's her own fault if she's not like me today, a good, healthy mother of 36, with a man and a boy. Besides, from the time she was 14 it was too late for that! Well, then, she was the daughter of Guybertaut, a minstrel on the boats at Reims, the same who played before King Charles VII at his coronation, when he went down our river Vesle from Sillery to Muison, and Madame the Maid* herself was in the boat. Her old father died while Paquette was still a small child; so all she had was her mother, the sister of Monsieur Mathieu Pradon, master brazier and coppersmith in Paris, in the rue Parin-Garlin, who died last year. So you can see that she came of good family. Her mother was a good, simple soul,

unfortunately, and taught Paquette nothing but a bit of
sewing, haberdashery and mercery, which didn't stop the
little girl growing very tall and remaining very poor. The
two of them lived in Reims by the riverside, in the rue de
Folle-Peine. Note that; I think that's what brought misfortune on Paquette. In '61, the year of the coronation of our
King Louis XI, whom God preserve, Paquette was so gay
and pretty that she was known everywhere just as la Chantefleurie. Poor girl!—she had beautiful teeth, and liked to
laugh to show them off. Now, a girl who likes to laugh is
on the way to tears: beautiful teeth are the ruin of beautiful
eyes. So she was la Chantefleurie. She and her mother just
scraped a living. They had fallen on hard times since
the minstrel's death. Their haberdashery brought them in
scarcely more than 6 *deniers* a week, that's not quite 2 *liards-
à-l'aigle*. Where were the days when father Guybertaut
could earn 12 *sols parisis* with a song at a single coronation?
One winter—it was that same year, '61—when the two
women hadn't a stick of wood to burn, and it was very cold,
it gave la Chantefleurie such a pretty colour that men would
call out to her: "Paquette!" and more than one called
"Pâquerette!",* and she was lost.—Eustache don't let me
see you biting that cake!—We could see straight away she
was lost one Sunday when she came to church with a gold
cross round her neck—at 14, just imagine! First it was the
young vicomte de Cormontreuil, whose church tower is
three-quarters of a league from Reims; then Messire Henri
de Triancourt, the King's master of horse; then, going
down, Chiart de Beaulion, sergeant-at-arms; then, still
going down, Guery Aubergeon, the king's carver; then
Macé de Frépus, Monsieur le Dauphin's barber; then
Thévenin Le Moine, the king's cook; then, going down all
the time, less and less young, less and less noble, she fell
as low as Guillaume Racine, fiddler, and Thierry de Mer,
lamplighter. By then, poor Chantefleurie, she was fair game
for anyone. She was down to the last *sou* of her gold piece.
What more can I say, mesdamoiselles? At the coronation,
that same year, '61, it was she who made the king of the
ribalds' bed! That same year.'

Mahiette sighed and wiped a tear from her eye.

'That's not such a very unusual story,' said Gervaise, 'and I don't see anything in it to do with gypsies or children.'

'Patience!' Mahiette went on; 'as for a child, you are going to see one. In '66—it will be sixteen years ago* this month come St Paul's day—Paquette gave birth to a little girl. Poor wretch! She was overjoyed. She had been wanting a child for a long time. Her mother, a simple soul who had never known anything better than to keep her eyes closed, her mother was dead. Paquette had no one left in the world to love, no one to love her. In the five years since she had gone astray la Chantefleurie had become a poor creature. She was alone, all alone in the world, pointed at, shouted at in the street, beaten by the sergeants, jeered at by ragged little boys. And then, she had reached the age of 20; and 20 is old age for loose women. Her wantonness was beginning to bring her in no more than the haberdashery used to; each new wrinkle meant a crown lost; she was finding winter hard again, once more she seldom had wood in her grate or bread in her bin. She couldn't work any more, because her life of sensual pleasure had made her idle, and she suffered much more, because as she became idle she had become more sensual—at least that's how Monsieur le curé of Saint-Rémy explains why such women feel the cold and hunger more than other poor women when they grow old.'

'Yes,' observed Gervaise, 'but what about the gypsies?'

'Just a moment, Gervaise!' said Oudarde, whose attention was not so impatient. 'What would there be at the end if everything came at the beginning? Go on, Mahiette, please. Poor Chantefleurie!'

Mahiette continued:

'So she was very unhappy, very miserable, and her cheeks were furrowed with tears. But in her shame, her wantonness, and her abandonment, it seemed to her that she could be less shameful, less wanton, less abandoned if there was something or someone in the world whom she could love and who could love her. It had to be a child, because only a child could be innocent enough. She had realized that after

trying to love a robber, the only man who might have
wanted her; but after a little while she saw that the robber
despised her. These women who live by love need a lover
or a child to fill their hearts. Otherwise they are very unhappy. Since she could not have a lover, she turned completely to wanting a child, and as she had never stopped
being devout, that was what she constantly prayed God for.
So God took pity on her and gave her a little girl. I won't
tell you how delighted she was. She was in a frenzy, crying,
fondling, kissing it. She fed the child herself, made it swaddling clothes out of her blanket, the only one she had on
her bed, and no longer felt cold or hunger. It brought back
her beauty. An old maid becomes a young mother. Men
took an interest again, Chantefleurie once more had callers,
she found customers for her wares, and from all these
horrors she made baby clothes, bonnets, and bibs, lace vests
and little satin caps, without even a thought of buying
herself another blanket.—Monsieur Eustache, I've already
told you once not to eat the cake.—Little Agnès—that was
the child's name, her baptismal name, for Chantefleurie
hadn't had a family name for a long while—for sure and
certain was wrapped up in more ribbons and embroidery
than a dauphiness of Dauphiné! Among other things she
had a pair of little shoes! King Louis XI has certainly never
had the like! Her mother had sewn and embroidered them
herself, she had put into it all her needleworking skills and
enough spangles for a Holy Virgin's robe. They were certainly the two daintiest little pink shoes you ever saw. At
most they were as long as my thumb, and you had to see
the baby's little feet come out of them to believe that they
could ever have got them on. It's true that those little feet
were so tiny, so pretty, so pink! pinker than the satin shoes!
When you have children, Oudarde, you will know that
there's nothing prettier than such tiny hands and feet.'

'I ask for nothing better,' said Oudarde with a sigh,
'but I'm waiting on the good pleasure of Monsieur Andry
Musnier.'

'Besides,' Mahiette went on, 'Paquette's baby didn't only
have pretty feet. I saw her when she was only four months

old. She was a real darling! Her eyes were bigger than her
mouth. And she had the sweetest fine dark hair, which was
already curling. She would have been a lovely brunette at
16! Her mother doted on her more fondly every day. She
would caress her, kiss her, tickle her, dress her up, almost
eat her! She was crazy about her, and kept thanking God
for her. The pretty pink feet especially never ceased to
amaze her and send her into transports of delight! She was
always pressing her lips to them and couldn't get over how
tiny they were. She would slip them into the little shoes,
take them out, admire them, marvel at them, look at the
light through them, feel sorry when she tried walking them
across her bed, and would gladly have spent the rest of her
life on her knees covering and uncovering those feet as if
they had belonged to a baby Jesus.'

'The story is all very fine,' Gervaise said in an undertone,
'but where does Egypt come in?'

'Now,' Mahiette replied. 'There came to Reims one day
a very odd lot of riders. They were beggars and truands
travelling through those parts, led by their duke and their
counts. They were swarthy, with crinkly hair and silver
rings in their ears. The women were even uglier than
the men. Their faces were even darker, and always uncovered, they wore a ragged sort of smock over their body,
an old cloth woven from cord tied on their shoulders, and
their hair done up in horsetails. The children sprawling
about their legs would have scared a monkey. A band of
excommunicates! The whole lot came straight from Lower
Egypt to Reims by way of Poland. The Pope had confessed
them, so it was said, and as a penance had told them to
travel around for seven years without stopping, and never
sleeping in a bed. So they were called Penitents and they
stank. It seems that they had formerly been Saracens, which
means they believed in Jupiter, and they claimed 10 *livres
tournois* from all archbishops, bishops, and abbots with
cross and mitre. A papal bull granted them that right.
They had come to Reims to tell fortunes in the name of the
King of Algiers and the Emperor of Germany. You can
imagine that that was all it took for them to be forbidden

entry into the town. So the whole band cheerfully pitched camp near the Porte de Braine, on that hill where there's a windmill, next to the old chalkpits. And everyone in Reims raced off to see them. They read your hand and told you the most amazing prophecies. They were quite capable of telling Judas he would become pope. But there were nasty rumours going round about them stealing children and cutting purses and eating human flesh. Sensible folk told foolish ones "Don't go," and secretly went themselves. So it was all the rage. The fact is that they said things to make a cardinal gasp. Mothers made a great to-do over their children once the gypsy women had read in their hands all manner of miracles written in heathen or Turkish. One mother had an emperor, another a pope, another a captain. Poor Chantefleurie was seized with curiosity. She wanted to know what she had, and whether her pretty little Agnès might not one day be Empress of Armenia or something. So she took her to the gypsies; and the gypsy women were all over the child, admiring her, fondling her, kissing her with their black mouths, and marvelling over her little hand. Alas! to the great delight of the mother. They made a special fuss over the pretty feet and the pretty shoes. The child was not yet one year old. She was already lisping, laughed at her mother like a little mad thing, was plump and chubby, and had lots of sweet little gestures like an angel from paradise. She was very frightened by the gypsy women and cried. But her mother only kissed her the more and went off delighted by the fortune the soothsayers foretold for her Agnès. She would be a beauty, a virtue, a queen. So she returned to her garret in the rue Folle-Peine, full of pride at bringing home a queen. Next day she took advantage of a moment when the child was asleep on her bed, for she always put it to sleep with her, very quietly left the door ajar, and hurried to tell one of the neighbours in the rue de la Séchesserie that the day would come when her daughter Agnès would be served at table by the King of England and the Archduke of Ethiopia, and lots of other surprising things. On her return, hearing no crying as she went up the stairs, she said to herself: "Good! the child is still asleep." She found the door open wider than she had left it, but went in all the same, the poor mother, and ran to the bed . . . . The child was not there any more, the place was empty. There was no trace of the baby left, except for one of her pretty little shoes. She rushed out of the room, hurtled down the stairs, and began banging her head against the wall as she cried: "My baby! Who has got my baby? Who's taken my baby?" The street was deserted, the house isolated; no one could tell her anything. She went round the town, searched all the streets, ran to and fro all day long, crazy, distraught, terrible, sniffing at doors and windows like a wild animal that has lost its young. She was panting, dishevelled, a frightening sight, and the fire blazing in her eyes dried up any tears. She stopped people passing by and cried: "My daughter! my daughter! my pretty little daughter! If anyone gives me back my daughter I'll be his servant, his dog's servant, and he can eat my heart if he wants to." She met Monsieur le curé of Saint-Rémy and told him: "Monsieur le curé, I'll plough the earth with my fingernails, but give me back my child!"—It was heart-rending, Oudarde; and I saw one very hard man, Maître Ponce Lacabre, the prosecutor, weeping. Ah! the poor mother! In the evening she returned home. During her absence a neighbour had seen two gypsy women sneak up there with a bundle in their arms, then come down again, closing the door behind them, and run away. Since they had gone, something like a child crying had been heard coming from Paquette's room. The mother burst out laughing, flew up the stairs as if she had wings and crashed the door open as though with a cannonball, and went in. . . . Something awful, Oudarde! Instead of her sweet little Agnès, so rosy and fresh, who was a gift from God, a kind of little monster, hideous, lame, one-eyed, misshapen, was dragging itself across the floor squawking. She covered her eyes in horror. "Oh!" she said, "can the sorceresses have changed my daughter into this dreadful animal?" They hastily took the little clubfoot away. He would have driven her mad. It was the monstrous child of some gypsy woman who had given herself to the devil. He seemed to be about

4 years old, and spoke in what was no human language; the words were just not possible. Chantefleurie had pounced on the little shoe, all that remained to her of everything she had loved. She stayed so long without moving, without speaking, without breathing, that they thought she was dead. Suddenly she trembled in every limb, covered the relic with frantic kisses, and burst out sobbing as though her heart had broken. I assure you that we were all weeping too. She kept saying: "Oh! my little daughter! my pretty little daughter! where are you?"—It was heart-rending. I still weep when I think of it. Our children, you see, are the very marrow of our bones.—My poor Eustache! you are such a lovely boy! If you only knew what a good boy he is! Yesterday he told me: "I want to be a soldier." Oh Eustache! if I were to lose you!—Chantefleurie got up all of a sudden and began running round Reims crying: "To the gypsy camp! to the gypsy camp! Sergeants to burn the witches!" The gypsies had gone. It was pitch dark. They couldn't go after them. Next day, two leagues from Reims, on a heath between Gueux and Tilloy, they found the remains of a big fire, some ribbons which had belonged to Paquette's child, some drops of blood, and some goat droppings. The night just past was precisely a Saturday. There was no more room for doubt; the gypsies had held their sabbath on that heath, and had devoured the child in the company of Beelzebub, as the Mohammedans do. When Chantefleurie learned these horrible details she did not weep, she moved her lips as though to speak, but could not. Next day her hair had gone grey. The day after that she had disappeared.'

'That is indeed a frightful story,' said Oudarde, 'enough to make a Burgundian weep!'

'I'm not surprised any more,' added Gervaise, 'that you are so obsessed with fear of gypsies!'

'And when you ran off just now with your Eustache,' Oudarde went on, 'you were all the better advised, because these are gypsies from Poland too.'

'No they aren't,' said Gervaise, 'they are said to come from Spain and Catalonia.'

'Catalonia? Maybe,' answered Oudarde. 'Poland, Catalonia, Valogne,* I always confuse those three provinces. What is certain is that they are gypsies.'

'And their teeth are certainly long enough,' added Gervaise, 'to eat little children. And I wouldn't be surprised if la Smeralda ate a bit too, for all her simpering ways. Her white goat is up to too many mischievous tricks; there must be some sort of debauchery behind it all.'

Mahiette walked on in silence. She was absorbed in the kind of daydream that somehow prolongs a painful story, and stops only when it has spread the shockwave, vibration by vibration, to the innermost fibres of the heart. However, Gervaise spoke to her: 'And did they ever find out what became of la Chantefleurie?' Mahiette did not answer. Gervaise repeated her question, shaking Mahiette by the arm and calling out her name. Mahiette seemed to awaken from her thoughts.

'What became of la Chantefleurie?' she said, mechanically repeating the words whose impression was fresh in her ear; then, making an effort to turn her attention to the sense of those words: 'Ah!' she went on quickly, 'no one ever knew.'

She added after a pause:

'Some said they had seen her leave Reims at dusk by the Porte Fléchembault; others at dawn by the old Porte Basée. A poor man found her little golden cross hung on the stone cross in the field where they hold the fair. That was the jewel that caused her downfall, in '61. It was a gift from the handsome vicomte de Cormontreuil, her first lover. Paquette would never part with it, however great her need. She clung to it as to her very life. So when we saw that she had given up that cross we all thought she was dead. However, some people at Cabaret-les-Vantes said they had seen her go by on the Paris road, walking barefoot on the stones. But then she would have had to have left by the Porte de Vesle, and that doesn't fit in. Or rather, I believe that she did in fact leave by the Porte de Vesle, but left this world.'

'I don't understand,' said Gervaise.

'The Vesle,' Mahiette answered with a sad smile, 'is the river.'

'Poor Chantefleurie!' said Oudarde with a shudder, 'drowned!'

'Drowned,' Mahiette went on, 'and who could have told good old Guybertaut as he drifted down under the bridge at Tinqueux, singing in his boat, that one day his dear little Paquette would drift under that bridge too, but without a song or a boat?'

'And the little shoe?' asked Gervaise.

'Vanished with the mother,' Mahiette replied.

'Poor little shoe!' said Oudarde.

Oudarde, a plump, sentimental woman, would have been very happy to sigh along with Mahiette. But Gervaise, with more curiosity, had not done with her questions.

'And the monster?' she suddenly asked Mahiette.

'What monster?' the latter asked.

'The little gypsy monster that the witches left in Chantefleurie's room in exchange for her daughter. What did you do with it? I hope you drowned it too.'

'No,' Mahiette answered.

'What! well, burned it then? In fact that would be more fitting. An infant sorcerer!'

'Neither of those things, Gervaise. The archbishop took an interest in the gypsy child, he exorcised it, blessed it, carefully drove the devil out of its body, and sent it to Paris to be put out on the wooden bed at Notre-Dame as a foundling.'

'Those bishops!' grumbled Gervaise. 'Because they are learned they don't behave like other people. I ask you, Oudarde, putting the devil with the foundlings! For it's quite certain that the little monster was the devil. Well then, Mahiette, what did they do with him in Paris? I reckon that no charitable person wanted anything to do with him.'

'I don't know,' answered their friend from Reims. 'That was just the time my husband bought the tabellionage* of Beru, two leagues from the town, and we didn't concern ourselves with the story any more; and on top of that there are the two hills of Cernay lying in front of Beru which block the view of the towers of Reims cathedral.'

As they talked the three worthy women had reached the place de Grève. They were so preoccupied that they had gone past the public breviary at the Tour-Roland without stopping and were making their way without thinking towards the pillory around which the crowd was constantly growing. It is quite likely that the spectacle which at that moment was attracting every eye would have made them completely forget the Rat-hole and the halt they had intended to make there if plump, 6-year old Eustache, whom Mahiette was dragging along, had not suddenly reminded them of its purpose: 'Mother,' he said, as if some instinct warned him that the Rat-hole was behind him, 'now may I eat the cake?'

If Eustache had been shrewder, that is less greedy, he would have waited longer, and only when they were back home in the University, at Maître Andry Musnier's house in the rue Madame-la-Valence, with the two arms of the Seine and the five bridges of the City between the Rat-hole and the cake, would he have ventured to ask timidly: 'Mother, now may I eat the cake?'

That question, ill-advised at the moment that Eustache put it, revived Mahiette's attention.

'By the way,' she exclaimed, 'we are forgetting the recluse! Show me your Rat-hole, then, so I can give her her cake.'

'Right away,' said Oudarde. 'It's a charity.'

That was not how Eustache saw it.

'Hey! my cake!' he said, bumping each ear in turn against his shoulders, which in such a situation is the ultimate sign of dissatisfaction.

The three women retraced their steps, and when they were near the house of the Tour-Roland, Oudarde said to the other two: 'We mustn't all look into the hole at the same time in case we frighten the *sachette*. You two must pretend to be reading *dominus* in the breviary while I have a peep through the window. The *sachette* knows me slightly. I'll let you know when you can come near.'

She went by herself to the window. The moment she saw what was inside, a profound pity was depicted on all her features, and her cheerful, open face changed expression and colour as abruptly as if it had gone from sunshine to moonlight. Her eyes grew moist, her mouth puckered as when one is about to weep. A moment later she put a finger to her lips and beckoned to Mahiette to come and look.

Mahiette came, very moved, in silence and on tiptoe, as one does approaching a deathbed.

It was indeed a sad spectacle that the two women had before their eyes as they looked, without moving or breathing, through the barred window of the Rat-hole.

The cell was narrow, wider than it was deep, with a pointed vault, and from inside rather resembled the alveole of a large episcopal mitre. On the bare flagstones which formed the floor, in a corner, a woman sat, or, rather, crouched. Her chin rested on her knees, which her two crossed arms held tightly against her chest. Huddled like that, wearing brown sacking that wholly covered her in its wide folds, her long grey hair swept forward, falling over her face and legs down to her feet, she looked at first sight like a strange shape, silhouetted against the gloomy background of the cell, a kind of blackish triangle, which the ray of daylight coming through the window crudely divided into two shades, one dark, the other light. It was one of those spectres, half light, half shade, such as one sees in dreams and in Goya's extraordinary works, pale, motionless, sinister, crouched on a grave or leaning against the bars of a dungeon. It was neither woman nor man, nor living creature, nor definite shape; it was a figure; a sort of vision where reality and fantasy intersected like darkness and daylight. Beneath her hair, which spread out down to the ground, a harsh and wasted profile could just be discerned; from her robe just the tip of a bare foot protruded, clenched on the freezing, unyielding stone. What little could be glimpsed of human shape beneath that envelope of mourning made one shudder.

This figure, which looked as though it were fixed to the floor, seemed to be without movement, thought or breath. Under that thin canvas sack, in January, lying naked on a granite floor, without a fire, in the shadows of a dungeon whose slanting window let in from outside only the icy wind and never the sun, she did not seem to be suffering, or even to feel. It was as if she had turned into stone like her cell, ice like the season. Her hands were clasped together, her eyes fixed. At first sight she could be taken for a spectre, at a second look, for a statue.

However, at intervals her blue lips parted in a breath, and quivered, but as lifelessly and mechanically as leaves shifting in the wind.

However, in her dull eyes a look would pass, a look ineffable, profound, mournful, unwavering, constantly fixed on a corner of the cell which could not be seen from outside; a look which seemed to link all the gloomy thoughts of that soul in distress to some mysterious object.

Such was the creature who took from her abode the name 'recluse' and from her garment the name '*sachette*'.

The three women, for Gervaise had now joined Mahiette and Oudarde, looked through the window. Their heads blocked the feeble light in the cell, without the wretched being thus deprived apparently taking any notice of them. 'We must not disturb her,' Oudarde said in a low voice; 'she is in her ecstasy, she's praying.'

Meanwhile Mahiette was gazing with growing anxiety at that gaunt, withered, dishevelled head, and her eyes filled with tears. 'That would be most strange,' she murmured.

She passed her head through the window bars, and managed to see into the corner on which the unfortunate woman's eyes were invariably fixed.

When she withdrew her head from the window her face streamed with tears.

'What do you call that woman?' she asked Oudarde.

Oudarde answered: 'We call her Sister Gudule.'

'Well,' Mahiette went on, 'I call her Paquette la Chantefleurie.' Then, putting her finger to her lips, she made a sign to the astounded Oudarde to put her head through the window and look.

Oudarde looked, and saw in the corner on which the recluse's eyes were fixed in such sombre ecstasy, a little, pink, satin shoe embroidered with hundreds of gold and silver spangles.

Gervaise looked in after Oudarde, and then the three women, gazing at the unhappy mother, began to weep.

Neither their looking in nor their tears, however, had distracted the recluse. Her hands remained clasped, her lips speechless, her eyes fixed, and for anyone who knew her story it was heart-breaking to see her staring like that at the little shoe.

The three women had so far not uttered a word; they did not dare to speak, even in a low voice. The absolute silence, absolute grief, absolute oblivion in which all had vanished but for this one thing had the same effect on them as a high altar at Easter or Christmas. They kept quiet, they collected their thoughts, they were ready to go down on their knees. It seemed to them as though they had just gone into a church for Tenebrae in Holy Week.

At length Gervaise, the most inquisitive of the three, and consequently the least sensitive, tried to get the recluse to speak: 'Sister, Sister Gudule!'

She repeated her call three times, more loudly each time. The recluse did not stir. Not a word, not a look, not a sigh, no sign of life.

Oudarde in her turn, more gently and tenderly, said: 'Sister! Sister Sainte-Gudule!'

The same silence, the same immobility.

'A strange woman!' exclaimed Gervaise, 'she wouldn't be stirred by a bombard!'

'Perhaps she is deaf,' Oudarde said with a sigh.

'Perhaps blind,' added Gervaise.

'Perhaps dead,' Mahiette put in.

It is certain that if the soul had not yet left this inert, somnolent, lethargic body, it had at least withdrawn to hide in depths to which the perceptions of external organs no longer penetrated.

'We'll have to leave the cake on the window ledge, then.' said Oudarde. 'Some fellow will take it. What can we do to rouse her?'

Eustache, who up to that moment had been distracted by a little cart pulled by a large dog, which had just gone by, suddenly noticed that his three guides were looking at something through the window and, seized with curiosity in his turn, he got up on a marker stone, stood on tiptoe and stuck his fat, red face in the opening as he cried: 'Mother, do let me see then!'

At the sound of this childish voice, clear, fresh, resonant, the recluse started. She turned her head with the sharp, abrupt movement of a steel spring, her two long, skinny hands came up to push the hair back from her forehead, and she looked at the boy in bitter, hopeless amazement. This look lasted only for a flash.

'O God!' she suddenly cried, hiding her head in her lap, and it seemed as though her hoarse voice tore her chest as it came out, 'at least don't show me those of others!'

'Good-day, madame,' said the boy gravely.

However, the shock had, so to speak, roused the recluse. A long shudder ran through her whole body from head to foot, her teeth chattered, she half raised her head, and, pressing her elbows tightly against her hips and taking her feet in her hands as if to warm them, she said: 'Oh! how bitter cold it is!'

'Poor woman,' said Oudarde, full of pity,' would you like a bit of fire?'

She shook her head in refusal.

'All right,' Oudarde went on, offering her a flask, 'there's some hippocras to warm you up. Go on, drink.'

She shook her head again, stared at Oudarde and answered: 'Water.'

Oudarde was insistent: 'No, sister. That's no drink for January. You must drink a little hippocras and eat this maize cake we've baked for you.'

She rejected the cake that Mahiette offered her, and said: 'Black bread.'

'Come now,' said Gervaise, feeling charitable in her turn, and undoing her woollen smock,' here's a coat that's a bit warmer than yours. Put that over your shoulders.'

She refused the coat as she had refused the flask and cake, and answered: 'A sack.'

'But you must surely realize,' went on kindly Oudarde, 'that yesterday was a holiday.'

'I do realize,' said the recluse. 'It's two days since I ran out of water in my pitcher.'

She added after a silence: 'It's a holiday, people forget me. They are quite right to do so. Why should the world think of me when I don't think of it? Dead coals go with cold ash.'

And as though wearied by so much talk, she let her head drop back on her knees. Simple, charitable Oudarde, who took her last words to mean that she was still complaining of the cold, answered in all innocence: 'Then you would like a bit of fire?'

'Fire!' said the *sachette* in a strange voice: 'and will you make a bit too for the poor little girl who's been under the ground for the past fifteen years?'

She trembled in every limb, her voice shook, her eyes shone, she had risen to her knees. Suddenly she stretched out her wan skinny hand towards the child who looked at her in amazement: 'Take that child away!' she cried. 'The gypsy girl is going to pass by!'

Then she fell with her face to the ground, and her forehead struck the flags with the sound of stone on stone. The three women thought she was dead. A moment later she stirred, and they saw her drag herself on knees and elbows to the corner where the little shoe lay. Then they did not dare look, they could no longer see her, but they heard kisses and sighs without number mixed with heart-rending cries and dull thuds as of a head banging against a wall. Then, after one of these thuds, so violent that it made all three of them reel, they heard nothing more.

'Could she have killed herself?' said Gervaise, venturing to pass her head through the bars. 'Sister! Sister Gudule!'

'Sister Gudule!' repeated Oudarde.

'Oh, my God! she's not moving!' went on Gervaise. 'Is she dead?—Gudule! Gudule!'

Mahiette, so overcome up till then that she could not speak, made an effort. 'Wait,' she said. Then leaning towards the window: 'Paquette!' she said. 'Paquette la Chantefleurie!'

A child innocently blowing on the flickering fuse of a petard, and having it explode in his face, could not have been more appalled than Mahiette at the effect produced by this name abruptly cast into Sister Gudule's cell.

The recluse's whole body shook, she stood up on bare feet and sprang at the window with such blazing eyes that Mahiette, Oudarde, the other woman, and the boy retreated as far as the parapet on the quay.

Meanwhile the sinister face of the recluse appeared, pressed against the window bars. 'Oh! oh!' she cried with a terrifying laugh, 'it's the gypsy woman calling me!'

At that moment the scene round the pillory caught her frantic eye. Her brow wrinkled with horror. She stuck two skeletal arms out of her cell, and cried out in a voice like a death-rattle: 'So it's you, daughter of Egypt! You calling me, child-stealer! All right! Curses on you! curses! curses! curses!'

IV

A TEAR FOR A DROP OF WATER

THESE words were, so to speak, the point of intersection of two scenes which had up to then developed in parallel, simultaneously, each on its own stage; the one, which you have just read, at the Rat-hole, the other, which you are about to read, on the ladder of the pillory. The only witnesses to the first were the three women whose acquaintance the reader has just made; the spectators of the second were all the people whom we saw earlier, collecting in the Place de Grève around the pillory and the gibbet.

That crowd had been led to expect some sort of execution from the presence of the four sergeants posted since nine in the morning at each corner of the pillory, doubtless not a hanging, but a whipping, an ear-cropping, in a word, something; that crowd had swollen so rapidly that the four sergeants, hemmed in too closely, had more than once needed to 'compress' it, as the expression then went, by laying about them with their cudgels and backing their horses into it.

This mass of people, well trained in waiting for public executions, were not showing signs of undue impatience. They amused themselves looking at the pillory, a very simple sort of monument consisting of a cube of masonry some ten feet high, hollow inside. A very steep set of rough stone steps, known as the 'ladder' *par excellence*, led to the upper platform, on which could be seen a horizontal wheel of solid oak. The victim was fastened on to this wheel, kneeling, with his arms behind his back. A timber shaft, activated by a capstan concealed inside the small structure, set the wheel rotating, always fixed in a horizontal plane, and thus presented the condemned man's face to each corner of the square in succession. This was termed 'turning' a criminal.

As you can see, the pillory in the Grève was a long way from affording all the entertainment of the pillory in the

Halles. Nothing architectural. Nothing monumental. No roof of iron crosses, no octagonal lantern, no slender columns rising to spread out on the edge of the roof into capitals of acanthus and flowers, no chimerical and monstrous waterspouts, no carved timbers, no delicate sculpture deeply cut into the stone. One had to be content with these four rubble walls and two sandstone backplates, and a mean stone gibbet, meagre and bare, beside it.

It would have been a poor treat for lovers of Gothic architecture. It is true that no one was less interested in monuments than our good onlookers of the Middle Ages, and they cared very little about the beauty of a pillory.

The victim arrived at last, tied to the tail of a cart, and when he had been hoisted on to the platform, when he could be seen from every corner of the square bound with ropes and straps on to the pillory wheel, a prodigious booing, mixed with laughter and cheering, broke out in the square. They had recognized Quasimodo.

It was indeed he. It was a strange reversal. Pilloried in the selfsame square where only the day before he had been greeted, acclaimed, and adjudged Pope and Prince of Fools, in procession with the Duke of Egypt, the King of Tunis, and the Emperor of Galilee. One thing is certain: there was not a mind in the crowd, not even his, in turn hero and victim, which could draw any clear conclusion from this connection. Gringoire and his philosophy were missing from this spectacle.

Soon Michel Noiret, sworn trumpeter of our lord the King, had the churls brought to silence and proclaimed the sentence, in accordance with the ordinance and command of Monsieur the Provost. Then he withdrew behind the cart with his men in their liveried tunics.

Quasimodo, impassive, did not blink. All resistance had been made impossible for him by what was then termed, in the style of the criminal chancellery, 'the vehemence and firmness of his bonds', which means that the thongs and chains were probably cutting into his flesh. That in any case is one tradition of the gaols and galleys which has not been abandoned, and which handcuffs still preciously preserve among us, a civilized, gentle, humane people (hard labour and the guillotine in parentheses).

He had let himself be led and pushed, carried, perched, bound and bound again. All that could be read on his face was the astonishment of a savage or an idiot. He was known to be deaf, it was as though he were also blind.

He was made to kneel on the circular planks, he let them do it. They stripped him of shirt and doublet down to his waist, he let them do it. They trussed him up in a new system of straps and buckles, he let them buckle and bind him. He merely snorted noisily from time to time, like a calf with its head hanging and jolting over the side of the butcher's cart.

'The dolt,' Jehan Frollo du Moulin said to his friend Robin Poussepain (for the two students had followed the victim, as might be expected); 'he doesn't understand any more than a cockchafer shut up in a box!'

The crowd could not control their mirth when they saw Quasimodo's naked hump, his camel's chest, his calloused, shaggy shoulders. While all this merriment was going on, a short sturdy-looking man in the town's livery climbed up on to the platform and stood by the victim. His name ran quickly through the public. It was Maître Pierrat Torterue, sworn torturer of the Châtelet.

He began by setting down in one corner of the pillory a black hourglass, whose upper cup was filled with red sand which filtered through to the lower one. Then he took off his parti-coloured surcoat, and they saw hanging from his right hand a thin, slender whip of long, white, shiny, knotted, plaited thongs, armed with metal hooks. With his left hand he casually rolled up his shirt sleeve round his right arm up to the armpit.

Meanwhile Jehan Frollo raised his fair curly head above the crowd (climbing on Robin Poussepain's shoulders to that end) and cried: 'Come and look, ladies and gentlemen! They are about to give a peremptory flogging to Maître Quasimodo, bell-ringer to my brother, Monsieur the Archdeacon of Josas, a weird bit of oriental architecture, with a dome for a back, and twisted columns for legs!'

And the crowd laughed, especially the children and the girls.

At length the torturer stamped his foot. The wheel began to turn. Quasimodo staggered in his bonds. The stupefaction suddenly depicted on his deformed features provoked renewed gusts of laughter all round.

Suddenly, just as the rotating wheel presented Quasimodo's mountainous back to Maître Pierrat, the latter raised his arm. The slender thongs hissed sharply through the air like a bunch of snakes and came down furiously on the poor wretch's shoulders.

Quasimodo jerked up as if suddenly roused from sleep. He was beginning to understand. He writhed in his bonds; a violent spasm of surprise and pain distorted the muscles of his face; but he uttered not a sigh. He merely turned his head backwards, to the right, then to the left, swinging it about like a bull stung on its flank by a horsefly.

A second blow followed the first, then a third, and another, continously. The wheel did not stop turning nor the blows raining down. Soon the blood spurted, and could be seen trickling in countless streams over the hunchback's black shoulders, and the slender thongs as they whirled slashing through the air sprinkled drops of it over the crowd.

Quasimodo had resumed, at least apparently, his original impassivity. He had first tried silently and with no great outward effort to burst his bonds. They had seen his eye blaze, his muscles tense, his limbs gather themselves, and the straps and chains stretch. The effort was mighty, prodigious, desperate; but the provostry's old restraints held out. They creaked, and that was all. Quasimodo fell back in exhaustion. The stupefaction written on his features gave way to a mood of bitter, profound dejection. He closed his one eye, let his head drop on to his chest and looked as if he were dead.

From then on he did not stir. Nothing could force the slightest movement out of him. Not his blood, which flowed incessantly, nor the blows which fell with redoubled frenzy, nor the fury of the torturer who was working himself up and becoming intoxicated with his work of execution, not the sound of the dreadful thongs whistling through the air shriller than a cloud of mosquitoes.

At last an usher from the Châtelet dressed in black, riding a black horse, who had been stationed beside the ladder since the execution began, stretched out his ebony rod towards the hourglass. The torturer stopped. The wheel stopped. Quasimodo slowly opened his eye.

The flogging was over. The assistants of the sworn torturer washed the victim's bloody shoulders, rubbed them with some ointment or other which at once closed up all the wounds, and threw over his back a kind of yellow wrap shaped like a chasuble. Meanwhile Pierrat Torterue was shaking out over the pavement the thongs of his whip, all reddened and soaked with blood.

All was not over for Quasimodo. He still had to undergo the extra hour in the pillory which Florian Barbedienne had so judiciously added on to the sentence of Messire Robert d'Estouteville; all to the greater glory of the old physiological and psychological wordplay of John Comenius:* *surdus absurdus* [deaf, absurd].

So the hourglass was turned the other way up and the hunchback was left bound to the plank so that justice should be done to the very end.

The common people, especially in the Middle Ages, are to society what the child is to the family. As long as they remain in this state of primal ignorance, moral and intellectual minors, it may be said of them as of the child: 'That age is without pity.'* We have already shown that Quasimodo was generally detested, for more than one good reason, it is true. There was hardly a spectator in this crowd who did not have, or believe he had, cause for complaint against the evil hunchback of Notre-Dame. There had been universal delight at seeing him appear in the pillory; and the harsh punishment which he had just undergone, and the pitiful state in which it had left him, far from moving the populace to pity, had made their hatred more spiteful by sharpening it with an occasion for merriment.

So, once the *vindicte publique* [public vengeance] was satisfied, as the jurists of our own day still put it in their

legal jargon, it was the turn of countless private venge-
ances. Here, as in the Great Hall, it was especially the
women who burst out. They all bore him some grudge,
some for his malice, others for his ugliness. The latter were
the most violent.

'Oh! mask of Antichrist!' said one.

'Broomstick-rider!' cried another.

'What a fine tragic grimace,' yelled a third; 'it would
make you Pope of Fools if today were yesterday!'

'That's good,' went on an old woman. 'That's his pillory
face. When do we see his gallows one?'

'When will you have your great bell stuck on your head
and put a hundred feet under the ground, cursed ringer?'

'Yet it's this devil who rings the Angelus!'

'Oh! you deaf! one-eyed! hunchbacked! monster!'

'There's a face would bring about an abortion better than
any medicines or pharmatics!'

And the two students, Jehan du Moulin and Robin Poussepain, sang at the top of their voices the popular old refrain:

> A halter for the gallows-bird,
> A faggot for this monkey face!

Countless other insults rained down on him, with boos,
and imprecations, and roars of laughter, and now and
then stones.

Quasimodo was deaf, but he could see clearly enough,
and the people's fury was written no less vigorously on their
faces than in their words. Besides, the stones that hit him
explained the laughter.

He stuck it out at first. But gradually his patience, hardened under the torturer's whip, bent and gave way before
all these insect bites. The Asturian bull, unmoved by the
picador's attacks, is irritated by the dogs and banderillas.

He began by looking round the crowd threateningly. But
trussed as he was, his look was quite unable to drive away
these flies biting at his wound. Then he struggled in his
bonds, and his frenzied convulsions made the old pillory
wheel creak on its boards. All that only increased the cat-
calls and jeers.

Then the poor wretch, unable to burst the bonds which chained him like a wild animal, grew quiet again. Only intermittently did a groan of rage swell every cavity in his chest. His face showed no sign of shame or blushes. He was too far from the social state and too near the state of nature to know what shame was. Besides, with such a degree of deformity, is infamy something that can be felt? But anger, hatred, despair slowly covered that hideous face with a cloud that grew darker and darker, full of more and more electricity which burst out as incessant lightning flashes from that Cyclops' eye.

However, this cloud lightened momentarily as a mule passed through the crowd with a priest on its back. At his first distant sight of this mule and this priest the poor victim's face softened, the fury contracting it gave way to a strange smile, full of ineffable gentleness, docility, and affection. As the priest drew nearer this smile became clearer, more distinct, more radiant. It was as though the poor wretch was greeting the arrival of a saviour. However, just as the mule came close enough to the pillory for its rider to recognize the victim, the priest dropped his eyes, abruptly turned back, spurred his mule as though in a hurry to avoid humiliating recriminations and most unwilling to be greeted and recognized by a poor devil in such a situation.

This priest was the archdeacon, Dom Claude Frollo.

The cloud returned blacker than ever to Quasimodo's brow. The smile still mingled with it for a time, but now bitter, dejected, profoundly sad.

Time went by. He had been there for at least an hour and a half, lacerated, abused, mocked without respite, and almost stoned to death.

Suddenly he struggled again in his chains in renewed desperation, which shook the whole framework supporting him, and breaking the silence which he had obstinately kept so far, he cried in a hoarse, furious voice, more like a bark than a human cry, and rising above the noise of jeers: 'A drink!'

This exclamation of distress, far from exciting compassion, was added entertainment for the good Parisian people round the ladder and who, it must be said, taken in the mass and as a multitude, were then scarcely less cruel and less brutalized than that horrible tribe of truands to whom we have already introduced the reader, and who were quite simply the lowest stratum of the people. Not one voice was raised around the unhappy victim but to mock him for his thirst. Certainly at that moment he was even more grotesque and repulsive than pitiable, with his streaming, purple face, his distraught eye, his mouth frothing with rage and pain, his tongue half lolling out. It must be said too that had there been in the throng any charitable soul, any respectable man or woman of the town, who might have felt tempted to bring a glass of water to this wretched creature in distress, there reigned about the infamous steps of the pillory such a prejudice of shame and ignominy as would have repelled the good Samaritan.

After a few minutes Quasimodo looked round the crowd despairingly, and repeated in a still more heart-rending voice: 'Drink!'

And they all laughed.

'Drink this!' cried Robin Poussepain, throwing into his face a sponge that had been dragged through the gutter. 'Here, you deaf rascal! I am in your debt.'

A woman hurled a stone at his head: 'That'll teach you to wake us up at night with your damned ringing!'

'Hey there, lad!' shouted a cripple as he tried hard to hit him with his crutch, 'will you go on casting spells on us from the top of the towers of Notre-Dame?'

'Here's a drinking bowl,' went on another man, hitting him in the chest with a broken pitcher. 'Just going by in front of my wife you made her give birth to a child with two heads!'

'And made my cat have a kitten with six paws,' yelped an old woman, throwing a tile at him.

'Drink!' Quasimodo gasped for the third time.

At that moment he saw the people draw aside. A strangely dressed girl came out from the throng. She was accompanied by a little white goat with gilded horns, and carried a tambourine in her hand.

Quasimodo's eye flashed. It was the gypsy girl whom he had tried to abduct the previous night, an assault for which he dimly felt he was being punished at that very moment; which anyhow was not remotely the case, since he was being punished only for the misfortune of being deaf and having come before a deaf judge. He did not doubt that she too had come for her revenge and would add her blow like everyone else.

In fact he saw her spring quickly up the ladder. Anger and frustration choked him. He would have liked to be able to bring the pillory crashing to the ground, and if the lightning in his eye could have struck her, the gypsy would have been reduced to dust before reaching the platform.

Without a word she approached the victim who twisted about in vain to escape her, and taking a gourd from off her belt, she gently brought it to the poor wretch's parched lips.

Then from that eye, which up to then had been so dry and burnt up, a big tear could be seen slowly rolling down that misshapen face, so long distorted by despair. It was perhaps the first tear the unfortunate creature had ever shed.

Meanwhile he forgot about drinking. The gypsy girl made her little pout of impatience, and pressed the neck of the gourd to Quasimodo's tusky mouth. He drank a long draught. His thirst was burning.

When he had finished, the poor wretch extended his black lips, no doubt to kiss the lovely hand that had just come to his aid. But the girl, perhaps somewhat wary, remembering the violent attempt of the night before, withdrew her hand with the frightened gesture of a child afraid of being bitten by an animal.

Then the poor deaf creature gave her a reproachful look, filled with inexpressible sadness.

It would have been a touching spectacle anywhere, this beautiful girl, fresh, pure, charming and at the same time so weak, coming thus piously to the help of so much misery, deformity, and malice. On a pillory the spectacle was sublime.

All the people in this crowd were themselves struck by it, and began to clap their hands and shout: 'Noël! Noël!'

It was at that moment that the recluse caught sight of the gypsy on the pillory through the window of her Rat-hole and hurled at her the sinister imprecation: 'May you be accursed, daughter of Egypt! accursed! accursed!'

V

THE STORY OF THE CAKE
(CONCLUDED)

LA ESMERALDA went pale, and came down unsteadily from the pillory. The recluse's voice still pursued her. 'Down, down, you go! thief from Egypt, you will be going up there again!'

'The *sachette* is in one of her crazy moods,' the people murmured; and that was as far as it went. For women of that kind were feared, and that made them sacred. In those days people were not keen to attack someone who prayed night and day.

The time had come to take Quasimodo back. They untied him and the crowd dispersed.

Near the Grand-Pont Mahiette, coming away with her two companions, suddenly stopped: 'That reminds me, Eustache! What have you done with the cake?'

'Mother,' said the boy,' while you were talking to that lady in the hole a big dog came and took a bite of my cake. So I ate some too.'

'What, sir,' she went on, 'you've eaten it all up?'

'Mother, it was the dog. I told him not to, he didn't listen, so then I had a bite too, you see!'

'What a terrible child,' said the mother, smiling and scolding at the same time. 'Do you know, Oudarde, he ate all the cherries off the tree in our orchard at Charlerange, all by himself. So his grandfather says he'll be a captain— just let me catch you again, Monsieur Eustache. Come on, you big lion!'

BOOK SEVEN

I

OF THE DANGER OF CONFIDING YOUR
SECRET TO A GOAT

SEVERAL weeks had passed.

It was early March. The sun, which du Bartas,* that classic ancestor of the periphrasis, had not yet named 'the grand duke of candles', was no less radiant and joyful for that. It was one of those spring days so sweet and lovely that all Paris fills the squares and promenades to celebrate as if it were a Sunday. On such bright, warm, tranquil days there is a certain hour especially for admiring the portal of Notre-Dame. That is the moment when the sun, already declining in the west, faces the cathedral almost directly. Its rays, becoming ever more horizontal, slowly withdraw from the pavement of the Place and travel up the perpendicular façade, making the countless carvings stand out roundly from their shadows, while the great central rose-window blazes like a Cyclops' eye afire with reflections from the forge.

It was that time now.

Opposite the tall cathedral stained red by the setting sun, on the stone balcony built over the porch of a handsome Gothic mansion, standing on the corner of the Place and the rue du Parvis, some lovely young girls were laughing and chatting in the most delightful and light-hearted manner. From the length of the veil which fell from the top of their pointed head-dress, all wound about with pearls, down to their heels, from the delicacy of the embroidered chemisette covering their shoulders and revealing, in the attractive fashion of the times, the cleavage of their beautiful maidenly bosoms, from the opulence of their underskirts, even more costly than their topcoats (a wonderful refinement!), from the gauze, the silk, and the velvet lavished on all this, above all from the whiteness of their hands, which betokened leisure and idleness, it was easy to guess that these were rich and noble heiresses. They were in fact Damoiselle Fleur-de-Lys de Gondelaurier and her companions Diane de Christeuil, Amelotte de Montmichel, Colombe de Gaillefontaine, and the little de Champchevrier; all girls of good family, at that moment gathered together at the house of the widowed Dame de Gondelaurier, on account of Monseigneur de Beaujeu and his lady wife, who were due to come to Paris in April to choose the maids of honour to accompany Madame the Dauphine Marguerite, when they went to Picardy to receive her from the hands of the Flemings. Now all the country squires for thirty leagues around were soliciting this favour for their daughters, and a good many of them had already brought or sent the girls to Paris. They had been entrusted by their parents into the discreet and venerable keeping of Madame Aloïse de Gondelaurier, widow of a former master of the King's crossbowmen, now living a retired life with her only daughter in her house on the place du Parvis Notre-Dame in Paris.

The balcony on which these girls were sitting opened on to a room richly hung with fawn-coloured Flanders leather, printed with gold foliage. The parallel beams running across the ceiling amused the eye with hundreds of strange sculptures, painted and gilded. On carved chests splendid enamels gleamed here and there; a boar's head in faience crowned a magnificent dresser, whose two steps proclaimed that the mistress of the house was wife or widow of a knight banneret. At the end, beside a tall chimney breast emblazoned with coats of arms from top to bottom, in a sumptuous red velvet armchair, sat the Dame de Gondelaurier, whose 55 years were written no less clearly on her clothes than on her features. Beside her stood a young man of somewhat proud demeanour, though a little vain and swaggering, one of those good-looking boys on whom all women are agreed, although serious men with some knowledge of physiognomy shrug their shoulders at them. The young cavalier wore the dazzling uniform of captain of archers of the ordinance of the King, much too closely resembling Jupiter's costume, which the reader has already been able to admire in the opening book of this story, for us to inflict on him a second description.

The young ladies were sitting, some inside, some on the balcony, some on cushions of Utrecht velvet with gold corner pieces, others on oaken stools carved with flowers and figures. Each of them held on her knees a section of a great needlework tapestry, on which they were working together, while a goodly length of it trailed over the matting covering the floor.

They were talking together in whispers, with stifled laughter, like any collection of girls with a young man in their midst. The young man, whose presence was enough to excite all this female vanity, seemed for his part to take very little interest in it, and while these lovely girls vied with each other to attract his attention, he seemed mainly occupied in polishing up his belt buckle with his kid glove.

From time to time the old lady addressed him in an undertone, and he replied as best he could with a clumsy and constrained sort of politeness. From the smiles, the little signs of complicity of Madame Aloïse, the winks she directed at her daughter Fleur-de-Lys as she spoke quietly to the captain, it was obvious that the subject at issue was some betrothal already confirmed, some marriage doubtless forthcoming, between the young man and Fleur-de-Lys. And from the officer's embarrassed lack of enthusiasm it was obvious that, at least on his part, love no longer came into it. His whole bearing expressed a feeling of discomfort and tedium which our modern subalterns on garrison duty would render admirably by: 'What a frightful chore!'

The good lady, quite obsessed by her daughter, like any poor mother, did not notice the officer's lack of enthusiasm, and was taking great pains to point out to him in whispers the infinite perfection with which Fleur-de-Lys plied her needle or wound her thread.

'There now, young cousin,' she said, tugging at his sleeve so that she could speak in his ear. 'Look at her! See how she is bending over.'

'Indeed,' the young man answered; and relapsed into his icy and abstracted silence.

A moment later he had to lean over again, and Dame Aloïse said: 'Have you ever seen a more attractive and cheerful figure than your betrothed? Could anyone be more white and fair? Aren't her hands just perfect? And doesn't she move that neck quite charmingly, like a swan? How I envy you sometimes! And how fortunate you are to be a man, you wicked young libertine! Isn't it true that my Fleur-de-Lys is adorably beautiful and you are madly in love with her?'

'Without question,' he answered, his thoughts elsewhere.

'Go over and talk to her, then,' Madame Aloïse said suddenly, pushing him by the shoulder. 'Say something to her. You have become very shy.'

We can assure our readers that shyness did not belong either to the captain's virtues or his failings. He tried, however, to do as he was asked.

'Fair cousin,' he said, approaching Fleur-de-Lys, 'what is the subject of this piece of tapestry you are working on?'

'Fair cousin,' Fleur-de-Lys answered in vexed tones, 'I've told you three times already. It's Neptunus' grotto.'

It was evident that Fleur-de-Lys saw much more clearly than her mother through the captain's cold and abstracted behaviour. He felt the need to make conversation.

'And for whom is all this Neptunery intended?' he asked.

'For the abbey of Saint-Antoine-des-Champs,' said Fleur-de-Lys without looking up.

The captain picked up a corner of the tapestry: 'Who, fair cousin, is this stout soldier blowing a trumpet with all his might?'

'It's Triton,' she answered.

There was still a somewhat sulky tone in Fleur-de-Lys's brief words. The young man realized that it was essential to say something in her ear, some piece of nonsense, gallantry, anything. So he leaned over, but could devise nothing more tender or intimate than these words: 'Why does your mother still wear a kirtle with her coat of arms on it like our grandmothers in Charles VII's time? Do tell her, fair cousin, that it's out of fashion today, and that her blazon of hinge [*gond*] and laurel [*laurier*] embroidered on her dress makes her look like a walking chimneypiece. No one sits on their banner any more like that today, I swear.'

Fleur-de-Lys looked up at him reproachfully with her beautiful eyes: 'Is that all you swear to me?' she said in a low voice.

Meanwhile good Dame Aloïse, delighted to see them leaning together whispering like this, said as she played with the clasps of her book of hours: 'What a touching love scene!'

The captain, feeling more and more ill at ease, fell back on the tapestry: 'That really is a charming piece of work!' he exclaimed.

In that connection Colombe de Gaillefontaine, another beautiful fair-skinned blonde in a high-necked blue damask dress, shyly ventured a remark which she addressed to Fleur-de-Lys in the hope that the handsome captain would reply to it: 'My dear Gondelaurier, have you seen the tapestries in the Hôtel de la Roche-Guyon?'

'Isn't that the hôtel enclosing the garden belonging to the wardrobe-mistress of the Louvre?' asked Diane de Christeuil with a laugh; she had beautiful teeth, and consequently laughed at the slightest thing.

'And where there is that huge old tower from the ancient walls of Paris,' added Amelotte de Montmichel, a pretty, fresh-looking girl with dark curly hair, who had a habit of sighing as the other one laughed, without really knowing why.

'My dear Colombe,' put in Dame Aloïse, 'don't you mean the hôtel which used to belong to Monsieur de Bacqueville in Charles VI's time? There are indeed some quite superb high-warp tapestries there.'

'Charles VI! King Charles VI!' muttered the young captain, twirling his moustache. 'Goodness! What a memory the good lady has for bygone things!'

Madame de Gondelaurier went on: 'Beautiful tapestries, indeed. Work so highly regarded as to be considered unique!'

At that moment Bérangère de Champchevrier, a slender little girl of 7, who was looking down into the square through the trefoil apertures of the balcony, exclaimed: 'Oh! look, godmother Fleur-de-Lys, look at that pretty dancing girl, dancing there on the paving, playing her tambourine in the middle of those common townsfolk!'

They could indeed hear the resonant thrumming of a tambourine.

'Some gypsy girl from Bohemia,' said Fleur-de-Lys, casually turning round towards the square.

'Let's see! let's see!' cried her lively companions; and they all rushed to the edge of the balcony, while Fleur-de-Lys, preoccupied with her fiancé's coolness, slowly followed them and he, relieved by this incident which cut short an uncomfortable conversation, went back inside the apartment with the contented look of a soldier whose duty is over. Yet being on duty with the beautiful Fleur-de-Lys was pleasant and delightful, and so it had formerly appeared to him; but the captain had become gradually bored with it; the prospect of a forthcoming marriage cooled his ardour more every day. Besides, he was a man of changeable moods and, need it be said? of somewhat vulgar tastes. Although of most noble birth, he had in the course of his military service contracted more than one of the common soldiery's habits. He enjoyed the tavern, and what came next. He only felt at ease with coarse language, a soldier's approach to women, easy beauties, and easy conquests. Yet he had received from his family some education and some manners; but he was too young when he had started to roam the country, too young when he had begun garrison duty, and with every day more of the gentlemanly veneer was rubbed away by the harsh pressure of his soldier's baldric. While he still paid her occasional visits, from some remnant of human respect, he felt doubly uncomfortable with Fleur-de-Lys; first, because as a result of scattering his affections in all sorts of places he had kept back very little for her; then because in the midst of so many stiff, starched, and proper lovely ladies he went in constant fear lest his mouth, so accustomed to bad language, might suddenly take the bit between its teeth and run off into the language of the tavern. Imagine what an effect that would have!

For the rest, this all went with great pretensions to elegance, fine clothes, and handsome demeanour. Put it all together as best you may. I am only a historian.

He had been standing there for a few minutes, thinking or unthinking, leaning in silence against the carved mantelpiece, when Fleur-de-Lys, suddenly turning round, spoke to him. After all, the poor girl only sulked at him with great reluctance.

'Fair cousin, didn't you tell us about some little gypsy girl you rescued from the hands of a dozen robbers one night two months ago, when you were on the counterwatch?'

'Yes, I think I did, fair cousin,' said the captain.

'Well,' she went on, 'perhaps it was that gypsy girl dancing down there in the Parvis. Come and see whether you recognize her, fair cousin Phoebus.'

A secret desire for reconciliation came through in this gentle invitation to join her and in her careful use of his name. Captain Phoebus de Châteaupers (for it is he at whom the reader has been looking since the beginning of this chapter) slowly approached the balcony.

'There,' Fleur-de-Lys said, tenderly putting her hand on Phoebus' arm, 'look at that girl dancing there in that circle. Is she your gypsy?'

Phoebus looked and said: 'Yes. I recognize her by her goat.'

'Oh! isn't it a pretty little goat!' said Amelotte, clasping her hands in admiration.

'Are its horns really made of gold?' asked Bérangère.

Without stirring from her chair, Dame Aloïse spoke up: 'Isn't it one of those gypsies who came in last year by the Porte Gibard?'

'Mother dear,' Fleur-de-Lys said gently, 'that gate is called Porte d'Enfer nowadays.'

Mademoiselle de Gondelaurier knew how her mother's outdated way of speaking grated on the captain. Indeed he had begun to snigger as he muttered between his teeth: 'Porte Gibard! Porte Gibard! That's for Charles VI to go through!'

'Godmother,' cried Bérangère, whose constantly roving eyes had suddenly looked up at the top of the towers of Notre-Dame, 'who's that man in black up there?'

All the girls looked up. There was indeed a man leaning on the topmost balustrade of the north tower, looking on to the Grève. He was a priest. They could clearly make out his costume and his face resting on his hands. For the rest he was as motionless as a statue. He was gazing down into the square.

His immobility had something of the hawk who has just discovered a sparrows' nest and is watching it.

'It's the archdeacon of Josas,' said Fleur-de-Lys.

'You must have good eyesight if you can recognize him from here!' remarked the Gaillefontaine girl.

'How he stares at the little dancing girl!' put in Diane de Christeuil.

'The Egyptian girl had better look out!' said Fleur-de-Lys, 'he doesn't like gypsies.'

'It's a real shame that man is looking at her like that,' added Amelotte de Montmichel, 'she's a marvellous dancer.'

'Fair cousin Phoebus,' suddenly said Fleur-de-Lys, 'as you know that little gypsy, signal to her to come up. That will be fun for us.'

'Oh yes!' cried all the girls, clapping their hands.

'But that's silly,' answered Phoebus. 'She has probably forgotten me, and I don't even know her name. However, since that is your wish, mesdemoiselles, I'll try.' And leaning over the balcony balustrade he began shouting: 'Little girl!'

The dancer was not playing her tambourine at that moment. She turned her head in the direction of the call, her shining eyes fixed on Phoebus, and she stopped dead.

'Little girl!' the captain repeated, and beckoned her up.

The girl looked at him again, then she flushed as though a flame had risen in her cheeks, and tucking her tambourine under her arm, she made her way through the astonished onlookers towards the door of the house from which Phoebus had called to her, slowly, unsteadily, and with the troubled look of a bird surrendering to the fascination of a snake.

A moment later the door-hanging was raised and the gypsy girl appeared in the doorway, red-faced, dismayed, out of breath, not daring to take another step.

Bérangère clapped her hands.

Meanwhile the dancer stayed motionless in the doorway. Her appearance had had a singular effect on this group of girls. Undoubtedly a vague, indeterminate desire to please the handsome officer animated them one and all, his splendid uniform was the target for all their coquetry, and ever since he had been there, there had been a certain secret rivalry between them, which they scarcely admitted even to themselves, but which was none the less continually manifested in their gestures and words. Nevertheless, as they all shared more or less the same degree of beauty, they were competing on an equal footing, and each of them might hope to win. The gypsy's arrival abruptly upset that balance. She was of such exceptional beauty that the moment she appeared at the entrance to the apartment she seemed to radiate a kind of light that was all her own. In this enclosed space, in this sombre setting of hangings and panelling, she was incomparably more beautiful and radiant than in a public square. The effect was like that of a torch brought from broad daylight into the shadows. The noble young ladies were dazzled despite themselves. Each of them felt somehow injured in her own beauty. So their battlefront, if we may be permitted the expression, changed immediately, without a single word being spoken between them. But they understood one another wonderfully well. Women understand and respond to each other's instincts more swiftly than men to each other's intellects. A common enemy had just arrived; they all felt it, they all rallied together. One drop of wine is enough to turn a whole glass of water red; to tinge with a certain ill-humour a whole collection of pretty women, it is enough for a still prettier woman to turn up—especially when there is only one man.

Thus the gypsy's reception was extraordinarily glacial. They looked her up and down, then looked at each other, and it had all been said. They had understood one another.

Meanwhile the girl waited for someone to speak to her, so overcome that she did not dare to raise her eyelids.

The captain was the first to break the silence: 'Upon my word,' he said in his fearlessly fatuous voice, 'what a charming creature she is! What do you think of her, fair cousin?'

This remark, which a more delicate admirer would at least have uttered in a low voice, was not of a kind to dispel the feminine jealousies keeping a keen look-out on each other in the gypsy's presence.

Fleur-de-Lys answered the captain with a sugary affectation of disdain: 'Not bad.'

The others were whispering.

At length Madame Aloïse, who was no less jealous than the rest because she was jealous for her daughter, addressed the dancer: 'Come here, little girl.'

'Come here, little girl,' Bérangère repeated with comical dignity, she who did not come up to her waist.

The gypsy approached the noble lady.

'Fair child,' said Phoebus pompously, taking a few steps towards her himself, 'I do not know if I have the supreme good fortune to be recognized by you . . .'

She interrupted him with a smile and a look full of the utmost sweetness: 'Oh! yes,' she said.

'She has a good memory,' observed Fleur-de-Lys.

'Well, now,' Phoebus went on, 'you got away very smartly the other evening. Do I frighten you?'

'Oh! no,' said the gypsy.

In the tone of that 'oh! no', coming after the 'oh! yes', there was some ineffable quality which made Fleur-de-Lys feel hurt.

'In your place you left me, my fair one,' went on the captain, whose tongue was loosened now that he was speaking to a girl from the streets, 'a pretty surly rascal, one-eyed and hunchbacked, the bishop's bell-ringer, as I believe. I'm told he is an archdeacon's bastard and born of the devil. He has some funny name, Ember Days, Palm Sunday, Shrove Tuesday, I don't recall! The name of some big feast-day, anyhow! So he was taking the liberty of abducting

you, as if you were made for beadles! That's a bit much.
What the devil did he want with you then, that screech-owl?
Eh, tell me!'

'I don't know,' she replied.

'Can you imagine such insolence! A bell-ringer abducting
a girl, like a viscount! A peasant poaching noblemen's
game! That's uncommon cheek. Anyhow he paid dearly for
it. Maître Pierrat Torterue is the roughest groom who ever
curried a rogue, and I can tell you, if that gives you any
pleasure, that your bell-ringer's hide got a proper tanning
at his hands.'

'Poor man!' said the gypsy, for whom these words revived
memories of the scene at the pillory.

The captain roared with laughter: '*Corne de bœuf!* your
pity is about as well placed as a feather in a pig's arse! May
I be as pot-bellied as a pope if . . .'

He stopped short: 'I beg your pardon, ladies! I think I
was about to come out with something silly.'

'Fie on you, sir!' said la Gaillefontaine.

'He talks to that creature in her own language!' Fleur-de-
Lys added in an undertone, her resentment growing with
every moment. That resentment did not lessen when she
saw the captain, enchanted by the gypsy and above all with
himself, spin on his heel as he repeated with the crude,
naïve gallantry of a soldier: 'A lovely girl, upon my soul!'

'Dressed pretty much as a savage,' said Diane de Christeuil, showing off her beautiful teeth as she laughed.

That remark was a beam of light for the others. Unable
to carp at her beauty, they pounced on her attire.

'That's true enough, little girl,' said la Montmichel. 'Where
did you learn to run about the streets like that without a
wimple or a gorget?'

'That's a fearfully short skirt,' added la Gaillefontaine.

'My dear,' Fleur-de-Lys continued rather acidly, 'you'll
get yourself picked up by the sergeants of the *douzaine* for
that gilt belt of yours.'

'Little girl, little girl,' la Christeuil went on with an implacable smile, 'if you wore decent sleeves on your arms
they wouldn't get so sunburnt.'

It was truly a sight worthy of a more intelligent spectator than Phoebus to see how these lovely girls, with their poisonous, angry tongues, coiled, slithered, and twisted round the street dancer. They were at once cruel and graceful. They probed and pried with their malicious words into her poor outlandish costume of sequins and gaudy rags. They never stopped their mocking, ironic, humiliating comments. Sarcasms, patronizing benevolence, spiteful glances rained down upon the gypsy. It was like watching those young Roman ladies who would amuse themselves by sticking gold pins into the breast of some beautiful slave girl. It was like a pack of elegant greyhounds circling, with flaring nostrils and blazing eyes, round some poor woodland doe which their master's eye forbids them to devour.

After all, what was a wretched dancer of the public squares to these girls of noble family? They seemed to ignore her presence, and spoke about her, in front of her, directly to her, aloud, as if she were something rather grubby, rather despicable, and rather pretty.

The gypsy was not indifferent to these pinpricks. From time to time a flush of shame, a flash of anger, inflamed her eyes or her cheeks; a disdainful word seemed to tremble on her lips; she made her little grimace of contempt, with which the reader is familiar; but she kept silent. Unmoving, she fixed on Phoebus a look of sad, gentle resignation. There was happiness and affection too in that look. It was as though she was containing herself for fear of being driven away.

As for Phoebus, he laughed and took the gypsy's part with a mixture of impertinence and pity.

'Let them talk, little girl!' he repeated, jangling his spurs, 'no doubt your dress is a bit eccentric and wild; but with a girl as charming as you, what does that matter?'

'Good heavens!' cried fair-haired Gaillefontaine, straightening her swan-like neck and smiling bitterly, 'I see that messieurs the archers of the King's ordinance are easily set alight by beautiful gypsy eyes.'

'Why not?' said Phoebus.

At this reply, casually tossed away by the captain like a stray stone whose fall one does not bother to observe,

Colombe began to laugh, and Diane, and Amelotte, and Fleur-de-Lys, to whose eyes a tear came at the same time.

The gypsy, who had dropped her eyes to the ground at Colombe de Gaillefontaine's words, raised them, radiant with joy and pride, and gazed again at Phoebus. She was very beautiful at that moment.

The old lady, who was watching the scene, felt offended and did not understand.

'Holy Virgin!' she suddenly cried out, 'what's that moving against my legs? Oh! the nasty animal!'

It was the goat that had just arrived in search of its mistress and, as it rushed towards her, had begun by getting its horns caught in the pile of material which the noble lady's clothes heaped up over her feet when she was sitting down.

It caused a diversion. The gypsy, without speaking a word, freed the goat.

'Oh! there's the little goat with golden hooves!' cried Bérangère, jumping for joy.

The gypsy crouched down on her knees, and rested the goat's head against her cheek as it caressed her. It was as though she was asking forgiveness for leaving it like that.

Meanwhile Diane had leaned over into Colombe's ear. 'Eh! Goodness! Why didn't I think of it before? She's the gypsy with the goat. They say she's a witch, and that her goat performs quite miraculous tricks.'

'Very well,' said Colombe, 'the goat must entertain us in its turn and do a miracle for us.'

Diane and Colombe eagerly spoke to the gypsy. 'Little girl, get your goat to do a miracle for us.'

'I don't know what you mean,' the dancer replied.

'A miracle, a piece of magic, witchcraft, you know.'

'I don't know.' And she went back to stroking the pretty creature, saying over and over: 'Djali! Djali!'

At that moment Fleur-de-Lys noticed a little embroidered leather bag hanging from the goat's neck. 'What's that?' she asked the gypsy.

The gypsy raised her large eyes towards her and answered gravely: 'That's my secret.'

'I would very much like to know what your secret is,' thought Fleur-de-Lys.

Meanwhile the good lady had stood up irritably. 'Well then, young gypsy, if neither you nor your goat have any dancing to show us, what are you doing in here?'

The gypsy, without replying, went slowly towards the door. But the nearer she came to it, the slower her steps. An irresistible magnet seemed to be holding her back. Suddenly she turned her eyes, wet with tears, on Phoebus and stopped.

'God's truth!' cried the captain, 'you can't go off like that. Come back and dance something for us. By the way, my lovely, what's your name?'

'La Esmeralda,' said the dancer, without taking her eyes off him.

At this strange name the girls burst out into uncontrollable mirth.

'That,' said Diane, 'is a terrible name for a young lady!'

'You can see,' Amelotte put in, 'that she's an enchantress.'

'My dear,' Dame Aloïse exclaimed solemnly, 'your parents never fished up that name for you from the baptismal font.'

Meanwhile, for the past few minutes, unnoticed, Bérangère had enticed the goat into a corner of the room with a bit of marzipan. In a moment they had become great friends. The inquisitive child had removed the bag from round the goat's neck, opened it and emptied the contents on to the matting. It was an alphabet with each letter separately inscribed on a little boxwood block. No sooner had the toys been spread out on the matting than the child was surprised to see the goat, one of whose 'miracles' this no doubt was, pull out certain letters with its gilded hoof, and gently push them so as to arrange them in a certain order. After a moment this made a word which the goat had seemingly been trained to write, for it composed it with so little hesitation, and Bérangère suddenly cried out, clasping her hands together in wonder:

'Godmother Fleur-de-Lys, come and see what the goat has just done!'

Fleur-de-Lys ran to her and gave a start. The letters arranged on the floor composed the word: 'PHOEBUS'.

'Did the goat write that?' she asked in a changed voice.

'Yes, godmother,' answered Bérangère.

No doubt was possible; the child could not write.

'So that's the secret!' thought Fleur-de-Lys.

Meanwhile the child's cry had brought everyone running, the mother, the girls, the gypsy, and the officer.

The gypsy saw the folly that the goat had just committed. She went red, then pale, and began trembling like a guilty thing in front of the captain, who looked at her with a smile of pleasure and amazement.

'*Phoebus!*' the girls whispered, dumbfounded; 'that's the captain's name!'

'You have a wonderful memory!' Fleur-de-Lys said to the petrified gypsy. Then bursting into sobs: 'Oh!' she stammered in her grief, hiding her face in her lovely hands, 'She's a magician!' And she heard a still more bitter voice tell her in her inmost heart: 'She's a rival!'

She fell down in a faint.

'My daughter! my daughter!' cried the terrified mother. 'Be off with you, you gypsy from hell!'

La Esmeralda picked up the ill-fated letters in an instant, beckoned to Djali, and went out by one door as Fleur-de-Lys was carried out by the other.

Captain Phoebus, left alone, hesitated for a moment between the two doors; then followed the gypsy girl.

II

A PRIEST AND A PHILOSOPHER ARE
TWO DIFFERENT THINGS

THE priest whom the girls had noticed on top of the north tower, leaning out over the square and so intently watching the gypsy's dance, was indeed archdeacon Claude Frollo.

Readers will not have forgotten the mysterious cell that the archdeacon had reserved for himself in that tower. (I am not sure, be it said in passing, that it is not the same into which you can still look today through a little square window, open to the east at a man's height, on the platform from which the towers spring: a squalid chamber, at present bare, empty and dilapidated, the peeling plaster of the walls decorated here and there at the moment with a few sorry engravings of cathedral façades. I assume that this hole is jointly inhabited by bats and spiders, and is consequently the scene of a double war of extermination against flies.)

Every day, an hour before sunset, the archdeacon would climb the tower stairs and shut himself up in this cell, sometimes staying there all night. On that day, just as he arrived outside the low door of the cubby-hole and was inserting in the lock the intricate little key which he always carried with him in the wallet hanging by his side, the sound of tambourine and castanets reached his ear. That sound came from the Place du Parvis. The cell, as already mentioned, had only one window, giving on to the rear of the church. Claude Frollo hurriedly extracted the key, and a moment later was standing on top of the tower in the attitude of sombre meditation in which the young ladies had noticed him.

He stood there grave and motionless, absorbed by one look and one thought. The whole of Paris lay at his feet, with the countless spires of its buildings and its circle of gentle hills on the horizon, with its river winding under the bridges and its people flowing through the streets, with the cloud of smoke rising from its chimneys, with its steep roofs pressing round Notre-Dame in a close-knit chain. But in this whole town the archdeacon was looking at a single point on the ground: the Place du Parvis; in all that crowd, at a single figure: the gypsy girl.

It would be hard to say what kind of look it was, or the source of the flame that sprang from it. The look was fixed, yet turbulent and stormy. And seeing the profound stillness of his whole body, barely stirring at intervals in an involuntary shudder, like a tree in the breeze, his elbows, set more stiffly than the marble on which they rested, the petrified smile contorting his features, one would have said that nothing was still alive in Claude Frollo except his eyes.

The gypsy danced. She whirled her tambourine round on her fingertips, threw it into the air as she danced Provençal sarabands; nimble, light, and joyous, unaware of the fearful look plunging so heavily straight down on to her head.

The crowd was teeming around her; from time to time a man got up in a red and yellow tabard would push them into a circle, then go back and sit on a chair a few feet from the dancer, and take the goat's head in his lap. This man seemed to be the gypsy's companion. From the height where he stood, Claude Frollo could not make out his features.

The moment the archdeacon noticed this unknown man his attention seemed to be divided between the dancer and him, and his expression grew darker and darker. Suddenly he straightened up and his whole body trembled. 'Who is that man?' he muttered. 'I have always seen her alone before!'

Then he dived back under the twisting vault of the spiral staircase and went down again. As he passed by the door of the ringing chamber, which stood ajar, he saw something that struck him; he saw Quasimodo, leaning at an opening of those slate louvres which look like huge venetian blinds, also looking down on to the square. He was rapt in such profound contemplation that he was unaware of his adoptive father passing by. His wild eye bore a singular expression; a look both enchanted and gentle. 'That's odd!' murmured Claude. 'Is it the gypsy he's looking at like that?'

He continued on his way down. After a few minutes the worried archdeacon emerged into the square by the door at the bottom of the tower.

'What's happened to the gypsy?' he said, joining the group of onlookers which had been attracted by the tambourine.

'I don't know,' replied one of his neighbours. 'She has just disappeared. I think she's gone to dance some fandango in that house opposite, where they called her in.'

In the gypsy's place, on the same carpet whose pattern of arabesques had been concealed a moment before by the capricious movements of her dance, all the archdeacon could see was the man in red and yellow who, to earn a few coins in his turn, was parading round the circle, elbows on hips, head thrown back, face scarlet, neck extended, with a chair held between his teeth. On the chair he had tied a cat, lent by a woman nearby, which was swearing with terror.

'By Our Lady!' cried the archdeacon just as the tumbler, sweating profusely, passed him with his pyramid of chair and cat, 'what is Maître Pierre Gringoire doing there?'

The archdeacon's stern voice threw the poor devil into such a commotion that he lost his balance, and his whole edifice with it, so that chair and cat fell pell-mell on the bystanders' heads, amid an inextinguishable chorus of boos.

It is likely that Maître Pierre Gringoire (for it was indeed he) would have had an awkward score to settle with the cat's owner, and all the bruised and scratched faces surrounding him, if he had not hastened to take advantage of the uproar to seek refuge in the church, whither Claude Frollo had beckoned him to follow.

The cathedral was already dark and deserted. The side-aisles were plunged in gloom, and the lamps in the chapels were beginning to twinkle like stars, so black had the vaults above become. Only the great rose-window of the façade, whose innumerable colours were bathed in a horizontal ray from the setting sun, sparkled in the shadows like a pile of diamonds, and reflected its dazzling spectrum against the far end of the nave.

When they had taken a few steps, Dom Claude leaned against a pillar and gazed at Gringoire. It was not the sort of look that Gringoire had been fearing, ashamed as he was of having been caught unawares in this clownish costume by a grave and learned person. There was nothing mocking or ironic in the priest's glance; it was serious, calm and piercing. The archdeacon was the first to break the silence.

'Come now, Maître Pierre. You are going to explain a lot of things to me. And first of all, how is it that we haven't seen you for nearly two months now, and then find you again in the street, handsomely turned out, to be sure—half yellow and half red like a Caudebec apple?'

'Messire,' said Gringoire piteously, 'it is indeed an amazing rig and makes me feel more foolish than a cat with a calabash jammed on its head. It's quite wrong, I know, to expose the sergeants of the watch to the risk of thrashing beneath this tabard the humerus of a Pythagorean philosopher. But it can't be helped, my reverend master. I blame my old jerkin which abandoned me in the most cowardly way at the start of winter, on the pretext that it was falling to shreds and needed a rest in the ragman's basket. Civilization has not yet reached the point where one can go about naked, as old Diogenes wanted. On top of that a very cold wind was blowing, and January is not the month for a successful attempt at getting mankind to take this new step forward. This tabard was on offer. I took it, and left off my old black smock, which for a hermetist like me was not at all hermetically closed. So here I am then in actor's garb, like Saint Genestus.* What could I do? It is an eclipse. But Apollo himself served as herdsman to Admetus.'

'That's a fine trade you are following!' the archdeacon put in.

'I agree, master, that it's better to philosophize and poeticize, blow the flame in the furnace or receive it from heaven, than to carry cats in triumph. So when you addressed me I felt as silly as an ass in front of a roasting-jack. But what's to be done, messire? One has got to stay alive, and the finest Alexandrines don't appease hunger like a piece of Brie cheese. Well, I composed that famous epithalamium for Madame Marguerite of Flanders, as you know, and the Town won't pay me, on the pretext that it was not

of the highest quality, as if anyone could turn out a So-
phocles tragedy for 4 crowns. So I was going to starve to
death. Fortunately I found that my jaws were pretty strong,
and I told the said jaws: "Perform some feats of strength
and balance, provide your own food. *Ale te ipsum.*" A pack
of beggars, who have become good friends of mine, taught
me twenty kinds of Herculean tricks, and now every evening I give my teeth the bread they have earned during the
day by the sweat of my brow. After all, *concedo*, I grant that
it's a poor way to use my intellectual faculties, and that man
was not made to spend his life banging a tambourine and
biting chairs. But, reverend master, it's not enough to
spend your life, you've got to earn it.'

Dom Claude listened in silence. Suddenly his deep-set
eyes took on such a shrewdly penetrating expression that
Gringoire felt, so to speak, probed in his innermost soul by
that look.

'Very good, Maître Pierre, but how does it come about
that you are now in the company of that dancer from Egypt?'

'My goodness!' said Gringoire, 'because she is my wife
and I am her husband.'

The priest's eyes blazed. 'Could you have done such a
thing, you wretch?' he cried, furiously seizing Gringoire by
the arm; 'could you have been so forsaken by God as to lay
hands on that girl?'

'By my share of paradise, monseigneur,' Gringoire replied, trembling in every limb, 'I swear to you that I have
never touched her, if that's what is worrying you.'

'And what is this talk, then, of husband and wife?' said
the priest.

Gringoire hastened to give him as succinct an account as
possible of all that the reader already knows, his adventure
in the Court of Miracles and his marriage ceremony with
the broken pitcher. It seems that this marriage ceremony
had so far had no result, and that every evening the gypsy
girl found some way of tricking him out of a wedding night
as she had on that first day. 'It's disappointing,' he said in
conclusion, 'but it's due to the fact that I was unlucky
enough to marry a virgin.'

'What do you mean?' asked the archdeacon, who had gradually calmed down during this account.

'It's rather hard to explain,' the poet answered. 'It's a superstition. My wife, according to what I was told by an old ruffian whom our people call the Duke of Egypt, my wife is a foundling, or a stray, which comes to the same thing. She wears an amulet round her neck which, they maintain, will one day enable her to meet her parents, but which would lose its virtue if the girl lost hers. It follows that we have both remained very virtuous.'

'So,' Claude put in, his brow steadily clearing, 'it's your belief, Maître Pierre, that this creature has never been approached by a man?'

'What do you expect a man to do with a superstition, Dom Claude? She's got it into her head. I reckon that it's rare, right enough, that anyone should stay as fiercely pure as a nun in the midst of those gypsy girls who are so easily tamed. But she's got three means of protection: the Duke of Egypt, who has taken her under his wing, perhaps counting on selling her to some lord abbot; the whole tribe, who hold her in singular veneration, like a Virgin Mary; and a certain dainty dagger which the young spark always keeps somewhere on her person, in spite of the Provost's ordinances, and which you can bring leaping into her hands just by squeezing her waist. She's a real wasp, I can tell you!'

The archdeacon questioned Gringoire closely.

La Esmeralda, in Gringoire's judgement, was a delightful, inoffensive creature, pretty apart from a way of pouting peculiar to herself; an innocent, passionate girl, ignorant of everything and enthusiastic about everything; not yet aware of the difference between men and women, even in her dreams; made like that; crazy about dancing, noise, open air; a sort of bee-woman, with invisible wings on her feet, living in a whirlwind. She owed that nature to the wandering life she had always led. Gringoire had managed to find out that when she was still very small she had travelled through Spain and Catalonia and as far as Sicily; he thought she had been taken, in the Zingari caravan of which she was part, to the kingdom of Algiers, a country situated in

Achaea, the said Achaea bordering on one side Lesser Albania and Greece, and on the other the Sicilian sea, which is the way to Constantinople. The Bohemians, said Gringoire, were vassals of the King of Algiers, in his capacity as head of the nation of white Moors. What was certain was that la Esmeralda had come to France, still very young, by way of Hungary. From all these countries the girl had brought back scraps of weird jargons, songs, and outlandish ideas, which made her way of speaking as motley as her costume, half Parisian, half African. For the rest, the people in the districts she frequented loved her for her gaiety, her kindness, her lively ways, her dancing and singing. In the whole town she believed herself to be disliked by only two persons, about whom she often talked with dread: the *sachette* of the Tour-Roland, a nasty old recluse who bore some unknown grudge against gypsy women, and cursed the poor dancer whenever she went by her window; and a priest who never encountered her without looking and speaking to her in a way that frightened her. This last detail much disturbed the archdeacon, though Gringoire took no great notice of this reaction; two months had been quite enough to make the carefree poet forget the peculiar details of the evening when he had first met the gypsy girl, and the archdeacon's presence on that occasion. Otherwise the little dancer feared nothing; she did not tell fortunes, which kept her safe from the charges of sorcery so frequently brought against gypsy women. And then Gringoire was like a brother to her, if not like a husband. All in all the philosopher put up very patiently with this sort of platonic marriage. It meant that he always had a bed and some bread. Every morning he left the truands' quarters, usually with the gypsy girl, he helped her collect the harvest of *targes* and *petits-blancs* at the street crossings; every evening he went home with her under the same roof, let her bolt herself in her little room, and slept the sleep of the just. A very pleasant existence, all things considered, he said, and very conducive to musing. And then, in his soul and conscience, the philosopher was not too sure that he was madly in love with the gypsy girl. He was almost as fond of the goat. It was a delightful animal, gentle, intelligent, witty, a performing goat. Nothing was more common in the Middle Ages than those performing animals which provoked the greatest wonder and frequently led their trainers to the stake. However, the sorceries of the golden-hooved goat were quite innocent bits of mischief. Gringoire explained them to the archdeacon, who seemed keenly interested in these details. In most cases it was enough to present the tambourine to the goat in such and such a way to obtain from it the desired trick. The goat had been trained to do this by the gypsy, who had such a rare gift for these delicate tasks that two months had sufficed for her to teach the goat to write the word *Phoebus* with movable letters.

'*Phoebus!*' said the priest; 'why *Phoebus?*'

'I don't know,' answered Gringoire. 'Perhaps it's a word which she thinks is endowed with some magic and secret virtue. She often repeats it to herself in an undertone when she thinks she is alone.'

'Are you sure,' Claude continued with his penetrating gaze, 'that it's only a word and not a name?'

'Whose name?' said the poet.

'How do I know?' said the priest.

'This is what I imagine, messire. These gypsies are a bit like the Zoroastrians and worship the sun. Hence Phoebus.'

'That doesn't seem as clear to me as it does to you, Maître Pierre.'

'Anyhow, it doesn't matter to me. Let her mumble her Phoebus as much as she likes. What is sure is that Djali is already almost as fond of me as of her.'

'Who is this Djali?'

'That's the goat.'

The archdeacon put his chin in his hand, and seemed to be reflecting for a moment. Suddenly he turned round towards Gringoire. 'And you swear you have never touched her?'

'Who?' said Gringoire. 'The goat?'

'No, the woman.'

'My wife? I swear I haven't.'

'And you are often alone with her?'

'Every evening, for a good hour.'

Dom Claude frowned. 'Oh! oh! *solus cum sola non cogita-buntur orare Pater noster* [a man and a woman alone together will not be assumed to be saying the Our Father].'

'Upon my soul, I could say the *Pater* and the *Ave Maria*, and the *Credo in Deum omnipotentem* [I believe in God the Father almighty] without her taking any more notice of me than a hen of a church.'

'Swear on your mother's womb,' the archdeacon repeated violently, 'that you haven't laid so much as a finger on that creature.'

'I'd swear it on my father's head too, for the two things are connected in more than one way. But, reverend master, allow me a question in my turn.'

'Speak on, sir.'

'What's all this to you?'

The archdeacon's pale face blushed as red as a young girl's cheek. He remained for a moment without answering. Then, in obvious embarrassment: 'Listen, Maître Pierre Gringoire. You are not damned yet, as far as I know. I take an interest in you and wish you well. Now, the slightest contact with that devil's gypsy would put you in thrall to Satan. You know that it is always the body that ruins the soul. Woe betide you if you approach that woman! That's all.'

'I tried once,' said Gringoire, scratching his ear. 'It was on the first day, but I got stung.'

'You had that much effrontery, Maître Pierre?' And the priest's brow clouded over again.

'Another time,' the poet continued, smiling, 'I looked through her keyhole before going to bed, and, believe me, I saw the most delightful lady in a shift that ever made a bedframe creak beneath her naked foot.'

'Go to the devil!' cried the priest with a terrible look, and pushing the astonished Gringoire by the shoulders, he strode away under the darkest arcades of the cathedral.

III

THE BELLS

SINCE the morning in the pillory, it had seemed to the people living near Notre-Dame that they could detect a considerable cooling-off in Quasimodo's ardour for ringing the bells. Previously they had rung out for any and every occasion, long aubades lasting from Prime to Compline, peals from the belfry for a High Mass, rich scales up and down the smaller bells for a wedding or a christening, mingling in the air like an embroidery of all kinds of delightful sounds. The old church, all vibrating and resonant, lived in a perpetual rejoicing of bells. One felt there the abiding presence of a spirit of noise and caprice singing out through all those bronze mouths. Now that spirit seemed to have disappeared; the cathedral seemed dreary and only too glad to be silent. The bells rang for festivals and funerals, starkly and without frills, what the ritual demanded and no more. Of the twin sounds that a church makes, the organ within, the bells without, only the organ was left. Yet Quasimodo was still there. What then had come over him? Was it that the shame and despair of the pillory still lingered in the depths of his heart, that the lash of the torturer's whip still endlessly reverberated in his soul, that his misery at such treatment had extinguished every spark within him, even his passion for the bells? Or was it that Marie had a rival in the heart of the bell-ringer of Notre-Dame, and that the great bell and her fourteen sisters were being neglected for something more beautiful and worthy of love?

It happened that in that year of grace 1482 the Annunciation fell on a Tuesday, 25 March. On that day the air was so pure and light that Quasimodo felt some renewal of his affection for his bells. So he climbed up inside the north tower, while down below the beadle was opening wide the church doors, which at that time were huge panels of stout wood covered in leather, bordered with gilded studs and set in a framework of 'most skilfully worked' sculptures.

Once up in the lofty cage of the bell chamber, Quasimodo, sadly shaking his head, contemplated for a time the six bells there, as if bemoaning some alien intruder which had interposed itself in his heart between them and himself. But once he had set them swinging, when he felt this cluster of bells move beneath his hand, when he saw, for he could not hear, the palpitating octave go up and down on this scale of sound like a bird hopping from branch to branch, when the musical devil, that demon who shakes a dazzling bunch of *stretti*, trills, and arpeggios, had taken possession of the poor deaf creature, then he became happy again, he forgot everything, and his swelling heart brought a beam to his face.

He went to and fro, clapping his hands, running from one rope to another, he urged on the six singers by voice and gesture, like the conductor of an orchestra spurring on intelligent virtuosi.

'Go on,' he said,' go on, Gabrielle. Pour all your sound out into the square. It's a feast day today.—Thibauld, no slacking. You're slowing down. Come on, come on then! Have you gone rusty, you lazybones?—That's fine! Quick! quick! don't let them see the clapper. Make them all as deaf as I am. That's it, Thibauld, splendid! Guillaume! Guillaume! you're the biggest, and Pasquier's the smallest, and Pasquier's doing best. I wager that those who are listening can hear him better than you.—Good! good! Gabrielle, loud, louder!—Hey! what are you doing up there, Sparrows? I can't see you making the slightest noise—what are those bronze mouths that look as though they are yawning when it's singing that's wanted? Come on, to work! It's the Annunciation. It's a lovely sunny day. We want a lovely peal.—Poor Guillaume! you're quite out of breath, old fellow!'

He was wholly absorbed in spurring on his bells, all six of them leaping as hard as they could go and shaking their gleaming rumps like a noisy team of Spanish mules goaded now and then by the driver's rude yells.

Suddenly, looking down between the broad scales of slate which cover the perpendicular wall of the bell tower up to a certain height, he saw in the square a girl in a strange outfit stop, spread out on the ground a carpet on which a little goat came to stand, and a group of onlookers collecting all around. This sight abruptly changed his train of thought, and congealed the flow of his musical enthusiasm as a puff of wind congeals molten resin. He stopped still, turned his back on the bells, and squatted behind the slate canopy, gazing at the dancer in that dreamy, tender, and gentle way which had once before astonished the archdeacon. Meanwhile the bells, now forgotten, suddenly all fell silent at the same time, to the great disappointment of the lovers of bell-ringing, who were listening to the peal in all good faith from the Pont-au-Change, and went away as bewildered as a dog who has been shown a bone and given a stone.

IV

'ANAΓKH

IT so happened that one fine morning in that same month of March, I think it was Saturday the 29th, Saint Eustache's day,* our young student friend, Jehan Frollo du Moulin, noticed as he got dressed that his breeches, which contained his purse, emitted no clink of metal. 'Poor purse!' he said, pulling it out from his fob. 'What? not the least little *parisis*? How cruelly dice, pots of beer, and Venus have gutted you! Look at you now, all empty, wrinkled, and limp! You look like a Fury's breast! I ask you, messer Cicero and messer Seneca, whose dog-eared works I see scattered over the floor, what is the use of my knowing better than a director of the mint or a Jew on the Pont-aux-Changeurs that a gold *écu* with a crown on it is worth 35 *unzains* of 25 *sols* 8 *deniers parisis* each, and that an *écu* with a crescent is worth 36 *unzains* of 26 *sols* and 6 *deniers tournois* apiece if I don't have a wretched black *liard* to risk on the double six! Oh! consul Cicero! That's not the sort of calamity you can get out of with periphrases like *quemadmodum* [in such a way] or *verum enim vero* [but in point of fact].'

He dressed gloomily. A thought had occurred to him as he was lacing up his boots, but at first he rejected it; however, it came again, and he put his waistcoat on back to front, an obvious sign of violent inner struggle. Finally he threw his cap roughly to the ground and exclaimed: 'Too bad! Come of it what may, I'll go to my brother. I'll get a sermon, but I'll get an *écu* too.'

Then he hurried to put on his tabard with its padded shoulders, picked up his cap, and went out like a man in despair.

He went down the rue de la Harpe towards the Cité. As he passed by the rue de la Huchette, the smell from those wonderful spits ceaselessly turning there came to tickle his olfactory organs, and he looked lovingly at the Cyclopean

roaster which one day wrung from the Franciscan Calatagi-
rone the pathetic exclamation: *'Veramente, queste rotisserie
sono stupende!'* [Truly, these roasters are something amazing!]
But Jehan did not have the price of a meal, and sighing
deeply plunged beneath the porch of the Petit Châtelet, a
huge double clover-leaf of massive towers guarding the
entrance to the Cité.

He did not even take a moment as he passed by to throw
a stone, as was customary, at the wretched statue of that
Périnet Leclerc who had delivered up to the English the
Paris of Charles VI, a crime which his effigy, the face
crushed with stones and soiled with mud, expiated for three
centuries at the corner of the rue de la Harpe and the rue
de Bussy, as if on an eternal pillory.

Crossing the Petit-Pont, and striding over the rue Neuve-
Sainte-Geneviève, Jehan de Molendino found himself in
front of Notre-Dame. Then he was seized again with indecision, and spent a few minutes walking round the statue
of Monsieur Legris, repeating to himself in anguish: 'The
sermon is certain, the *écu* is doubtful.'

He stopped a beadle who was coming from the cloister:
'Where is the archdeacon of Josas?'

'I think he's in his hiding-place in the tower,' said the
beadle, 'and I don't advise you to disturb him, unless you
have come on behalf of someone like the Pope or the King.'

Jehan clapped his hands: 'The devil! here's a marvellous
chance to see the famous little cubby-hole of sorcery!'

This reflection decided him, and he plunged resolutely
under the little black doorway and began climbing the
Saint-Gilles spiral staircase leading to the upper floors of
the tower. 'I'm going to see it!' he said to himself on the
way. 'By the *corbignolles* of the Blessed Virgin! There must
be something really curious about this cell that my reverend
brother hides like his pudendum! They say that he lights
up the fires of hell in there and cooks the philosophers'
stone on a high flame. *Bédieu!* The philosophers' stone
means no more to me than a pebble, and I'd rather find an
omelette of Easter egg and bacon on his furnace than the
biggest philosophers' stone in the world!'

When he reached the gallery of colonnettes, he stopped for a moment to get his breath, and cursed the interminable stairs by I don't know how many millions of cartloads of devils; then went on climbing, through the narrow door in the north tower, nowadays closed to the public. A few moments after passing the bell cage, he came upon a little landing, inserted into a recess in the side wall, and under the vault a low, pointed door. A loophole pierced in the circular staircase wall opposite enabled him to see its huge lock and mighty iron frame. Anyone today curious to visit this door will recognize it from the following inscription, carved in white letters on the black wall: 'I ADORE CORALIE 1823. SIGNED UGÈNE.'* The word 'signed' is in the text.

'Whew!' said the student; 'this must be it.'

The key was in the lock. The door was right beside him. He gave it a gentle push and stuck his head through the opening.

The reader will surely be familiar with the admirable works of Rembrandt, that Shakespeare of painting. Among so many wonderful engravings, there is one etching in particular representing, so it is supposed, Doctor Faustus, which any viewer must find quite dazzling. It shows a gloomy cell. In the middle is a table laden with hideous objects—skulls, spheres, alembics, compasses, hieroglyphic parchments. The doctor is in front of this table, wearing his heavy greatcoat and his fur cap pulled down over his forehead. Only his upper half can be seen. He has half risen from his immense armchair, his clenched fists are resting on the table and he is gazing, curious and terrified, at a great luminous circle, composed of magic letters, shining on the far wall, like the solar spectrum in a camera obscura. This cabalistic sun seems to tremble as one looks and fills the pale cell with its mysterious rays. It is at once horrible and beautiful.

Something rather similar to Faust's cell presented itself to Jehan's eyes when he ventured to put his head round the half-open door. There was the same gloomy, dimly lit recess. There too was a big armchair and a big table, compasses, alembics, animal skeletons hanging from the ceiling,

a sphere rolling on the floor, horse-heads all mixed up with
jars containing quivering gold leaves, skulls lying on sheets
of vellum, covered with a medley of figures and letters,
thick manuscripts lying open, piled up, heedless of the
brittle corners of the parchment, in short all the rubbish of
science, and lying everywhere on this jumble a layer of dust
and cobwebs; but there was no luminous circle of letters,
no doctor in ecstasy gazing at the flaming vision as an eagle
looks at the sun.

The cell was not, however, deserted. A man was sitting
in the armchair, bent over the table. Jehan, on whom his
back was turned, could see only his shoulders and the back
of his skull; but he had no difficulty recognizing that bald
head on which nature had imposed an eternal tonsure, as
if wanting to mark by some outward symbol the archdeacon's irresistible clerical vocation.

Jehan then recognized his brother. But the door had
opened so quietly that nothing had made Dom Claude
aware of his presence. The inquisitive student took advantage of this to spend a few minutes examining the cell at his
leisure. A large furnace, which he had not noticed at first,
stood on the left of the chair, under the window. The ray
of light admitted by this aperture filtered through a circular
spider's web, which tastefully inscribed its delicate rose-
tracery in the pointed window arch, and at its centre the
insect architect sat motionless like the hub of this lacy
wheel. On the furnace were heaped in disorder all kinds of
vessels, stone flasks, glass retorts, charcoal matrasses. Jehan
observed with a sigh that there was no saucepan. 'The pots
and pans aren't too fresh!' he thought.

For the rest there was no fire in the furnace, and indeed
it looked as though none had been lit for a long time. A
glass mask, which Jehan noticed among the alchemical
utensils, and which served no doubt to protect the archdeacon's face while he was concocting some fearsome substance, lay in a corner, covered in dust, as though forgotten.
Beside it lay an equally dusty pair of bellows, its upper leaf
bearing the legend, incrusted in brass letters: SPIRA, SPERA
[breathe, hope].

There were a great many other legends written on the walls, according to the practice of the hermetics; some traced in ink, others incised with a metal point. For the rest, Gothic, Hebrew, Greek, and Roman letters all jumbled together, inscriptions overflowing haphazardly, some on top of others, the most recent obliterating the older ones, all tangled together like branches of undergrowth or pikes in a mêlée. It was, in fact, a rather confused mêlée of all the philosophies, daydreams, wisdoms of mankind. Here and there one shone out above the others like a flag among spearheads. Most of the time it was some brief Latin or Greek motto, such as the Middle Ages were so good at formulating: *unde? inde?* [whence? thence?]; *Homo homini monstrum* [man is a monster for man]; *Astra, castra, nomen, numen* [stars, camp, name, divinity]; μέγα βιβλίον, μέγα κακόν [great book, great evil]; *sapere aude* [dare to know]; *Flat ubi vult* [it bloweth where it listeth], etc.; sometimes a word devoid of any obvious sense: ἀναγχοφαγία, perhaps concealing some bitter allusion to the regime of the cloister; sometimes a simple maxim of clerical discipline formulated as a regular hexameter: *Cœlestium dominum, terrestrem dicito domnum* [call the Lord of Heaven 'dominus', of earth 'domnus']. There were also, *passim*, Hebrew scribbles, of which Jehan, who had very little Greek, understood nothing, and it was all crossed, here, there, and everywhere by stars, human or animal figures, and intersecting triangles, which went quite a long way to making the wall of the cell, covered in scrawls, look like a sheet of paper over which a monkey had been tracing a pen full of ink.

In any case, the chamber as a whole gave a general impression of neglect and decay; and the poor state of the utensils led one to suppose that its master had for quite some time been distracted from his work by other concerns.

That master, however, bent over an enormous manuscript, decorated with strange paintings, seemed tormented by some idea which constantly intruded on his meditations. At least that is how Jehan judged it as he heard him cry, with the reflective pauses of a visionary dreaming aloud:

'Yes, Manou* said and Zoroaster taught, the sun is born of fire, the moon born of the sun. Fire is the soul of the great whole. Its elemental atoms pour and stream continuously over the world in infinite currents. At the points where the currents intersect in the heavens, they produce light; at their points of intersection within the earth they produce gold. Light, gold, the same thing. Fire in its concrete state—the difference between the visible and the palpable, the fluid and the solid, for the same substance, from steam to ice, that's all. Those aren't just dreams—it is the general law of nature. But how are we to extract from science the secret of that general law? Why! This light bathing my head is gold! These same atoms dilated according to a certain law only have to be condensed according to a certain other law! How can it be done? Some have had the idea of burying a sunbeam. Averroes—yes, it is Averroes—Averroes buried one beneath the first pillar on the left of the sanctuary of the Koran, in the Grand Mosque at Cordoba; but the vault can only be opened to see if the operation succeeded in eight thousand years' time.'

'Devil!' said Jehan to himself, 'that's a long time to wait for a gold *écu*!'

'Others have thought,' the archdeacon continued pensively, 'that it would be better to work with a beam from Sirius. But it's very difficult to get this beam pure, because of the simultaneous presence of the other stars which get mixed up in it. Flamel considers that it is easier to work on terrestrial fire. Flamel! what a predestined name. *Flamma*! Yes, fire. That's all. The diamond is in the coal, gold is in fire,—but how to extract it? Magistri asserts that there are certain women's names so sweet and so mysterious that it is enough to pronounce them during the operation . . . Let's read what Manou says about it: "Where women are honoured, the divinities are overjoyed; where they are despised, it is no use praying to God. . . . A woman's mouth is constantly pure; it is running water, a sunbeam. . . . A woman's name must be pleasing, sweet, imaginative; it must end in long vowels, and resemble words of benediction." '

'Yes, the sage is right indeed. Maria, Sophia, Esmer . . . Damnation! always that thought!'

And he closed the book violently.

He passed his hand over his brow as if to drive away the idea obsessing him. Then from the table he took a nail and a small hammer with cabalistic letters curiously painted on the shaft.

'For some time now,' he said with a bitter smile,' all my experiments have failed! I am possessed by this fixed idea, and it is making my brain wither like dried clover. I haven't even been able to discover the secret of Cassiodorus, whose lamp burned without wick or oil. Yet that's simple enough!'

'Plague on it!' Jehan muttered in his beard.

' . . . so a single wretched thought,' the priest went on, 'is enough to make a man feeble and mad! Oh! how Claude Pernelle would laugh at me, she who couldn't divert Nicolas Flamel for a moment from pursuing the great work! Why! I hold in my hand Ezekiel's* magic hammer! With every blow that the fearsome rabbi struck on this nail with this hammer, in the depths of his cell, one of his enemies whom he had condemned, even if he were two thousand leagues away, was driven down a cubit into the earth which swallowed him up. The King of France himself, for knocking thoughtlessly one evening on the thaumaturge's door, sank up to his knees into his own Paris pavement—that happened less than three hundred years ago. Very well! I have the hammer and the nail, and those implements are no more fearsome in my hands than a mallet in the hands of a cutler—yet all that is needed is to find the magic word that Ezekiel pronounced when he hit the nail.'

'Fiddlesticks!' thought Jehan.

'Come then, let's try,' the archdeacon went on eagerly. 'If I succeed I'll see the blue spark fly from the head of the nail. Emen-hetan! Emen-hetan!—that's not it. Sigeani! Sigeani!—may this nail open the grave to anyone bearing the name Phoebus! Curse it! Always, again, endlessly the same idea!'

And he angrily threw away the hammer. Then he slumped so low over the chair and table that Jehan could not see him behind the huge chair-back. For a few minutes all he could see was his hand clenched convulsively on a book. Suddenly Dom Claude rose, took a compass and silently incised on the wall in capital letters the Greek word: 'ANÁΓKH.

'My brother is off his head,' Jehan said to himself, 'it would have been much simpler to write *Fatum*. Everyone is not obliged to know Greek.'

The archdeacon came back to sit in his chair, and laid his head in his hands like a sick man whose brow feels heavy and burning.

The student observed his brother in surprise. He did not know, he who wore his heart on his sleeve, who observed no other law in the world than the good law of nature, who let his passions flow according to his inclinations, and in whom the lake of violent emotions was always dry, from the many new ways he drained it every morning, he did not know how furiously the sea of human passions seethes and boils when it is denied any outlet, how it piles up, swells, overflows, how it scours the heart, bursts out in inward sobs and silent convulsions, until it has breached its dykes and burst its bed. The austere, icy exterior of Claude Frollo, that chill surface of rugged, inaccessible virtue, had always deceived Jehan. The merry student had never thought that there is boiling lava raging deep beneath the snow-capped peak of Etna.

We do not know if he suddenly realized all these ideas, but featherbrained as he was, he understood that he had seen what he ought not to have seen, that he had just surprised his elder brother's soul in one of its most secret attitudes, and that Claude must never suspect this. Seeing that the archdeacon had relapsed into his former immobility, he withdrew his head very quietly and made a noise as of footsteps behind the door, like someone coming and announcing his arrival.

'Come in!' cried the archdeacon from inside the cell, 'I was expecting you. I left the key in the door on purpose. Come in, Maître Jacques.'

The student boldly entered. The archdeacon, very embarrassed by such a visit in such a place, started in his chair.

'What! It's you, Jehan?'

'It's still a J,' said the cheeky, red-faced, cheerful student.

Dom Claude's face had assumed its stern expression again. 'What have you come here for?'

'Brother,' answered the student, striving to achieve a decent, piteous, and modest demeanour, turning his cap round in his hands with an air of innocence,' I was coming to ask you . . .'

'What?'

'For a much-needed moral lesson.' Jehan did not dare add aloud: 'And a little money which I need even more.' That last part of his sentence remained unspoken.

'Sir,' said the archdeacon coldly,' I am much displeased with you.'

'Alas!' sighed the student.

Dom Claude turned his chair through a quarter of a circle, and stared hard at Jehan: 'I am very glad to see you.'

It was a daunting exordium. Jehan prepared for a rude clash.

'Jehan, every day people bring me complaints about you. What is this fight you had which left a young Vicomte Albert de Ramonchamp all bruised from your drubbing?'

'Oh!' said Jehan, 'that was nothing much! A nasty little page amusing himself spattering students by riding his horse through the mire!'

'What about this Mahiet Fargel,' went on the archdeacon, 'whose gown you tore? *Tunicam dechiraverunt* says the complaint.'

'Oh that! a rotten little Montaigu cappette,* wasn't it?'

'The complaint says *tunicam* not *cappettam*. Don't you know Latin?'

Jehan did not answer.

'Yes!' the priest went on, shaking his head, 'that's what learning and letters have come to now. The Latin tongue is scarcely understood, Syriac unknown, Greek so detested that it's not accounted ignorance when the most learned scholars skip a Greek word without reading it, and people say: "*Graecum est, non legitur* [It is Greek, it is not to be read]." '

The student resolutely raised his eyes: 'Brother, would you like me to explain to you in good French parlance that Greek word written on the wall over there?'

'Which word?'

' 'ANÁΓKH.'

The archdeacon's sallow cheeks flushed slightly, like a puff of smoke outwardly proclaiming the secret commotions of a volcano. The student hardly noticed,

'All right, Jehan,' the elder brother managed with difficulty to stammer, 'what does that word mean?'

'Fatality.'

Dom Claude paled again, and the student casually went on: 'And that word underneath, incised with the same hand, 'Aναγνεία means "impurity". You see, we know our Greek.'

The archdeacon remained silent. This Greek lesson had made him thoughtful. Young Jehan, who had all the acuteness of a spoilt child, judged this a favourable moment for venturing his request. So he adopted an extremely gentle tone, and began: 'Good brother, do you dislike me so much that you scowl at me for a few slaps and punches dealt out in fair fight to some boys and brats, *quibusdam marmosetis*? You see, good brother Claude, we know our Latin.'

But all this wheedling hypocrisy did not produce its usual effect on the stern big brother. Cerberus would not nibble at the honey cake. Not a wrinkle on the archdeacon's brow was smoothed away.

'What are you trying to say?' he asked drily.

'Very well! I'll come to the point now!' Jehan boldly replied. 'I need money.'

At this shameless declaration the archdeacon's features took on an entirely pedagogic and paternal expression.

'You know, Monsieur Jehan, that our fief of Tirechappe brings in only, taking altogether the quit-rents and income from the twenty-one houses, 39 *livres* 11 *sols* 6 *deniers parisis*. That's half as much again as in the time of the Paclet brothers, but it is not a lot.'

'I need money,' said Jehan stoically.

'You know that the official has decided that our twenty-one houses depended on the bishopric in full fief, and that we could only redeem that homage by paying the reverend bishop 2 *marcs* of silver-gilt to the value of 6 *livres parisis*. Now, as regards the 2 *marcs*, I haven't yet been able to get them together. You know that.'

'I know that I need money,' Jehan repeated for the third time.

'But what do you intend to do with it?'

This question brought a gleam of hope into Jehan's eyes. He resumed his tone of cajoling, honeyed persuasion.

'Look, dear brother Claude, I would not come to you with any dishonourable intentions. It's not a question of showing off in the taverns with your *unzains* and strutting around the streets of Paris all tricked out in gold brocade, with my lackey—*cum meo laquasio*. No, brother, it's for a good work.'

'What good work?' asked Claude in some surprise.

'Two of my friends would like to buy baby clothes for the child of a poor *haudriette** widow. It's a charity. It will cost 3 florins, and I'd like to contribute my share.'

'What are the names of your two friends?'

'Pierre l'Assommeur [Slaughterman] and Baptiste Croque-Oison [Chaw-Gosling].'

'Hm!' said the archdeacon, 'those names are as fitting for a good work as a bombard on a high altar.'

Jehan had certainly made a very bad choice of names for his two friends. He realized it too late.

'And then,' Claude went on shrewdly, 'what sort of children's clothes are going to cost 3 florins? And for a *haudriette*'s child? Since when have *haudriette* widows had infants in swaddling clothes?'

Jehan broke the ice once more: 'All right, then. I need money to go and see Isabeau la Thierrye this evening at the Val d'Amour.'

'Filthy wretch!' cried the priest.

' ʾΑναγνεία,' said Jehan.

This quotation which the student borrowed, perhaps to make mischief, from the cell's wall, had a singular effect on the priest. He bit his lip, and his anger died down as he flushed.

'Be off with you,' he then said to Jehan. 'I am expecting someone.'

The student made one more attempt: 'Brother Claude, at least give me one little *parisis* for some food.'

'Where have you got to in Gratian's *Decretals*?' asked Dom Claude.

'I've lost my notebooks.'

'Where have you got to in Latin humanities?'

'Someone stole my copy of Horace.'

'Where have you got to in Aristotle?'

'My word, brother, which Church Father was it, then, who said that the errors of heretics through the ages have always had their lair in the tangled undergrowth of Aristotle's metaphysics? A fig for Aristotle! I don't want to wreck my religion on his metaphysics!'

'Young man,' went on the archdeacon, 'the last time the king made a solemn entry there was a gentleman called Philippe de Commines, who bore embroidered on his horse's housing his motto, which I advise you to meditate upon: *Qui non laborat non manducet* [He who does not work, let him not eat].'

The student remained silent for a moment, his finger in his ear, his eyes fixed on the ground, his expression cross. Suddenly he turned towards Claude as swiftly and nimbly as a wagtail:

'So, good brother, you refuse me a *sol parisis* to buy a crust from a hedge-baker?'

'*Qui non laborat non manducet.*'

At this answer from the inflexible archdeacon, Jehan buried his head in his hands, like a woman sobbing, and cried out with an expression of despair:' ''Οτοτοτο-τοτοί!'

'What's the meaning of this, sir?' asked Claude, surprised at the outburst.

'Well, what?' said the student, looking up at Claude with impudent eyes, which he had been pressing with his fists to make them look red, as though from weeping. 'It's Greek! It's an anapaest from Aeschylus which is the perfect expression of grief.'

And at that point he broke into so comical and boisterous a roar of laughter that he made the archdeacon smile. It was indeed Claude's fault; why had he spoiled the boy so much?

'Oh! good brother Claude,' Jehan went on, encouraged by that smile, 'look at the holes in my boots. What buskin in the world could be more tragic than a boot with its sole hanging off?'

The archdeacon had promptly resumed his original severity: 'I'll send you some new boots. But no money.'

'Just one little *parisis*, brother,' Jehan persisted with his entreaty. 'I'll learn Gratian off by heart, I'll really believe in God, I'll be a proper Pythagoras of science and virtue. But one little *parisis* for pity's sake! Do you want starvation to seize me in its jaws, gaping there in front of me, blacker, deeper, more noisome than Tartarus or a monk's nose?'

Dom Claude shook his wrinkled head: '*Qui non laborat . . .*'

Jehan did not let him finish.

'All right,' he cried, 'to the devil! Three cheers for fun! I'll go round the taverns, I'll fight, I'll break pots, and I'll visit the girls!'

Whereupon he hurled his cap at the wall and clicked his fingers like castanets.

The archdeacon looked at him gloomily.

'Jehan, you have no soul.'

'In that case, according to Epicurius [*sic*], I lack something or other made of something else that has no name.'

'Jehan, you must think seriously of mending your ways.'

'So,' cried the student, looking alternately at his brother and the alembics on the furnace, 'so everything here is askew, the ideas as well as the bottles.'

'Jehan, you are on a very slippery slope. Do you know where you are going?'

'To the wineshop,' said Jehan.

'The wineshop leads to the pillory.'

'That's as good a lantern as any, and with that one Diogenes might have found his man.'

'The pillory leads to the gallows.'

'The gallows is a pair of scales with man at one end and the whole earth at the other. It's a fine thing to be the man.'

'The gallows leads to hell.'

'That's a pretty big fire.'

'Jehan, Jehan, this will have a bad end.'

'The beginning will have been good.'

At that moment the sound of footsteps came from the stairs.

'Silence!' said the archdeacon, putting a finger to his lips, 'here comes Maître Jacques. Listen, Jehan,' he added in a low voice, 'be sure you never speak of what you see and hear here. Quickly, hide under this furnace and don't breathe.'

The student huddled under the furnace. Then a fruitful idea occurred to him.

'By the way, brother Claude, a florin for not breathing.'

'Silence! I promise you one.'

'You must give it to me.'

'Take it then!' said the archdeacon, angrily throwing his purse to him. Jehan burrowed back under the furnace, and the door opened.

V

THE TWO MEN IN BLACK

THE person who entered wore a black robe and a gloomy expression. What instantly struck our friend Jehan (who, as one might expect, had so disposed himself in his corner that he could see and hear everything just as he wished) was the absolute dreariness of the newcomer's dress and features. There was, however, a certain air of gentleness about that face, but the gentleness of a cat or a judge, an affected gentleness. He was very grey, wrinkled, not far off 60, with blinking eyes, white eyebrows, drooping lip and large hands. When Jehan saw that that was all there was to it, that this man was no doubt a physician or a magistrate, and that his nose was a long way from his mouth, a sign of stupidity, he curled up again in his hole, in despair at having to spend an indefinite time in such an uncomfortable position and in such poor company.

The archdeacon, however, had not even stood up for this person. He had bidden him with a sign to sit down on a stool by the door, and after a few moments' silence, which seemed to be the continuation of some previous meditation, he said somewhat patronizingly: 'Good-day, Maître Jacques.'

'Greetings, maître!' the man in black answered.

In the two ways of pronouncing respectively 'Maître Jacques' and the deferential 'maître' there was the same difference as that between *monseigneur* and *monsieur*, *domine* and *domne*. This was clearly a meeting between master and disciple.

'Well,' the archdeacon went on after a fresh silence, which Maître Jacques took care not to disturb, 'are you having any success?'

'Alas, master,' the other said with a sad smile, 'I keep on at my bellows. All the ash I could wish. But not a sparkle of gold.'

Dom Claude gestured impatiently. 'I'm not talking about that, Maître Jacques Charmolue, but about the case of your magician. Didn't you say his name was Marc Cenaine, the butler from the audit office? Has he confessed to his magic? Did you succeed with putting the question under torture?'

'Alas, no,' Maître Jacques replied, still smiling sadly. 'We have not had that consolation. The man's like a stone. We could boil him alive at the Marché-aux-Pourceaux before he said anything. However, we shall spare no pains to get at the truth. His body is already all broken. We have tried everything we've got, as the old comedian Plautus has it:

> *Advorsum stimulos, laminas, crucesque, compedesque,*
> *Nervos, catenas, carceres, numellas, pedicas, boias.*

[Against goads, red-hot irons, crosses and shackles, fetters, chains, prisons, hobbles, foot-chains, iron collars.]

'All to no effect. I'm completely nonplussed.'

'You haven't found anything new in his house?'

'Yes, we have,' said Maître Jacques, rummaging in his wallet. 'This parchment. There are some words on it that we can't understand. Monsieur Philippe Lheulier, the criminal advocate, knows a bit of Hebrew though, which he learned in that business with the Jews in the rue Kantersteen in Brussels.'

As he spoke Maître Jacques unrolled a parchment. 'Give it to me,' said the archdeacon. And running his eyes over the document: 'Pure magic, Maître Jacques!' he cried. '*Emen-hetan!* is what the vampires cry when they arrive at the witches' sabbath. *Per ipsum, et cum ipso, et in ipso** [through him, with him and in him] is the command which locks the devil up in hell again. *Hax, pax, max!* that's medicine—a formula against the bite of rabid dogs. Maître Jacques, you are the King's attorney in the ecclesiastical court, this parchment is an abomination!'

'We'll put the man to the question again. Here's something else,' added Maître Jacques, rummaging again in his satchel, 'we found in Marc Cenaine's house.'

It was a vessel of the same kind as those lying on top of Dom Claude's furnace. 'Ah!' said the archdeacon, 'an alchemist's crucible.'

'I must confess,' Maître Jacques went on with his shy, awkward smile, 'that I have tried it on the furnace, but I had no better result than with my own.'

The archdeacon began examining the vessel. 'What has he engraved there on his crucible? *Och! och!* The word for getting rid of fleas! This Marc Cenaine is an ignoramus! I can quite believe that you won't make gold with this. It would do for putting by your bed in the summer, and that's all!'

'Talking about mistakes,' said the King's attorney, 'I was just studying the doorway down below before I came up; is your reverence quite sure that it is the opening of the book of physics that is represented on the side facing the Hôtel-Dieu, and that among those seven naked figures at the feet of Our Lady the one with wings on his heels is Mercury?'

'Yes,' the priest answered. 'So Augustin Nypho writes, that Italian doctor whose bearded demon taught him everything. In any case, we'll go down, and I'll explain it to you from the text.'

'Thank you, master,' said Charmolue, bowing down to the ground. 'By the way, I was forgetting! When would you like me to have that little enchantress picked up?'

'What enchantress?'

'That gypsy, as you know, who comes to the Parvis every day to dance, despite the official's prohibition. She has a goat which is possessed, with devil's horns; it can read and write, and knows as much mathematics as Picatrix, and would be enough to hang the whole of Bohemia. The case is all ready. It will soon be done, I can tell you! A pretty creature, upon my soul, that dancer is! The loveliest black eyes! Two carbuncles from Egypt. When do we start?'

The archdeacon had gone extremely pale.

'I'll let you know,' he stammered in a barely articulate voice. Then went on with an effort: 'You take care of Marc Cenaine.'

'Don't worry,' Charmolue said with a smile. 'I'll have him buckled back on the leather bed when I get back. But he's a devil of a man. He tires out Pierrat Torterue himself, and his hands are bigger than mine. As our good Plautus says:

Nudus vinctus, centum pondo, es quando pendes per pedes.

[Trussed up naked, you weigh a hundred pounds when you are hanging by your feet.]

The question with the pulley! that's the best we've got. He'll have a taste of that.'

Dom Claude seemed to be plunged in gloomy abstraction. He turned towards Charmolue.

'Maître Pierrat . . . I mean Maître Jacques, you take care of Marc Cenaine.'

'Yes, yes, Dom Claude. Poor fellow! He will have suffered like Mummol. But what an idea to go to the sabbath! A butler of the audit office, who ought to know Charlemagne's text *Stryga vel masca* [vampire or wanton]. As for the little one—Smelarda as they call her—I shall await your orders. Ah! as we go under the portal you can also explain to me the meaning of that painted gardener that you see as you go into the church. It's the Sower, isn't it?—eh, master, what's on your mind?'

Dom Claude, sunk deep in his own thoughts, was no longer listening. Charmolue, following the direction of his eyes, saw that they had fixed mechanically on the big spider's web hanging over the window. At that moment a silly fly, looking for the March sun, blundered into the net and became stuck there. The movement of its web made the huge spider suddenly shoot out of its central cell, then with one bound it pounced on the fly, bending it in two with its front antennae, while its hideous trunk scooped out the head. 'Poor fly!' said the King's attorney in ecclesiastical courts, and lifted a hand to rescue it. The archdeacon, as though waking up with a start, held back his arm with convulsive violence.

'Maître Jacques,' he cried, 'let fate do its work!'

The attorney turned round aghast. He felt as though iron pincers had gripped his arm. The priest's eyes were fixed, haggard, blazing, and remained riveted to the horrible little group of the fly and the spider.

'Oh! yes,' the priest continued, in a voice which seemed to come from his innermost heart, 'there is a symbol of it all. She flies, she's happy, she's just been born; she seeks the spring, the open air, freedom; oh! yes, but then she hits the fatal rosace. The spider emerges, hideous spider! Poor dancer! poor foredoomed fly! Maître Jacques! let it be! it's fatality!—Alas! Claude, you are the spider. Claude, you are the fly too!—you were flying towards knowledge, the light, the sun, your only concern was to reach the open air, the broad daylight of eternal truth; but in your rush towards the dazzling window that opens on to that other world, the world of clarity, intelligence, and knowledge, blind fly, demented doctor, you did not see the subtle spider's web stretched by destiny between the light and you, you rushed into it headlong, wretched fool, and now you struggle, with your head smashed in and your wings ripped off, in the iron grip of fate's antennae!—Maître Jacques! Maître Jacques! let the spider get on with it!'

'I assure you,' said Charmolue, looking at him but not understanding, 'that I won't touch it. But, master, I beg you, let go of my arm, you have a grip of iron.'

The archdeacon did not hear him. 'Oh! what madness!' he went on, never taking his eyes off the window. 'If only you could break that dreadful web with your gnat's wings, you think you could reach the light! Alas! that pane of glass beyond, that transparent obstacle, that wall of crystal harder than bronze separating all philosophical systems from the truth, how would you get past that? Oh! the vanity of science! How many sages come fluttering from afar only to dash their heads against it! How many systems clash in confusion as they buzz against that eternal window pane!'

He fell silent. These last ideas, which had imperceptibly led him away from himself to science, seemed to have calmed him. Jacques Charmolue brought him fully back to reality by asking him: 'Well then, master, when are you coming to help me make gold? I long to succeed.'

The archdeacon nodded his head with a bitter smile. 'Maître Jacques, read Michael Psellos,* *Dialogus de energia et operatione daemonum*. What we are doing is not wholly innocent.'

'Not so loud, master! I suspect as much,' said Charmolue. 'But you've got to practise a bit of hermetics when you are only King's attorney in ecclesiastical courts, at 30 *écus tournois* a year. Just let's keep our voices down.'

At that moment a sound of jaws engaged in mastication coming from under the furnace caught Charmolue's anxious ear.

'What's that?' he asked.

It was the student who, very bored and uncomfortable in his hiding place, had managed to discover an old crust of bread and a wedge of mouldy cheese, and had begun eating the lot without more ado, by way of consolation and breakfast. Ravenous as he was, he was making a lot of noise, and loudly stressed each mouthful, and this it was that had alerted and alarmed the attorney.

'It's a cat of mine,' the archdeacon said quickly, 'treating himself to a mouse or something under there.'

This explanation satisfied Charmolue. 'Indeed, master,' he answered with a respectful smile, 'all the great philosophers have had their familiar animal. You know what Servius says: *Nullus enim locus sine genio est* [For there is no place without its spirit].'

Meanwhile Dom Claude, fearing some new outburst from Jehan, reminded his worthy disciple that they had some figures on the portal to study together, and they both left the cell, to a loud 'Whew!' from the student, who had begun to be seriously afraid that his knee was going to take on the imprint of his chin.

VI

THE EFFECT THAT CAN BE PRODUCED BY SEVEN OATHS UTTERED IN THE OPEN AIR

'*Te Deum laudamus!*' exclaimed Maître Jehan as he came out of his hole, 'the two screech-owls have gone. *Och! och! Hax! pax! max!* Fleas! mad dogs! The devil! I have had enough of their conversation! My head is ringing like a belfry. Mouldy cheese into the bargain! Come on! let's go on down, take our big brother's wallet and convert all these coins into bottles!'

He cast an affectionate and admiring glance inside the precious wallet, straightened his clothes, rubbed his boots, dusted his poor padded sleeves, all grey with ash, whistled a tune, spun a caper, looked to see if there was anything else left in the cell for him to take, picked up here and there on the furnace some glass amulets good enough to present to Isabeau la Thierrye as jewellery, finally pushed the door, which his brother had left open as a final piece of indulgence, and which he left open in his turn as a final piece of mischief, and went hopping down the circular stairway like a bird.

In the darkness of the spiral stairs his elbow bumped into something which withdrew with a grunt; he presumed it was Quasimodo, and found that so funny that he went down the rest of the stairs holding his sides with laughter. He was still laughing as he emerged into the square.

He stamped his foot once he was back on the ground. 'Oh!' he said, 'good honourable Paris paving! That cursed staircase would make the angels on Jacob's ladder gasp for breath! What was I thinking of, sticking my nose into that stone gimlet that goes boring up into the sky; all to eat some whiskery cheese and see the steeples of Paris through a little window!'

He walked on a few steps, and noticed the two screech-owls, that is Dom Claude and Maître Jacques Charmolue, absorbed in contemplation before a sculpture in the portal. He approached them on tiptoe, and heard the archdeacon say in a very low voice to Charmolue: 'It was Guillaume de Paris who had a Job carved on that lapis-lazuli coloured stone, with gilded edges. Job appears on the philosophers' stone, which must also be tried and tormented to become perfect, as Raymond Lull* says: *Sub conservatione formae specificae salva anima* [under the conservation of the specific form the soul is safe].'

'It's all the same to me,' said Jehan, 'I'm the one who has the purse.'

At that moment he heard a loud, resonant voice behind him uttering a formidable string of oaths: 'God's blood! God's belly! *Bédieu!* God's body! Beelzebub's navel! Name of a pope! Horn and thunder!'

'Upon my soul,' exclaimed Jehan, 'that can only be my friend Captain Phoebus!'

This name 'Phoebus' reached the archdeacon's ear just as he was explaining to the King's attorney the dragon hiding its tail in a bath from whence smoke and a king's head emerge. Dom Claude gave a start, broke off, to Charmolue's great astonishment, turned round, and saw his brother Jehan accosting a tall officer at the door of the Gondelaurier residence.

It was indeed Captain Phoebus de Châteaupers. He was leaning against the corner of his fiancée's house, swearing like a heathen.

'My word, Captain Phoebus,' said Jehan, taking him by the hand, 'you swear with admirable vigour.'

'Horn and thunder!' replied the captain.

'Horn and thunder yourself!' retorted the student. 'Well now, gentle captain, what has brought on such a spate of eloquence?'

'Forgive me, good comrade Jehan,' cried Phoebus, shaking his hand, 'a horse doesn't pull up short when it's got the bit between its teeth, and I was swearing at full gallop. I have just left the company of those prudes, and when I come away from them my throat's always full of oaths; I've got to spit them out or I'd choke, belly and thunder!'

'Would you like to come for a drink?' asked the student.
That proposal calmed the captain.

'Gladly, but I don't have any money.'

'But I have.'

'Bah! let's see!'

Jehan displayed the wallet, simply and majestically, for
the captain to see. Meanwhile the archdeacon, who had left
Charmolue in utter amazement, had come close to them,
stopping a short way off, and was observing the two of them
without their being aware of him, so deeply absorbed were
they in contemplation of the wallet.

Phoebus exclaimed: 'A purse in your pocket, Jehan, is
like the moon in a bucket of water. You can see it, but it
isn't there. There's only its shadow. By God! let's bet those
are pebbles!'

Jehan coldly replied: 'Here are the pebbles I pave my
fob with.'

And without another word he emptied the wallet on to a
marker-stone nearby with the air of a Roman saving
his country.

'God's truth!' muttered Phoebus, '*targes, grands blancs,
petits blancs, mailles* at a *tournois* for two, *deniers parisis*, real
liards with the eagle! It's dazzling!'

Jehan remained dignified and impassive. A few *liards* had
rolled into the mud; the captain, in his enthusiasm, stooped
to pick them up. Jehan restrained him: 'Shame on you,
Captain Phoebus de Châteaupers!'

Phoebus counted the coins, and turning solemnly to
Jehan: 'Do you know, Jehan, there are 23 *sols parisis* there!
Who did you rob last night in the rue Coupe-Gueule?'

Jehan threw back his fair, curly head and said disdainfully
with eyes half closed: 'We have a brother who is an archdeacon and an idiot.'

'God's horn!' cried Phoebus, 'the worthy man!'

'Let's go and drink,' said Jehan.

'Where shall we go?' said Phoebus. 'To the Pomme d'Ève?'

'No, captain. Let's go to the Vieille Science. An old
woman [*vieille*] sawing a jug [*scie-anse*]. It's a rebus. I
like that.'

'Blow rebuses, Jehan! The wine is better at the Pomme d'Ève. Anyway, beside the door there's a vine in the sun that cheers me up when I'm drinking.'

'All right! let's settle for Eve and her apple,' said the student; then, taking Phoebus by the arm: 'By the way, my dear captain, a moment ago you mentioned the rue Coupe-Gueule. That's a most improper way to speak. We are not so barbaric nowadays. We say rue Coupe-Gorge.'*

The two friends set off for the Pomme d'Ève. Needless to say, they picked up the money first, and the archdeacon followed them.

The archdeacon followed them, gloomy and haggard. Was this the Phoebus whose accursed name, ever since his interview with Gringoire, kept cropping up in his thoughts? He did not know, but at any rate he was *a* Phoebus, and that magical name was enough to make the archdeacon stealthily follow the two carefree friends, listening to what they said and watching their slightest gesture with anxious attention. However, it was only too easy to hear everything they said, they were talking so loudly, quite unconcerned about letting passers-by into half their secrets. They were talking about duels, girls, drink, wild pranks.

At a bend in the street the sound of a tambourine came to them from a crossroads nearby. Dom Claude heard the officer say to the student:

'Thunder! let's walk faster.'

'Why, Phoebus?'

'I'm afraid of the gypsy girl seeing me.'

'What gypsy?'

'The girl with the goat.'

'La Smeralda?'

'That's right, Jehan. I always forget her infernal name. Let's get a move on, she would recognize me. I don't want that girl accosting me in the street.'

'Do you know her, Phoebus?'

At this, the archdeacon saw Phoebus snigger, bend over into Jehan's ear, and whisper a few words. Then Phoebus roared with laughter and wagged his head with a triumphant look.

'Really?' said Jehan.

'Upon my soul!' said Phoebus.

'This evening?'

'This evening.'

'Are you sure she'll come?'

'Are you crazy, Jehan? Does one doubt such things?'

'Captain Phoebus, you're a lucky soldier!'

The archdeacon heard the whole of this conversation. His teeth chattered. A visible shudder went right through his body. He stopped for a moment, leaned against a marker-stone like a drunken man, then again took up the trail of the two merry rascals.

Just as he caught up with them, they had changed the subject. He heard them bawling out the old refrain:

> Children from the Petits-Carreaux*
> Like calves to the gallows go.

VII

THE BOGEYMAN-MONK

THE illustrious tavern of the Pomme d'Ève was situated in the University, on the corner of the rue de la Rondelle and the rue du Bâtonnier. It was a room at street level, quite spacious and very low, with a vaulted ceiling whose central springing rested on a massive wooden pillar painted yellow. There were tables everywhere, gleaming pewter jugs hanging on the wall, always a crowd of drinkers, plenty of girls, a window on to the street, a vine by the door, and over the door a gaudy metal sheet, with an apple and a woman painted on it, rusted by rain and swinging in the wind on an iron shaft. This sort of weathercock overlooking the street was the inn-sign.

Night was falling. The crossroads were dark. The tavern, bright with countless candles, blazed from afar like a forge in the shadows. The sound of glasses, feasting, swearing, and quarrelling could be heard through the broken window panes. The warmth of the room had misted over the glass front, but through it could be seen scores of hazy figures milling about, and breaking out now and then with a burst of resounding laughter. Passers-by going about their business did not look in through this turbulent window. Only at intervals some ragged urchin would stretch up on tiptoe to reach the window sill and shout into the tavern the mocking old cry with which drunkards were then harried: '*Aux Houls*, drunk, drunk, drunk!'*

One man, however, was walking imperturbably up and down in front of the rowdy tavern, constantly looking inside and straying from it no further than a pikeman from his sentry-box. He had a cloak pulled up to his nose. He had just bought this cloak from the secondhand-clothes dealer near the Pomme d'Ève, no doubt as protection against the cold March evenings, perhaps to conceal his dress. From time to time he would stop in front of the clouded casement with its lead lattice, look, listen, and stamp his feet.

At length the tavern door opened. This seemed to be what he was waiting for. Two drinkers came out. The beam of light shining from the doorway glowed red for a moment over their merry faces. The man in the cloak went to take up an observation post beneath a porch on the other side of the street.

'Horn and thunder,' said one of the two drinkers. 'It's going to strike seven. That's the time of my appointment.'

'I tell you,' his companion put in, slurring his words, 'I don't live in the rue des Mauvaises-Paroles, *indignus qui inter mala verba habitat* [unworthy the man who dwells amid evil words]. My lodgings are in the rue Jean-Pain-Mollet, *in vico Johannis-Pain-Mollet*—you are cornier than a unicorn if you say otherwise. Everyone knows that once you've ridden a bear you're cured of fear, but you have a nose for a dainty morsel, like Saint-Jacques de l'Hôpital.'

'Jehan, my friend, you're drunk,' the other said.

His friend replied, staggering along: 'You like saying so, Phoebus, but it has been proved that Plato had the profile of a hunting-dog.'

The reader has doubtless already recognized our two fine friends, the captain and the student. The man spying on them from the shadows had also recognized them, apparently, for he slowly followed all the zigzags which the student imposed on the captain, who as a more seasoned drinker had kept a perfectly cool head. Listening to them attentively, the man in the cloak was able to pick up the whole of the following interesting conversation:

'*Corbacque!* Try and walk straight, Monsieur the Bachelor of Arts. You know I've got to leave you. There's seven o'clock. I have an appointment with a woman.'

'Leave me alone then, will you! I'm seeing stars and fiery spears. You are like the château of Dampmartin falling apart with laughter.'

'By my grandmother's warts, Jehan, that's pushing nonsense too far. By the way, Jehan, don't you have any money left?'

'Monsieur le Recteur, it's no one's fault, the small shambles, *parva boucheria*.'

'Jehan, Jehan, my friend! you know I've arranged to meet this girl at the end of the Pont Saint-Michel. The only place I can take her is to la Falourdel's, the bawd on the bridge, and I'll have to pay for the room. The old trull with her white whiskers won't give me credit. Jehan! for pity's sake have we really drunk away all the reverend's wallet? Haven't you a single *parisis* left?'

'The knowledge that the other hours have been well spent is a just and savoury condiment for the table.'*

'Belly and bowels! give your nonsense a rest! Tell me, you devil's own Jehan, have you any money left? Give it here, by God, or I'll search you, be you as leprous as Job or scabby as Caesar!'

'Monsieur, the rue Galiache* is a street running at one end into the rue de la Verrerie, and at the other into the rue de la Tixanderie.'

'That's right, my good friend Jehan, my poor comrade, the rue Galiache, that's right, quite right. But in heaven's name, get hold of yourself. I only need one *sol parisis*, and I need it for seven o'clock.'

'Silence all round, and attend to the chorus:

> When rats eat cats,
> The king will rule in Arras;
> When the sea, stretching far and wide,
> is frozen hard at Midsummertide,
> You will see upon the ice
> The people fleeing from Arras.'

'All right, student of Antichrist, may you be strangled with your mother's guts!' cried Phoebus, and roughly shoved the drunken student, who slid down the wall and fell limply on Philip-Augustus's paving-stones. Moved by some remnant of that fellow-feeling which never forsakes a drinker's heart, Phoebus rolled Jehan with his foot on to one of those poor men's pillows which providence keeps ready at the corner of every marker-stone in Paris, and which the rich contemptuously brand with the name of muck-heaps. The captain arranged Jehan's head on an inclined plane of cabbage stalks, and straight away the student began snoring in a magnificent bass-baritone. Some resentment, however, still smouldered in the captain's heart: 'Too bad if the devil's muck-cart picks you up as it goes by!' he said to the poor sleeping clerk, and went off.

The man in the cloak, who had never ceased to follow him, stopped for a moment before the recumbent student, as if in the throes of indecision; then, heaving a deep sigh, he too went off, after the captain.

Like them we shall leave Jehan sleeping under the kindly gaze of the stars, and will follow too, if it please the reader.

As he came out into the rue Saint-André-des-Arcs Captain Phoebus realized that he was being followed. He saw, as he chanced to look round, a kind of shadow creeping along the walls behind him. He stopped, the shadow stopped. He walked on, the shadow walked on. This caused him very little concern. 'Bah!' he said to himself, 'I haven't a *sou.*'

He halted before the façade of the Collège d'Autun. It was at this college that he had embarked on what he called his studies and from a habit acquired as an irreverent student and never given up, he never went by the façade without inflicting on the statue of Cardinal Pierre Bertrand, carved to the right of the gate, the kind of affront of which Priapus complains so bitterly in Horace's satire: *Olim truncus enim ficulus* [I was once the trunk of a fig tree]. He had gone about it with such enthusiasm that the inscription *Eduensis episcopus* [Bishop of Autun] had been almost obliterated. He stopped, then, in front of the statue as usual. The street was quite deserted. Just as he was casually tying up his laces* again, his head in the clouds, he saw the shadow approaching slowly, so slowly that he had plenty of time to observe that this shadow wore a cloak and a hat. When it had come up close to him, it stopped, and stayed as motionless as the statue of Cardinal Bertrand. Meanwhile it fixed on Phoebus two staring eyes full of that vague luminosity given off at night by the pupils of a cat's eyes.

The captain was a brave man and would have been scarcely upset by a robber with a rapier in his hand. But this walking statue, this man turned to stone, made his blood run cold. At the time some kind of stories were circulating about a bogeyman-monk prowling the streets of Paris by night, and he vaguely recalled them. He remained dumbfounded for some moments, finally breaking the silence with an attempt at laughter.

'Monsieur, if, as I hope, you are a thief, you make me think of a heron attacking a walnut-shell. I am the son of an impoverished family, my dear fellow. Try next door. In the college chapel there is a piece of the true cross, in a silver case.'

The shadow's hand came out from beneath the cloak and fell upon Phoebus' arm as heavily as an eagle's talon. At the same time the shadow spoke: 'Captain Phoebus de Châteaupers!'

'What the devil!' said Phoebus. 'You know my name?'

'I don't just know your name,' the man in the cloak went on in his sepulchral voice. 'You have an appointment this evening.'

'I have,' answered Phoebus, quite astounded.

'At seven o'clock.'

'In a quarter of an hour.'

'At la Falourdel's place.'

'Just so.'

'The bawd of the Pont Saint-Michel.'

'Saint Michael the archangel, as the Paternoster* puts it.'

'Impious fellow!' muttered the spectre. 'With a woman?'

'*Confiteor* [I confess].'

'By the name of . . .'

'La Smeralda,' Phoebus said gaily. All his insouciance had gradually returned.

At that name the shadow's claw shook Phoebus' arm furiously. 'Captain Phoebus de Châteaupers, you are lying!'

Anyone who could have seen the captain's face blaze at that moment, the way he sprang backwards, so violently that he broke loose from the pincer grip that had seized him, the haughty expression with which his hand flew to his sword hilt, and faced so angrily the bleak immobility of the man in the cloak, anyone who had seen that would have been terrified. It was not unlike the struggle between Don Juan and the statue.

'Christ and Satan!' cried the captain, 'that's a word that seldom assaults the ears of a Châteaupers! You would never dare repeat it.'

'You are lying,' said the shadow coldly.

The captain ground his teeth. Bogeyman-monk, phantom, superstitions, all was forgotten at that moment. All he could see was a man and an insult.

'Ha! That's the way!' he spluttered in a voice choking with rage. He drew his sword, then stammering, for anger makes one tremble as much as fear: 'Here! now! go to! Swords! swords! Blood on these cobbles!'

Meanwhile the other did not stir. When he saw his adversary on guard and ready to lunge: 'Captain Phoebus,' he said in a tone vibrant with bitterness, 'you are forgetting your appointment.'

The rages of men like Phoebus are like heated milk which a drop of cold water can take off the boil. Those simple words brought down the sword glinting in the captain's hand.

'Captain,' the man continued, 'tomorrow, the day after, in a month, in ten years, you will find me again, ready to cut your throat; but first go to your appointment.'

'Indeed,' said Phoebus, as though looking for some accommodation with himself, 'to encounter a sword or a girl are both delightful assignations; but I don't see why I should give up one for the other when I can have both.'

He sheathed his sword again.

'Go to your appointment,' the stranger went on.

'Monsieur,' Phoebus answered in some embarrassment, 'many thanks for your courtesy. There will in fact still be time tomorrow for us to cut slashes and buttonholes in each other's birthday suits. I am grateful to you for letting me spend another pleasant quarter of an hour. I was fully hoping to lay you out in the gutter and still arrive in time for the lady, all the more so, as it's good form to keep a woman waiting a bit in such cases. But you look pretty powerful, and it's safer to put off the contest until tomorrow. So I'll be off to my appointment. It's for seven o'clock, as you know.' Here Phoebus scratched his ear—'Ah! *Corne-Dieu!* I was forgetting! I haven't a *sou* to pay the charge for the garret, and the old crone will want to be paid in advance. She doesn't trust me.'

'Here's something to pay with.'

Phoebus felt the stranger's cold hand slip a large coin into his own. He could not stop himself taking the money and shaking the hand.

'God's truth!' he cried, 'you're a good chap!'

'One condition,' the man said. 'Prove that I was wrong and that you were telling the truth. Hide me in some corner where I can see whether this woman really is the one whose name you mentioned.'

'Oh!' Phoebus replied, 'it's all the same to me. We'll take the Sainte-Marthe room. You'll be able to see all you want from the dog kennel next to it.'

'Come along then,' the shadow went on.

'At your service,' said the captain. 'I don't know if you aren't Messer Diabolus in person. But let's be friends this evening. Tomorrow I'll pay off all my debts of purse and sword.'

They set off again at a rapid pace. After a few minutes the sound of the river told them that they were on the Pont Saint-Michel, at that time all built up with houses. 'First of all I'm going to let you in,' Phoebus told his companion, 'then I'll go and find my lovely who is supposed to be waiting for me by the Petit Châtelet.'

His companion made no reply. Since they had been walking side by side he had not said a word. Phoebus stopped in front of a low door and knocked at it roughly. A light appeared at the cracks in the door. 'Who is it?' cried a toothless voice.

'God's body! God's head! God's belly!' the captain answered.

The door opened at once and revealed to the newcomers an old woman and an old lamp, both trembling. The old woman was bent double, dressed in rags, a duster over her doddery head, with little slit eyes; she was wrinkled all over, on hands, face, neck; her lips sank in under her gums, and all round her mouth she had tufts of white hairs which made her look like a contented cat. The inside of the hovel was no less decrepit than she was. The walls were chalk, the beams on the ceiling were black, there was a broken-down fireplace, spiders' webs in every corner, in the middle a rickety flock of unsteady tables and stools, a dirty child in the ashes, and at the back a staircase, or rather a wooden ladder, going up to a trapdoor in the ceiling. As he penetrated this den, Phoebus' mysterious companion pulled his cloak up to his eyes. Meanwhile the captain, swearing the while like a Saracen, hastened 'to make the sun shine on a gold piece' as our admirable Régnier puts it. 'The Sainte-Marthe room,' he said.

The old woman treated him like a lord, and put the gold piece away in a drawer. It was the coin the man in the black cloak had given Phoebus. While her back was turned, the ragged, long-haired little boy who was playing in the ashes came deftly up to the drawer, took out the coin and in its place put a dry leaf that he had torn off a faggot.

The old woman beckoned to the two noble gentlemen, as she called them, to follow her, and preceded them up the ladder. When she reached the upper floor, she put the lamp on a chest, and Phoebus, as one used to the ways of the house, opened a door giving on to a dark closet.

'Go in there, my dear fellow,' he said to his companion. The man in the cloak obeyed without answering a word. The door fell back behind him. He heard Phoebus bolt it shut, and a moment later go back downstairs after the old woman. The light had vanished.

VIII

OF THE USEFULNESS OF WINDOWS LOOKING OUT ON TO THE RIVER

CLAUDE FROLLO (for we presume that the reader, more intelligent than Phoebus, has seen in all this adventure no other bogeyman-monk than the archdeacon), Claude Frollo groped about for a moment or two in the dark recess where the captain had bolted him in. It was one of those nooks and crannies which architects sometimes provide where the roof and the supporting wall meet. The vertical section of this kennel, as Phoebus had so aptly described it, would have made a triangle. For the rest it had no windows or skylight, and the sloping angle of the roof made it impossible to stand up inside. So Claude crouched down in the dust and lumps of plaster which crumbled beneath him. His head was on fire. Rummaging around with his hands he found on the floor a piece of broken window-glass which he pressed to his forehead and whose coldness provided some relief.

What was going on at that moment in the archdeacon's dark soul? Only God and he could know.

In what fatal order had he ranged in his mind la Esmeralda, Phoebus, Jacques Charmolue, his beloved young brother, whom he had abandoned in the mire, his archdeacon's cassock, perhaps his reputation, dragged along to la Falourdel's, all these images, all these adventures? I could not say. But it is certain that these ideas composed a dreadful pattern in his mind.

He had been waiting for a quarter of an hour; he felt as though he had aged by a hundred years. Suddenly he heard the boards of the wooden staircase creaking. Someone was coming up. The trapdoor opened, a light reappeared. There was quite a wide crack in the worm-eaten door to his hole. He pressed his face to it. In this way he could see everything that was going on in the next room. The cat-faced old woman came up from the trapdoor first, then Phoebus, twirling his moustache, then a third person, the beautiful and graceful figure of la Esmeralda. The priest saw her emerge from below like some dazzling apparition. Claude trembled, a cloud came over his eyes, the blood pounded in his arteries, a buzzing filled his ears, everything was spinning around. He saw and heard nothing more.

When he came to, Phoebus and la Esmeralda were alone, sitting on the wooden chest beside the lamp, which lit up sharply before the archdeacon's eyes these two youthful figures and a wretched pallet at the far end of the garret.

Beside the pallet was a window, its glass caved in like a spider's web battered by rain, and through the broken lattice could be seen a patch of sky and the moon in the distance, resting on an eiderdown of woolly clouds.

The girl was flushed, confused, quivering with emotion. Her long eyelashes were lowered, shading her crimson cheeks. The officer, on whom she did not dare raise her eyes, was beaming. Mechanically, and with a charmingly awkward gesture, she was tracing random patterns on the seat with her fingertip and looking at her finger. Her foot was hidden by the little goat crouching on top of it.

The captain was very smartly dressed, with knots of braid at collar and cuffs—the height of elegance at the time.

With some difficulty Dom Claude managed to hear what they were saying through the pounding of the blood in his temples.

(Love talk is a somewhat trite affair. It is one perpetual 'I love you'—a very bare and insipid musical phrase for the uninvolved listener unless embellished with some *fioriture*. But Claude was no uninvolved listener.)

'Oh!' the girl was saying, without raising her eyes, 'do not despise me, Monseigneur Phoebus. I feel that what I am doing is wrong.'

'Despise you, lovely child!' the officer replied with an air of superior and distinguished gallantry, 'despise you, God's head! whatever for?'

'For following you.'

'On that score, my beauty, we don't agree. I ought not to despise but hate you.'

The girl looked at him in alarm: 'Hate me! But what have I done?'

'For having needed so much persuading.'

'Alas!' she said, 'the fact is I am breaking a vow . . . . I'll never find my parents again . . . . The amulet will lose its virtue—but what of it? What need have I now of father and mother?'

Thus saying, she gazed at the captain with her large black eyes moist with joy and affection.

'The devil if I understand you!' cried Phoebus.

La Esmeralda stayed silent for a moment, then a tear fell from her eyes, a sigh from her lips, and she said: 'O my lord, I love you.'

The girl was surrounded with such an aura of chastity, such a spell of virtue, that Phoebus did not feel wholly at ease with her. However, these words made him bolder. 'You love me!'

He said in rapture, and flung his arm round the gypsy's waist. He had only been waiting for this opportunity.

The priest saw him, and with his fingertip tested the point of a dagger which he kept hidden on his breast.

'Phoebus,' the gypsy continued, gently removing the captain's tenacious hands from round her waist, 'you are kind, you are generous, you are handsome. You saved me, me, a poor lost child in Bohemia. I have long dreamed of an officer saving my life. I was dreaming of you before I knew you, my own Phoebus. The man in my dreams had a fine uniform like you, a grand demeanour, a sword. You are called Phoebus, it is a beautiful name. I love your sword. Draw your sword, Phoebus, so that I can see it.'

'Child!' said the captain, and unsheathed his rapier with a smile. The gypsy looked at the hilt, the blade, examined with adorable curiosity the cipher on the guard, and kissed the sword, telling it: 'You are the sword of a brave man. I love my captain.'

Phoebus once more seized the opportunity to bestow on her lovely neck as it bent over a kiss which made the girl straighten up, scarlet as a cherry. The priest ground his teeth in the dark.

'Phoebus,' the gypsy went on, 'let me talk to you. Walk about a bit so that I can see how tall you are and hear your spurs jangle. How handsome you are!'

The captain stood up to oblige her, scolding her with a self-satisfied smile. 'How childish you are! By the way, charming lady, have you seen me in my ceremonial tunic?'

'Alas! no,' she answered.

'That's a really handsome sight!'

Phoebus came to sit beside her again, but much closer than before.

'Listen my dear . . .'

The gypsy gave him a few little taps on the mouth with her pretty hand, playfully childish, graceful, and gay. 'No, no, I won't listen. Do you love me? I want you to tell me if you love me.'

'Do I love you, angel of my life!' cried the captain, half kneeling. 'I am all yours, body, blood, soul, all is for you! I love you and I've never loved anyone else but you.'

The captain had repeated that phrase so many times, in so many similar situations that he declaimed it all in one breath, with flawless accuracy. At this passionate declaration, the gypsy looked up at the dingy ceiling which took the place of heaven with eyes full of angelic happiness. 'Oh!' she murmured, 'this is the moment when one should die!' Phoebus found 'the moment' suitable for stealing another kiss, adding to the torment of the wretched archdeacon in his corner.

'Die!' cried the amorous captain. 'What are you talking about, beautiful angel? This is the time for living, or Jupiter is just a rogue! Die when something so sweet is just starting? *Corne de bœuf*, what a joke! That's not right. Listen, my dear Similar . . . Esmenarda—forgive me, but you have such a prodigiously Saracen name that I can't get it out straight. It's such a tangle that it stops me in my tracks.'

'Goodness,' said the poor girl, 'and I thought it was a pretty name because it was so unusual! But since you don't like it, I don't mind being called Goton.'

'Ah! let's not cry over such a little thing, my lovely! It's a name one has to get used to, that's all. Once I know it by heart, it will come quite naturally. Listen then, my dear Similar, I adore you passionately. I truly love you so much that it's a miracle. I know one girl who is dying of rage because of it . . .'

The jealous girl interrupted him: 'Who's that?'

'What does that matter to us?' said Phoebus. 'Do you love me?'

'Oh!' she said.

'Well! that's all. You'll see how I love you too. May the great devil Neptune stick his fork in me if I don't make you the happiest creature in the world. We'll have a pretty little nest somewhere. I'll have my archers parade beneath your window. They are all mounted and have no time for Captain Mignon's lot. There are halberdiers, crossbowmen, and culverineers. I'll take you to the Parisians' great musters at the barn at Rully.* It's really magnificent. Eighty thousand armed men; thirty thousand white harnesses, jacks, or brigandines; the seventy-seven guild banners; the standards of the Parliament, the audit office, the treasurers-general, and the mint; the very devil of an army in fact! I'll take you to see the lions of the Hôtel du Roi; they're wild animals. Women all love that.'

For some moments, the girl, absorbed in her delightful thoughts, had been dreaming to the sound of his voice without taking in the meaning of his words.

'Oh! you will be so happy!' the captain continued, at the same time gently unbuckling the gypsy's belt.

'What are you doing?' she said sharply. This 'assault' had jerked her out of her reverie.

'Nothing,' Phoebus answered. 'I was just saying you'll have to give up this wild street-corner outfit when you're with me.'

'When I'm with you, my Phoebus!' the girl said tenderly. She relapsed into a thoughtful silence.

The captain, emboldened by her docility, put his arm round her waist without meeting any resistance, then began very quietly unlacing the poor child's bodice, and disarranged her gorget to such an extent that the priest, breathing heavily, saw the gypsy's bare shoulder emerge from the gauze, round and brown, like the moon rising on a misty horizon.

The girl let Phoebus have his way. She did not seem to notice. The bold captain's eyes sparkled.

She suddenly turned to him: 'Phoebus,' she said with an expression of boundless love, 'teach me about your religion.'

'My religion!' the captain exclaimed, with a roar of laughter. 'Me, teach you about my religion! Horn and thunder! What do you want with my religion?'

'It's so that we can get married,' she replied.

The captain's face took on an expression of mixed surprise, disdain, nonchalance, and passionate lust. 'Bah!' he said, 'does marriage come into it?'

The gypsy paled, and sadly let her head drop on her breast.

'My loving beauty,' Phoebus went on tenderly, 'what's all this nonsense? Marriage is a great song and dance! Are we any less loving for not having spouted a bit of Latin in a priest's shop?'

As he said this in his gentlest voice, he came extremely close to the gypsy girl, his fondling hands resumed their position around that delicate, supple waist, his eyes grew brighter and brighter, and all the evidence proclaimed that Monsieur Phoebus was clearly on the brink of one of those moments when Jupiter himself commits such follies that good Homer is obliged to enlist the aid of a cloud.

Dom Claude, however, could see everything. The door was made of rotten puncheon staves, which left wide cracks through which his predatory gaze could pass. This broad-shouldered, brown-skinned priest, hitherto condemned to the austere virginity of the cloister, shivered and seethed at this scene of love, darkness, and sensuality. The beautiful young girl surrendering in disarray to this ardent young man sent molten lead coursing through his veins. Extraordinary reactions stirred within him. His jealous and lascivious eye delved deep beneath all those undone pins. To anyone seeing the unhappy man's face at that moment pressed against the worm-eaten bars, it would have looked like the face of a tiger watching from the depths of its cage a jackal devouring a gazelle. His pupils blazed like candles through the cracks in the door.

Suddenly Phoebus snatched off the gypsy's gorget. The poor child, who had remained pale and dreamy, came awake with a start. She abruptly drew away from the adventurous officer, and casting a glance at her naked bosom and shoulders, red with confusion and speechless with shame, she crossed her lovely arms over her breast to cover it. But for the fiery blush on her cheeks, seeing her thus silent and motionless, one would have taken her for a statue of modesty. Her eyes remained cast down.

Meanwhile the captain's gesture had uncovered the mysterious amulet that she wore round her neck. 'What's that?' he said, seizing this pretext to come closer again to the lovely creature whom he had just frightened away.

'Don't touch it!' she said sharply. 'It's my guardian. It is what will enable me to find my family again if I remain worthy of it. Oh! let me be, Monsieur le capitaine! My mother! my poor mother! mother! where are you? Help me! Please, Monsieur Phoebus, give me back my gorget!'

Phoebus stepped back and said coldly: 'Oh! mademoiselle! I see clearly that you don't love me!'

'Not love him!' exclaimed the poor unhappy child, at the same time clinging to the captain and making him sit beside her. 'I not love you, my Phoebus! What are you saying, wicked man, trying to break my heart? Oh! go on! take me, take all I have! Do what you will with me. I am yours. What does the amulet matter to me? What does my mother matter? You are my mother, since I love you! Phoebus, my beloved Phoebus, do you see me? It's me, look at me. This is the little girl you won't reject, who has come, come in person, to find you. My soul, my life, my body, my person, all is yours, captain. All right, no! we shan't get married, that annoys you. Anyhow, what am I? A worthless girl from the gutter, while you, my Phoebus, you are gentry. A fine thing indeed! A dancer marrying an officer! I was crazy. No, Phoebus, no, I'll be your mistress, for your amusement, pleasure, whenever you like, a girl who'll be yours, that's all I was made for, soiled, despised, dishonoured, but, what of it?—loved. I'll be the proudest and most joyful of women. And when I'm old or ugly, Phoebus, when I am no longer fit to love you, my lord, you'll still put up with me as a servant. Others will embroider sashes for you. I'll be the servant, who will take care of them. You'll let me polish your spurs, brush your tunic, dust your riding boots. Won't you, my Phoebus, won't you have pity on me? Until then, take me! Look, Phoebus, all this belongs to you, just love me! That's all we gypsy women need, fresh air and love.'

So saying she threw her arms round the officer's neck, looked up at him beseechingly and smiling beautifully amid her tears, her delicate breasts rubbed against his woollen doublet and its rough braid. She writhed, with her lovely body half naked on his knees. The captain, drunk with desire, pressed his ardent lips on those lovely African shoulders. The girl, staring vacantly at the ceiling, bent backwards, trembling and palpitating beneath that kiss.

Suddenly, above Phoebus' head, she saw another head, a livid, green, convulsed face, with the eyes of a damned soul. Beside that face was a hand holding a dagger. The face and the hand were the priest's. He had smashed down the door and was there. Phoebus could not see him. The girl stayed motionless, frozen, speechless before the terrifying apparition, like a dove raising its head just as the round-eyed osprey looks into the nest.

She was unable even to utter a cry. She saw the dagger strike down at Phoebus and come up again reeking. 'Curses!' said the captain, and fell.

She fainted.

Just as her eyes closed, when all feeling was drifting away, she thought she felt a fiery touch imprinted on her lips, a kiss more searing than the executioner's red-hot iron.

When she recovered her senses, she was surrounded by soldiers of the watch. The captain's body, drenched in his own blood, was being carried away, the priest had vanished, the window at the back of the room, looking on to the river, stood wide open, someone was picking up a cloak, supposing it to belong to the officer, and she heard them say around her: 'She's a witch who has stabbed a captain.'

BOOK EIGHT

I

THE GOLD *ÉCU* TURNED INTO A DRY LEAF

GRINGOIRE and everyone in the Court of Miracles were desperately worried. For a good month now no one had known what had happened to la Esmeralda, much to the distress of the Duke of Egypt and his friends the *truands*, or to the goat, which intensified Gringoire's grief. One evening the gypsy girl had disappeared, and had given no signs of life since then. All attempts to find her had been in vain. Some teasing *sabouleux** told Gringoire that they had come across her that evening in the vicinity of the Pont Saint-Michel, going off with an officer; but this bohemian-style husband was a sceptical philosopher, and besides he knew better than anyone how absolutely his wife had preserved her virginity. He had been able to judge how impregnable was the modesty resulting from the combined virtues of the amulet and the gypsy, and he had worked out mathematically to the power of two the resistance of that chastity. So he was not concerned on that score.

Thus he could find no explanation for her disappearance. It grieved him deeply. It would have caused him to lose weight, had that been possible. It drove everything else from his mind, even his literary interests, even his great work '*De figuris regularibus et irregularibus*' ['On Regular and Irregular Figures'], which he intended to have printed as soon as he was next in funds. (For he had been going on about printing ever since he had seen Hugh of Saint-Victor's *Didascalon** printed in the celebrated characters of Wendelin of Speyer.)

One day, as he was walking gloomily past the Tour Crimi-nelle, he noticed quite a crowd at one of the doors of the Palais de Justice.

'What's going on?' he asked a young man who was coming out.

'I don't know, monsieur,' the young man replied. 'They say a woman is on trial for murdering a soldier. As there seems to be some sorcery involved in the affair, the bishop and his official have intervened in the case and my brother, who is archdeacon of Josas, spends all his time on it. Now I wanted a word with him, but I couldn't get to him because of the crowd, and that is most annoying, because I'm in need of some money.'

'Alas, monsieur,' said Gringoire, 'I'd like to be able to lend you some; but if there are holes in my breeches it's not gold pieces that have made them.'

He did not dare tell the young man that he knew his brother the archdeacon, whom he had not been back to see since the scene in the church, an omission which embarrassed him.

The student went his way, and Gringoire began to follow the crowd going up the stairs to the Great Chamber. He reckoned that there is nothing like the spectacle of a criminal trial for driving away melancholy, entertaining as the judges' stupidity usually is. The people whom he had joined were walking and jostling each other in silence. After a slow, tedious tramp through a long, gloomy corridor, which wound its way inside the palace like the intestinal canal of the old building, he arrived at a low door opening on to a hall which his height enabled him to scan over the swaying heads of the throng.

The hall was spacious and gloomy, which made it look all the more spacious. Daylight was fading; the long Gothic windows now let in only a pale beam of light which died out before reaching as far as the vaulted ceiling, an immense trellis of carved timbers, whose countless figures seemed to be moving vaguely in the shadows. There were already several candles burning here and there on the tables, casting their beams over the heads of clerks slumped over piles of paper. The front part of the hall was occupied by the public; to left and right were lawyers sitting at tables; at the back, on a dais, numerous judges, their back rows buried in the shadows: sinister faces without movement. The walls were sprinkled with countless fleurs-de-lys. A large figure of Christ could be vaguely discerned above the judges, and everywhere were pikes and halberds, their ends tipped with fire reflected from the candlelight.

'Monsieur,' Gringoire asked one of his neighbours, 'who are all those people sitting in rows over there like prelates at a conclave?'

'Monsieur,' said the neighbour, 'on the right are the counsellors of the Great Chamber, and on the left the counsellors of the *chambre des enquêtes*; the *maîtres* are in black robes, the *messires* in red ones.'

'There, sitting above them,' Gringoiure went on, 'who is that stout, red-faced man all in a sweat?'

'That is Monsieur le Président.'

'And those sheep behind him?' continued Gringoire, who, as already mentioned, had no love for the magistracy, which might have had something to do with the grudge he had borne the Palais de Justice ever since his dramatic misadventure.

'Those are the *maîtres des requêtes** of the king's household.'

'And that wild boar in front of them?'

'That's the clerk to the court of Parliament.'

'And, on the right, that crocodile?'

'Maître Philippe Lheulier, advocate extraordinary to the King.'

'And on the left, that big black cat?'

'Maître Jacques Charmolue, the King's attorney in ecclesiastical courts, with the gentlemen from the officiality.'

'Well now, monsieur,' said Gringoire, 'what are all these good people doing here?'

'They are judges in the trial.'

'Who is on trial? I don't see anyone in the dock.'

'It's a woman, monsieur. You can't see her. She has her back to us, and she's hidden by the crowd. Look, there she is, where you see that bunch of halberds.'

'Who is this woman?' asked Gringoire. 'Do you know her name?'

'No, monsieur. I've only just arrived. I'm only assuming that it's to do with witchcraft, because the official is present at the trial.'

'Well then!' said our philosopher, 'we're going to see all these legal gentlemen eating human flesh. It's as good a show as any.'

'Monsieur,' observed his neighbour, 'don't you think Maître Jacques Charmolue has a very gentle look to him?'

'Hm!' Gringoire answered. 'I don't trust the sort of gentleness that has pinched nostrils and thin lips.'

At this point those nearby made the two chatterers keep quiet. An important deposition was being heard.

'My lords,' said an old woman in the middle of the hall, her face so concealed by her clothing that she looked like a walking pile of rags, 'my lords, the thing is as true as it's true that I am la Falourdel, established for the past forty years on the Pont Saint-Michel, and regularly paying my rents, dues, and quit-rents, the door opposite the house of Tassin-Caillard, the dyer, which is on the side of the bridge facing upstream. A poor old woman now, but used to be a pretty girl, my lords. They had been telling me for the past few days: "La Falourdel, don't work too hard at your spinning-wheel in the evenings, the devil likes to comb old women's distaffs with his horns. There's no doubt that the bogey-monk, who was over by the Temple last year, is now prowling about in the Cité. Take care, la Falourdel, that he doesn't bang on your door." One evening I had my spinning-wheel going, there's a bang at my door. I ask who it is. Someone swears. I open up. In come two men. A man in black with a handsome officer. All you could see of the man in black was his eyes. Two live coals. The rest of him was all cloak and hat. Then they say to me: "The Sainte-Marthe room." That's my room upstairs, my lords, my best room. They give me an *écu*. I put the coin away in my drawer and say: "That will do to buy some tripe tomorrow from the flayers at la Gloriette." We go upstairs. When we get to the upper room, while I have my back turned, the man in black vanishes. That rather amazes me. The officer, who was as handsome as a noble lord, comes down again with me. He goes out. By the time I've spun a quarter of a skein he's back with a lovely young girl, a real doll who could have shone as bright as the sun if she had had her hair properly done. She had a he-goat with her, a big one, black or white, I forget now. That gave me something to think about. The girl, she's none of my business, but the goat!—I don't like those creatures, they have a beard and horns, they look so like a man. Besides, they have a whiff of the sabbath about them. Still, I don't say anything. I had my gold *écu*. That's fair enough, isn't it, Monsieur le juge? I show the girl and the captain to the upstairs room, and I leave them on their own, that is, with the goat. I come down again and go back to my spinning. I must explain that my house has a ground floor and one above; at the back it looks out on to the river, like the other houses on the bridge, and the window on the ground floor and the one on the upper floor open on to the water. So there I was at my spinning-wheel. I don't know why, but I was thinking of the bogey-monk that the goat had put me in mind of, and anyhow the lovely young girl's get-up was a bit weird. Suddenly I hear a cry from upstairs, and something falling on the floor, and the window opening. I hurry over to my window, which is just underneath, and I see a black shape go past my eyes and fall into the water. It was a phantom dressed as a priest. The moon was shining bright. I saw it quite clearly. It was swimming towards the Cité. Then, all of a tremble, I called the watch. The gentlemen of the *douzaine* come in, and right from the start, not knowing what it was all about, and being in high spirits, they knocked me about. We go up, and what do we find? My poor room with blood all over it, the captain stretched out full length with a dagger in his neck, the girl acting dead, and the goat quite terrified. "Right," I say, "it'll take me more than a couple of weeks to wash that floor clean. It'll have to be scraped, it'll be an awful job." They took away the officer, poor young man! and the girl, not even properly dressed. Wait. The worst of it was that next day when I went to get the *écu* to buy my tripe, I found a dry leaf in its place.'

The old woman fell silent. A murmur of horror ran through the audience. 'That phantom, that he-goat, that all smells of magic,' said one of Gringoire's neighbours. 'And that dry leaf!' added another. 'No doubt about it,' put in a third, 'she's a witch who has dealings with the bogey-monk so as to rob officers.' Gringoire himself was not far from finding the whole business frightening and probable.

'Mistress Falourdel,' said Monsieur le Président majestically, 'have you nothing more to tell the court?'

'No, my lord,' the old woman replied, 'except that in the report they described my house as a stinking, dilapidated old hovel, which is most offensive language. The houses on the bridge don't look all that fine, because they are so crammed with people, but all the same that doesn't stop the butchers living there, and they are rich men married to fine women as clean as could be.'

The magistrate who had put Gringoire in mind of a crocodile rose: 'Silence!' he said. 'I ask you, messieurs, not to lose sight of the fact that a dagger was found on the accused woman. Mistress Falourdel, have you brought the dry leaf into which the *écu* given you by the demon was changed?'

'Yes, my lord,' she answered, 'I found it again. Here it is.'

An usher handed over the dead leaf to the crocodile who gave a lugubrious nod and passed it to the president who dispatched it to the King's attorney in ecclesiastical courts, so that it went all round the room. 'It is a birch leaf,' said Maître Jacques Charmolue; 'further evidence of magic.'

A counsellor spoke up: 'Witness, two men went up your stairs at the same time, the man in black whom you saw first vanish, then swimming in the Seine in priest's clothing, and the officer—which of them handed you the *écu*?'

The old woman reflected for a moment and said: 'The officer.' A murmur ran through the crowd.

'Ah!' thought Gringoire, 'that rather shakes my conviction.'

Meanwhile Maître Philippe Lheulier, advocate extraordinary to the King, intervened again: 'May I remind you, messieurs, that in the deposition taken down at his bedside, the murdered officer, while declaring that the thought had vaguely occurred to him at the moment when the man in black accosted him that he might very well be the bogey-monk, added that the phantom had keenly pressed him to enter upon familiar relations with the accused, and on his observing, I mean the captain, that he had no money, had given him the *écu* with which the said officer had paid la Falourdel. So the *écu* is a coin from hell.'

This conclusive remark seemed to dispel all doubts in the mind of Gringoire and other sceptics in the audience.

'You have the dossier of evidence, messieurs,' the King's advocate added as he sat down, 'and you can consult the statement of Phoebus de Châteaupers.'

At that name the accused stood up. Her head rose clear of the crowd. Gringoire was appalled to recognize la Esmeralda.

She was pale, her hair, once so gracefully plaited and spangled with sequins, fell loose in disorder; her lips were blue; her sunken eyes frightening. Alas!

'Phoebus!' she said, distraught. 'Where is he? Oh my lords! before you kill me, I beg you, tell me if he is still alive!'

'Be quiet, woman,' the president answered. 'That's not our business.'

'Oh! for pity's sake, tell me if he is alive!' she went on, clasping her lovely, wasted hands, and her chains could be heard rattling against her dress.

'Very well,' the King's advocate said drily, 'he's dying. Are you satisfied?'

The wretched girl fell back on her seat, without a word, without a tear, white as a waxwork figure.

The president bent over to a man at his feet, wearing a gold cap and a black robe, a chain round his neck, and a staff in his hand. 'Usher, bring in the second accused.'

Every eye turned to the small door which opened and, to the thumping of Gringoire's heart, admitted a pretty she-goat with gilded horns and hooves. The elegant animal stopped for a moment in the doorway, stretching out its neck as if, standing on some rocky peak, it had a vast horizon before its eyes. It suddenly caught sight of the gypsy girl, and jumping over the table and the clerk's head, in two leaps was at her knee. Then it curled up gracefully over its mistress's feet, inviting a word or a caress: but the accused stayed motionless, and poor Djali herself was spared not a glance.

'Eh! but . . . that's my nasty animal,' said old Falourdel, 'and I recognize both of them right enough!'

Jacques Charmolue intervened: 'If it please you, messieurs, we shall proceed with the interrogation of the goat.'

It was indeed the second accused. At that time nothing could be simpler than putting an animal on trial for sorcery. You will find among others in the Provostry accounts for 1466 a curious detail of the expenses incurred in the trial of Gillet-Soulart and his sow, 'executed for their demerits at Corbeil'. Everything is there, the cost of digging pits to put the sow in, the five hundred bundles of sticks collected from the harbour at Morsant, the three pints of wine and the bread, the victim's last meal, fraternally shared with the executioner, down to the eleven days of guarding and feeding the sow at 8 *deniers parisis* a day. Sometimes they went even further than animals. The capitularies of Charlemagne and Louis the Debonair inflict heavy punishments on fiery phantoms which take the liberty of appearing in the air.

Meanwhile the attorney in ecclesiastical courts had cried: 'If the demon possessing this goat, which has resisted all attempts at exorcism, persists in its wickedness, and if it shocks the court thereby, we warn it that we shall be compelled to require the gallows or the stake for it.'

Gringoire was in a cold sweat. Charmolue picked up the gypsy's tambourine from a table and, presenting it to the goat in a certain way, asked it: 'What time is it?'

The goat looked at him shrewdly, lifted a gilded hoof and knocked seven times. It was indeed seven o'clock. A movement of terror went through the crowd.

Gringoire could not stand it.

'She's damning herself!' he shouted loudly. 'You can see very well that she doesn't know what she is doing.'

'Silence, the churls at the end of the hall!' the usher called sharply.

Jacques Charmolue, with the help of similar manœuvres with the tambourine, made the goat perform a number of other tricks, the day's date, the month of the year and so on, which the reader has already witnessed. And by an optical illusion peculiar to judicial proceedings, those same spectators who had perhaps more than once applauded Djali's innocent tricks at street corners, were terrified by them under the vaulting of the Palais de Justice. The goat was definitely the devil.

It was much worse when the King's attorney emptied on to the floor a certain leather pouch full of movable letters which Djali wore round her neck, and they saw the goat pull out with her hoof from the scattered alphabet the fateful name: PHOEBUS. The spells of which the captain had been the victim seemed to be irresistibly demonstrated, and, in the eyes of all, the gypsy girl, that delightful dancer who had so often dazzled passers-by with her grace, was just a horrible vampire.

For the rest she gave no sign of life. Neither Djali's graceful movements, nor the lawyers' threats, not the muffled imprecations of the audience, nothing reached her mind any more.

A sergeant had to shake her mercilessly, and the president had to raise his voice solemnly, to arouse her:

'Girl, you are of Bohemian race, given to malefices. You have, acting in complicity with the bewitched goat implicated in the charge, on the night of 29 March last, murdered and stabbed, in league with the powers of darkness, with the help of charms and practices, a captain of the archers of the King's ordinance, Phoebus de Châteaupers. Do you persist in your denial?'

'Horrors!' cried the girl, burying her face in her hands. 'My Phoebus! Oh! this is hell!'

'Do you persist in your denial?' the president asked coldly.

'Yes, I deny it!' she said in a terrible voice, standing up with flashing eyes.

The president continued bluntly: 'Then how do you explain the facts with which you are charged?'

She replied in broken tones: 'I have already said, I don't know. It's a priest. A priest I don't know. An infernal priest who is pursuing me!'

'That's right,' the judge went on. 'The bogey-monk.'

'O my lords! have mercy! I am only a poor girl . . .'

'From Egypt,' said the judge.

Maître Jacques Charmolue spoke up gently: 'In view of the painful obstinacy of the accused, I call for the question to be applied.'

'Granted,' said the president.

The wretched girl trembled in every limb. She stood up, however, at an order from the guard, and walked quite steadily, preceded by Charmolue and the priests from the officiality, between two rows of halberds, to a side door, which opened suddenly and closed behind her, making the dejected Gringoire think of horrible jaws which had just devoured her.

When she disappeared a plaintive bleating was heard. It was the little goat crying.

The hearing was suspended. When one councillor remarked that they were all tired and it would be a long time to wait until the torture was finished, the president replied that a magistrate must be ready to sacrifice himself to his duty.

'What a tiresome, disagreeable hussy,' said one old judge, 'having them apply the question to her when we have not yet had supper!'

II

THE GOLD *ÉCU* TURNED INTO A DRY LEAF
(CONTINUED)

AFTER going up and down steps in corridors so gloomy that they were lit by lamps even in daytime, la Esmeralda, still surrounded by her mournful procession, was pushed by the palace sergeants into a sinister chamber. This chamber, circular in shape, occupied the ground floor of one of those massive towers which still in our own day break through the layer of modern buildings with which new Paris has covered the old. This cellar had no windows, no other opening than the entrance, low and closed by an enormous iron door. There was, however, no shortage of light. A furnace was set into the thickness of the wall. A massive fire burned within it, the reflection of its red glare filling the cellar and depriving a wretched candle standing in a corner of any radiance. The iron portcullis used to close the furnace was raised for the moment, and revealed only, at the mouth of the hole flaming out from the dark wall, the lower end of its bars, like a row of sharp, black teeth, with spaces in between, making the furnace look like one of those dragons' mouths which belch out flame in legend. By its light the prisoner could see all around the room dreadful instruments of which she did not understand the use. In the middle a leather mattress lay almost touching the ground, and hanging above it was a strap with a buckle, fastened to a brass ring held in the jaws of a flat-nosed monster carved on the keystone of the vault. There was a clutter of tongs, pincers, great ploughshares inside the furnace, all reddening together on the coals. All that the blood-red glow from the furnace lit up throughout the room was a jumble of horrible things.

This Tartarus was simply called 'the question-chamber'.

On the bed Pierrat Torterue, the sworn torturer, sat nonchalantly. His assistants, two square-faced gnomes, in leather aprons and canvas breeches, were moving the iron-ware about on the coals.

The poor girl had summoned up her courage in vain. As she entered this room she was struck with horror.

The sergeants of the palace bailiff lined up on one side, the priests from the officiality on the other. A clerk, a writing case, and a table were in a corner. Maître Jacques Charmolue approached the gypsy, smiling very gently: 'My dear child,' he said, 'do you persist then in your denial?'

'Yes,' she answered in an already dying voice.

'In that case,' Charmolue went on, 'it will grieve us deeply to question you more insistently than we should like. Kindly take the trouble to sit on that bed. Maître Pierrat, make room for mademoiselle and shut the door.'

Pierrat stood up grumbling: 'If I shut the door,' he muttered, 'my fire will go out.'

'All right, my dear fellow,' rejoined Charmolue, 'leave it open.'

Meanwhile la Esmeralda remained standing. That leather bed, on which so many poor wretches had writhed, appalled her. Terror froze the marrow of her bones. She stood there aghast and stupefied. At a sign from Charmolue, the two assistants took her and sat her down on the bed. They did not hurt her, but when these men touched her, when the leather touched her, she felt all her blood run back into her heart. She looked round the room distraught. She imagined she saw moving and advancing from every side towards her, so as to clamber along her body and bite and pinch her, all those shapeless instruments of torture, which were, among all the instruments of every kind which she had seen up till then, what bats, millipedes, and spiders are among insects and birds.

'Where is the doctor?' asked Charmolue.

'Here,' answered a black robe she had not noticed before. She shuddered.

'Mademoiselle,' went on the caressing voice of the attorney in ecclesiastical courts, 'for the third time, do you persist in denying the facts of which you are accused?'

This time she could only nod her head. Her voice failed her.

'You persist?' said Jacques Charmolue. 'Then, I'm desperately sorry, but I must fulfil the duties of my office.'

'Monsieur the King's attorney,' Pierrat said brusquely, 'what shall we start with?'

Charmolue hesitated for a moment with the ambiguous frown of a poet searching for a rhyme. 'The boot,' he said in the end.

The unfortunate girl felt so thoroughly abandoned by God and man that her head fell on her breast like some inert thing with no strength of its own.

The torturer and the doctor came up to her together. At the same time the two assistants began rummaging through their hideous arsenal.

At the jangling of these frightful irons the wretched child started like a dead frog being galvanized. 'Oh!' she murmured, so softly that no one heard her, 'oh, my Phoebus!' Then she sank back into her immobility and marmoreal silence. Such a sight would have rent the heart of anyone but a judge. It was like some poor, sinful soul being questioned by Satan beneath the crimson wicket-gate of hell. The wretched body to which that dreadful swarm of saws, wheels, and racks was about to cling, the being about to be handled by the rough hands of executioners and their pincers, was this gentle, fair, fragile creature. Poor grain of millet given over by human justice to be ground in the fearful mills of torture!

Meanwhile the calloused hands of Pierrat Torterue's assistants had brutally stripped the charming leg, the dainty foot which had so often filled passers-by with wonder at their grace and beauty in the streets of Paris.

'It's a pity,' growled the torturer as he looked at such graceful and delicate limbs. If the archdeacon had been present he would surely have remembered his symbolic spider and fly. Soon the unfortunate creature saw through the cloud spreading over her eyes the boot approaching, soon she saw her foot enclosed between the iron-bound boards and disappear into the fearful apparatus. Then terror gave her back her strength. 'Take that off!' she cried in a rage. And, sitting up all dishevelled: 'Mercy!'

She sprang off the bed to throw herself at the feet of the King's attorney, but her leg was caught in the heavy block of oak and iron, and she collapsed over the boot, more broken than a bee with a damaged wing.

At a sign from Charmolue, she was put back on the bed, and two huge hands secured round her delicate waist the strap hanging from the vaulting.

'For the last time, do you admit the facts of the case?' Charmolue asked with his imperturbable benignity.

'I am innocent.'

'Then, mademoiselle, how do you explain the circumstances with which you are charged?'

'Alas, my lord! I don't know.'

'So you deny it?'

'Everything!'

'Go ahead,' said Charmolue to Pierrat.

Pierrat turned the handle of the screw, the boot tightened, and the unfortunate girl let out one of those terrible screams for which no human language has a written equivalent.

'Stop,' Charmolue told Pierrat. 'Do you confess?' he said to the gypsy.

'Everything!' cried the wretched girl. 'I confess! I confess! mercy!'

She had miscalculated her strength in facing the question. Poor child, whose life up till then had been so joyful, so smooth, so sweet, the first pain had overcome her.

'Humanity obliges me to tell you,' observed the King's attorney, 'that by confessing you must expect the death penalty.'

'I hope so,' she said. And fell back on the leather bed, dying, bent double, letting herself hang from the strap buckled over her chest.

'Up there, my beauty, hold yourself up a bit,' said Maître Pierrat as he raised her. 'You look like that golden sheep the Duke of Burgundy wears round his neck.'

Jacques Charmolue raised his voice. 'Clerk, write: Young Bohemian girl, you confess that you have taken part in the agapes, sabbath, and malefices of hell, with larvae, masks, and vampires? Answer.'

'Yes,' she said so quietly that the word was covered by her breathing.

'You admit to seeing the ram that Beelzebub makes appear in the clouds to convene the sabbath, and is seen only by sorcerers?'

'Yes.'

'You confess to worshipping the heads of Bophomet, the Templars' abominable idols?'*

'Yes.'

'To having had habitual dealings with the devil in the form of a familiar she-goat, jointly charged with you?'

'Yes.'

'Finally, you admit and confess to having, with the help of the demon, and the phantom commonly known as the bogey-monk, on the night of 29 March past, murdered and assassinated a captain named Phoebus de Châteaupers?'

She looked up at the magistrate with her large, staring eyes, and answered like a machine, without tension or tremor: 'Yes.' It was obvious that everything in her was shattered.

'Write, clerk,' said Charmolue. And, addressing the torturer: 'Have the prisoner unfastened and brought back to the hearing.'

When the prisoner was 'unshod', the attorney in ecclesiastical courts examined her foot, still numb from the pain. 'Come along!' he said, 'there's no great harm done. You cried out in time. You would still be able to dance, my beauty!'

Then he turned to his acolytes from the officiality: 'There at last justice is enlightened! It is a relief, messieurs! Mademoiselle will testify to the fact that we acted with all possible gentleness.'

III

END OF THE GOLD *ÉCU* TURNED INTO A DRY LEAF

WHEN she came back into the courtroom, pale and limping, she was greeted by a general murmur of pleasure. On the audience's part there was the feeling of impatience rewarded which one experiences in the theatre at the end of the last interval in the play, when the curtain goes up and the end is about to begin. On the judges' part it was the hope of being soon able to sit down to supper. The little goat too bleated with delight. It tried to run to its mistress, but it had been tied to the bench.

It was now completely dark. The candles, whose number had not been increased, gave so little light that one could not see the walls of the hall. Darkness wrapped every object in a kind of haze. The apathetic faces of some of the judges just barely emerged. Facing them, at the end of the long hall, they could see a vague white blur standing out against the gloomy background. It was the accused.

She had dragged herself to her place. When Charmolue had installed himself magisterially in his, he sat down, then stood up again and said, without betraying too much vanity at his success: 'The accused has admitted everything.'

'Bohemian girl,' the president put in, 'you have admitted all your acts of magic, prostitution, and murder against Phoebus de Châteaupers?'

Her heart constricted. She could be heard sobbing in the shadows. 'Whatever you will,' she answered feebly, 'but kill me quickly.'

'Monsieur the King's attorney in ecclesiastical courts,' said the president, 'the court is ready to hear your requisitions.'

Maître Charmolue displayed an intimidating register, and began reading with a wealth of gesture and the exaggerated accents of advocacy a Latin oration in which all the evidence of the charges was stacked upon Ciceronian periphrases flanked by quotations from Plautus, his favourite comic author. We regret being unable to offer our readers this remarkable piece. The orator delivered it with a marvellous range of actions. Before he had even finished his exordium the sweat was already running off his brow and his eyes were bulging. Suddenly, right in the middle of a period, he broke off, and his expression, usually quite gentle and even stupid, became thunderous: 'Messieurs,' he cried (this time in French, for it was not in his text), 'Satan is so much involved in this affair that there he is, present at our proceedings and aping their majesty. Look!'

So saying he pointed to the little goat, who, seeing Charmolue gesticulate, had indeed thought it appropriate to do the same, and had sat down on its rump, copying as best it could with its forelegs and bearded face the emotional pantomime of the King's attorney in ecclesiastical courts. This was, you may remember, one of the goat's most charming talents. This incident, this last *proof*, produced a great effect. They tied the goat's hooves together, and the King's attorney resumed the thread of his eloquence.

It took a very long time, but the peroration was admirable. Here is the final sentence; add to it Maître Charmolue's hoarse voice and breathless gestures:

Ideo, Domni, coram stryga demonstrata, crimine patente, intentione criminis existente, in nomine sanctae ecclesiae Nostrae-Dominae Parisiensis, quae est in saisina habendi omnimodam altam et bassam justitiam in illa hac intemerata Civitatis insula, tenore praesentium declaramus nos requirere; primo, aliquandam pecuniariam indemnitatem; secundo, amendationem honorabilem ante portalium maximum Nostrae-Dominae, ecclesiae cathedralis; tertio, sententiam in virtute cujus ista stryga cum sua capella, seu in trivio vulgariter dicto la Grève, *seu in insula exeunte in fluvio Sequanae, juxta pointam jardinis regalis, executae sint!*

[Therefore, gentlemen, in the presence of a proven vampire, the crime being patent, the criminal intention existent, in the name of the holy church of Notre-Dame de Paris, which is seized of the right of exercising justice of all kinds, high and low, in that undefiled island of the Cité, by the tenor of these presents we declare that we demand: first, some pecuniary indemnity; second, public penance before the great portal of the cathedral church of Notre-Dame; thirdly, a sentence by virtue of which this vampire, together with her goat, either in the square commonly called la Grève, or where the island comes to a point in the river Seine, beside the tip of the royal gardens, be executed.]

He put his cap on again and sat down.

'*Eheu!*' Gringoire sighed, heartbroken, '*bassa latinitas* [Alas! what low Latin].'

Another man in a black robe stood up by the accused. It was her advocate. The judges, still fasting, began to murmur.

'Advocate, be brief,' said the president.

'Monsieur le Président,' replied the advocate,' since the defendant has confessed her crime, I have only one word to say to these gentlemen. Here is a text from the Salic law: "If a vampire has eaten a man, and been convicted of it, she shall pay a fine of 8,000 *deniers* which makes 200 gold *sous*." May it please the court to condemn my client to that fine.'

'The text has been abrogated,' said the advocate extraordinary to the King.

'*Nego* [I deny that],' retorted the advocate.

'Put it to the vote!' said a counsellor. 'The crime is patent and the hour is late.'

They proceeded to vote without leaving the hall. The judges voted by raising their caps, they were in a hurry. Their hooded heads could be seen in the shadows being uncovered one after the other as the president put the lugubrious question to them in a low voice. The poor accused seemed to be watching, but her blurred eyes no longer saw.

Then the clerk began writing; then he handed the president a long parchment scroll.

At that the wretched girl heard the people stirring, pikes clashing, and an icy voice saying:

'Bohemian girl, on such a day as may please our lord the King, at the hour of noon, you will be taken in a tumbril, wearing a shift, barefoot, a rope round your neck, before the great portal of Notre-Dame, and there you will do public penance with a wax torch of two pounds' weight in your hand, thence you will be taken to the Place de Grève, where you will be hanged and strangled on the town gibbet; likewise your goat; and you will pay the official 3 *lions* of gold in reparation for the crimes committed and confessed by you of witchcraft, magic, lechery, and murder against the person of Monsieur Phoebus de Châteaupers. May God have mercy on your soul!'

'Oh! I'm dreaming!' she murmured, and felt rough hands taking her away.

IV

IN the Middle Ages, once a building was completed there
was almost as much of it in the ground as outside. Unless
it was built on piles, like Notre-Dame, a palace, a fortress,
a church, always had a double bottom. In cathedrals it was,
as it were, another cathedral underground, low, dark, mysterious, blind and dumb, beneath the upper nave flooded
with light and resounding day and night with organ and
bells; sometimes it was a sepulchre. In palaces, in fortresses,
it was a prison, sometimes again a sepulchre, sometimes
both together. These mighty buildings, whose method of
formation and 'vegetation' we have discussed elsewhere, did
not simply have foundations but, so to speak, roots, whose
ramifications extended into the soil as chambers, galleries,
stairways, like the building constructed above. Thus churches, palaces, fortresses had earth up to their waists. A building's cellars were another building, in which you went down
instead of up, and whose underground storeys joined on beneath the pile of external storeys of the structure, like those
forests and mountains reflected upside-down in the waters
of a lake beneath the forests and mountains on its shore.

At the Bastille Saint-Antoine, at the Palais de Justice in
Paris, at the Louvre, these underground constructions were
prisons. The storeys of these prisons, as they plunged
deeper into the earth, became darker and more cramped.
They amounted to so many zones on a graduated scale of
horror. Dante could find no better scheme for his Inferno.*
These funnels of cells usually ended in a sump-like dungeon, where Dante put his Satan, and where society put
those condemned to death. Once a wretched being had
been buried down there it meant farewell to daylight, fresh
air, life, *ogni speranza* [all hope]. It came out only for the
gallows or the stake. Sometimes it rotted away down there.

Human justice called that 'forgetting'.* Between mankind
and himself the condemned person felt weighing down on
his head an accumulation of stones and gaolers, and the
whole prison, the massive fortress, was just an immense,
complex lock shutting him out from the world of the living.

It was in just such a sump, in the oubliettes excavated by
St Louis, in the *in pace* of the Tournelle, that they had,
doubtless for fear of an escape, deposited la Esmeralda,
condemned to the gallows, with the colossal Palais de Justice over her head. Poor fly who could not have budged the
smallest of its stones!

Providence and society had surely been equally unjust;
such a profusion of misery and torture was not needed to
shatter so frail a creature.

She was there, lost in the darkness, buried, interred,
walled up. Anyone who could have seen her in such a state,
after seeing her laughing and singing in the sunlight, would
have shuddered. Cold as night, cold as death, no longer a
breath of air through her hair, no human sound in her ear,
no gleam of daylight in her eyes, broken in half, crushed
with chains, squatting by a pitcher and a loaf of bread on
a bit of straw amid the pool of water formed beneath her
by the dampness oozing from the dungeon, unmoving, almost unbreathing; she was no longer even capable of suffering. Phoebus, the sunshine, noonday, fresh air, dancing
to applause, sweet prattling of love with the officer, all that
indeed still ran through her mind, sometimes as a golden,
lilting vision, sometimes as a shapeless nightmare; but now
it was just a vague, horrible struggle fading into the darkness, or distant music playing up there above ground, no
longer audible at the depths to which the unfortunate girl
had fallen.

Since she had been down there she had been neither
awake nor asleep. In such misfortune, in such a dungeon,
she could no longer distinguish sleeping from waking,
dream from reality, day from night. It was all mixed up,
broken, drifting, scattered in confusion in her mind. At
most she dreamed. Never had a living creature come so
close to nothingness.

Thus numb, chilled, petrified, she had hardly noticed on two or three occasions the sound of a trapdoor opening somewhere above her, without letting in even a chink of light, and through it a hand throwing her a crust of black bread. This was, however, the sole human contact remaining to her—the gaoler's periodic visit.

Just one thing still automatically caught her ear: above her head the dampness seeped through the mouldering stones of the vault, and at regular intervals a drop of water broke away. She listened in a daze to the sound of each drop falling into the pool beside her.

This drop of water falling into the pool was the only thing that still stirred around her, the only clock to mark the time, the only sound to reach down to her out of all the sounds being produced on the earth's surface.

In point of fact she also felt from time to time, in this cloaca of mire and darkness, something cold pass here and there over her foot or her arm, and she shivered.

How long she had been there, she did not know. She remembered a death sentence being pronounced somewhere against someone, then being taken away, and waking up in blackness and silence, frozen. She had dragged herself along on her hands, then iron rings had cut into her ankles and there had been a clanking of chains. She had realized that there was a wall all round her, that beneath her was a flagstone covered with water and a bundle of straw. But no lamp and no airhole. So, she had sat down on the straw and sometimes, to change her position, on the bottom step of some stone stairs which there were in the dungeon. For a while she had tried to count the black minutes measured out by the drops of water, but soon this dismal labour of a sick brain had broken off of its own accord in her head and left her in a stupor.

One day finally, or one night (for midday and midnight were the same colour in this tomb) she heard above her a louder noise than that usually made by the warder when he brought her her jug and her bread. She looked up and saw a reddish beam shine through the cracks in the kind of door or trap set into the ceiling of the *in pace*. At the same time the heavy ironwork creaked, the trap grated on its rusty hinges, then turned, and she saw a lantern, a hand, and the lower part of the bodies of two men, the door being too low for her to see their heads. The light hurt so badly that she closed her eyes.

When she opened them again the door was once more shut, the torch set down on one of the steps; one man, on his own, stood before her. A black cowled robe fell to his feet, a *caffardum** of the same colour hid his face. Nothing could be seen of his body, neither his face nor his hands. He was like a long black shroud standing upright, beneath which something could be perceived moving. She stared for a few minutes at this kind of spectre. Meanwhile neither she nor he spoke. They looked like two statues facing each other. Only two things seemed to be alive in the cellar: the wick of the lantern, sputtering from the dampness in the atmosphere, and the water dripping from the ceiling which punctuated the irregular crepitation with its own monotonous splash and made the light from the lantern tremble in concentric ripples on the oily water of the pool.

At last the prisoner broke the silence: 'Who are you?'

'A priest.'

The word, the accent, the sound of his voice made her shudder.

The priest went on in muffled tones: 'Are you prepared?'

'For what?'

'To die.'

'Oh!' she said, 'will it be soon?'

'Tomorrow.'

Her head, which had been raised in joy, sank back on her chest. 'That's a long time yet!' she murmured; 'what difference would it make to them to do it today?'

'So you are very unhappy?' the priest asked after a silence.

'I'm very cold,' she answered.

She took her feet in her hands, a habitual gesture of unhappy creatures who are cold, already observed in the recluse of the Tour-Roland, and her teeth chattered.

The priest seemed to be looking round the dungeon, his eyes concealed beneath his hood.

'No light! no fire! in a pool of water! It's horrible!'

'Yes,' she replied with the stunned look that misfortune had given her. 'Daylight belongs to everyone. Why do they give me only night?'

'Do you know,' the priest went on after a further silence, 'why you are here?'

'I think I once knew,' she said, rubbing her skinny fingers over her eyebrows as though to help her remember, 'but I don't know now.'

Suddenly she began weeping like a child: 'I want to get out of here, monsieur. I'm cold, I'm afraid, and there are creatures that climb over my body.'

'Very well, follow me.'

So saying the priest took her by the arm. The wretched girl was frozen to the marrow, yet that hand felt cold to her.

'Oh!' she murmured, 'it's the icy hand of death,—who are you, then?'

The priest lifted up his hood. She looked. It was the sinister face which had been pursuing her for so long, that demon's head which had appeared at la Falourdel's above the beloved head of her Phoebus, that eye which she had last seen glinting beside a dagger.

This apparition, which had always been so fateful for her and had driven her from misfortune to misfortune as far as the torture chamber, roused her from her torpor. It seemed to her that the sort of veil which had shrouded her memory was being rent asunder. All the details of her dismal adventure, from the nocturnal scene at la Falourdel's down to her condemnation at the Tournelle came back to her mind all at once, not vague and confused as they had been up till then, but distinct, raw, clear-cut, lifelike, terrible. Those half-erased memories, almost wiped away by an excess of suffering, were revived by the sombre figure before her, just as invisible letters traced with sympathetic ink stand out bold and fresh on blank paper when brought close to a fire. It seemed to her that all the wounds in her heart had re-opened at once, and were bleeding.

'Ha!' she cried, her hands over her eyes, trembling convulsively, 'it's the priest!'

Then she dropped her arms in dejection, and remained sitting, with head bowed, eyes fixed on the ground, mute, continuing to tremble.

The priest looked at her with the eye of a kite which has long been hovering in circles high up in the sky around a poor lark cowering in the corn, which has long been silently contracting the formidable circles of its flight, has suddenly fallen upon its prey like lightning, and holds it quivering in its claws.

She began murmuring very softly: 'Finish it! finish it! the final blow!' And in terror buried her head between her shoulders, like a sheep waiting for the butcher's club to fall.

'So you find me abhorrent?' he said at last.

She did not answer. 'Do you find me abhorrent?' he repeated.

Her lips contracted as if she were smiling. 'Yes,' she said; 'the executioner mocks the condemned man. For months now he has been pursuing me, threatening me, frightening me! But for him, my God, how happy I should have been! He's the one who cast me into this abyss. Oh heavens! He's the one who killed . . . he's the one who killed him! my Phoebus!'

At this, bursting into sobs and looking up at the priest: 'Oh! you wretch! Who are you? What have I done to you? Do you hate me then? Alas, what have you got against me?'

'I love you!' cried the priest.

Her tears suddenly ceased. She looked at him like an idiot. He had fallen to his knees and gazed longingly at her with blazing eyes.

'Do you hear? I love you!' he cried once more.

'What a love!' the unfortunate girl said, shuddering.

He went on: 'The love of a damned soul!'

They both remained silent for some minutes, crushed by the weight of their emotions, he out of his mind, she in a daze.

'Listen,' the priest said at last, strangely calm again. 'You are about to learn everything. I'm going to tell you what up till now I hardly dared to tell myself when I furtively examined my conscience during those deep hours of the night

when it is so dark that it seems as though God can no longer
see us. Listen. Before I met you, girl, I was happy . . .'

'So was I!' she sighed weakly.

'Don't interrupt. Yes, I was happy, I thought I was, at
least. I was pure, my soul was filled with limpid brightness.
No one raised his head more proudly and radiantly than I.
Priests consulted me on chastity, learned doctors on doc-
trine. Yes, knowledge meant everything to me. It was like
a sister, and a sister was enough for me. It's not that other
ideas did not come to me with age. More than once my
flesh was excited by a woman's form passing by. That force
of sex and blood in the grown man which, as a foolish youth
I thought I had stifled for life, had more than once convulsively shaken the iron chain of vows binding me, poor
wretch, to the cold stones of the altar. But fasting, prayer,
study, the mortifications of the cloister, had restored to the
spirit mastery over the flesh. Anyhow, I avoided women.
Besides, I had only to open a book for all the impure
vapours of my brain to be dispelled before the splendour
of knowledge. In a few minutes I felt gross earthly things
recede into the distance, and I was calm, dazzled, and
serene again in the presence of the tranquil radiance of
eternal truth. As long as the demon sent to attack me only
the vague shadows of women passing occasionally before
my eyes in church, in the street, in the fields, and rarely
returning in my dreams, I easily overcame him. Alas! if the
victory has not remained mine, it is God's fault for not
creating man and the devil with equal strength.—Listen.
One day . . .'

Here the priest stopped, and the prisoner heard rending
sighs come from his chest like a death-rattle.

He went on: 'One day, I was leaning at the window of
my cell . . . . What was I reading? Oh! it's all spinning
round in my head!—I was reading. The window overlooked
a square. I heard the sound of music and a drumbeat.
Annoyed at this disturbance to my reverie, I looked out on
to the square. What I saw was being seen by others as well,
and yet it was not a sight intended for human eyes. There,
in the middle of the pavement—it was noon—bright sun-

shine—a creature was dancing. So beautiful a creature that God would have preferred her to the Virgin, and chosen her for his mother and wanted to be born of her if she had existed when he was made man! Her eyes were dark and splendid, in the midst of her black hair a few loose strands shone as bright as gold thread where the sun had penetrated. Her feet moved so swiftly that they became blurred like the spokes of a rapidly revolving wheel. Round her head, in her black tresses, were metal plates sparkling in the sun and forming on her brow a starry crown. Her sequined dress sparkled blue and star-spangled like a summer night. Her supple brown arms twined and untwined round her waist like two sashes. The shape of her body was of astonishing beauty. Oh! that resplendent figure standing out like something luminous in the light of the sun itself! Alas! girl, it was you. Surprised, intoxicated, spellbound, I let myself go on looking at you. I looked at you so hard that I suddenly shivered with terror, I felt in the grip of fate.'

The priest, overcome, stopped again for a moment. Then he went on:

'Already half fascinated, I tried to cling to something to halt me in my fall. I remembered the ambushes Satan had already laid for me. The creature I had before my eyes had that more than human beauty which can come only from heaven or hell. This was no ordinary girl made from a handful of clay, dimly lit within by the flickering beam of a woman's soul. It was an angel! but of darkness, of flames, and not of light. At the very moment that I was thinking thus, I saw a goat beside you, a beast from the sabbath, looking at me and laughing. The noonday sun gave it horns of fire. Then I glimpsed the demon's snare, and I doubted no more that you had come from hell and had come thence for my damnation. So I believed.'

Here the priest looked directly at the prisoner and added coldly:

'I still believe so. Meanwhile the spell was gradually working, your dance whirled round in my brain, I felt the mysterious malefice taking effect within me, all that should have been vigilant in my soul fell asleep, and like those who

die in the snow I enjoyed letting sleep come. Suddenly you
began to sing. What could I do, wretch that I am? Your
singing was even more enchanting than your dancing. I
tried to flee. I could not. I was pinned, rooted to the
ground. It seemed to me that the marble floor slabs had
risen up to my knees. I had to stay to the end. My feet were
like ice, my head was boiling. At last, you felt sorry for me,
perhaps, you stopped singing, you disappeared. The reflection of that dazzling vision, the echo of that enchanting
music gradually faded from my eyes and ears. Then I fell
down in the window embrasure, stiffer and weaker than a
dislodged statue. The bell for vespers roused me. I rose, I
fled, but, alas! something in me had fallen and could not
be raised again, something had come upon me from which
I could not flee.'

He paused once more, then continued:

'Yes, from that day on there was a man in me whom I
did not know. I tried to use all my remedies, the cloister,
the altar, work, books. Madness! Oh! how hollow science
rings when one desperately bangs a head filled with passions against it! Do you know, girl, what from then on I
would see between the book and me? You, your shadow,
the image of the luminous apparition which had one day
crossed the space before me. But that image was no longer
the same colour; it was gloomy, funereal, dark as the black
circle which long dogs the sight of anyone who has been
unwise enough to stare at the sun.

'Unable to get rid of it, hearing your song always ringing
in my heart, seeing your feet always dancing over my breviary, feeling always in my dreams at night the smooth
touch of your shape upon my flesh, I tried to see you again,
to touch you, to find out who you were, to see if I would
find you anything like the ideal image of you which had
remained with me, perhaps to break my dream with the
reality. In any case I hoped that a new impression would
wipe out the original one, and that first impression had
become unbearable. I looked for you. I saw you again.
Disaster! When I had seen you twice, I wanted to see you
a thousand times, I wanted to see you always. Then—how

can one check the hellish slide?—then I was no longer
my own master. The other end of the string that the devil
had fastened to my wings he had tied to your foot. I wan-
dered aimlessly like you. I waited for you in doorways,
I spied on you at street corners, I watched out for you
from the top of my tower. Each evening I came back into
myself more spellbound, more desperate, more bewildered,
more damned!

'I had found out who you were, gypsy, Bohemian, gitane,
Zingara, what doubt could there be that magic was involved? Listen. I hoped that bringing you to trial would
release me from the spell. A sorceress had bewitched Bruno
of Asti, he had her burned and was cured. I knew that. I
wanted to try that remedy. I tried first to have you banned
from the Parvis Notre-Dame, hoping to forget you if you
did not come back any more. You realized that. You came
back. Then the idea occurred to me of abducting you. One
night I made an attempt. There were two of us. We already
had you in our grasp when that wretched officer turned up.
He rescued you. In doing so he began your misfortunes,
and mine, and his own. Finally, no longer knowing what to
do or what would become of me, I denounced you to the
official. I thought that I would be cured, like Bruno of Asti.
I also thought in a confused way that a trial would deliver
you into my hands, that I could hold you in a prison, I
would have you, that you would not be able to escape me
there, that you had possessed me long enough for me to
possess you in my turn. In doing wrong one must go the
whole way. It's crazy to stop half-way in what is monstrous!
The extreme in crime brings delirious joy. A priest and a
witch can melt in transports of delight on the straw of a
dungeon floor!

'So I denounced you. It was then that I terrified you when
we met. The plot that I was hatching against you, the storm
that I was piling up over your head, broke out from me in
threats and glances like lightning. However, I still hesitated.
My plan had frightening aspects which held me back.

'Perhaps I would have given it up, perhaps my hideous
idea would have withered in my brain without bearing fruit.

I believed that it would always depend on me whether to continue or interrupt this case. But every evil thought is inexorable and tries to become a deed; but where I believed myself omnipotent, fate was more powerful than I. Alas! alas! it is fate that took you and delivered you up to the dreadful mechanism of the apparatus that I had secretly constructed! Listen—I am nearly at an end.

'One day—another day of bright sunshine—I saw a man pass by who spoke your name, and laughed, and whose eyes were full of lust. Damnation! I followed him. You know the rest.'

He fell silent. The girl could find only one word: 'Oh, my Phoebus!'

'Not that name!' said the priest, gripping her violently by the arm. 'Don't say that name! Oh! wretches that we are, that is the name that has ruined us! Or rather we have all ruined each other through the inexplicable play of fatality! You are suffering, aren't you? You are cold, the darkness makes you blind, the dungeon envelops you, but perhaps you still have some light in your innermost depths, even if it is only your childish love for that hollow man who toyed with your heart! Whereas I carry my dungeon within me, within me is winter, ice, despair. I have dark night in my soul. Do you know all that I have suffered? I was present at your trial. I sat on the official's bench. Yes, beneath one of those priestly hoods were the writhings of a damned soul. When they brought you in, I was there; when they interrogated you, I was there. Den of wolves!—it was my crime, my gallows that I saw built up slowly over your head. Each witness, each piece of evidence, each lawyer's speech, I was there; I could count every step you took along the *via dolorosa*; I was even there when that wild beast . . . Oh! I hadn't foreseen torture! Listen. I followed you into the chamber of pain. I saw you undressed and handled half naked by the torturer's infamous hands. I saw your foot, that foot for which I would have given an empire to kiss just once and die, that foot which I should have been so over-joyed to feel crushing my head, I saw that foot clamped in that horrible boot which turns the limbs of a living creature into bloody mush. Oh! wretch that I am! While I saw that, I had a dagger under my shroud with which I was gashing my breast. When you cried out I dug it into my flesh; if you had cried a second time it would have gone into my heart! Look. I think it is still bleeding.'

He opened his cassock. His breast was indeed lacerated as though by a tiger's claw, and in his side was a large wound which had not properly closed.

The prisoner recoiled with horror.

'Oh!' said the priest, 'have pity on me, girl! You think you are unhappy, alas! alas! you don't know what unhappiness is. Oh! to love a woman! to be a priest! to be hated! to love her with all the frenzy in one's soul, to feel that for the least of her smiles one would give one's blood, one's entrails, reputation, salvation, immortality and eternity, this life and the next; to regret not being a king, emperor, archangel, god, so that she could have a greater slave at her feet; to embrace her night and day in dreams and thoughts; and see her in love with a soldier's uniform! and to have nothing to offer her but a dingy priest's cassock which would fill her with fear and disgust! To be there, jealous and furious, while she lavishes on this wretched swaggering fool treasures of love and beauty! To see that body whose shape makes you burn, that breast so soft and sweet, that flesh thrill and flush under another's kisses! O heavens! To love her foot, her arm, her shoulder, think about her blue veins, her brown skin, to the point of writhing all night on your cell's stone floor, and then to see all the caresses you dreamed of end up as torture! To have succeeded only in laying her down on the leather bed! Oh! there are the real pincers made red-hot in hell-fire! Oh! happy is he who is sawn between two planks, torn apart by four horses! Do you know what it is to undergo the torment inflicted during long nights by seething arteries, bursting heart, splitting head, teeth biting at your hands; relentless torturers who turn you over and over unceasingly, as on a burning grid-iron, on a thought of love, jealousy, despair! Mercy, girl! a moment's truce! a few ashes on the coals! Wipe away, I beseech you, the great drops of sweat streaming from my brow! Child! torture me with one hand, but caress me with the other! Have pity, girl; have pity on me!'

The priest was rolling on the ground in the water and banging his skull on the corners of the stone steps. The girl listened to him, looked at him. When he fell silent, exhausted and panting, she repeated faintly: 'Oh! my Phoebus!'

The priest dragged himself towards her on his knees. 'I beseech you,' he cried, 'if you have feelings, do not reject me! Oh! I love you! I am a wretch! When you say that name, unhappy creature, it is as though you were crushing every fibre in my heart between your teeth! Mercy! If you have come from hell, I am going there with you. I have done everything to that end. Hell with you there is my heaven, the sight of you is more delightful than that of God! Oh! tell me! won't you have anything to do with me, then? The day a woman spurned such a love I should have thought the mountains would move. Oh! if you were willing! Oh! how happy we could be! We would run away—I would make you run away—we would go somewhere, look for the place on earth with the most sunshine, the most trees, the most blue sky. We should love each other, pour out our two souls into each other, and feel insatiable thirst for each other, slaking it together and unceasingly from this cup of ever-flowing love.'

She interrupted him with a loud and terrible laugh. 'Just look, father! you have blood on your nails!'

The priest stayed as though petrified for a few moments, his gaze fixed on his hand.

'Very well, yes!' he went on at last, strangely gentle, 'insult me, mock me, crush me! But come, come. We must make haste. It's for tomorrow, I tell you—the gibbet on the Grève, you know? It's always ready. It's horrible! to see you step into that tumbril! Oh! mercy!—I had never realized as I do now how much I loved you—Oh! follow me. You can take your time loving me after I have saved you. You can hate me for as long as you like. But come! Tomorrow! tomorrow! the gibbet! your execution! Oh! save yourself! spare me!'

He seized her arm, he was distraught, he tried to drag her along.

She stared at him fixedly: 'What has become of my Phoebus?'

'Ah!' said the priest, letting go of her arm, 'you are pitiless!'

'What has become of Phoebus?' she repeated coldly.

'He's dead!' the priest cried.

'Dead!' she said, still glacial and unmoving; 'then why do you talk to me of living?'

He was not listening to her: 'Oh! yes,' he said, as though talking to himself, 'he must surely be dead. The blade went in very deep. I think I touched his heart with the tip. Oh! I was alive right down to the tip of the dagger!'

The girl hurled herself upon him like a raging tigress, and thrust him on to the stairs with supernatural strength. 'Go, monster! Go, murderer! Let me die! May the blood of us both stain your brow eternally! Be yours, priest? Never! never! Nothing will unite us, not even hell! Go, curses on you! Never!'

The priest had stumbled to the stairs. In silence he freed his feet from the folds of his robe, picked up his lantern and began slowly climbing the steps up to the door; he opened the door once more and went out.

Suddenly the girl saw his head reappear, a terrifying expression on his face, and he cried with a groan of rage and despair: 'I tell you he is dead!'

She fell face down on the ground; and there was no other sound now to be heard in the dungeon but the sigh of the water dripping and sending ripples through the pool in the darkness.

V

THE MOTHER

I DO not think that there can be anything in the world happier than the thoughts awakened in a mother's heart at the sight of her child's little shoe. Above all if it is the shoe for special occasions, Sundays, christening, the shoe embroidered even under the sole, a shoe in which the child has not yet taken a step. That shoe is so tiny and graceful, it is so impossible for it to walk, that for the mother it is as if she were seeing her child. She smiles at it, kisses it, talks to it. She wonders if a foot can really be so small; and if the child is not there, the dainty shoe is enough to bring back before her eyes the soft and fragile creature. She imagines she can see him, she does see him, all of him, living, joyful, with his delicate hands, round head, pure lips, untroubled eyes with the whites still tinged with blue. If it is winter, he is there, crawling on the carpet, clambering laboriously on to a stool, and his mother is fearful in case he goes too near the fire. If it is summer, he is creeping about in the yard, in the garden, pulling up grass from between the paving stones, looking innocently at the big dogs, the big horses, quite unafraid, playing with the ornamental shells, the flowers, and making the gardener grumble at finding sand in the flowerbeds and soil on the paths. Everything around him is as smiling, beaming, radiant as himself, down to the breath of wind and the ray of sunlight frolicking in rivalry through his downy curls. The shoe shows the mother all this and makes her heart melt like wax before a fire.

But when the child is lost, these countless images of joy, delight, tenderness crowding round the little shoe become so many objects of horror. The pretty embroidered shoe is now just an instrument of torture everlastingly crushing the mother's heart. It is still the same fibre vibrating, the deepest and most sensitive one; but instead of an angel stroking it, it is a demon who plucks it cruelly.

One morning, when the May sun was rising on one of those dark blue skies against which Garofalo* likes to set his *Descents from the Cross*, the recluse of the Tour-Roland heard the sound of wheels, horses, and clanking iron from the Place de Grève. It hardly roused her, but she tied her hair over her ears to shut it out and went back to gazing on bended knees at the inanimate object which she had been worshipping for the past fifteen years. This little shoe, as already related, was the whole world for her. Her thoughts were locked up in it, never to leave it until her death. What bitter imprecations, pathetic laments, prayers, and sobs she had raised to heaven over the charming pink satin bauble only the gloomy hole in the Tour-Roland knew. Never has more despair been lavished on a more graceful and dainty object.

On that morning it seemed that her grief was bursting out even more violently than usual, and she could be heard from outside lamenting in a loud, monotonous voice which pierced the heart.

'Oh! my daughter!' she was saying, 'my daughter! My poor dear little child! So I shall never see you again. So it's all over! It still seems as if it happened yesterday! O God, God, it would have been better never to have given her to me at all if you were going to take her back so soon. Don't you know, then, that our children come from our wombs, and that a mother who has lost her child no longer believes in God?—Ah! wretch that I am to have gone out that day!—Lord! Lord! to have taken her from me like that, you can never have watched me with her, when I warmed her at my fire and she was so happy, when she smiled at me as she sucked at my breast, when I walked her little feet all the way up my chest to my lips! Oh! if you had seen that, God, you would have had pity on my joy, you would not have taken from me the only love left in my heart! Was I then such a miserable creature, Lord, that you couldn't look at me before condemning me? Alas! alas! here is the shoe, but where's the foot? Where is the rest? Where is the child? My daughter, my daughter! What have they done with you? Lord, give her back to me! I have scraped my knees raw praying to you for fifteen years, God, isn't that enough? Give her back to me for a day, an hour, a minute, one minute, Lord! And then cast me to the demon for all eternity! Oh! if I knew where the hem of your garment was trailing, I should cling to it with both hands, and you would have to give me back my child! Her pretty little shoe, Lord, have you no pity for it? Can you condemn a poor mother to fifteen years of such torture? Good Virgin! good Virgin in heaven! my own baby Jesus is what they have taken from me, stolen from me, they've eaten my baby on some heath, drunk her blood, chewed her bones! Good Virgin, have pity on me! My daughter! I need my daughter! What is it to me that she is in paradise? I don't want your angel, I want my child! I am a lioness, I want my cub. Oh! I shall writhe on the ground, break stone with my forehead, damn myself, and curse you, Lord, if you keep my child from me! You can see how I have gnawed at my arms, Lord! Has the good God no pity?—Oh! give me nothing but salt and black bread if I may only have my daughter to warm me up like a sun! Alas! Lord God, I am only a vile sinner; but my daughter made me pious. I was full of religion for love of her; and I saw you through her smile as though through an opening in the heavens.—Oh! if only I could just once, once more, once only, put this shoe on her pretty little pink foot, I would die, good Virgin, blessing you!—Ah! fifteen years! She would be grown up now! Unfortunate child! Why! it's quite true then, I shall never see her again, not even in heaven! for I shan't go there. Oh! what misery! to think that her shoe is there and that's all!'

The unhappy woman had flung herself upon this shoe, her consolation and despair for so many years, and her heart was racked with sobs as on the first day. For it is always the first day for a mother who has lost her child. That grief never grows old. The mourning weeds may wear out and fade; the heart stays black.

At that moment the fresh, joyous sound of children's voices passed by the cell. Every time children caught her eye or her ear the poor mother would rush to the darkest corner of her tomb, and it was as if she was trying to bury her head in the stone so that she would not hear them. This time, on the contrary, she sat up as if with a start and listened eagerly. One of the boys had just said: 'It's because they are going to hang a gypsy woman today.'

With the sudden pounce of the spider which we saw hurling itself on the fly when its web was shaken, she rushed to the window which, as we know, looked out on to the Place de Grève. A ladder had indeed been set up by the permanent gibbet, and the executioner was busy adjusting the chains, rusted by the rain. A few people stood around.

The laughing band of children was already far off. The *sachette* looked out for some passer-by to question. Right beside her cell she noticed a priest, pretending to read the public breviary, but much less concerned with the 'iron-latticed lectern' than with the gallows, on which he cast from time to time a gloomy and forbidding glance. She recognized Monsieur the Archdeacon of Josas, a saintly man.

'Father,' she asked, 'who are they going to hang there?'

The priest looked at her and did not answer; she repeated her question. Then he said: 'I don't know.'

'Some passing children were saying it was some gypsy woman,' the recluse went on.

'I think that is so,' said the priest.

Then Paquette la Chantefleurie burst out laughing like a hyena.

'Sister,' said the archdeacon, 'do you really hate gypsy women then?'

'Do I hate them?' cried the recluse; 'they are vampires, child-stealers! They ate my little girl, my child, my only child! I have no heart left. They ate it up.'

She was terrifying; the priest looked at her coldly.

'There is one I specially hate, and whom I have cursed,' she went on; 'she's a young one. The same age that my daughter would be if her mother hadn't eaten my daughter. Every time that young viper goes past my cell, she makes my blood curdle!'

'Well, sister, you should rejoice,' said the priest, glacial as a statue on a tomb, 'she's the one you are going to see die.'

His head fell upon his breast, and he slowly went away.

The recluse hugged herself with joy. 'I told her she would go up there! Thank you, priest,' she cried.

And she began pacing up and down before the bars of her window, dishevelled, eyes blazing, banging her shoulder against the wall, with the wild look of a caged she-wolf which has long been hungry and feels feeding time draw near.

VI

THREE MEN'S HEARTS DIFFERENTLY MADE

PHOEBUS, however, was not dead. Men of that kind have nine lives. When Maître Philippe Lheulier, advocate extra-ordinary to the King, had told poor Esmeralda: 'He is dying', he was in error or jesting. When the archdeacon had repeated to the condemned girl: 'He's dead', the truth is that he did not know, but believed it to be so, was relying on the fact, did not doubt it, very much hoped it was so. It would have been much too hard for him to give the woman he loved good news of his rival. In his place any man would have done the same.

It was not that Phoebus' wound had been anything but serious, but it had been less serious than the archdeacon was pleased to think. The master-surgeon, to whose house the soldiers of the watch had carried him in the first instance, had feared for his life for a week, and had even told him so in Latin. Youth, however, had gained the upper hand; and, as often happens, notwithstanding prognoses and diagnoses, nature had amused herself by saving the patient to spite the doctor. It was while he was still lying on a sickbed at the surgeon's house that he had undergone the first interroga-tion of Philippe Lheulier and the official's inquisition, which he had found very tiresome. So, one fine morning, feeling better, he had left his golden spurs as payment for the pharmacopolist, and made himself scarce. This, however, caused no problems for the preparation of the case. Jus-tice at that time was very little concerned with precision and propriety in criminal trials. Provided the accused was hanged, that was all that was required. Now, the judges had enough evidence against la Esmeralda. They had believed Phoebus to be dead, and there was no more to be said.

Phoebus, for his part, had not fled very far. He had simply gone back to rejoin his company, in garrison at Queue-en-Brie,* in the Île-de-France, a few stages from Paris.

After all, it did not suit him to appear in person at this trial. He had a vague feeling that he would look ridiculous. In fact he was not too sure what to make of the whole affair. Irreligious and superstitious, like any soldier who is only a soldier, when he questioned himself about this adventure, he was not happy about the goat, about the odd way he had first met la Esmeralda, about the equally strange manner in which she had revealed to him the secret of her love, finally about the bogey-monk. He suspected much more magic than love in this story, probably a witch, perhaps the devil; a piece of theatre, in short, or, to speak the language of the time, a most unpleasant mystery play, with him playing a very clumsy part, the butt for beatings and ridicule. The captain felt very sheepish about it. He experienced the kind of shame which our La Fontaine has so admirably defined: 'Ashamed as a fox caught by a hen'.*

He hoped anyway that the affair would not become public, that in his absence his name would hardly be mentioned, and would in any case not send echoes beyond the proceedings at the Tournelle. In that he was not mistaken, there was no *Gazette des Tribunaux** in those days, and as hardly a week went by without some forger being boiled alive, or some witch hanged, or some heretic burned at one of the innumerable 'justices' of Paris, people were so used to seeing at every crossroads the old feudal Themis,* sleeves rolled up and arms bare, doing her job at the gallows, ladders, and pillories, that they took hardly any notice. The high society of the time scarcely knew the name of the victim passing by at the corner of the street, and it was at most only the common people who regaled themselves with such coarse fare. An execution was a regular occurrence on the public thoroughfare, like the baker's brazier or the flayer's slaughteryard. The executioner was only a rather darker kind of butcher than the others.

Phoebus, then, quickly put his mind at rest concerning the enchantress Esmeralda, or Similar, as he called her, the stabbing by the gypsy or the bogey-monk (it mattered little to him which), and the outcome of the trial. But as soon as his heart was vacant on that score, the image of Fleur-de-Lys returned. Captain Phoebus' heart, like the physics of the time, abhorred a vacuum.

Queue-en-Brie was in any case a very dull place to be stationed, a village of blacksmiths and cow-girls with chapped hands, a long ribbon of mean hovels and cottages strung along both sides of the highway for half a league; in short a *queue*, or tail.

Fleur-de-Lys was his last passion but one, a pretty girl, with a delightful dowry; so one fine morning, completely cured, and fully supposing that after two months the affair of the gypsy girl must be over and forgotten, the amorous cavalier pranced up to the door of the Gondelaurier mansion.

He paid no attention to a rather numerous throng gathering in the Place du Parvis, in front of the portal of Notre-Dame; he remembered that it was May, assumed it was some procession, some Pentecost, some feast day, tied up his horse to the ring in the porch and went cheerfully upstairs to his lovely fiancée.

She was alone with her mother.

Fleur-de-Lys still had weighing on her heart the scene with the witch, her goat, the cursed alphabet, and Phoebus' long absences. However, when she saw her captain come in, she found him looking so fine, with his new acton,* his gleaming baldrick, his passionate air, that she blushed with pleasure. The noble damsel herself was more charming than ever. Her magnificent fair hair was arranged in the most ravishing plaits, she was dressed from head to foot in that sky-blue which suits fair-skinned women so well, a coquetry learned from Colombe,* and her eyes glistened with that amorous languor that suits them even better.

Phoebus, who as far as beauty was concerned had seen nothing since the cowherds of Queue-en-Brie, was intoxicated by Fleur-de-Lys, which made our officer so gallant and attentive that his peace was made straight away. Madame de Gondelaurier herself, still sitting maternally in her big armchair, did not have the strength to scold him. As for Fleur-de-Lys's reproaches, they died away in tender cooings.

The girl was sitting by the window, still embroidering her Neptune's grotto. The captain stood leaning on the back of her chair, and in a low voice she grumbled at him affectionately:

'But what have you been up to these past two months and more, you wicked man?'

'I swear,' answered Phoebus, a little embarrassed by the question, 'that you are beautiful enough to give an archbishop dreams.'

She could not help smiling.

'That will do, sir, that will do. Leave my beauty alone, and answer. A fine beauty indeed!'

'All right! dear cousin, I have been recalled to garrison duty.'

'And where might that be, if you please? And why didn't you come and say goodbye to me?'

'At Queue-en-Brie.'

Phoebus was delighted that the first question helped him evade the second.

'But that's no distance, sir. How is it that you haven't once been to see me?'

Here Phoebus was quite seriously at a loss. 'The fact is . . . duty . . . and, besides, charming cousin, I have been ill.'

'Ill!' she repeated in alarm.

'Yes . . . wounded.'

'Wounded!'

The poor girl was quite overcome.

'Oh! nothing to be frightened at,' Phoebus said casually, 'it's trifling. A quarrel, a sword-thrust; what is it to you?'

'What is it to me?' exclaimed Fleur-de-Lys, looking up with her lovely eyes brimming with tears. 'Oh! you are not thinking what you are saying when you say that. What's this about a sword-thrust? I want to know all about it.'

'Very well! dear lovely lady, I had a row with Mahé Fédy, you know? lieutenant of Saint-Germain-en-Laye, and we tore a few strips of skin off each other. That's all.'

The mendacious captain knew very well that an affair of honour always enhances a man's standing in a woman's eyes. Indeed Fleur-de-Lys was looking straight at him, deeply moved by fear, pleasure, and admiration. She was not, however, fully reassured.

'As long as you are completely cured, my Phoebus!' she said. 'I don't know your Mahé Fédy, but he's a nasty man. And what was this quarrel about?'

Here Phoebus, not gifted with a specially creative imagination, began to wonder how on earth to extricate himself from his supposed feat of arms.

'Oh! I don't really know . . . a trifle, a horse, a remark! . . . Fair cousin,' he exclaimed, to change the subject, 'what's all that noise in the Parvis?'

He went to the window: 'Oh! good heavens, fair cousin, the square is full of people!'

'I don't know,' said Fleur-de-Lys; 'it seems that a witch is going to do public penance this morning in front of the church and then be hanged.'

The captain was so sure that the affair of la Esmeralda was over that he hardly reacted to Fleur-de-Lys's words. He put a question or two to her all the same.

'What is this witch's name?'

'I don't know,' she replied.

'And what is she said to have done?'

This time too she shrugged her white shoulders. 'I don't know.'

'Oh! my God, Jesus!' said the mother, 'there are so many sorcerers about nowadays that I think they burn them without knowing their names, You might as well try to know the name of every cloud in the sky. After all, there's nothing to worry about. God keeps his own list.' At this the venerable lady stood up and went to the window. 'Lord!' she said, 'you are right, Phoebus. That is a huge mob of people. Some of them, blessed be God!, are even up on the rooftops. Do you know, Phoebus, that reminds me of my young days, the entry of King Charles VII, when there was such a crowd too—I don't recall the year any more. When I talk to you about that, it strikes you, doesn't it, as something old, and me as something young?—Oh! it was a very much finer crowd than nowadays. Some of them were even up on the machicolations of the Porte Saint-Antoine. The King had the Queen riding pillion, and after their highnesses came all the ladies riding pillion behind all the lords. I remember there was a lot of laughter because next to Amanyon de Garlande, who was very short, was Sir Matefelon, a knight of gigantic stature, who had killed heaps of Englishmen. It was really fine. A procession of all the gentlemen of France, with their oriflammes blazing red for all to see. Some of them had pennons and some banners. Let me see: Lord de Calan, pennon; Jean de Châteaumorant banner; Lord de Coucy, banner, richer than any of the others, except the duc de Bourbon . . . Alas! how sad it is to think that all that once existed and now there's nothing of it left!'

The two lovers were not listening to the venerable dowager. Phoebus had returned to lean on the back of his fiancée's chair, a delightful position, from which his licentious eye could see down into all the openings of Fleur-de-Lys's collaret. This *gorgerette* gaped open so conveniently, allowing him to see so many exquisite things and to guess at so many more, that Phoebus, dazzled by such satin-smooth skin said inwardly: 'How could one love anything but a fair-skinned blonde?' They both kept silence. The girl looked up at him now and then with eyes full of sweet delight, and their hair mingled in a ray of spring sunshine.

'Phoebus,' Fleur-de-Lys suddenly murmured, 'we are to be married in three months' time, swear that you have never loved any other girl but me.'

'I swear it, fair angel!' Phoebus answered and his passionate gaze accompanied the ring of sincerity in his voice to convince Fleur-de-Lys. At that moment he may even have believed himself.

Meanwhile the good mother, delighted to see the betrothed pair getting on so admirably together, had just left the apartment to attend to some domestic detail. Phoebus noticed this, and the fact that they were now alone so emboldened the adventurous captain that some very strange ideas came into his head. Fleur-de-Lys loved him, he was her betrothed, she was alone with him, his former feelings for her had reawakened, not quite as freshly as before, but just as ardently; after all, it is no great crime to pluck an ear or two before the corn is ripe; I do not know if such thoughts ran through his mind, but what is certain is that Fleur-de-Lys was suddenly frightened by the expression in his eyes. She looked around, and could no longer see her mother.

'Goodness me!' she said, flushed and anxious, 'I do feel warm!'

'I think indeed,' Phoebus replied, 'that it's not far off noon. The sun is becoming a nuisance. We have only to draw the curtains.'

'No, no!' cried the poor girl, 'on the contrary, I need air.'

And like a hind catching the scent of the hounds, she stood up, hurried to the window, opened it, and rushed on to the balcony.

Phoebus, quite put out, followed.

The Place du Parvis Notre-Dame, over which the balcony looked out, as we know, presented at that moment a strange and sinister sight that abruptly changed the nature of the shy Fleur-de-Lys's terror.

An immense crowd, which flowed back into all the adjacent streets, blocked the Place proper. The low wall surrounding the Parvis at waist height would not have sufficed to keep it clear had it not been reinforced by a solid rank of sergeants of the *onze-vingts* and hackbuteers, culverin in hand. Thanks to this thicket of pikes and arquebuses, the Parvis was empty. The entrance to it was guarded by a body of halberdiers wearing the bishop's arms. The great doors of the church were closed, in contrast to the countless windows round the square, which, open right up to the gables, revealed thousands of heads heaped up something like piles of cannonballs in an artillery park.

The surface of this throng was grey, dirty, muddy. The spectacle it was awaiting was obviously one of those which are privileged to bring out and attract the lowest dregs of the population. Nothing could be more hideous than the noise emanating from that swarm of yellow caps and filthy hair. In that crowd there was more laughter than shouting, more women than men.

From time to time some shrill vibrant voice would pierce the general hubbub . . .

'Hey there, Mahiet Baliffre, is that where they're going to hang her?'

'Don't be so silly! Here is where she does her public penance, in a shift! God will cough some Latin in her face! That always happens here, at noon. If it's the gallows you want, go off to the Grève.'

'I'll go afterwards.'

. . . .

'Tell me, la Boucanbry, is it true she has refused a confessor?'

'It seems so, la Bechaigne.'

'There's a proper heathen!'

. . . .

'Monsieur, it's the custom. The Palais bailiff is obliged to deliver the malefactor after sentence to be executed, if it's a lay person to the Provost of Paris; if a clerk, to the bishop's official.'

'I thank you, monsieur.'

. . . .

'O heavens!' said Fleur-de-Lys, 'the poor creature!'

At that thought, the eyes she was running over the populace filled with grief. The captain, much more occupied with her than with that heap of riff-raff, was amorously rumpling her waist-band from behind. She turned round, begging him with a smile: 'Please leave me alone, Phoebus! If my mother came back she would see your hand!'

At that moment the clock of Notre-Dame slowly struck noon. A murmur of satisfaction broke out among the crowd. The last vibration of the twelfth stroke had scarcely died away when all the heads rippled like waves in a gust of wind, and an immense cry rose from the pavement, windows and roofs: 'There she is!'

Fleur-de-Lys put her hands over her eyes so that she would not see.

'Charming lady,' Phoebus said to her, 'do you want to go inside?'

'No,' she answered; and the eyes she had just closed out of fear she opened again out of curiosity.

A tumbril, drawn by a powerful Norman horse, and completely surrounded by cavalry in violet uniform with white crosses, had just come out on to the Place from the rue Saint-Pierre-aux-Bœufs. The sergeants of the watch cleared a way for it through the crowd with great sweeps of their *boullayes*. Beside the tumbril rode some officers of the police and the law, recognizable by their black costumes and their awkwardness in the saddle. Maître Jacques Charmolue paraded at their head.

In the fateful cart sat a girl, arms bound behind her back, but no priest beside her. She wore a shift, her long, black hair (it was then the custom to cut it off only at the foot of the gallows) fell loose over her breast and her half-uncovered shoulders.

Across that undulating, hair, darker than a raven's wing, could be seen twisting and knotting a thick grey, coarse rope, chafing her delicate collarbones and twining round the poor girl's charming neck like an earthworm on a flower. Under the rope sparkled a little amulet decorated with green glass beads, which she had been allowed to keep, no doubt because nothing is refused to those about to die. The spectators in the windows could see at the bottom of the tumbril her bare legs which she was trying to tuck out of sight beneath her as though from a last feminine instinct. At her feet lay a little goat all trussed up. The condemned girl held up in her teeth the shift which had not been properly fastened. It was as though even in her misery it pained her to be thus exposed almost naked to every eye. Alas! modesty was not intended for shuddering like hers.

'Jesus!' Fleur-de-Lys said sharply to the captain. 'Look, fair cousin! It's that horrid gypsy girl with the goat!'

So saying, she turned round to Phoebus. He had his eyes fixed on the tumbril. He was very pale.

'What gypsy with the goat?' he stammered.

'What!' went on Fleur-de-Lys; 'don't you remember?'

Phoebus interrupted her; 'I don't know what you mean.'

He took a step to go inside. But Fleur-de-Lys, whose jealousy, so keenly aroused only recently by the same gypsy girl, had just been reawakened, gave him a penetrating and mistrustful glance. At that moment she vaguely remembered hearing something about a captain mixed up in the trial of this witch.

'What's the matter?' she said to Phoebus. 'Anyone would think that woman has upset you!'

Phoebus tried hard to laugh it off. 'Me! not a bit of it. Ah! well, yes!'

'Then stay here,' she went on imperiously, 'and let's watch to the end.'

The unfortunate captain was obliged to stay. He was somewhat reassured by the fact that the condemned girl did not take her eyes off the floor of the tumbril. It was only too genuinely la Esmeralda. Reduced to this bottom rung of ignominy and misfortune she was still beautiful, her large dark eyes seemed larger still because her cheeks were so wasted, her livid profile was pure and sublime. She bore the same resemblance to what she had been as a Virgin by Masaccio* to a Virgin by Raphael: frailer, thinner, more gaunt.

There was nothing in her, moreover, which was not in some sense being tossed about and which, but for modesty, she had not abandoned to chance, so profoundly was she shattered by stupor and despair. Her body bounced with every jolt of the tumbril like a thing dead or broken. Her gaze was dull and demented. A tear still showed in her eyes, but it did not move and was so to speak frozen.

Meanwhile the dismal cavalcade had passed through the crowd amid cries of joy and people straining to see. We must, however, say, for the sake of historical fidelity, that seeing her so lovely and in such distress many had been moved to pity, even some of the hardest hearts. The tumbril had entered the Parvis.

In front of the central portal it stopped. The escort lined up on either side. The crowd fell silent, and amid that silence, both solemn and anxious, the two halves of the great door turned, as if of their own accord, on their hinges, which creaked as shrilly as a fife. Then the church could be seen in all its length, stretching into the deep interior, dark, hung with mourning, dimly lit by a few candles twinkling in the distance on the high altar, opening like a cave mouth in the middle of a square filled with dazzling light. Right at the back, in the shadows of the apse, a gigantic silver cross could just be made out, spread out over a black drape hanging from the vaulting to the pavement. The nave was completely deserted. However, the heads of a few priests in the distant choir-stalls could vaguely be seen moving about, and at the moment when the great door opened there came from the church the sound of a grave, sonorous, and monotonous chant, casting over the condemned woman's head, as it were, in one gust after another, fragments of dismal psalms.*

'*Non timebo millia populi circumdantis me: exsurge, Domine; salvum me fac, Deus!*' [Ps. 3: 6—I will not be afraid of ten thousands of people that have set themselves against me round about. Arise, O Lord; save me, O my God!]

'. . . *Salvum me fac, Deus, quoniam intraverunt aquae usque ad animam meam.*' [Ps. 69: 1—Save me, O God, for the waters are come in unto my soul.]

'. . . *Infixus sum in limo profundi; et non est substantia.*' [Ps. 69: 2—I sink in deep mire, where there is no standing.]

At the same time another voice, separate from the choir, intoned from the steps of the high altar this melancholy offertory:

'*Qui verbum meum audit, et credit ei qui misit me, habet vitam aeternam et in judicium non venit; sed transit a morte in vitam.*' [John 5: 24—He that heareth my word and believeth on him that sent me, hath everlasting life, and shall not come into condemnation; but is passed from death into life.]

This chant, which some old men lost in the distant darkness were chanting over this beautiful creature, full of youth and life, caressed by the warm air of springtime, bathed in sunshine, was the mass for the dead.

The people listened devoutly.

The bewildered, unfortunate girl seemed to have lost all sight and reason within the dark interior of the church. Her bloodless lips moved as though in prayer, and when the executioner's assistant came up to help her down from the tumbril, he heard her repeating in an undertone the word: *Phoebus*.

Her hands were untied, she was made to get down, accompanied by her goat, which had been also untied and was bleating with joy at feeling free, and they made her walk barefoot over the hard pavement to the foot of the steps of the portal. The rope round her neck trailed behind her. It was like a snake following her.

Then the chant in the church broke off. A great golden cross and a line of candles moved off in the shadows. The halberds of the colourfully dressed beadles rang on the floor, and a few moments later a long procession of priests in chasubles and deacons in dalmatics, chanting as they advanced gravely towards the condemned girl, came within her sight and the eyes of the crowd. But her gaze fixed on the one walking at the head, immediately after the crucifer. 'Oh!' she whispered, shuddering, 'it's him again! The priest!'

It was indeed the archdeacon. On his left he had the succentor, on his right the precentor armed with his staff of office. He came on, head thrown back, eyes staring and open wide, chanting in a loud voice:

'*De ventre inferi clamavi, et exaudisti vocem meam, et projecisti me in profundum in corde maris, et flumen circumdedit me.*' [Jonah 2: 2–3—out of the belly of hell cried I, and thou heardest my voice, for thou hadst cast me into the deep, in the midst of the seas; and the floods encompassed me.]

When he appeared in full daylight under the high Gothic portal, wrapped in a huge silver cope, emblazoned with a black cross, he was so pale that more than one of those watching in the crowd thought that it was one of those marble bishops, kneeling on the tombstones in the choir, who had risen and was coming to receive on the threshold of the grave one who was about to die.

She, equally pale and equally like a statue, had hardly noticed that someone had put a heavy, lighted, yellow wax candle into her hand; she had not listened to the clerk's yapping voice reading out the fateful tenor of the public penance; when she had been told to answer '*Amen*', she had answered '*Amen*'. To give her back some life and strength it took the sight of the priest bidding the guards step back and then advancing on his own towards her.

Then she felt the blood seething in her head, and a last spark of indignation kindled in her already numb and chilled soul.

The archdeacon slowly came up to her. Even in this extremity she saw him stare at her nakedness with an eye glittering with lust, jealousy, and desire. Then he said to her aloud: 'Girl, have you asked God's forgiveness for your faults and failings?' He bent over to speak in her ear and added (the spectators thought he was hearing her last confession): 'Will you have me? I can still save you!'

She fixed her eyes on him: 'Away with you, demon! or I'll denounce you.'

He began to smile a horrible smile: 'They won't believe you—you would only be adding a scandal to a crime—answer quickly! Will you have me?'

'What have you done with my Phoebus?'

'He's dead,' said the priest.

At that moment the miserable archdeacon raised his head automatically and saw, at the far end of the square, on the balcony of the Gondelaurier mansion, the captain standing next to Fleur-de-Lys. He swayed, passed his hand over his eyes, looked again, muttered a malediction, and all his features contracted violently.

'Very well! Die then!' he said between his teeth. 'No one will have you.'

Then lifting his hand over the gypsy he cried in a funereal voice:

'*I nunc, anima anceps, et sit tibi Deus misericors!*' [Go now, dubious soul, and may God be merciful to you.]

This was the fearsome formula which customarily concluded these sombre ceremonies. It was the agreed signal from the priest to the executioner.

The people knelt.

'*Kyrie Eleison*,' said the priests who had remained beneath the arched doorway.

'*Kyrie Eleison*,' repeated the crowd in a murmur running over their heads like water lapping in a choppy sea.

'*Amen*' said the archdeacon.

He turned his back on the condemned girl, his head sank back on to his chest, he folded his hands, rejoined his procession of priests, and a moment later he was seen disappearing, with the cross, candles, and copes, beneath the hazy arches of the cathedral; and his sonorous voice gradually died away in the choir as he chanted the despairing verse:

'*Omnes gurgites tui et fluctus tui super me transierunt!*' [Jonah 2: 3—All thy billows and thy waves passed over me.]

At the same time the intermittent clanging of the iron-tipped shafts of the beadles' halberds, gradually fading away beneath the bays of the nave, sounded like the hammer of a clock striking the condemned's last hour.

Meanwhile the doors of Notre-Dame had stayed open, revealing the church empty, desolate, in mourning, without candles and without voices.

The condemned girl stayed unmoving where she was, waiting for them to dispose of her. One of the sergeants of the wand had to draw Maître Charmolue's attention to this, for, throughout this scene, he had been busy studying the bas-relief of the main doorway which represents, according to some, Abraham's sacrifice, according to others the alchemists' process, portraying the sun by the angel, the fire by the faggots, the operator by Abraham.

With considerable difficulty he was torn away from this contemplation, but at last he turned round, and at a sign from him two men in yellow, the executioner's assistants, came up to the gypsy to fasten her hands again.

The unfortunate girl, just as she was going back into the fateful tumbril on her way to her final destination, was seized, perhaps, by some anguished longing for life. She raised her dry, bloodshot eyes to the sky, the sun, the silvery clouds broken here and there by trapezoid and triangular patches of blue, then lowered them to look around her, at the ground, the crowd, the houses . . . Suddenly, while the man in yellow was binding her elbows, she uttered a terrible cry, a cry of joy. On the balcony, over there in the corner of the square, she had just caught sight of him, him, her friend, her lord, Phoebus, the other apparition in her life! The judge had lied! The priest had lied! It was really him. There could be no doubt about it, there he was, handsome, alive, dressed in his dazzling uniform, plume on head, sword at side!

'Phoebus!' she cried, 'my Phoebus!'

And she tried to stretch out her arms to him, trembling with love and rapture, but they were bound.

Then she saw her captain frown, and a beautiful girl, who was leaning back on him, look at him with scornful lip and angry eye, then Phoebus spoke some words, which did not reach her, and the two of them hurriedly disappeared behind the balcony window, which closed behind them.

'Phoebus!' she cried frantically, 'do you believe it?'

A monstrous thought had just occurred to her. She remembered that she had been convicted of murder against the person of Phoebus de Châteaupers.

She had endured everything up till then. But this final blow was too harsh. She fell to the pavement inert.

'Come,' said Charmolue, 'carry her on to the cart and let's get this finished!'

No one had yet noticed in the gallery of the statues of the kings, carved immediately above the arches of the doorway, a strange spectator who had so far been observing everything so impassively, his neck so outstretched, his face so deformed, that but for his costume, half red and half violet, he could have been taken for one of those stone monsters through whose jaws the cathedral's long gutters have been discharging for six hundred years. This spectator had missed nothing of what had been going on since midday before the portal of Notre-Dame. And from the very first moments, without anyone thinking of watching him, he had firmly secured to one of the colonnets of the gallery a stout knotted rope, its end trailing down on the steps below. With that done, he had been calmly watching, whistling from time to time when a blackbird passed by. Suddenly, at the moment when the executioner's assistants were preparing to carry out Charmolue's phlegmatic order, he climbed over the balustrade of the gallery, gripped the rope with feet, knees and hands, then they saw him slither down the façade, like a raindrop sliding along a window pane, run towards the two executioners as swiftly as a cat fallen from a roof, lay them low with his two huge fists, pick up the gypsy in one hand, like a child with its doll, and in a single bound leap back into the church, lifting the girl over his head and crying in a formidable voice: 'Asylum!'

This all happened so fast that had it been night time, everything could have been seen by the light of a single flash of lightning.

'Asylum! asylum!' the crowd repeated, and the clapping of ten thousand hands made Quasimodo's one eye sparkle with joy and pride.

The shock brought the girl back to her senses. She opened an eye, looked at Quasimodo, then abruptly closed it again, as if terrified by her saviour.

Charmolue remained dumbfounded, as did the executioners and the escort. Within the precincts of Notre-Dame, the condemned girl was in fact inviolable. The cathedral was a place of refuge. All human justice expired on its threshold.

Quasimodo had stopped beneath the great portal. His broad feet seemed to stand as solidly on the pavement of the church as the heavy Romanesque pillars. His massive shaggy head was sunk on his shoulders like a lion's; they too have a mane and no neck. He held the trembling girl, hanging from his calloused hands like some white drapery; but he carried her so carefully that he seemed to be afraid of breaking or withering her. It was as though he felt that she was something delicate, exquisite, and precious, made for other hands than his. At times he looked as though he did not dare to touch her, not even with his breath. Then, all of a sudden, he would clasp her tightly in his arms, against his angular breast, as his property, as his treasure, as this child's mother would have done; his gnome's eye, looking down on her, showered her with tenderness, grief, and pity, and suddenly looked up again, flashing. Then the women laughed and cried, the crowd stamped with enthusiasm, for at that moment Quasimodo truly had a beauty of his own. He was beautiful, he, the orphan, the foundling, the reject, he felt august and strong, he looked society in the face, that society from which he had been banished, and in which he was intervening so powerfully, that human justice whose prey he had snatched, all these tigers forced to chew on emptiness, those police agents, those judges, those executioners, all that royal might, which he had just broken, he the lowliest of the low, with the might of God.

Besides it was very affecting, this protection coming from so deformed a creature upon so unhappy a being, a girl condemned to death rescued by Quasimodo. It was two extremes of wretchedness, of nature and of society, meeting and helping each other.

Meanwhile, after some minutes of triumph, Quasimodo had abruptly plunged into the church with his burden. The people, enthusiastic about any daring deed, tried to spy him in the darkness of the nave, regretting that he had so soon removed himself from their applause. Suddenly they saw him reappear at one end of the gallery of the kings of France, he ran along it like a man demented, raising his conquest in his arms and shouting: 'Asylum!' The crowd broke into fresh applause. When he reached the end of the gallery, he plunged back inside the church. A moment later he reappeared on the upper platform with the gypsy still in his arms, still running like a madman, still shouting: 'Asylum!' And the crowd applauded. Finally he made a third appearance, on top of the great bell's tower; from there he seemed to be displaying proudly to the whole town the girl whom he had rescued and his thunderous voice, the voice that was so seldom heard by anyone, and which he himself could never hear, repeated three times, in a frenzy, up into the clouds: 'Asylum! asylum! asylum!'

'Noël! Noël!' cried the people for their part, and this immense acclamation could be heard on the opposite bank of the Seine, amazing the crowd on the Grève and the recluse who was still waiting with eyes fixed on the gibbet.

BOOK NINE

I

FEVER

CLAUDE FROLLO was no longer in Notre-Dame when his adoptive son so abruptly cut through the fatal knot in which the unhappy archdeacon had trapped the gypsy girl and trapped himself. On his return to the sacristy he had ripped off alb, stole, and cope, tossed the lot into the hands of the astonished beadle; he had made his escape through the concealed door into the cloister, ordered a boatman from the Terrain to take him across to the left bank of the Seine, and had plunged into the steep streets of the University, without any idea where he was going, at every step running into bands of men and women gleefully hurrying towards the Pont Saint-Michel in the hope of 'getting there in time' to see the witch hanged; he was pale, distraught, more confused, more blind, more unapproachable than a night bird released and pursued by a pack of children in broad daylight. He no longer knew where he was, what he was thinking about, whether he was dreaming. He went on, walking, running, taking any street at random, making no choice, simply driven on all the time by the Grève, by the horrible Grève, which he vaguely felt lay behind him.

He thus passed round the Montagne Sainte-Geneviève, and finally left the town by the Porte Saint-Victor. He continued to flee for as long as he could see, when he turned his head, the ring of the University's towers and the scattered houses of the suburbs, but when at last a fold in the ground completely hid that hateful Paris from his sight, when he could feel that he was a hundred leagues away, in the country, in a desert, he stopped and seemed able to breathe again.

Then dreadful thoughts crowded into his mind. He saw clearly again into his soul, and shuddered. He thought of the unfortunate girl who had caused his ruin, and whom he had ruined. He cast a haggard eye over the tortuous double path which fatality had made their two destinies follow up to their point of intersection, where fatality again had smashed them mercilessly against each other. He thought of the folly of eternal vows, the futility of chastity, science, religion, virtue, the pointlessness of God. He indulged these evil thoughts to his heart's content, and as he plunged ever deeper he felt breaking out within him a burst of satanic laughter.

As he thus delved into his soul, when he saw what spacious provision nature had made in it for passions, he laughed all the more bitterly. He stirred up all the hatred, all the malice in his innermost heart, and recognized, with the cool eye of a physician examining a patient, that this hatred and malice was nothing but vitiated love; that love, source of every human virtue, could, in a priest's heart, turn into something horrible, and that a man constituted like him, by becoming a priest became a devil. Then he gave a dreadful laugh, and suddenly paled again as he contemplated the most sinister aspect of his fatal passion, of that corrosive, poisonous, hateful, implacable love whose only outcome had been the gallows for one of them, hell for the other: she condemned, he damned.

And then he laughed again, at the thought that Phoebus was still alive, that after all the captain was living, was merry and contented, had finer actons than ever, and a new mistress whom he was taking to see the old one hang. His mirth increased as he reflected that of all the living beings whose death he had wanted, the gypsy, the only creature he did not hate, was the only target he had not missed.

Then, from the captain his thoughts passed to the people, and an unprecedented kind of jealousy came over him. He thought how the people too, the whole crowd, had seen with their very eyes the woman he loved, in a shift, almost naked. He writhed at the thought that this woman, whose figure half seen in the shadows by him alone would have brought him supreme happiness, had been delivered up in broad daylight, at high noon, to the whole multitude of people, dressed as though for a night of sensual delight. He wept with rage over all these mysteries of love, now profaned, soiled, exposed, withered for ever. He wept with rage as he imagined how many prurient watchers had found satisfaction in the loosely fastened shift; and in the thought that this lovely girl, this virgin lily, this cup of modesty and delights to which he would only have dared to bring his lips in fear and trembling, had just been transformed into a kind of public trough, at which the meanest rabble in Paris, thieves, beggars, lackeys, had come to drink in common their shameless, impure, and depraved pleasure.

And when he tried to picture to himself the happiness he might have found on earth if she had not been a gypsy and he had not been a priest, if Phoebus had not existed, and she had loved him; when he imagined that a life of serenity and love might have been possible even for him, that at that very moment here and there on earth there were happy couples, absorbed in long conversations under orange-trees, beside running brooks, in the presence of a setting sun, of a starry sky; and that if God had so wished he could have formed with her one of those blessed couples, his heart melted with tenderness and despair.

Oh! her! it's her! This was the fixed idea which kept continually returning, torturing him, eating away at his brain, tearing at his vitals. He had no regrets, he was not sorry; all he had done, he was ready to do again; he would rather see her in the executioner's hands than on the captain's arm, but he was suffering; suffering so much at times that he tore out handfuls of hair to see whether it had gone white.

There was one moment among others when it occurred to him that at that very minute the hideous chain he had seen that morning might be tightening its iron noose around that neck, so slender and graceful. The thought made the sweat gush from his every pore.

There was another moment when, while laughing diabolically at himself, he simultaneously pictured Esmeralda as he had first seen her, lively, carefree, joyful, all dressed up, dancing, winged, harmonious, and the Esmeralda of her

last day, in a shift, the rope round her neck, slowly climbing, barefoot, the sharp steps up to the gibbet; this double
image was so vivid that he let out a terrible cry.

While this hurricane of despair shattered, smashed, tore
up, bent, uprooted everything in his soul, he looked at
nature around him. At his feet a few hens were pecking as
they foraged in the undergrowth, enamelled beetles ran
about in the sunshine; above his head a few clusters of
dappled-grey clouds were scudding across a blue sky; on
the horizon the steeple of the abbey of Saint-Victor thrust
its slate-covered obelisk across the curving contour of the
hillside, and the miller of the Butte Copeaux whistled as he
watched the sails of his windmill diligently spinning round.
All this active, organized, tranquil life, reproduced around
him in countless forms, upset him. He embarked once more
on flight.

He hurried thus across country until evening. This flight
from nature, life, himself, mankind, God, from everything,
lasted all day. Sometimes he would throw himself face
downwards on the ground and tear up the young corn with
his fingernails. Sometimes he would stop in some deserted
village street, and his thoughts were so unbearable that he
would clutch his head in both hands and try to rip it from
his shoulders and smash it on the paving-stones.

About the time the sun was going down he examined
himself afresh, and found that he was almost mad. The
storm which had raged in him from the moment when he
had lost all hope and will to save the gypsy had left in his
consciousness not a single sane idea, not a single thought
still upright. His reason lay there, almost wholly destroyed.
There were only two distinct images left in his mind: la
Esmeralda and the gallows. All the rest was darkness. These
two images brought together confronted him with a terrifying group, and the more he concentrated on them what
remained of his powers of attention and thought, the more
he saw them grow, in a fantastic progression, the one in
grace, charm, beauty, light, the other in horror, so that in
the end la Esmeralda appeared to him as a star, the gibbet
as a huge fleshless arm.

It is worthy of note that during all this torment the idea of dying never seriously occurred to him. That was how the wretch was made. He clung to life. Perhaps he really did see hell beyond.

Meanwhile daylight continued to fade. The living being which still existed in him vaguely thought of going back. He believed he was a long way from Paris; but, taking his bearings, he realized that he had simply been circling round the wall of the University. The steeple of Saint-Sulpice and the three tall spires of Saint-Germain-des-Prés rose above the horizon to his right. He made off in that direction. When he heard the abbot's men-at-arms crying out their challenges around the crenellated circumvallation of Saint-Germain, he turned aside, took a path he found between the abbey mill and the leper house of the village, and after a few moments found himself on the edge of the Pré-aux-Clercs. This Pré, or meadow, was famous for the uproar which went on there day and night; it was the 'hydra' of the poor monks of Saint-Germain, *quod monachis Sancti-Germani pratensis hydra fuit, clericis nova semper dissidiorum capita suscitantibus* [which was the hydra of the monks of Saint-Germain-des-Prés, since the clerks were always raising new heads of disagreement]. The archdeacon was afraid of meeting someone there; he feared every human face; he had just avoided the University and the Bourg Saint-Germain, he did not want to return to the streets until the last possible moment. He skirted the Pré-aux-Clercs, took the deserted path separating it from the Dieu-Neuf, and finally arrived at the water's edge. There Dom Claude found a boatman who, for a few *deniers parisis*, took him back up the Seine as far as the tip of the Cité, and set him down on that abandoned strip of land where the reader has already seen Gringoire dreaming, and which extended beyond the king's gardens, parallel to the island of the *passeur-aux-vaches* [cow-ferryman].

The monotonous rocking of the boat and the lapping of the water had somehow numbed the unhappy Claude. When the boatman had taken himself off, he remained standing on the bank in a stupor, looking straight ahead and now seeing objects only through magnifying oscillations which turned everything into a kind of phantasmagoria. It is not unusual for the weariness caused by extreme grief to have this effect on the mind.

The sun had gone down behind the lofty Tour de Nesle. It was the moment of half-light. The sky was white, the river water was white. Between these two patches of white, the left bank of the Seine, at which he was gazing, thrust forth its dark mass, and dwindling steadily in perspective, plunged into the hazy horizon like a black arrow. It was laden with houses, of which only the dark silhouette could be made out, boldly picked out in black against the light background of sky and water. Here and there windows were beginning to sparkle like glowing embers. This huge black obelisk thus isolated between the two white sheets of sky and river, very broad at that spot, made a peculiar impression on Dom Claude, comparable to that which a man would experience if he were to lie on the ground, on his back, at the foot of the steeple of Strasbourg and look up at the huge spire above his head plunging into the shadowy twilight. Only here it was Dom Claude who was upright and the obelisk which was recumbent; but as the river, reflecting the sky, prolonged the abyss below him, the immense promontory seemed to be soaring as boldly into the void as any cathedral spire; and the impression was the same. What was strange and profound about this impression was that it was indeed the Strasbourg steeple, but a Strasbourg steeple two leagues high, something incredible, gigantic, immeasurable, a structure such as had been seen by no human eye, a Tower of Babel. The chimneys of the houses, the crenellations of the walls, the carved roofgables, the spire of the Augustins, the Tour de Nesle, all these projections indenting the profile of the colossal obelisk, added to the optical illusion with their weird simulation of the jagged carvings of some fantastic, luxuriant sculpture. Claude, in the state of hallucination in which he found himself, thought he was seeing with his living eyes the steeple of hell; the countless lights distributed along the whole height of the horrifying tower appeared to him like so many openings into the huge inner furnaces; the voices and murmurs coming from it, like so many cries, so many death-rattles. Then he felt afraid, he put his hands over his ears so that he should hear no more, turned his back so that he should see no more, and strode away from the fearful vision.

But the vision was within him.

When he came back to the streets, the passers-by jostling in the glow from the shop fronts appeared to him like spectres going everlastingly to and fro around him. There was a strange roaring in his ears, extraordinary fantasies disturbed his mind. He did not see houses, or pavements, or carts, or men and women, but a chaotic jumble of indeterminate objects merging at the edges into one another. On the corner of the rue de la Barillerie there was a grocer's shop, whose awning, in accordance with immemorial custom, was decorated all round with tin hoops with a circle of wooden candles hanging from them, clashing together like castanets in the wind. He thought that what he heard banging together in the shadows was the bundle of skeletons at Montfaucon.*

'Oh!' he murmured, 'the night wind is blowing them together, mingling the sound of their chains with that of their bones! Perhaps she is there among them!'

Distraught, he did not know where he was going. After a few steps he found himself on the Pont Saint-Michel. There was a light in one of the ground-floor windows. He came closer. Through a cracked pane of glass he saw a sordid room, which awoke a confused memory in his mind. In that room, poorly lit by a meagre lamp, was a fresh, merry-looking, fair young man embracing, with great bellows of laughter, a girl most shamelessly attired. And by the lamp was an old woman spinning and singing in a quavering voice. As the young man did not laugh all the time, the old woman's song reached the priest in snatches. It was something unintelligible and awful:

> Grève bay, Grève rumble!
> Spin, my distaff spin.
> Spin the rope for the hangman,

Whistling there in the prison yard.
Grève bay, Grève rumble.

Fine hempen rope!
Sow hemp and not corn
In the fields both far and wide.*
No thief has ever stolen
Fine hempen rope.

Rumble Grève, bay Grève!
To see the harlot swing
From the bleary gallows,
Windows are your eyes.
Rumble Grève, bay Grève!

Wheupon the young man laughed and fondled the girl.
The old woman was la Falourdel; the girl a common whore;
the young man, his young brother Jehan.

He went on looking. This show was as good as any other.

He saw Jehan go to a window at the back of the room,
open it, look out on to the quay where hundreds of lighted
casements shone in the distance, and heard him say as he
closed the window again: 'Upon my soul! It's dark already.
The townsfolk are lighting their candles and God lights up
his stars.'

Then, Jehan went back to the wench, and broke a bottle
which was on a table, exclaiming:

'Empty already, *corbœuf!* and I've no money left! Isabeau,
my dear, I shan't be pleased with Jupiter until he changes
your two white tits into two black bottles, from which I can
suck Beaune wine day and night.'

This witty sally made the wench laugh, and Jehan left.

Dom Claude just had time to fling himself to the ground
to avoid a meeting, face to face, with his brother and being
recognized by him. Fortunately the street was dark, and the
student drunk. He noticed the archdeacon, however, lying
in the mire on the roadway.

'Oh! oh!' he said, 'here's one who's been making merry
today.'

With his foot he pushed Dom Claude, who was holding
his breath.

'Dead drunk,' Jehan went on. 'Come on then, he's full.
A proper leech pulled off a barrel. He's bald,' he added,

stooping down; 'he's an old man! *Fortunate senex!* [Fortunate old man!]'*

Then Dom Claude heard him go off, saying: 'It's all the same, reason's a fine thing, and my brother the archdeacon is indeed a lucky man to be wise and have money too.'

The archdeacon got up then, and hurried without pausing for breath towards Notre-Dame, whose enormous towers he could see looming in the darkness above the houses.

At the moment when he arrived panting at the Place du Parvis he recoiled and did not dare look up at the fatal building. 'Oh!' he said in a low voice, 'can it really be true that such a thing took place here, today, this very morning!'

However, he risked a look at the church. The façade was dark. The sky behind sparkled with stars. The crescent moon, which had just taken off above the horizon, stopped at that moment on top of the right-hand tower and seemed to be perching, like some luminous bird, on the edge of the balustrade, with its pattern of cut-out trefoils.

The cloister door was closed. But the archdeacon always had on him the key to the tower where his laboratory was. He used it to enter the church.

The church he found as dark and silent as a cave. From the great shadows which fell on all sides in wide patches he realized that the hangings from that morning's ceremony had not yet been taken down. The great silver cross glimmered in the depths of the darkness, sprinkled with a few points of twinkling light, like the Milky Way of that sepulchral night. The tall windows of the choir revealed above the black drapes the upper extremities of their pointed arches, and the stained glass in them displayed in the light of a passing moonbeam only the dubious colours of the night, a violet, a white, and a blue of a shade to be found only on the face of the dead. The archdeacon, as he remarked all round the choir the pallid tips of these lancets, thought he was seeing the mitres of bishops consigned to damnation. He closed his eyes, and when he opened them again he thought there was a circle of pale faces watching him.

He began to flee through the church. Then it seemed to him that the church too was shaking, moving, stirring, coming alive, that every massive column had become an enormous foot striking the ground with its broad stone spatula, that the gigantic cathedral had become nothing but a sort of prodigious elephant breathing and walking with pillars for feet, the two towers for trunks, and the huge black drapery for caparison.

Thus the unfortunate man's fever or madness had reached such a degree of intensity that the outside world had become for him nothing but a kind of visible, palpable, terrifying apocalypse.

For a moment he felt relieved. As he plunged into the side aisles he saw, behind a cluster of pillars, a reddish gleam. He ran to it as to a star. It was the mean lamp which day and light lit up the public breviary of Notre-Dame, beneath its iron mesh. He pounced eagerly upon the holy book, in the hope of finding there some consolation or encouragement. The book lay open at this passage from Job [4: 15] which he scanned with staring eyes: 'Then a spirit passed before my face; I heard a small breath; the hair of my flesh stood up.'*

Reading this dismal text his sensations were those of a blind man when he feels himself pricked by the stick he has just picked up. His knees gave way from under him, and he collapsed on the pavement, thinking of her who had died that day. He felt so many monstrous fumes pass and discharge into his brain that his head seemed as if it had become one of the chimneys of hell.

Apparently he stayed in that posture for a long time, no longer thinking, shattered and passive under the demon's hand. At length, regaining some strength, he thought of going to seek refuge in the tower near his faithful Quasimodo. He stood up, and as he was afraid, took the breviary lamp to light his way. That was sacrilege; but he was past caring about such trifles.

He slowly climbed the tower staircase, filled with secret terror which must have communicated itself to the rare passers-by in the Parvis by the mysterious light from his lamp going up at so late an hour from one loophole to the next to the top of the bell tower.

He suddenly felt a coolness on his face and found himself beneath the door of the topmost gallery. The air was chill; clouds swept across the sky, in white streaks, overflowing one upon the other, crushing away the corners, looking like winter ice breaking up in a river. The crescent moon, stranded amid the clouds, seemed like some heavenly ship caught in these aerial ice-floes.

He looked down and for a moment contemplated, between the grid of colonnettes joining the two towers, in the distance, through a haze of mist and smoke, the silent throng of Paris roofs, pointed, innumerable, packed and small as the ripples of a calm sea on a summer night.

The moon's feeble beams gave sky and earth an ashen hue.

At that moment the clock raised its shrill, cracked voice. It struck midnight. The priest thought of midday. It was twelve o'clock come round again. 'Oh!' he murmured to himself, 'she must be cold by now!'

Suddenly a puff of wind blew his lamp out, and at almost the same time he saw appearing, at the opposite corner of the tower, a shadow, a patch of white, a shape, a woman. He shuddered. By the woman's side was a little goat, its bleating mingling with the final bleat of the clock.

He found the strength to look. It was her.

She was pale, she was sombre. Her hair fell over her shoulders as it had that morning. But there was no longer a rope round her neck, her hands were no longer bound. She was free, she was dead.

She was dressed in white, and had a white veil over her head.

She came towards him, slowly, looking at the sky. The supernatural goat followed her. He felt as if he were made of stone, too heavy to flee. With each step she took forward, he took one back, and that was all. He thus returned beneath the dark vaulting of the staircase. He went ice-cold at the thought that she might perhaps come there too; if she had done so, he would have died of terror.

She did indeed arrive in front of the staircase door, stopped there for a few moments, gazed into the darkness, but apparently without seeing the priest, and went on past. She looked taller to him than when she had been alive; he saw the moon through her white robe; he heard her breathing.

When she had gone by he started down the stairs again, moving as slowly as he had seen the spectre move, believing himself to be a spectre, haggard, hair standing on end, his hand still holding the extinguished lamp; and as he went down the spiral stairs, he distinctly heard in his ear a voice laughing and repeating: 'A spirit passed before my face; I heard a small breath; the hair of my flesh stood up.'

II

HUNCHBACKED, ONE-EYED, LAME

EVERY town in the Middle Ages, and up until Louis XII*
every town in France, had its places of asylum. These places
of asylum, amid the deluge of penal laws and barbaric
jurisdictions which flooded the city, were like islands rising
above the level of human justice. In a suburb there were
almost as many places of asylum as of execution. It was the
abuse of impunity side by side with the abuse of punishment, two evils each trying to correct one another. The
king's palaces, princely residences, churches especially had
the right of asylum. Sometimes a whole town which needed
repopulating was temporarily made a place of refuge. Louis
XI made Paris an asylum in 1467.

Once the criminal had set foot in an asylum he was
sacred, but he had to take care not to leave it. One step
outside the sanctuary and he fell back into the water. The
wheel, the gibbet, the strappado, kept a keen watch around
the place of refuge, lying ceaselessly in wait for their prey
like sharks around a ship. There were cases of condemned
persons growing white-haired in a cloister, on the steps of
a palace, in the fields of an abbey, under a church porch;
in that respect asylum was a prison like any other. It sometimes happened that a solemn decree of Parliament violated
the asylum and delivered the condemned back to the executioner; but that was rare. Parliament was wary of bishops,
and when it came to a clash between the two robes, the
magistrate's cimarra was not evenly matched against the
cassock. At times, however, as in the case of the killers of
Petit-Jean, the Paris executioner, and in that of Emery
Rousseau, Jean Valleret's murderer, secular justice went
over the Church's head and proceeded to execute its sentence; but short of a parliamentary decree, woe betide
anyone who violated a place of asylum by force of arms! It
is well known how Robert de Clermont, Marshal of France,

and Jean de Châlons, Marshal of Champagne, died; and yet all that was at issue was a certain Perrin Marc, a money-changer's lad, a wretched murderer; but the two marshals* had broken down the doors of Saint-Méry. That was the enormity.

Asylums were hedged about with such respect that, according to tradition, it extended at times even to animals. Aymoin tells of a stag, hunted by Dagobert, which sought refuge by the tomb of Saint-Denys; the hounds stopped dead, still baying.

Churches usually had a small cell ready to receive suppliants. In 1407 Nicolas Flamel had built for them, over the vaulting of Saint-Jacques-de-la-Boucherie, a room which cost him 4 *livres* 6 *sols* 16 *deniers parisis*.

At Notre-Dame it was a cell constructed in the roof space of the side-aisles beneath the flying buttresses, facing the cloister, exactly at the spot where the wife of the present concierge of the towers has contrived for herself a garden, which is to the hanging gardens of Babylon what a lettuce is to a palm tree, or a porter's wife to Semiramis.

There it was that Quasimodo, after his frantic and triumphant dash over the towers and galleries, had set down la Esmeralda. As long as that headlong course lasted, the girl had been unable to regain full consciousness; half comatose, half awake, all she had felt was going up in the air, floating, flying, being carried off by something above the earth. Now and then she heard the bellowing laughter, the loud voice of Quasimodo in her ear; she half opened her eyes; then beneath her she had a confused view of Paris, inlaid with its thousands of slate and tile roofs like a red and blue mosaic, and above her head the frightening, gleeful face of Quasimodo. Then her eyelids closed again; she thought it was all over, that she had been executed while she was in a faint, and that the deformed spirit which had presided over her destiny had caught her again and was carrying her off. She did not dare to look at him and just lay inert.

But when the bell-ringer, dishevelled and panting, put her down in the cell of refuge, when she felt his great hands undo the cord which was bruising her arms, she experienced the kind of shock which wakes up passengers with a start when their ship grounds in the middle of a dark night. Her thoughts awoke too, and came back one by one. She saw that she was in Notre-Dame, she remembered being snatched from the hands of the executioner, that Phoebus was alive, that Phoebus did not love her any more; and those two ideas, the one casting so much bitterness over the other, coming into her mind together, she turned to Quasimodo, who was standing before her and frightened her. She said to him: 'Why did you rescue me?'

He looked at her anxiously as if trying to guess what she was saying. She repeated her question. Then he gave her a look of profound sadness and fled.

She remained astounded.

A few moments later he came back, bringing a package that he cast at her feet. In it were clothes which some charitable women had left for her at the entrance to the church. Then she looked down at herself, saw she was almost naked and blushed. Life was coming back.

Quasimodo seemed to feel some of the same modesty. He veiled his eyes with a large hand and went away again, but slowly.

She hurried to get dressed. There was a white robe with a white veil. A novice's habit from the Hôtel-Dieu.

She had scarcely finished when she saw Quasimodo returning. He carried a basket under one arm and a mattress under the other. In the basket was a bottle, some bread, and some provisions. He put the basket on the ground and said: 'Eat.' He laid the mattress out over the stone floor, and said: 'Sleep.' It was his own meal, his own bed, that the bell-ringer had gone to fetch.

The gypsy looked up at him to thank him, but could not utter a word. The poor devil looked truly horrible. She lowered her head with a shudder of fright.

Then he said: 'I frighten you. I am very ugly, aren't I? Don't look at me. Just listen. During the day you will stay here; at night you can go wherever you like in the church. But don't leave the church day or night. You would be done for. They would kill you and I should die.'

Touched by this, she raised her head to answer. He had disappeared. She was alone again, musing on the singular words of this almost monstrous creature, and struck by the sound of his voice, so raucous and yet so gentle.

Then she examined her cell. It was a room of some six square feet, with a little window and a door on to the gently inclined plane of the roof of flat stones. Several waterspouts with animal faces seemed to be leaning out round her, craning their necks to see her through the window. At the edge of her roof she could see the tops of countless chimneys from which rose, as she watched, the smoke from all the fires in Paris. A cheerless sight for the poor gypsy girl, a foundling, condemned to death, an unhappy creature, without a country, without a family, without a home.

At the moment when the thoughts of her isolation thus came over her, more poignantly than ever, she felt a shaggy, bearded head slip into her hands, over her knees. She shuddered (everything frightened her now) and looked. It was the poor goat, the agile Djali, who had escaped after her, just as Quasimodo was scattering Charmolue's brigade, and who had been lavishing caresses on her feet for the best part of an hour without being able to get so much as a glance from her. The gypsy smothered her with kisses. 'Oh! Djali,' she said, 'how I had forgotten you! So you still think of me! Oh! you are not the one who is ungrateful!' At the same time, as if an invisible hand had lifted the weight which had for so long been holding down the tears in her heart, she began to weep; and as the tears flowed, she felt all that was most sharp and bitter in her grief going away with them.

With the coming of evening she found the night so beautiful, the moon so sweet, that she walked all the way round the lofty gallery encircling the church. The walk brought her some relief, so calm did the earth appear seen from that height.

III

DEAF

NEXT morning she realized when she woke up that she had been asleep. This singular fact amazed her. For so long she had grown unaccustomed to sleep. A joyful beam from the rising sun came in through the window and fell upon her face. At the same time as the sun she saw at the window an object which frightened her; the unfortunate face of Quasimodo. Involuntarily she closed her eyes again, but in vain; she still thought she could see through her rosy eyelids that gnome's mask, one-eyed and gap-toothed. Then, as she kept her eyes closed, she heard a rough voice saying very gently: 'Don't be afraid. I am your friend. I came to look at you sleeping. It does you no harm, does it, if I come and look at you sleeping? What does it matter to you if I am there when your eyes are closed? Now I'm going away. There, I've put myself behind the wall. You can open your eyes again.'

Even more plaintive than these words was the tone in which they were uttered. Touched, the gypsy opened her eyes. He was indeed no longer at the window. She went to it and saw the poor hunchback huddled into a corner of the wall, in an attitude of sorrowful resignation. She made an effort to overcome the revulsion he inspired in her. 'Come,' she said to him gently. From the movement of her lips Quasimodo thought she was sending him off: so he stood up and limped away, slowly, hanging his head, not even daring to look up at the girl with his eye full of despair. 'Come here, then,' she cried. But he continued to retreat. Then she rushed out of the cell, ran after him and took him by the arm. When he felt her touch upon him, Quasimodo trembled in every limb. He looked up with a beseeching eye, and seeing that she was drawing him close to her, his whole face radiated joy and tenderness. She tried to make him enter her cell, but he stayed obstinately in the doorway. 'No, no,' he said, 'the owl does not enter the lark's nest.'

Then she squatted gracefully on her bed with the goat asleep at her feet. Both stayed for a few moments without moving, silently contemplating, he so much grace, she so much ugliness. With every moment she discovered some new deformity in Quasimodo. Her eyes ranged from his knock-knees to his humped back, from his humped back to his single eye. She could not understand how a creature so awkwardly designed could exist. Yet over it all lay so much sadness and gentleness that she began to get used to it.

He was the first to break the silence: 'So you were telling me to come back?'

She nodded assent and said: 'Yes.'

He understood her nod. 'Alas,' he said as if hesitating to finish the phrase: 'the fact is . . . I'm deaf.'

'Poor man!' exclaimed the gypsy with an expression of kindly pity.

He gave a sorrowful smile. 'You think that was the only item lacking, don't you? Yes, I'm deaf. That's how I am made. It's horrible, isn't it? And you are so beautiful!'

In the wretched man's tone there was so profound a sense of his wretchedness that she did not have the strength to say a single word. Besides he would not have heard. He went on. 'I have never before seen my ugliness as I do now. When I compare myself with you, I feel really sorry for myself; poor unfortunate monster that I am! I must look like some sort of animal to you, don't I?—you are a ray of sunshine, a drop of dew, the song of a bird!—while I am something dreadful, neither man nor beast, something harder, more downtrodden, more misshapen than a pebble!'

Then he laughed, and his laugh was the most heart-rending sound imaginable. He continued:

'Yes, I'm deaf. But you can speak to me in signs and gestures. I have a master who talks to me like that. And anyhow, I will soon know what you want from the movement of your lips and your eyes.'

'Very well,' she replied with a smile, 'tell me why you rescued me.'

He watched her attentively while she was speaking.

'I understand,' he answered. 'You ask why I rescued you. You have forgotten a wretch who tried to abduct you one night, a wretch to whom you brought succour the very next day on that shameful pillory of theirs. A drop of water and a little pity, that's more than I could repay with my life. You have forgotten that wretch; but he remembered.'

She listened, deeply touched. A tear welled up in the bell-ringer's eye, but did not fall. He seemed to make it a point of honour to swallow it.

'Listen,' he went on, once he was no longer afraid that the tear might fall, 'we have very high towers over there, and anyone falling from one would be dead before he reached the pavement; if you would ever like me to fall, you won't even have to say a word, a glance will do.'

Then he stood up. This strange creature, unhappy though the gypsy's plight was, still aroused in her a feeling of compassion. She signed to him to stay.

'No, no,' he said. 'I mustn't stay too long. I don't feel comfortable with you looking at me. It's out of pity that you don't turn your eyes away. I'm going somewhere where I can see you without you seeing me. That will be better.'

He took a little metal whistle out of his pocket. 'Here,' he said, 'when you need me, when you want me to come, when you won't feel too revolted at the sight of me, you can whistle with this. That is a sound I can hear.'

He laid the whistle on the ground and fled.

IV

EARTHENWARE AND CRYSTAL

DAY after day went by.

Calm gradually returned to la Esmeralda's soul. Excessive pain, like excessive joy, is something violent that does not last. The human heart cannot long remain at an extreme. The gypsy girl had suffered so much that all that now remained was astonishment.

With the sense of security, hope had returned to her. She was outside society, outside life, but she vaguely felt that it might not be impossible to come inside again. She was like a dead person holding in reserve a key to her tomb.

She felt the terrible images which had obsessed her for so long gradually becoming more remote. All the hideous phantoms, Pierrat Torterue, Jacques Charmolue, faded from her mind, all of them, even the priest.

And then Phoebus was alive, she was sure of it. She had seen him. Phoebus' life, that meant everything. After the series of fatal shocks which had brought her soul to total collapse, the one thing, the one feeling which she found still standing in her soul was her love for the captain. The fact is that love is like a tree, it grows of its own accord, strikes deep roots throughout our being, and continues to put out leaves on a heart in ruins.

And what defies explanation is that the blinder the passion, the more tenacious it is. It is never more solid than when it lacks all reason.

No doubt la Esmeralda could not think of the captain without bitterness. No doubt it was awful that he too had been mistaken, that he should have believed that impossible thing, that he should have believed a dagger thrust to have come from someone who would have given her life a thousand times over for him. Still, one must not hold too much against him: had she not confessed 'her crime'? Had she not given in, weak woman that she was, to torture? It was

all her fault. She should have let them pull out her nails
rather than extract such words from her. Anyhow, if she
could see Phoebus just once more, just for a minute, it
would take but one word, one look, to put him right, to
bring him back. She had no doubt about it. She dulled her
feelings too over a number of strange facts—Phoebus
chancing to be present on the day of her public penance,
the girl he had been with. It was no doubt his sister. An
unreasonable explanation, but one she was content to accept, since she needed to believe that Phoebus still loved
her and no one else. Had he not sworn so to her? What
more did she need, naïve and credulous as she was? And
then, in this matter, did not appearances tell much more
against her than against him? So she waited. She hoped.

We may add that the church, that vast church which
enveloped her on every side, guarding her, saving her, was
itself a sovereign tranquillizer. The solemn lines of the
architecture, the religious attitude of all the objects around
the girl, the devout and severe thoughts given off, so to
speak, by every pore of the stonework, acted on her without
her knowing. The building had its sounds too, so full of
benediction and majesty that they lulled that ailing soul.
The monotonous chant of those saying the offices, the
people's response to the priest, sometimes a mumble,
sometimes thunderous, the harmonious vibration of the
stained glass, the organ blaring out like a hundred trum-
pets, the three bell towers humming like hives of huge bees,
that whole orchestra, over which a gigantic musical scale
leaped without cease up and down from congregation to
bell tower, deadened her memory, her imagination, her
pain. The bells above all soothed her. It was as if these huge
machines poured over her some powerful magnetism.

So each sunrise found her more at peace, breathing more
easily, less pale. As her inner wounds healed, so her grace
and beauty flowered again on her face, but more thoughtful
now and calmer. Her former character came back too, even
some of her gaiety, her pretty pout, her love for her goat,
her taste for singing, her modesty. She was careful in the
morning to dress in the corner of her cell, for fear that

someone living in the neighbouring attics might see her through the window.

When thinking about Phoebus left her time, the gypsy sometimes thought of Quasimodo. He was the only link, the only connection, the only communication remaining to her with human kind, with the living. Unhappy girl! She was more cut off from the world than Quasimodo! She understood nothing about this strange friend whom chance had given her. She often reproached herself for not having enough gratitude to make her blind to his defects, but she could absolutely not accustom herself to the poor bell-ringer. He was too ugly.

The whistle he had given her she had left lying on the ground. That did not stop Quasimodo reappearing from time to time those first few days. She did her utmost not to turn away with too much revulsion when he came to bring her the basket of provisions or the jug of water, but he always noticed the least movement of that kind, and would then go away sadly.

Once he turned up just as she was fondling Djali. He stayed pensive for a few moments before the graceful pair of goat and gypsy girl. At length, shaking his heavy, mis-shapen head, he said: 'It's my misfortune still to look too much like a man. I'd like to be wholly animal, like that goat.'

She looked up at him in astonishment.

He answered her look: 'Oh! I know very well why.' And went away.

Another time he arrived at the entrance to the cell (he never went in) just as la Esmeralda was singing an old Spanish ballad, of which she did not understand the words, but which had remained in her ear because the gypsy women had lulled her to sleep with it when she was a little child. At the sight of that ugly face appearing in the middle of her song, the girl broke off with an involuntary gesture of fright. The unfortunate bell-ringer dropped to his knees in the doorway, and clasped his great shapeless hands be-seechingly: 'Oh!' he said sorrowfully, 'I beg you, go on and don't send me away.' She did not want to hurt him, and trembling all over went on singing her romance. Gradually, however, her fright abated, and she gave way completely to the impression of the melancholy, drawn-out tune she was singing. He had remained kneeling, hands folded as though in prayer, attentive, scarcely breathing, eyes fixed steadily on the gypsy's shining pupils. It was as though he were hearing the song through her eyes.

Yet another time he came to her looking awkward and shy. 'Listen', he said with an effort, 'I have something to tell you.' She made a sign to show that she was listening. Then he began sighing, half opened his mouth, seemed for a moment to be about to speak, then looked at her, shook his head, and slowly withdrew, with his hand to his forehead, leaving the gypsy astounded.

Among the grotesque figures carved on the wall was one of which he was particularly fond, and with which he often seemed to be exchanging fraternal looks. Once the gypsy heard him say to it: 'Oh! why am I not made of stone like you!'

One day, finally, one morning, la Esmeralda had come right up to the edge of the roof and was looking down at the square over the pointed roof of Saint-Jean-le-Rond. Quasimodo was there behind her. He took up that position of his own accord, so as to spare the girl as much as possible the unpleasantness of seeing him. Suddenly the gypsy started, a tear and a flash of joy shone at the same time in her eyes, she kneeled on the edge of the roof and stretched out her arms in anguish towards the square, crying: 'Phoebus! Phoebus! come! come! one word, a single word, in Heaven's name! Phoebus! Phoebus!'—her voice, her face, her movements, her whole person bore the heart-rending expression of a shipwrecked mariner making distress signals to the ship merrily passing in the distance in a ray of sunshine on the horizon.

Quasimodo leaned out over the square and saw that the object of this frantic, tender appeal was a young man, a captain, a handsome horseman, with gleaming weapons and finery, who was caracoling by at the far end of the square, and taking off his plumed hat to a lovely lady smiling on her balcony. In any case, the officer did not hear the unhappy girl calling him. He was too far away.

But the poor deaf ringer heard. His chest heaved with a deep sigh. He turned round. His heart was brimming with all the tears he was choking back, his two fists, clenched convulsively, struck his head, and when he withdrew them each held a handful of reddish hair.

The gypsy was paying no heed to him. Grinding his teeth he muttered in a low voice: 'Damnation! So that's how you've got to be! You need only to be handsome on the outside!'

Meanwhile she had remained kneeling and was crying out in a state of extraordinary agitation: 'Oh! there he is dismounting!—he's about to go into that house!—Phoebus!—he can't hear me! Phoebus!—how unkind of that woman to speak to him at the same time as me!—Phoebus! Phoebus!'

Deaf Quasimodo looked at her. He understood her mime. The poor bell-ringer's eyes filled with tears, but not one did he let fall. Suddenly he tugged gently at the edge of her sleeve. She turned round. He had assumed an air of calm. He said: 'Do you want me to go and fetch him?'

She let out a cry of joy: 'Oh! go, go on! hurry! quickly! That captain! that captain! bring him to me! I'll love you.' She embraced his knees. He could not help shaking his head sorrowfully. 'I'll go and bring him to you,' he said in a faint voice. Then he turned his head and strode hurriedly to the staircase, choking with sobs.

When he reached the square all he could see was the fine horse tethered to the door of the Gondelaurier mansion. The captain had just gone inside.

He looked up at the roof of the church. La Esmeralda was still there, in the same place, the same posture. He nodded to her sadly. Then he leaned against one of the stone bollards in the Gondelaurier porch, determined to wait until the captain came out.

In the Gondelaurier mansion it was one of those gala days which precede a wedding. Quasimodo saw a lot of people go in but he saw no one come out. From time to time he looked up at the roof. The gypsy girl had stirred no more than he had. A groom came to untie the horse and led it away to the stables.

The whole day went by like that, Quasimodo at his stone bollard, la Esmeralda on the roof, Phoebus no doubt at Fleur-de-Lys's feet.

At last night fell: a moonless night, a dark night. In vain did Quasimodo keep his eyes fixed on la Esmeralda. Soon there was nothing there but a patch of white in the half-light; then nothing. Everything was wiped out, everything was black.

Quasimodo saw the windows of the Gondelaurier mansion light up from top to bottom of the façade. He saw the other casements in the square light up one after the other; he saw their lights go out too, down to the last one. For he stayed at his post all evening. The officer did not come out. When the last passers-by had gone home, when all the windows in the other houses had gone dark, Quasimodo remained alone, all by himself in total darkness. At that time there was no lighting in the Parvis de Notre-Dame.

The windows of the Gondelaurier mansion, however, stayed lit up, even after midnight. Quasimodo, motionless and watchful, saw a host of lively, dancing shadows pass over the many-coloured window glass. If he had not been deaf, as the murmur of slumbering Paris died away, he would have heard more and more distinctly, from within the Gondelaurier mansion, the sound of revelry, laughter, and music.

At about one o'clock in the morning the guests began to leave. Quasimodo, wrapped in darkness, watched them pass by under the torch-lit porch. None of them was the captain.

Gloomy thoughts filled his mind. At times he looked up into the air, as people do when they are bored. Great, dark clouds, heavy, ragged, torn, hung like crêpe hammocks from the starry arch of night. They looked like cobwebs on heaven's vault.

At one such moment he suddenly saw opening mysteriously the French window to the balcony whose stone balustrade was silhouetted above his head. The flimsy glass door let through two figures, and then closed silently behind them. They were a man and a woman. With some difficulty Quasimodo managed to recognize in the man the handsome captain, and in the woman the young lady whom he had seen that morning, welcoming the officer from that very same balcony. The square was in total darkness, and a double crimson curtain which had dropped back behind the door just as it closed again hardly let through on to the balcony any light from inside the apartment.

The young man and the girl, as far as our deaf watcher could judge without being able to hear a single word they said, appeared to be indulging in a most affectionate tête-à-tête. The girl seemed to have allowed the officer to put both arms round her waist, and was gently resisting a kiss.

From below, Quasimodo watched this scene, a sight all the more charming for not being meant to be seen. He observed such happiness, such beauty, with bitterness. After all, nature was not dumb in the poor devil, and his spinal column, dreadfully misshapen though it was, was no less sensitive to excitement than anyone else's. He thought of the wretched lot dealt him by Providence, how women, love, sensual delight would everlastingly pass before his eyes, how he would only ever see the bliss of others. But what he found most heart-rending in this spectacle, what added indignation to his frustration, was the thought of how the gypsy girl must be suffering if she could see it. True, the night was very dark, la Esmeralda, if she had stayed where she was (and he did not doubt that she had) was a good way off, and it was as much as he could do himself to make out the lovers on the balcony. That consoled him.

However, their conversation was becoming increasingly animated. The young lady appeared to be begging the officer to make no further demands on her. From all this Quasimodo could make out only fair hands clasped together, smiles mingled with tears, the girl's eyes raised to the stars, the captain's eyes lowered ardently on her.

Fortunately, for the girl's resistance was beginning to become only faint, the balcony door suddenly opened, an old lady appeared, the fair young lady seemed embarrassed, the officer looked put out, and all three went back inside.

A moment later a horse stamped the ground under the porch and the dazzling officer, wrapped in his night cloak, went rapidly by in front of Quasimodo.

The bell-ringer let him turn the street corner, then began running after him, nimbly as a monkey, shouting: 'Hey! Captain!'

The captain stopped. 'What does this rascal want with me?' he said, spying in the darkness a lopsided sort of figure jerkily running towards him.

Quasimido, meanwhile, had reached him, and boldly seized the horse's bridle: 'Follow me, captain! There's someone wants a word with you.'

'*Cornemahom!*' muttered Phoebus, 'here's a nasty, scruffy customer I seem to have seen somewhere before! Hey there! my man, will you kindly let go of my horse's bridle?'

'Captain,' answered the deaf man, 'aren't you going to ask who it is?'

'I tell you, let go of my horse,' Phoebus replied, losing patience. 'What does he want, this rascal hanging on to my charger's reins? Do you take my horse for a gallows?'

Quasimodo, far from loosing the horse's bridle, was getting ready to make it turn round. Unable to account for the captain's resistance, he hastened to tell him: 'Come on, captain, there's a woman waiting for you.' He added, with an effort: 'A woman who loves you.'

'A rare scoundrel!' said the captain, 'to think I'm obliged to go and call on all the women who love me! or say they do!—And supposing by chance she looks like you, with your screech-owl face?—tell the one who sent you that I'm about to get married, and she can go to the devil!'

'Listen,' exclaimed Quasimodo, thinking he would overcome this hesitation with a word, 'come, my lord! It's the gypsy you know about!'

That word did indeed make a great impression on Phoebus, but not what the deaf man had expected. It will be remembered that our gallant officer had withdrawn with Fleur-de-Lys a few moments before Quasimodo had rescued the condemned woman from Charmolue's hands. Since then, on all his visits to the Gondelaurier mansion, he had been very careful to make no further mention of that woman, whose memory, after all, was a painful one for him; and for her part Fleur-de-Lys had not judged it politic to tell him that the gypsy girl was still alive. So Phoebus believed poor 'Similar' to be dead, and that already since a month or two back. Moreover, it may be added, the captain had been thinking for the past few moments of the deep darkness of the night, of the supernatural ugliness, the sepulchral tones of the strange messenger, that it was past midnight, that the street was as deserted as it had been that evening when the bogey-monk had accosted him, and that his horse snorted when it looked at Quasimodo.

'The gypsy!' he exclaimed, almost in fright. 'What then, do you come from the other world?'

And his hand went to the hilt of his dagger.

'Quick, quick,' said the deaf man, trying to drag the horse along. 'This way.'

Phoebus planted a mighty kick in his chest with his boot.

Quasimodo's eye sparkled. He made as if to lunge at the captain. Then he stiffened and said: 'Oh! how lucky you are to have someone who loves you!'

He stressed the word 'someone', and loosing the horse's bridle said: 'Off with you!'

Phoebus spurred away, swearing. Quasimodo watched him plunge off down the street into the murk. 'Oh!' the poor deaf creature whispered, 'fancy refusing that!'

He returned to Notre-Dame, lit his lamp and climbed back up the tower. As he had supposed, the gypsy was still in the same place.

As soon as she saw him coming, she ran to him. 'Alone!' she cried, clasping her lovely hands sorrowfully.

'I couldn't find him,' Quasimodo said coldly.

'You should have waited all night!' she went on furiously.

He saw her angry gesture, and understood her reproach. 'I'll keep a better look out for him another time,' he said, hanging his head.

'Go away!' she said.

He left her. She was displeased with him. He had preferred to be rebuked by her rather than distress her. He had
kept all the pain for himself.

From that day on, the gypsy saw him no more. He
stopped coming to her cell. At most she would sometimes
catch a glimpse of the bell-ringer's face at the top of a
tower, mournfully gazing at her. But as soon as she noticed
him he would vanish.

It has to be said that she was not too upset by this
voluntary absence of the poor hunchback. In her inmost
heart she was grateful to him for it. Besides, Quasimodo
had no illusions on that score.

She did not see him any more, but she felt the presence
of a kindly spirit round her. Her provisions were replen-
ished by an invisible hand while she was asleep. One morning she found a birdcage on her window. Above her cell
was a sculpture which frightened her. She had shown as
much more than once in front of Quasimodo. One morning
(for all these things happened at night), she could no longer
see it. Someone had shattered it. Whoever had climbed up
to that sculpture must have risked his life.

Sometimes, in the evening, she would hear a voice hidden
under the louvres of the bell tower singing a sad, strange
song, as if to lull her to sleep. The lines had no rhyme, and
were such as a deaf man might make up:

> Look not at the face,
> Young girl, look at the heart.
> The heart of a handsome young man is often misshapen.
> There are hearts where love does not last.

> Young girl, the pine tree is not beautiful,
> Not beautiful like the poplar,
> But it keeps its leaves in winter.

> Alas! what's the good of saying that?
> Whatever is without beauty is wrong to exist,
> Beauty only loves beauty,
> April turns her back on January.

> Beauty is perfect,
> Beauty can do anything,
> Beauty is the only thing that does not live by halves.

The crow flies only by day,
The owl flies only by night
The swan flies both by night and day

One morning, she saw, as she awoke, two vases filled with flowers on her window. One was a crystal vase, very fine and brilliant, but cracked. It had let all the water with which it had been filled run out, and the flowers in it were withered. The other was an earthenware pot, crude and common, but it had kept all its water, and the flowers in it had stayed fresh and bright red.

I do not know if it was intentional, but la Esmeralda took the faded bunch, and wore it all day on her breast.

That day she did not hear the voice from the tower singing.

She was not much concerned about that. She spent her days fondling Djali, keeping a watchful eye on the Gondelaurier mansion, talking to herself about Phoebus, and crumbling bread for the swallows.

She had, moreover, quite ceased seeing, or hearing, anything of Quasimodo. The poor bell-ringer seemed to have disappeared from the church. One night, however, as she was not asleep but dreaming of her handsome captain, she heard someone sighing near her cell. Frightened, she got up and saw in the moonlight a shapeless mass lying across her doorway. It was Quasimodo sleeping there on the stone.

V

THE KEY TO THE RED DOOR

MEANWHILE the archdeacon had learned from general rumour how the gypsy had been miraculously rescued. When he learned that, he did not know what to feel. He had come to terms with la Esmeralda's death. In that way he had set his mind at rest, he had plumbed the depths of all possible grief. The human heart (Dom Claude had meditated on such matters) can contain only a certain amount of despair. Once the sponge is saturated, the sea can pass over it without adding one drop more.

Now, with la Esmeralda dead, the sponge was saturated. For Dom Claude the last word had been spoken on this earth. But knowing her to be alive, and Phoebus too, meant the tortures beginning again, the shocks, the alternatives, life itself. And Claude was tired of it all.

When he learned the news, he shut himself up in his cell in the cloister. He did not appear at chapter conferences, nor at services. He closed his door to everyone, even the bishop. He stayed walled up like this for several weeks. People thought he was ill. Indeed he was.

What did he do shut up like that? With what thoughts did the unfortunate man wrestle? Was he putting up a last struggle against his dreadful passion? Was he contriving a final plan, of death for her and damnation for himself?

His Jehan, his beloved brother, his spoilt child, came to his door more than once, knocked, swore, said a dozen times who he was. Claude did not open.

He spent whole days with his face pressed against his window panes. From that window, located in the cloister, he could see la Esmeralda's cell; he often saw her, herself, with her goat, sometimes with Quasimodo. He observed how attentive the ugly, deaf creature was, how obedient, how delicate and submissive his behaviour to the gypsy. He recalled, for he had a good memory, and memory is the torturer of the jealous, the peculiar way the bell-ringer had looked at the dancer one particular evening. He wondered what motive could have driven Quasimodo to rescue her. He witnessed countless little scenes between the gypsy and the deaf man, whose pantomime, seen from a distance and commented on by his own passion, seemed most affectionate. He distrusted the odd ways of women. Then he vaguely felt waken within him a jealousy he had never expected, a jealousy which made him go red with shame and indignation.

'The captain's one thing, but him!' The thought overwhelmed him.

His nights were awful. Ever since he had known the gypsy to be still alive, the chilling thoughts of spectre and tomb which had obsessed him for one whole day had vanished, and the flesh came back to goad him. He writhed on his bed at the knowledge that the brown-skinned girl was so near.

Each night his delirious imagination depicted la Esmeralda to him in all the attitudes which had most set fire coursing through his veins. He saw her stretched out over the captain after the stabbing, her lovely bare breast covered in Phoebus' blood, at that moment of ecstasy when the archdeacon had printed on those pale lips that kiss, which the unfortunate girl, although half dead, had felt searing her. He saw her again, undressed by the brutal hands of the torturers, letting them strip and then fix in the iron-screwed boot her little foot, her slender, shapely leg, her supple, white knee. He saw once more that ivory knee, alone remaining outside Torterue's horrible apparatus. Finally he pictured to himself the girl wearing a shift, a rope round her neck, shoulders bare, feet bare, almost naked, as he had seen her on that last day. These sensual images made him clench his fists and sent a shiver down his spine.

One night in particular they so cruelly set on fire the blood running in his arteries, virginal and priestly though it was, that he bit his pillow, leaped out of bed, threw a surplice over his nightshirt and left his cell, lamp in hand, half naked, distraught, eyes blazing.

He knew where to find the key of the Red Door connecting the cloister to the church, and he always had on him, as we know, a key to the tower staircase.

The Key to the Red Door 442

He knew where to find the key of the Red Door giving on to the cloister of the church, and he always had on him, as we know, a key to the tower staircase.

VI

THE KEY TO THE RED DOOR (CONTINUED)

THAT night la Esmeralda had gone to sleep in her cell, filled with oblivion, hope, and sweet thoughts. She had been asleep for some time, dreaming as always of Phoebus, when she seemed to hear a noise near her. She slept as lightly and restlessly as a bird; the least thing woke her up. She opened her eyes. The night was very dark. She saw, however, at the window a face looking at her. A lamp lit up this apparition. The moment the figure realized that la Esmeralda had seen it, it blew out the lamp. Nevertheless the girl had had time to catch a glimpse. Her eyes closed again in terror. 'Oh!' she said in a faint voice, 'the priest!'

All her past misfortunes came back to her in a flash. She fell back on her bed, ice-cold.

A moment later she felt a touch along her body which made her shudder so violently that she sat up fully awake and furious.

The priest had just slipped in beside her. He had both arms round her.

She tried to scream, but could not.

'Go away, monster! Go away, murderer!' she said in a low voice, trembling with anger and terror.

'Mercy! mercy!' murmured the priest, pressing his lips to her shoulders.

She seized his bald head in both hands by his remaining hair, and strove to ward off his kisses as if they had been bites.

'Mercy!' the wretched man repeated. 'If you knew what my love for you is like! It's fire, molten lead, thousands of knives in my heart!'

And he held her arms still with superhuman strength. Distraught, she said: 'Let me go, or I'll spit in your face!'

He let her go: 'Degrade me, hit me, be vicious! Do whatever you like! But mercy! love me!'

Then she hit out at him in childlike rage. She made her lovely hand taut so that she could bruise his face: 'Go away, you devil!'

'Love me! love me! Have pity!' the poor priest cried, rolling on top of her and responding to her blows with caresses.

Suddenly she felt him get the better of her. 'We must put an end to this!' he said, grinding his teeth.

She was subjugated, quivering, shattered, in his arms, at his mercy. She felt a lascivious hand straying over her. She made one last effort and began to cry: 'Help! help me! A vampire! a vampire!'

No one came. Only Djali was awake, bleating in distress. 'Be quiet!' panted the priest.

Suddenly, as she struggled, crawling on the floor, the gypsy's hand touched something cold and metallic. It was Quasimodo's whistle. She seized it with a convulsion of hope, put it to her lips and blew with all her remaining strength. The whistle made a clear, shrill, piercing sound.

'What's that?' said the priest.

Almost at the same moment he felt himself being lifted up by a powerful arm; the cell was dark, he could not clearly make out who was holding him like that; but he could hear teeth chattering with rage, and there was just enough light scattered in the darkness for him to see a large cutlass blade glinting above his head.

The priest thought he could discern the form of Quasimodo. He supposed that it could only be him. He remembered stumbling as he had come in against a bundle lying across the doorway outside. However, as the newcomer did not utter a word, he did not know what to think. He threw himself at the arm holding the cutlass crying: 'Quasimodo!' He had forgotten at this moment of distress that Quasimodo was deaf.

In less than no time the priest was laid low, and felt a knee pressing on his chest like a lead weight. From the angular imprint of that knee he recognized Quasimodo. But what could he do? How could he make Quasimodo recognize him? The dark night made the deaf man blind.

He was lost. The girl, pitiless as an angry tigress, did not intervene to save him. The cutlass came closer to his head. The moment was critical. Suddenly his adversary seemed to be seized with hesitation. 'No blood on her!' he said in a muffled voice.

It was indeed the voice of Quasimodo.

Then the priest felt a huge hand dragging him by the foot out of the cell. That was where he was to die. Fortunately for him, the moon had just come up in the last few moments.

Once they were outside the cell, a pale moonbeam fell on the priest's face. Quasimodo looked at him, was seized with trembling, let go of the priest and drew back.

The gypsy, who had come as far as the entrance to the cell, saw with surprise the roles abruptly changed. Now it was the priest who was threatening, Quasimodo who was begging.

The priest, who was heaping gestures of anger and rebuke on the deaf man, bade him with a violent sign to withdraw.

The deaf man bowed his head, then went to kneel in front of the gypsy's door. 'My lord,' he said in grave and resigned tones, 'afterwards you can do what you like; but kill me first.'

So saying he held out his cutlass to the priest. The priest, beside himself, pounced for it, but the girl was quicker. She tore the knife out of Quasimodo's hands, and burst out into furious laughter. 'Come closer!' she said to the priest.

She was holding the blade up high. The priest stayed undecided. She would certainly have struck. 'You wouldn't dare come any closer now, you coward!' she cried at him. Then she added with a pitiless expression, knowing full well that it would send a thousand red-hot irons through the priest's heart: 'Ah! I know that Phoebus isn't dead!'

The priest sent Quasimodo sprawling to the ground with a kick, and shaking with rage plunged back under the staircase vault.

When he had gone, Quasimodo picked up the whistle which had just saved the gypsy. 'It was getting rusty,' he said as he gave it back to her. Then he left her on her own.

The girl, overcome by this violent scene, fell exhausted on her bed, and began weeping and sobbing. Her horizon was again ominous.

For his part, the priest had groped his way back to his cell.

It was done. Dom Claude was jealous of Quasimodo! He repeated thoughtfully his fateful words: 'No one will have her!'

BOOK TEN

I

GRINGOIRE HAS SEVERAL GOOD IDEAS IN SUCCESSION IN THE RUE DES BERNARDINS

ONCE Pierre Gringoire had seen how this affair was turning out and that there would definitely be rope, hanging, and sundry other bits of unpleasantness for the main actors in this play, he no longer cared to be mixed up in it. The truands, with whom he had remained, judging that in the last analysis they offered the best company in Paris, the truands had continued to take an interest in the gypsy girl. He had found that quite natural on the part of people who, like her, had no prospect other than Charmolue and Torterue, and who did not ride like him in the realm of the imagination between Pegasus' two wings. He had learned from their remarks that his bride of the broken pitcher had found refuge in Notre-Dame, and he was very glad she had. But he was not even tempted to go and see her there. He sometimes thought of the little goat, and that was all. For the rest, by day he performed feats of strength for a living, and at night he was working on a paper against the Bishop of Paris, for he remembered being soaked by the bishop's mill-wheels, and still bore him a grudge. He was also busy writing a commentary on the fine work of Baudry the Red, Bishop of Noyon and Tournai, *De cupa petrarum* [On Stonecutting], which had filled him with a violent enthusiasm for architecture; an interest which had replaced in his heart his passion for hermeticism, of which it was in any case merely the natural corollary, since there is a close link between hermetics and masonry. Gringoire had passed from the love of an idea to love of the form of that idea.

One day he had stopped near Saint-Germain-l'Auxerrois, at the corner of a house called le For-l'Evêque, which stood opposite another called le For-le-Roi. This For-l'Evêque had a charming fourteenth-century chapel with an apse giving on to the street. Gringoire was reverently examining its external sculptures. It was for him one of those moments of selfish, exclusive, supreme delight when the artist sees in the world only art and sees the world in art. Suddenly he felt a hand laid gravely on his shoulder. He turned round. It was his old friend, his old master, the archdeacon.

He was quite astounded. It had been a long time since he had last seen the archdeacon, and Dom Claude was one of those solemn, passionate men an encounter with whom always upsets the balance of a sceptical philosopher.

The archdeacon stayed silent for a few moments, during which Gringoire had leisure to observe him. He found Dom Claude much changed, pale as a winter's morning, hollow-eyed, hair almost white. It was the priest who finally broke the silence, saying in calm, but icy, tones: 'How are you, Maître Pierre?'

'My health?' Gringoire replied. 'Eh! middling, one might say. But on the whole quite good. I don't overdo anything. You know, master, the secret of good health, according to Hippocrates, *id est cibi, potus, somnii, Venus, omnia moderata sint* [that is, all things in moderation, food, drink, sleep, Venus].'

'So you have no worries, Maître Pierre?' the archdeacon went on, staring at Gringoire.

'My word, no.'

'And what are you doing now?'

'As you see, master. I am studying the way these stones have been cut, and the undercutting of this bas-relief.'

The priest began to smile, one of those bitter smiles which lift up only one corner of the mouth. 'And you enjoy that?'

'It's paradise!' exclaimed Gringoire. And leaning over the carvings with the dazzled look of someone demonstrating living phenomena: 'Don't you think, for example, that this metamorphosis in *basse-taille* has been executed with much skill, delicacy, and patience? Look at that little column. Have you ever seen a capital with more tender leaves around it, or more finely stroked by the chisel? Here are three sculptures in the round by Jean Maillevin. They are not that great genius's finest work. Nevertheless the simplicity, the sweetness of the faces, the gaiety of the attitudes and the draperies, and that indefinable charm which is blended with all the defects, make these figurines very cheerful and delicate, even perhaps too much so—don't you find that entertaining?'

'Indeed I do!' said the priest.

'And if you saw the inside of the chapel!' the poet went on, voluble with enthusiasm. 'Sculptures everywhere. It's as densely packed as a cabbage heart! The apse is in a most devotional style, and so unusual that I've never seen its like anywhere else!'

Dom Claude interrupted him: 'You are happy then?'

Gringoire answered enthusiastically: 'Upon my honour, yes! First I loved women, then animals. Now I love stones. They are just as entertaining as animals and women, and not so treacherous.'

The priest put his hand over his brow. It was a habitual gesture of his. 'Really!'

'Look!' said Gringoire, 'there's real enjoyment to be had!' He took the arm of the priest, who made no demur, and led him into the stair turret of the For-l'Evêque. 'There's a staircase for you! Every time I see it I feel happy. This flight of steps is the simplest and most uncommon in Paris. All the steps are hollowed out underneath. Its beauty and simplicity lie in the treads, a foot or so wide, which are interlaced, interlocked, fitted together, interlinked, embedded, morticed one inside the other, and make a really firm and attractive joint!'

'And you have no desires?'

'No.'

'And no regrets?'

'Neither regrets nor desires. I have arranged my life . . .'

'What men arrange,' said Claude, 'things disarrange.'

'I am a Pyrrhonist* philosopher,' Gringoire replied, 'and I keep everything in equilibrium.'

'And how do you earn your living?'

'Now and then I still compose epics and tragedies, but what brings me in most is that industry you have seen me at, master—carrying pyramids of chairs in my teeth.'

'A crude job for a philosopher.'

'It's still equilibrium,' said Gringoire. 'Once you have an idea you find it again everywhere.'

'I know,' the archdeacon answered.

After a silence, the priest went on: 'All the same you are still quite poorly off?'

'Poor, yes; unhappy, no.'

At that moment came the sound of horses, and our two interlocutors saw a company of archers of the King's ordinance riding by at the end of the street, lances raised, with their officer at their head. It was a glittering cavalcade, and made the roadway ring.

'How intently you are looking at that officer!' Gringoire said to the archdeacon.

'It's because I think I recognize him.'

'What is he called?'

'I think,' said Claude, 'his name is Phoebus de Châteaupers.'

'Phoebus! A curious name! There's also a Phoebus, comte de Foix.* I remember once knowing a girl who only ever swore by Phoebus.'

'Come along,' said the priest. 'I have something to tell you.'

Since the troop had ridden past, the archdeacon betrayed a certain agitation beneath his icy exterior. He began to walk. Gringoire followed, used to obeying him, like everyone else who had ever approached this commanding character. In silence they reached the rue des Bernardins, which was more or less deserted. Dom Claude stopped.

'What do you have to tell me, master?' asked Gringoire.

'Don't you think,' the archdeacon answered with an air of profound reflection, 'that the riders we have just seen are dressed more handsomely than you or I?'

Gringoire shook his head. 'My word! I prefer my yellow and red surcoat to those iron and steel scales. What sort of pleasure is it to clank about when you walk like a scrap-iron dump in an earthquake?'

'So, Gringoire, you have never felt envious of those handsome lads in their military actons?'

'Envious of what, Monsieur the Archdeacon? Their strength, their armour, their discipline? Better philosophy and independence in rags. I'd rather be a fly's head than a lion's tail.'

'That's odd,' the priest said thoughtfully. 'A fine uniform is fine all the same.'

Gringoire, seeing him sunk in thought, left him and went to admire the porch of a house nearby. He came back clapping his hands. 'If you were less preoccupied with the fine clothes of the army, Monsieur the Archdeacon, I would ask you to go and look at that door. I have always said Sieur Aubry's house has the most superb entrance in the world.'

'Pierre Gringoire,' said the archdeacon, 'what have you done with that little gypsy dancer?'

'La Esmeralda? That's a very abrupt change of subject.'

'Wasn't she your wife?'

'Yes, with the help of a broken pitcher. We were to have four years' worth. By the way,' Gringoire added, looking at the archdeacon, half mockingly, 'you still think of her, then?'

'What about you, don't you think of her any more?'

'Not much—I have so many things—goodness, what a pretty little goat that was!'

'Didn't the gypsy once save your life?'

'That's true, by God.'

'Well! what's become of her? What have you done with her?'

'I can't tell you. I believe they hanged her.'

'You believe?'

'I'm not sure. Once I saw they were intending to hang someone, I threw in my hand.'

'That's all you know about her?'

'Wait a moment. I was told she had taken refuge in Notre-Dame, and that she was safe there, and I'm delighted, and I haven't been able to discover whether the goat got away with her, and that's all I know about it.'

'I'm going to tell you more,' cried Dom Claude, and his voice which had been up till then quiet, slow, and almost muffled, had become thunderous. 'She has indeed taken refuge in Notre-Dame. But in three days' time justice will take her back from there and she will be hanged in the Grève. There's a decree of Parliament.'

'That's awkward,' said Gringoire.

The priest, in a flash, had become cold and calm again.

'But who the devil,' the poet went on, 'had nothing better to do than apply for a decree of reintegration? Couldn't they leave Parliament alone? What does it matter if a poor girl shelters under the flying buttresses of Notre-Dame beside the swallows' nests?'

'There are satans in the world,' the archdeacon replied.

'That's a devilish bad start,' Gringoire observed.

The archdeacon went on after a silence: 'So she saved your life?'

'When I was with my good friends the truands. I came within a hair's breadth of being hanged. They would be upset today if I had been.'

'Wouldn't you like to do something for her?'

'I should like nothing better, Dom Claude. But suppose it meant getting all tangled up with something nasty round my body?'

'What does that matter?'

'Ha! what does that matter! You are too kind, master! I have two major works already begun.'

The priest struck his forehead. Despite the calm he affected a violent gesture revealed from time to time his inner turmoil. 'How is she to be saved?'

Gringoire said to him: 'Master, my answer to you is *Il padelt*, which is Turkish for *God is our hope!*'*

'How can she be saved?' Claude repeated thoughtfully.

Gringoire in his turn smote his forehead.

'Listen, master, I'm a man with imagination. I'll find expedients for you—suppose we asked the King for a pardon?'

'Louis XI? Pardon?'

'Why not?'

'Try taking a bone away from a tiger!'

Gringoire started looking for fresh solutions. 'All right! Wait—would you like me to address a request to the matrons with a declaration that the girl is pregnant?'

That brought a glint to the priest's sunken eyes.

'Pregnant! you rascal! Have you any knowledge of that?'

Gringoire was frightened by his expression. He said hastily: 'Oh! not me! Our marriage was a real *foris maritagium* [marriage to an outsider]. I stayed outside. But at least we'd get a stay of execution.'

'Madness! Infamy! Hold your tongue!'

'You're wrong to lose your temper,' muttered Gringoire. 'We get a stay. That does no one any harm, and it makes 40 *deniers parisis* for the matrons, who are poor women.'

The priest was not listening to him. 'She must get out of there, all the same!' he murmured. 'The decree has to be executed within three days! Besides, even if there were no decree, that Quasimodo! Women have the most depraved tastes!' He raised his voice: 'Maître Pierre, I have given much thought to it; there's only one way to save her.'

'What's that? I can't see one.'

'Listen, Maître Pierre, remember that you owe her your life. I'll tell you my idea quite frankly. The church is watched day and night. No one is allowed out but those who have been seen going in. So you'll be able to get in. You'll go there. I'll take you in to her. You'll change clothes with her. She'll take your doublet, you'll take her skirt.'

'Fine so far,' observed the philosopher. 'And then?'

'And then? She'll go out in your clothes; you'll stay behind in hers. Maybe they'll hang you, but she'll be saved.'

Gringoire scratched his ear with a very serious look.

'Well now,' he said, 'that's an idea which would never have occurred to me just like that.'

At Dom Claude's unexpected proposal, the poet's open, kindly face had suddenly darkened, like some smiling Italian landscape when an untimely gust of wind blows up and blots out the sun with a cloud.

'Well, Gringoire? What do you say to my scheme?'

'What I say, master, is that they won't hang me maybe, but will hang me indubitably.'

'That's not our concern.'

'Plague on it!' said Gringoire.

'She saved your life. You'll be paying off a debt.'

'There are plenty of other debts I haven't paid!'

'Maître Pierre, it simply has to be done.'

The archdeacon spoke with authority.

'Listen, Dom Claude,' the poet replied in consternation, 'you are keen on this idea, and you're wrong. I don't see why I should have myself hanged in another person's place.'

'What do you have that makes you so attached to life?'

'Ah! innumerable reasons!'

'Such as, if you please?'

'Such as? Air, sky, morning, evening, moonlight, my good friends the truands, taunting the drabs with them, the beauties of Paris architecture to study, three big books to write, one of them against the bishop and his watermills, I don't know what else. Anaxagoras used to say that he was in the world to admire the sun. Moreover, I am fortunate enough to spend all my days from morning to evening with a man of genius, namely myself, and that's most agreeable.'

'Scatterbrain,' muttered the archdeacon. 'Eh! tell me, this life that you make so delightful for yourself, who preserved it for you?' Whom do you have to thank for breathing this air, seeing that sky, and being still able to amuse your lark's brain with frivolities and follies? But for her, where would you be? Do you want her to die then, she through whom you are alive? Let her die, that lovely, sweet, adorable creature, needful for the light of the world, more divine than God? While you, half wise and half foolish, empty sketch of something or other, some kind of vegetable being which believes it can walk and think, while you go on living the life of which you robbed her, useless as a candle at noonday? Come along, a little pity, Gringoire—be generous in your turn. It was she who did so first.'

The priest was vehement. Gringoire listened to him at first with an undecided look, then he softened, and ended by pulling a tragic grimace which made his wan face look like that of a newborn baby with colic.

'You are very moving,' he said, wiping away a tear. 'All right! I'll think about it. That's a very odd idea of yours. After all,' he went on after a silence, 'who knows? Perhaps they won't hang me. It's not every engagement which ends with a wedding. When they find me in that cell, got up so grotesquely in skirt and coif, perhaps they'll just roar with laughter. Anyhow, if they do hang me, all right! The rope is a death like any other, or, to be more precise, it is not like any other death. It is a death worthy of the sage who has spent his whole life oscillating, a death which is neither flesh nor fowl, like the mind of the true sceptic, a death stamped all over with Pyrrhonism and hesitation, half-way between heaven and earth, which leaves you in suspense. It's a philosopher's death, and perhaps that's what I was predestined for. It's a splendid thing to die as one has lived.'

The priest interrupted: 'Is it agreed, then?'

'What is death, when you come down to it?' Gringoire continued in a state of exaltation. 'A bad moment, a toll, a transition from not much to nothing at all. When someone asked Cercidas of Megalopolis if he would die gladly, he answered: "Why not? for after my death I shall see those great men, Pythagoras among philosophers, Hecataeus among historians, Homer among poets, Olympus among musicians." '

The archdeacon held out his hand to him: 'That's settled then? You'll come tomorrow.'

The gesture brought Gringoire back to reality. 'Ha! my goodness, no!' he said in the tone of a man just waking up. 'To be hanged! it's too absurd. I won't do it.'

'Farewell, then!' And the archdeacon added between his teeth: 'I'll find you again!'

'I don't want that devil of a man to find me,' thought Gringoire, and ran after Dom Claude. 'Come now, Monsieur the Archdeacon, no ill feeling between old friends! You have an interest in this girl, in my wife, I mean, that's fine. You have thought up a stratagem for getting her out of Notre-Dame safely, but your plan is extremely unpleasant for me, for Gringoire. Suppose I had another plan!— I warn you that at this very instant a most luminous inspiration has occurred to me,—suppose I had an expedient idea for extricating her from this predicament without compromising my neck with the slightest slip-knot? What would you say to that? Wouldn't that be enough for you? Is it absolutely necessary to make you happy that I should be hanged?'

The priest was ripping buttons off his cassock with impatience. 'A running stream of words!—What's your plan?'

'Yes,' Gringoire went on, talking to himself and touching his nose with his index finger to indicate deep thought. 'That's it! The truands are good lads. . . . The tribe of Egypt is very fond of her. . . . They will rise up at a word. . . . Nothing easier—a sudden raid—under cover of the disorder, she can easily be snatched away. . . . By tomorrow evening . . . they'll be only too pleased.'

'The plan! Tell me,' said the priest, shaking him.

Gringoire turned to him majestically. 'Let me be! You can see that I am putting it together.' He reflected for a few more minutes. Then he began to clap his hands at what he had thought up, crying: 'Admirable! Sure to work!'

'The plan!' Claude went on angrily.

Gringoire was radiant. 'Come here, let me whisper it to you. It's a really bold countermine, and it will solve the problem for all of us. You must agree that I'm no fool.'

He broke off: 'Oh yes! Is the little goat with the girl?'

'Yes. Devil take you.'

'And they would have hanged it too, wouldn't they?'

'What's that to me?'

'Yes, they would have hanged her. They hanged a sow right enough last month. The executioner likes that. He eats the animal afterwards. Hang my pretty Djali! Poor little lamb!'

'Curses!' exclaimed Dom Claude. 'You're the one who is the executioner. What way of saving her have you thought up then, you rogue? Has it got to be dragged out of you with forceps?'

'Steady there, master! Here you are.'

Gringoire leaned over and whispered in the archdeacon's ear, glancing anxiously up and down the street, though no one was passing by. When he had finished, Dom Claude took him by the hand and said to him coldly: 'All right. Until tomorrow then.'

'Till tomorrow,' repeated Gringoire. And while the archdeacon went off one way, he took himself off in another, saying to himself in an undertone: 'This is a fine business, Maître Pierre Gringoire. Never mind. Just because you are only a little man it doesn't mean you'll be scared of taking on something big. Bito* carried a great bull on his shoulders; wagtails, warblers, and wheatears fly across the ocean.'

II

BECOME A TRUAND!

ON his return to the cloister the archdeacon found waiting at the door of his cell his brother Jehan du Moulin, who had been whiling away his boredom while he waited by making a charcoal sketch on the wall of his older brother's profile enhanced by an outsize nose.

Dom Claude hardly looked at his brother. He had other things on his mind. The cheerful scamp's face, whose sunny beams had so often brought serenity back to the priest's sombre countenance, was now quite powerless to dispel the mist which lay denser every day over that corrupt, mephitic, stagnant soul.

'Brother,' Jehan said timidly, 'I've come to see you.'

The archdeacon did not even look up at him. 'So?'

'Brother,' the hypocrite went on, 'you are so kind to me, and give me such good advice, that I always come back to you.'

'And?'

'Alas! brother, you were so right when you told me: "Jehan, Jehan, *cessat doctorum doctrina, discipulorum disciplina* [the teaching of the teachers, the discipline of the disciples has slackened off]. Jehan, be good, Jehan, be studious, Jehan don't spend the night out of college without lawful occasion and the master's leave. Don't beat the Picards, *Noli, Joannes, verberare picardos*. Don't rot away like an illiterate donkey on the straw of the lecture-room floor. Jehan, accept your punishment at your master's discretion. Jehan, go to chapel every evening and sing an anthem with verse and prayer to Our Lady the glorious Virgin Mary." Alas! what most excellent advice that was!'

'Well?'

'You see before you, brother, a guilty man, a criminal, a wretch, a libertine, a heinous person! Brother, Jehan has treated your gracious counsels like straw and dung to be trampled underfoot. I have been well punished for it, and God has been extraordinarily just. As long as I had money, I feasted, led a wild and merry life. Oh! how debauchery, so delightful in prospect, turns out ugly and sour in retrospect! Now I don't have a farthing left, I've sold my tablecloth, my shirt, and my towel, no more making merry! The good wax candle has gone out, and all I have left is a nasty tallow wick smoking in my nose. The girls laugh at me. I drink plain water. I am racked by remorse and creditors.'

'The rest?' said the archdeacon.

'Alas! dearest brother, I'd like to settle down to a better life. I come to you full of contrition. I'm penitent. I confess my sins. I beat my breast with heavy blows. You are quite right to want me one day to become a graduate and submonitor of the Collège de Torchi. I now feel a splendid vocation for that way of life. But I've no ink left. I must buy some more; no quills left, I must buy some more; no paper, no books, I must buy some more. To do so I badly need a little financial support. And I come to you, brother, with a heart full of contrition.'

'Is that all?'

'Yes,' said the student. 'A little money.'

'I don't have any.'

At that the student said, looking at once grave and resolute: 'All right, brother, I'm sorry to have to tell you that I have received from other quarters some very handsome offers and proposals. You won't give me any money?—no?—in that case I'm going to become a truand.'

As he uttered those monstrous words, he assumed the air of Ajax, expecting to see a thunderbolt come down on his head.

The archdeacon said coldly: 'Become a truand.'

Jehan bowed low to him, and went back down the cloister stairs whistling.

Just as he was passing in the cloister garth beneath his brother's cell window, he heard that window open, raised his head and saw the archdeacon's stern face looking out through the opening. 'Go to the devil!' said Dom Claude, 'this is the last money you will get from me.'

At the same time the priest threw a purse at Jehan which raised a big lump on the student's forehead, and left him both amazed and pleased as he went away, like a dog pelted with marrow-bones.

III

THREE CHEERS FOR PLEASURE!

THE reader may perhaps not have forgotten that part of
the Court of Miracles was enclosed by the ancient town
wall, a good number of whose towers were beginning at
that time to fall into ruin. One of these towers had been
converted by the truands into a place of entertainment.
There was a tavern in the lower room, and the rest on the
floors above. This tower was the most lively, and thus the
most hideous, spot in the truanderie. It was a sort of monstrous hive, humming day and night. At night, when all the
rest of the beggars' realm was asleep, when not one window
in the grubby façades of the square remained lit, when there
was not a cry to be heard from the hundreds of households,
those swarms of thieves, harlots, and stolen or bastard
children, the pleasure tower could always be identified by
the noise coming from it and from the scarlet glare which,
radiating at once from air-vents, windows, and fissures in
the cracked walls, leaked out, so to speak, from all its pores.

The cellar, then, was the tavern. The way down to it was
by a low door and stairs as steep and rigid as a Classical
Alexandrine. On the door, by way of a sign, there was a
monstrous daub representing newly minted *sols* and
slaughtered chickens, with this pun underneath: *Aux sonneurs pour les trépassés* [At the ringers for the dead].*

One evening, just as the curfew was ringing out from all
the belfries in Paris, the sergeants of the watch, had they
been granted admission to the fearsome Court of Miracles,
might have noticed that the uproar in the truands' tavern
was even greater than usual, that there was more drinking and more swearing. Outside in the square a good number of groups were talking together in low tones, as when
some great scheme is afoot, and here and there a rascal
squatted down, sharpening some sorry iron blade on a
paving-stone.

Meanwhile in the tavern itself, wine and gambling provided so powerful a distraction from the thoughts occupying the minds of the truanderie that evening, that it would have been hard to guess from the drinkers' remarks what it was all about. They just looked merrier than usual, and all of them could be seen polishing up some weapon held between their legs, a billhook, an axe, a big two-edged sword, or the hook of an old arquebus.

The room, circular in shape, was very spacious, but the tables were so crowded together and the drinkers so numerous, that the whole contents of the tavern, men, women, benches, beer jugs, those drinking, sleeping, gambling, the fit and the cripples, seemed all to be piled up one on top of the other in as orderly and harmonious a fashion as a heap of oyster shells. There were a few tallow candles burning on the tables; but the real source of light in the tavern, fulfilling there the role of a chandelier in an opera house, was the fire. This cellar was so damp that the fire in the hearth was never allowed to go out, even at the height of summer; an immense fireplace with a carved mantel, bristling with heavy iron firedogs and cooking equipment, with one of those huge fires of mixed wood and peat, which in village streets at night cast on the walls opposite so red a reflection from the windows of the forge. A large dog, solemnly sitting in the ashes, was turning a spit laden with meat before the glowing embers.

Great as the confusion was, after the first glance you could distinguish in the throng three main groups, crowding round three personages whom the reader has already met. One of these, garishly attired in much oriental glittering finery, was Mathias Hungadi Spicali, Duke of Egypt and Bohemia. The rogue was sitting on a table, with legs crossed, finger raised, loudly imparting his knowledge of magic, white and black, to many of those standing around him with mouths agape. Another crowd was growing around our old friend the valiant King of Tunis, who was armed to the teeth. Clopin Trouillefou, looking very serious and keeping his voice down, was controlling the plundering of an enormous cask full of weapons, which stood smashed wide open in front of him, and from which spilled a mass of axes, swords, bassinets, coats of mail, plate armour, spear and pike heads, arrows and bolts for crossbows, like apples and grapes from a horn of plenty. Everyone took something from the pile, one a helmet, another a rapier, a third a misericord, a dagger with a cross-shaped hilt. The very children were arming themselves, and even the legless cripples, in bard and cuirass, scuttled between the drinkers' legs like huge beetles.

Lastly, a third audience, the noisiest, jolliest, and most numerous, jammed the benches and tables in the midst of which a shrill voice was perorating and swearing from beneath a set of heavy armour, complete from helmet to spurs. The individual who had thus screwed a whole panoply on to his body was so completely hidden beneath his battle order that nothing could be seen of him but an impudent, snub, red nose, a lock of fair hair, a pink mouth and bold eyes. His belt was crammed with daggers and poniards, he had a great sword by his side, a rusty crossbow on his left, and a huge jug of wine in front of him, not to mention a thick-set, dishevelled girl on his right. All the mouths around him were laughing, swearing, and drinking.

Add a score of secondary groups, serving maids and lads rushing about with jugs on their head, gamblers squatting over their billiards, marbles, dice, *vachettes*, the exciting game of *tringlet*, quarrels in one corner, kisses in another, and you will have some idea of the whole scene, over which the brightness of a great blazing fire flickered, making a thousand distorted and grotesque shadows dance over the tavern walls.

As for the noise, it was like being inside a bell in full peal.

A shower of fat crackled in the dripping pan, filling up with its constant sputtering the gaps in the hundreds of dialogues going on across the room from one end to the other.

Amid all the noise, at the far end of the tavern, on the seat inside the fireplace, a philosopher was meditating, his feet in the ashes and his eyes on the burning brands. It was Pierre Gringoire.

'Come along, quick there! Hurry up, arm yourselves! We're off in an hour!' Clopin Trouillefou was saying to his argoteers.

A girl was humming:

> Good-night father, good-night mother!
> Last to go put out the fire.

Two card-players were arguing: 'Knave!' cried the more rubicund of the two, shaking his fist at the other, 'I'll mark you in clubs. You'll be able to replace Mistigri,* as an extra knave of clubs in our lord the King's pack of cards.'

'Ugh!' shouted a Norman, recognizable by his nasal accent, 'we are as closely packed here as the saints at Caillouville!'*

'Lads,' the Duke of Egypt was telling his audience in falsetto tones, 'the witches in France go to their sabbath without a broomstick, without any grease, without anything to ride on, just with a few magic words. The witches in Italy always have a he-goat waiting at their door. They are all obliged to go out up the chimney.'

The voice of the young rascal armed from head to foot rose over the hubbub. 'Noël! Noël!' he cried. 'My first arms to day! Truand! I'm a truand, Christ's belly! Pour me a drink! My friends, my name is Jehan du Moulin, and I'm a gentleman. It's my opinion that if God were a soldier, he'd become a looter. Brothers, we are going off on a fine expedition. We are a valiant lot. Lay siege to the church, smash down the doors, take out the beautiful girl, save her from the judges, save her from the priests, wreck the cloister, burn the bishop in his palace, we'll do it in less time than it takes a burgomaster to eat a spoonful of soup. Our cause is just, we'll sack Notre-Dame, and that will be that. We'll hang Quasimodo. Do you know Quasimodo, mesdemoiselles? Have you ever seen him panting upon the great bell on some high Whitsun holiday? *Corne du Père!* It's a very fine sight! like a devil astride a gaping muzzle. My friends, listen to me, I am a truand to the bottom of my heart, I'm an argoteer in my very soul, I was born a *cagou*. I was once very rich, and I spent all I had. My mother wanted to make me an officer, my father a sub-deacon, my aunt a counsellor at the appeal court, my grandmother a royal protonotary, my great-aunt a treasurer of the short robe. As for me, I've become a truand! I told my father, who spat his curse in my face, my mother, and the old lady fell to weeping and drooling like that log on the firedog. Three cheers for pleasure! I'm a proper wrecker! Landlady, my love, some other wine! I've still got enough to pay for it. I don't want any more of that wine from Suresnes. It upsets my throat. I'd just as soon, *corbœuf*, gargle with a basket!'

Meanwhile the crowd applauded, with roars of laughter, and seeing the tumult increasing around him, the student exclaimed: 'Oh! what a lovely noise! *Populi debacchantis populosa debacchatio!* [popular revelry of a people revelling!]' Then he began to sing, with a faraway look as if in ecstasy, in the tones of a canon chanting vespers: '*Quae cantica! quae organa! quae cantilena! quae melodiae hic sine fine decantantur! Sonant melliflua hymnorum organa, suavissima angelorum melodia, cantica canticorum mira!* [What canticles! what instruments! what songs, what melodies are endlessly sung here! The mellifluous instruments of the hymns sound out, the angels' sweetest melodies, the wondrous song of songs!]'*

He broke off: 'You, you devil's own barmaid, bring me some supper!'

There was a moment of near silence during which the shrill voice of the Duke of Egypt rose in its turn, instructing his gypsies: '. . . the weasel is called Aduine, the fox Blue-Foot or Wood-Ranger, the wolf Grey-Foot or Gold-Foot, the bear the Old Man or Grandfather. A gnome's cap makes you invisible, and shows up invisible objects. Every toad that is baptized should be dressed in red or black velvet, with a little bell round its neck and another on its feet. The godfather holds its head, the godmother its rump. It is the demon Sidragasum who has the power to make girls dance stark naked.'

'By the mass!' Jehan interrupted, 'I'd like to be the demon Sidragasum.'

Meanwhile the truands went on arming themselves and whispering at the other end of the tavern.

'That poor Esmeralda!' one gypsy said. 'She's our sister—we must get her out of there.'

'Is she still in Notre-Dame then?' went on a Jewish-looking *marcandier*.

'Yes, by God.'

'Very well, comrades,' cried out the *marcandier*, 'on to Notre-Dame! It makes it even better that in the chapel of Saints Ferreol and Ferrution there are two statues, one of Saint John the Baptist and the other of Saint Antony, of solid gold, weighing altogether 17 gold *marcs* 15 *esterlins*, and the silver-gilt pedestals 17 *marcs* 5 ounces. I know. I'm a goldsmith.'

Here they served Jehan his supper. He shouted, sprawled over the bosom of the girl beside him:

'By the Holy Face of Lucca, which the people call Saint Goguelu,* I am completely happy. There's an idiot in front of me looking at me with a face as hairless as an archduke. There's another on my left with such long teeth that they hide his chin. And then I'm like the maréchal de Gié at the siege of Pontoise, my right is resting on a little bulge in the contours. Mahomet's belly, comrade! You look like a tennis-ball pedlar, and you come and sit next to me! I am a noble, my friend. Trade is incompatible with nobility. Off with you!—Hey! you there! don't fight! What, Baptiste Croque-Oison, with your fine nose, are you going to risk it against that lout's great fists! Idiot! *Non cuiquam datum est habere nasum* [It is not given to everyone to have a nose]— you're truly divine, Jacqueline Ronge-Oreille! a pity you haven't any hair—hallo! my name's Jehan Frollo, and my brother is an archdeacon. May the devil take him! Everything I'm telling you is the truth. By becoming a truand I cheerfully gave up half of a house in paradise that my brother promised me—*dimidiam domum in paradiso** [half a house in paradise/the Parvis]. I quote from the text. I own a fief in the rue Tirechappe, and all the women are in love with me, as true as it's true that Saint Éloy was an excellent goldsmith, and that the five trades of the good town of Paris are the tanners, the tawers, the baldric makers, the purse makers, and the cordwainers, and that Saint Lawrence was grilled on eggshells. I swear to you, comrades:

> Spiced wine won't pass my lips
> For one full year if now I lie.

My charmer, the moon shines bright, just look through the vent up there at the wind ruffling the clouds. As I'm doing with your gorget—Girls! snuff out the children and the candles. Christ and Mahomet! Whatever am I eating, Jupiter! Hey! you old trull! The hairs that are missing from your whores' heads we find in your omelettes. Old woman! I like my omelettes bald. May the devil squash your nose!— This is a fine Beelzebub's tavern where the wenches use the forks for combs!'

So saying he smashed his plate on the floor and began singing at the top of his voice:

> I'm a man, by God's blood,
> who has no faith, no law,
> no hearth, no home,
> no king, no God!

Meanwhile Clopin Trouillefou had finished distributing the arms. He came up to Gringoire, who seemed to be sunk in profound reverie, his feet up on a firedog. 'Pierre, my friend,' said the King of Tunis, 'what the devil are you thinking about?'

Gringoire turned round with a melancholy smile. 'I like fire, my dear lord. Not for the banal reason that fire warms our feet or cooks our soup, but because it gives off sparks. I discover countless things in those stars sprinkled over the black fireback. Those stars are worlds too.'

'Blast it if I understand you!' said the truand. 'Do you know what time it is?'

'No, I don't,' Gringoire replied.

Clopin then went up to the Duke of Egypt. 'Comrade Mathias, we've chosen a bad time. They say King Louis XI is in Paris.'

'All the more reason for getting our sister out of his clutches,' the old gypsy answered.

'Spoken like a man, Mathias,' said the King of Tunis. 'Besides, we'll be quick about it. We've no resistance to fear in the church. The canons are as timid as hares, and we'll be there in force. The men from the Parliament will be properly caught tomorrow when they come to fetch her! By the Pope's bowels! I don't want them to hang that pretty girl!'

Clopin left the tavern.

During this time, Jehan was crying hoarsely: 'I'm drinking, I'm eating, I'm drunk, I'm Jupiter!—Hey! Pierre l'Assommeur, if you give me another look like that, I'll give your nose a dusting with a few flicks of my fingers.'

For his part Gringoire, torn from his meditations, had begun observing the scene of clamorous excitement around him, muttering between his teeth: '*Luxuriosa res vinum et tumultuosa ebrietas* [Wine is a mocker, strong drink is raging].* Alas! how right I am not to drink and how excellently Saint Benedict puts it: *Vinum apostatare facit enim sapientes* [Wine makes even wise men go astray].'* At that moment Clopin came back and cried in a thunderous voice: 'Midnight!'

At that word, which had the same effect as the order to mount on a halted regiment, all the truands, men, women, children, rushed in a body out of the tavern with a great clatter of arms and old iron.

The moon had gone in.

The Court of Miracles lay in total darkness. There was not a light to be seen. It was, however, far from being deserted. A crowd of men and women, talking together in low tones, could be made out. One could hear them murmuring and see the gleam of all kinds of arms in the darkness. Clopin climbed on to a big stone. 'Fall in, Argot!' he cried. 'Fall in, Egypt! Fall in, Galilee!' There was movement in the shadows. The immense multitude seemed to be forming itself into a column. After a few minutes, the King of Tunis spoke up again: 'Now, silence as we cross Paris! The password is: *Little blade on the prowl!* No torches to be lit until we reach Notre-Dame! Forward, march!'

Ten minutes later the horsemen of the watch were fleeing in terror before a long procession of dark, silent men going down towards the Pont-au-Change, through the winding streets which cut in every direction through the dense quarter of les Halles.

IV

AN AWKWARD FRIEND

THAT same night Quasimodo was not asleep. He had just done his last rounds in the church. He had not noticed, as he closed its doors, the archdeacon passing close by him and showing some annoyance when he saw him carefully bolt and padlock the enormous iron armature which made their broad panels as solid as a wall. Dom Claude looked even more preoccupied than usual. Besides, ever since the nocturnal incident in the cell, he had been continually harsh to Quasimodo; but no matter how he abused him, sometimes even striking him, nothing could shake the submissiveness, patience, devoted resignation of the faithful bell-ringer. From the archdeacon he would endure anything, insults, threats, blows, with no murmur of reproach, without complaint. At the very most he would watch anxiously when Dom Claude went up the tower staircase, but the archdeacon had of his own accord refrained from appearing again before the gypsy's eyes.

That night, then, Quasimodo, after glancing at his poor neglected bells, Jacqueline, Marie, Thibault, had gone right up to the top of the north tower, and there, putting down on the leads his firmly closed dark lantern, had begun looking out over Paris. The night, as already mentioned, was extremely dark. Paris which had, so to speak, no lighting at that period, offered to the eye a confused collection of dark masses, broken here and there by the whitish curve of the Seine. The only light that Quasimodo could see was at the window of a distant building, whose vague and sombre profile stood out well above the roof-tops, over towards the Porte Saint-Antoine. There too someone was awake.

While he let his solitary eye drift over this misty, dark horizon, the bell-ringer felt within himself an inexpressible disquiet. For several days now he had been on his guard. He kept seeing, prowling ceaselessly around the church, sinister-looking men who never took their eyes off the girl's place of refuge. He thought that some plot was being hatched against the unfortunate refugee. He imagined that there was a feeling of popular hatred against her as there was against himself, and that it might well be that something was soon about to happen. So he kept to his bell tower, on the alert, 'musing in his musery' as Rabelais has it, his eye alternately on the cell and on Paris, keeping careful watch, like a faithful dog, his mind filled with mistrust. Suddenly, as he swept the great city with that one eye which, by way of compensation, nature had made so piercing that it could almost make up for the other organs which Quasimodo lacked, it seemed to him that there was something odd about the outline of the Quai de la Vieille Pelleterie, that something was moving at that point, that the line of the parapet, standing out black against the whiteness of the water, was not straight and still like that of the other quays, but rippling as he watched like waves on a river or the heads of a marching crowd.

That seemed odd. He looked even more intently. The movement seemed to be coming towards the Cité. No lights though. It lasted for a while on the quay, then gradually disappeared, as if whatever it was was going into the interior of the island, then it ceased altogether, and the line of the quay became once more straight and motionless.

Just as Quasimodo was exhausting himself in conjectures, he seemed to see the movement reappear in the rue du Parvis, which runs into the Cité at right angles to the front of Notre-Dame. At length, dense though the darkness was, he saw the head of a column debouching from that street, and in an instant a crowd spreading out over the square, of which all that could be made out in the darkness was that it was a crowd.

This sight had its own terror. It is likely that this strange procession, which seemed so keen to conceal itself in profound darkness, was observing an equally profound silence. However, some sort of noise must have issued from it, even if it were no more than the tramp of feet. But not even that sound reached our deaf man, and that great multitude which he could barely see and could not hear at all, moving and marching none the less so close to him, gave him the impression of a concourse of the dead, mute, impalpable, lost in a vapour. He seemed to see advancing towards him a fog full of men, shades moving in the shadows.

Then his fears came back. The idea of some attempt against the gypsy girl returned to his mind. He vaguely felt that he was approaching a violent situation. At that critical moment, he took counsel within himself, with a better and speedier line of reasoning than might have been expected of so ill-organized a brain. Should he rouse the gypsy? Help her escape? Which way? The streets were invested, the church backed on to the river. No boat! No way out!— There was only one option, fight to the death at the entrance to Notre-Dame, at least resist until help came, if help was to come, and not disturb la Esmeralda's sleep. The unhappy girl would in any case be woken soon enough to die. Once he had taken that decision, he began to examine the *enemy* more calmly.

The crowd in the Parvis seemed to be growing thicker every moment. He assumed, however, that it must be making very little noise, since the windows in the streets and the square remained closed. Suddenly a light shone out, and in an instant seven or eight lighted torches cast their light over the heads, their tufts of flame flickering in the shadows. Then Quasimodo saw distinctly milling about in the Parvis a frightening flock of ragged men and women armed with scythes, pikes, billhooks, and partisans, their hundreds of points all sparkling. Here and there black pitchforks added horns to hideous faces. He vaguely remembered this popular mob, and thought he recognized all the heads which, a few months earlier, had hailed him Pope of Fools. A man with a torch in one hand and a cudgel in the other got up on to a marker-stone and seemed to be haranguing them. At the same time the strange army performed some manœuvres, as if taking up position round the church. Quasimodo picked up his lantern and went down on to the platform between the towers for a closer view and to work out some means of defence.

Clopin Trouillefou, having arrived before the lofty portal of Notre-Dame, had indeed formed his troops into battle order. Although he did not expect any resistance, as a prudent general, he wanted to maintain a formation which would allow him, if need arose, to stand up to any sudden attack by the watch or the men of the *onze-vingts*. Thus he had disposed his brigade in such a way that, seen from above and at a distance, it recalled the Roman triangle at the battle of Ecnoma,* Alexander's pig's head, or the famous wedge of Gustavus Adolphus. The base of the triangle rested on the far end of the square, so as to block the rue du Parvis; one side faced the Hôtel-Dieu, the other the rue Saint-Pierre-aux-Bœufs. Clopin Trouillefou had placed himself at the apex, with the Duke of Egypt, our friend Jehan, and the boldest of the *sabouleux*.

Such an enterprise as the truands were at that moment attempting against Notre-Dame was by no means rare in medieval towns. What we call 'police' today did not then exist. In populous, and especially capital, cities there was no one, central, regulating authority. Feudalism had constructed these great communes in the most peculiar way. A city was a collection of hundreds of lordships which divided it into compartments of every shape and size. Hence there were hundreds of contradictory forms of policing, that is to say none at all. In Paris, for example, independently of the hundred and forty-one lords claiming quit-rent, there were twenty-five claiming justice and quit-rent, from the Bishop of Paris, who had a hundred and five streets, to the prior of Notre-Dame-des-Champs, who had four. All these feudal justiciaries gave only nominal recognition to the paramount authority of the king. They all had rights over the public highway. They were all their own masters. Louis XI, that tireless workman who began the widespread demolition of the feudal edifice, continued by Richelieu and Louis XIV to the advantage of the monarchy, and completed by Mirabeau to the advantage of the people, Louis XI had indeed tried to break up this network of lordships which covered Paris, by forcibly imposing right across it two or three ordinances of general police. Thus, in 1465, the inhabitants were ordered at nightfall to light candles in their windows and keep their dogs shut in, under pain of the halter; the same year, came the order to close streets every evening with iron chains, and a prohibition on carrying daggers or offensive weapons at night in the streets. But in a short time all these attempts at communal legislation fell into disuse. The burghers let the wind blow out the candles in their windows, and let their dogs stray; the iron chains were only put up when the city was under siege; the prohibition on carrying daggers changed nothing but the name of the rue Coupe-Gueule which became the rue Coupe-Gorge,* an obvious sign of progress. The old framework of feudal jurisdictions remained standing; the huge accumulation of bailiwicks and lordships cutting across each other over the town, hindering, tangling, muddling each other, snarling up and encroaching on each other; a useless thicket of watches, under-watches, counter-watches, through which brigandry, rapine, and sedition passed by force of arms. In such a disorderly situation it was thus by no means unknown for part of the population to make such raids on a palace, a mansion, a house, in the most densely populated quarters. In most cases the neighbours became involved only if looting actually reached their doorstep. They blocked their ears to the shooting, closed their shutters, barricaded their doors, let the dispute be settled with or without the watch, and next day people in Paris would tell each other: 'Last night they broke into Étienne Barbette's house.'—'The maréchal de Clermont was hauled off bodily'—and so on. Thus not only royal residences, the Louvre, the Palais, the Bastille, the Tournelles, but houses belonging simply to lords, the Petit-Bourbon, the Hôtel de Sens, the Hôtel d'Angoulême, etc., etc., had battlemented walls and machicolations over the doors. The churches had their sanctity to protect them. A few, however, which did not include Notre-Dame, were fortified. The abbot of Saint-Germain-des-Prés had battlements like a baron, and spent more on bronze for bombards than for bells. His fortress was still to be seen in 1610. Today barely his church remains.

To return to Notre-Dame.

When the first preparations were complete, and it must be said to the honour of truand discipline that Clopin's orders were carried out in silence and with admirable precision, the worthy leader of the band climbed on to the parapet of the Parvis and raised his gruff, raucous voice, standing turned towards Notre-Dame and waving his torch, the light from which, blown about by the wind and continually obscured by its own smoke, made the reddish façade of the church alternately appear and disappear from sight.

'To you, Louis de Beaumont, Bishop of Paris, counsellor in the court of Parliament, I, Clopin Trouillefou, King of Tunis, Grand Coësre, Prince of Argot, Bishop of Fools, say: Our sister, wrongly convicted of magic, has taken refuge in your church; you owe her asylum and safekeeping; now the court of Parliament intends to take her thence, with your consent; with the result that she would be hanged tomorrow in the Grève were God and the truands not present. So we come to you, bishop. If your church is sacred, so is our sister; if our sister is not sacred, neither is your church. That is why we call on you to hand the girl over to us if you want to save your church, otherwise we shall take the girl and sack your church. Which will be quite right. In witness thereof I hereby set up my banner, and may God keep you, Bishop of Paris.'

Quasimodo was unfortunately not able to hear these words, pronounced with a kind of wild and sombre majesty. A truand presented the banner to Clopin, who solemnly set it up between two paving-stones. It was a pitchfork, with a quarter of bloody carrion hanging from its prongs.

That done, the King of Tunis turned round and ran his eyes over his army, a ferocious multitude whose eyes gleamed almost as brightly as their pikes. After a moment's pause: 'Forward, lads!' he cried. 'To work, bully boys!'

Thirty stalwart fellows, square-limbed, with the look of locksmiths, stepped out from the ranks with hammers, pincers, and iron bars on their shoulders. They made for the church's main door, went up the steps and could all soon be seen squatting under the arch, working at the door with pincers and levers. A crowd of truands followed to provide help or simply to watch. The eleven steps up to the portal were packed with them.

However, the door stood firm: 'Devil take it! It's tough and stubborn!' one man said. 'It's old, and its cartilages have hardened,' said another. 'Don't lose heart, comrades!' Clopin went on. 'I'll wager my head against a slipper that you will have opened that door, taken the girl and stripped the high altar before even one of the beadles has woken up! I think the lock's breaking.'

Clopin was interrupted by a fearful crash resounding at that moment behind him. He turned round. An enormous beam had just fallen from the skies, crushing a dozen truands on the steps up to the church, and rebounded on the pavement with the noise of a cannon going off, breaking another leg or two in the crowd of beggars, who were pulling back with cries of terror. In the twinkling of an eye the enclosed area of the Parvis was empty. The 'bully boys', though protected by the deeply recessed arches of the doorway, abandoned the door, and Clopin himself fell back to a respectful distance from the church.

'That was a near thing!' cried Jehan. 'I felt the draught from it, *tête-bœuf!* But Pierre l'Assommeur [the Slaughterman] has been slaughtered!'

No words can describe the amazement mixed with fright which fell with this beam upon the bandits. They stood for some moments gazing upward, thrown into more dismay by this piece of timber than by twenty thousand of the King's archers. 'Satan!' muttered the Duke of Egypt, 'that smacks of magic!'

'It was the moon that threw that log at us,' said Andry the Red.

'What's more,' went on François Chanteprune, 'they say the moon is the Virgin's friend!'

'A thousand popes!' exclaimed Clopin, 'you are all a lot of idiots!' But he could find no explanation for the timber falling.

Meanwhile there was nothing visible on the façade, the light from the torches not reaching as far as the top. The heavy baulk lay in the middle of the Parvis, and they could hear the groans of the wretches who had taken its first impact and had their bellies sliced in two against the sharp edges of the stone steps.

The King of Tunis, once his initial amazement was past, finally found an explanation which seemed plausible to his companions. 'God's teeth! are the canons defending themselves? Right then, sack the place! sack it!'

'Sack it!' the mob repeated with a frenzied cheer. And a salvo from crossbows and arquebuses was fired at the front of the church.

This detonation woke up the peaceful occupants of the houses round about, several windows could be seen opening, and nightcaps and hands holding candles appeared at the casements. 'Shoot at the windows,' cried Clopin. The windows closed again forthwith, and the poor burghers, who had scarcely had time to cast an appalled glance on this scene of flaring lights and uproar, went back to lie sweating with fear beside their wives, wondering if the witches' sabbath was being held now in the Parvis Notre-Dame, or if the Burgundians were attacking as in '64. The husbands thought of rapine, the wives of rape, and they all trembled.

'Sack it!' the Argoteers kept repeating. But they did not dare to come closer. They looked at the church, they looked at the beam. The beam did not stir. The building maintained its calm, deserted air, but something froze the truands' courage.

'To work then, bully boys!' cried Trouillefou. 'Go on, force the door.'

No one moved.

'Beard and belly!' said Clopin, 'here are men afraid of a joist.'

An old bully addressed him. 'Captain, it's not the joist that's bothering us, it's the door, laced all over with iron bars. The pincers don't work on it.'

'What do you need then to break it down?' asked Clopin.

'Oh! we'd need a battering ram.'

The King of Tunis ran boldly to the formidable beam and set his foot on it. 'Here's one,' he cried; 'sent to you

by the canons.' And making a derisive bow in the direction
of the church: 'Thank you, canons!'

This bravado had the right effect: the beam's spell was
broken. The truands took heart again; soon the heavy
beam, picked up like a feather by two hundred strong arms,
was hurled furiously against the great door which they had
already tried to shift. Seen thus, in the half-light cast over
the square by the truands' few torches, the long beam
carried by this mass of men running to hurl it against the
church made one think of some monstrous beast with hundreds of feet charging head down against the giant of stone.

At the impact of the beam the half-metal door resounded
like an enormous drum; it did not give way, but the entire
cathedral shuddered, and rumblings could be heard from
its hollow depths. At the same moment a shower of huge
stones began dropping from the top of the façade on to the
attackers. 'The devil!' cried Jehan, 'are the towers shaking
off their balustrades on to our heads?' But the impetus had
been provided, the King of Tunis setting an example—it
was surely the bishop defending himself, and that only
made them batter at the door the more furiously, despite
the stones which were shattering skulls to right and left.

Remarkably enough these stones were all falling one after
another; but they were falling in close succession. The
Argoteers always felt two coming at once, one at their legs,
the other on their heads. Few stones failed to strike a target,
and already the dead and wounded lay bleeding and twitch-
ing in a wide layer under the feet of the attackers, who,
now infuriated, constantly filled up their ranks afresh. The
long beam continued to batter the door at regular intervals
like the clapper of a bell, the stones to rain down, the
door to boom.

The reader has no doubt already guessed that this unexpected resistance which had exasperated the truands came
from Quasimodo.

Chance had unfortunately aided the deaf man.

When he came down on to the platform between the
towers, his ideas were all mixed up in his head. For a few
minutes he had run up and down along the gallery like a

madman, seeing from above the packed mass of truands ready to rush upon the church, asking the devil, or God, to save the gypsy girl. It had occurred to him to climb the south tower and sound the tocsin; but before he could have got the bell swinging, before Marie's voice could have rung out even once, would there not have been time for the door of the church to be broken down ten times over? This was at the precise moment when the 'bully boys' were advancing on it with their implements. What was he to do?

Suddenly he remembered that masons had been working all day to repair the wall, the timber framework and the roofing of the south tower. This was a ray of light. The wall was stone, the roofing lead, the framework timber—that prodigious framework, so dense and complex that it was called 'the forest'.

Quasimodo hurried to that tower. The lower rooms were indeed full of materials. There were piles of building stones, sheets of lead in rolls, stout joists already notched by the saw, heaps of rubble. A complete arsenal.

Time pressed. The crowbars and hammers were working away below. With a strength increased tenfold by the sense of danger he raised one of the beams, the heaviest and longest, pushed it out through a window slit, then grasping it again from the outside of the tower, slid it along the edge of the balustrade running round the platform, and dropped it into the void. The enormous piece of timber, as it fell 160 feet, scraping the wall, breaking the carvings, turned over several times like a windmill sail spinning all by itself through space. Finally it hit the ground, a terrible cry went up, and the black beam, rebounding from the pavement, looked like a snake springing.

Quasimodo saw the truands scatter as the beam fell like ash blown by a child. He took advantage of their terror, and while they gazed superstitiously at the club fallen from the sky, and shot out the eyes of the stone saints in the portal with a volley of arrows and buckshot, Quasimodo silently went about piling up rubble, stones, building stone, even the masons' tool bags, on the edge of the balustrade from which the beam had already been hurled.

So, as soon as they began battering the great door, the hail of stones began to fall, and it seemed to them as if the church was demolishing itself of its own accord upon their heads.

Anyone who could have seen Quasimodo at that moment would have been struck with terror. Independently of the missiles that he had piled up on the balustrade, he had built up a heap of stones on the platform itself. As soon as the lumps of stone amassed on the outer edge were exhausted, he took more from the heap. Then he bent down, stood up, bent down, stood up again in incredible activity. His huge gnome's head would lean out over the balustrade, then an enormous stone would fall, then another, then yet another. From time to time he would follow some fine big stone with his eye, and when it killed its man, would say: 'Ha!'

However, the beggars were not losing heart. More than a score of times already the massive door which they were assaulting so furiously had shaken beneath the weight of their oaken battering ram multiplied by the strength of a hundred men. The panels cracked, the carvings flew in splinters, at each shock the hinges jumped on their hooks, the planks were dislodged, the wood was falling, ground into sawdust, between the iron ribbing. Fortunately for Quasimodo there was more iron than wood.

He sensed, however, that the great door was becoming shaky. Although he could not hear, every blow from the battering ram was echoed both in the cavernous church and in his own inner depths. From above he could see the truands, triumphant and furious, shaking their fists at the shadowy façade, and he envied, for the gypsy and for himself, the wings of the owls who were flying away in flocks over his head.

His shower of stones was not enough to repel the attackers.

At that moment of anguish he noticed, a little lower than the balustrade from whence he had been crushing the Argoteers, two long stone rainspouts which discharged immediately above the main door. The internal opening of these spouts was in the floor of the platform. An idea occurred to him. He ran to fetch a faggot from his bell-ringer's cubby-hole, piled on to the faggot numerous bundles of lathes and rolls of lead, munitions which he had not yet employed, and having arranged this pyre right in front of the hole to the two spouts, set fire to it with his lantern.

During this time, since the stones had ceased to fall, the truands had stopped looking upwards. The bandits, panting like a pack of hounds hunting the boar down in his lair, were crowding tumultuously round the great door, battered out of shape by the ram, but still standing. They were waiting with a shudder of excitement for the ultimate blow, the one that would rip it open. Each of them was striving to be nearest so that they could be first to rush, once it was open, into this opulent cathedral, a vast repository in which the riches of three centuries had come to be accumulated. They reminded each other, with roars of greedy delight, of the fine silver crosses, the fine brocade copes, the fine silver-gilt tombs, the great splendours of the choir, the dazzling festivals, Christmas sparkling with torches, Easter brilliant with sunshine, all those spendid solemnities at which shrines, candlesticks, ciboria, tabernacles, reliquaries made the altars look as though embossed with a covering of gold and diamonds. At this fine hour, *cagoux* and malingerers, henchmen and *rifodés* were certainly thinking much less about freeing the gypsy than plundering Notre-Dame. We should even be willing to believe that for a good number of them la Esmeralda was merely a pretext, if robbers had any need of pretexts.

Suddenly, as they were all grouping together round the battering ram for a final effort, each man holding his breath and flexing his muscles so as to lend his whole strength to the decisive blow, a screaming even more awful than that which had broken out and then expired beneath the beam, went up from their midst. Those who were not crying out, those who were still alive, looked—two streams of molten lead were falling from the top of the building on to the densest part of the crowd. This sea of men had just collapsed beneath the boiling metal, which, at the two points where it fell, had made two black, steaming holes in the crowd, like hot water falling on snow. The dying could be seen writhing, half charred to ashes, roaring with pain. Round the two main streams drops of this terrible rain were being sprinkled over the attackers, penetrating their skulls like gimlets of flame. It was heavy fire which riddled these wretches with a hail of countless burning drops.

The clamour was heart-rending. They fled in disorder, throwing the beam on top of the corpses, the boldest and the most fearful alike, and the Parvis lay empty a second time.

All eyes were raised to the top of the tower. What they saw was extraordinary. On the top of the highest gallery, higher than the central rose-window, rose a great flame between the two bell towers with swirls of sparks, a great, ragged, furious flame, from which at times the wind would snatch a strip into the smoke. Beneath this flame, beneath the sombre balustrade with its cut-out trefoils glowing with fire, two spouts in the form of monstrous gargoyles unceasingly spewed out this burning rain, whose silvery trickle stood out against the darkness of the lower part of the façade. As they came nearer the ground, the two jets of liquid lead spread out into showers of spray, like water spurting from the countless holes of a watering can. Above the flame, the enormous towers, each showing two sharply distinct faces, one all black, the other all red, seemed bigger still with the immensity of the shadow they projected right up to the sky. Their innumerable carvings of devils and dragons took on a macabre appearance. The restless brightness of the flame made them move before one's eyes. There were wyverns which looked as though they were laughing, gargoyles which one seemed to hear yelping, salamanders blowing on to the fire, tarasques sneezing in the smoke. And among those monsters roused from their stone slumbers by the flame, by the noise, was one walking about, who could be seen from time to time passing across the blazing front of the pyre like a bat in front of a candle.

No doubt this strange beacon would awaken in the distance the woodman of the Bicêtre hills, terrified at seeing the gigantic shadow of the towers of Notre-Dame wavering over his heath.

A terrified silence fell upon the truands, during which all that could be heard were the cries of alarm from the canons shut up in their cloister, more scared than horses in a burning stable, the stealthy sound of windows opening quickly and closing more quickly still, the commotion inside the houses and the Hôtel-Dieu, the wind on the flame, the last gasps of the dying, and the continual crackling of the shower of lead on the pavement.

Meanwhile the chief truands had withdrawn beneath the porch of the Gondelaurier mansion and were holding a council of war. The Duke of Egypt, sitting on a marker-stone, was gazing with religious dread at the fantastic bonfire blazing two hundred feet up in the air. Clopin Trouillefou was chewing his huge fists with rage. 'No way to get in!' he muttered between his teeth.

'Old witch of a church!' growled the old Bohemian Mathias Hungadi Spicali.

'By the Pope's whiskers!' put in a grizzled old rogue who had served in the army, 'those church waterspouts spit out molten lead better than the machicolations of Lectoure!'*

'Do you see that demon going to and fro in front of the fire?' exclaimed the Duke of Egypt.

'By God,' said Clopin, 'it's that damned bell-ringer, it's Quasimodo.'

The Bohemian shook his head. 'I tell you, it's the spirit Sabnac,* the great marquis, the demon of fortifications. He has the form of an armed soldier, and a lion's head. Sometimes he rides a hideous horse. He turns men into stones and builds towers with them. He commands fifty legions. It's him all right. I recognize him. Sometimes he's dressed in a fine golden robe figured in the Turkish fashion.'

'Where's Bellevigne de l'Étoile?' asked Clopin.

'He's dead,' answered one of the truand women.

Andry the Red was laughing like an idiot: 'Notre-Dame is making work for the Hôtel-Dieu,' he said.

'So there's no way to force that door?' cried the King of Tunis, stamping his foot.

The Duke of Egypt sadly pointed out to him the two streams of boiling lead which continuously streaked down the black façade, like two long distaffs charged with phosphorus. 'It's been known for churches to defend themselves like that,' he observed with a sigh, 'Saint Sophia in Constantinople, forty years ago now,* threw Mahomet's crescent to the ground three times in succession by shaking its domes, which are like its heads. William of Paris, who built this one, was a magician.'

'Does that mean we've got to beat a shameful retreat, like footboys* on the highway,' said Clopin, 'and leave our sister here for those wolves in their hooded robes to hang tomorrow?'

'And the sacristy, where there is gold by the cartload,' added a truand, whose name we regrettably do not know.

'Mahomet's beard!' cried Trouillefou.

'Let's try once more,' went on the truand,

Mathias Hungadi shook his head. 'We'll never get in through the door. We must find some chink in the old witch's armour. A hole, a false postern, some joint or other.'

'Who's for it?' said Clopin. 'I'm going back there—by the way, where's that little student Jehan who had all that scrap-iron round him?'

'He's probably dead,' someone replied. 'We don't hear his laugh any more.'

The King of Tunis frowned. 'That's too bad. There was a stout heart under all that scrap-iron. And Maître Pierre Gringoire?'

'Captain Clopin,' said Andry the Red, 'he dodged off when we'd only got as far as the Pont-aux-Changeurs.'

Clopin stamped his foot. 'God's teeth! He's the one who pushed us into it, and now he just walks out on us in the middle of the job! Cowardly blabbermouth, with a slipper for a helmet!'

'Captain Clopin,' cried Andry the Red, who was looking along the rue du Parvis, 'here's the little student.'

'Pluto be praised!' said Clopin. 'But what the devil is he pulling behind him?'

It was indeed Jehan, running up as fast as his heavy paladin's costume and a long ladder, which he was valiantly dragging along the pavement, would allow, more out of breath than an ant harnessed to a blade of grass twenty times longer than itself.

'Victory! *Te Deum!*' cried the student. 'Here's the stevedores' ladder from the Port Saint-Landry.'

Clopin came up to him. 'Boy! what are you intending to do, by God's horn, with this ladder?'

'I've got it,' Jehan answered, panting. 'I knew where it was—under the shed of the lieutenant's house—I know a girl there who thinks I'm as handsome as Cupido—I used her to get the ladder, and now I've got the ladder, *Pasque-Mahom!*—The poor girl came to let me in just in her nightshirt.'

'Yes,' said Clopin, 'but what do you intend to do with this ladder?'

Jehan gave him a knowing, capable look, and clicked his fingers like castanets. He was sublime at that moment. On his head was one of those overloaded fifteenth-century helmets, which would scare the enemy with the monsters on their peak. His bristled with ten iron beaks, so that Jehan could have challenged Nestor's Homeric ship for the redoubtable epithet δεκέμβολος [ten-beaked].

'What do I intend to do with it, august King of Tunis? Do you see that row of idiotic-looking statues there above the three doorways?'

'Yes. Well?'

'That's the gallery of the kings of France.'

'What do I care?' said Clopin.

'Wait a moment. At the end of that gallery is a door, which is only ever closed on the latch; with this ladder I climb up there, and I'm inside the church.'

'Boy, let me be first to go up.'

'No, comrade, the ladder's mine. Come on, you'll be second up.'

'May Beelzebub strangle you!' said Clopin, gruffly displeased, 'I don't want to come after anyone.'

'All right, Clopin, go and find a ladder!'

Jehan began running across the square, pulling his ladder and crying: 'To me, lads!'

In a moment the ladder was set up, resting on the balustrade of the lower gallery, above one of the side doorways. The crowd of truands, cheering loudly, pressed around its foot to go up. But Jehan maintained his right and was first to put his foot on the rungs. It was a rather long climb. The gallery of the kings of France today stands about sixty feet above the pavement. The eleven steps leading up to the door made it still higher then. Jehan climbed slowly, somewhat impeded by his heavy armour, holding the rungs with one hand and his crossbow with the other. When he was half-way up the ladder he cast a melancholy glance down on the poor dead Argoteers strewn over the steps. 'Alas!' he said, 'there's a heap of corpses worthy of the fifth canto of the *Iliad*!' Then he went on up. The truands followed him. There was one on each rung. That line of armoured backs rippling upward in the dark looked like some steel-scaled serpent rising up against the church. Jehan whistling at its head completed the illusion.

The student finally reached the balcony of the gallery, and swung over very nimbly to the applause of all the truandery. Thus master of the citadel, he let out a yell of joy, and suddenly stopped, petrified. He had just noticed, behind one of the royal statues, Quasimodo hiding in the darkness, his eye glittering.

Before a second besieger could set foot on the gallery, the formidable hunchback sprang to the head of the ladder, without saying a word, grasped the end of the two uprights in his powerful hands, lifted them, pushed them away from the wall, for a moment, amid cries of anguish, balanced the long, flexible ladder, packed with truands from top to bottom, and suddenly, with superhuman strength, threw this cluster of men back down into the square. The ladder, hurled backwards, for an instant stayed straight and upright, seemed to waver, swayed, then suddenly, describing a terrifying arc 80 feet in radius, crashed down on the pavement with its load of bandits more swiftly than a drawbridge when its chains snap. There was an immense cry of imprecation, then everything went quiet, and a few unfortunate victims crawled mutilated from under the pile of dead.

A murmur of grief and anger succeeded the besiegers' earlier cries of triumph. Quasimodo looked on impassively, leaning with both elbows on the balustrade. He looked like a shaggy old king at his window.

As for Jehan Frollo, he was in a critical situation. He found himself in the gallery with the fearsome bell-ringer, alone, separated from his companions by a vertical wall 80 feet high. While Quasimodo had been making sport with the ladder, the student had run to the postern which he thought was open. It was not. As the deaf man came into the gallery, he had locked it behind him. Then Jehan had hidden himself behind one of the stone kings, not daring to breathe, staring at the monstrous hunchback with a look of terror, like the man who, paying court to the wife of a menagerie keeper, went one night to keep a tryst, climbed over the wrong wall and suddenly found himself confronting a polar bear.

To begin with, the deaf man paid no attention to him, but finally he turned his head and suddenly straightened up. He had just caught sight of the student.

Jehan prepared for a violent clash, but the deaf man stayed motionless; he had simply turned towards the student and was looking at him.

'Ho! ho!' said Jehan, 'why are you looking at me with your one eye so mournfully?'

And as he spoke the young rascal was stealthily getting his crossbow ready. 'Quasimodo!' he cried, 'I'm going to change your nickname. You'll be called the blind man.'

The shot went off. The feathered bolt whistled and stuck in the hunchback's left arm. Quasimodo was no more affected by it than if it had scratched King Pharamond.* He put a hand on the arrow, tore it from his arm, and calmly snapped it over his huge knee. Then he dropped, rather than threw down, the two bits. But Jehan had no time for a second shot. When he had broken the arrow, Quasimodo gave a noisy snort, sprang like a grasshopper, and fell upon

the student, whose armour was flattened against the wall
by the blow.

Then, in the half-light from the wavering torches something dreadful could be dimly seen.

Quasimodo had gripped both Jehan's arms in his left
hand; Jehan felt so utterly lost that he did not struggle. With
his right hand the deaf man removed, in silence and with
sinister deliberation, one by one, every piece of his armour—
sword, daggers, helmet, breastplate, brassards. He looked
like a monkey peeling a nut. Quasimodo threw down at his
feet, bit by bit, the student's iron shell.

When the student saw himself disarmed, stripped, weak,
and naked in those redoubtable hands, he did not try to
speak to the deaf man, but began laughing insolently in his
face and singing in the carefree, dauntless way of a lad of
16, the currently popular song:

> The town of Cambrai,
> Is all in fine array.
> Marafin sacked it . . .

He did not finish. They saw Quasimodo standing on the
parapet of the gallery, holding the student by the feet in
one hand and whirling him over the abyss like a sling. Then
they heard a noise like a bone box bursting against a wall,
and saw something fall, until it was caught a third of the
way down on a projection of the architecture. It was a dead
body which remained hanging there, bent in half, back
broken, skull empty.

A cry of horror went up from the truands. 'Vengeance!'
cried Clopin. 'Sack the church!' answered the multitude.
'Assault! assault!' Then came a prodigious yell, in which
every language, every dialect, every accent mingled. The
poor student's death filled the crowd with burning fury.
They felt seized with shame, and anger, at having been kept
in check for so long before the church by a hunchback.
Their rage found them ladders, increased the number of
torches, and after a few moments Quasimodo was distraught at the sight of this terrifying swarm of ants climbing
up on every side to assault Notre-Dame. Those who did

not have ladders had knotted ropes, those who did not have ropes used the reliefs of the sculptures to clamber up. They hung on to each other by their rags. There was no way to resist the rising tide of frightening faces. Fury made these savage faces gleam; their grubby foreheads streamed with sweat; their eyes flashed. Quasimodo was besieged by all these contorted faces, all this ugliness. It looked as if some other church had sent to the assault of Notre-Dame its gorgons, its mastiffs, its dragons, its demons, its most fantastic sculptures. It was like a layer of living monsters on top of the stone monsters of the façade.

Meanwhile the square sparkled with a thousand torches. This scene of disorder, buried up till then in darkness, had suddenly flared up with light. The Parvis was resplendent and projected its radiance into the sky. The pyre alight on the platform still blazed, and lit up the town in the distance. The enormous silhouette of the two towers, extending far over the rooftops of Paris, scooped out of all this brightness a broad patch of shadow. The town seemed to be roused. Distant tocsins sounded their plaints. The truands yelled, panted, cursed, climbed, and Quasimodo, helpless against so many enemies, trembling for the gypsy girl, seeing the furious faces come ever closer to his gallery, asked heaven for a miracle, wringing his arms in despair.

V

THE PRIVATE RETREAT WHERE MONSIEUR
LOUIS OF FRANCE SAYS HIS HOURS

THE reader may not have forgotten that a moment before catching sight of the truands' nocturnal band, Quasimodo, inspecting Paris from the top of his bell tower, had seen only one light still shining, twinkling like a star in a window of the top storey of a tall, gloomy building, near the Porte Saint-Antoine. That building was the Bastille. The star was Louis XI's candle.

King Louis XI had in fact been in Paris for two days. He was due to leave again in two days' time to go back to his citadel of Montilz-les-Tours. His appearances in his good town of Paris were only ever brief and rare, because he did not feel that there were enough trapdoors, gallows, and Scottish archers around him there.

He had come that day to spend the night at the Bastille. The great bedchamber of 5 square *toises** which he had in the Louvre, with its great chimney-piece, laden with twelve huge beasts and thirteen major prophets, and his great bed, measuring 11 by 12 feet, was not much to his liking. He felt lost amid all that grandeur. This good bourgeois king preferred the Bastille with a little bedroom and a little bed. Moreover, the Bastille was stronger than the Louvre.

This 'little bedroom' which the King had kept for himself in the famous State prison was still spacious enough, and occupied the top floor of a turret set into the keep. It was a redoubt, circular in shape, carpeted with mats of gleaming straw, the ceiling beams embellished with fleurs-de-lys of gilded tin and the space in between painted, panelled with ornate woodwork sprinkled with rosettes of white tin, and painted a beautiful bright green, made of orpiment and fine indigo.

There was only one window, a long lancet latticed with brass wire and iron bars, further obscured by fine glass

painted with the arms of the King and Queen, each pane
costing 22 *sols*.

There was only one entrance, a modern door, set in a
surbased arch, furnished on the inside with a tapestry, and
on the outside with one of those Irish wood porches, frail
structures of curiously worked joinery, which one could still
see a hundred and fifty years ago in many old houses.
'Although they disfigure and clutter up the place,' says
Sauval in despair, 'our old men will not get rid of them and
keep them in spite of everyone.'

None of the furniture of an ordinary apartment was to be
found in this room, no benches, no trestles, no forms, no
common box stools, no fine stools supported on pillars and
counter-pillars at 4 *sols* each. All that was to be seen was a
very splendid folding armchair: the wood was painted with
roses on a red background, the seat was of scarlet Cordovan
leather, decorated with long silver fringes and studded with
countless gold nails. The isolation of this chair showed that
one person only had the right to be seated in the room.
Next to the chair, right by the window, stood a table
covered by a cloth with a pattern of birds; on the table an
inkhorn stained with ink, a few parchments, a few quills,
and a goblet of chased silver. A little further away there was
a food-warmer, and a prie-dieu in crimson velvet, set
off with small gold studs; finally, at the far end, a simple
bed of pink and yellow damask, with no tinsel or braid;
the fringes quite plain. This was the bed, famous for having borne Louis XI sleeping or sleepless, on which one
could still gaze two hundred years ago in the home of
a State counsellor, where it was seen by Madame Pilou,
celebrated in *Cyrus** under the name of 'Arricidie' and
'Living morality.'

Such was the room known as: 'the private retreat where
Monsieur Louis of France says his hours'.

At the moment when we introduced the reader to it, this
little room was very dark. Curfew had sounded an hour
before, night had fallen, and there was only a flickering wax
candle on the table to provide light for five individuals
variously grouped around the room.

The first on whom the light fell was a nobleman superbly dressed in doublet and hose of scarlet striped with silver, and a cloak with padded shoulders in cloth of gold with patterns in black. This spendid costume, where the light played on it, seemed glazed with flame in every fold. The man wearing it bore his coat of arms embroidered on his chest in bright colours: a chevron accompanied in point by a deer passant. The escutcheon was supported on the right by an olive branch, on the left by a deer's horn. On his belt this man wore a costly dagger, with a silver-gilt handle chased in the shape of a helmet crest, surmounted by a count's coronet. He looked evil, haughty, and stiff-necked. At first glance one saw arrogance in his face, at the second, cunning.

He stood bare-headed, holding a long scroll, behind the armchair on which sat, inelegantly doubled up, knees crossed, elbow on the table, a very meanly turned-out individual. Picture to yourself in fact, on this seat of rich Cordovan leather, two knock-knees, two skinny thighs shabbily dressed in black woollen knitted hose, a torso wrapped in a fustian cloak with a fur trimming showing more hide than hair; finally, to crown it all, a greasy old hat of the meanest black cloth with a circular band of lead figurines running round it. That, with a grimy skullcap which barely let a single hair show, was all that could be made out of the person seated. He kept his head bent so low on his chest that there was nothing to be seen of his face, covered in shadow, but for the tip of his nose, on which a ray of light fell and which must have been a long one. From his skinny, wrinkled hand one could guess that he was an old man. It was Louis XI.

Some distance behind them two men dressed in the Flemish cut conversed in low tones, and they were not so hidden in the shadows that anyone who had been present at the performance of Gringoire's mystery play could have failed to recognize in them two of the principal Flemish envoys, Guillaume Rym, the shrewd pensionary from Ghent, and Jacques Coppenole, the popular hosier. It will be remembered that these two men were involved in Louis XI's secret policies.

Finally, right at the back, near the door, there stood in the dark, still as a statue, a sturdy, thick-set man, in military equipment, and an emblazoned tunic, whose square face, with eyes sticking out from his head, split by a huge mouth, ears concealed beneath two wide screens of flattened hair, with no forehead, took after both dog and tiger.

All, except the King, had their heads uncovered.

The nobleman standing by the King was reading out to him some kind of lengthy memorandum to which His Majesty seemed to be listening attentively. The two Flemings were whispering.

'By the Rood!' Coppenole grumbled, 'I am tired of standing. Isn't there a chair here?'

Rym answered with a negative gesture, accompanied by an anxious smile.

'By the Rood!' Coppenole went on, most unhappy at being thus obliged to lower his voice, 'I feel a great itch to sit on the floor, legs crossed like a hosier, as I do in my own shop.'

'Mind you don't, Maître Jacques!'

'Huh! Maître Guillaume! So you can only stay on your feet here?'

'Or on your knees,' said Rym.

At that moment the King raised his voice. They fell silent.

'Fifty *sols* for our servants' robes, and 12 *livres* for the clerks of our crown for their cloaks!* That's right! Pour out gold by the ton! Are you crazy, Olivier?'

As he spoke, the old man had raised his head. Round his neck could be seen gleaming the golden cockleshells of the collar of Saint-Michel. The candle lit up fully his morose and emaciated profile. He snatched the papers from the other man's hands.

'You are ruining us!' he cried, running his sunken eyes over the register. 'What's all this? Why do we need such a prodigious household? Two chaplains at 10 *livres* each a month, and a chapel clerk at 100 *sols*! A groom of the bedchamber at 90 *livres* a year! Four kitchen clerks at 120 *livres* a year each! A roaster, a pottinger, a sauce-maker, a chief cook, an armoury-keeper, two sumptermen at 10 *livres* a month each! Two scullions at 8 *livres*! A groom and two assistants at 80 *livres* a month! A porter, a pastrycook, a baker, two carters, each at 60 *livres* a year! And the head farrier 120 *livres*! And the master of our exchequer, 1200 *livres*, and the comptroller 500! And what more, I ask you!—it's madness! The wages of our servants are plundering France! All the hidden treasures in the Louvre will melt away in such a blaze of expense! We'll be selling off our plate! And next year, if God and Our Lady (here he raised his hat) grant us life, we'll be drinking our tisane out of a pewter mug!'

As he said that he glanced at the silver goblet sparkling on the table. He coughed and continued:

'Maître Olivier, princes who rule over great lordships, like kings and emperors, must not allow extravagance to breed in their households, because from there the fire spreads through their provinces. So, Maître Olivier, take this as said. Our expenses increase every year. This displeases us. Why, *Pasque-Dieu!* until '79 the sum did not exceed 36,000 *livres*. In '80 it reached 43,619 *livres*—I have the figures in my head—in '81 66,680 *livres*; and this year, by the faith of my body! it will reach 80,000 *livres*! Doubled in four years! Monstrous!'

He stopped, out of breath, then went on, beside himself: 'All I see around me are people getting fat from my leanness! You suck gold pieces out of me from every pore!'

They all stayed silent. It was one of those tempers that are best left alone. He continued:

'It is like this Latin petition from the nobility of France, asking us to restore what they call the great offices or charges of the Crown. Charges indeed! Crushing charges! Ah! gentlemen! you say that we are not a king for reigning *dapifero nullo, buticulario nullo* [without carver or butler]. We'll show you, *Pasque-Dieu*, whether we are a king or not!'

At this he smiled with the sense of his power, his ill-humour abated, and he turned to the Flemings:

'Do you see, Compère Guillaume? The great pantler, the great butler, the great chamberlain, the great seneschal are not worth the lowliest servant,—remember this, Compère

Coppenole—they serve no purpose. Standing around the King uselessly like that they put me in mind of the four evangelists round the dial of the great clock in the Palais, which Philippe Brille has just renovated. They are gilded and they don't show the time; and the hands can do without them.'

He remained pensive for as moment, and added, nodding his old head: 'Ho! ho! ho! by Our Lady, I'm not Philippe Brille, and I'm not going to regild the great vassals. I agree with King Edward:* save the people and kill the lords—go on, Olivier.'

The person whom he designated by that name took back the register from his hands and began again reading aloud:

'To Adam Tenon, clerk to the keeper of the seals of the Provostry of Paris, for the silver, working, and engraving of the said seals, because the previous ones, on account of being so old and worn, could no longer properly be used— 12 *livres parisis*.

'To Guillaume Frère, the sum of 4 *livres* 4 *sols parisis* for his pains and wages in looking after and feeding the doves in the two dovecotes of the Hôtel des Tournelles, during the months of January, February, and March of this year; and for this provided 7 *setiers* of barley.

'To a Cordelier friar for hearing a criminal's confession, 4 *sols parisis*.'

The King listened in silence. From time to time he would cough. Then he would bring the goblet to his lips, and pull a face as he swallowed from it.

'In this year fifty-six cries to the sound of a trumpet have been made by judicial order at the crossroads in Paris— account to be settled.

'For digging and searching in certain places, both in Paris and elsewhere, for treasure said to be hidden, but without finding anything—45 *livres parisis*.'

'Burying a gold piece to unearth a *sol*!' said the King.

'For fitting six panes of white glass at the Hôtel des Tournelles in the place where the iron cage is—13 *sols*. For making and delivering, by the King's command, on the day of the musters four escutcheons with the arms of the said lord, enchased with garlands of roses all the way round—6 *livres*. For two new sleeves on the King's old doublet—20 *sols*. For a box of grease for greasing the King's boots—15 *deniers*. A new sty for keeping the King's black swine—30 *livres parisis*. Several partitions, planks, and trapdoors made for the lions' enclosure near Saint-Paul—22 *livres*.'

'They are expensive animals,' said Louis XI. 'No matter! It's a fine way for a king to be lavish. There is one big tawny lion I really like for his tricks—have you seen him, Maître Guillaume?—princes need to have some of these wonderful animals. For us kings, our dogs must be lions and our cats tigers. Greatness goes with the crown. In the days of Jupiter's pagans, when the people offered up in the churches a hundred oxen and a hundred ewes, the emperors would give a hundred lions and a hundred eagles. That was something very fine and savage. The kings of France have always had wild beasts roaring round their thrones. All the same it must be admitted, to do me justice, that I spend even less money on that than they did, and have a more modest collection of lions, bears, elephants, and leopards—go on now, Maître Olivier. We wanted to tell our friends the Flemings about it.'

Guillaume Rym made a deep bow, while Coppenole, with his surly expression, looked like one of those bears His Majesty had been speaking about. The King did not notice. He had just wet his lips at the goblet, and spat the liquid out again, saying: 'Ugh! horrible tisane!' The man reading continued:

'For feeding a rogue and vagabond shut up for the past six months in the cell at the flayers' yard, while waiting to learn what to do with him—6 *livres* 4 *sols*.'

'What's that?' the King interrupted. 'Feed what should be hanged! *Pasque-Dieu!* I won't give another *sol* for his food. Olivier, settle the matter with Monsieur d'Estouteville, and this very evening make the preparations for marrying this rascal to a gallows. Go on.'

Olivier made a thumbmark at the article on 'the rogue and vagabond' and proceeded.

'To Henriet Cousin, master executioner of the justice of Paris, the sum of 60 *sols parisis*, taxed and ordered to him by my lord the Provost of Paris, for purchasing, on the orders of the said Monsieur the Provost, one large broadsword to be used for executing and beheading those persons condemned by justice for their misdeeds, and providing it with a scabbard and all appurtenances; and likewise refurbishing and renovating the old sword, which had been splintered and chipped in carrying out sentence on Messire Louis de Luxembourg,* as may appear more fully . . .'

The King interrupted: 'That's enough. I gladly authorize the sum. Those are expenses I don't examine. I have never regretted the money. Next.'

'For making a great new cage . . .'

'Ah!' said the King, gripping the arms of his chair with both hands, 'I knew I had come here to the Bastille for something. Wait, Maître Olivier. I want to see the cage for myself. You can read out to me what it cost while I examine it. Messieurs the Flemings, come and see this. It's quite curious.'

Then he rose, leaned on his interlocutor's arm, signed to the sort of mute standing in front of the door to precede him, to the two Flemings to follow, and left the room.

At the door of the room the royal party recruited men-at-arms weighed down with iron, and slim pages carrying torches. It wended its way for some while through the inside of the sombre keep, riddled with stairways and corridors running even in the thickness of the walls. The captain of the Bastille walked at their head and had the wickets opened to the sickly, stooping old King, who coughed as he walked.

At each wicket, they all had to bow their heads, except the old man, bent with age. 'Hm!' he said between his gums, for he had no teeth left, 'we are quite prepared now for the door of the sepulchre. To pass through a low door you must needs stoop.'

Finally, having passed through a last wicket with such a complexity of locks that it took quarter of an hour to open it, they came into a high, spacious, vaulted room, in the centre of which could be made out by the glow of the torches a huge, massive cube of masonry, iron, and timber.

It was one of those famous cages for prisoners of State known as 'the King's little girls'. There were two or three little windows in its walls, so densely latticed with thick iron bars that the glass could not be seen. The door was a great flat slab of stone, as in a tomb. Such doors are only ever used for entrance. Only, here, the corpse was alive.

The King began walking slowly round the little structure, carefully examining it, while Maître Olivier, who was following him, read out the memorandum aloud:

'For making a great new wooden cage with big joists, ribs and string-pieces, 9 feet long by 8 feet broad, 7 feet high between the boards, smoothed and bolted with large iron bolts, which has been installed in a room, belonging to one of the towers of the fortress of Saint-Antoine, in the which cage is kept and detained, by command of our lord the King, a prisoner who lived previously in an old, worn-out and decrepit cage—in the making of the said new cage there have been used 96 horizontal joists and 52 upright ones, 10 string pieces 3 *toises* long; and 19 carpenters have been employed in squaring, working, and shaping all the aforesaid wood in the yard of the Bastille for twenty days . . .'

'Pretty fine heart of oak,' said the King, thumping the frame work with his fist.

'. . . into this cage,' went on the other, 'have gone 220 large iron bolts, of 9 feet and 8 feet, the rest of medium length, with the rowels, pommels, and counterbands serving the said bolts. The said iron weighing in all 3,735 *livres*; besides 8 large iron braces serving to fasten the said cage, with clamps and nails weighing together 218 *livres* of iron, not counting the iron lattice over the window of the room where the cage has been placed, the iron bolts of the door to the room, and various other items . . .'

'That's a lot of iron,' said the King, 'to contain the lightness of a spirit!'

'The total comes to 317 *livres* 5 *sols* 7 *deniers*.'

'*Pasque-Dieu!*' exclaimed the King.

At this oath, Louis XI's favourite one, someone seemed to be waking up inside the cage, chains scraped noisily across the floor, and a feeble voice was raised, which seemed to come from the grave: 'Sire! sire! mercy!' The speaker could not be seen.

'317 *livres* 5 *sols* 7 *deniers*!' Louis XI went on.

The lamentable voice issuing from the cage had chilled all those present, even Maître Olivier himself. Only the King appeared not to have heard it. At his order Olivier resumed his reading, and His Majesty coldly continued his inspection of the cage.

'. . . beside which, to a mason who made the holes for setting in the grills over the windows, and the floor of the room where the cage is, because the floor would not have been strong enough to bear the cage because of its weight, 27 *livres* 14 *sols parisis* . . .'

The voice began groaning again:

'Mercy! Sire! I swear it was the Cardinal of Angers who committed the treason, not I.'

'The mason's a rough one!' went on the King. 'Go on, Olivier.'

Olivier went on: 'To a joiner, for windows, bed, close-stool, and other items, 20 *livres* 2 *sols parisis*.'

The voice went on too: 'Alas! Sire! will you not hear me? I protest that it was not I who wrote that to my lord of Guyenne, but Monsieur the Cardinal Balue!'*

'The joiner is expensive,' observed the King. 'Is that all?'

'No, sire—to a glazier, for the windows of the said room, 46 *sols* 8 *deniers parisis*.'

'Have mercy, sire! Is it not enough that all my property has been given to my judges, my plate to Monsieur de Torcy, my library to Maître Pierre Doriolle, my tapestry to the governor of Roussillon? I am innocent. I have been shivering now for fourteen years in an iron cage. Have mercy, sire! You will be repaid in heaven.'

'Maître Olivier,' said the King, 'the total?'

'367 *livres* 8 *sols* 3 *deniers parisis*.'

'By Our Lady!' cried the King, 'that's an outrageous cage!'

He snatched the register from Maître Olivier's hands, and began counting up for himself on his fingers, studying in turn the paper and the cage. Meanwhile they could hear the prisoner sobbing. This sounded most doleful in the dark, and their faces paled as they looked at one another.

'Fourteen years, sire! It's fourteen years now! Since April 1469. In the name of the Holy Mother of God, sire, listen to me! All that time you have enjoyed the warmth of the sun. Shall I, wretch that I am, never see daylight again? Mercy, sire! be merciful. Clemency is a fine royal virtue and stems the flow of anger. Does Your Majesty believe that at the hour of death it is a great satisfaction for a king to have let no offence go unpunished? Besides, sire, I did not betray Your Majesty, it was my lord of Angers. And on my foot is a very heavy chain, with a great iron ball at the end of it, much heavier than it need be. Ah! sire! Have pity on me!'

'Olivier,' said the King, shaking his head, 'I notice that I've been charged 20 *sols* a barrel for plaster that is only worth 12. Do this memorandum over again.'

He turned his back on the cage and prepared to leave the room. The wretched prisoner judged that the King was going from the fact that the torches and noise were growing more distant. 'Sire! sire!' he cried in despair. The door closed. He saw nothing more, and all he heard was the gaoler's raucous voice singing in his ear the song:

> Maître Jean Balue
> Has lost from sight all his sees;
> Monsieur of Verdun
> Has been left without one;
> They've all been despatched.

The King went back up to his retreat in silence, and his train followed him, terror-struck at the condemned man's final groans. Suddenly His Majesty turned to the governor of the Bastille. 'By the way,' he said, 'was there not someone in that cage?'

'By God, sire!' answered the governor, staggered at the question.

'Who was it then?'

'Monsieur the Bishop of Verdun.'

The King knew that better than anyone. But it was an obsession.

'Ah!' he said with an innocent look, as if it was the first time he had thought of it, 'Guillaume de Harancourt,* the friend of Monsieur the Cardinal Balue. A good fellow for a bishop!'

A few moments later the door of the retreat opened and then closed again on the five individuals whom the reader saw there at the beginning of this chapter, and who had now gone back to their places, their subdued conversations, and their attitudes.

During the King's absence some dispatches had been laid on the table, and he himself broke their seals. Then he began promptly to read them, one after the other, made a sign to 'Maître Olivier', who appeared to be acting as his minister, to take up a pen, and without informing him of the contents of the dispatches, began in a low voice to dictate answers to them, which Olivier wrote down, kneeling somewhat uncomfortably in front of the table.

Guillaume Rym watched.

The King spoke so quietly that the Flemings could not hear anything of his dictation except occasional isolated scraps like: '. . . Maintain fertile areas by trade, and infertile ones by manufacture . . . Show the English lords our four bombards, the London, the Brabant, the Bourg-en-Bresse, the Saint-Omer . . . Artillery is the reason why war is waged now more judiciously . . . To Monsieur de Bressuire, our friend . . . Armies cannot be maintained without tribute . . . etc.'

Once he raised his voice: '*Pasque-Dieu!* Monsieur the King of Sicily seals his letters with yellow wax, like a king of France. Perhaps we are wrong to permit him to do so. My fair cousin of Burgundy did not grant arms on a field of gules. The greatness of a house is assured by keeping the integrity of its prerogatives. Note that, Compère Olivier.'

Another time: 'Oh! oh!' he said, 'what a big letter! What is our brother the Emperor asking for?' And running his eyes over the missive, punctuating his reading with interjections: 'To be sure! The Germanies are so great and powerful that it is scarcely credible! But we haven't forgotten the old proverb: the fairest county is Flanders; the fairest duchy, Milan; the fairest kingdom, France—is that not so, Messieurs the Flemings?'

This time Coppenole bowed with Guillaume Rym. The hosier's patriotism was flattered.

One last despatch made Louis XI frown: 'What's this?' he exclaimed. 'Complaints and grievances against our garrisons in Picardy! Olivier, write without delay to Monsieur the maréchal de Rouault.—That discipline is growing slack.—That the men-at-arms of the ordinances, the nobles of the ban, the free archers, the Swiss are causing endless trouble to the inhabitants.—That the soldiers, not satisfied with the property they find in the farmworkers' houses, force them, by beating them with staves and spears, to go into town and look for wine, fish, spices and other extravagances.—That Monsieur the King knows this.—That we intend to keep our people from harassment, theft, and pillage.—That such is our will, by Our Lady!—That furthermore it is not our pleasure that any minstrel, barber, or servant-at-arms should dress like a prince in velvet, silk and gold rings.—That such vanities are hateful to God.—That we content ourselves, we who are gentlemen, with a doublet of cloth at 16 *sols* the Paris ell.—That messieurs the camp-followers can very well come down to that too.—Order and command.—To Monsieur de Rouault, our friend.—Right.' He dictated this letter aloud, in firm tones and in bursts. Just as he was finishing, the door opened and admitted a new personage, who rushed into the room in great alarm, crying: 'Sire! sire! There is an an uprising of the people in Paris!'

Louis XI's grave features contracted, but what could be seen of his emotion passed in a flash. He contained himself, and said with calm severity: 'Compère Jacques, you come in very abruptly!'

'Sire! sire! There's a revolt!' Compère Jacques went on, breathlessly.

The King, who had risen, took him roughly by the arm and said in his ear, so that no one else could hear, with concentrated anger and a sidelong glance at the Flemings: 'Hold your tongue or keep your voice down!'

The newcomer understood, and began in a low voice to give a most terrified account, to which the King listened quite calmly, while Guillaume Rym pointed out to Coppenole the face and dress of the newcomer, his fur-trimmed hood, *caputia fourrata*, his short cloak, *epitogia curta*, his black velvet robe, which indicated a president of the court of accounts.

This personage had scarcely given the King some explanation when Louis XI burst out laughing and exclaimed:

'Really! Speak more loudly, Compère Coictier! What's the matter with you that you're whispering like that? Our Lady knows we have nothing to hide from our good Flemish friends.'

'But, sire . . .'

'Speak up!'

Compère Coictier stayed dumb with surprise.

'So,' the King went on, 'speak, sir. There is a disturbance of the people in our good town of Paris?'

'Yes, sire.'

'And you say it is directed against the bailiff of the Palais de Justice?'*

'Apparently so,' the compère answered, stammering, still quite dazed at the abrupt and inexplicable change which had just taken place in the mind of the King.

'Where did the watch encounter the mob?'

'On the way from the Grande-Truanderie to the Pont-aux-Changeurs. I ran into them myself as I was coming here on Your Majesty's orders. I heard some of them shouting: "Down with the bailiff of the Palais!" '

'And what grievance do they have against the bailiff?'

'Ah!' said Compère Jacques, 'that he is their lord.'

'Really!'

'Yes, sire. They are rogues from the Court of Miracles. They have been complaining for a long time now about the bailiff, whose vassals they are. They won't recognize his rights either as justiciary or over the highways.'

'Well, well!' the King replied with a smile of satisfaction that he tried in vain to disguise.

'In all their petitions to Parliament,' Compère Jacques went on, 'they claim that they have but two masters, Your Majesty and their God, who is, I believe, the devil.'

'Ha! ha!' said the King.

He was rubbing his hands together and laughing with that inward laughter which makes the face beam. He was unable to conceal his delight, though he tried from time to time to compose himself. No one understood it at all, not even 'Maître Olivier'. The King remained silent for a moment, looking thoughtful, but pleased.

'Are they in force?' he asked suddenly.

'Yes, indeed, sire,' Compère Jacques answered.

'How many?'

'At least six thousand.'

The King could not stop himself saying: 'Good!' He went on: 'Are they armed?'

'With scythes, pikes, hackbuts, picks. All sorts of most violent weapons.'

The King appeared quite unperturbed by such a display. Compère Jacques thought he should add: 'If Your Majesty does not send help to the bailiff quickly, he is a lost man.'

'We shall send it,' said the King with a false appearance of seriousness. 'Right. Certainly we shall send help. Monsieur the Bailiff is our friend. Six thousand! They are determined rascals. Their boldness is quite amazing, and angers us greatly. But we have few people around us tonight—it will be time enough tomorrow morning.'

Compère Jacques protested: 'Straight away, sire! There'll be time for them to sack the bailiff's residence twenty times over, violate his authority, and hang the bailiff. For God's sake, sire! send help before morning!'

The King looked straight at him: 'I said tomorrow morning.'

It was one of those looks which brook no reply.

After a silence, Louis XI again spoke up. 'Compère Jacques, you should know. What was . . .'; he corrected himself: 'What is the bailiff's feudal jurisdiction?'

'Sire, the bailiff of the Palais has the rue de la Calandre up to the rue de l'Herberie, the Place Saint-Michel and the places commonly called les Mureaux, situated near the church of Notre-Dame-des-Champs' (here Louis XI raised the brim of his hat), 'which mansions are thirteen in number, plus the Court of Miracles, plus the leper-house called the Banlieue, plus the whole of the highway beginning at the leper-house and ending at the Porte Saint-Jacques. In all these different places he enjoys rights over thoroughfares, high, middle, and low justice, and is fully lord.'

'Is he indeed?' said the King, scratching his left ear with his right hand. 'That makes quite a fair portion of my town! Ah! Monsieur the Bailiff *was* king of all that!'

This time he did not correct himself. He continued, musing and as though talking to himself: 'Very nice, Monsieur the Bailiff! You had your teeth into a very decent bit of our Paris!'

Suddenly he exploded: '*Pasque-Dieu!* Who are all these people who claim to have rights over highways, to be justiciaries, lords and masters in our domain? Who set up their tolls all over the countryside, their justice and their executioner at every crossroads among our people? So that as the Greek believed he had as many gods as he had fountains, and the Persian as many as he could see stars, the Frenchman reckons he has as many kings as he can see gibbets! By God! That's all wrong, and such confusion displeases me. I'd very much like to know if it is God's grace that there should be in Paris anyone else with highway rights but the King, any other justice than our Parliament, any other emperor than us in this empire! By the faith of my soul! The day must surely come when in France there will be only one king, one lord, one judge, one headsman, just as in paradise there is only one God!'

He raised his cap again, and went on still musing, with the look and tone of a huntsman urging on and launching his pack: 'Good! my people! Boldly done! Smash these false lords! Do your job! Go on! go on! Plunder them, hang them, sack them! Ha! You want to be kings, my lords? Go to it! My people! Go!'

Here he abruptly broke off, bit his lip, as if to retrieve an idea that had escaped him, fixed his piercing gaze in turn on each of the five persons around him, and suddenly grasping his hat in both hands and looking directly at it, he said: 'Oh! I'd burn you if you knew what I have in my head!'

Then, looking around him again as intently and anxiously as a fox returning stealthily to its earth: 'No matter! We'll help Monsieur the Bailiff. Unfortunately we have only a small force here at the moment against such numbers of the people. We'll have to wait until tomorrow. Order will be restored in the Cité and anyone caught will be hanged without more ado.'

'That reminds me, sire!' said Compère Coictier, 'I forgot to say in my initial confusion that the watch picked up two stragglers from the band. If Your Majesty wishes to see these men, they are here.'

'If I wish to see them!' cried the King. 'What! *Pasque-Dieu!* you forgot something like that! Hurry, quick, you, Olivier! go and fetch them.'

Maître Olivier went out and came back a moment later with the two prisoners, surrounded by archers of the ordinance. The first had a big, stupid face, drunk and dumbfounded. He was dressed in rags, and was walking with one knee bent and the foot dragging. The second was a pale, smiling figure already known to the reader.

The King studied them for a moment without saying a word, then, abruptly addressing the first one:

'What's your name?'

'Gieffroy Pincebourde.'

'Your trade?'

'Truand.'

'What were you going to do in this damnable sedition?'

The truand looked at the King, swinging his arms with a dazed expression. He had one of those ill-adapted heads in which intelligence is about as comfortable as light under a snuffer.

'I don't know,' he said. 'People were going, I went.'

'Were you not going to assault and pillage quite outrageously your lord the bailiff of the Palais?'

'I know they were going to take something from somebody's house. That's all.'

A soldier showed the King a pruning hook which had been found on the truand.

'Do you recognize this weapon?' the King asked.

'Yes, it's my pruning hook. I'm a vine-dresser.'

'And do you recognize this man as your companion?' Louis XI added, pointing to the other prisoner.

'No, I don't know him.'

'That's enough,' said the King, beckoning to the silent individual standing motionless by the door, to whom we have already drawn the reader's attention.

'Compère Tristan, here's a man for you.'

Tristan l'Hermite bowed. He gave an order in an undertone to two archers who took the truand away.

Meanwhile the King had come up to the second prisoner, who was sweating heavily: 'Your name?'

'Sire, Pierre Gringoire.'

'Your trade?'

'Philosopher, sire.'

'How can you take the liberty, you rascal, of going to besiege our friend Monsieur the Bailiff of the Palais, and what have you to say about this popular disturbance?'

'Sire, I was not part of it.'

'How now! Scoundrel, were you not apprehended by the watch in that bad company?'

'No, sire, there's a mistake. It is fatality. I compose tragedies. Sire, I beseech Your Majesty to hear me. I am a poet. It's the melancholy lot of men of my profession to walk the streets at night. I was passing by there this evening. It was pure chance. I was arrested in error. I am innocent of this civil tempest. Your Majesty has seen that the truand did not recognize me. I beg Your Majesty . . .'

'Hold your tongue!' said the King between two sips of tisane. 'Your babbling makes us tired.'

Tristan l'Hermite came forward, and pointing to Gringoire: 'Sire, may this one be hanged too?'

'Hm!' the King answered casually. 'I don't see any objection.'

'But I do, I see a lot of objections!' said Gringoire.

Our philosopher at that moment had turned as green as an olive. He saw from the King's cold and indifferent expression that the only course left to him was something most pathetic, and flung himself at Louis XI's feet, crying out with a gesture of despair:

'Sire! Your Majesty will deign to hear me. Sire! do not break out into thunder over such a nonentity as myself. God's great thunderbolts are not for bombarding lettuces. Sire, you are a most mighty, august monarch, have pity on a poor, honest man, as incapable of stirring up a revolt as an icicle is of striking a spark! Most gracious sire, mildness is a virtue in lions and kings. Alas! severity only strikes terror into people's minds, the violent gusts of the north wind would never make the traveller lay aside his cloak, the sun's rays gradually warm him so that he will go about in shirt-sleeves. Sire, you are the sun. I protest to you, my sovereign lord and master, I am not a companion of truands, thieving and disorderly. Revolt and brigandage have no part in Apollo's company. I am not one for rushing headlong into those clouds which break out in rumbles of sedition. I am Your Majesty's faithful vassal. The same jealousy that a husband feels for his wife's honour, a son's appreciation of his father's love, a good vassal must feel for the glory of his king, he must drain himself dry in zeal for his house, in the increase of his service. Any other passion which might transport him would just be frenzy. These, sire, are my maxims of State. So do not judge me guilty of sedition and pillage because my clothes are out at the elbows. If you show me mercy, sire, I shall wear them out at the knees too, praying God night and morning for you! Alas! I am not exceptionally rich, it's true. In fact I am rather poor. But not vicious on that account. It's not my fault. Everyone knows that great wealth is not to be gained from literature, and those who are most accomplished at writing good books do not always enjoy much of a fire in winter. The legal profession takes all the wheat for itself and leaves only the chaff for the other learned professions. There are forty most excellent proverbs about the philosopher's ragged cloak. Oh! sire! clemency is the only virtue which can light up the inside of a great soul. Clemency carries the torch ahead of all the other virtues. Without it they are blind men groping about in their search for God. Mercy, which is the same as clemency, makes for loving subjects, a prince's most powerful bodyguard. What difference does it make to you, Your Majesty, by whom every eye is dazzled, that there should be one more poor man on earth? A poor innocent philosopher, floundering in the darkness of calamity, with his empty fob ringing upon his hollow belly? Besides, sire, I am a man of letters. Great kings add a jewel to their crown by being patrons of letters. Hercules did not scorn the title of Musagetes.* Matthias Corvinus* showed favour to Jean de Monroyal,* the ornament of mathematics. Now, hanging men of letters is a poor way of being a patron of letters. What a blot on the name of Alexander if he had had Aristotle hanged! Such an act would not just have been a small patch on the face of his reputation to embellish it, but a malignant ulcer to disfigure it. Sire! I composed a most suitable epithalamium for Mademoiselle of Flanders and Monseigneur the most august Dauphin. That doesn't go with incitement to rebellion. Your Majesty can see that I am no ignorant scribbler, that I am highly educated, and that I have natural eloquence. Grant me mercy, sire. In so doing you will be performing a most noble act for Our Lady, and I swear to you that I am very frightened at the idea of being hanged.'

So saying, the desolate Gringoire kissed the King's slippers, and Guillaume Rym whispered to Coppenole: 'He does well to crawl on the ground. Kings are like the Cretan Jupiter, they have ears only in their feet.' And without concerning himself with Cretan Jupiter the hosier answered with a heavy smile, eyes fixed on Gringoire: 'Oh! That's really good! It makes me think I'm hearing Chancellor Hugonet* begging me for mercy.'

When Gringoire finally stopped, quite out of breath, he looked up trembling at the King, who was scratching with his nail a patch on the knee of his hose. Then His Majesty began to drink from the goblet of tisane. For the rest, he did not breathe a word, and the silence was torment for Gringoire. At length the King looked at him. 'What a dreadful one for bawling!' he said. Then, turning to Tristan l'Hermite: 'Bah! let him go!'

Gringoire fell on his backside, quite appalled with joy.

'Go free?' grumbled Tristan. 'Wouldn't Your Majesty like him to be kept in a cage for a bit?'

'Compère,' retorted Louis XI, 'do you think it's for birds like him that we have cages made costing 367 *livres* 8 *sols* 3 *deniers*—release the whoremonger right away' (Louis XI was fond of that word, which with *Pasque-Dieu!* made up his stock of joviality), 'and send him out with a drubbing!'

'Phew!' exclaimed Gringoire, 'there's a great King!'

And for fear of a countermand he rushed to the door which Tristan opened for him with somewhat bad grace. The soldiers came out with him, pushing him before them with hard punches, which Gringoire endured as a true Stoic philosopher.

The King's good humour, ever since he had been informed of the revolt against the bailiff, came through in everything. His unwonted clemency was a by no means unimportant sign of it. Tristan l'Hermite in his corner had the disgruntled expression of a mastiff which has seen but not had.

The King meanwhile was cheerfully beating out with his fingers on the arm of his chair the Pont-Audemer march. He was a secretive prince, but he was much better at hiding his sorrows than his joys. These outward manifestations of joy at any piece of good news sometimes went to great lengths: thus, on the death of Charles the Bold, to the point of promising silver balustrades to Saint-Martin at Tours; on his accession to the throne, to the point of forgetting to arrange his father's obsequies.

'Ha! sire!' suddenly exclaimed Jacques Coictier, 'what has become of that stabbing pain for which Your Majesty had me summoned?'

'Oh!' said the King, 'I am really in great pain, Compère. There's a whistling in my ears, and burning rakes scraping my chest.'

Coictier took the King's hand, and began to take his pulse with the look of an expert.

'Look, Coppenole,' Rym said in an undertone, 'there he is between Coictier and Tristan. That's his whole court. A physician for him, an executioner for everyone else.'

As he felt the King's pulse, Coictier looked more and more alarmed. Louis XI watched him with some anxiety. Coictier's face was visibly darkening. The good man had no other fields to cultivate but the King's ill health. He made the most of it.

'Oh! oh!' he murmured finally, 'this is serious indeed.'

'Is that so?' said the King anxiously.

'*Pulsus creber, anhelans, crepitans, irregularis* [rapid pulse, gasping, rattling, irregular],' the doctor continued.

'*Pasque-Dieu!*'

'In less than three days it can carry a man off.'

'Our Lady!' exclaimed the King. 'And the remedy, compère?'

'I'm thinking about it, sire.'

He made Louis XI put his tongue out, shook his head, pulled a face, and in the middle of this performance: 'By God, sire,' he said suddenly, 'I must tell you that there's a receivership vacant of ecclesiastical revenues due to the Crown, and I have a nephew.'

'I'll give my receivership to your nephew, Compère Jacques,' the King replied; 'but take away this burning in my chest.'

'Since Your Majesty is so kind, he will not refuse me a little help in the construction of my house in the rue Saint-André-des-Arcs.'

'Hm!' said the King.

'I've come to the end of my financial resources,' the doctor went on, 'and it would really be a pity if the house did not have a roof. Not for the sake of the house, which is plain and quite unpretentious, but for Jehan Fourbault's* paintings, which brighten up the wainscotting. There is a Diana flying in the air, but so outstanding, so tender, so delicate, her action so artless, her hair so beautifully dressed, crowned with a crescent, her flesh so white that it leads into temptation those who look at it with too much curiosity. There is also a Ceres. She is another very beautiful divinity. She is sitting on wheatsheaves, and has a handsome garland round her head of ears of corn interwoven with salsify and other flowers. You've never seen anything more amorous than her eyes, more rounded than her legs, more noble than her attitude, better draped than her skirt. It is one of the most innocent and perfect beauties ever produced by a painter's brush.'

'Hangman!' grumbled Louis XI, 'what are you getting at?'

'I need a roof over those paintings, sire, and although it's only a trifle, I have no money left.'

'How much is it, this roof of yours?'

'Well . . . a copper roof, figured and gilded, 2,000 *livres* at most.'

'Ah! murderer!' cried the King. 'He never pulls a tooth from me but it turns out to be a diamond.'

'Do I get my roof?' said Coictier.

'Yes! and go to the devil, but cure me.'

Jacques Coictier bowed deeply and said: 'Sire, what will save you is a repercussive. We shall apply to the small of your back the great defensive, consisting of cerate, bole armenie, white of egg, oil, and vinegar. You will continue with your tisane, and we shall answer for Your Majesty.'

A shining candle does not attract just one moth. Maître Olivier, seeing the king in generous mood and thinking the moment favourable, came up in his turn: 'Sire . . .'

'What is it now?' said Louis XI.

'Sire, Your Majesty knows that Simon Radin is dead?'

'Well?'

'The fact is that he was King's counsellor for the jurisdiction of the treasury.'

'Well?'

'Sire, his place is vacant.'

As he spoke, Maître Olivier's haughty face dropped its arrogant expression for a servile one. It is the only change a courtier's face can register. The King looked him straight in the eye and said drily: 'I understand.'

He went on:

'Maître Olivier, Marshal de Boucicaut* used to say: "The only good gift comes from the King, the only good fishing from the sea." I see that you are of Monsieur de Boucicaut's opinion. Now listen to this. We have a good memory. In '68 we made you Groom of the Bedchamber; in '69 Warden of the castle of the bridge of Saint-Cloud at a salary of 100 *livres tournois* (you wanted *livres parisis*). In November '73, by letters given at Gergeole, we appointed you Keeper of the Forest of Vincennes, in place of Gilbert Acle, squire; in '75, Verderer of the Forest of Rouvray-lez-Saint-Cloud, in place of Jacques le Maire; in '78 we graciously settled on you, by letters patent sealed on double label of green wax, an annuity of 10 *livres parisis*, for you and your wife, on the Place aux Marchands, situated at the École Saint-Germain; in '79 we made you Verderer of the Forest of Senart, in place of poor Jehan Daiz; then Captain of the castle at Loches; then Governor of Saint-Quentin; then Captain of the Bridge of Meulan, of which you call yourself count. From the fine of 5 *sols* paid by every barber who shaves on a feast day, 3 *sols* go to you, and we have what's left. We were kind enough to change your name from le Mauvais [the bad], which is too much like your appearance. In '74 we granted you, to the great displeasure of our nobility, a coat of arms of countless colours which makes your chest look like a peacock's. *Pasque-Dieu!* haven't you had your fill? Isn't the draught of fishes fine and miraculous enough? And aren't you afraid that one extra salmon might capsize your boat? Pride will destroy you, compère. Pride always has ruin and shame hot on its heels. Think about all that and hold your tongue.'

These words, uttered with severity, brought back the insolent look to the resentful features of Maître Olivier. 'Right,' he murmured almost aloud, 'it is obvious that the King is unwell today. He gives everything to his doctor.'

Louis XI, far from being annoyed at this outburst, went on quite mildly: 'Oh yes, I was forgetting that I made you my ambassador at Ghent to Madame Marie. Yes, gentlemen,' the King added, turning to the Flemings, 'this man has been an ambassador. There now, compère,' he continued, addressing Maître Olivier, 'let's not fall out; we are old friends. It's very late now. We have finished our work. Shave me.'

Our readers have certainly not waited until now to recognize in 'Maître Olivier' that terrible Figaro whom Providence, that great dramatist, involved so artistically in the long bloody play of Louis XI. This is not the place to undertake the development of this strange character. This royal barber had three names. At court he was politely called Olivier le Daim; among the people, Olivier the Devil. His real name was Olivier le Mauvais [the Bad].

So Olivier the Bad stayed motionless, sulking at the King and looking askance at Jacques Coictier: 'Yes, yes! the doctor!' he said between his teeth.

'Oh! yes, the doctor,' Louis XI went on, strangely good-humoured, 'the doctor enjoys even more credit than you. It's perfectly simple. He has a hold on our entire body, and you hold us only by the chin. Come, my poor barber, things will even out. What would you say then, and what would become of your office, if I were a king like King Chilperic, whose habit it was to hold his beard in his hand? Come along, compère, see to your duties, shave me. Go and fetch what you need.'

Olivier, seeing that the King had decided to treat everything as a joke, and there was no way even to make him lose his temper, went out grumbling to carry out his orders.

The King stood up, went over to the window, and suddenly opened it in extraordinary agitation: 'Oh! yes!' he cried, clapping his hands, 'there's a red glow in the sky over the Cité. It's the bailiff burning. It can't be anything else. Ah! my good people! So you're helping me at last to bring down the lordships!'

Then, turning to the Flemings: 'Messieurs, come and look at this. Isn't that a fire glowing?'

The two men from Ghent came up.

'A great fire,' said Guillaume Rym.

'Oh!' Coppenole added, 'that reminds me of when the lord of Hymbercourt's house was burned down. It must be a really big revolt over there.'

'Do you think so, Maître Coppenole?' And Louis XI looked almost as delighted as the hosier. 'It will be hard to resist it, will it not?'

'By the Rood sire! Your Majesty would get quite a few companies of soldiers mauled doing it!'

'Ah! I would! That's different,' replied the King. 'If I wanted . . .'

The hosier boldly answered: 'If this revolt is what I assume, you would want in vain, sire.'

'Compère,' said Louis XI, 'two companies of my men-at-arms and a volley from the serpentines would make short work of a mob of the common people.'

The hosier, despite the signals that Guillaume Rym was sending him, appeared determined to stand up to the King.

'Sire, the Swiss were commoners too. Monsieur the Duke of Burgundy was a great noble, and he despised such rabble. At the battle of Grandson,* sire, he cried: "Gunners! fire on those knaves!" and swore by Saint George. But the *avoyer* Scharnachtal* rushed on the fine duke with his club and his people, and when they clashed with these peasants in their buffalo skins, the shining Burgundian army shattered like a pane of glass hit by a stone. A good many knights were killed there by knaves; and Monsieur de Château-Guyon, the greatest lord in Burgundy, was found dead with his great grey horse in a little marshy field.'

'My friend,' the King retorted, 'you are speaking of a battle. Here it is an insurrection. And I can put an end to it whenever I choose to put on a frown.'

The other replied with indifference: 'That may be so, sire. In that case it is because the people's hour has not come.'

Guillaume Rym thought he should intervene: 'Maître Coppenole, you are talking to a mighty king.'

'I know,' the hosier answered gravely.

'Let him have his say, Monsieur Rym, my friend,' said the King. 'I like such plain speaking. My father Charles VII used to say that truth was ailing. For my part, I used to think that truth was dead, and had not found a confessor. Maître Coppenole is putting me right.'

Then, laying his hand familiarly on Coppenole's shoulder: 'You were saying then, Maître Jacques?'

'I say, sire, that you may be right, that the hour of the people has not yet come in your kingdom.'

Louis XI gave him a penetrating look. 'And when will that hour come, Maître?'

'You'll hear it strike.'

'From which clock, if you please?'

Coppenole, with his calm, homely composure, brought the King over to the window. 'Listen, sire! Here we have a keep, a tower with an alarm bell, cannon, citizens, soldiers. When the alarm bell booms, when the cannons roar, when the keep tumbles down with a great crash, when citizens and soldiers yell and kill each other, that will be the hour striking.'

Louis's face became sombre and thoughtful. He remained silent for a moment. Then he gently patted the thick wall of the keep, like someone stroking a charger's crupper. 'Oh! no!' he said. 'You won't tumble down so easily, will you, my good Bastille?'*

And turning with an abrupt gesture to the bold Fleming: 'Have you ever seen a revolt, Maître Jacques?'

'I have made them,' said the hosier.

'How,' said the King, 'do you go about making a revolt?'

'Ah!' Coppenole answered; 'it's not very difficult. There are lots of ways. First of all people in the town must be dissatisfied. That's nothing unusual. And then there's the character of the inhabitants. Those of Ghent are easily brought to revolt. They always like the prince's son, never the prince. Very well! One morning, let us suppose, someone comes into my shop and says: "The Lady of Flanders wants to save her ministers, the high bailiff is doubling the tax on vegetables, or something. Whatever you like. I stop work, go out of my hosier's shop into the street, and shout "Pillage!" There's always some broken cask lying around. I get up on it, and say out loud the first thing that occurs to me, what I have at heart; and when you're one of the people, sire, you've always got something at heart. Then they gather together, shout, the tocsin is sounded, the people get arms by disarming the soldiers, the folk from the market join in, and you're off! And it will always be like that, so long as there are lords in the lordships, townsfolk in the towns, and country folk in the country.'

'And whom do you rebel against like that?' asked the king. 'Against your bailiffs? Against your lords?'

'Sometimes, It all depends. Against the duke too, sometimes.'

Louis XI went back to his seat, and said with a smile: 'Ah! here they've only got as far as bailiffs!'

At that moment Olivier le Daim came back. He was followed by two pages carrying the King's toilet articles and clothes; but what struck Louis XI was the fact that he was also accompanied by the Provost of Paris and the captain of the watch, who appeared quite dismayed. The resentful barber too wore a look of dismay, but with underlying satisfaction. He it was who spoke up: 'Sire, I beg Your Majesty's pardon for the calamitous news I bring.'

The King turned round so sharply that he scraped the floor matting with the legs of his chair. 'What does that mean?'

'Sire,' continued Olivier le Daim with the malicious expression of a man delighted at having to strike a violent blow, 'it is not at the bailiff of the Palais that this popular uprising is directed.'

'At whom then?'

'At you, sire.'

The old king stood up, straight and upright as a young man. 'Explain yourself, Olivier! explain yourself! And keep a good hold on your head, my compère, for I swear to you by the cross of Saint-Lô* that if you lie to us now, the sword which cut off Monsieur de Luxembourg's head is not so chipped that it can't saw yours off as well!'

The oath was a formidable one. Louis XI had sworn only twice in his life by the cross of Saint-Lô.

Olivier opened his mouth to answer: 'Sire . . .'

'Down on your knees!' the King violently interrupted. 'Tristan, keep your eyes on this man!'

Olivier knelt down, and said coldly: 'Sire, a witch has been condemned to death by your court of Parliament. She has taken refuge in Notre-Dame. The people are trying to recover her by force. Monsieur the Provost and Monsieur the captain of the watch, who have just come from the riot, are there to give me the lie if that is not the truth. It is Notre-Dame the people are besieging.'

'Indeed!' said the King in a low voice, pale and trembling with rage. 'Notre-Dame! They are laying siege to Our Lady, my good mistress, in her own cathedral!—Get up, Olivier. You are right. I give you Simon Radin's office. You are right—it's me they are attacking. The witch is under the safeguard of the church, the church is under my safeguard. And there was I thinking it was all to do with the bailiff! It's against me!'

Then, rejuvenated by fury, he began striding up and down. He was not laughing any more, he was terrible, pacing up and down, a fox turned into a hyena, he seemed to be so choked that he could not speak, his lips moved, and his bony fists clenched. Suddenly he raised his head, his sunken eyes seemed to be full of light, and his voice rang out like a bugle. 'Cut them down, Tristan! Cut these rogues down! Go, Tristan my friend! Kill! kill!'

When this eruption was over, he sat down again, and said with cold, concentrated rage:

'Here, Tristan!—here with us in the Bastille there are the vicomte de Gif's fifty lances,* which makes three hundred horse; take them. There is also Monsieur de Châteaupers' company of archers of our ordinance; take them too. You are Provost-Marshal, you have the men of your Provostry; take them. At the Hôtel Saint-Pol you will find forty archers of Monsieur the Dauphin's new guard, take them; and with all those men hasten to Notre-Dame. Ha! messieurs, you common people of Paris! So you pit yourselves against the Crown of France, the sanctity of Notre-Dame, and the peace of this realm! Exterminate them, Tristan! exterminate them! And let not one of them get away except to the gallows of Montfaucon.'

Tristan bowed. 'Very good, sire!'

After a silence he added: 'And what shall I do with the witch?'

The question gave the King thought. 'Ah!' he said, 'the witch!—Monsieur d'Estouteville, what were the people wanting to do with her?'

'Sire,' the Provost of Paris answered, 'I suppose that as the people have come to snatch her out of her asylum in Notre-Dame, they are offended by her impunity and want to hang her.'

The King appeared to be deep in reflection, then, addressing Tristan l'Hermite: 'Very well! Compère, exterminate the people and hang the witch.'

'That's right,' Rym whispered to Coppenole, 'punish the people for wanting, and do what they wanted.'

'That's enough, sire,' Tristan answered. 'If the witch is still in Notre-Dame, should she be seized there in spite of the asylum?'

'*Pasque-Dieu!* the asylum!' said the King, scratching his ear. 'The woman must be hanged all the same.'

At that, as if suddenly struck by an idea, he fell hurriedly to his knees in front of his chair, took off his hat, placed it on the seat, and gazing devoutly at one of the lead amulets with which it was loaded: 'Oh!' he said, hands clasped together, 'Our Lady of Paris, my gracious patroness, forgive me. I shall do it only this once. This criminal must be punished. I assure you, my Lady the Virgin, my good mistress, that she is a witch who is not worthy of your kind protection. You know, madame, that many most pious princes have trespassed against the privilege of churches for the glory of God and the needs of the state. Saint Hugh,* an English bishop, allowed King Edward to seize a magician in his church. Saint Louis of France, my master, transgressed the church of Monsieur Saint Paul* for the same purpose; and Monsieur Alphonse, the King of Jerusalem's son, even the church of the Holy Sepulchre. Forgive me then this time, Our Lady of Paris. I shall not do it again, and I will give you a beautiful silver statue, like the one I gave last year to Our Lady of Ecouys. Amen.'

He made the sign of the cross, stood up, put on his hat again and said to Tristan: 'Be quick about it, compère. Take Monsieur de Châteaupers with you. Have the tocsin rung. Crush the people. Hang the witch. That's settled. And I mean the execution to be performed by you. You will give me an account of it.—Come on, Olivier, I won't be going to bed tonight. Shave me.'

Tristan l'Hermite bowed and went out. Then the King dismissed Rym and Coppenole with a gesture: 'God keep you, messieurs, my good friends the Flemings. Go and rest a while. The night is far advanced and we are closer to morning than evening.'

They both withdrew, and as they went to their apartments escorted by the captain of the Bastille, Coppenole said to Guillaume Rym: 'Hm! I've had enough of that king and his coughing! I saw Charles of Burgundy drunk; he was not as nasty as Louis XI sick.'

'Maître Jacques,' Rym replied, 'that's because wine is less cruel to kings than tisane.'

VI

LITTLE BLADE ON THE PROWL

LEAVING the Bastille, Gringoire went down the rue Saint-Antoine with the speed of a runaway horse. When he came to the Porte Baudoyer he made straight for the stone cross standing in the middle of the square, as if he had been able to distinguish in the darkness the figure of a man dressed and hooded in black sitting on the steps of the cross. 'Is that you, master?' said Gringoire.

The man in black stood up. 'Death and passion! You make me boil, Gringoire. The man on the tower at Saint-Gervais* has just called out half-past one in the morning.'

'Oh!' retorted Gringoire, 'it's not my fault, but that of the watch and the King. I have just had a very narrow escape! I always just miss being hanged. That is my predestination.'

'You just miss everything,' the other said. 'But let's go quickly. Do you have the password?'

'Just imagine, master, I've seen the King. I've just come from there. He wears fustian breeches. It was quite an adventure.'

'Oh! you and your word-spinning! What do I care about your adventure? Do you have the truands' password?'

'Yes, I have. Don't worry. *Little blade on the prowl.*'

'Good. Otherwise we'd never be able to get through to the church. The truands are blocking the streets. Fortunately they seem to have met with some resistance. We may still get there in time.'

'Yes, master. But how will we get into Notre-Dame?'

'I have the key to the towers.'

'And how will we get out?'

'Behind the cloister there's a little door giving on to the Terrain, and from there on to the water. I've taken the key to it, and moored a boat there this morning.'

'I came jolly near being hanged!' Gringoire went on.

'Quick! come on!' said the other.

They both went off striding down towards the Cité.

VII

CHÂTEAUPERS TO THE RESCUE!

THE reader may recall the critical situation in which we left Quasimodo. The worthy deaf man, assailed on every side, had lost, if not all heart, at least all hope of saving, not himself, he had no thought of himself, but the gypsy girl. He was running about on the gallery quite distraught. Notre-Dame was about to be captured by the truands. Suddenly a great galloping of horses filled the neighbouring streets, and with a long line of torches and a dense column of riders, riding with bridles dropped and lances ready, furious sounds swept through the square like a hurricane: 'France! France! Cut the knaves to pieces! Châteaupers to the rescue! Provostry! Provostry!'

The truands turned about in alarm.

Quasimodo, who could not hear, saw the naked swords, the torches, the pikeheads, all this cavalry, at whose head he recognized Captain Phoebus; he saw the truands, thrown into confusion, the terror of some, the agitation of the best of them, and this unhoped-for aid so revived his strength that he hurled off the church the first attackers who were already stepping over the gallery.

It was in fact the King's troops arriving.

The truands put up a brave fight. They defended themselves like desperate men. Caught on the flank by the rue Saint-Pierre-aux-Bœufs, and in the rear by the rue du Parvis, driven back against Notre-Dame, which they were still assaulting and Quasimodo was defending, at once besiegers and besieged, they were in the singular situation in which, at the famous siege of Turin in 1640, comte Henri d'Harcourt found himself, between Prince Thomas of Savoy whom he was besieging and the marquis de Leganez who was blockading him, *Taurinum obsessor idem et obsessus** as his epitaph puts it.

It was a fearsome struggle. Wolf's flesh needs dogs' teeth, as P. Matthieu* says. The King's horsemen, in the midst of whom Phoebus de Châteaupers bore himself valiantly, gave no quarter, and the edge of the sword cut down any who escaped the thrust. The poorly armed truands foamed at the mouth and bit. Men, women, and children threw themselves at the cruppers and chests of the horses and clung on like cats with tooth and nail, by hands and feet. Others rammed torches into the archers' faces. Others again stuck iron hooks into the riders' necks and pulled them off. They tore to shreds those who fell.

One in particular had a great gleaming scythe for a long time mowing at the horses' legs. He was frightening. He sang a nasal song, he swept the scythe ceaselessly out and back. With each slash he traced around him a ring of severed limbs. He advanced like that into the thick of the cavalry, with the calm, slow pace, the swaying head and regular hard breathing of a harvester cutting into a field of corn. It was Clopin Trouillefou. He was laid low by an arquebus.

Meanwhile windows had opened again. The neighbours, hearing the war cries of the royal troops, had taken a hand in the business and musket balls rained down on the truands from every storey. The Parvis was full of dense smoke which musket volleys streaked with fire. Through it the façade of Notre-Dame could dimly be made out, and the crumbling Hôtel-Dieu, with a few wan-looking patients looking down from the top of its roof, covered with dormer windows like scales.

At last the truands gave in. Exhaustion, lack of proper weapons, the fright caused by the surprise, the musketry from the windows, the stout charge of the King's men, everything overwhelmed them. They broke through the attackers' line, and began to flee in every direction, leaving the Parvis heaped with their dead.

When Quasimodo, who had never for a moment stopped fighting, saw this rout, he fell to his knees and raised his hands to Heaven; then, drunk with joy, he ran, he went up as swiftly as a bird to the cell whose approaches he had so dauntlessly defended. He had only one thought left now, and that was to kneel down in front of her whom he had just saved for the second time.

When he entered the cell, he found it empty.

gave no quarter; and the edge of the sword cut down any
who escaped the first. The poorly armed inmates foamed
at the mouth and bit. Men, women, and children flung
themselves at the choppers and the iron of the horses and
clung on like cats with tooth and nail, by hands and feet.
Others ranged torches into the archers' faces. Others
again stuck iron hooks into the rafters' necks, and pulled
them off. They tore to shreds those who fell.

One in particular had a great gleaming scythe for mowing
time, mowing at the horses' legs. He was terrifying. He
sang a nasal song, he swept the scythe ceaselessly out and
back; with each slash he traced around him a ring of severed
limbs. He advanced like that into the thick of the cavalry,
with the calm, slow pace, the swaying head and regular hard
breathing of a harvester cutting into a field of corn, Jewin
Choprat Trouilleton. He was laid low by an arquebus.

Meanwhile windows had opened again. The neighbours,
hearing the exercise of the royal troops, had taken a hand;
in the batteries and musket balls rained down on the infants
from every storey. The Barria was full of dense smoke
which musket volleys streaked with fire. Throughout, the
facade of Notre-Dame could dimly be made out, and the
quibbling Hôtel-Dieu, with a few wan-looking patients
looking down from the top of its roof, covered with donkeys
window-while squea.

At long the inmates gave up. Exhaustion, lack of proper
weapons, the fright caused by the surprise, the musketry
from the windows, the stout charge of the King's men,
carrying, overwhelmed them. They broke through the
guards' line, and began to flee in every direction, leaving
the Barria heaped with their dead.

When Quasimodo, who had never for a moment stopped
fighting, saw this rout, he fell to his knees and raised his
hands to heaven, then drunk with joy, he ran like wind up
as swiftly as a bird to the cell whose approach he had so
dauntlessly defended. He had only one thought left now,
and that was to kneel down in front of her whom he had
just saved for the second time.

When he entered the cell, he found it empty.

BOOK ELEVEN

I

THE LITTLE SHOE

AT the moment when the truands launched their assault on the church, la Esmeralda was sleeping.

Soon the ever-increasing uproar round the building and the anxious bleating of her goat, which had already woken up, roused her from sleep. She sat up, listened, looked, and then, frightened by the glow and the noise, rushed out of the cell and went to look. The appearance of the square, the sight astir there, the disorder of this night attack, the hideous crowd, hopping up and down like a horde of frogs, dimly spied in the darkness, the hoarse croaking of this multitude, the few red torches speeding along and passing each other against the background of shadow, like the fires to be seen at night streaking over the misty surface of marshes, the whole scene looked to her like some mysterious battle being waged between the phantoms of a witches' sabbath and the stone monsters of the church. Imbued from childhood with the superstitions of the Bohemian tribe, her first thought was that she had surprised at their evil spells the strange beings of the night. So she ran back in terror to cower in her cell, asking her pallet for a nightmare less full of horror.

Gradually, however, the first vapours of fear cleared away; the noise, constantly increasing, and several other signs of reality, made her realize that her besiegers were not spectres but human beings. This did not increase her fright, but transformed it. She thought about the possibility of a popular insurrection to snatch her from her refuge. The idea of yet again losing life, hope, Phoebus, whom she still glimpsed in her future, the absolute void in which her weakness left her, all escape cut off, unsupported, abandoned, isolated, all these thoughts and countless others overwhelmed her. She fell to her knees, her head on the bed, hands clasped upon her head, filled with anxiety and trembling, and though a gypsy, idolatrous and pagan, she began sobbing to beg mercy of the good Christian God and to pray to Our Lady, her hostess. For, even if one believes in nothing, there are moments in life when one always holds the religion of the temple closest to hand.

She remained prostrate like that for a very long time, trembling, in truth, rather than praying, chilled as the breath of the raging multitude came nearer and nearer, understanding nothing of their frenzy, knowing nothing of what was planned, what they were doing, what they intended, but filled with a premonition of some dreadful outcome.

Then, in the midst of her anguish she heard footsteps nearby. She turned round. Two men, one carrying a lantern, had just entered her cell. She let out a feeble cry.

'Don't be afraid,' said a voice not unknown to her, 'it's me.'

'Who? Who are you?' she asked.

'Pierre Gringoire.'

The name reassured her. She looked up, and indeed recognized the poet. But next to him was a figure dressed in black and veiled from head to foot who struck her dumb.

'Ah!' Gringoire went on reproachfully, 'Djali recognized me before you did!'

The little goat had indeed not waited for Gringoire to announce his name. He had barely come in before she was fondly rubbing against his knees, covering the poet with caresses and white hairs, for she was moulting. Gringoire returned her caresses.

'Who's that with you?' the gypsy said in a low voice.

'Don't worry,' Gringoire answered. 'It's a friend of mine.'

At that the philosopher, setting his lantern on the floor, crouched down on the flagstones and exclaimed enthusiastically as he hugged Djali in his arms: 'Oh! what a graceful animal, no doubt more notable for her cleanliness than her size, but ingenious, subtle, and as well lettered as a grammarian! Let's see, my Djali, have you forgotten any of your pretty tricks? How does Maître Jacques Charmolue go . . .?'

The man in black did not let him finish. He came up to Gringoire and pushed him roughly by the shoulder. Gringoire stood up. 'It's true,' he said, 'I was forgetting that we are in a hurry—but that's no reason, master, to rage at people so. My dear, fair child, your life is in danger, and so is Djali's. They want to hang you again. We are your friends, and we have come to save you. Follow us.'

'Is that true?' she cried, quite overcome.

'Yes, quite true. Come quickly!'

'I will,' she stammered. 'But why doesn't your friend speak?'

'Ah!' said Gringoire, 'it's because his father and mother were whimsical people who gave him a taciturn disposition.'

She had to be content with that explanation. Gringoire took her by the hand, his companion picked up the lantern and walked in front. The girl was stunned by fear. She let herself be led. The goat skipped after them, so happy to see Gringoire again that she kept making him stumble by sticking her horns between his legs. 'That's life!' said the philosopher each time he just missed falling; 'it's often our best friends who cause our downfall!' They hurried down the tower stairs, crossed the church, all dark and lonely, but echoing with the uproar, which made a dreadful contrast, and came out into the cloister garth by the Red Door. The cloister was abandoned, the canons had fled to the bishop's palace to pray there together; the garth was empty, with a few terrified servants hiding in dark corners. They made for the door giving on to the Terrain from this courtyard. The man in black opened it with a key he had. Our readers know that the Terrain was a spit of land enclosed by walls on the Cité side, belonging to the chapter of Notre-Dame, and it formed the eastern tip of the island behind the church. They found this enclosure completely deserted. There the noise of tumult in the air was already fainter. The sounds of the truands' attack reached them more confusedly and with less clamour. The cool breeze blowing downstream stirred the leaves of the single tree planted at the tip of the Terrain quite audibly. However, they were still very close to danger. The nearest buildings to them were the bishop's palace and the church. There was obviously a great commotion going on inside the palace. Its dark mass was all crisscrossed with lights hurrying from one window to another; just as, when you have been burning paper, there remains a dark pile of ash through which live sparks run in countless peculiar patterns. Next to it, the enormous towers of Notre-Dame, seen thus from behind with the long nave over which they rise, silhouetted in black against the vast, red glow filling the Parvis, looked like the two gigantic firedogs of a Cyclopean fire.

What could be seen of Paris on every side wavered as one looked in a blend of light and shade. Some of Rembrandt's pictures have that sort of background.

The man with the lantern walked straight to the tip of the Terrain. There, at the very edge of the water, were the decaying remains of a fence made of stakes with laths laid across them to which a low vine clung with a few meagre branches sticking out like the fingers of an open hand. Behind, in the shadow cast by this trellis, a small boat lay hidden. The man beckoned to Gringoire and his companion to get into it. The goat followed. The man stepped in last. Then he cut the boat's moorings, pushed it away from the bank with a long hook, and seizing a pair of oars, sat down in the bows, rowing with all his might towards the open water. The Seine runs very fast at that spot, and he had some trouble clearing the tip of the island.

Gringoire's first concern on getting into the boat was to take the goat on his knees. He installed himself in the stern, and the girl, in whom the stranger inspired an indefinable anxiety, came to sit pressed closely against the poet.

When the philosopher felt the boat moving, he clapped his hands and kissed Djali between her horns. 'Oh!' he said, 'now all four of us are safe.' He added, with the expression of a profound thinker: 'One is obliged, sometimes to fortune, sometimes to cunning, for the happy outcome of great enterprises.'

The boat moved slowly towards the right bank. The girl watched the stranger with secret terror. He had carefully stopped up the light from his dark lantern. He could be dimly seen in the bows of the boat, like a spectre in the dark. His hood, still lowered, had the effect of a kind of mask, and each time he opened his arms as he rowed, with the wide black sleeves hanging down, they looked like two huge batwings. For the rest, he had still not said a word, let out a breath. There was no other sound in the boat but the oars going in and out, mingled with the constant rippling of the water against the sides.

'Upon my soul!' Gringoire suddenly exclaimed, 'we are as bright and cheerful as [if we had all been changed into owls like] Ascalaphus!* We are observing silence like so many Pythagoreans or fish! *Pasque-Dieu!* my friends, I'd like someone to speak to me—the human voice comes as music to the human ear. It's not I who say so, but Didymus of Alexandria, and they are famous words—to be sure, Didymus of Alexandria is no mean philosopher. A word, my lovely child! speak a word to me, I beseech you! That reminds me, you had a funny way of making a special little pout; do you still do it? Do you know, my dear, that Parliament has full jurisdiction over places of asylum, and that you were in great danger in your cell in Notre-Dame? Alas! the little trochilus bird makes its nest in the crocodile's mouth. Master, there's the moon coming out again—I only hope no one spots us! We are performing a laudable act by rescuing mademoiselle, yet they'd hang us by order of the King if they caught us. Alas! there are two ways of taking human actions. I am condemned for what earns you a prize. The man who admires Caesar blames Catilina. Isn't it so, master? What do you say to such philosophy? For my part I possess the philosophy of instinct, of nature, *ut apes geometriam* [as bees do geometry].* Come on! no one answers me. What a tiresome mood you're both in! I'll have to talk all by myself. In tragedy it's what we call a monologue. *Pasque-Dieu!*—I warn you that I've just been seeing King Louis XI and it's from him that I've caught that oath—*Pasque-Dieu!* then! They are still making the devil of a row in the Cité. He's a nasty evil old king. He's all wrapped up in furs. He still owes me money for my epithalamium, and he came within an ace of having me hanged this evening, which

I should have found most embarrassing. He's stingy with men of merit. He really ought to read the four books of Salvian of Cologne *Adversus avaritiam* [*Against Avarice*]. Truly! he is anything but generous in his treatment of men of letters, and he goes in for the most barbaric cruelties. He's a sponge for soaking up money laid upon the people. His savings are like the spleen, which swells up as all the other parts grow lean. So complaints against the rigours of the times become murmurings against the prince. Under this mild and pious lord the gallows creak with all those hanged, the headsman's blocks go rotten with blood, the prisons burst like overstuffed bellies. This king grabs with one hand and hangs with the other. He is procurator to Dame Gabelle* and my lord Gibbet. The great are stripped of their dignities, and the small ceaselessly burdened with new exactions. He's a monstrous prince. I don't like this monarch. What about you, master?'

The man in black let the garrulous poet run on. He continued to struggle against the violent, compressed current separating the prow of the Cité from the poop of the Île Notre-Dame, which today we call the Île Saint-Louis.

'By the way, master,' Gringoire suddenly went on, 'as we came out on to the Parvis through those crazy truands, did your reverence notice the poor little devil whose brains your deaf man was busy dashing out against the balustrade of the gallery of kings? I'm shortsighted and couldn't recognize him. Do you know who it might be?'

The stranger did not answer a word. But he stopped rowing abruptly, his arms gave way as if they were broken, his head slumped on his breast, and la Esmeralda heard him heave a convulsive sigh. She trembled too. She had heard someone sigh like that before.

The boat, left to itself, drifted for a moment or two with the stream. But the man in black finally straightened up, gripped the oars again, and continued upstream. He rounded the tip of the Île Notre-Dame, and made for the landing stage at the Port-au-Foin.

'Ah!' said Gringoire, 'there's the Logis Barbeau over there. Look, master, see, that group of dark roofs at peculiar angles, there, beneath that heap of low, ragged, dirty, smeared clouds, where the moon looks all squashed and spread out like an egg yolk when the shell is broken—it's a fine mansion. There's a chapel crowned by a little vault full of nicely carved decorations. Above it you can see the very delicately pierced bell tower. There's also a pleasant garden, consisting of a pond, an aviary, an echo, a mall, a maze, a wild animal house, and a good many leaf-shaded walks most agreeable to Venus. There's also a rascally tree they call "the lecher", because it served for the pleasures of a famous princess and a gallant and witty constable of France,—alas! we poor philosophers are to a constable what a bed of cabbages and radishes is to the garden of the Louvre. What does it matter after all? Human life for the great as for us is a mixture of good and bad. Grief is always next to joy, the spondee next to the dactyl. Master, I must tell you the story of the Logis Barbeau. It ended tragically. It was in 1319, in the reign of Philippe V,* the longest of any king of France. The moral of the story is that the temptations of the flesh are pernicious and malignant. Let us not look too hard at our neighbour's wife, however susceptible our senses may be to beauty. Fornication is a most licentious thought. Adultery is curiosity about the sensual pleasure of another . . . Oh! the noise is louder than ever over there!'

The uproar was indeed increasing around Notre-Dame. They listened. Cries of victory could be clearly heard. Suddenly a hundred torches, which made the soldiers' helmets sparkle, spread over the church, at every height, on the towers, on the galleries, under the flying buttresses. The torches seemed to be searching for something; and soon the distant shouts reached the fugitives distinctly: 'The gypsy! The witch! Death to the gypsy!'

The unfortunate girl dropped her head into her hands, and the stranger began rowing furiously towards the bank. Meanwhile our philosopher reflected. He hugged the goat in his arms, and very gently moved away from the gypsy, who was huddling closer and closer to him, as her sole remaining refuge.

Gringoire was, to be sure, cruelly perplexed. He was thinking that the goat too 'according to existing legislation' would be hanged if recaptured; that that would be a great pity, poor Djali! that to have two females condemned to death clinging to him like this was really too much; that anyhow his companion would be only too happy to take on the gypsy. A violent conflict raged in his mind, in which, like Jupiter in the *Iliad*, he weighed up the gypsy and the goat in turn; and he looked at them, one after the other, his eyes moist with tears, as he said between his teeth: 'Yet I can't save you both.'

A sudden jolt told them at last that the boat had reached the bank. The sinister hubbub still filled the Cité. The stranger stood up, came over to the gypsy and tried to take her arm to help her to alight. She pushed him away and clung to Gringoire's sleeve, while he, in his turn, busy with the goat, almost pushed her away. So she jumped down from the boat by herself. She was so upset that she did not know what she was doing, or where she was going. She stayed for a moment in a daze, watching the water flow by. When she recovered her senses a little she was alone on the landing stage with the stranger. Gringoire had apparently taken advantage of the moment of landing to slip away with the goat into the block of houses in the rue Grenier-sur-l'Eau.

The poor gypsy shuddered at seeing herself alone with this man. She tried to speak, to cry out, to call Gringoire; her tongue lay inert in her mouth, and no sound came from her lips. Suddenly she felt the stranger's hand upon her own. It was a cold, strong hand. Her teeth chattered, she went paler than the moonlight shining upon her. The man did not say a word. He began striding up towards the Place de Grève, holding her by the hand. At that moment she had a vague feeling that destiny is an irresistible force. She had no energy left, she let herself be pulled along, running while he walked. The quay at that point ran upwards. It seemed to her, however, that she was going down a slope.

She looked in every direction. Not a soul passing by. The quay was absolutely deserted. She could hear no sound, detect no sign of human movement save from the Cité, in uproar and glowing red, separated from her only by an arm of the Seine, and from whence her own name reached her mixed with cries of death. The rest of Paris lay spread out around her in great blocks of shadow.

The stranger, meanwhile, was still pulling her along as silently and swiftly as ever. She did not recognize from her memory any of the places where she was walking. As she went past a lighted window, she made an effort, stiffened up abruptly, and cried: 'Help!'

The citizen whose window it was opened it, appeared in his nightshirt with his lamp, looked at the quay bemusedly, said a few words she could not catch, and closed his shutter again. Her last glimmer of hope was extinguished.

The man in black did not utter a syllable; he held her firmly and stepped out again more quickly. She offered no further resistance, and followed him, shattered.

From time to time she gathered up a little strength and said in a voice made jerky from the unevenness of the cobbles and their breathless rush: 'Who are you? Who are you?' He did not answer.

So they arrived, always following the quay, at a quite large square. There was a little light from the moon. It was the Grève. Standing in the middle a kind of black cross could be made out. It was the gibbet. She recognized it and saw where she was.

The man stopped, turned to her and raised his hood. 'Oh!' she stammered, petrified, 'I knew it was him again!'

It was the priest. He looked like his own ghost. Moonlight has that effect. By that light one seems to see only the spectres of things.

'Listen,' he said, and she shuddered at the sound of that voice of ill omen which she had not heard for so long. He continued. He spoke in short, gasping bursts, revealing the tremors deep within. 'Listen. We are here. I'm going to talk to you. This is the Grève. It is an extreme point. Destiny has delivered us up to one another. I'm going to decide your life; you, my soul. Beyond this place and this night there is nothing to be seen. So listen to me. I'm going to tell you. . . . First of all don't talk to me about your Phoebus.' (As he said that, he walked to and fro, like a man who cannot stand still, pulling her after him.) 'Don't talk about him. You see? If you utter that name, I don't know what I shall do, but it will be terrible.'

With that said, like a body returning to its centre of gravity, he became motionless once more. But his words revealed just as much agitation. His voice sank lower and lower.

'Don't turn your head away like that. Listen to me. This is a serious matter. First of all, this is what has happened—it won't be anything to laugh about, I swear—what was I saying then? Remind me! Ah!—there's a decree of Parliament sending you back to the scaffold. I've just pulled you out of their hands. But there they are, pursuing you. Look!'

He stretched out his arm towards the Cité. The search did indeed appear to be continuing there. The rumblings were coming closer. The tower of the lieutenant's house, opposite the Grève, was full of noise and lights, and soldiers could be seen running along the quay opposite with torches, shouting: 'The gypsy! Where's the gypsy? Death! death!'

'You see, they are after you, and I'm not lying. I love you—don't open your mouth, or rather don't speak if it's just to say you hate me. I'm determined to hear no more of that. I've just saved you—let me finish first—I can save you completely. I have got everything ready. It's for you to wish it. As you wish, so I can do.'

He interrupted himself violently: 'No, that's not what I must say.'

Then hurrying, and making her hurry, for he did not let her go, he made straight for the gibbet, and, pointing it out to her with his finger: 'Choose between the two of us,' he said coldly.

She tore herself from his grasp and fell at the foot of the gibbet, clasping the funereal support. Then she half turned her lovely head and looked at the priest over her shoulder. She was like a Holy Virgin at the foot of the Cross. The priest had remained motionless, finger still pointing at the gibbet, holding his gesture, like a statue.

At last the gypsy said to him: 'That does not fill me with as much loathing as you do.'

At that he slowly lowered his arm, and looked at the pavement in deepest despondency. 'If those stones could speak,' he murmured, 'yes, they would say: "There is a most unhappy man." '

He went on. The girl kneeling before the gibbet, covered by her long, flowing hair, let him speak without interruption. His tone was now sorrowful and gentle, contrasting painfully with the lofty harshness of his features.

'Yes, I love you. Oh! yet it is quite true. So nothing shows outwardly of the fire burning my heart! Alas! girl, night and day, yes, night and day, does that deserve no pity? The love goes on night and day, I tell you, torture! Oh! I am suffering too much, my poor child!—it is something worthy of compassion, I assure you. You see that I am talking to you gently. I want you to stop loathing me so much—anyhow, if a man loves a woman, it's not his fault! O God! What! will you never forgive me then—will you always hate me? So it's finished! That's what makes me evil, you see, and loathsome to myself! You won't even look at me! You are thinking of something else perhaps while I stand talking to you, shivering on the brink of the eternity that faces us both! Above all don't talk to me about that officer! Why! I could cast myself at your knees; why! I could kiss, not your feet, you wouldn't want that, but the ground beneath your feet; why! I could sob like a child, I could rip from my breast not just words, but my heart and my entrails to tell you I love you, but it would all be in vain, all of it! And yet you have nothing in your soul but affection and mildness, you radiate the most lovely sweetness, you are wholly gentle, kind, merciful, and delightful. Alas! your spite is reserved for me alone! Oh! what a fatality!'

He buried his face in his hands. The girl heard him weeping. It was the first time. Standing like that, shaken by sobs, he was more wretched and imploring than on his knees. He wept like that for a while.

'Well now!' he continued, once these first tears were over, 'I am lost for words. And yet I had thought out what I was going to say to you. Now I'm trembling and shivering, I'm failing at the decisive moment, I feel something supreme enfolding us, and I stammer. Oh! I shall fall to the pavement if you don't take pity on me, pity on yourself. Don't condemn us both. If you only knew how much I love you! What kind of heart is mine! Oh! all virtue forsaken! my own self abandoned in despair! Learned doctor, I make mock of learning; gentleman, I besmirch my name; priest, I use the missal as a pillow for lust, I spit in the face of my God! All for you, enchantress—to be more worthy of your hell! And you want nothing to do with a man damned! Oh! I must tell you all! Still more, something even more horrible, oh! more horrible!'

As he uttered those last words, his manner became quite distraught. He fell silent for a moment, then went on, as though talking to himself, in a loud voice: 'Cain, what have you done with your brother?'

There was another silence, then he continued: 'What have I done with him, Lord? I took him in, I brought him up, I fed him, I loved him, I idolized him, and I killed him! Yes, Lord, they have just now dashed his head before my eyes against the stones of your house, and it is because of me, because of this woman, because of her. . . .'

He was wild-eyed. His voice fading away, he repeated several times more, mechanically, at quite long intervals, like a bell drawing out its last vibrations: 'Because of her . . . because of her . . . !' Then his tongue stopped forming any perceptible sound, but his lips still continued to move. Suddenly he collapsed like something falling to pieces, and remained motionless on the ground, his head between his knees.

The girl's light touch as she withdrew her foot from under him made him come round. He ran his hand slowly over his sunken cheeks, and looked for a few moments in amazement at his fingers, which were damp. 'Why!' he murmured, 'I've been crying!'

And abruptly turning to the gypsy in indescribable anguish: 'Alas! you watched coldly as I wept! Child, do you know that those tears are burning lava? Is it really true

then—nothing can move us in a man we hate? If you saw
me dying you would only laugh. Oh! I don't want to see
you die! One word! A single word of forgiveness! Don't tell
me you love me, just tell me you are willing, that will be
enough, I'll save you. Otherwise . . . Oh! time is passing, I
beg you by all that is sacred, don't wait for me to become
stone again like that gibbet which claims you too! Just think
that I hold our two destinies in my hand, that I am out of
my mind—this is dreadful—that I may let everything fall,
and that beneath us is a bottomless abyss, unhappy girl,
down which my fall will follow yours through all eternity!
One kind word! Say one word! just one word!'

She opened her mouth to answer. He flung himself to his
knees before her to receive in adoration the word, perhaps
of pity, about to come from her lips. She said: 'You are
a murderer!'

The priest in a frenzy took her into his arms and began
to laugh an abominable laugh: 'All right then, yes! murderer!' he said, 'and I shall have you. You won't have me
as your slave, so you'll have me as your master. I'll have
you! I have a lair and I'll drag you there. You'll follow me,
you'll have to follow me, or I'll hand you over to them! You
must die, my lovely, or be mine! Be the priest's! the apostate's! the murderer's! This very night, do you hear? Come
now! joy! come! Kiss me, foolish girl! The grave or my bed!'

His eyes flashed with lust and rage. His lascivious mouth
left red marks on the girl's throat. She struggled in his arms.
He covered her with slavering kisses.

'Don't bite me, monster!' she cried. 'Oh! vile, loathsome
monk! let me go! I'll tear out your horrid grey hair in
handfuls and throw it in your face.'

He went red, he went white, then he loosed her and looked
at her with a sombre expression. She thought she had won,
and continued: 'I tell you I belong to my Phoebus, it's
Phoebus I love, it's Phoebus who is so handsome! You,
priest, you are old! you are ugly! Go away!'

He let out a violent cry, like a wretch being burned by
the red-hot iron. 'Die then!' he said through grinding teeth.
She saw his frightful look and tried to flee. He seized her,

shook her, threw her to the ground, and hurried towards the corner of the Tour-Roland, dragging her behind him over the pavement by her lovely hands.

Once there, he turned to her: 'One last time, will you be mine?'

She replied forcefully: 'No.'

At that he cried loudly: 'Gudule! Gudule! here's the gypsy girl! Take your revenge!'

The girl felt her elbow roughly seized. She looked. It was an emaciated arm coming out of the window slit in the wall and holding her in a grip of iron.

'Hold her tight!' said the priest. 'It's the gypsy who escaped. Don't let her go. I'll go and fetch the sergeants. You'll see her hang.'

From inside the wall a throaty laugh responded to these bloodthirsty words. 'Ha! ha! ha!' The gypsy saw the priest run off in the direction of the Pont Notre-Dame. A troop of riders could be heard from over there.

The girl had recognized the spiteful recluse. Panting with terror she tried to pull free. She twisted about, heaved convulsively several times in agony and despair, but the other held her with extraordinary strength. The lean, bony fingers which were bruising her clutched her flesh and met round it. It was as though that hand were riveted to her arm. It was more than a chain, more than a shackle, more than an iron ring: it was living, intelligent pincers emerging from a wall.

Exhausted, she fell back against the wall, and then the fear of death took hold of her. She thought of all the beauty in life, youth, the sight of the sky, aspects of nature, love, Phoebus, of all that was fleeing away from her and all that was coming closer, the priest denouncing her, the executioner who was coming, the gibbet standing there. Then she felt horror rise to the roots of her hair, and she heard the dismal laugh of the recluse whispering: 'Ha! ha! you're going to be hanged!'

Half dead she turned to the window, and saw the *sachette*'s wild face through the bars. 'What have I done to you?' she said almost unconscious.

The recluse did not answer, but began mumbling in a singsong tone, angry and mocking: 'Daughter of Egypt! daughter of Egypt! daughter of Egypt!'

The unfortunate Esmeralda dropped her head beneath her hair, realizing that she was not dealing with a human being.

Suddenly the recluse cried out, as though the gypsy's question had taken all that time to get through to her mind: 'What have you done to me? you say! Ah! what have you done to me, gypsy woman! All right! listen. I had a child, yes I did, do you see? I had a child! a child, I say!—a pretty little girl!—my Agnès,' she went on, distraught, kissing some object in the shadows. 'Well! do you see, daughter of Egypt? They took my child away, they stole my child, they ate my child. That's what you've done.'

The girl answered, like the lamb in the story: 'Alas! I may not even have been born then!'

'Oh yes!' retorted the recluse, 'you must have been born. You were one of them. She would be your age! So—for fifteen years now I've been here, fifteen years I've been suffering, fifteen years I've been praying, fifteen years I've been banging my head against these four walls. I tell you, it's the gypsy women who stole her from me, do you hear? and ate her with their teeth. Do you have a heart? Imagine what it's like, a child playing, a child feeding at the breast, a child sleeping. It's so innocent! Well! that's what they took from me, what they killed! The good Lord knows! Today it's my turn, I'm going to eat gypsy!—Oh! how I'd bite you if the bars didn't get in the way. My head's too big!—Poor little thing! while she was asleep! And if they woke her up when they took her, it was no good her crying, I wasn't there!—Ah! you gypsy mother, you've eaten my child! Come and see yours!'

Then she started to laugh, or grind her teeth, the two looked much the same in that ferocious face. Day was beginning to break. An ashen glint dimly lit up this scene, and the gibbet stood out more and more distinctly in the square. In the other direction, over towards the Pont Notre-Dame, the poor condemned girl thought she could hear the sound of cavalry coming closer.

'Madame!' she cried, hands clasped, down on her knees, dishevelled, distraught, wild with fright, 'madame! have pity. They are coming. I have done nothing to you. Do you want to see me die so horribly before your eyes? You can feel pity, I'm sure. It's too awful. Let me run away! Loose me! Mercy! I don't want to die like that!'

'Give me back my child!' said the recluse.

'Mercy! mercy!'

'Give me back my child!'

'Loose me, in heaven's name!'

'Give me back my child!'

This time the girl fell back once more, exhausted, broken, her eyes already glazed like someone in the grave. 'Alas!' she stammered, 'you are looking for your child. I am looking for my parents.'

'Give me back my little Agnès!' Gudule continued. 'You don't know where she is? Die then!—I'm going to tell you. I was a loose woman, I had a child, they took my child from me—it was the gypsy women. You can see that you must die. When your gypsy mother comes to claim you, I'll tell her: "Mother, look at that gibbet!" Or give me back my child—do you know where my little girl is? Wait, I'll show you. Here's her shoe, all that I have left of her. Do you know where the matching one is? If you know, tell me, and if it's only the other end of the world, I'll go and fetch it walking on my knees.'

As she said this, with her other arm stretched out of the window she showed the gypsy the little embroidered shoe. It was already light enough to make out its shape and colours.

'Show me that shoe,' said the gypsy, giving a start. 'God! God!' And at the same time, with her free hand, she swiftly opened the little bag decorated with green glass beads which she wore round her neck.

'Go on! go on!' muttered Gudule, 'rummage in your devilish amulet!' Suddenly she broke off, trembled in every limb, and cried out in a voice which came from her innermost depths: 'My daughter!'

The gypsy had just pulled out of the bag a little shoe exactly matching the other one. Attached to this little shoe was a scrap of parchment on which was written this verse:

> When you find the pair to this shoe,
> Your mother will stretch out her arms to you.

Quicker than a flash of lightning, the recluse had compared the two shoes, read the inscription on the parchment, and pressed her face, radiant with heavenly joy, to the window bars, crying out: 'My daughter! my daughter!'

'Mother!' answered the gypsy.

Here we give up any attempt at description.

The wall and the iron bars stood between them.

'Oh! the wall!' cried the recluse. 'Oh! to see her and not embrace her! Your hand! your hand!'

The girl passed her arm through the window, the recluse threw herself upon that hand, fastened her lips to it and stayed, plunged in that kiss, showing no other sign of life than a sob which made her body heave from time to time. Meanwhile she wept torrents, in silence, in darkness, like rainfall at night. The poor mother poured out in streams over this adored hand the deep, black well of tears within her, into which all her grief had filtered drop by drop for fifteen years.

Suddenly she stood up, pushed her long grey hair away from her forehead and without saying a word began shaking the bars of her cell with both hands more furiously than a lioness. The bars held firm. Then she went to fetch from a corner of the cell a big paving-stone which served her as a pillow, and hurled it at the bars so violently that one broke in a shower of sparks. A second blow completed the collapse of the old iron crossbar which blocked the window. Then using both hands she finished breaking and pushing clear the rusty stumps of the bars. There are moments when a woman's hands have superhuman strength.

Once a way through had been cleared, and that took less than a minute, she seized her daughter round the waist and pulled her into the cell. 'Come! let me fish you back from the abyss!' she murmured.

When her daughter was inside the cell, she gently laid her on the ground, then picked her up again, and carrying her in her arms as though she was still the baby Agnès, walked up and down in the harrow cell, intoxicated, out of her mind with joy, shouting, singing, kissing her daughter, talking to her, roaring with laughter, bursting into tears, all at the same time, in a frenzy.

'My daughter, my daughter!' she said. 'I've got my daughter! Here she is. The good Lord has restored her to me. Hey you! come here all of you! Is there anyone there to see that I've got my daughter? Lord Jesus, how beautiful she is! You kept me waiting fifteen years, merciful God, but that was so she would be beautiful when you gave her back. So the gypsy women had not eaten her! Who told me so? My little girl! my little girl! kiss me. Those good gypsy women! I love gypsy women. It's really you. So that's why my heart leaped each time you went by. But there was I taking that for hatred! Forgive me. Agnès, forgive me. You thought I was very spiteful, didn't you? I love you.—That little mark on your neck, do you still have it? Let's see. She's still got it. Oh! you are beautiful! You got those great big eyes from me, mademoiselle. Kiss me. I love you. I don't mind other mothers having children, I don't care about them now. They have only to come here. Here's mine. There's her neck, her eyes, her hair, her hand. Try and find anything as beautiful as that! Oh! I can assure you that she'll have lots of men in love with her, that one! All my beauty has gone, and passed to her. Kiss me!'

She said countless other extravagant things to her, to which the tone alone lent beauty, disarranged the poor girl's clothing to the point of making her blush, smoothed out her silken hair with her hand, kissed her foot, her knee, her forehead, her eyes, went into raptures about everything. The girl submitted to it all, repeating at intervals, very softly and with infinite gentleness: 'Mother!'

'You see, my little girl,' the recluse went on, punctuating each word with kisses, 'you see, I'll love you dearly. We'll go away from here. We're going to be really happy. I've inherited something at Reims, the part of the country we come from. Reims, you know? Ah! no, you don't know it, you were too small! If you knew how pretty you were at four months! Such tiny feet that people came to see them out of curiosity from Épernay, and that's seven leagues distant! We'll have a field, a house, I'll have you sleep in my bed. My goodness! my goodness! Who would ever believe it? I've got my daughter!'

'O mother!' the girl said, finally finding enough strength to speak in her emotion, 'the gypsy woman did tell me. There was a good gypsy woman of our people who died last year, and always cared for me like a foster mother. She was the one who put that little bag round my neck. She always used to say to me: "Little one, look after this jewel. It's a treasure. It will enable you to find your mother again. You are wearing your mother round your neck." She had foretold it, that gypsy had.'

The *sachette* once more hugged her daughter. 'Come here, let me kiss you! You say that so nicely. When we are back home, we'll put those little shoes on an Infant Jesus in one of the churches. We certainly owe that to the good Holy Virgin. Goodness, what a pretty voice you have! When you were talking to me just now it was like music! Oh! my Lord God! I have found my child! But who would ever believe such a story? Nothing is going to make us die, for I haven't died of joy!'

Then she started clapping her hands again, laughing and shouting: 'We are going to be happy!'

At that moment the cell rang with the clanking of weapons and the noise of galloping horses which seemed to emerge from the Pont Notre-Dame and to be approaching nearer and nearer along the quay. The gypsy flung herself in anguish into the *sachette*'s arms.

'Save me! save me! mother! They are coming!'

The recluse went pale.

'Oh! heavens! What are you saying? I had forgotten! They are pursuing you! But what have you done?'

'I don't know,' the unhappy child replied, 'but I have been condemned to death.'

'To death!' said Gudule, staggering as though struck by a thunderbolt. 'To death!' she went on slowly, staring fixedly at her daughter.

'Yes, mother,' the girl went on, quite distraught, 'they want to kill me. They are coming now to take me. That gallows is for me! Save me! save me! They're coming! Save me!'

The recluse stood quite still for a few moments as if turned to stone, then shook her head doubtingly, and suddenly let out a roar of laughter, but with her mad, terrifying laugh which had come back: 'Oh! oh! no! it's a dream that you're telling me. Ah, yes! I lose her, and that lasts fifteen years, then I find her again and that lasts one minute! And they are going to take her away again! And it's now that she is beautiful, grown up, talking to me, loving me, it's now they come to devour her, before my eyes, I, her mother! Oh no! Such things are not possible. The good God doesn't allow things like that.'

Now the cavalcade appeared to halt, and a distant voice could be heard saying: 'Over here, Messire Tristan! The priest says we'll find her at the Rat-hole.' The sound of horses began again.

The recluse stood upright with a desperate cry. 'Flee, flee, my child! It all comes back to me. You are right. It is your death! Horrors! malediction! flee!'

She put her head out of the window and quickly withdrew it.

'Stay,' she said, in a low voice, curt and mournful, convulsively squeezing the hand of the gypsy, who was more dead than alive. 'Stay! don't breathe! There are soldiers everywhere. You can't go out. It's too light.'

Her eyes were dry and burning. She stayed for a moment without speaking. She just strode about the cell, stopping periodically to rip out handfuls of grey hair, and then tore them with her teeth.

Suddenly she said; 'They are coming closer. I'll talk to them. Hide in that corner. They won't see you. I'll just tell them you escaped, that I let you go.'

She put her daughter down, for she was still carrying her, in a corner of the cell which could not be seen from outside.

She made her crouch down, carefully arranging her so that neither her hand nor her foot emerged from the darkness, undid her black hair and spread it over her white dress to conceal it, and put the pitcher and paving-stone, the only furniture she had, in front of the girl, imagining that the pitcher and paving stone would hide her. When that was done, now calmer, she knelt down and prayed. Day, which was only just breaking, still left plenty of dark corners in the Rat-hole.

At that moment the priest's voice, that voice out of hell, passed right by the cell, shouting: 'Over here, Captain Phoebus de Châteaupers!'

At that name, that voice, la Esmeralda, crouching in her corner, made a movement. 'Don't stir!' said Gudule.

She had scarcely finished speaking before a tumult of men, swords, and horses halted round the cell. The mother quickly stood up and took up a position in front of the window to block it. She saw a great body of armed men, on foot and on horseback, drawn up on the Grève. Their commander dismounted and came over to her. 'Old woman,' said this man, who had a most cruel face, 'we are looking for a witch to hang her; we've been told you had her.'

The poor mother put on the most casual air she could, and answered: 'I'm not sure what you mean.'

The other went on: 'God's head! What was that tale that archdeacon was making all that fuss about then? Where is he?'

'My lord,' a soldier said, 'he's vanished.'

'Now then, you crazy old woman,' the commander continued, 'don't lie to me. You were given a witch to guard. What have you done with her?'

The recluse did not want to deny everything, for fear of arousing suspicion, and replied in a tone of surly sincerity: 'If you're talking about a tall girl they gave me to hold just now, I can tell you that she bit me and I let her go. There. Leave me in peace.'

The commander made a grimace of disappointment.

'Don't go lying to me, you old spectre,' he went on. 'My name is Tristan l'Hermite and I'm the King's *compère*. Tristan l'Hermite, do you hear?' He added, looking around him at the Place de Grève: 'It's a name with echoes around here.'

'Even if you were Satan l'Hermite,' Gudule replied, regaining hope, 'I wouldn't tell you any different and I wouldn't be afraid of you.'

'God's head!' said Tristan, 'what an old harridan! Ah! so the witch girl escaped! Which way did she go?'

Gudule answered in a tone of indifference: 'The rue du Mouton, I think.'

Tristan turned his head, and signalled to his troop to prepare to move off again. The recluse breathed again.

'My lord,' one of the archers said suddenly, 'ask the old hag why the bars on her window are all broken like that.'

The question brought anguish back into the wretched mother's heart. She did not, however, lose all presence of mind: 'They've always been like that,' she stammered.

'Oh no!' retorted the archer, 'only yesterday they formed a fine black cross which gave people pious thoughts.'

Tristan cast a sidelong look at the recluse. 'I think the old girl is getting upset!'

The luckless woman realized that everything depended on putting on a bold face, and with death in her heart she began to snigger. Mothers have that kind of strength. 'Tush!' she said, 'the man's drunk. More than a year ago the tail of a cart carrying stones hit my window and smashed in the grating. I can tell you, I gave the carter a piece of my mind!'

'That's true,' said another archer, 'I was there.'

There are always people everywhere who have seen everything. The unhoped-for testimony of the archer put new spirit into the recluse for whom this interrogation was like crossing over an abyss on a knife-edge.

But she was condemned to continual alternation of hope and alarm.

'If a cart did that,' the first soldier retorted, 'the stumps of the bars should be pushed inwards, whereas they are bent outwards.'

'Ha! ha!' Tristan said to the soldier, 'you've got a nose like an investigator at the Châtelet. Answer what he says, old woman!'

'For goodness' sake!' she cried, feeling cornered, and in a tearful voice despite herself, 'I swear to you, my lord, that it was a cart that broke those bars. You've heard that this man saw it. Anyhow, what's that got to do with your gypsy?'

'The devil!' went on the soldier, flattered by the Provost's praise, 'the breaks in the iron are quite fresh!'

Tristan nodded. She went pale. 'How long ago, do you say, was this cart business?'

'A month, maybe two weeks, my lord. I don't remember.'

'First of all she said more than a year,' observed the soldier.

'That's suspicious!' said the Provost.

'My lord,' she cried, still pressed up against the window, trembling with fear lest suspicion should prompt them to stick their heads through and look into the cell, 'my lord, I swear to you that it was a cart broke this grating. I swear by the holy angels in paradise. If it was not a cart, may I be eternally damned and I deny God.'

'You're putting a lot of warmth into that oath!' said Tristan with his inquisitorial look.

The poor woman felt her assurance slipping away more and more. She had begun making blunders, and realized with terror that she was not saying what she should have said.

At this point another soldier arrived, shouting: 'My lord, the old hag is lying. The witch didn't escape by the rue du Mouton. The chain has been stretched across the street all night, and the chain-keeper has seen no one go by.'

Tristan, whose expression was becoming more sinister every moment, addressed the recluse: 'What do you have to say to that?'

She tried once more to face up to this new incident. 'I don't know, my lord, I may have been mistaken. I think she crossed the water, in fact.'

'That's in the opposite direction,' said the Provost. 'It's not very likely, though, that she'd want to go back to the Cité where they were pursuing her. You're lying, old woman!'

'Anyhow,' added the first soldier, 'there isn't a boat on this side of the water or on the other.'

'She must have swum across,' replied the recluse, defending her ground inch by inch.

'Can women swim?' asked the soldier.

'God's head! old woman! you're lying! you're lying!' Tristan angrily went on. 'I've a good mind to drop this witch hunt and take you in. Perhaps a quarter of an hour of the question will drag the truth out of you. Come on! You'll come along with us.'

She seized on his words eagerly—'As you wish, my lord. Go on. Go on. The question, I don't mind. Take me along. Quick! quick! Let's go right away.' During that time, she was thinking, my daughter can escape.

'God's death!' said the Provost, 'how greedy she is for the rack! I can't make head nor tail of this mad old woman.'

A grizzled old sergeant of the watch stepped forward and addressed the Provost: 'Mad, indeed, my lord! If she let the gypsy go, it's not her fault, for she has no liking for gypsies. I've done fifteen years in the watch, and every evening I've heard her cursing gypsy women and calling down endless execrations on them. If the one we are after is, as I believe, the little dancer with the goat, she hates her above all.'

Gudule made an effort and said: 'Above all that one.'

The unanimous testimony of the men of the watch confirmed the old sergeant's words for the Provost. Despairing of getting anything out of the recluse, Tristan l'Hermite turned his back on her and with inexpressible anxiety she saw him walk slowly towards his horse. 'Come on,' he said between his teeth, 'on our way! Resume the search. I shan't sleep until the gypsy girl has been hanged.'

He still hesitated a while, however, before mounting his horse. Gudule palpitated between life and death as she watched him scanning the square with the restless look of a hunting-dog that senses the quarry's lair nearby and is reluctant to move away. At last he shook his head and swung into the saddle. Gudule's heart, so horribly com-

pressed, now dilated, and she murmured, casting a glance
at her daughter whom she had not yet dared to look at since
the men's arrival: 'Saved!'

The poor child had stayed in her corner all that time
without breathing or stirring, the image of death standing
before her. She had missed nothing of the scene between
Gudule and Tristan, and each of her mother's fits of anguish had found an echo in her. She had heard each successive strain. On the thread holding her suspended over
the abyss, a score of times she had thought she was about
to see it snap, and she was at last beginning to breathe again
and feel her feet on firm ground. Just then she heard a voice
saying to the Provost:

'*Corbœuf!* Monsieur the Provost, I'm a soldier and it's not
my business to hang witches. The rabble has been put
down. Allow me to rejoin my company, because it's without
its captain.' The voice was that of Phoebus de Châteaupers.
What took place within her defies description. So he was
there, her friend, protector, support, refuge, her Phoebus!
She stood up, and before her mother could stop her, she
hurled herself at the window, crying: 'Phoebus! come to
me, my Phoebus!'

Phoebus was no longer there. He had just galloped off
round the corner of the rue de la Coutellerie. But Tristan
had not gone yet.

The recluse rushed at her daughter roaring. She pulled
her back violently, digging her nails into the girl's neck. A
mother tigress is not too particular about such details. But
it was too late. Tristan had seen.

'Ha! ha!' he cried, with a laugh that bared his teeth and
made his face look like a wolf's muzzle, 'two mice in the
mouse-hole!'

'I suspected as much,' said the soldier.

Tristan clapped him on the shoulder: 'You make a good
cat! Come on,' he added, 'where's Henriet Cousin?'

A man who had neither the dress nor the bearing of the
soldiers stepped out of their ranks. He wore a particoloured
outfit, half grey, half brown; he had straight hair, leather
sleeves, and a bundle of rope in his huge fist. This man was

constantly in Tristan's company, as Tristan was constantly in that of Louis XI.

'My friend,' said Tristan l'Hermite, 'I presume that's the witch we've been looking for. You'll hang it for me. Have you got your ladder?'

'There's one over in the shed at the Maison-aux-Piliers,' the man answered. 'Is that the gallows we're going to use for the job?' he continued, pointing to the stone gibbet.

'Yes.'

'Ho! ho!' the man went on, with a coarse laugh even more bestial than the Provost's, 'we shan't have far to go.'

'Get a move on,' said Tristan. 'You can laugh afterwards.'

Meanwhile, ever since Tristan had seen her daughter and all hope was lost, the recluse had not uttered a word. She had flung the poor gypsy, half dead, into the corner of the cellar, and had resumed her position at the window, both hands resting on the corner of the ledge like a pair of talons. They saw her in this attitude fearlessly eyeing all those soldiers with a gaze which had become once more wild and crazy. When Henriet Cousin approached the cell she made such a savage face at him that he fell back.

'My lord,' he said returning to the Provost, 'which one am I to take?'

'The young one.'

'That's good, for the old one looks troublesome.'

'That poor little dancer with her goat!' said the old sergeant of the watch.

Henriet Cousin went back back to the window. The look in the mother's eyes made him lower his own. He said rather timidly:

'Madame . . .'

She interrupted in a very low, furious voice: 'What do you want?'

'Not you,' he said, 'the other one.'

'What other one?'

'The girl.'

She began to shake her head and shout: 'There's no one here! There's no one here! There's no one here!'

'Yes, there is,' the hangman went on, 'as you know very well. Let me take the girl. I don't want to hurt you.'

She said with an odd sort of giggle: 'Ah! you don't want to hurt me!'

'Let me take the other one, madame; that is the wish of Monsieur the Provost.'

She repeated crazily: 'There's no one here.'

'I tell you there is!' replied the hangman. 'We've all seen that there are two of you.'

'Take a look!' jeered the recluse. 'Stick your head through the window.'

The hangman studied the mother's fingernails and did not dare.

'Hurry up!' shouted Tristan, who had just posted his troops in a circle round the Rat-hole, and was waiting on horseback beside the gibbet.

Henriet went back to the Provost once more, wholly at a loss. He had put down his rope on the ground, and was awkwardly rolling his hat in his hands. 'My lord,' he asked, 'how do I get in?'

'Through the door.'

'There isn't one.'

'Through the window.'

'It's too narrow.'

'Widen it,' Tristan said angrily. 'Don't you have any picks?'

From the depths of her cave the mother, still in the same position, was watching. She no longer had any hope, she no longer knew what she wanted, but she did not want them to take her daughter away from her.

Henriet Cousin went to fetch the hangman's box of tools from the shed at the Maison-aux-Piliers. He also took from there the double ladder, which he set up right against the gibbet. Five or six men from the Provostry armed themselves with picks and crowbars, and Tristan made his way with them to the window.

'Old woman,' said the Provost in a stern tone, 'hand over that girl to us without any fuss.'

She looked at him like someone failing to understand.

'God's head!' Tristan went on, 'what's wrong with you, trying to prevent the witch from being hanged at the King's pleasure?'

The wretched woman began to laugh her wild laugh. 'What's wrong with me? She's my daughter.'

The tone in which she uttered that word made even Henriet Cousin shudder.

'I'm sorry about that,' the Provost replied. 'But such is the King's good pleasure.'

With her terrible laugh growing even louder she cried: 'What does your king matter to me? I tell you she's my daughter!'

'Break through the wall,' said Tristan.

To make a wide enough opening they had only to dislodge one course of stone underneath the window. When the mother heard the picks and crowbars sapping her fortress, she let out a frightful scream, then began racing round her cell at terrifying speed, a habit of wild animals which she had acquired from being caged up. She did not say anything more, but her eyes blazed. The soldiers' blood ran cold.

Suddenly she picked up her paving stone, laughed, and flung it with both hands at the men working. The stone, badly aimed, for her hands were trembling, did not hit anyone, and came to rest under the hooves of Tristan's horse. She ground her teeth.

Meanwhile, although the sun was not yet up, it was broad daylight, a fine rosy tint brightened up the rotten old chimneys of the Maison-aux-Piliers. It was the hour when the first early-morning windows in the great city open cheerfully upon the roofs. A few peasants, a few fruiterers going to market on their donkeys, were beginning to cross the Grève. They stopped for a moment in front of this body of soldiers massed around the Rat-hole, gazed in amazement, and went on their way.

The recluse had gone to sit down by her daughter, putting her own body in front of her as a shield, her eyes staring, listening to the poor child who did not stir and whose only utterance was a low murmur: 'Phoebus!

Phoebus!' As the work of demolition seemed to be making progress, the mother automatically moved back, pressing the girl more and more tightly against the wall. The recluse suddenly saw the stone shift (for she was standing guard and never took her eyes off it), and heard Tristan's voice encouraging the workmen. At that, she emerged from the state of collapse into which she had fallen for a few moments, and cried out, and while she spoke her voice at one moment rent the ear like a saw, at the next stammered as if every possible malediction had crowded upon her lips to burst out simultaneously. 'Oh! oh! This is horrible! You are brigands! Are you really going to take my daughter from me? I tell you she's my daughter! Oh! you cowards! hangman's lackeys! miserable murdering churls! Help! Help! Fire! But are they going to take my child from me just like that? Who is it they call the good God, then?'

Then, foaming at the mouth, wild-eyed, on all fours like a panther, bristling all over, she addressed Tristan: 'Come a bit nearer to take my daughter! Can't you understand that this woman is telling you it's her daughter? Do you know what it is to have a child? Eh, you lynx, haven't you ever lain with your mate? Haven't you ever had a cub? And if you do have little ones, isn't there something inside you that is stirred when they howl?'

'Lower the stone,' said Tristan; 'it's loose now.'

The crowbars raised the heavy stone course. It was, as we have said, the mother's last rampart. She threw herself upon it, tried to hold it back, dug her nails into the stone, but the massive block, set moving by six men, escaped from her and slid gently to the ground along the iron bars.

When the mother saw that they had now made a way in, she fell across the opening, barricading the breach with her body, wringing her arms, banging her head against the stone floor, and crying in a barely audible voice made hoarse by exhaustion: 'Help! fire! fire!'

'Now take the girl,' said the ever-impassive Tristan.

The mother gave the soldiers such a fearful glare that they felt more like retreating than advancing.

'Go on, then,' the Provost went on. 'You, Henriet Cousin!'

No one moved.

The Provost swore: 'Christ's head! my soldiers! scared of a woman!'

'My lord,' said Henriet, 'do you call that a woman?'

'She has a lion's mane!' said another.

'Go on!' the Provost retorted, 'the opening is wide enough. Go in three abreast, as at the breach at Pontoise. Let's have done, Mahomet's death! The first man who falls back, I'll cut him in two!'

Caught between the Provost and the mother, both threatening, the soldiers hesitated a moment, then, making up their minds, advanced on the Rat-hole.

When the recluse saw that, she abruptly knelt upright, pushed her hair away from her face, then let her torn, skinny hands drop on to her thighs. Then great tears fell from her eyes one by one, and ran down her furrowed cheeks like a torrent in the bed it has scoured out. At the same time she began to speak, but in tones so beseeching, so gentle, so submissive and so harrowing, that around Tristan more than one old sergeant who would have eaten human flesh was wiping his eyes.

'My lords! messieurs the sergeants, one word! There's something I must tell you. She's my daughter, do you see? The dear little daughter I had lost! Listen. It's quite a story. I am well acquainted with messieurs the sergeants, believe me. They were always kind to me at the time when little boys used to throw stones at me because I led a life of shame. You see? you'll let me keep my child when you know! I'm a poor harlot. It was the gypsy women who stole her from me. I've even kept her shoe these fifteen years. Look, here it is! That was her little foot. At Reims! Chantefleurie! rue Folle-Peine! You may have known it. That was me. When you were young, those were good times. We had some merry moments. You'll have pity on me, won't you my lords? The gypsies stole her from me, they hid her from me for fifteen years. I thought she was dead. Imagine, my good friends, I thought she was dead. I've spent fifteen years in this cellar, without a fire in winter. That's hard, that is. Poor dear little shoe! I cried out so much that the good Lord heard me. Last night he gave me back my daughter. It was a miracle from the good Lord. She wasn't dead. You won't take her from me, I'm sure. Now, if it was me, I wouldn't say that, but her, a child of 16! Let her have time to see the sun! What's she done to you? Nothing at all. Nor have I—if only you knew that she's all I've got, that I am old, that she's a blessing sent to me by the Holy Virgin. And then you are all so kind! You didn't know she was my daughter, but you know now. Oh! I love her! Monsieur the High Provost, I'd rather have a hole in my insides than see a scratch on her finger. You are someone who looks like a kind lord! What I'm telling you explains it all, doesn't it? Oh! if you ever had a mother, my lord! You are the captain, let me keep my child! Look at me praying to you on my knees as one prays to Jesus Christ! I'm not asking anything from anyone, but I want my child! Oh! I want to keep my child! The good Lord, who is the master, didn't give her back to me for nothing! The King! the King, you say! He won't get much pleasure from having my little girl killed! And he's a kind king too! She's my daughter! my daughter, mine! She doesn't belong to the King! She's not yours! I want to go away! We want to go away! Come now, when two women are passing by, one mother, the other daughter, you let them through! Let us through! We're from Reims. Oh! you're very kind, messieurs the sergeants, I love you all. You won't take my dear little daughter from me, you can't! It's quite impossible, isn't it? My child! my child!'

We shall not attempt to give any idea of her gestures, her tone, the tears she swallowed as she spoke, the way she clasped and then wrung her hands, her heart-rending smiles, her tearful glances, the groans, the sighs, the chilling cries of misery mingled with her muddled, crazy, incoherent words. When she fell silent, Tristan l'Hermite frowned, but that was to hide a tear welling up into his tigerish eye. He overcame that weakness, however, and said curtly: 'It is the King's will.'

Then he bent over Henriet Cousin's ear and whispered: 'Get it over quickly!' Perhaps even the formidable Provost felt his heart failing him.

The hangman and the sergeants entered the cell. The mother offered no resistance, she just dragged herself over to her daughter and threw herself headlong over her. The gypsy saw the soldiers approaching. The horror of death revived her. 'Mother!' she cried in tones of indescribable distress, 'mother! They're coming! Defend me!'

'Yes, my love, I'll defend you!' her mother answered in a feeble voice, and hugging her tightly in her arms smothered her with kisses. The two of them lying like that upon the ground, the mother on top of her daughter, made a pitiable sight.

Henriet Cousin grasped the girl round the middle, under her lovely shoulders. When she felt his hand she gasped: 'Ugh!' and fainted. The hangman, shedding great tears on her, drop by drop, tried to pick her up in his arms. He attempted to pull the mother loose, for she had, so to speak, knotted both hands around her daughter's waist, but she clung to the child so tenaciously that it was impossible to separate them. So Henriet Cousin dragged the girl out of the cell, with her mother behind her. The mother too kept her eyes closed.

The sun was coming up just at that moment, and there was already a considerable crowd of people gathered in the square, watching from a distance to see who it was being dragged like that over the pavement to the gibbet. For such was Provost Tristan's custom at executions. He had a mania for preventing curious spectators from coming anywhere near.

There was no one at the windows, only in the distance, on top of the tower of Notre-Dame that overlooks the Grève, two men could be seen, standing out in black against the clear morning sky, apparently watching.

Henriet Cousin stopped at the foot of the fatal ladder with what he was dragging, and hardly breathing, so moved to pity was he, put the rope round the girl's adorable neck. The unfortunate child felt the horrible touch of the hemp.

She opened her eyes, and saw the gaunt arm of the stone
gibbet stretched out above her head. Then she shook herself, and cried out in a loud, heart-rending voice: 'No! no!
I don't want to!' The mother, whose head was buried and
hidden beneath her daughter's clothes, did not say a word;
but her whole body could be seen to shudder and she could
be heard kissing her daughter more intensely than ever. The
hangman took advantage of that moment swiftly to break
the grip of the arms with which she clasped the condemned
girl. Either from exhaustion or despair, she let him do it.
Then he slung the girl over his shoulder, whence the charming creature hung down gracefully, bent double over his
massive head. Then he put his foot on the ladder to go up.

At that moment the mother, lying huddled on the paving,
fully opened her eyes. She did not utter a cry, but stood up
straight with a terrible expression and then hurled herself,
like a beast at its prey, upon the hangman's hand and bit
him. It happened in a flash. The hangman howled with
pain. Some men rushed up. With difficulty they pulled his
bleeding hand free from the mother's teeth. She maintained
a profound silence. They pushed her away quite brutally,
and noticed that her head fell back heavily on the paving.
They picked her up again. Again she fell back. She was, in
fact, dead.

The hangman, who had not loosed the girl, started up
the ladder again.

II

LA CREATURA BELLA BIANCO VESTITA (DANTE)*
[THE LOVELY CREATURE ROBED IN WHITE]

WHEN Quasimodo saw that the cell was empty, that the
gypsy was no longer there, that while he was defending her
she had been abducted, he gripped his hair with both hands
and stamped the ground in surprise and grief. Then he
began running all over the church, looking for his gypsy,
bellowing strange cries at every corner of the walls, scattering his red hair over the pavement. It was exactly at this
moment that the King's archers made their victorious entry
into Notre-Dame, also looking for the gypsy. Quasimodo
helped them, never suspecting, poor deaf creature, their
fatal intentions; he believed the gypsy girl's enemies were
the truands. He himself led Tristan l'Hermite to all the
possible hiding places, opened secret doors for him, false
altar backs, inner sacristies. Had the unfortunate girl still
been there, he would have been the one to deliver her up.
When Tristan, weary at never finding anything, gave up in
discouragement, and he was not easily discouraged, Quasimodo continued the search by himself. He went all round
the church, twenty, a hundred times, back and forth, from
top to bottom, climbing, descending, running, calling,
shouting, sniffing, ferreting, rummaging, poking his head
into every hole, pushing a torch under every vault, crazy
with despair. A male animal who had lost its mate could
not have roared more loudly nor been more frantic. At last,
when he was sure, quite sure, that she was no longer there,
that it was finished, that someone had stolen her from him,
he went back slowly up the tower staircase, that staircase
he had scaled in such excitement and triumph the day he
had rescued her. He passed by the same places, his head
drooping, without speaking, without weeping, almost without breathing. The church was once more deserted and
plunged into silence. The archers had left it to hunt down

the witch in the Cité. Quasimodo, remaining on his own in the vastness of Notre-Dame, a moment before under such tumultuous siege, made his way back to the cell where the gypsy had slept for so many weeks with him as her guard. As he approached it he imagined that he might perhaps find her there. When, at a bend in the gallery overlooking the roof of the side-aisles, he saw the narrow cell with its little window and little door, huddled under a huge flying buttress like a bird's nest under a branch, the poor man's heart failed him, and he leaned against a pillar to stop himself falling. He imagined that she might perhaps have returned, that some good spirit had no doubt brought her back, that the little cell was too peaceful, too safe, too delightful for her not to be there, and he dared not take another step for fear of shattering his illusion. 'Yes,' he told himself, 'she may be asleep, or praying. Let's not disturb her.'

He finally gathered up his courage, advanced on tiptoe, looked, and went in. Empty! the cell was still empty. The unhappy deaf man went round it slowly, lifted up the bed and looked underneath, as if she might be hidden between the floor and the mattress, then shook his head and stayed bemused. All of a sudden he furiously stamped out his torch, and without a word or a sigh rushed full tilt to hit his head against the wall and fell unconscious to the floor.

When he came to, he flung himself on the bed, rolled about on it, frantically kissed the place, still warm, where the girl had slept, stayed motionless there for a few minutes as if he was about to expire, then stood up, pouring with sweat, panting, out of his mind, and began banging his head against the walls with the frightening regularity of one of his bell clappers and the determination of a man wanting to break his own skull. At length he fell down a second time, exhausted; he dragged himself out of the cell on his knees, and crouched down facing the door in an attitude of astonishment. He stayed like that for over an hour without stirring, his eye fixed on the deserted cell, more gloomy and pensive than a mother sitting between an empty cradle and a full coffin. He did not utter a word; only, at long intervals, a sob violently shook his whole body, but it was a sob without tears, like summer lightning which makes no sound.

It was apparently then that, as he was trying to work out in the depths of his desolate reflections who could so unexpectedly have abducted the gypsy, he thought of the archdeacon. He remembered that Dom Claude was the only person with a key to the staircase leading to the cell, he recalled his nocturnal attempts on the girl, the first of which Quasimodo had assisted, the second prevented. He recalled countless details, and soon no longer doubted that the archdeacon had taken the gypsy from him. However, such was his respect for the priest, his gratitude, devotion, love for the man were so deeply rooted in his heart that they held out even at that moment against the claws of jealousy and despair.

He reflected that the archdeacon had done this thing, and the bloody, murderous anger which he would have felt against anyone else turned, once Claude Frollo was involved, into an increase in the poor man's grief.

Just when his thoughts were thus fixed upon the priest, as dawn whitened the flying buttresses, he saw on the upper storey of Notre-Dame, at the angle in the outer balustrade which runs round the apse, a figure walking. This figure was coming in his direction. He recognized it. It was the archdeacon. Claude was pacing slowly and solemnly. He was not looking ahead as he walked, he was making for the north tower, but his face was turned to the side, towards the right bank of the Seine, and he held his head high, as though he were trying to see something over the rooftops. Owls often present this oblique attitude. They fly in one direction and look towards another—the priest thus passed by above Quasimodo without seeing him.

The deaf man, who had been petrified by this sudden apparition, saw him disappear under the doorway to the north tower staircase. The reader knows that it is from this tower that one can see the Hôtel de Ville. Quasimodo rose and followed the archdeacon.

Quasimodo climbed the tower stairs for the sake of climbing them, to find out why the priest was climbing them.

For the rest, the poor bellringer did not know what he, Quasimodo, would do, what he would say, what he wanted. He was filled with fury, and filled with fear. The arch-deacon and the gypsy clashed in his heart.

When he reached the top of the tower, before coming out of the shadows of the staircase and going on to the plat-form, he looked cautiously to see where the priest was. The priest had his back to him. There is an open-work balus-trade running round the bell-tower platform. The priest was gazing down upon the town, with his chest resting on that one of the four sides of the balustrade which looks out on the Pont Notre-Dame.

Quasimodo came up stealthily behind him to see what he was looking at. The priest's attention was so taken up elsewhere that he did not hear the deaf man's steps behind him.

Paris is a splendid and attractive sight, the Paris of those days especially, seen from the top of the tower of Notre-Dame in the fresh light of a summer dawn. That day it might have been July. The sky was perfectly clear. A few lingering stars were fading out at various points, and there was one very brilliant one in the east in the brightest part of the sky. The sun was about to come up. Paris was beginning to stir. A very pure, white light brought out vividly to the eye all the different planes which the hundreds of houses present to the east. The gigantic shadow of the church towers went from roof to roof, from one end of the great city to the other. Some districts were already talking and making a noise. Here a bell rang out, there a hammer, over there the complex clatter of a moving cart. Already here and there smoke poured out over this whole surface, as though from the fissures of some immense sulphur field. The river, water ruffling against the arches of so many bridges, the tips of so many islands, was all a-shimmer with silvery pleats. Round the city, outside the ramparts, the eye was lost in a great ring of fluffy vapours through which one could dimly discern the indefinite line of the plains and the graceful swelling of the hills. All sorts of sounds drifted and scattered all over the city, now half awake. Over to the east the morning breeze chased across the sky a few white shreds of cottonwool torn from the hazy fleece covering the hills.

Down in the Parvis some good women, carrying their milk-jugs, pointed out to each other in astonishment the strangely dilapidated state of the main door of Notre-Dame, and two congealed streams of lead between the cracks in the sandstone. That was all that remained of the previous night's tumult. The pyre that Quasimodo had lit between the towers had gone out. Tristan had already cleaned up the square and had the dead thrown into the Seine. Kings like Louis XI take care to wash down the pavement quickly after a massacre.

Beyond the tower balustrade, exactly beneath the spot where the priest had stopped, there was one of those fancifully carved stone waterspouts which bristle all over Gothic buildings, and in a crevice of this spout, two pretty wallflowers in bloom, shaking and almost brought alive by the breeze, were greeting each other with playful bows. Above the towers, far up in the sky, faint bird-cries could be heard.

But the priest was neither listening nor looking at any of this. He was one of those men for whom there are no mornings, no birds, no flowers. In all that vast horizon, with such diverse aspects all around him, his contemplation was concentrated on a single point.

Quasimodo was burning to ask him what he had done with the gypsy. But at that moment the archdeacon seemed not to be of this world. He was obviously at one of those violent moments in life when one would not feel the earth crumble. With his eyes fixed unwaveringly on a certain spot, he remained motionless and silent; and there was something about this silence and immobility so fearsome that the savage bell-ringer trembled before it and did not dare risk a clash. All he did, and it was another way of interrogating the archdeacon, was to follow the direction of his line of sight, and in that way the eye of the unfortunate deaf man fell on the Place de Grève.

Thus he saw what the priest was looking at. The ladder had been put up beside the permanent gibbet. There were a few of the people in the square and a lot of soldiers. A man was dragging over the pavement something white to which something black was attached. The man stopped at the foot of the gibbet.

Here something took place that Quasimodo could not see clearly. It was not that his single eye was any less able to see at long range, but there was a mass of soldiers preventing him from making out everything. Besides, at that moment the sun appeared and such a flood of light overflowed the horizon that it was as though every pointed projection in Paris—spires, chimneys, gables—caught fire at once.

Meanwhile the man began climbing the ladder. Now Quasimodo could see him distinctly. He carried a woman over his shoulder, a girl dressed in white, and the girl had a noose round her neck. Quasimodo recognized her. It was *her*!

Thus the man reached the top of the ladder. There he adjusted the noose. At that point the priest knelt down on the balustrade to have a better view.

The man suddenly pushed the ladder away with a sharp kick of his heel, and Quasimodo, who had been holding his breath for some moments, saw swaying at the end of the rope, some twelve feet above the ground, the unfortunate child with the man crouching with his feet on her shoulders. The rope spun round several times and Quasimodo saw the gypsy's body seized with horrible convulsions. The priest for his part, craning his neck, was gazing with bulging eyes at the dreadful tableau of man and girl, spider and fly.

At the moment of greatest horror, a diabolical laugh, a laugh possible only for one who is no longer human, burst out from the priest's livid face. Quasimodo could not hear the laugh, but he saw it. The bell-ringer retreated a step or two behind the archdeacon, and suddenly, rushing at him furiously, pushed him in the back with both his huge hands, down into the abyss over which Dom Claude was leaning.

The priest cried: 'Damnation!' and fell.

The rainspout above which he had been leaning broke his fall. He clung to it with desperate hands, and just as he opened his mouth to cry out a second time, he saw passing over the balustrade, above his head, the fearsome, vengeful face of Quasimodo. So he was silent.

The abyss lay beneath him. A fall of more than two hundred feet, and the pavement. In this terrible situation the archdeacon spoke not one word, let out not one groan. He simply writhed about on the spout in the most incredible efforts to climb up again. But his hands had no hold on the granite, his feet just scratched the blackened wall without getting a grip. Those who have climbed up the towers of Notre-Dame know that there is a bulge in the stonework immediately beneath the balustrade. It was on this re-entrant angle that the wretched archdeacon was exhausting himself. He did not have a vertical wall to deal with, but one sloping away under him.

Quasimodo would have needed only to stretch out his hand to haul him back from the gulf, but he simply did not look at him. He was looking at the Grève. Looking at the gibbet. Looking at the gypsy. The deaf man was leaning with his elbows on the balustrade in the place where the archdeacon had been a moment before, and there, never taking his eyes off the only object there was for him in the world at that moment, he stayed unmoving and dumb like a man struck by a thunderbolt, and a long stream of tears flowed silently from that eye which until then had only ever shed a single tear.

Meanwhile the archdeacon was panting. His bald forehead ran with sweat, his nails bled on the stonework, his knees were rubbing raw on the wall. He could hear his cassock, which had caught on the rainspout, tearing and coming unstitched every time he gave a jerk. As a crowning misfortune, the spout ended in a lead pipe which was bending under the weight of his body. The archdeacon could feel this pipe slowly giving way. He told himself, wretched man, that once his hands became too tired to hold on, once his cassock was completely torn, once the lead pipe finally gave way, he must inevitably fall, and terror gripped his bowels. At times he looked wildly at a kind of narrow ledge some ten feet below, formed by chance in the sculptures, and he begged heaven from the depths of his soul in distress that he might finish out his life on that space of two square feet, even if it were to last a hundred years. Once he looked beneath him, into the abyss; when he raised his head again his eyes were closed and his hair standing on end.

The silence of these two men was frightening. While the archdeacon faced death so horribly a few feet away, Quasimodo wept and looked at the Grève.

The archdeacon, seeing that all his violent efforts served only to weaken the one fragile support left to him, had decided not to move any more. There he was, clasping the spout, hardly breathing, no longer stirring, left with no other movement than that contraction of the belly we experience in dreams when we think we are falling. His staring eyes were open, with a look in them of sickly amazement. Gradually, though, he was losing ground, his fingers were slipping on the spout, he felt more and more how weak his arms were and how heavy his body, how the curved lead pipe holding him up was bending all the time a notch closer to the abyss. He saw beneath him a terrifying sight: the roof of Saint-Jean-le-Rond no bigger than a playing card folded in half. He looked successively at the impassive sculptures of the tower, like him suspended over the precipice, but feeling no terror for themselves nor pity for him. All around him was stone; before his eyes the gaping monsters; below, at the very bottom, in the square, the pavement; above his head Quasimodo weeping.

In the Parvis there were a few groups of honest bystanders, calmly trying to guess who the madman might be who was amusing himself in such a peculiar way. The priest heard them say—for their voices reached up to him, loud and shrill: 'But he'll break his neck!'

Quasimodo wept on.

At length the archdeacon, foaming with rage and terror, realized that it was all to no purpose. However, he gathered up all the strength remaining to him for one last effort. He stiffened up on the spout, pushed away from the wall with both knees, clung by his hands to a crack between the stones, and managed to climb up a foot, perhaps; but this commotion caused the lead spout supporting him suddenly to bend over. At the same time the cassock ripped apart. At that, feeling everything give way beneath him, with only his stiff and weakening hands still holding on to anything, the unfortunate man closed his eyes and let go of the spout. He fell.

Quasimodo watched him fall.

A fall from such a height is seldom perpendicular. As he was launched into the void, the archdeacon at first fell with head down and both hands extended, then turned over several times. The wind drove him on to the roof of a house where the unfortunate man's body was first smashed. However, he was not dead when he reached it. The bell-ringer saw him still trying to cling to the gable with his fingernails. But the slope was too steep, and he had no strength left. He slid rapidly over the roof like a tile coming off, and rebounded on the pavement. There he did not move again.

Quasimodo then looked up at the gypsy, whose body he could see in the distance, hanging from the gibbet, shuddering in her white dress in the last twitches of the death agony, then he looked down again at the archdeacon stretched out at the foot of the tower, no longer in human shape, and said with a sob that made his deep chest heave: 'Oh! all I have loved!'

III

PHOEBUS' MARRIAGE

TOWARDS evening on that day, when the bishop's judicial officers came to collect from the pavement of the Parvis the archdeacon's dislocated corpse, Quasimodo had disappeared from Notre-Dame.

Many rumours went round concerning this incident. There was no doubt in people's minds that the day had come when, in accordance with their pact, Quasimodo, that is the devil, was to carry off Claude Frollo, that is the sorcerer. It was supposed that he had shattered the body as he took the soul, as monkeys break the shell to eat the nut.

That is why the archdeacon was not interred in consecrated ground.

Louis XI died the following year, in August 1483.

As for Pierre Gringoire, he managed to save the goat and had some success as a writer of tragedy. It seems that after trying a taste of astrology, philosophy, architecture, hermetics, all sorts of follies, he came back to tragedy, the greatest folly of all. That is what he called 'coming to a tragic end'. On the subject of his dramatic triumphs, this is what we read under 1483* in the accounts of the ordinary: 'To Jehan Marchand and Pierre Gringoire, carpenter and composer, who made and composed the mystery performed at the Châtelet in Paris at the entry of Monsieur the Legate, ordering the characters, these being dressed and attired as was requisite for the said mystery, and likewise constructed the scaffolding which was necessary thereto; and for doing this, 100 *livres*.'

Phoebus de Châteaupers also came to a tragic end: he got married.

IV

QUASIMODO'S MARRIAGE

WE have just said that Quasimodo disappeared from Notre-Dame on the day of the gypsy's and the archdeacon's deaths. He was in fact never seen again, and no one knew what had become of him.

During the night following la Esmeralda's execution, the executioner's men had taken down her body from the gibbet and carried it, according to custom, into the cellar at Montfaucon.

Montfaucon was, as Sauval says, 'the most ancient and superb gibbet in the kingdom'. Between the suburbs of the Temple and Saint-Martin, about 160 *toises** from the walls of Paris, a few crossbow shots from la Courtille, could be seen on the top of a gentle, imperceptible eminence, high enough to be visible for several leagues around, a strangely shaped structure, somewhat resembling a Celtic cromlech, and where human sacrifices were also made.

Imagine, then, crowning a mound of plaster, a huge parallelepiped of masonry, 15 feet high, 30 feet wide, 40 feet long, with a door, an outside ramp and a platform: on this platform stand sixteen enormous pillars of rough stone, 30 feet high, arranged in a colonnade round three of the four sides of the massive structure supporting them, connected at the top by stout beams from which chains hang at intervals; on all these chains, skeletons; nearby on the plain, a stone cross and two secondary gibbets, which seem to be growing like shoots around the central fork; above it all, in the sky, crows perpetually circle. That is Montfaucon.

At the end of the fifteenth century the formidable gibbet, which dated from 1328, was already very dilapidated. The beams were worm-eaten, the chains rusty, the pillars green with mould. The courses of dressed stone were all cracked at their joins, and grass grew on the platform where feet never trod. This monument presented a horrible profile, standing out against the sky, especially at night, when a little moonlight fell upon the white skulls, or when the chill evening wind rattled the chains and skeletons and set everything moving in the dark. The presence of that gibbet was enough to impart to all its surroundings the most sinister air.

The block of stone which formed the base of this repulsive structure was hollow. A huge cellar had been excavated within, closed by an old, broken-down iron grating, and into it were thrown not only the human remains which came off the chains at Montfaucon, but the bodies of all the wretches executed at the other permanent gibbets in Paris. In this deep charnel house where the dust of so many human beings and so many crimes rotted away together, many of the great of this world, many of the innocent too, came in turn to add their bones, from Enguerrand de Marigni, who inaugurated Montfaucon as victim, and was a just man, down to Admiral de Coligny,* who closed it, and was a just man.

As for Quasimodo's mysterious disappearance, all we have been able to discover is this.

About two years, or eighteen months, after the events which conclude this history, when they came to the cellar to look for the corpse of Olivier le Daim, who had been hanged two days before,* and to whom Charles VIII granted the favour of being buried at Saint-Laurent in better company, they found among all these hideous carcasses two skeletons, one clasping the other in a strange embrace. One of these two skeletons, that of a woman, still wore some tatters of a dress of a material which had once been white, and round the neck they saw a necklace of adrezarach seeds with a little silken bag, decorated with green glass beads, which was open and empty. These objects were of so little value that the hangman had no doubt not wanted them. The other skeleton, which held the first in close embrace, was that of a man. They noticed that the spinal column was curved, the head down between the shoulder blades, and one leg shorter than the other. Moreover, there was no fracture of the vertebrae of the neck, and it was obvious that he had not been hanged. The man to whom the skeleton belonged had therefore come there himself, and died there. When they tried to remove it from the skeleton it embraced, it fell to dust.

NOTE ON MONEY

REFERENCES in the book to money and coins are so frequent that a general explanation may be found more helpful than piecemeal notes. Especially, but not exclusively, in depicting the character of the notoriously avaricious Louis XI, Hugo quotes exact details of the cost of such items as buildings, repairs, even executions, as well as of emoluments, rents, tolls, dues of various kinds. Many of these details come from fifteenth-century account books, particularly that published by Sauval, and are all expressed in *livres*, *sous* (or *sols*), *deniers*, the familiar pre-metric £. *s. d.* system ultimately going back to Latin *libra*, *sestertii*, *denarii*. This money of account, with 12*d.* = 1*s.*, and 20*s.* 1*l.* (£), originally represented relative weights of silver, but the value of actual coins struck, expressed in *l. s. d.*, was subject to frequent change, in France effected by royal decree. By the end of the Hundred Years War two principal moneys of account coexisted within the boundaries of the kingdom (and other regional ones of dwindling importance): the *livre tournois* (from Tours), the more common, and the *livre parisis*, the more valuable, because it was associated with central government and the monarchy. By 1482 the *livre parisis* had for some time been fixed at 25 per cent more than the *tournois* (e.g. 16 *parisis* = 20 *tournois*). This distinction explains, for instance, why at the beginning of Book Five, Ch. I, Coictier parries Frollo's recital of his supposed wealth by complaining that his tolls bring in only a modest sum in *livres*, 'and not even *parisis*'.

As it happens, immediately following that remark of Coictier's there comes a reference to gold *écus*, a coin which plays a vital role in the story. This large coin, whose value had been first fixed by an ordinance of Charles VII (quoted by Jehan at the beginning of Book Seven, Ch. IV) and whose value then varied according to its design—the most recent in 1482 bearing a sun, following issues bearing a crown or a crescent—was worth from 36*s.* in 1487 and constantly appreciated. It is the transformation of such a coin into a dry leaf that motivates the charge of witchcraft against Esmeralda.

Other humbler coins are mentioned when referring to the takings from street performances, or the contents of the purse begged by Jehan Frollo from his brother. *Blanc* (white) indicates substantial silver content, *noir* (black) copper or brass; a *maille* was half a *denier*, a *liard* 3 *deniers*, or a quarter of a *sou*, a *grand blanc* or *gros* a whole *sou*, a *petit blanc* half that, or 6 *deniers*; an *unzain* was 11 *deniers*, a *douzain* 12 deniers. Lists of coins are often quoted verbatim from such sources as Sauval.

EXPLANATORY NOTES

7 *ΑΝΑΓΚΗ*: the word means rather more than the 'fatality' by which Hugo translates it in the novel; 'force', 'constraint', 'necessity' are the basic meanings, but it could also be used for actual torture.

10 *Currit rota . . .*: what Horace actually wrote in the *Ars poetica* was: *currente rota, cur urceus exit?* [as the wheel turns, why does a pot emerge?]

11 *archbishop's palace*: throughout the Middle Ages the diocese of Paris was ruled by a bishop under the Archbishop of Sens, but in 1622 a new province was created under its own archbishop. His palace dated from the late seventeenth century.

Daumesnil: governor, and successful defender under Napoleon, of the fortress of Vincennes, where the chapel in question was located.

Palais Bourbon: built in the eighteenth century as a royal residence. Since the Revolution of 1789 it has been used for the National Assembly.

Saint-Jacques-de-la-Boucherie: the church was destroyed in 1797, but the tower still survives, despite Hugo's gloomy prediction.

Saint-Germain-des-Prés: in the course of restoration the church lost two of its three steeples in 1822.

Saint-Germain-l'Auxerrois: across the street from the Louvre. Badly damaged in riots in 1831, there was indeed talk of demolition, but it was eventually restored.

green coats: the distinctive uniform of Academicians.

Philibert Delorme: a major architect (died 1570), who designed the Palace of the Tuileries, eventually destroyed by the Commune in 1871. The nineteenth-century link between the Louvre and the Tuileries survives.

13 *three hundred and forty-eight years . . . ago today*: 25 July 1830, the date when Hugo began this novel.

Picards . . . Burgundians: as in 1465.

Laas: a vineyard on the left bank, extending towards Saint-Germain-des-Prés, inevitably a scene of student disturbances.

13 *Jean de Troyes*: in fact Jean de Roye, author of a history of Louis XI, commonly known as *Chronique scandaleuse*.

Epiphany . . . Feast of Fools: 6 January is indeed Twelfth Night, or Epiphany, but it is Hugo who combines it with the Feast of Fools.

Braque: a person, not a place, founder of the chapel which was next to the rue des Haudriettes (who play an important role in the story) and near the present Hôtel des Archives.

14 *camlet*: a rough, woollen material, originally derived from camel hair.

16 *Pharamond*: legendary ancestor of the Merovingians (AD 420–8); the do-nothing, or *fainéant*, kings were the Merovingians after Dagobert, from 639.

Du Breul: Father Jacques Du Breul (1528–1614), author of *Théâtre des antiquités de Paris*, one of Hugo's main sources.

Ravaillac: assassinated Henri IV in 1610.

17 *Théophile*: the libertine poet Théophile de Viau (1590–1626); the 'épices' were originally presents in kind, spices, to judges, and then came to mean simply 'bribes', while the word 'palais' meant both palace and palate.

Philippe le Bel: Philippe IV (the Fair: died 1314).

Benedict: Pierre de Luna, anti-pope 1394–1423.

18 *Biscornette*: responsible for the ironwork on the doors of Notre-Dame.

Du Hancy: a carpenter, of the sixteenth century.

de Brosse: Salomon de Brosse, died 1627.

Patrus: Olivier Patrus, a lawyer and Academician, died 1681.

20 *King of Sicily*: René of Anjou, died 1480; he was King of Sicily only in name, and also comte de Provence, whither he retired.

23 *rue Thibautodé*: or Thibaut-Odet; pun on 'dé', dice.

24 *Saturnalitias . . .*: the quotation is from Martial.

disputations, the regular ones and the occasional ones: the normal test for a student; 'occasionals' or '*quodlibetales*' were originally displays of virtuoso skill improvised on any subject by masters, but by the fifteenth century formed part of student testing.

Sainte-Geneviève: the great abbey of canons regular stood where the Panthéon and the Lycée Henri IV are today, on the mount of the same name.

25 *Post equitem . . .*: Horace, *Odes*, iii. I.

27 *Ne deus . . .*: Horace, *Ars poetica*, 21–2.

28 *charivari*: a serenade of pots and pans.

29 *Corneille*: quotation from his comedy *Le Menteur*, II. v.

30 *Legate*: the papal legate had made a solemn entry in 1480.

31 *bergerettes*: pastorals; the *wild men and women* belong to the same convention.

   hippocras: a medicated wine, a popular cordial of the time.

   Dieppe: Louis XI had captured Dieppe from the English in 1443, before becoming king.

32 *Pierre Gringoire*: for the full text of which this is a résumé, see penultimate chapter of the novel.

33 *cramignole*: see p. 43.

38 *Father Du Breul . . . no mean feat'*: he had dedicated his book on Paris in 1612 to the Prince de Conti, a member of the Bourbon family. The supposed derivation of the name Paris from the quite authentic Greek word was widely put forward by Renaissance humanists.

39 *The Florentine*: the author of the play (1685) was in fact Charles de Champmeslé, friend of La Fontaine.

40 *Nemours . . . Saint-Pol*: Jacques d'Armagnac, duc de Nemours and Louis de Luxembourg, Constable, comte de Saint-Pol, were executed for treachery against Louis XI in 1476 and 1475 respectively.

42 *Saint Louis*: Saint Louis IX, reigned 1226–70, had enacted the most severe measures against blasphemers.

   . . . would last: the marriage never took place; Marguerite eventually married Don John of Austria in 1497, and on his death the Duke of Savoy; the Dauphin Charles, soon to be Charles VIII, married Duchess Anne of Brittany in 1491.

   Edward IV: died in April 1483; there is no foundation for the story that Louis XI (died August 1483) was in any way responsible.

43 *. . . parchons*: the dialect word for 'portions' or the court responsible for fair distribution of estates. The list comes

straight from Commines, himself a Fleming, and Hugo exploits it for its outlandish sound to a French ear.

46 *Hymbercourt . . . Hugonet*: executed in 1477 by the citizens of Ghent in defiance of Mary, for supposed double-dealing with France.

51 *vera . . .*: Virgil, *Aeneid*, i. 405.

53 *Timanthes*: a Greek painter of the fourth century BC.

55 *Germain Pilon*: a sculptor (1537–90).

David Teniers: the younger, a painter (1610–70).

Salvator Rosa: a painter (1615–73).

56 *Sauveur . . . Biot*: Joseph Sauveur (1653–1716), physicist and acoustics specialist; J.-B. Biot (1774–1862), pioneer of electromagnetism.

58 *great man*: the name of Napoleon figures clearly in the manuscript, but not in the final version.

59 *douzain*: a (then) newly introduced silver coin worth a *sou*.

63 *Naso*: the poet P. Ovidius Naso, Ovid, died in exile on the Black Sea coast.

66 *May bundle*: like the maypole, a festive rather than a seasonal object, essentially a bundle of sticks.

69 *Boccador*: Italian architect who died in Paris *c.* 1549. The Hôtel de Ville was destroyed by the Commune of 1871.

Saint-Vallier: Jean de Poitiers, comte de Saint-Vallier, father of Diane, mistress of the future Henri II, was condemned to death for conspiracy against François I in 1524, but later reprieved.

71 *Besos para Golpes*: bad Spanish for 'kisses for blows'; the linguistic oddities throughout the chapter indicate that Hugo deliberately put 'para' for 'por'.

72 *salamander*: a creature whose natural element was fire.

Bacchante from Mount Maenalus: the Bacchantes, or Maenads, danced in a frenzy inspired by Bacchus; Mount Maenalus is sacred to Pan, and the first syllable has nothing to do with Bacchus. One of countless examples of Gringoire's wide and inaccurate erudition.

74 *grands blancs etc.*: see Note on Money.

75 *sachette*: explained later from the fact that she wore a sack.

camichon: apparently a version of *cramiche*, a kind of bun or cake; cf. *cramique*, a sort of fruit-loaf, in Belgium today.

76 '*Un cofre . . . echar*': 'A chest of great value/ They found in a pillar/Inside new banners/ With frightening figures/Arab riders/Sitting immobile/With swords, and round their necks/Crossbows which shot well.' The poem comes from a collection of Spanish *Romanceros* published in 1821 by Abel Hugo, Victor's brother.

77 *courtauds . . . dogs*: the list and definitions of these sturdy beggars comes from Sauval, writing nearly two hundred years later. It should be taken to represent what Hugo was happy to pass on, rather than as historically accurate. A fuller description follows in the text, pp. 96–8.

courtauds—winter beggars; *coquillarts*—alleged pilgrims wearing their badge of scallop shells; *hubins*—persons bitten by rabid dogs seeking a cure at Saint-Hubert; *sabouleux*—supposed epileptics, foaming at the mouth with soap; *calots*—ringworm sufferers; *francs-mitoux*—wearing bandages round their heads; *polissons*—thieving children; *pières*—beggars on crutches; *capons*—cutpurses; *malingreux*—fakers of running sores or dropsy; *rifodés*—supposedly made homeless through fire; *marcandiers*—supposed victims of theft; *narquois*—supposed wounded soldiers; *archisuppôts, cagoux*—the chief officers, often hooded for anonymity; *coësre*—Argot word for their King.

Galilee: the association of clerks from the counting-house.

basoche: those from the High Court of Parliament.

78 *Sainte-Geneviève*: patron of Paris, whose reliquary was borne in procession round the city in times not only of plague but of flood, storm, or any other disaster.

balafos: an African percussion instrument.

re–la–mi: the reference is to the hexachord associated with Guido d'Arezzo in the eleventh century. It was a very restrictive form, and by the time of the Renaissance was replaced by the system more familiar today.

82 *Celestine*: a monastic order, part of the Benedictine family, much in honour in France in the fifteenth century, but defunct since the eighteenth (before the Revolution). An oblate is a lay associate.

84 *archers . . . King's troop*: these troops were first formed by Charles VII as the nucleus of a standing army, and provided

mounted patrols for the watch in Paris. Originally bowmen, they kept the name all though the *ancien régime* long after they adopted other arms, and 'archer' became a synonym for policeman.

84 *gendarme*: literally 'man of war', a mounted soldier.

86 '*and what . . . but dream?*': quotation from La Fontaine's fable *The Hare and the Frog*.

Maître Nicolas: the celebrated alchemist Nicolas Flamel: see Book Four, Ch. V, below.

87 *Belleforêt, Father Le Juge, and Corrozet*: François de Belleforêt, Pierre Le Juge, and Gilles Corrozet published contributions to the history of Paris in 1580, 1586, and 1532 respectively.

88 *Sainte-Opportune*: the church did not survive the Revolution.

90 *Salve*: one of the most ancient and popular hymns to the Virgin Mary is '*Ave maris stella*', dating from the ninth century; hardly less famous is the antiphon '*Salve Regina*' of the eleventh century; neither is part of the litany. Gringoire's Classical erudition has already been shown to be unreliable; his knowledge of liturgy is clearly no better.

buona mancia: the usual meaning is in fact 'tip' in Italian.

91 *Señor . . .*: to show the reader that from Italian we have switched to Spanish.

Vendidi . . .: a fair measure of Gringoire's, rather than Cicero's, Latin!

95 *Michelangelo . . . Callot*: the first lived from 1475 to 1564, Jacques Callot, a prolific and realistic engraver, especially of low life, from 1592 to 1635.

96 *God's leg*: because it brings in a good income. Rabelais in the Fourth Book of *Pantagruel* confirms (and condemns) the expression (ch. 1).

Benserade: the poet Isaac de Benserade (1612–91) was a regular producer of court entertainments.

100 *petite flambe*: a small curved knife used for cutting purses; the Argoteers collectively were the people of the *petite flambe* and the word comes in the password mentioned in Book Ten.

franche-bourgeoisie: that is, exempt from taxes. The modern rue des Francs-Bourgeois commemorates a poorhouse set up in the early fifteenth century, but Trouillefou is clearly not thinking of anything so charitable.

105 *Burington*: more correctly Daines Barrington, *Observations on the Statutes . . .* (1766).

110 *Despréaux*: the name by which the poet Boileau, friend of Racine and Molière, was known. Boileau's *Satire X* on women (1692) no doubt earned him this description.

112 *Raphael*: 1483–1520.

113 *Quando . . .*: another fragment from Abel Hugo's *Romanceros*.

117 *Micromegas*: eponymous giant hero of Voltaire's tale (1752).

119 *Charlemagne . . . Philip Augustus*: Charlemagne reigned 742–814, Philip-Augustus 1180–1223.

 Tempus edax . . .: the quotation is adapted from Ovid, *Metamorphoses*, xv.

120 *quae mole . . .*: the chronicler is Du Breul.

 Childebert: son of Clovis, reigned AD 511–58.

121 *Hercandus*: Bishop of Paris in Charlemagne's time; Louis XIII had vowed to repair the altar, but it was completed only sixty years later by his son Louis XIV.

 Constable de Bourbon's treason: this time Charles de Bourbon, who joined the Imperial forces against France in 1523 and died during the sack of Rome in 1527.

122 *Catherine . . . Dubarry's boudoir*: Catherine de' Medici, wife of Henri II, died 1589; Madame Dubarry, mistress of Louis XV, executed 1793.

123 *Vitruvius*: Roman architect of the first century BC, the most important authority on the art for the Renaissance.

 Vignolo: died 1573, author of an authoritative treatise on the five orders of architecture. Note that 'Goths and Vandals' were often bracketed together by the humanists, while only the latter term has retained its original pejorative sense.

 Erostratus: an otherwise obscure Ephesian who set fire to the temple there so that his name would live for ever. The quotation comes from Du Breul.

125 *Gregory VII*: Pope 1073–85.

 pendent opera interrupta: Virgil, *Aeneid*, iv. 88.

126 The note is by Hugo, the quotation from Ovid, *Metamorphoses*, ii.

129 *Julian the Apostate*: about the mid-fourth century AD.

130 '*Le mur . . .*: 'the wall ringing Paris makes Paris ring with murmuring.'

136 *Bernardins*: another name for the Cistercians, whose important college was situated in the place indicated.

142 *Place Royale*: now Place des Vosges, and site of the Victor Hugo Museum.

143 *unfinished*: not even begun until 1508.

145 *guilloched*: a form of ornamentation consisting of intersecting curved bands.

   Saint-Ladre: or Saint-Lazare.

146 *Montfaucon*: for a detailed description, see the last chapter of the novel.

147 *Voltaire . . . four fine monuments*: what he actually wrote, in the introduction to his *Siècle de Louis XIV*, was 'did not possess four fine monuments', and in ch. xxxii he particularly praises the new Louvre and the Luxembourg Palace.

   Mignards: Pierre Mignard (1612–75) was a portrait painter loaded with honours by Louis XIV.

148 *Year III . . . Messidor style*: in the Revolutionary calendar, year III ran from 1796 to 1797, Messidor, the tenth month, from late June to late July.

152 *stretta*: a compression and acceleration announcing the end of a piece of music; there is also *stretto*, essentially a device at the end of a fugue where parts overlap rather than follow each other.

   Ave-Maria: a Franciscan house founded by Louis XI in 1471, near the Hôtel de Ville, from which the Angelus was rung three times a day.

153 *Haudry*: Étienne Haudry founded this charitable institution for women in 1306, whence the familiar name *haudriettes*. The other details come via Sauval and Du Breul from authentic documents.

154 *Laetare Sunday*: mid-Lent or Refreshment Sunday, that is, five weeks earlier than Low or Quasimodo Sunday.

155 *Phlegethon*: river of flame in Hades.

157 *Collège de Torchi*: or Torci, better known as Collège de Lisieux.

158 '*Master of the Sentences*': Peter Lombard; the 'sentences' in question formed the basis for theological study for most of the Middle Ages. The remainder of the list includes the collection of civil statutes known as the *Capitularies*, Gratian's twelfth-century work on canon law, the *Decretum*, and various collections of decretals, that is rulings on canon law given by popes, which then had the force of law.

 Jacques d'Espars . . . Richard Hellain: actual members of the medical faculty at the time.

159 *all four faculties*: Arts, and the three higher faculties—Theology, Law, and Medicine.

 Jean de Troyes: Jean de Roye; see p. 13.

160 *age of* 20: officially he should have waited until 25, the age of legal majority.

162 *more or less*: Quasimodo in Latin means rather 'as it were'.

163 *Immanis . . .*: the chapter heading is an adaptation from Virgil, *Bucolics*, v. 44, replacing the original '*formosi*' ('comely') with its opposite, '*immanis*'.

 Josas: one of three archdeaconries of Paris, Josas lay to the south-west.

166 *Hobbes*: Thomas Hobbes (1588–1679), English philosopher who wrote in Latin and English.

167 *Montagu*: beheaded in 1409.

169 *Astolfo*: a brave and amiable character in Ariosto's *Orlando Furioso*, who travels far and wide on the hippogriff, a winged horse with a griffin's head.

 tarasques: the tarasque was a dragon reputedly slain at Tarascon in Provence by St Martha, sister of Lazarus; like the dogs and wyverns, a gargoyle.

173 *machicots*: full-time singers at Notre-Dame, lay clerks.

 Paul the Deacon: an eighth-century Lombard historian, also known as Warnefrid.

174 *classic*: there is a pun on 'classic' and the Latin for trumpet, '*classicum*'.

 rue de Glatigny: the street of recognized brothels.

175 *Claude Pernelle*: wife of Nicolas Flamel.

176 *Pacifique*: a Capuchin friar of the seventeenth century.

Legris: 'Mr Grey'.

180 *Régnier . . .* : he had in fact not written 'songbirds' (*fauvettes*) but 'screech-owls' (*chouettes*).

Claudius . . .: the name 'Claudius' in Latin is etymologically connected with the word '*claudus*', lame or limping, and provides an obvious pun.

181 *powder of projection*: a sort of alchemist's catalyst, supposedly able to turn metals on to which it was cast into gold.

182 ABRI-COTIER: means apricot-tree, and is yet another pun, formed from *abri* = shelter and *cotier*, a recognizable variant of Coictier.

183 *livres . . .* : see Note on Money.

184 *Compère*: means something like 'good friend' and was well known as Louis XI's usual form of address to his intimates. The mysterious stranger's identity would be immediately spotted by any reader, but it is typical of Hugo to make a pseudo-mystery of it until the end of the chapter,

Aesculapius: the Greek god of medicine, used here for a medical authority.

JAMBLICHUS: neo-Platonist of the fourth century AD, author of a life of Pythagoras.

185 *emprosthotonos . . . opisthotonos*: violent muscular contractions bending the body forwards after it has been bent backwards.

186 *Credo . . . Dominum nostrum*: 'I believe in God, Our Lord . . .'

187 *Epidaurus . . . Chaldea*: referring to medicine and astrology respectively.

boustrophedon . . . ziruph . . . zephirod: terms from the Kabbala, referring to ways of deciphering the Hebrew alphabet.

Clavicula: magic book attributed to King Solomon.

cyprinidae: carp, goldfish, etc.

189 *Eklinga*: in Sanskrit means the 'one, or unique, *lingam*'. in Hindu mythology the *linga(m)* was the phallic symbol representing the generative power of the god Siva; there is a temple of some importance with the same name near Udaipur, built by a Rajput prince, but nothing to show what Hugo may have read or believed.

Sikra: the summit or crest of a pagoda.

peristera: the word normally means 'dove, pigeon', but it also seems to have referred to the sacred plant verbena, used in peace-making rituals.

193 *Moses*: according to Exodus 20: 25, it was forbidden to use 'hewn stone' for altars.

195 *Gregory VII*: this pope, mentioned several times, humbled the Emperor by obliging him to do penance at Canossa (1077).

196 *Jacqueries, Pragueries, Leagues*: the first was a peasants' revolt in the fourteenth century, used by analogy for other peasant risings; the second a revolt against Charles VII, in which his son, the future Louis XI, took part, so called because of a recent revolt in Prague by the Hussites; the League was the party of extreme Catholics, led by the Guise family and supported by Spain, in the sixteenth-century Wars of Religion in France.

Quia . . . leo: the quotation is from Phaedrus' *Fables*.

197 *Guillaume de Paris*: previous references are here made clear by the mention of the thirteenth century. Guillaume is also known as Guillaume d'Auvergne. Bishop of Paris from 1228 until his death in 1249, he was a prolific and important writer on theology and philosophy.

testudo: 'tortoise': the Roman formation of shields overlapping like scales to give the soldiers underneath maximum protection.

203 *Quatre-Nations*: now the Institut de France, across the Seine from the Louvre.

204 *Glaber Radulphus*: the monastic chronicler Raoul Glaber, writing in the eleventh century.

column . . . cannon: the column in the Place Vendôme.

205 *Vyasa*: Hindu ascetic, traditional author of the *Mahabharata*.

206 *Rétif de la Bretonne*: a printer who wrote literally hundreds of novels about the life of the poor in his day.

Moniteur: the newspaper *Le Moniteur universel*, founded in 1789 on the model of contemporary English papers.

207 *Robert d'Estouteville*: he died, in fact, in 1479 and was succeeded by his son.

207 *marriage*: Jeanne married Louis de Bourbon in 1465.

208 '*League of the public weal*': formed 1464–5 against Louis, with Burgundian help.

entry in 14[67]: in 1467; the two last figures are omitted by Hugo.

Montlhéry: the rebel forces defeated the royal army there in 1465.

209 *Constable*: that is, Saint-Pol.

212 *our rector*: Thibaut, already introduced as a notorious gambler.

215 *Conservancy*: the court which dealt with cases relating to University privileges.

221 *Puits-qui-parle*: more prosaically known today as Puits de l'Ermite (Hermit's Well).

222 *Trou-aux-Rats*: here, and elsewhere, the omission of the 'r' sound in popular speech in Paris of the day is exploited for the sake of wordplay. Thus, 'tu ora' sounded to the Parisian ear like 'Trou-aux-Rats'.

225 *eighteen years ago*: the coronation of Louis XI was indeed in 1461, but there is no way that the Reims chronology can be squared with the other events of the story, laid in 1482. Esmeralda is about 16, Quasimodo about 20 in 1482, but the revelations of Mahiette at this point in the story have to be accepted as they are told. After all, the discrepancy of some four years is minor compared to that of twenty in the case of Gringoire. It will be seen in the course of this chapter that the time scale is repeatedly mentioned, but what is important is the age at which the *sachette* began her brief life of shame—14; she saw a chance of true love with the birth of her daughter, lost it with the baby's disappearance (and the substitution of the little monster 'about 4 years old'), and has been trying to atone for the past sixteen years.

clairet: a light red wine; the word 'claret' comes from it, but refers to the wines of the Bordeaux region rather than to the colour, and to speak of claret from Beaune today would be absurd.

demi-queues: vessels containing '27 *septiers* of 8 Parisian pints each'.

cinquantenier: one who has charge of fifty men.

226 *Espérance*: the Bourbon motto.

227 *Madame the Maid*: Joan of Arc, in 1429.

228 *Pâquerette*: the diminutive of her name, presumably implying familiarity; both words were then used for 'daisy'.

229 *sixteen years ago*: this time the chronology agrees with the Parisian side of the story, that is, the *sachette*'s own testimony.

235 *Poland* . . .: in French, *Pologne, Catalogne, Valogne* makes her confusion more intelligible.

236 *tabellionage*: the office of scrivener.

248 *John Comenius*: pioneer educationalist (1592–1670); born in Moravia, died in Amsterdam.

   That age . . .: quotation from La Fontaine's fable *The Two Pigeons*.

255 *du Bartas*: Guillaume du Bartas, poet (1540–90).

273 *Saint Genestus*: an actor reputedly converted to Christianity in the course of an anti-Christian play and martyred under Diocletian. Best known through Rotrou's tragedy of the same name (1646).

282 *Saint Eustache's day*: apparently a misprint for Eustase. The obscure abbot of that name is commemorated on 29 March, and his name appears in Hugo's manuscript. The much better known Eustache has 20 September as his feast day. Hugo wanted the events to take place on a Saturday (sabbath) for the association with witchcraft.

284 *1823 . . . UGÈNE*: Eugène Hugo, Victor's brother, was certified insane in 1823—a private joke?

287 *Manou*: for Manes, from whom Manicheism is named?

288 *Ezekiel*: according to Sauval, who tells the story, a rabbi in the thirteenth century.

290 *Montaigu cappette*: the very short cloaks for which the poor scholars of the Collège de Montaigu were ridiculed gave them their nickname.

292 *haudriette*: see the beginning of Book Four.

297 *per ipsum* . . .: the conclusion of the solemn prayer in the canon of the mass. Frollo is saying what Hugo had found in the *Dictionnaire infernal* under various headings.

300 *Psellos*: Byzantine statesman and Platonist of the eleventh century. His *Dialogue on the Energy and Operation of Daemons*

was translated into Latin by Ficino before 1479, and became an important source for Renaissance poets.

303 *Raymond Lull*: Catalan mystic philosopher, died 1316.

305 *Coupe-Gueule . . . Coupe-Gorge*: both words mean 'throat', but *gueule* is more vulgar; the change in name actually took place.

306 *Petits-Carreaux*: the rue des Petits Carreaux still exists, near the Halles (and the Court of Miracles).

307 *Aux Houls . . .*: the word for 'drunk', *saoul*, sounded like the word for 'bear'; thus the rue aux Houls, or Ours, invited the mocking jingle.

309 '*The knowledge . . . table*': an anachronistic quotation from the *Essays* of Montaigne (1533–92).

   rue Galiache: the word just used for 'scabby' was *galeux*, whence Jehan's drunken association of ideas.

310 *laces*: the equivalent of buttoning up his flies.

311 *Paternoster*: Phoebus drunkenly includes St Michael in the Lord's Prayer, when his name in fact comes into the formula for confession.

319 *Rully*: now Reuilly; Hugo quotes details from an account of such a muster held in 1467.

323 *sabouleux*: see note to p. 77.

   Hugh of Saint Victor's Didascalon: twelfth-century treatise, properly *Didascalion*, on arts and theology.

325 *maîtres des requêtes*: counsellors reporting directly to the king, whose role became increasingly important under the monarchy.

337 *Bophomet . . . Templars*: the Templars had been suppressed in the fourteenth century on charges of witchcraft, supported by evidence extorted by torture. Hugo is once again using the *Dictionnaire infernal*.

342 *Inferno*: the chapter heading comes from the device inscribed on the gates of hell, according to Dante.

343 '*forgetting*': whence *oubliette*.

345 *caffardum*: a kind of hood.

357 *Garofalo*: Benvenuto Tisi, died 1559.

361 *Queue-en-Brie*: there really is such a village, some 22 kilometres east of Paris, but Seebacher shows in a detailed note

that the description applies more accurately to a village called la Queue-les-Yvelines, some 50 kilometres west of Paris, where Hugo is known to have stayed in 1821 and where he became involved in a duel.

362 *La Fontaine*: in his fable *The Fox and the Stork*.

Gazette des Tribunaux: Court Reports.

Themis: goddess of justice.

363 *acton*: a padded leather jacket worn under a coat of mail.

Colombe: her friend, de Gaillefontaine.

370 *Masaccio*: Florentine artist (1401–28), precursor of Raphael.

371 *dismal psalms*: the Latin text is from the Vulgate, but the English text and references are all to the Authorized Version, which varies slightly.

385 *Montfaucon*: for a full description, see the final chapter.

386 *In the fields . . .*: the original specified the villages (now suburbs) of Issy and Vanves to rhyme with *chanvre*, hemp.

387 *Fortunate senex*: Virgil, *Bucolics*, i. 46.

388 *Job . . .*: the middle phrase of the quotation is the latter part of verse 12, inserted between two parts of verse 15.

391 *Louis XII*: reigned 1498–1515.

392 *two marshals . . .*: the incident took place in 1358; Hugo confuses several details.

419 *Pyrrhonist*: Gringoire has already been described as a sceptical philosopher; Pyrrho (died 276 BC) was the best-known exponent of the attitude and immensely influential in the Renaissance.

420 *Phoebus, comte de Foix*: Froissart gives a detailed, and famous, description of Gaston Phoebus, comte de Foix (1331–91).

422 *Il padelt*: not Turkish, but Gringoire's erudition is always suspect.

427 *Bito*: Gringoire seems to be confused again. Bito and his brother Cleobis replaced two missing bulls to draw their mother's chariot to the temple so that she could do her duty as priestess of Hera.

431 *Aux sonneurs . . .*: the pun, and many others in this book, depend on a systematized version of Parisian speech

at the time, where the sound 'r' and many plurals were silent; thus *sols neufs* sounded like *sonneurs*, and *pour les* like *poulets*.

434 *Mistigri*: the knave of clubs in some card games.

Caillouville: near the abbey of Saint-Wandrille in Normandy, it was famous for the dense rows of saints in the church.

435 *Quae cantica . . .*: the words are from St Augustine.

436 *Saint Goguelu*: the Holy Face was a full-size wooden statue of Christ in the cathedral at Lucca. Known as *Volto santo*, it had been put there in the eleventh or twelfth century and was much venerated. A copy was placed in the Paris church of Saint-Sépulcre and was known as Saint-Voult de Lucques. This soon became corrupted into Vaudelu, to Godelu, until finally it took a form the people recognized, Goguelu, meaning 'braggart'. Linguistically this footnote contributed by Jehan is interesting enough, but, drunk as he is, sounds hardly realistic.

in paradiso . . .: the word 'parvis' really does come from the Latin *paradisum*, but apart from the pun, there is an uneasy parody of Christ's promise to the penitent thief about paradise (Luke 23: 43).

438 *Luxuriosa res . . .*: Proverbs 20: 1.

Vinum . . .: Rule of St Benedict, ch. 40.

443 *Ecnoma*: Roman naval victory off Sicily over the Carthaginians in 256 BC; Alexander and Gustavus Adolphus (King of Sweden 1611–32) used the wedge formation on land.

444 *rue Coupe-Gueule*: see note to p. 305.

453 *Lectoure*: in Armagnac; besieged in 1473 by royal troops.

Sabnac: as for most of Spicali's demonology, Hugo quotes from the *Dictionnaire infernal*.

454 *forty years ago now*: the Turks took Constantinople in 1453, thirty years ago.

footboys . . .: at the time the word 'laquais', here translated footboy, simply meant a foot soldier, rather than a flunkey, and the number of discharged troops roaming the countryside after the Hundred Years War had become a proverbial nuisance; it is likely that this is what Hugo had in mind.

457 *Pharamond*: one of the kingly statues.

460 *toises*: a variable measure, usually about 6 feet.

461 *Cyrus*: the very fashionable novel *Le Grand Cyrus* (1653) was said to include Madame Pilou as stated, but Louis XI's bed is nothing to do with it.

463 *Fifty sols . . . cloaks*: all the facts and figures which so annoy the king come from account books published by Sauval and others, but dates are, as usual, random; the Palais clock, for example, was renovated in 1472.

465 *King Edward*: Edward IV of England.

467 *Louis de Luxembourg*: the comte de Saint-Pol, already mentioned, executed in 1475.

469 *Cardinal Balue*: Jean de la Balue (1421–91), Bishop of Evreux, then of Angers, was imprisoned in such a cage (which he is reputed to have designed, though not for his own use) at Loches in 1469, for allegedly conspiring with Louis XI's enemies. He was released in 1480. Many of the details in fact apply to him rather than to the unfortunate Bishop of Verdun.

471 *Guillaume de Harancourt*: or Haraucourt, of a leading family in Lorraine. Made Bishop of Verdun in 1456, he was arrested with Balue and caged in the Bastille in 1469, but released in April 1482 on agreeing to accept the see of Ventimiglia. He eventually was allowed back to Lorraine, where he died in 1500.

473 *bailiff of the Palais de Justice*: the post was held by Coictier himself at the time, though Hugo seems conveniently to have forgotten.

479 *Musagetes*: 'leader of the Muses'.

   Matthias Corvinus: King of Hungary and Bohemia, died 1490.

   Monroyal: French version of Regiomontanus, 'from Kønigsberg' (Franconia, not Prussia), as Johann Müller, a noted astronomer, was known.

   Hugonet: see p. 46.

481 *Jehan Fourbault*: he is mentioned at the end of Book Two, Ch. I, as having contributed banners to the decorations.

482 *Boucicaut*: died in 1367.

485 *Grandson*: battle in 1476.

avoyer Scharnachtal: an *avoyer* was a chief magistrate; in the case of Scharnachtal, of Berne.

486   *Bastille*: the irony is not just the implicit reference to its fall in 1789, but to the fact that by the time Hugo wrote the words, the Bourbons had just been evicted again by the July Revolution.

487   *Saint-Lô*: although Hugo twice wrote the name of this Norman town, in which there was an abbey called Sainte-Croix, it seems that the true reference is to the castle chapel of Saint-Laud at Angers (pronounced the same).

488   *lances*: a lance was a troop of six horsemen.

489   *St Hugh*: the only English Bishop Hugh to be canonized was Hugh of Avalon, a Carthusian monk who became Bishop of Lincoln; he died in 1200, well before the first King Edward came to the throne (1274), and the allusion remains obscure.

    Saint Paul: the church of that name in Paris.

491   *Saint-Gervais*: Gringoire has rushed all the way back to the town centre; Saint-Gervais is near the Hôtel de Ville.

492   *Taurinum obsessor . . .* : the epitaph has just been translated: 'at once besieger and besieged at Turin'.

    P. Matthieu: *Histoire de Louis XI* (1628), a major source for Book Ten.

499   *Ascalaphus*: son of Acheron; Hugo does not explain the allusion, but Gringoire must have been thinking of his metamorphosis.

    geometry: in the original sense of measuring distances and directions by instinct, not solving abstract problems.

500   *Gabelle*: the much-resented salt tax.

501   *Philippe V*: known as Philippe the Long; his reign was from 1316 to 1322, but the position of the adjective in the original is deliberately ambiguous.

528   *Dante*: Hugo himself gives Dante as the source for this chapter heading, actually referring to the angel of humility in *Purgatorio*, xii. 89–90. Unlike the universally familiar title to Book Eight, Ch. IV, this is by no means a well-known quotation.

537   *1483*: in fact from the accounts for 1502; see p. 32.

    160 toises: some 330 yards outside the walls.

539 *Marigni . . . Coligny*: the first was executed in 1315, the other was one of the chief victims of the massacre of St Bartholomew's Day, 1572.

Olivier le Daim . . . before: executed in May 1484. The church of Saint-Laurent is near the site of Montfaucon (and today near the Gare de l'Est).